Helmi

To Jeanette From Dar

Review
by Rabia Tanveer, *Reader's Favorite*
Review Rating: ★★★★★

This was such a fulfilling novel to read. Helmi is like that lovable grandma who sits beside you and tells you stories that have you riveted. She is spunky, sassy, incredibly hard-working and a fighter. I loved the way she lived her life. I enjoyed how the author created this gem of a character and allowed her to make room in the hearts of readers. The pace is not too fast or too slow; the author allows the reader to settle into Helmi's world, get to know her and then jump into one adventure after the other along with her. This novel is a whole experience, the full treatment where you get a fantastic character, amazing entertainment, great plot development and exceptionally well-crafted situations that just make you fall in love with Helmi.

Helmi

Dar Bagby

Published by Dar Bagby

Copyright 2019 by Dar Bagby

ALL RIGHTS RESERVED. No part of this book may be reproduced or transmitted in any form by any means, electronic or mechanical, including photocopying, scanning and recording, or by any information storage and retrieval system, except as may be expressly permitted in writing by the publisher. (darbagby@gmail.com)

Cover design by Dar Bagby
Manufactured and written in the United States of America

Published by Dar Bagby

First Edition
Printed in the United States of America

ISBN 13: 978-1-0878-0693-8

Library of Congress Control Number: 2019915986

The opinions in this book are the author's opinions only and are freely offered. They are not meant to be offensively portrayed.

DEDICATION

I dedicate this book to the first man I ever loved.
I miss you, Daddy.

ACKNOWLEDGEMENTS

It is because of my sister, Janet, that I decided to undertake the writing of this book. She was my inspiration. She has overcome severe difficulties, physically and emotionally, throughout her life. But in spite of the obstacles, she has never allowed her talents to be buried; they may have been placed on the back burner every once in a while, but they have always returned to the forefront. *Thank you, little sister, for fueling my incentive in this endeavor.*

I owe most of what is in this book to my family and friends, those still with me and those who have departed. The majority of the chapters herein are either direct representations of actual occurrences in my life or ones that were inspired by other incidents that touched me in some way. *My heartfelt thanks to all who contributed.*

During the writing of this book, I was amazed at how my husband, Ken, managed to carry on some semblance of normal life and keep slogging away while I may have ignored him. *Forgive me, if that's the case; it wasn't intentional, Bagman.*

It may seem odd to thank my miniature dachshund, Hammie, but for at least seventy-five percent of my time at the keyboard, he was lying beside me, keeping me calm and centered on the task at hand. The other twenty-five percent was spent protecting me from possible ravages by squirrels, chipmunks, the mail delivery truck, and all large vehicles passing by our house. *Thank you, little buddy, for sticking with me and for keeping me safe.*

Thank you to Connie, whose expertise in her field of layout and design was paramount in making the appearance of this book, both inside and out, even better than I imagined. *It's not easy to tell you how much you mean to me as both a coworker and a friend.*

A special thank you goes to Shirley, my cheerleader. When I was at my lowest point, she spent hours encouraging and inspiring me. Without her, I might not have seen my way clear to share this story with those who choose to travel through Helmi's life along with me. *Thank you for your loving and caring friendship, which I cherish.*

O love that wilt not let me go…

…I give thee back the life I owe.

George Matheson

PROLOGUE

Here it is, early 2020, and I'm still alive, be it only by the skin of my teeth. It appears that my body has a mind of its own; my cognition and attitude have no further say in the matter. These old bones will soon be telling my brain to turn off the ignition. I can honestly say, however, that it certainly doesn't come as a surprise, considering I'm only a few months away from completing a century of life.

Lately I've been dealing with memories that pop into my head from so far back in time I can barely recall the details. The ones from my earliest days may be distorted, and that's what I like about them. They're probably not a hundred percent accurate, but most are the way I like to remember them.

I've rubbed elbows countless times with Old Man Death throughout my life, so he's no stranger knocking at my door now. But I haven't determined that it's time to invite him into my parlor just yet. I need to finish this race I've been running for ninety-nine-plus years, and that's going to take a little longer. So he can just cool his heels and move on to someone who's presently closer to the finish line than I am. Did you hear that, Old Man?

I struggle through the conquest of coming to terms with whether I'm lucky that my brain has outlived my body. I've seen it go both ways: my aunt in Chicago, who was dumb as a box of rocks but as strong as any athlete, died of Alzheimer's disease at only 63, but one of my sisters, smart as a whip, died at an early age of Lou Gehrig's disease. Brain versus body: seems to me, when push comes to shove, it's a toss-up.

Britta Bonbright, my attorney, sits in a chair at the foot of my hospital bed. Quite the alliterative moniker (poor thing), probably brought on by marriage. I can't imagine parents being so vindictive as to intentionally beleaguer a child with such a name. She is currently updating *The Wilhelmina Butcher Revocable Trust*.

I smile and simultaneously ignore most of her effervescent prattle. But Britta is demanding that I pay attention now so we can finish this Herculean task. I begrudgingly answer her questions and listen to what she reads back to me, grasping only a small percentage of what it all means; I am not a connoisseur of legalese. She tells me it must be done, however, so I'll swallow the unsavory task and make the best of it—meaning I'll do what I can for whomever I leave behind, trusting that Britta knows best.

I've chosen to donate my body to science. I feel strongly that science needs a century-old body for research. A noble premise, perhaps, but one I'm compelled to fulfill. Who knows? Maybe the medical world will discover what has made me tick for so long and will be able to duplicate it for mankind's greater good, if expanding human longevity is a good thing, or even ethical.

I've answered all of Britta's tedious questions. Now she can go away and work her magic, and I'll try to stick around long enough to sign on the dotted line. Meanwhile, I want to savor the reminiscences of a lifetime. Then I can willingly cross the finish line and, with one last deep-cleansing breath, open my door to the Old Man and invite him in.

MY SHORT SPAN AS AN ONLY CHILD

Granny Nan's face was the first that met me when I came into this world, just as mine was the last to bid her adieu when she left it. She was a wise old bird with a high-spirited love for life that seemed lacking in just about everyone else I ever knew. Ours was a special bond, the kind only a fortunate few have the joy of encountering during their existence: some with a relative, some with a friend, some with a partner. I could talk to Granny Nan about anything. Almost anything. But I only had her around for my first 21 years. She was already ancient when she gave me that hearty slap on the backside, causing me to suck in my first breath.

I know babies cannot see clearly when they are only seconds old, but I am sure I could see Granny Nan's eyes smiling down at me as she bundled me in a piece of an old blanket and handed me to Mama. It is a story she told me over and over, enough times to convince me that I might truly recall that exact moment. And who is to say for sure? Maybe I can.

My Granny Nan told me Papa was the proudest man alive the day I was born. "Why, he kicked up his heels and did a little jig when he heard his firstborn bellow. And bellow you did!" She would always stop there momentarily and chuckle, the creases at the corners of her eyes growing more pronounced. She also said I stopped bellowing the minute Mama took me and held me close. "Your Mama gave one of her giggles, you know, the kind that made a tinkling sound like little pieces of glass bumping together in the wind, as she watched her crazy husband dance around the room like he had lost all semblance of sanity. He was the father of a brand spanking new baby girl, and he wanted the entire world to know she was going to be someone special."

Big shoes for a newborn to fill.

My first home, humble to say the least, was in the eastern Oklahoma panhandle, about 30 miles west of Beaver City (population 920 according to the 1920 census). We had a small herd of cattle that ranged within fences on some acres of land surrounding our one-room cabin, a mare named Trot that Papa loved and rode around the perimeter of the homesite two or three times a week, two Jersey cows that provided milk and occasional calves (when our neighbor loaned us one of his bulls), three sheep that grew enough wool for clothing, and a henhouse full of chickens for eggs and meat. We had a patch of dirt to scratch in; it yielded barely enough vegetables to feed us. And we had each other's company to keep ourselves entertained.

The short span of my life as an only child began on November 13, 1920. It was mostly uneventful. On the journey from infant to toddler I observed and learned the things every growing child does. But once, while sitting on Granny Nan's lap, she told me, "You are the most level-headed, intelligent, talented, and spirited young lady I have ever encountered. You are eager to learn, sometimes to a fault."

She was right. I was walking by myself at eight months. I savored everything that occurred both in and around our home on the prairie, and I did it with ferocity and a voraciousness to learn. I did my best to avoid letting something go on without my knowing about it. And that was never more apparent than the time I scared the bejeebies out of Mama and Granny Nan when I was ten months old.

Papa was riding Trot somewhere out on the property, chasing our cattle and checking our fences. Granny Nan had fallen asleep in front of the fire after cleaning up the dishes following the midday meal. Mama's back was to me as she sat in her rocking chair, darning socks, unwittingly humming a familiar tune, probably a hymn. I was on the braided rag rug, appearing to be concentrating deeply on building new worlds with some sticks I had found in the yard a couple of days prior and had painstakingly carried inside, one by one, trip after trip. However, something special—something other than stick construction—was occupying my mind. An ulterior motive involving a heretofore unexplained event was foremost in my thoughts.

Every night Mama and Papa disappeared up a ladder into the loft. I knew this because I slept with Granny Nan beneath the loft. The loft itself was enclosed behind a patchwork curtain; Mama and Granny Nan had sewn it together and hung it from some braided-together baling twine that ran from one side of the ceiling to the other. The curtain hung down to the hand-hewn beam that supported whatever was at the top of that ladder…whatever was in that secret place only Mama and Papa occupied after the sun went down. With the dim light from the carefully banked fire behind them, I could just make out their silhouettes climbing up every night, so I assumed it was where they slept, but I had a driving urge to be certain. I imagined maybe there was a whole other existence up that ladder and behind that curtain. I could be missing out on something exciting!

Several years after the fact, Mama told me, "I was paying no attention to your babbling behind me. But when my mind became less intent on my mending and more aware of the strange noises you made, I realized the sounds originated not only behind me, but also from above me. I turned and saw you perched on the edge of the loft, your little legs dangling over the beam, your arms waving like the wings of some crazed bird, and a smile as wide as the Beaver River on your face. You were just about to pop with pride.

"My heart jumped into my throat, but I stifled a scream, as I feared it would startle you and Granny Nan. I quietly put down my darning, stood up, and walked toward you, cooing softly to you the whole way. When I reached the point directly under you, I snatched you by a leg and held on for dear life."

I had cut loose with a shriek and managed to wiggle loose from Mama's grip and clamber onto their sleeping pallet, all the while squealing with excitement over this fun new game. Granny Nan (at age 70 but with the dexterity of a teenager) was awake and at the top of that ladder before I had a chance to blink. She sat down on the pallet beside me and told me what a wonderful acrobat I had become. "You climb better than a little monkey." I was ecstatic.

Neither she nor Mama ever scolded me for climbing up there that day. They simply learned to put the ladder up on the platform and out of my reach in the daytime. And I have come to wonder here of late if, when Papa saw the ladder, they told him I had made it to the top, or if they merely suggested to him that I was reaching an age where I had begun to show some interest in the ladder, so it would probably be prudent to keep it out of my reach. I will never know.

Granny Nan took me on long walks. She pointed out wildflowers, occasional clouds, birds, the sun's twinkling reflection in the slow-moving water of the little creek that passed through our property. Over and again she would say, "See how pretty?" And "pretty" became my first word.

I did not associate the word with people at that point in my life, only with things. Looking back, I recall that the people I was exposed to *weren't* pretty. None of the women or girls I saw were any different from me, Mama, or Granny Nan. Faces were plain, more often than not browned by the sun and deeply lined. Lips were un-curved, straight lines that indicated no particular emotion, and frequently chapped. Eyes were either brown, gray, or blue, revealing the strain of hard work, nothing more. Hair was always drab and straight. Clothes were sewn-together flour sacks or worn-out linens stained by sweat or dust or both and not giving any indication of the figure that dwelt underneath.

Over the next few months I took an interest in watching everyone's faces as they talked. I wanted to talk, too, so I imitated as many words and facial expressions as I could, and before long, Granny Nan said it was impossible to shut me up. At that same time, I discovered my eyebrows, nose, chin, and ears. We did not have a mirror, so I was on my own at imagining how I looked by comparison.

❖❖❖

One day Mama told me I was going to go to church with Granny Nan and her, but I had to promise them I would be real quiet and sit still.

"Papa go?" I asked.

"No, he has to stay home and take care of things here. But since you will not be here to help him Sunday next, he will have to work extra hard."

Up to that point in time, I had stayed home with Papa while the women went to church. I relished learning new things, and I continued the quiet observation that served to teach me so much about the world around me. I could always tell which day of the week it was by the routine everyone followed.

The routine for Sunday was: Mama and Granny Nan put on a clean dress; a wagon that had other people in it came to our cabin, and Mama and Granny Nan climbed up into it; they all greeted one another very pleasantly. I watched them and waved to them until the wagon disappeared in the distance, then Papa scooped me up in his big strong arms and took me with him to the barn. We did lots of chores until Mama and Granny Nan came home in time to fix the midday meal.

We did not own a wagon, only a buckboard. I found out later that it was our neighbors to the south who came by and picked up Mama and Granny Nan every Sunday. Those people later played a big role in our lives.

I do remember going to the church once before I learned to talk; I think it was probably a covered-dish get-together, as Granny Nan carried out a basket full of bread and a crock of freshly churned butter covered with a kitchen towel. I was very timid at that age, not having seen a lot of outsiders. I remember that I liked the ordeal, especially the wagon ride and the food, but I did not like the way everyone came up and poked at me or got so close to my face when they talked to me. And it had not been on a Sunday. It was all rather confusing yet thrilling at the same time.

So now I was going to go to church on a Sunday. "Food at church?"

Mama smiled. "No, not this time. We will be in God's house, so you have to be on your best behavior."

"Who is God?" I asked innocently. Mama and Granny Nan looked at each other with strange expressions on their faces. They must have realized neither of them had ever tried to explain God to me.

It was Papa who cleared up the issue. "That is vhat you go to church for," he said in his obvious German accent, "to learn who Gott is."

Papa was a man of few words, but in my opinion, his wisdom exceeded that of the most intelligent men throughout creation. His answer to that profound question made perfect sense to me. Still does. I continued going to church for much of my early life, but I remain at a loss to explain exactly who God is.

One day in the spring of 1922 I found myself staring at Mama's belly and thought it looked big. "Your belly is fat!" I announced to her, as if it were an astounding fact. She was, by then, eight months pregnant.

She looked down at the obvious bulge and said to me, "I think you are right."

"There must be something in there," Granny Nan said, acting surprised. "What do think it could be?"

"Food," I suggested matter-of-factly. My eyes widened, and I said, "Maybe air." They laughed at my conclusion, and I was totally befuddled by their reaction. When I ate beans or cabbage, I got air in my belly, so it made perfect sense to me.

Granny Nan said, "I guess we will have to wait and see if something comes out of your Mama's belly."

I pointed my finger at Mama and wagged it back and forth in a scolding motion. "No fart."

"Where did you learn that word?" Mama asked, wide eyed, turning to look directly at Papa. She and Papa and Granny Nan struggled to stifle their laughter.

Thinking I had been funny, I said, "Fart, fart, fart, fart," as I danced around the room.

Papa stopped me in my tracks. "Do not use that vord around other people, young lady," he said. "It is just betveen you and me." He winked at Granny Nan.

Mama chimed in, "So that is what she has been learning from you on Sundays. It is a good thing she is going to go to church with us."

Granny Nan smiled and winked back at Papa.

I had never heard Mama and Granny Nan "have words" until...

One day I was playing at the table just before supper. Without any hesitation or concern, I grunted, became red-faced, and pooped in my diaper.

Granny Nan told Mama, "I think she is ready to be toilet trained."

Mama's voice went up about two octaves, and the volume went from pianissimo to fortissimo. "No, no, NO! The doctor said no baby should be toilet trained until the age of two, and Helmi will not turn two until…"

"I know how old she is and when she will have a birthday," Granny Nan said, agitation obvious in her voice. "But she has done everything else before it was 'the right time.' She walked and climbed before her first birthday, she talks like she is five years old, and she sits and *thinks*. Have you not seen her do that? A far-away look overtakes her face…"

"Yes, I have seen her do that, and it amazes me, but we are not talking about thinking here. We are talking about her…her…other habits. Doc Weiser said it is the newest finding. They have studied what happens to children who are trained too early, and their findings indicate…"

"Findings! Studies! Indications! I have news for you, Violet. You were put on a gusunda when you were fifteen months old, and it did not create any horrible problems with you. How do you think it could hurt a mentally advanced child like Helmi?"

Mama went silent, and her brows furrowed. "A guh…guh…"

"Gusunda. The word is gusunda."

"What beneath God's Heaven is a gusunda?"

"The pot that goes under the bed. Goes under. Gusunda the bed. Gusunda."

Mama stared at Granny Nan, her mouth hanging slack. "Why have I never heard that word before?"

"I do not know. I suppose because we always referred to it as the…"

"The bowl. You always called it 'the bowl.' I used to hide my face and stifle a laugh when I had to set the table because you told me to be sure and put out the plates and *bowls*."

Granny Nan snorted, which she often did when something struck her as extra funny—one of the numerous things I always loved about her—and she reflexively put her hand over her mouth.

Mama put her hands on her hips. "And to set the record straight, we now call it a 'potty'." She could not maintain her angry façade. They both burst out laughing.

We did not have beds at our house, only sleeping pallets on the floor and in the loft. So it stands to reason that I had never seen or heard of a gusunda either, nor a potty, nor the bowl. Like an untrained puppy, I simply did my business whenever and wherever the urge struck. There was a tiny building a ways off to the side of our cabin that was specifically off-limits to me. It had a door on the side that faced away from the cabin, and there was a piece of wood nailed next to the door, way up high where I could not reach; that piece of wood swiveled sideways to keep the door shut, or it stayed in an up-and-down position when someone went in. Mama, Granny Nan, and Papa all went in there during the day, but because Mama had made it a point to warn me that I might disappear and never come back if I went in there, I kept a safe distance between it and me. I knew it did not catch and keep adults—they always came out after a while—but it certainly was not meant for little people like myself. And besides, it smelled bad. And it smelled especially bad if the wind was blowing toward our cabin, so I was not very interested in it. It was the one thing that did not capture my curiosity.

The laughing finally calmed down. "I just think she is too small to be taken out there and made to do her business," Mama finally said, pointing in the direction of the little building.

Granny Nan shook her head and sighed. "She is your child, Violet, so you have the final say."

That night, just before dark, Mama took me on my first trip to the outhouse. I did not understand what was going on. Mama said nothing to me the whole way from the cabin to the little building. I was beyond confused; I was terrified. Had I done something so bad that Mama was going to get rid of me? If she put me in there, I knew I would disappear and not come back; she had told me so. I cried and screamed. I pulled against the hand that held me—my own mother's hand—as she dragged me to my doom. What would meet me as she opened the door to that little building? What fate awaited me? I was just a tiny person. I had not had a chance to grow up. I thought, *Oh, someone please save me!* I wailed at the top of my lungs.

Then I had an idea: I went completely limp, just dangled from Mama's hand. I knew that, any second, she would look down at me and burst into tears. She would say, "What have I done to my baby?" But she continued to drag me toward the place I most feared. Had she no compassion? Could she feel no guilt? "No, Mama! No! Not go!"

She stopped. She looked up at the sky and said, "God, please forgive me." Then she looked back at our cabin. Granny Nan was standing outside the door with her arms crossed over her chest. *She will save me!*

Mama picked me up, hugged me, and we walked back to the cabin. Not a word was spoken between the two most important women in my life. But I looked up at Mama's face as we went through the door. She was smiling.

I realized later in life that Mama was trying to make a point to Granny Nan, but neither of them had tried to reason with *me* before the event. Why would I *not* be scared to death, being dragged to a place I feared more than any other in the world? I know Mama eventually saw the error of her ways. But she had won her battle: I was not introduced to the concept of toilet training until after my second birthday, which may have been due in part to the birth of my sister, Josephina, in April of that year. Mama and Granny Nan were busy taking care of a new baby instead of being concerned with my toilet habits.

THE ARRIVAL OF YOSIE

Papa loved citing profound quotes (and even authoring his own) for every situation. He had always been interested in names, so much so that he had formulated his own adage about them and often recited it with his German accent spilling into the words: "If you vant a man to be famous, he must be given a name that vill prompt the eventual achievement of fame." Mama said he was polite enough to ask her opinion regarding their children's names, but when push came to shove, her opinion did not mean squat.

Papa's given name was Heinrich, and his papa's name had been Wilhelm. Papa came from "goot Deutsch stock," and he wanted his offspring to perpetuate that. While I was still in the womb, he had determined I was going to be a boy, destined to carry on his German heritage; therefore, my name was to be Wilhelm (with the W pronounced as a V) in honor of my grandfather. Mama told me that only once did she suggest I might be a girl, but Papa would hear none of it.

Thus, I became Wilhelmina, Helmi for short. Mama said she started calling me Willie, but Papa said that degraded his father's reputation. So Granny Nan stepped up to the plate. "You do not like Willie as a nickname," she stated matter-of-factly to Papa. "So what do you suggest we call her? I am not going to say 'Vilhelmina' every time I want to get her attention; that is too big a mouthful." Papa did not answer, so Granny Nan began calling me Helmi, and it stuck. Even Papa called me by that name, but only at home, never in public.

❖❖❖

If opposites truly do attract, then Mama and Papa fit the bill. Mama, whose name was Violet, was easy-going and fun-loving and, befitting to her name, a true flower child, though that term was not coined until about eighty years after her birth on January 20, 1891. She loved nature, just like Granny Nan, but after marrying Papa, Mama did not have the opportunity to roam the outdoors as much as she would have liked. She did have a flower garden, in name only, which was a patch of ground about three feet square. She was only able to coax a few species of wildflowers up through the dirt every spring. They consisted mostly of stems with a few tiny malformed leaves and even fewer buds and blooms. Papa told her she was wasting both her time and water on the poor, scraggly specimens, but she went to the creek and got a pitcher of water every day—sometimes twice a day (probably just to get out of the house)—to keep them growing. She once said to Papa, "Even one flower makes the whole place look prettier. Do you not think so, Heinrich?"

Papa only grumbled in German.

Granny Nan (Nancy) was not only Mama's mother but also her backbone. I assumed that Granny Nan's husband (and therefore, my grandfather), Buster, had died long before I was born, and that was why I did not know much about him. And Granny Nan did not offer up any information about him, either. As a child I respected that. I could only guess what he had been like in his youth. I asked Mama about her father once, but she said, "We do not talk about him, dear." And that was that. Things were just that way in the early post World War I days. And I accepted it.

I used to make up stories about Buster. After all, he was an enigma, so I could think of him any way I wanted. Sometimes I thought of him as a brave soldier in France or Belgium or England or Germany, fighting in the trenches or commanding his armies. I pretended I was Granny Nan and would swoon when I saw him coming home from the war, decorated with ribbons and medals. Or I would break down in make-believe tears when he was reported as wounded, or worse. Sometimes I pictured him as a poor dirt farmer with a wife and children who needed him at home, so he was sad because he could not go to war. And sometimes I pictured him as an outlaw in the Kansas Territory, a man with a wild heart who could not stand the confines of a farm, so he left his family behind and became a gunslinger, shooting people and robbing banks or trains.

❖❖❖

My papa wanted one thing in his life: sons. After his disappointment with me not being a Wilhelm but a Wilhelmina, he was ready and waiting for Joseph (he pronounced it YO-zef) when Mama gave birth on April 18, 1922. Joseph was, instead, Josephina (yo-zef-EE-na).

Yosie was everything I was not—calm, quiet, satisfied simply to exist. She seldom cried, loved to be carried around and molly-coddled, and to top it off, she had natural dark brown curls and a smile that could light up a room. What a charmer!

I can recall a few things about the morning she was born. I was still asleep on the pallet where Granny Nan and I slept under the loft. The sun had only begun to appear over the horizon, so the cabin was barely lit when I heard Mama scream. I thought she was being butchered by some wild Indian, so I covered my head and tried to lie very still and become as flat as I could, as if I were merely a bump in the linens. Then I heard Granny Nan ask Mama, "Do you want Heinrich to be here? I can send Helmi out to the barn to get him."

I lowered the comforter ever so slowly and quietly, and I looked over at Mama, who was bent over the table, holding herself up with both hands. Granny Nan had one arm around Mama's shoulders. She glanced in my direction for a fraction of a second.

I was frantic and began bawling and wailing, "Mama sick? Mama? Mama!" By now I was up and stumbling toward my mother, my face wet with tears and my heart pounding.

Granny Nan let go of Mama and calmly walked toward me with her hands held out. "You do not need to be afraid. This is a joyful time, Helmi."

I stopped dead in my tracks and looked up at her, my innocence trusting that whatever she said must be true. She picked me up, and I took immediate comfort in her arms.

Mama said, "Nothing is wrong, Helmi. I am having a baby. Granny Nan is going to help you get dressed so you can go down to the barn and tell Papa."

The door opened, and Papa appeared. "I heard you all the vay down to the barn, Violet," he said to Mama. Then he looked at Granny Nan. "It is time, ja?" She nodded.

Everything from that moment on is blurred in my memory. I cannot even remember where Mama had the baby. I am guessing it was either on the pallet where Granny Nan and I slept, or maybe they moved our comforter to the table, and she had the baby there. I do not know if Mama did more screaming or if Granny Nan and Papa kept her quiet. I simply cannot remember. I only remember playing in front of the fireplace while the entire thing happened. I was oblivious to the whole event, whether due to fear or due to confidence in their ability to take care of it. I was in a self-concocted world, and I do not even remember how long the birthing took.

Some time later—hours or days—Mama asked me to sit down in the rocking chair Papa had made and given her on their wedding day, the "wedding rocker," as she called it. Then she bent down and handed me the tiny bundle that was Yosie. "That is what was in my belly," she said, her face beaming. I had never seen Mama look like that before. It was at that moment I realized a woman could be pretty. I smiled at her and then looked down at the baby who was red and wrinkled and smelled new and sweet, and I smiled a little bigger.

"Her name is Yosephina," Mama said softly.

"A girl?" I asked, not looking up.
"Yes. You have a beautiful sister."

I had no idea, of course, that Yosie's birth would be the first of many more to come. I was overjoyed at having a playmate. I planned to make up games that were all about her and me. I pretended we were going to a ball, and Mama had asked me to dress her up; I dreamed of finding a beautiful yellow dress in a hollowed-out tree, and the dress had jewels on it that sparkled in the sunshine. Or I pretended I was a queen, and Yosie was my daughter who had been stolen from me but was found in a nearby Indian village by a tracker who traded furs with the tribe and could speak their language. Or perhaps Yosie and I had both been captured by the Indians and did not understand why we could not go home, so we whispered to each other and figured out a way to escape when the Indians were not looking.

It is difficult to imagine that, when I was a child, there was a distinct fear of the natives who roamed the land around our Oklahoma panhandle home. Mama, Papa, and Granny Nan had only seen them once near our cabin before I was born; the natives were simply watching from a distance. But Indians were to be feared; Papa had heard and read stories about the "savages" who captured women and children and did horrific things to them, then turned their captives into Indians and never let them go back to their families.

Of course, it is also difficult to determine how much truth there had been in the tabloids of the mid-1800s. Granny Nan was terrified. She was far more fearful of the "red man" than Mama and Papa. I can only guess that, while having been raised in Indiana and making the trek to Oklahoma during her teens, she had witnessed some of the horrors that had been inflicted on the "white man" during her family's migration south and west.

Indiana had become a state in 1816, and in 1850, the year Granny Nan was born, Indiana was no longer considered a part of the American frontier. Instead, half of the population of that state already had either brick or frame houses, not log cabins. Much of the rural population (farmers) owned their holdings rather than renting from landowners. Moving to Oklahoma from Indiana in 1868, so soon after the end of the Civil War, had undoubtedly been a step down the social ladder for Granny Nan's family. I did not realize this until long after Granny Nan was gone, so I never had reason to ask her about it. Nevertheless, part of her strong constitution had been brought about by exposure to a land that was still considered wild when she became an Oklahoma Sooner. And she was not afraid to fill me with the same fear she had of the Native Americans.

I have lived near reservations throughout my nearly one hundred years of existence, and my feelings regarding the Native Americans have traveled through a myriad of emotions—fear, acceptance, pathos, respect. But when I look back on Granny Nan's feelings about them, I can understand how profoundly her lack of education about native customs could have shaped her feelings. Fear of the unknown holds a powerful weapon over one's head.

I wanted Yosie to be with me every minute of every day. Being an only child for a year-and-a-half had proven to have its advantages, but in my mind, having a playmate for life was a much greater opportunity—a dream I could make come true. I tried to get her to go to the barn with Papa and me; I wanted her to love the animals as I did. I wanted her to be there with me when I helped Mama gather eggs from the henhouse. I wanted her to talk to Papa the way I always had and to listen to his stories about Germany and the time he had spent in his homeland. But Yosie had other ideas.

From early on, it was obvious that Yosie was not interested in the things I was. At first it was difficult for me to accept. When Yosie made her mind up, there was no changing it. "That child is the most obstinate creature on God's Great Earth!" Granny Nan would say, pursing her lips and throwing her hands in the air in frustration when Yosie would glare at her, just daring Granny Nan to *make* her do whatever it was that she had no intentions of doing.

Yosie was a mama's girl. She loved being with Mama and only Mama. When she was a mere infant, she would lie in the cradle and intently watch Mama cook or mend or read or sing. If one of us tried to talk to Mama, Yosie fussed and fidgeted. If Granny Nan or Papa picked Yosie up, she cried. But when Mama picked her up, she cooed and smiled. She never cried when Mama rocked her in the cradle or held her and rocked her to sleep while sitting in the wedding rocker. But when anyone else tried to do the same, Yosie would have none of it.

Her preference for Mama continued throughout her childhood. She did everything Mama wanted her to do and nothing anyone else asked of her. And Mama seemed oblivious to how badly she was spoiling Yosie. I came to realize that Yosie's clinging to Mama created ill feelings from the rest of us toward the child, and a gap developed between Yosie and us.

I was jealous of her because she dominated Mama's attention and affection. Granny Nan had little to do with her, only completing the bare necessities when Mama asked, such as changing Yosie's diaper now and then or feeding her when Mama was busy with something else. Even then, Granny Nan had to fight with Yosie in order to accomplish such menial tasks. I can remember the alterations in Granny Nan's attitude and the sourness that appeared on her face when she was busy trying to take care of a child who obviously did not want anyone but Mama doing things for her.

After a while, Papa basically gave up trying to get close to Yosie. She had no intention of going to the barn with him; she turned her head and pouted when he talked to her; she refused to sit on his lap or ride with him on Trot. Yosie loved only one person, and to that one person she gave her all. But I think it made me closer to Papa and Granny Nan.

Yosie was a stunning child. I look back on her infancy and see her as a spitting image of the 1950s' Gerber baby: round face, rosy-cheeks, big twinkling eyes, chestnut brown curls, prominent dark pink lips. When she reached toddlerhood, she could have been the twin of Darla from the Little Rascals. I never saw another girl whose looks came close to matching those popular icons. When Yosie flashed her alluring smile, people melted.

I was not ugly, but I was not beautiful, either, with my mousy brown hair, gray eyes, and thin lips. I might have been somewhat attractive, but no man was ever going to write poetry about my face. I had no idea, of course, that in time Yosie's looks would be her downfall. Beauty is not all it is cracked up to be.

TWO BABIES AND BEAVER CITY

When Mama's belly got big again, I realized it meant I was going to have another sibling. I should have been excited, but because Yosie had not been the playmate I had hoped for, I had my doubts about another baby being any different. Oh, there was a glimmer of hope in the back of my mind, but even at age three I was not foolish enough to let that glimmer dominate my anticipation of a new brother or sister.

Mama was moving slower than she had when she was pregnant with Yosie, and her belly was a whole lot bigger. I was sure this was going to be a boy. In the stories Mama and Granny Nan read to Yosie and me, the males were always large and strong, the females tiny and helpless. I had not been exposed to any literature that presented the sexes in any other form. I was not sure how I fit in, because I was not big and muscular, though neither was I miniscule and defenseless. I pondered this a lot, but not enough to alter my attitude to match what I had been told. I was my own person, and no one was going to change that, no matter how often I heard the references regarding male stature versus that of a female.

On the afternoon of December 11, 1923, Mama went into labor. Papa made the comment, "There vill be two, Nancy. You can bet your life on it."

I was not sure what he meant. Two? Two what? I did not realize Mama was about to have twins. Unbeknownst to me, Papa's father had been a twin, so they ran in the family.

I was much more interested in Mama's delivery this time, since I had seen so many animal births taking place around the homestead. I discovered it was not much different for people, except that Mama did a lot more screaming and sweating than the cows or sheep or pigs. And I remember thinking that, until that precise moment, I had not taken into consideration the fact that chickens lay eggs which sometimes hatched into chicks, whereas the other animals had live babies that came out of their bodies. Life was becoming more and more fascinating.

My job throughout the birthing ordeal was to sit next to Mama and keep a cool cloth on her forehead while Granny Nan talked her through the events leading up to the actual delivery. And Granny Nan was in the right place to catch the baby when it came out. I felt extremely important; Granny Nan told me I had a big responsibility that required me to do my best. I was then, and continue to be, conscientious about my duties.

Isabella and Isadora (Bella and Dora) were born in the early morning of December 12, 1923. They both had red hair and fair skin, and they had enormous heads and skinny little bodies. I remember Granny Nan whispering to Papa, "Do you think they are all right?" I did not hear Papa's response, but I later found out that, according to Doc Weiser, Mama had probably been malnourished during her pregnancy, so the twins had not gotten as big as they should have. Their heads were of normal size, but because their bodies were so small, their heads appeared oddly enlarged.

To make matters more bizarre, Dora had a huge pinkish brown birthmark that covered most of her left cheek. It ran from her nose to her ear and was about two inches wide at the widest point, directly under her eye. It would become an important part of her adult life.

❖❖❖

Papa was quite the craftsman when it came to woodworking. He had built the "wedding rocker" for Mama and a cradle for any babies who came into their lives. He had had the foresight to build our cabin big enough to accommodate Mama and him and a couple of children, as well as provide enough room for Granny Nan. It was one of the few cabins out on the prairie that had an extra extension off the main building; this room was divided into a loft and a sleeping space under it.

By the time the twins were born, Granny Nan and I were no longer sleeping on a pallet on the floor; Papa had built us each a bed. Mama, Papa, and Yosie slept in the loft. In the sleeping space under it, Granny Nan slept in one bed and I in the other. The cradle, which contained the twins, was between our beds. A big open area between the kitchen and hearth room would render ample space for another bed for me when Yosie was old enough to move from the loft and sleep by herself under the loft with Granny Nan.

The way Papa constructed our beds was quite interesting. He only made one leg for each bed. Since each bed sat in a corner, the head and one side were nailed to heavy boards that were attached to the wall; the walls held the majority of the weight, and the single leg supported the bottom outside corner of each bed.

There was storage space under each bed which, of course, had not been there when the floor had been covered with Granny Nan's and my pallet. Mama and Granny Nan talked for several days before deciding what would be put in the space; they finally agreed to use it for extra blankets that had heretofore been stored in Granny Nan's wedding chest, which had a prominent place in the hearth room. The wedding chest graduated to holding their prized possessions—a large blue and white China platter and a beautiful hand-painted blue glass pitcher and drinking glasses that had belonged to Granny Nan's mother. The dishes had spent most of their "lives" wrapped up in flour sacks and stored in a makeshift cabinet in the barn. I had never even seen them. But when they came out of hiding, I was captivated by their beauty, and I still love beautiful dishes to this day. I wished at the time they could have been displayed on the mantle, but, out of necessity, the mantle held practical items instead.

Following the birth of the twins, more jobs were delegated to me. While Yosie's job was to sit around and look pretty, mine was to keep the cabin picked up and make sure it was presentable when people stopped by. That meant I was constantly retrieving the things Yosie threw on the floor and returning them to their respective places. If Papa left his boots out on the stoop, I made sure he cleaned the mud off them, then I put them where they belonged—on the small welcome mat just inside the door. If Mama left the everyday dishes to dry after being washed, I put them in the cupboard under the pump. If she or Granny Nan dropped a clothespin when they took the washing off the line, I was the one who was to put the clothespin back in the clothespin bag (funny how they seemed to drop at least one every time they gathered the clothes off the line). But the biggest job of all was that I had become solely responsible for feeding the chickens. Mama still had to help me gather eggs, though.

When I was not working my fingers to the bone (all that responsibility for a girl who was only three), I spent time with Papa in the barn or with Granny Nan learning to do embroidery and some sewing or with Mama working in the garden or her flower bed. Otherwise, Yosie and the twins kept them busy.

One day I was watching Mama make bread. "Mama, can I have a baby?"

"You want one of the twins?"

"No. *Have* one."

"Ohhh. Do you mean now or when you grow up?"

"Now."

"Why do you want one? Are Yosie and the twins not enough?"

"Um...I want mine."

"I see." She stopped kneading and looked at me for a long time. "You have a lot of things to do around the cabin. Are you sure you would have time to do all of your chores if you have to take care of your own baby?"

That had never occurred to me. I had been selfishly wishing I could have someone my own age to play with. "Well...a baby in my belly (I was thinking on my feet here) could get old as me before it comes out. We do my jobs, then we play."

Granny Nan, who had been listening to our conversation while making some yarn at our spinning wheel, spoke up. "Violet, how many children her age have the wisdom to work through something like that in their minds? She has it all figured out. It may have some loopholes, but the concept is *genius*." I had no idea what "genius" meant, but I could tell it was something good, just by the way Granny Nan had spoken the word. She turned to me; she was all smiles. "You are too smart for your own good," she said to me. "But how would you go about keeping a baby inside you so it could grow to be old enough to help you when it came out?"

I was stumped.

Mama said, "Why not think about it for a while, Helmi, and let us know when you have an answer."

"How does a baby get in here?" I poked myself in the stomach.

"God will put one there when your body is ready," Mama said, and she went back to kneading the dough she was preparing for two loaves of bread.

Yosie, realizing she was no longer the center of attention, grunted and spat out a little cry. Mama immediately turned her attention to Yosie. Granny Nan looked at Mama, pursed her lips, and went back to her spinning, vigorously pumping the foot treadle as if it needed to be punished for not turning the wheel faster.

I went over to the cradle where the twins were sleeping feet-to-feet, Bella with her head at the top of the cradle and Dora with her head at the bottom. It was easy to tell them apart because of Dora's birthmark.

"Will it go away?" I asked.

"Will what go away, Helmi?" Granny Nan responded before Mama had a chance to speak.

"That...her face." I pointed to Dora's face.

"No, dear. It is called a birthmark. It will be there from the day she was born until the day she leaves this earth."

"Looks like Betsy's face." Betsy was a scraggly, long-haired, brown and white spotted dog Papa had found abandoned along the road on his way home from Beaver City one day about a year back.

She did, in fact, have a large brown spot on one side of her face.

"Helmi!" Mama shouted at me. Her voice made me jump, "You are NOT to say un-nice things about your sister."

Now I was confused. I had not meant to be un-nice; I was just stating a fact. In no way had I intended it to be taken as an insult. I loved Betsy, and I did not think the spot on her face made her look odd or bad or funny anymore than I thought such a thing about Dora's birthmark.

I started to cry, and Granny Nan came to my rescue. She took me by the hand and led me out onto the stoop, closing the door behind her. "Helmi," she said quietly, "your mama is very concerned about the mark on Dora's face. She is afraid it will make Dora's life difficult because she will look different from other children." She held me close and whispered in my ear, "You must be certain you never mention it again."

"Does the mark hurt?"

"No. Dora does not even know it is there. But one day someone who sees it might possibly say something about it to Dora that would make her cry."

"I like it. She should not cry."

"You have a special heart, Helmi. But please do not say anything about it in front of Mama."

"Mama not likes it?"

"Mama thinks it is pretty, too, but she worries that someone will hurt Dora's feelings about it one day. Not everyone is as understanding as you, Helmi."

I did not understand. But I knew I would never talk to Mama about it again.

Regarding the lack of contractions in Mama's, Papa's, and Granny Nan's speech…

It is a known fact that contractions were used as far back as Roman times. But because Papa was German, he had learned to speak "the King's English," which came without contractions. Nancy's family seldom used them because Nancy's grandfather was of the opinion that contractions made a person sound unrefined, hailing as he did from New England society. Although he moved the family to Indiana where contractions were commonly used in everyday language, he stuck to his guns about retaining the family image as upper echelon, so it merely became a habit for Nancy to speak the same way. And since she spoke with the absence of contractions, her daughters followed suit.

Papa took me to Beaver City for the first time soon after the twins were born. "Since you are such a goot helper, I vill take you tomorrow." Mama usually went with him. Occasionally Granny Nan would go, but Mama needed to be home to feed Bella and Dora, and she did not want to "wrestle" with them on the trip. She also needed Granny Nan's help with things I was not able to do, so Papa said he would take me instead. I was filled with pride at being asked to do such a huge and important job.

I was used to being with Papa, since I had spent so much time with him in the barn. I knew how to help him hook up the draft horse to the buckboard, which means I could hand him the right pieces of equipment at the right time. Some of the leather pieces, like the reins, were long and heavy, but he had shown me how to loop them over my head and shoulder so I could carry their weight. There were bells on one of the straps, and I loved hearing them jingle when the horse was trotting or when it shook its head.

The horse was a Percheron, an extremely large creature with gargantuan feet, especially through the eyes of a three-year-old. Percherons have the reputation of being gentle giants, as they tend not to have a mean bone in their bodies. Our Percheron's name was Ham. My entire body was hardly as big as his head, but when he lowered that head to sniff me, I patted him on the nose and gave him a kiss. I loved Ham, and he knew it. And Papa knew Ham loved me—and carrots.

Part of our garden plot consisted of two rows of carrots. When they were harvested, Papa made sure half of them were kept whole in the root cellar so he always had one to give Ham as a reward whenever he came back to the barn after working, and that included completing a trip to and from Beaver City. I hoped I would be allowed to give Ham his carrot after we got back late that evening.

Beaver City was thirty miles to the east of our farm. Papa said, "It vill take a long time to get there, Helmi, and a long time to come back home." Most of the times Mama and Papa went there, they took something to sell or trade. This time we were taking five dozen eggs that Mama and I had gathered over the last three days. It being December, the root cellar was plenty cool and had kept them from spoiling. They would bring us enough money, or enough in trade, to get the groceries and some other things we needed. It might even be enough for me to get a lollipop or a strawberry taffy cream or maybe even a stick of horehound. But I knew I had to be very "goot" for that to happen.

The sun had just risen above the horizon when we left. Papa had loaded the buckboard the night before (except for the eggs and our dinner). He had made sure to tie everything down tightly since we had so far to go and did not know what to expect along the roads. "You vill need to help me look for holes and bumps," Papa warned me as we crossed our yard and headed toward the two-track. "Sometimes they are hiding and do not show up until you are almost on top of them."

"Ham watches, too," I informed him.

"And you know this to be a fact?" he asked me.

"Yes. Ham is a smart horse."

"Ja, that he is." I saw the corners of his mouth turn up in a smile, though he did not look at me. That's one of the things I liked best about Papa. He treated me like an equal instead of a child. I knew it was a grown-up thing that people did not always look at each other when they talked. But most grown-ups seemed to think they had to look right at children when they spoke to them.

On the way to town Papa and I talked about a lot of things: the lack of the color green, the sun low in the sky, not like in summer when the sun was much higher and warmer, the depth of the ruts in the road, some of which had been made by motor cars. Papa told me Ford automobiles were becoming more popular in the towns and cities around us, and that someday he hoped he could afford one. On our way to Beaver City, two motor cars passed us. I had never seen one before. I could not believe my eyes—there was no horse pulling them! They made Ham a little bit nervous; he stopped, knickered, and raised his head up and down when each of them passed us.

"It is goot that the livery stable is on the vest side of town," Papa said after the second motor car passed us. "Do you think so too, Helmi?"

I nodded my head in agreement.

"Helmi, do you think so, too?"

"Yes, Papa. I told you with my head."

"I did not hear you," he said.

"Again, I nodded."

"Vell, I cannot hear the rocks rolling around in your head. You need to *speak* to me instead."

I giggled.

We reached Beaver City and dropped off the buckboard and horse at the stable. Papa picked up the basket of eggs and checked to make sure none had broken. Then he handed me a can that contained our dinner. I set the can on the ground, pulled off the lid, and took out one of the packets.

"Vhat are you doing?" he asked me.

"Dinner," I said and looked at him as if he were simple. (In the early 1920s, the three meals of the day were breakfast, dinner or midday meal, and supper.)

"Not here. I know a goot place. Put that back. Ve vill have a picnic." He helped me put the packet back in the can, took me by the hand, and we walked to Main Street.

I looked one way and then the other, and my mouth dropped open. Motor cars were racing back and forth. Stores with fancy, brightly painted signs lined the street as far as I could see…both ways. Men and women, and even children, were walking on raised boardwalks in front of all the stores, and all the people were dressed in Sunday clothes. Some of the shopkeepers with white aprons were leaning against the doorways, and people greeted each other and the shopkeepers as they walked past. Some of the stores had giant windows, and there were things in the windows. The store directly across from us had a woman wearing a dress, but she did not have a head or arms or legs! It was the scariest thing I had ever seen.

"Wilhelmina, you are shaking!" Papa laughed. "Are you excited?"

I could not answer; my mouth just hung open, and I was breathing extra fast, my heart pounding so hard in my ears I could not hear. The dinner can fell from my arm, and I was too terrified to reach down and pick it up. I started to cry.

"Wilhelmina, sveetie. Vhat is the matter?" He swept me up and hugged me.

I was sure I was going to die. I latched onto his collar with both hands. He would have to pry my dead fingers from it. I was finally able to spit out, "Scared. Scared, Papa."

"I am right here, and you can hang on tight to me until you are no longer afraid." He began to walk slowly to the left, away from the awful image of that headless, limbless woman in the window across the street.

"Papa, wait! Dinner!" I pointed back at the can I had dropped, and he turned back toward it.

"You vill have to help me," he said, "because I can only carry two things: either the eggs and you, or the eggs and the dinner can. Vhat vill it be, Wilhelmina?"

I could not let Papa down. I had to be brave. I pointed to the can again. "You pick it up. I carry it, but you carry me, too." I had figured out an alternate plan that neatly fit my agenda.

Papa looked at me, then he threw his head back and laughed. "You are such a smart vun. All right, I carry you and the eggs, and you carry the dinner can." He bent down and grabbed the can, which he handed to me, and the four of us—Papa, eggs, dinner can, Helmi—

went down the sidewalk with Papa laughing and shaking his head.

"Heinrich! Wie geht's?" (How's it going?) a man shouted at us.

Papa looked ahead and shouted, "Sehr gut!" (Very good!) He picked up his pace a bit.

After passing three more stores, I spotted the man who had shouted; he was standing in a doorway and was wearing an apron covered in blood! What was this place? Was he going to kill me? Had I died and gone to Hell? Mama and Granny Nan and the preacher at church had all said we go there if we do bad things. I did not remember being bad, but maybe I had been bad without knowing it.

"Johann!" Papa said, put down the basket of eggs, and shook the man's hand. The blood did not seem to bother Papa at all.

"Wer ist das?" (Who is this?) the man asked, looking at me.

"Meine Tochter." (My daughter.)

"Wie heißt?" (Her name?) Johann asked.

"Wilhelmina. Sie ist nach meinem Vater benannt." (She is named after my father.)

"Ah, gut, gut." (Ah, good, good.) "Aber sie ist kein Sohn." (But she is not a son.)

"Ja, das ist richtig. Aber ich habe mehr Zeit, Söhne zu haben. Ich bin noch nicht tot!" (Yes, that is correct. But I still have time to have sons. I am not dead yet!) Both men laughed. I stared at the man's apron. His eyes followed mine.

"I am sorry, little one. I am a butcher, and blood goes with butchering." I continued to stare at his apron.

"Wilhelmina? Can you say hello to Johann?" Papa asked softly. My eyes did not move. He shook me up and down on his hip to break my gaze, and my eyes traveled from the man's apron to his face. He had a nice face; it was smiling. His whole face smiled, not just his lips.

"Hello," I said softly. I hardly had enough breath left to speak.

"Ist das Ihre erste Reise in die Stadt?" (Is this her first visit to the city?) he asked Papa.

"Ja," Papa said.

"Well, little one, I am happy to meet you. There are many things to see and do here in the city. I see you have a dinner can. Are you going to have a picnic?"

I nodded; it was the best I could manage.

"Come, then. We go to the park." He shouted something in German to another man in the butcher shop, then he untied his apron and pulled it up over his head. He hung the apron on a hook just inside the door and picked up the basket of eggs. "These should go in the cooler." He disappeared for half a minute and returned with something wrapped in white paper. Then he, Papa, and I walked a little farther down the street to where there was an opening between two buildings. In that opening was the park. It had two trees and a tiny pond, and there were two tables with benches attached to them. Johann sat down on one side of one of the tables and motioned for us to sit on the other side. "You have been on the road a long time if you came in that horse-drawn buckboard of yours. You are ready to eat, Ja?"

Papa took the dinner can from me, sat me down, then opened the can and passed a fried chicken leg to me that Mama or Granny Nan had wrapped in paraffine paper. There were two pieces of chicken for Papa and a boiled egg for each of us, along with a piece of bread, which Papa divided between us. "Ve vill get something to drink vhen ve are finished," Papa said. "I know a place that sells root beer."

I looked at him like he was crazy. "Root beer?" It sounded awful to me. I wondered what kind of root was used to make beer. And why would he want me to drink it? I was too young for beer.

"Oh, ja," Johann said. "You will like it. Have you ever had sassafras?"

I was completely lost. Root beer? Sassafras? What were they talking about? I would have been perfectly happy with a glass of nice cold water. But Papa could be trusted, so if he wanted me to have root beer, I guess I would have root beer.

Johann opened the package wrapped in white paper, which turned out to be a sandwich made with some kind of meat and cheese. We rarely had sandwiches at home; Mama said it was a waste of bread, because a sandwich used double the amount of bread a person should eat at any one meal. Johann pulled a tomato out of his pocket and ate it like an apple. We continued to eat, and Papa and Johann talked in German to one another.

I turned around on the bench and saw some ducks walking toward the pond. "Papa, look!" I pointed to them. I had seen pictures of ducks, and I had seen real live ducks flying overhead, but none of them had ever landed close enough for me to inspect. They were beautiful. Their feathers were slick and reflected blues and greens. Their eyes were round and looked in every direction as they walked. Their legs were dull yellow, and their feet were flat with little toenails that curved downward. They waddled, just the way I had pictured them when Granny Nan had read to me about them from one of the books she kept beside her bed. I was enraptured. I wanted a duck. I would have to think about how I could manage to get one. "Can I pet it?"

Johann said, "You can try, but they don't usually like being touched by people."

I looked at Papa for permission to get up from the table. "Go on," he said, "but do not fall into the pond. You have no dry clothes other than vhat you are vearing."

Johann had been right. I could not come within ten feet of it before it flew a short distance away from me. I tried and tried to call it and talk softly to it, but it avoided me. *Maybe a duck would not be such a good pet after all*, I thought.

When it was time to go back into the butcher shop, I was much less afraid. I knew now what a butcher was—I had figured it out. We butchered our own animals, so the blood on Johann's apron was no longer a mystery. Johann said he could definitely use the eggs, and he asked Papa, "Do you want to sell them to me, or do you want to make a trade?"

"I do not need meat this time, Johann. Ve butchered a sheep, so the root cellar is full of mutton. I vill take vhatever money you can give me for the eggs, though. You alvays treat me fairly."

Papa and Johann finished their business, and Papa and I moved on. I was still in awe of all the people and stores, and I was hoping we did not have to go to the store with the headless, limbless woman in the window. Papa took my hand, and we continued walking in the direction we had been going until we reached a general store. Papa stood back away from the counter while he perused the shelves, checking the prices. Finally, we went up to the woman who was standing behind the counter.

There, right in front of me, was a candy jar full of horehound sticks. My mouth began to water. I lost all contact with the world around me, save for that jar. I was picking out the exact stick I wanted, when I heard Papa say to the woman, "...and a horehound stick."

The woman picked up the jar and pulled one from it. *Could it be the one I had decided would be the perfect stick? The stick I had waited for my whole life? The one that would taste better than any of the others in that jar?* I could not make out which one she had chosen for me. My shoulders drooped. I would have to take the one she handed me. I reached for it, ready to thank her. "That is it!" I shouted. I recognized it as the one I had had my eye on, because it had an extra little bump next to the stick.

I reached for it, but Papa intercepted it in mid-air. "You have to choose, Wilhelmina. Do you vant this now and forego the root beer, or do you vant to try some of that root beer I promised you and eat the horehound on your vay home?"

Why, oh why does it have to be a choice? My mouth could already taste the candy. *But if I eat it now, I will not get to try the root beer Papa promised.* I sighed. "Wrap it up," I said to the woman behind the counter. She smiled.

Papa leaned down close to my ear and said, "Goot choice."

We crossed the street and continued to go to other stores, the post office, and the book shop. I had to help Papa carry some of the packages he bought, and they had gotten heavier by the time we reached the store with the headless, limbless woman in the window. I came to a dead halt; Papa went on. After a few steps, he realized I was not beside him. He turned to me and said, "Come, Wilhelmina."

I shook my head.

"Vhat is wrong?"

I pointed to the window, not moving my arm, only my index finger.

Papa looked in the window, turned back to me, and said, "I do not understand. Do you vant something you see inside?"

Again, I shook my head. My knees were knocking, and my breathing was shallow. Did he not see the poor dead woman, nothing but her body covered in that dress? I was frozen to the spot, could not move.

Papa looked in the window again. "Do you vant that dress?"

Why would I want that dress? The dress of a dead woman? What is he thinking? Has he lost his mind? My eyes must have grown three times their normal size.

He came back to me and bent down. "Vhat is wrong?"

He must have been temporarily blinded. "That woman," I whispered. "No legs or arms. No head!"

He looked at the dress form on which the dress was displayed, and the answer finally sunk in. He started to laugh but stifled it as best he could. "Wilhelmina. That is not a voman. It is called a dress form. It is nothing but fence vire underneath in the shape of a voman. The store owner uses it to show off how goot a seamstress she is. She makes dresses for mamas and suits for papas, and she vants the people passing by to see them. Come. Look closer." He walked right up to the window and motioned for me to come stand beside him.

I had to do what he said. Papa had never put me in danger. I gulped. Then I closed my eyes and walked toward him. When I felt him in front of me, I grabbed his pants leg and stopped. It took every ounce of trust I had in him to look up and see the form in the window. I was short enough to be able to see underneath it, and Papa had been right. The dress was hanging on wire that had been shaped to look like a woman's body. And right behind it was another form that the seamstress was covering with a man's suit. I had been scared to death by fence wire! My cheeks were burning, and I knew they were red; I was so embarrassed.

We continued—without going into that store—to one that had a sign sitting in front of it on the boardwalk. Painted on the sign was a big glass with a handle; it was filled with a brown liquid and was overflowing with something that looked like cream. "What that say, Papa?" I asked as I pointed.

"It says, 'Root Beer, Right Here.' I think ve have found the right place."

We went inside, and the place smelled wonderful. It was a sweet smell, and as my eyes adjusted, I was able to see a counter that had seats in front of it. The seats were round, backless, and sat atop silver posts. The tops of the seats were covered with shiny red material. Papa stepped aside, bowed, and motioned with his hand for me to pick out a seat. I went right to the middle of the counter and tried to climb up onto one of the seats, but I was a bit too short, so Papa helped me.

After positioning myself and smoothing my skirt, I allowed my eyes to wander. What I took in was awe-inspiring. There were jars and jars of tiny candies and nuts lining the shelves on the wall behind the counter. There were rows of tall glass dishes that were wide at the top and tapered at the bottom. There were large heavy glasses stacked on top of each other, and they looked just like the one on the sign out front. And beside all the dishes and glasses was a jar that held spoons with extra-long handles.

A young man with a funny-looking white hat came up to us on the other side of the counter, leaned on his elbows right in front of me, and asked, "What'll ya have?" His face had no hair on it, and his sun-browned skin was smooth. He had black hair that hung out from under the front of the hat and curved around his forehead. He smelled really good, but not sweet like the air in the room. His eyes were the lightest shade of blue I had ever seen, and they were topped with long dark eyelashes. He looked at me and winked. I was in love.

"Ve vould like two root beers, please," Papa said.

"Two RB's, comin' right up."

I watched him grab two of the big, thick glasses with handles and flip them up into the air. They each did a complete rotation, and he caught them by their handles. He put one of the glasses under a spigot (only it was much smaller than the spigot on our pump at home), and he pulled on a handle above the spigot. That rich brown liquid flowed into the glass. As the glass filled, a tan foam formed on the top of the root beer, and before the young man let go of the handle above the spigot, he allowed a little bit of the foam to run over the side of the glass, just like on the sign outside.

I did not even realize I was grinning when he brought the root beers to us. I knew I was going to like it. How could it not be wonderful? I reached for the glass, but I was unable to budge it. Had the young man glued it to the counter? I looked up at Papa.

The young man said, "Kind of heavy?" He winked at me. "I'll help you out." He reached into a box behind him and handed me a long thin paper tube. I took it from him and stared at it. Papa reached over and guided it into the glass, then he lifted the glass down to my level and said, "Suck through the straw."

The only kind of straw I knew was the kind we put in the stalls in the barn for the animals to lie on. I wasn't going to suck through it.

"Vatch me," Papa said. He motioned for the young man to give him one of the tubes, then he put it into his own glass, put his lips around it, and sucked up the root beer; I watched the level of the brown liquid go down in his glass. When he had swallowed it, his eyes rolled back into his head, he smacked his lips, and he said, "Ahhhh!"

Okay. My turn. I put my mouth around the straw, sucked up some of the root beer, then swallowed, wiped my mouth with the back of my hand, and said, "Ahhhh!" Papa and the young man both laughed. And I said, "Ahhhh!" after I finished each slurp. I had discovered the tastiest thing on the face of the planet. And to this day, I still prefer root beer to any other soda pop.

The sun was halfway between the middle of the sky and the western horizon. It was time to head home. We went back to the stable, and Papa tied down the packages we had procured that day. My eyelids were so heavy, I was blinking at half speed. Ham seemed happy to see us, and he held extra still while Papa hitched him to the buckboard. I did not help; I only watched.

When Papa put me up on the seat of the buckboard, he gave me a blanket and a cushion stuffed with wheat straw. I knew exactly what to do with them: I wrapped myself up in the blanket and lay down on the seat, putting the cushion under my head. I do not remember any of the ride home, but it was dark when we got there. Papa carried me into the cabin and handed me to Granny Nan. I had forgotten all about the horehound stick and Ham's carrot.

TWO LETTERS AND A TWISTER

Papa's only brother, Herrmann, lived in Flint, Michigan, where he worked for the auto industry. According to Papa, Herrmann had never felt satisfied being a farmer. It seems he had a "wild hair" (or, to hear Papa say it, a "vild hairrr") and wanted to see other places and do other things. Because Herrmann preferred construction to farming, he moved all around the eastern states doing small building projects until, one day, a big-time construction company manager in Ohio hired him on as an apprentice.

The story goes that Herrmann didn't like the way a building was being erected, so he went to the head of the company and suggested an alternative. "It's not going to remain standing if we build it the way the foreman says we must. Frankly, I don't think he has even considered that there might be a flaw on the blueprint," he told the boss man.

"And just what do *you* propose?" the executive asked him—either he was in an exceptionally good mood, or he had some "dirt" on the foreman; otherwise, he would never have granted this know-nothing apprentice an appointment. "I have every faith in my foreman, son, but I'm open to suggestions."

Herrmann unfolded a copy of the blueprint (which he had essentially stolen from the job site) and explained the fault in the designer's engineering. Turns out, Herrmann was absolutely right! So the current foreman was demoted, and Herrmann took his place. Herrmann continued to climb straight up the corporate ladder for the next two years.

"Managing a construction company is no different from managing a farm," Herrmann wrote to Papa in one of his letters. "Same bad actors, just on a different stage. I want to create something, but I want someone else to be in charge."

The automobile was becoming popular, so in 1918, just ten years after General Motors had become incorporated, Herrmann moved to Flint and became a GM engineer. A couple of years later, he was next in line for a promotion that would earn him almost half again as much as he was currently making, but he turned it down so he could continue doing the thing he loved without having to be a boss.

❖❖❖

"Violet, ve need to talk," Papa said to Mama one night after supper. That meant the rest of us had to find somewhere to be other than in the cabin. It was a pleasant summer evening in 1924, so being outdoors, watching the sunset and waiting for the stars to come out, was fine by me. I had no idea what Papa wanted to talk about, but it had to be something important. The only thing I could even think it might be associated with was that Papa had gotten a letter from Uncle Herrmann a week prior. This would normally have been of no concern, as Papa and Uncle Herrmann communicated at least once a month. But I had seen Papa reading Uncle Herrmann's latest letter over and over when we were in the barn. When he thought I was busy with my chores, he would take it out of his pocket, unfold it, and read it slowly and carefully. Then he would refold it and put it back in his pocket, but his brow became more furrowed after each reading.

❖❖❖

I had gone to Beaver City several more times with Papa, so it had become old hat to me. Our usual schedule was to make the trip every other week. One of the stops in town was always at the post office. We received our mail via general delivery, which means we did not have an actual mailbox. Our mail was addressed to: Heinrich Schnier, Beaver City, Oklahoma c/o General Delivery. That was all. No numbers, no street. Most of the farmers who lived within fifty miles of the city picked up their mail at the same address, the only difference being that their name was on the envelope.

Doc Weiser, who had cared for our family for countless years, owned the property that backed up against ours. The difference between his land and ours was that he owned four times the acres we did. He and Papa had become good friends from the first time they had met. The Weisers were the ones who picked up Mama, Granny Nan, and me each Sunday on their way to church because they had a wagon. Their wagon differed from our buckboard in that it had side walls and could haul loose things, like field corn or grain. Each Sunday Doc put bales of straw in the wagon so everyone had a place to sit. On the Sundays when it was raining or threatened rain—few and far between in the panhandle—he added side extensions and an oilcloth cover to keep us dry. I loved being in the wagon under the cover; the rain made a pitter-patter sound that was not unlike that on the roof of our cabin or the barn. To me, that sound was calming medicine.

Doc and Papa had worked it out to go to town on alternate weeks. This meant that one or the other was in Beaver City every week. If we had a letter to go out and were not scheduled to go to town for another week, Papa would ride over to Doc's place and give him the letter to mail, and vice versa. They also did the same when picking up the mail, so we actually "received" our mail every week. Since the Beaver City postmaster knew us, he allowed us to pick up each other's mail when we were in town. We always picked up a newspaper for each other, too. It was a good system, and it kept us from receiving news only every two weeks.

The letter Papa had received from his brother was not even a week old when he had announced to Mama that they needed to talk. He had not shown her the letter, so it was a surprise when he presented it to her. Mama later said she had to read it three times before she understood it. I heard the gist of its contents three weeks later...

I was playing with Betsy behind the cabin. There was a window above the counter in the kitchen beside the pump, and it was open that day. We rarely opened the windows because of so much dust in the air and because the cabin stayed cooler when kept closed. But today the temperature had dropped a little, and the cabin needed to be "aired out." It was a Saturday, and I could hear Mama and Granny Nan talking through the open window. I thought little of it to begin with, as they talked to each other a lot, mostly about church things, the neighbors, Yosie and the twins, or the status of the garden and the root cellar and what needed to be picked and canned.

As usual, Yosie was on the kitchen floor watching Mama work—she could not be more than a few feet from Mama at any given moment without a fuss. The twins were napping in the cradle, and Granny Nan was at the table ironing the clothes she had taken down off the line. I heard Mama say, "I think Heinrich is going to talk to the people at the land office on Monday."

"Does Herrmann have an idea about what the place is worth?" Granny Nan asked.

"He only knows what we are paying monthly and how many months we have paid," Mama answered.

"And the buildings? We own them outright, you know."

"Yes, and along with them, we own our equipment, whatever it is worth. The livestock, the buildings and the equipment are our only assets," Mama said. "The way Heinrich and I understand it, our land will go back to the county and be sold without us seeing any profit from it. But Herrmann says we must be sure to check with a lawyer, because the laws about owning land in Oklahoma have changed."

There was a long pause in the conversation. What were they talking about? Were we getting rid of our cabin and barn? And what did "...our land will go back to the county..." mean? I had no clue. I had heard Mama and Papa whispering to each other lately, more than usual, when they were in the loft, but I had not been able to make out much of what they had said. I was usually too tired to care anyway and fell asleep quickly. But I did realize there had been an abundance of tension in the cabin for the last few weeks.

Sunday came, and Mama told me she and Papa were going to drive the buckboard to church. I was to stay at home and help Granny Nan care for Yosie and the twins. She gave me no explanation and no alternatives. I later realized they were going to try to find a buyer for the buckboard and Ham.

On Monday, Papa and I made our usual trip to Beaver City. Our first stop was at an office called *Torvin Setters, Attorney at Law*. I could not read it, of course; Papa told me what it said when I asked. It was really nice inside. There were heavy flowered curtains at the front window, and a thick, round rug with flowers that matched the window curtains. Around the rug were plush chairs with padded arms, and in the middle of the rug was a round table that held magazines, a Bible, and a picture book about animals. Papa told me to sit down and be still, so I crawled up into one of the soft chairs, and Mr. Setters handed me the picture book to look at while he and Papa did business. I loved coming to the city; my life was much fuller because of it.

Our next stop was the post office, where we picked up a letter that was from Mama's sister and brother-in-law, my Aunt Lavern and Uncle Julius Gounaris, who lived in Chicago. Papa opened it as soon as we went out onto the boardwalk. Usually he waited until we got home to open our mail, but this must have been a very important letter; he did not share its contents with me. He did, however, share a photo that was included with the letter. It showed Aunt Lavern and Uncle Julius standing in front of a huge ship. They were not standing side by side; rather, they stood apart from one another, Aunt Lavern on one side of the photo and Uncle Julius on the other. Between them was some writing on the side of the ship. But I was not yet able to read, so I had no concept of the significance of that writing.

Papa simply thrust the photo in front of me and said angrily, "Your Aunt Lavern and Uncle Julius (he pronounced it with a Y-sound: Yulius). If you ever hear the vord 'pompous,' you should think of them." He put the photo away, grabbed me by the hand and took off down the boardwalk so fast I couldn't keep up. He dragged me a few feet before he realized what he was doing.

"Oh, Wilhelmina, I am so sorry. Papa vas angry and should not have shared his anger vit you." He picked me up and hugged me. "Please do not be angry vit your papa." Then he lapsed into German, and I was unable to make out a word of it. But no matter. I understood that he was not angry with me, only with our Chicago relatives. I did not know why, but I knew it was not my place to try and figure it out.

Lavern and Julius were quite wealthy. They lived in a mansion in one of Chicago's high-income neighborhoods. Julius worked for a shipping firm and had a lot of money invested in the stock market. I did not know what stocks were, but I figured they must have been sold at a very important store.

I could not help but wonder why Papa had gotten so angry. Was he jealous? Reverend Bryant told us we should never be jealous or want something other people have; that was a sin. But I did not dwell on Papa's reaction. It was what it was, and he went back to being himself. He even sang and laughed on the way back home that evening.

The next day came, and everyone did their assigned chores as usual. Following supper, however, Mama asked us all to stay at the table because she and Papa had some news. They stood up beside each other. Papa cleared his throat and, without further ado, announced, "Ve are moving to Michigan. The matter is closed. There vill be no more discussion."

I blinked a few times and then looked over at Granny Nan; her face was expressionless. Mama was not looking at anyone; she simply stared off into the distance.

I had a thousand questions, but I knew better than to open my mouth. My inquiries would have to wait to be answered. I did not think I should ask Papa about it the next day in the barn, either; I remembered how angry he had become over the photo of our Chicago relatives, and I did not want to ignite that wrath again. Somehow, I knew Granny Nan would be able to fill me in. I did not know when, but I knew she would be my confidante in the matter.

It was days before she and I had the opportunity to be alone together. We were in the garden picking lima beans when she said to me, "Helmi, you have been unusually quiet lately."

I nodded. "Keeps Papa happy," I said.

She sighed. "You have a right to know what is going on. But you have been wise to keep your questions to yourself, and I know you have many."

"Where is Mich…?"

"Michigan." She stood upright and pointed in a northeasterly direction. "It is that way, many, many miles. I used to live in Indiana. It took us three weeks to get from there to here, and Michigan is even farther away than that."

"Will we have a farm?"

"Yes. Your Uncle Herrmann says the farmland there is much better than here in Oklahoma—much more fertile. And he says there are lots of parcels of land that have streams running through them."

"Like ours?" I asked.

"Yes, like ours, only theirs seldom dry up. And he says the town that we will be closest to is called Mount Pleasant. Is that not the nicest name you ever heard for a new place to live?"

I thought about it for a little bit before answering. "Yes, but…"

"But what, dear?"

"Will we go on the buckboard?"

"No!" she said emphatically. "We will sell the buckboard and buy a Ford truck so we can all ride in comfort."

"Will Ham go? And Trot?"

"I am afraid not. But someone around here will take good care of them for us. Maybe Doc Weiser and his family."

"The other animals?"

"They will stay here, too."

"Even Betsy?"

"Well, we will have to see about her."

I started to cry. I had grown close to that scroungy old dog, and leaving her behind was not an option in my mind. "Betsy has to come."

Granny Nan had tears in her eyes, as well, and her lower lip was quivering. She stopped picking beans and sat down in the dirt. She swallowed hard and said, "There will only be enough room for a few things in the truck, but I will see to it that Betsy is one of them."

"Promise?" I asked, my voice barely audible.

"Promise." She extended her hand across the row of beans, and I reached across the row and shook it. I knew there was no doubt about it now.

The temperature continued to drop for a while, then some clouds moved in, and the humidity began to soar. I saw lightning in the distance.

"We need to get these beans inside. We will have to hull them tonight. Mama and I will be putting them up tomorrow. It looks like we will have a lot of quarts of them this year."

She gazed into the distance, toward the darkest part of the sky, and her face changed. "Hurry up, now, Helmi. Can you carry both buckets into the cabin for me? I need to talk to your papa." Before I could answer her, she was hustling among the rows of beans and carrots and onions on her way to the barn.

I carried the first bucket into the kitchen and went back for the second one. The wind had picked up in those few minutes, and the dust was swirling around me and getting in my eyes and nose. I struggled to haul the second bucket into the cabin. The wind caught the door, slamming it behind me. It startled me; I jumped and upset one of the buckets.

Mama was standing at the kitchen window looking out into the distance. Yosie was fussing, and the twins were both crying. "Helmi, where is your granny?" she spoke sharply to me. "Is she still in the garden?"

"No, Mama. The barn."

Without a word, she yanked the door open and went running in the direction of the barn. I started picking up the beans I had spilled.

Within seconds, Mama, Granny Nan, and Papa came scrambling into the house. Papa proceeded to close all the windows. Mama scooped up Bella and Dora and said to Yosie, "Get up! Right now!"

Yosie began to whimper, and Mama squelched it with a snap of her fingers (I was unaware that Mama could snap her fingers!) Yosie had never been reprimanded like that by Mama before. Her eyes got big, and she pushed herself up off the floor. She just stood there, looking forlorn.

I knew something was up, so I abandoned the beans, ran over to Yosie, and took her hand. Granny Nan was gathering up blankets, and Papa had begun pumping water into our galvanized pitcher. While it filled, he picked up a drinking glass and some forks and spoons and dumped them into a bowl. Granny Nan took the bread out of the bread box and wrapped it in one of the blankets. Mama put the twins on the floor, snatched the linens out of the cradle, spread them out on the table, and put the twins, kicking and wriggling, on them. She pulled four baby bottles of milk out of the icebox and put them in her apron pockets, along with two nipples, then she picked up a bundle of folded diapers and laid them on the cradle linens with the twins. Bella and Dora were screaming at the tops of their lungs. Mama shouted to Papa, "Heinrich, take the twins. Bundle them up with the diapers. Mother and I will get the rest of the things. Helmi, you and Yosie follow Papa to the root cellar. Get a roll of toilet paper from the outhouse on your way."

Are we moving already? Why is everyone in such a hurry? It had been getting darker and darker, and the lightning and thunder were getting closer. It had grown much cooler, too.

"Helmi! Go! GO!"

My feet were frozen to the floor. I stood there and stared at her. She walked over to me and gave my bottom a hefty wallop. That got me moving! By that time, Yosie was wailing and fighting me, so I grabbed her by the hair and pulled her toward the door. She must have gotten the message, because she finally shut up and went with me.

We stopped at the outhouse. The door was ajar, swinging and banging in the wind. I grabbed a roll of toilet paper, never letting go of Yosie, who had decided to stay outside the privy and keep the door from closing me inside. I remember thinking, *Maybe she is not totally useless.*

We got to the root cellar just as Papa was emerging. He had put the twins inside and was coming back up to help us. He lowered Yosie down into the darkness, then he did the same with me. Mama and Granny Nan were right on our heels and followed us in. Papa came in last, but before he could close the cover behind himself, the sky opened up, and rain pelted him like daggers. It did not start slowly and increase; it was as if God had said, "Rain NOW!" Papa was soaked instantly, but he had gotten the cover closed, so the rest of us were dry.

"Betsy," I said, breathing hard. "Ham and Trot."

"They vill be fine. They are used to taking care of themselves," Papa answered.

"They in the barn?"

"No," Mama said. "Papa turned them loose so they would not get trapped in there in case..." She did not finish her sentence.

I realized what was happening. A twister was coming. We had been through it a few times before, but there had never been such a rush to get everything done. The wind had never come up so fast, and the dust had never blown in every direction like it was doing this time. And the rain…

Papa took a few moments to get his breath, then he felt around in the dark until he found the candles and matches. He struck one of the matches, but it only flashed and went out. He tried again, but the same thing happened. "It is too vindy," he said. I had not noticed it, but there really was actual wind blowing *inside* the root cellar. That had never happened before.

"Ve vill have to be in the dark for a bit," he said, "but our eyes vill adjust. Now stop crying, Yosie. You need to help Mama take care of the tvins."

Yosie hiccupped a couple more sobs, then she felt her way to Mama and crawled up onto Mama's lap and sucked her thumb. I had never seen her do that before.

Granny Nan handed Dora to me, and she took Bella. I held Dora close and gently stroked her face. She was crying, but it was getting more and more difficult to hear her, or anything else for that matter, except for the roar outside that overpowered all other sounds. The cover over the root cellar began to shake. Papa grabbed it and pulled down on it. The pressure in my ears was nearly unbearable. I was more frightened than I had ever been.

The roar continued to grow louder and louder. There was a monumental thump on the cover. I nearly jumped out of my skin, the twins yelled at the tops of their lungs, and Yosie screeched. Mama and Granny Nan even let out yelps.

The rain continued to pound the cover and began to seep in around the edges; Mama saw it at the same time I did. "Oh, no!" She stood up, hitting her head on the low ceiling.

"Papa!" I yelled. Then it occurred to me that the cover was no longer shaking, even though the wind had not subsided. Papa was no longer holding it down, either. Whatever had thumped the cover was now holding it in place.

Time was playing tricks on me. I had no idea whether it had been seconds, minutes, or hours since Papa had pulled the cover closed. I only knew the sound was still deafening, and the rain was still beating down; it came in sheets that followed an irregular, arrhythmic pattern.

I continued to hold Dora as close to me as I could. Luckily, she was the smaller of the twins, but despite that, I became aware of the aching in my arms. And the storm raged on. I could hear Granny Nan singing, just barely. I wondered if she was doing it to calm Bella or to calm herself.

The roar slackened. The rain stopped as quickly as it had started. A tiny slit of light became visible in a spot along one edge of the cover. It was over.

Papa, who was shivering, turned toward us and lit a candle. No one made a sound, not even the twins. The silence was eerie.

Granny Nan was the first to interrupt the stillness. "Is everyone all right?" More silence. "Is anyone hurt?"

"Mama," I said, pointing to her head. There was a trickle of blood running down the right side of her face.

She reached up and felt it. "It is nothing," she said. "I bumped my head when I stood up; that is all. I am fine. Not to worry."

"Looks like everyone else is in one piece," Granny Nan said and smiled.

We all sat back and took a breath. There was not a sound from outside: no birds singing, no squeaks from the windmill; no moos or neighs; no baaing or barking.

Papa raised his arms up and pushed against the cover. It would not budge. He changed his position and tried again. No luck. He sighed heavily. "It seems ve vill be spending some time here in the root cellar. Somevun vill check on us. Do not vorry." This was the very reason we had carried as many goods as we could into that dark hole in the ground.

Mama handed Yosie to Papa. Yosie wound up to cry, but Mama shushed her, and Yosie settled onto Papa's lap with no more resistance.

"We need to thank God for sparing us," Mama said. Unbeknownst to the rest of us, Mama had smuggled a Bible out of the cabin and into the root cellar. She motioned for Papa to hand her the candle, and she read scripture to us until she had no voice left.

Ten hours later, we were discovered.

THE AFTERMATH

I could hear men's muffled voices outside and scuffling noises on the cover of the root cellar. There was pounding and scraping, and a dog was barking. I folded my hands and asked God to let it be Betsy.

After nearly an hour of hearing noises, someone knocked on the cover with a hammer. Papa unlatched it, and it flew open. Nighttime had set in. A lantern appeared over the opening to the root cellar, and a voice shouted, "Is everyone all right down there?"

Papa stood up and stuck his head through the opening. "Ve are certainly glad to see you, Amos. And you, Lucas." Papa shaded his eyes from the lantern light. "Is that you, Reverend Bryant?"

"Yes, and Lawrence and Howard are here, too. It's a good thing we all came, or you'd still be in that root cellar."

A woman's voice called out, "Violet? Nancy? Are you and the babies okay?"

"Ye…yes," Granny Nan called back, struggling to gain her legs after sitting for so long.

"We are fine," said Mama.

Papa crawled up out of the cellar, arched his back in a stretch, then turned and reached a hand back in. "Come on out."

Mama put Yosie down off her lap and stood up as far as she could without hitting her head on the ceiling again. Yosie pushed me out of the way and reached for Papa's hand. Papa raised her up by one arm and deposited her behind him.

"You next, Mama," I said. Mama looked down at me, bent over and kissed me on the head, then climbed out. Granny Nan and I handed the twins up to Mama and Papa, then we emerged. Betsy was there to greet us with sloppy dog kisses.

Helen, Lucas's wife, had brought us some cornbread and butter, along with a jug of milk. Mama and Granny Nan thanked her profusely, and Mama asked, "Did an angel send you?"

"I don't think so," Helen said. "We just knew something was wrong here because there was no lantern light. And when we got closer, we saw that there wasn't any barn."

"You're lucky you took shelter in the root cellar," Amos said. "It was just unfortunate that the roof beam landed on the cover." The main beam from the barn roof had positioned itself over the root cellar cover and was wedged between a fence post and the livestock's watering trough. The trough had been lifted from beside the barn and slammed into the ground hard enough to bury half of it. One end of the barn's roof beam was lodged inside the exposed portion of the trough, which was crumpled and mangled and wrapped around the beam, holding it in place. Fencing was wrapped around the other end of the beam and held it solidly in place up against a fence post. The weight of the beam on the root cellar cover was simply too great for Papa to lift due to the way it was being held immobile.

It finally occurred to me to look around. The moonlight revealed that the barn and everything that had been in it was gone. Completely gone. There was nothing but an occasional board that had once been part of a stall or the roof or siding. The roof beam was lying on the ground just on the other side of the opening to the root cellar where the five men had rolled it off the cover.

I was afraid to look in the direction of the cabin, but I curled my hands into fists and turned my head. There, with the moonlight on its roof, stood the silhouette of our cabin, as though nothing had happened only thirty yards away from the disaster that had once been our barn.

A hand grasped my shoulder.

"Helmi?" It was Granny Nan.

I reached up and put my hand on hers. "Are there twisters in Mich…Mich…" I tried to ask.

"Michigan," she said. "And I do not know. But I hope not."

At sunrise Papa climbed down the ladder from the loft and crept to the kitchen. I heard him retrieve the can of coffee from the cupboard and put a couple of scoops into the white granite coffee pot. Then he filled the pot with water and carried it to the fireplace. I watched him hang it on the hook at the end of a metal bar that could be swung out over the fire. He poked at the banked coals and added some kindling, and a small blaze erupted. He added small slivers of wood which, despite the mind-numbing devastation, he had had the foresight to bring into the cabin last night. When the fire was hot enough to boil the coffee, he swung the pot over the flames. The scraps of wood from our barn—at least the ones that were unusable for anything else—would allow us to continue to cook.

The twins stirred and, right on cue, Mama came down from the loft and tip-toed to the cradle between Granny Nan's and my beds. I waved my fingers at her from my snug little nest, and she smiled and waved back. I needed to make a trip to the outhouse, so I slipped on my shoes and walked to the door. The sunshine met me, but so did the reminders of yesterday's events. I stopped and stared.

"Go on, Helmi," Papa whispered. "Nothing is different except that our barn is no longer standing." He came over and hugged me to him with one hand, my head not even reaching the top of his leg. He was not a big man, but he was tall, especially from his feet to his hips. His torso was not proportionate; it was short and stocky. Mama always said, "Heinrich, you are all limbs." To me, that created a mental picture of him as a head with long arms and legs coming right out of his neck.

I went outside, and the sun, barely having risen in the sky, was already causing heat waves that wrinkled the horizon. I yawned. The outhouse was still standing, but there was no door. It did not matter much, since no one lived close enough to see me doing my business. I positioned myself over the hole and looked out. Standing at the site where our barn used to be was Ham, looking no worse for wear.

I finished and ran toward him. He turned and looked at me, but he seemed confused. Why would he not be? Unlike my home, *his* home was gone. I talked softly to him, and he lowered his head. I kissed him on the nose and patted his cheek. The buckboard and all the tack for it had been swept away. There was no familiar stall for him to retreat to, no bins of grain, stacks of hay in the mow, no straw to cushion his big feet. I felt so sorry for him.

Papa had evidently seen me with Ham. Sipping his coffee, he came toward us. "Whoa, Ham," he said as he approached; he did not want to startle the big horse. If Ham took one step toward me, his giant foot might inadvertently crush mine.

"Papa?"

"Ja."

"You look for Trot today?"

He nodded. "Should be the first priority."

"Take me?"

He looked at me with more tenderness in his eyes than I had ever seen before. "I vould love to have you come along." He took another swig of coffee. "Ve vill have to valk far. Ve have no reins for Ham, so he cannot help us."

"I can walk," I told him.

"Goot. Ve go right after breakfast."

I ate the last bite of my eggs and fried mutton and drank the last gulp of my milk. Then I put on my boots. Papa and I spent most of the morning traipsing about the property before Papa spotted a horse lying on its side. It was not moving. He and I looked at each other, then we both took off running toward it. The closer we got, the more

I realized it was the wrong color to be Trot. When we got closer, I saw a long board sticking out of the horse's side. The poor thing was still breathing, but its eyes were already dead; there was no spark in them.

"Vun of Doc's horses," he said.

"What we do, Papa?"

He stood there thinking. "It is in misery. It has lost a lot of blood and is too veak to stand. The sun vill be too hot for it, and ve cannot bring it enough vater to drink." He sighed deeply. "I know vhat Doc vould vant us to do." He reached into his pocket and drew out a handgun.

"Papa…?"

"Turn your head avay."

"But…"

"Do it, Helmi."

I did as I was told. I heard him put a bullet into the chamber and cock the pistol. I put my fingers in my ears, but it did not eliminate the sound.

We walked all the way to Doc Weiser's house. His son, Robert, answered the door and said, "Dad and Mom are caring for the people injured secondary to the twister. They've been out all night."

Papa told him about the horse, described it and the injury, and Robert thanked Papa for doing what had to be done. "I'll tell Dad what you had to do. He'll be b'holden to you."

When we left, I hoped we would not find Trot in the same shape. I was going to have trouble digesting what had already happened, and I was surely not looking forward to seeing it happen again, especially to our own horse.

We came to the stream that ran through ours and Doc Weiser's land. It originated a long way off, and it didn't run very fast by the time it reached our propertty. It usually dried up in the late spring and summer, but the rain from the twister was making it run full on. We stopped to take a much-needed drink, and there, not more than twenty yards downstream, stood Trot. She raised her head and came directly toward us, nickering, telling us she was as glad to see us as we were to see her.

Papa stepped up to her, put both hands on her neck, and said, "I do not have a halter, girl. You vill have no place to stay out of the sun vhen ve get home. Maybe you stay close to the stream, like now, only closer to home. I have no hay for you, either, but I vill see if a neighbor can give you some, along vit a bit of grain. I can give you a carrot, though." Papa reached into his pocket and produced a carrot. Trot was happy and followed us.

When we got to within a quarter of a mile of home, Papa asked me, "Vant to ride bareback?"

I had never done that on Trot before. Papa would occasionally lift me up onto Ham's back, which I could not even straddle—I practically had to do the splits in order to sit there—and Papa would lead Ham around the barn a couple of times. Trot was another story. Though she was used to being ridden, and I had no fear of climbing onto her back, I did not know how I was going to hold on; there were no reins.

"How I hang on?" I asked Papa.

"Scoot up closer to her neck and grab hold of her mane."

I did as Papa said, and we followed the stream back to our farm. Papa lifted me down from Trot's back and pulled another carrot out of his pocket. He handed it to me, and I gave it to Trot.

"You stay vit her vhile I get something to hobble her."

I was glad to have Trot back home. I knew Papa was overjoyed.

Doc Weiser and his wife, Naomi, were at our cabin when Papa and I got back. Papa told them about shooting the horse and talking to Robert. They arranged for Ham to stay in Doc's barn since there was now an open stall. Papa offered to pay rent or do something in trade, but Doc would hear none of it.

"That brings up another point," Doc said. "Nancy, Violet, Naomi, come on in here and sit down."

The three women had been outside with Yosie and the twins. Mama stuck her head in the door and said, "Helmi, will you…"

"Yes, Mama." I immediately took over the babysitting duties. Bella and Dora were loving the afternoon sun and were wriggling on a blanket. They seemed to be talking to one another in a language only they understood. Yosie broke into a fake cry when she realized Mama was not going to be within sight, but I was able to get her attention with a stone I had picked up at the stream. It sparkled in the sun. That provided a distraction, and I was able to listen to the grown-ups with one ear.

"How did the other neighbors fare?" Papa asked.

"Some good, some not so good," Naomi said. "Eber had to treat lots of lacerations, a few broken bones, and there was one death."

Papa gasped. "Who?"

Mama and Granny Nan bowed their heads in respect.

"Old Mr. Basham," Doc said. "We figure he must have fallen when he was rushing to get to his root cellar. Lawrence and Howard found him about three-quarters of the way there from his cabin. He had no wounds, but he had a history of a bad heart, so that's probably what took him. At least that's what it'll say on his death certificate."

Papa shook his head. "He lived alone. I hope he is vit family and friends in Heaven now."

"He has a son in Beaver City, but that's a long way for an old man to go for a visit, and it seems his son was always too busy to make the trip to the farm," Naomi said. "If you ask me, his son doesn't deserve anything his father left to him." She sounded bitter, but I guessed it was just because she had not had any sleep.

"I know you talked to a lawyer—Setters, wasn't it?" Doc asked Papa.

"Ja."

"Well, did he say it would be all right for me to buy your land?"

"No. He said it belongs to the county, but he said instead of us merely giving it back, the county vill buy it from us...but only for pennies."

"This is one of the best properties around because of that stream running through it," Doc said. "It's not every day decent land becomes available. And since my property butts up to yours, I'd be interested in buying it."

"But Setters says you can only buy it from them after they purchase it from me. You cannot buy it from me outright."

"I understand that," said Doc. "But I want this property. I know a way to keep us both from having to lose anything on it. You won't make as much as if you were able to sell it to me outright, but you *will* get more for it than if you settle only for the money the county is willing to pay you."

"Go on," Papa said.

"I am interested, too," Mama said.

"I want to hear more," Granny Nan added.

"You go ahead and let the county buy the property from you. Then I'll offer the county double for what they gave you. When I get it, I'll put it on the market for another sixty percent—still a bargain for a buyer since it's sought-after land, and I'll split that sixty percent with you. I'll still make a small profit, and you'll have what the county gave you plus the extra thirty percent. And I'm willing to gamble that it'll sell quickly, so you won't have to wait very long to get your money."

Mama said, "I am pretty good with figures, but that was a lot to cipher all at once. Put that in dollars for me, please, Doc."

"Okay," Doc said. "Let's say the county gives you one dollar per acre. You own fifty acres, right?"

"Ja," Papa said, "so ve get fifty dollars from the county."

"Right. Now I go to the county and offer them two dollars per acre—double what they paid for it—so they'll be getting one hundred dollars from me. Of course, they'll tell me the going rate is currently higher than that, but I'll remind them that they aren't in the real estate business, so why would they want to be bothered by trying to sell it. I guarantee they won't turn down my offer, because it'll reimburse them the fifty dollars they paid you and put them fifty dollars ahead, *and* they didn't have to advertise it to try and find a buyer. Are you with me so far?"

"Yes," Mama said, and Papa nodded.

"Now...I put the land on the market at three dollars and twenty cents per acre, which is only a few cents higher than the current going rate. My son, Robert deals in real estate, so he can do the footwork to get this property sold. He's good. He can sell ice to an Eskimo. The land goes for one hundred and sixty dollars, and I'll give you thirty dollars of that, which is half of the additional sixty percent I received."

Mama said, "That means we will actually get eighty dollars for the land, plus we will be getting a few dollars more for the cabin, our equipment, the horses, and the other livestock, because we will be selling those outright."

"And that brings up another point," Doc said. "If I'm lucky enough to find a buyer who wants to live on the property and not just use it for pasture, I'm sure Robert can bargain with the buyer for the cabin, and that profit will be all yours."

"How much does Robert charge for his sales services?" Granny Nan asked.

"He'll take one-and-a-half percent; that's what all the real estate dealers are getting right now. And he doesn't take it until the sale is final and the papers are signed."

Then there was silence. A long silence. Papa quietly asked, "Vhy vould you do this for us?"

"Can you name one reason I shouldn't?"

Granny Nan was sniffling, and Mama had tears in her eyes. Papa was speechless. That is just how good neighbors treated one another back then.

PREPARATIONS

Another month had passed, and it was late August. Our lives had changed: Papa rode to Beaver City with Doc Weiser every other week, so I did not get to go along. I missed those rides with Papa, especially since I did not get to spend any time with him in the barn.

I did not get to see Ham and give him carrots, either, because he was staying at Doc Weiser's place now. Papa had used whatever lumber he could find to make a lean-to for Trot, but he did not ride her around the property because he had no saddle; the twister had taken it, and no one had come forth to say they had found it. "For all ve know, it could be twenty miles from here," Papa said. He made a harness out of scraps of rope he had found, and he knotted the rest of the pieces together to make a tether, so at least Trot could not wander any farther than the length of the rope when Papa tied it to the lean-to. He led Trot out into the field to eat what little bits of dried-up grass were available and to the stream a couple of times every day, so at least the poor horse did not get bored. And of course, she got half a carrot every day. Because it was late summer, the garden had not produced much more, but the root cellar was full, so we ate well. Granny Nan even finished putting up the lima beans we had picked the day of the twister—the wind never touched them, not even the ones I had spilled.

I mostly played with Betsy and did my jobs around the cabin. I helped with the twins whenever Mama and Granny Nan needed me to, and I tried to do whatever else I could to make things go smoothly. But a nearly-four-year-old girl could not do a whole lot in that department. I figured it was best just to stay out of everyone's hair.

It was Monday, and Papa had left early to go with Doc to Beaver City. I spent the morning helping clean the woven rag-rug that covered the floor in the hearth room. Mama and Granny Nan lugged it outside and flung it over the clothesline. I stood on a wooden crate to help beat the dust out of it, and then I concentrated on scrubbing some of the worst spots. By mid-day the sun was so hot Mama made me go inside. I drank three glasses of water!

Mama had opened the sewing machine cabinet. It was usually

closed up with a lantern sitting on it, but she had asked Papa to bring home some pretty gingham and matching thread so she could make new dresses for us girls. That was exciting for me!

Papa planned to stop at the county courthouse to pick up the money we were getting for the property. We had found out that they only made pay-outs once a month because the property commission had to have a meeting where they voted on how much a property was worth, and those meetings only occurred monthly. They had met two Wednesdays ago, and we had gotten a letter—delivered to our cabin in person—telling us our money would be waiting for Papa to sign for it today. That was exciting for Mama, Papa, and Granny Nan.

At about 4:30 Mama, Granny Nan, and I stopped what we were doing and listened; it sounded like a motor car coming up to our cabin. I jumped up and ran to the door, and the "Ah-OOOO-Ga" of a horn blasted my ears.

"A truck! A truck!"

Mama and Granny Nan both came to the door. It was highly unusual to see a motor car going by on the road, but it was even more unusual to see a truck pulling up so close to our door. "Ah-OOO-Ga," the horn sounded again. Mama squinted, and Granny Nan shaded her eyes with her hand. The truck pulled right up to our cabin, but we were unable to see who was driving because the sun was in our eyes.

The engine stopped, and a man stepped out. It was Papa! He had his hat pulled down over his eyes at a jaunty angle, and he was whistling. He ambled up to Mama and said, "How do, ma'am. Can I interest you in a ride?"

"Heinrich! Where did you get that? Who did you get it from? Why do you have it?"

"No more qvestions until you answer mine."

Mama stuttered, "Wh…what do…do you mean?"

"Do you vant a ride or not?"

"Oh! Of course I do!"

Papa offered her his arm, and she slipped hers inside the crook of his elbow. He escorted her to the passenger side and helped her up into the seat. Then he went around the front of the truck, stopped and kicked up his heels, and walked on around and slid into the driver's side. The truck started without a crank!

Granny Nan was extremely quiet. She had not smiled, but she had not seemed angry, either. She simply went back into the cabin and sat down in the wedding rocker with Yosie. I did not quite know how to respond, so I just sat down on the stoop and waited for Mama and Papa to return. They were gone for twenty-five minutes, and Mama was giggling like a schoolgirl when they got back. She went flying past me without a word. "Mother! Mother, come and look."

"Shhh. I will see it eventually," Granny Nan whispered. "Yosie is asleep."

Papa was taking packages out of the back of the truck, so I ran to help.

"Vhat do you think, Helmi?"

"Is it ours?"

"Oh, ja. She is spiffy, eh?"

"Spiffy!" I repeated. "Are we rich?"

Papa threw his head back and guffawed. Then he scooped me up and sat me down behind the steering wheel. I grabbed it and bounced up and down on the seat and squealed, laughing with him. What a treat!

Papa had been worrying himself sick over how to get to Michigan without a truck. He knew that the states farther north and east frowned on horse-drawn vehicles on the main roads. His own brother had told him that. In one of his letters to Papa, Herrmann had written:

The automobile has rendered the horse obsolete. If you can possibly find a way to do it, get yourself a truck—or at least a car—for your travels.

Papa had taken his older brother's suggestion to heart.

Mama came back out and kissed Papa right on the mouth. I had never seen them so happy. The truck was a brand new 1924 Ford TT with an Express Body pickup bed. It had an electric starter motor and had been fit with a canopy, screens, and side curtains. It was beyond spiffy; it was the bee's knees!

I was oblivious to the details of our financial state back then, of course. No child my age would have been able to grasp any of it. I learned later in life that the county had paid Papa two-and-a-half dollars per acre, not one dollar, as he expected, so instead of getting fifty dollars for our land, we got one hundred and twenty-five dollars.

Papa and Doc Weiser met with Mr. Setters, the attorney, the same morning the county gave Papa the check. Papa and Doc explained their plan, but Setters provided information that changed their minds about the whole thing. Unbeknownst to either Doc or Papa, politics over the past twenty years had changed the national outlook regarding Oklahoma's economics. People were looking to find oil. Thousands of gushers were tempting them, just like gold had done in California, so Oklahoma's population was increasing while the farmers' income was decreasing. People moving to the Sooner state were willing to pay more for land that might yield oil than the state and county governments had originally anticipated.

Mr. Setters told Doc to buy the land from the county, just as he had previously intended. And Setters convinced Doc to buy our cabin, the horses, and the livestock; he should keep the livestock and horses for himself, then sell the cabin sitting on half of the property and absorb the remainder of what had been our land into his own land holdings. According to the lawyer, "People are willing to buy twenty-five acres to gamble on striking oil, but most won't put out the money to buy fifty acres. And if they get a cabin already built on the property they propose to buy, it'll sell much faster." That meant everything would be expedited, and both Doc and Papa would get their money quicker. They agreed it would make things much easier, and both would be making more money in the process.

After talking to the lawyer, Papa had gone to the bank where he had always done business and talked to a loan officer. He showed the banker his check from the county and the letter from his brother. He explained that Herrmann was an engineer at General Motors and probably knew more about the auto industry than the two of them put together. The banker, who was a young man, didn't hesitate to ask a senior partner to hear Papa's story; he wanted to make sure the bank did their best for Papa. They were willing, without any qualms, to finance a new vehicle for up to six hundred dollars for ten years. Papa said, "I vill be back." He left and walked to the Ford dealer there in Beaver City.

Within an hour Papa walked back to the bank. "I have found a new Ford truck for four-hundred and ninety-three dollars. Can ve vork out a deal?"

Papa signed the loan papers, and the bank gave him a check made out to the dealership for that full amount. They also gave him a "coupon book" which contained one coupon for each month for ten years. He was to include a coupon each time he mailed the bank a check. Papa said, "I vill be in Michigan. Does that matter?" They told him it didn't make any difference where he was, as long as he paid them the amount that appeared on the coupon when it was due. Then Papa walked back to the Ford dealer and handed them the bank check. After he signed some papers, they handed him the temporary title to the truck.

❖❖❖

That night Papa sat down and wrote a letter to Herrmann telling him all the details of the day. None of us knew it, but Herrmann had a friend, a real estate agent, in Mount Pleasant. Papa asked Herrmann to find out if there was any land available in the area that had accessible water for livestock, and if any of the properties had any buildings on them. He wrote:

I will not be raising more beef cattle than we can use for our own meat; I want to start a dairy farm, as you suggested, since dairy products are on the rise and the price of beef has been slowly declining nationwide. Violet and her mother deserve a real house, not a dilapidated cabin in a field of dust. It does not have to be a big house; I am willing to add on to a smaller one. My children need a good school, as Wilhelmina is already close to being four years old. I am able to pay up to $15 per month to buy a place we can call our home. If you can find something that fits the bill for me and my family, I will be forever in your debt.

The next day Papa and I drove the new truck to the post office in Beaver City to mail the letter he had written. He asked Granny Nan to go with us, but she claimed she had too much to do. "You seem to have forgotten that we are getting ready to move," she said to Papa. Then she turned her back to him and busied herself with some mundane thing in the kitchen.

"Have it as you vill," Papa said to her, but she did not acknowledge him. He took a deep breath, took me by the hand, and we walked to the truck.

It only took us a little less than an hour to get to the city. Papa drove the truck to a gasoline filling station and "gassed 'er up." I loved watching the little red balls bounce around in the top of the gas pump, and I loved the smell of the fuel. We bought a roast beef sandwich at Johann's butcher shop; we divided it and ate it at the park, then we shared a root beer float while sitting at the counter in the ice cream shop before starting home.

❖❖❖

The first two weeks of September were spent packing for our move. Mama spent most of the time sewing dresses: one for Yosie, one for me, and one for herself. Granny Nan had told her, "Be sure and make cute little matching dresses for the twins. You do not need to make one for me; I have a perfectly good dress that I only wore to church for special occasions." Mama agreed, but she made one for Granny Nan anyway without her knowing about it. Granny Nan's birthday was coming up, and Mama wanted to surprise her with it.

We kept trying to get Granny Nan to take a ride in the truck, but she continued to make excuses. Yosie would only go if Mama went, too. But I went every time I was offered the opportunity.

Finally, push came to shove, and Papa put his foot down. It was the morning of September 10, Granny Nan's birthday. Papa said to her, "Nancy, I vill not take no for an answer. You are coming vit me. Ve are going to the post office to see if Herrmann has found us a place to live near Mount Pleasant." Granny Nan immediately started to argue, but Papa held his hand up to her and said, "End of discussion."

Granny Nan could be pretty stubborn, but she did not hold a candle to Papa when he made his mind up about something. When I was older I learned that Granny Nan was scared to death of automobiles and trucks. Horses and wagons had been the only mode of transportation she had ever experienced, and that covered a lot of years. She had been born in 1850; she had been seventy years old when I was born; today she was "celebrating" 74 years. She had not shown any signs of aging between the time I first saw her face and now, but then I had seen her every day, so I did not realize any change. I must admit, I was shocked that she had reservations about traveling in the truck; I always saw her as fearless.

"All right, I will go. But I do not want you 'showing off' in that... machine. Straight there and straight back. It is not a race. Understand? You must promise me, Heinrich."

Papa had a smirk on his face.

"Heinrich? You hear me?"

"For you, Nancy, I vill do only tventy miles per hour, no faster."

Mama said to Granny Nan, "Before you go, you should have this." She handed Granny Nan something wrapped in a pillow linen and tied with a bow of gingham. "Happy Birthday, Mother."

"Happy Birthday!" I shouted and jumped up and down. Then I ran to Granny Nan and hugged her around the knees. She looked down at me, and I wiggled my index finger at her in a 'come here' fashion. She bent down, and I whispered in her ear, "Get a root beer." She stood back up, and I motioned for her to bend down again. She did, and I whispered, "A float."

A few minutes later, Granny Nan and Papa climbed into the truck. Granny Nan was wearing the new dress Mama had made for her, and she was all smiles. I think she was enjoying being the center of attention. Everyone needs to feel special now and then.

When Papa and Granny Nan returned a few hours later, Papa ran—actually ran—into the cabin shouting and waving an envelope. "Ve have it! Ve have it! Violet! Ve have a new home!"

"Oh, Heinrich. That is vunderbar!" Mama rarely used any German words, but she knew that one and used it when she really liked something. It made me laugh.

"Gott im Himmel. Wo ist mein Kopf?" ("God in Heaven. Where is my head?") Papa said under his breath and ran back out to the truck.

Granny Nan was sitting there with a smile on her face. "I wondered if you were going to remember me," she said to Papa, who was helping her climb out.

Papa walked with her to the cabin, apologizing all the way. As soon as he was sure she was all right, he turned his attention back to Mama, sweeping her up and spinning her around three times. "Ve are going to be Michiganders! This Gott-forsaken Oklahoma land has lost its potency. There is not enough fertilizer vit-in vun hundred miles to make up for the nutrients the ground has lost over the last few years. Our crops are not vorth the money ve spend to plant them in this unfertile soil."

I remember Granny Nan commenting, "If you ask me, this never was a very fertile part of the country," and under her breath, "…save for my daughter's womb." And she was spot on; I had been born in November 1920, Yosie in April 1922, and the twins in December 1923—four children in three years.

I had just finished feeding the chickens and was putting the scoop back into the feed bin and latching the lid when Mama joined me to help gather eggs. She held the basket while I reached under the hens to see if they had laid any. Usually the hens clucked, stood up, and maybe flapped their wings a couple of times, then they either jumped down or sat back down on the nest, even though their eggs were gone.

But there was one old "settin' hen" (as Granny Nan called our layers) that was as mean as a snake. She pecked me every time I tried to put my hand in the nest. I was scared of her, so Mama always shooed her away before I reached for her eggs. This hen was a big Rhode Island Red that gave us ample big brown eggs. We had lots of Rhodies and a few Orpingtons, all of which were pleasant and friendly, but that one Rhodie ruled the hen house.

We also had three roosters. One of them, the prominent or alpha, chased me at every opportunity. I did everything I could think of to keep from being pecked or spurred. I ran from him, I tried bluffing him by running back at him, I raised my arms and roared at him, and sometimes I even stood my ground and did not move. Nothing worked. He still chased me. Being only a few inches taller than that rooster made for some scary battles. He was tall enough that his head reached my chin, and if he craned his neck, he could reach my eyes. More than once, I went crying into the cabin with bleeding wounds from his sharp beak. I begged Papa to get rid of him, but Papa would not hear of it.

Papa kept all three roosters in a scratching pen by themselves most of the time, but they were out with the hens for a few days every month. The big one that chased me was an enormous Rhode Island Red with dark plumage—almost burgundy. He was robust and healthy, and he began crowing around four a.m. every day. The other two roosters followed suit in their pecking order. When Papa let the roosters out, that big Rhodie would search out a good patch of food or grit, lead the hens to it, and then stand guard over them while they pecked and ate. He was a top-notch rooster.

Our hens were free-range most of the time. They were gentle, and I really liked them (except for the leader of the hen house). I loved their soft clucking, cackling, and chucking. I had not realized that the fried chicken we ate came from our flock until one day when I overheard Mama telling Papa that one of the Orpingtons had not been laying for about three months. "She is old," Mama said. "I think it is her time."

"I vill get the axe," Papa said. "You catch her and put the vater on to boil."

I do not know how I had avoided seeing this happen until then. "Mama, why Papa gets the axe?"

She reached down and took my chin in her hand. "It is time to dress a chicken," she said.

I did not understand. Mama must have seen the bewildered look on my face. She bent down to my level. "Helmi, we eat our chickens when they get old and quit laying eggs. You like chicken, right?"

"Yes."

"Where do you think it comes from?"

I had never thought about it.

"You have seen us butcher sheep and cattle and pigs every so often. We also butcher chickens."

"But, I like them. I pet them."

"They are not pets, Helmi."

I was sad. Then I had an idea, and my face lit up. "Butcher the big rooster. I hate that rooster!"

"Helmi! It is not nice to *hate* anyone or anything. The Bible tells us that."

"That rooster hates me!"

She could not hold back a laugh. "You are right about that," she said. "But we need that rooster, and we do not need that old hen who will no longer lay eggs for us. Do you see?"

I did not, but I told her I did. "Mama, you put clothes on it?"

"What?"

"You said 'dress' the chicken."

"Oh. Yes, I did. 'Dressing' is another word for butchering."

"No clothes?"

"No clothes."

I watched my first chicken being dressed that day, but I did not participate. Mama caught it, Papa chopped it's head off and dropped the decapitated chicken on the ground. It flapped and jumped around, and I understood why people said, "He ran around like a chicken with his head cut off." Granny Nan dunked its body in the boiling water, and she and Mama plucked the feathers off. It was tough to watch, but I was a farm girl, so I took it all in stride. And that night, we had chicken and noodles for supper. I ate two helpings and loved every bite of it.

I never found the letter Papa had gotten from Uncle Herrmann saying that we had a place to live in Michigan, so I never knew the particulars of the arrangement. I heard Mama, Papa, and Granny Nan use words that were new to me: mortgage, property taxes, millage rate, assessment, income tax, sixteenth amendment, loan interest. I understood none of what they talked about, so I pretty much tuned them out when they had their discussions about the place that was to be our new home. I did, however, understand one thing they discussed—Aunt Lavern and Uncle Julius.

It seems that Mama had written her sister a letter explaining that we were moving. In turn, Mama had gotten a letter from Aunt Lavern asking us to visit them in Chicago on our way. Papa was vehemently against it, but Mama appeared to be suppressing her excitement about a visit with her sister.

One night, just before my bedtime, Papa, Mama, and Granny Nan were sitting around the table having a discussion about the visit.

"I vill not stand in your vay," Papa said. "But be assured, I vill not be a goot conversationist."

"Why not?" Mama asked.

"Because I do not vant to say something I vill regret. I am sorry I feel this vay; I know they are your family. But I am not blood relation; I am related only by marriage. I vill not be rude, but I cannot promise that I vill be overly friendly, either."

"Thank you, Heinrich," Mama said. "I know this will be hard for you. I appreciate your acceptance of their invitation."

Papa did not answer.

Mama said, "Now, we must decide what day we will be leaving."

"You are right, Violet. September is nearly gone, and Herrmann says vinter vill be coming soon in Michigan."

"There is not a lot left to do since we already have a buyer for the cattle and chickens," Granny Nan said. "It is just a matter of when the buyer can come to take them to their new homes."

"And the pigs vill be taken to Johann's butcher shop in Beaver City tomorrow," Papa said. "He prefers to do his own butchering, so ve need to deliver them alive."

Mama put her hand over Papa's. "It is a good thing we have that truck."

"That is the truth," Granny Nan added and winked at Papa.

"Doc said he and Robert vill come by early tomorrow and get Trot." He shook his head. "I vill miss that horse, but I know he vill be in good hands, and I think he vill be glad to see Ham."

That made me cry, but I did not want anyone to see me crying, so I quietly walked to my bed and lay down. I cried into my pillow until I fell asleep.

❖❖❖

The next morning I was awakened by the squeals and screams of our two pigs. My first thought was that someone was trying to butcher them, but then I remembered Papa saying he was taking them to Beaver City. I ran to the door and saw Mama and Papa chasing one of them. It had evidently gotten loose when they tried to get it into the truck; Papa had jury-rigged a ramp from a couple pieces of left-over barn siding. I could tell it was not going well; Mama and Papa were running around like two wild Indians; the pig seemed to think the whole thing was a game. And the pig was winning.

I called Granny Nan to come and watch. She and I laughed and laughed as Mama and Papa struggled. They did, finally, get the pig in the back of the truck, however. But not without a free-for-all.

Things were really hopping around the cabin. Looking back on it, it was like electrical sparks jumping from one person to another and from one job to the next. I had never lived with electricity. No wires ran to our cabin. Papa said we could have run electric off a generator, but one big enough to power our cabin would cost too much and use up too much fuel. But he said our new house would have electricity.

I was playing with the twins while Mama and Granny Nan packed up all the kitchen things: pots and pans, skillets, pitcher, coffee pot, dishes, eating and cooking utensils, canning items, etc. Dora was dozing off and on in the sunshine, but Bella was restless and kept swinging her arms and gurgling, blowing little saliva bubbles. She suddenly let out a blood-curdling scream. I nearly jumped out of my skin, and Mama came running.

As Mama picked her up, I saw what had caused the outburst. On Bella's neck, just below her left ear, was a huge hornet. It had obviously stung her. I cannot imagine how awful that would feel to a tiny little girl who was doing nothing more than enjoying the beautiful day. I had been stung several times by honeybees, but a hornet was a whole different story. Their stings had been known to inject enough poison to kill a small child.

"Mother!" Mama cried. But Granny Nan was already beside her

and had seen the hornet.

"Put her on the table," Granny Nan said. "and take that bonnet off her. I will get the soda."

I had never seen Granny Nan move that fast. She opened the cabinet door where all the spices and baking needs were kept, but it was empty. "Dear God," she whispered. Mama had already packed all those items in a blanket-lined crate. But which one? Granny Nan was frantic. She yanked a blanket out of one crate, spilling all its contents on the floor. No baking soda. She scrambled around the table to another crate and performed the same action. "Where is the damned soda?" she yelled.

Mama had batted the hornet off Bella's neck and was stamping it on the floor. I knew it was already dead, but that did not matter to Mama—she was going to reduce that critter to nothing more than a grease spot. I could see several sting marks under Bella's ear, too, and I knew this was serious.

"Get the stinger out!" Granny Nan yelled.

"I do not see one," Mama yelled back. (We did not know that hornets leave no stingers behind like honeybees do.) "Just hurry up with the soda." Mama now had Bella in her arms, softly saying to her, "It will be all right. Shh, shh, shh. I know it hurts. Poor thing. Shh. Just settle down now."

Granny Nan had found the baking soda and had mixed it with a small amount of water to make a paste. She told Mama to put Bella back down on the table, but Bella screamed even louder when Mama tried to lay her down. "Okay, okay. Just hold her still so I can put this on the sting."

As soon as Granny Nan touched the spots with some soda paste, Bella wailed and wiggled. "Hold her head still, Violet."

"Easier said than done," Mama replied. "I can only do so much while holding her, you know."

"Sit down, Mama," I said. "I can hold her head still."

Mama sat immediately, and I put my hands on both sides of Bella's head, holding it as still as I could. I knew I did not dare touch the top of her head, because Mama had warned me about the soft spot. I looked into Bella's eyes and talked softly to her, telling her she looked like a cute little furry bunny, and anything else that popped into my mind. Granny Nan was able to apply some of the paste, and Bella began to calm down. Within a few seconds, she was quiet. Too quiet.

"Bella? Bella? Mother!" Mama gently shook Bella. "Mother, she is limp."

Granny Nan grabbed the baby and turned her upside down, holding her by the ankles. She shook that child like she was shaking flour out of a sack. "Pat her on the back. Hard!" she told Mama.

That scared me. I did not know what to do. Now I was crying. "Is Bella going to die? Is she okay? Help her! Help her!"

Then Bella threw up. Granny Nan waited till Bella was no longer retching, then she put Bella on the table and picked her up, right side up. As soon as Bella was righted, she coughed, looked at Granny Nan, and babbled some baby talk. She tried to reach for the site where the hornet had stung her, but Mama grabbed her hand and, in a baby-talk voice, said, "You are going to be just fine, little punkin. Yes, you are. Who is Mama's big girl?" Bella smiled at her.

I felt like a limp rag.

A couple of hours after the hornet ordeal, and while helping Granny Nan re-pack the crates that had been emptied so unceremoniously, I asked Granny Nan, "When do we move?"

"Day after tomorrow," she said matter-of-factly, not looking up.

THE FIRST LEG OF THE MOVE

Granny Nan and Mama each held one of the twins and rode up front with Papa. Yosie and I rode in the back of the truck. Granny Nan had kept her word, and Betsy came with us, too, but she was close to the very back of the truck, tied to one side so she could not jump down or fall out while we were moving. I could not reach far enough to pet her, but I talked to her a lot, especially when Yosie was napping. At first, Yosie had been upset over not being on Mama's lap, but Papa put her in her place: "Young lady, I vill have no grousing from you. You vill sit in the back with Helmi and like it!"

I loved it. We had our own little space under the table, right up next to the back of the truck cab, probably so we could easily let someone know if we had to go potty. We sat on the doubled-up pallet that had once been my bed. We were surrounded by the wedding chair, the sewing machine, Granny Nan's wedding chest full of special dishes, and all the crates that had been packed full of our lives. I knew that no matter where we went, it would smell like home. Mama had seen to it that Yosie and I had plenty of things to keep us occupied: books, dolls, a pillow and blanket, and our own Thermos of water, of which I had been deemed "The Keeper." She knew how much I liked being in charge of things.

The church had given us a cold chest as a going-away present. Mama was so thankful to have a way to keep our food from spoiling. We stopped along the road to eat dinner when the weather was nice, but we always ate breakfast and supper in the truck while we were moving. Sometimes Yosie would cry between meals because she was hungry, but I did my best to distract her until mealtime arrived. Every so often we made stops at a grocery store to pick up things that would keep the longest and to replenish the ice. Some of the filling stations carried ice as well.

I can only guess at the route we took. I did not really care how we got to Michigan, I only cared that we got there. I knew we were going to make two special stops—one in Chicago to see Aunt Lavern and Uncle Julius, whom I had never met, and another in Flint to visit

Uncle Herrmann, also a new face for me. Other than that, I viewed the trip as an adventure, and I planned to tackle each leg of it as it happened.

I could not see much from the niche Yosie and I occupied because things were piled up around us and secured to the supports that held the canopy over the truck bed. I could smell trees and water when we passed them, and I was surprised at how different the wheels sounded on the roads as we went from dirt to gravel to pavement. I sang a lot of songs, some of which I made up, as we traveled. I even taught Yosie some of them. And sometimes I just closed my eyes and imagined what our new cabin—no, our new *house*—would look like inside and out.

The farther we went the colder it got as evening approached. We did not have any heavy winter coats, only jackets and sweaters, as the temperature rarely fell below freezing in the Oklahoma panhandle, and then it was only at night during December, January, or February. I had to ask Mama if we could have another blanket.

Mama and Granny Nan spent about half an hour one morning unwrapping and re-wrapping some items to provide us with an extra blanket so we would not be so cold. Of course, there were no hard windows in the truck, so Mama, Granny Nan, and Papa needed more on, too. They bundled the twins together to keep each other warm.

Papa made us get out and go to the bathroom whenever we stopped to get gasoline, whether we had to go or not. Some of the filling station outhouses were awful; they were dirty and smelled terrible. We went into one right at the Missouri state line—I could see the sign with the outline of Missouri on it. There was no knob on the door, just a hole that you had to put your fingers through to pull the door open. So, of course, there was no lock, either. Granny Nan took a couple of sheets of toilet paper (surprisingly, some was hanging there) and used them to keep from touching the door as she held it shut. Mama said to Granny Nan, "Does anyone ever take time to clean in here?" One of the mechanics happened to be passing by the ladies' room at the same time and must have heard Mama's comment. He was waiting when we came out.

"'Scuse me, ma'am. I hear you're unhappy with our facility."

Mama stared at his filthy clothes and grimy hands. "What?" she asked.

"I heard you say our privy's dirty." He had a toothpick in his mouth and was talking around it. He looked Mama up and down, from "stem to stern," as Papa would say. "You might be a little too dirty to be a-usin' it."

She straightened up and looked right at him. "I beg your pardon," she said politely.

"I know'd it! I know'd you'd be a-beggin' fer somethin'," he said and grinned, all three of his existing teeth yellowed with black stains at the gum line. "You filthy Okies ain't got the fetchin's up of a cur dog."

Granny Nan stepped in front of Yosie and me and took a place right beside Mama. "Excuse me, *sir*, but I kept my pig sties cleaner than you keep that poor excuse for a privy." And with that, she grabbed Mama by the arm and turned, pushing Yosie and me ahead of her.

I tried to look back to see what the man was doing, but Mama whispered, "Keep your eyes forward, Helmi. Do. Not. Look. Back!"

When we reached the truck, Papa was having a heated conversation with the man pumping the gas. "I gave you exactly vhat the pump said I owed you plus ten cents for a block of ice."

"But I checked the oil, too, you stinkin' Okie."

Papa shifted in his shoes. "I did not ask you to do so, and I vill not pay for something I did not ask for."

"Know what? You're *worse*'n a stinkin' Okie. You're a German stinkin' Okie. A *cheap* German stinkin' Okie. Cain't think of anything I hate more," the man said and spat on the ground at Papa's feet. I could not see whether it had hit Papa's shoes.

"Heinrich, let us be on our way," Mama said. She had practically thrown Yosie and me into the back of the truck, and Granny Nan was already in the front with both Dora and Bella on her lap.

Papa straightened up to his full height and stared at the man who had pumped the gas. The man was obviously getting nervous; Papa was a head-and-a-half taller and twice as muscular, as was obvious by his arms, the biceps of which were bulging and twitching. After what seemed like an eternity, Papa raised his hand (be it somewhat rapidly) to scratch his head; gas pump man jumped. Papa grinned and silently backed away from him. Never breaking eye contact with the man, Papa slid into the driver's seat and, still staring at him, started the truck, put it in gear, and drove away. Not a great first impression of the Show-Me state. But other than a couple of flat tires, that was the only trouble we had experienced so far on our trip.

St. Louis was a spectacle to behold. I had been impressed by how big Beaver City was: it took Papa and me an hour to walk from one end of Main Street to the other and back. But it took us *over* an hour to *drive* just *one way* through St. Louis. I did not know so many cars and trucks even existed. And the stores! I just knew there was not one thing that city did not have.

It was getting dark by the time we reached the northeast edge of the city. Mama had traded places with me; she was now in the back with Yosie. We began to notice a lot of cars and trucks parked in areas that had been cleared out along both sides of the road. There were no stores. We had crossed the Mississippi River a ways back, so people would not have been parked there to go fishing. We saw what appeared to be outhouses every half-mile or so. People were sitting on blankets on the ground or in their cars and trucks eating supper. There were groups of men or women standing around talking. No one seemed to be in a hurry. What were they doing?

Without a word, Papa pulled off the road and drove up beside a man walking along the row of vehicles. "Goot day to you, friend!" Papa said to the man. The man kept walking but tipped his hat to us. Papa kept the truck rolling at the same speed as the man was walking. "Vhat is going on here? Ve are not from this area and are curious." The man turned and looked at our truck, then he stopped walking. Papa stopped the truck.

"Looks like you're traveling," the man said.

"Ja. Ve are going to Michigan," Papa said. "Ve have a new farm vaiting for us there."

"Congratulations," the man said without any emotion. "I hope you have a good life." Then he began walking again.

Papa looked over at Granny Nan and whispered, "People are not so friendly here as back in Beaver City."

"Here comes a woman. I will ask her," Granny Nan said. She leaned out the window and said, "Hello there! Is something special going on here?"

The woman looked at our truck and asked, "Ya comin' from the south?"

"Beaver City, Oklahoma," Granny Nan answered.

"Where ya headed?"

"Michigan. We are moving to a new farm."

The woman acknowledged the answer with a nod of her head. "This here's a stop-over for those of us who cain't afford to stay at a inn. It ain't much, but it's better'n stoppin' where there ain't nobody else. Security in numbers, I guess. I'd keep an eye on my young 'uns and my goods, though, if'n I's you."

"Is somevun in charge?" Papa asked.

A single "Ha" erupted from the woman's mouth. "Ya just pull in wherever there's a space and go 'bout your business. Usually nobody bothers ya, and it's best if'n ya do the same." She started to move on but stopped and said over her shoulder, "A word to the wise…don't use the privies. They're crawlin' with flies and fleas, and I hate to think what else."

Papa and Granny Nan looked at each other.

"I think I can drive farther tonight," Papa said.

The stop-overs went on for miles. We could see lanterns lit at some of the sites, but most were dark. Papa drove until after midnight before pulling off the road and parking behind a big tree. I had to pee so bad, I only got about three feet from the truck before squatting.

Mama and Yosie had been sleeping. Mama asked, through a yawn, "Where are we now, Heinrich?"

"I do not know exactly. I only know I vanted to get as far from the stop-overs as I could. I vould not allow our children to spend even a second there, let alone a whole night. I just hope there is a filling station close by. Ve vill need fuel before ve go much farther."

"Things will look brighter tomorrow, Heinrich," Granny Nan said. "Right now, we need to feed these babies and ourselves and get some sleep." She got out of the truck. "Violet, I will sleep in the back tonight with Helmi. And we will have room for one of the twins with us. You and Yosie can sleep up here with Heinrich and the other twin."

Mama said, "Okay. I am not hungry." I think replying to Granny Nan used up all the energy she had left.

Not only did things look better in the daylight, the weather was beautiful—bright and sunny with only a light breeze blowing. The temperature had risen a bit, so we started the day without jackets or sweaters. We had not wakened up until after seven a.m., so Papa was afraid we'd fallen behind schedule. One of his favorite things to say was, "Not only does the early bird catch the vorm, he also gets to see the sunrise." We had missed it that morning.

While Granny Nan and Mama got things out for our mobile breakfast, I spiffed up our little niche under the table, and Papa studied the map. Within minutes we were back on the road. Papa said he had seen a filling station about a mile back, and he thought we had better backtrack to make sure we did not run out of gas. Turns out, it was a good idea, as the next station was over forty miles away.

The weather deteriorated as we progressed, and before it was time to eat dinner, it had started to rain. It was a cold rain, too. For the first time since our last winter in Oklahoma, I felt chilled. Granny Nan said, "Fall is in the air. It is almost October."

We did not stop to eat our mid-day meal; Papa just kept driving. I got really hungry, but I knew it was important for us to get as far as we could each day since the weather was changing. The rain finally stopped, and so did we. We ate our supper beside a river. It sounded so nice. Papa said we should probably not go any farther that night because the map showed lots of open spaces, and that meant it was probably private farmland; he did not want to trespass. I knew I would sleep well that night.

Things went on without any more unwanted events, except for another flat tire. Looking back on it, I do not know how Papa kept his spirits up. I slept more than usual, but Papa just kept plugging away. We were almost a week into the trip, and the twins were getting cranky. Yosie whimpered a lot. Betsy whined incessantly. Mama's temper had grown short, and Granny Nan was unusually quiet. But we sang, and we sometimes played games when I was riding up front, like "I went on a trip, and with me I took..." and you had to name something you would take. Then the next person did the same, but they had to say what you said first and then add something. The next person had to say everything that everyone else had said and then add another item. It went round and round like that until the game ended when someone forgot to name one of the items.

The roads were getting better and better, even between the towns and cities. One night we saw a soft light low in the sky. "Look," Papa said. "Chicago. And ve are still at least a half-a-day avay."

❖❖❖

St. Louis had been huge, but it did not hold a candle to Chicago. It was as if we had been transported to a different world. When we had gotten close, Papa stopped for gasoline and bought a Chicago map. It was too big to unfold all at once, so Papa took a look at it and folded it in fourths. Then he handed it to Mama and said, "You vill have to help me. I cannot look at the map and drive at the same time; there is too much other stuff I need to pay attention to. Can you figure out vhere ve are?"

Mama looked at the street signs on the corner, then she looked at the map. After turning it around a few times, she said, "We are right here." She pointed to a spot on the map and showed Papa.

He looked up at the signs and back down at the map and said, "You are absolutely right, Violet. You vill be our navigator."

"I am not going to do any navigating until I see where we are going." She would not let Papa move the truck until she had found the street on the map where Aunt Lavern and Uncle Julius lived. When she had located it, her mouth dropped open. "We will have to start at one end of their street and go to the other to find their house. The street is one, two, three, four, five, six, seven, eight, nine..." and she did not stop counting aloud until she reached twenty-four, "...twenty-four blocks long. I have no idea which end of the street the numbers start on, so I do not know which end Lavern and Julius are closest to. In her last letter, Lavern said their house number is 1846."

"Okay," Papa said. "Get me to the street."

It took us forty-five minutes just to find the right section of town. There were a lot of one-way streets, so that messed everything up for

Dar Bagby 67

us. It seemed impossible to go down a street and come back the right way on the one we wanted. We ended up going in circles over and over again. And sometimes the names on the street signs did not match what was on the map.

Papa was beginning to get frustrated. He pulled over to the side of the street. He and Mama were studying the map when a man in a blue suit with gold buttons and a strange flat blue hat with a gold band and a white bill came up to our truck. He was carrying a stick. He walked right up to Papa and said, "You can't stop here. This is a thoroughfare."

"A vhat?" asked Papa.

"There is no stopping allowed on this street. Don't you hear the people behind you honking? And see all of the cars whipping around you?"

"No, I did not. I vas concentrating on trying to find my vife's sister's house. Can you help me?"

Blue suit man sighed. "If you pull into that parking lot up ahead," he pointed to a big space where lots of cars were parked, "I can try and help you, but you'll have to move from here immediately."

"I vill. Vielen Dank." (Many thanks.)

The man went to the back of our truck and held his hand up to the cars that had lined up behind us. Then he came up to the front of our truck and motioned for Papa to pull out. Papa followed his directions and parked in the lot.

"Who is he?" I asked.

"That is a policeman," Mama said. "He helps people like us, and he arrests people who are doing bad things."

"What is 'arrests'?"

"I will tell you later. Right now, Papa and I have to talk to him and see if he can point us in the right direction."

"I like his suit," I said.

The policeman told Papa exactly how to get to 1846 Hanover Street. He said, "It's a one-way street, but luckily, you'll be on the right end of it." And within a few minutes, we had parked in front of Aunt Lavern and Uncle Julius's house.

A man in a suit and tie came out to meet us. I knew it was not Uncle Julius because this man's face was black! I had never seen a Negro in Beaver City; this was the first one I had ever laid eyes on. Granny Nan had told me about them being slaves and getting freed by President Abraham Lincoln after the Civil War, but I never thought about them participating in my life; I thought they only lived in the south, and I did not understand slavery.

He came to our car, opened the passenger door, and bowed. He held Mama's arm to help her out and then did the same for Granny Nan. He did not say a word. He started around to the driver's side, but Papa was already walking around the front of the truck. Mama helped Yosie and me over the side of the truck bed. Yosie took one look at the Negro, and her eyes got as big as saucers. She grabbed hold of Mama's hand and held on for dear life, staring at the man.

He bowed again and motioned for us to go through a gate in a wrought iron fence that was as tall as Papa, and we all walked up the red stone sidewalk that led to their front door. When we reached the steps up to the porch, the black man said, "Please," and motioned again for us to go to the door. I looked up, and there, in the doorway, was Uncle Julius; I recognized him from the photo Papa had shown me. He looked down at Yosie and said, "It's all right. I'm not going to eat you!" Then he offered his hand to Papa.

Papa shook it, nodded his head, and said, with his German accent, "Yulius." It all felt very awkward.

Aunt Lavern appeared in the doorway and said, "You have found us! Please, do come in." She went ahead of us and took us through a room as big as our cabin had been, but there was no furniture it, only some statues. The floor was covered with big squares of shiny, black and white swirly stone, and the walls were covered with little squares of different colors. Mirrors hung in huge frames on the two side walls. Until now, I had only ever seen my reflection in some of the store windows in Beaver City, and I could see my face in the rear-view mirror in our truck if I stood up on the seat. The ceiling was so high I felt like I was looking up at the sky…and it even had clouds painted on it. There was a thing hanging from the ceiling that looked like it was made of diamonds; it was round and huge and glistened in the light that was shining through a window above the door.

Uncle Julius, who was following us, turned to Granny Nan and asked, "Should Afton retrieve anything from your vehicle? Perhaps the children need something."

Aunt Lavern said, "I am sure you will want to change out of those dirt…uh, riding clothes for the evening meal."

Granny Nan said to Afton, "The twins' diapers should be changed. There is a pillowcase in the back of the truck, close to the cab. It contains what they will need." She turned toward Aunt Lavern and said, "The rest of us will be fine for now."

Aunt Lavern started to say something, but she frowned, took a deep breath, smiled an insincere smile, and said, "Of course." We passed through a large archway, and I could see a room filled with overstuffed chairs, small sofas (I had seen similar ones in the lawyer's office in Beaver City), and multiple tables—all tiny, some on very short legs—situated either beside the chairs or in front of the sofas. Some of the tables had electric lamps on them. Papa had told me all about electricity and had said, "Ve vill have it at our new farm, yust like you vill see at Aunt Lavern and Uncle Yulius's house." On the floor was a rug that was square and had fringe on two sides; it was at least three times the size of the one in the lawyer's office. The fireplace in the back of the room was much smaller than the one in our cabin, and it had the same little squares all around it that I had seen in the room with the mirrors and statues where we had first come into the house.

"It is such a lovely day, why not go out on the veranda? We can have some lemonade and get to know each other again," Aunt Lavern said.

"Good idea," Mama said.

Afton had returned with the pillow linen, which he handed to Aunt Lavern. Granny Nan relieved her of it and asked, "Where shall I go to change the twins' diapers?"

Aunt Lavern put her hand in the air and waved it. A woman with dark skin, but not a Negro, appeared from behind a large door made of dark wood. "Yes ma'am?" she said, her head down.

"Take the children and change the babies' diapers. The children can play in the nursery while we are on the veranda." Aunt Lavern turned to Mama and said, "Belinda will take the children and get them settled. Then she will come back for the babies."

Belinda was dressed in a white, collarless blouse tucked into a dark gray pleated skirt. Her hair, dark but streaked with gray, was pulled back and woven into a long braid. She looked up only enough to catch my eye, and I thought I saw her wink at me. "Come along," she said to Yosie and me. She had a nice voice. I looked up at Mama, and she nodded, so I went to Belinda, who was holding out her hand. I took it. Yosie, of course, wanted nothing to do with this stranger.

Mama bent down on one knee and said to Yosie, "It is perfectly fine, Yosie. Go with Helmi and Belinda. She has some fun things for you to do. Go on."

Yosie's eyes welled up with tears, and her lower lip pooched out. "No."

"Yosie, you will have fun. I promise," Mama said.

I looked up at Belinda, and she said to me, "Come on. We'll go and have a cookie. Yosie will miss out if she doesn't come with us." She turned, and we started toward the room with the big door. Yosie let go Mama's hand and came running to me. She took my other hand and, together, the three of us went into the room.

In the middle of the room sat a round table and chairs that had been made especially for little people, and in the middle of the table was a plate of cookies, two drinking glasses, and a glass pitcher filled with lemonade. Yosie let go my hand and went running to the table. "Cookie," she said and reached for one.

Belinda led me to a chair and pulled it out so I could sit down. Then she put a cookie on a small plate and placed it on the table in front of me, along with a napkin that had been folded into a triangle. She poured a glass of lemonade and placed it up and to the right of my plate.

"Thank you," I said, not yet reaching for either the cookie or the lemonade.

Belinda smiled and nodded, then she pulled out another chair, picked up Yosie, who was cramming a cookie into her mouth as fast as she could, crumbs falling every which way, and sat her down. She did not give Yosie a plate, only a napkin. Then she turned to me and asked, "Should I pour a glass for her?"

I said, "Yes, but I should help her."

Once again Belinda smiled and nodded. After pouring Yosie's lemonade, she left the room. So I took a bite of the cookie. It was light and airy, not like anything I had ever tasted. I could not identify the exact flavor, but it was nutty-tasting. Yosie was reaching toward the lemonade, opening and closing her fingers in a "give-me" gesture. I held the glass up to her lips and she took a drink. Her eyes squinted, her mouth puckered up, and she shuddered.

"Is it sour?" I asked her. She shoved it away.

Belinda came back with Bella in her arms, and she was followed by Mama, who was carrying Dora and the pillowcase full of baby things. They went into an alcove (at that point in my life I did not know that was what it was called) where there was a tall table with short railings built up around three sides of the top. It was a changing table. Belinda put Bella on the table. Without moving away from the front, she took Dora from Mama and placed her in a tall cradle beside the changing table. This cradle did not rock. I would one day learn that it was a bassinette. At six months old, Dora nearly filled it.

"Thank you," Belinda said to Mama. "Things here will be fine. You may join the others."

Mama just stood there for a moment, then she turned and left. It was the first time she had ever allowed anyone to take care of us other than Granny Nan or Papa.

I could hear Bella fussing a bit, and Belinda was singing—more like chanting. Her long braid was dangling over Bella, who began reaching for it. Dora was laughing, and I saw why: three tiny carved horses hung from the top of the bassinette's cover. Dora was reaching for them and making all sorts of giggly noises.

When I looked back, Yosie was clambering up onto the table, dead set on getting another cookie. I jumped up, grabbed her around the waist, and started pulling her back into her chair. She let loose a whoop, but Belinda never even turned to see the reason for it. She simply said, "Yosie, sit down."

Yosie stopped in mid screech and sat. There was something in that woman's voice that had struck a nerve with Yosie. I did not know whether it was the tone or the pitch, or if it was simply Yosie's understanding that she had better do what Belinda said. Or else. I wondered, *Does that woman possess some sort of magic?*

Belinda picked up Bella, slipped her into the bassinette beside Dora, and wiped the changing table. Then she scooped up Dora and changed her diaper, all the while chanting something to her, just as she had to Bella. Bella had fallen asleep, so Belinda brought Dora into the room, sat her on the floor, and gave her a doll to play with. Then she went back into the changing room and fastened a strap over the bassinette to keep Bella from falling out if she woke up without us hearing her.

I was mesmerized by the way Belinda had gone about taking care of us. Four children all at once, all of us strangers to her, had not seemed to ruffle her feathers in the slightest. She came over and sat down on a chair next to me. Her knees stuck up in the air because the chair was so short. "You have good manners," she said to me.

I did not know how to respond, so I just smiled.

"Your grandmother and mother have taught you well."

"And Papa," I said.

She laughed. "Of course, your papa."

"I like your hair. And the way you sing," I said.

"Now it is my turn to say 'thank you.'" She picked up the cookie plate and passed it to me. "Another?"

I shook my head. "It might ruin my supper."

She tilted her head back and laughed. "You might not want too much supper."

I did not understand. "Why?"

"Have you ever eaten a lobster?"

"A what?"

"It is a giant crawdad."

On a couple of occasions, I had seen crawdads in our stream in Oklahoma, but they certainly were not something I had ever considered eating. I wrinkled my nose and said, "Yuck!"

Yosie continued to stuff cookies into her face. She was totally oblivious to our conversation. She yawned and got down off her chair, came to me, and pointed to a big stuffed bear sitting on the floor in a corner of the room.

"Can Yosie play with that bear?" I asked Belinda.

"Of course. That is why he is here." She picked up Yosie and took her over to the bear.

"Pet," said Yosie.

Belinda picked up one of Yosie's hands and placed it on the bear's head. Then Yosie wriggled to get down.

Belinda came back over to me and again offered me the plate of cookies. I reconsidered and took one. She went to a bookcase that covered half of one wall in the room. "Do you like to read?"

"I cannot read yet. I will learn at my school in Michigan. But I know my letters. And I can count. Past forty."

"You are not only polite, you are smart," she said. "May I tell you a story?"

I nodded. Dora had abandoned the doll and crawled over to the stuffed bear. She had snuggled up to Yosie, and her eyes were blinking slowly and heavily.

Belinda sat on the floor with her legs underneath her. "This is the story of the Union of Corn and Bean.

Corn was a tall, slender, and very handsome plant. He stood in a choice section of the garden. Most of the time Corn was happy to look at his beautiful surroundings, like the sunrise and sunset. He loved to watch the animals as they scurried about their business. Sometimes he'd feel a little sad, although he didn't know why.

One evening as he watched the sunset change from orange to red to purple, he noticed two butterflies fluttering around each other. He noticed how they brushed each other's wings as they flew by. Suddenly, Corn knew what brought his occasional sadness. He missed the closeness and companionship of a family. He sang the song of loneliness as the sun slipped below the horizon.

As the morning sun awakened the world, Corn saw that the Squash Maiden had made her way towards him. She told him she had heard his song and came to offer her companionship. Corn immediately saw their differences and explained, 'You are a beautiful plant, but we cannot grow together. You must wander all over the ground while I must stand in one place. Your broad leaves block the sun from the young ones beneath you. I grow tall and thin to share the sunlight.

The slender Bean heard this and planted herself next to Corn. Her

slender threadlike vines spread out as if to feel for something to lean on. She touched Corn and wrapped herself around the stalk. They grew tall together. They knew this was the union that was meant to be. They promised to be together forever."*
*(Native Languages of the Americas website © 1998-2015)

    I looked up to see Granny Nan standing at the door. Her face was pale, and she was staring at Belinda with a strange expression. Finally, she said, "That was a beautiful story. Where did you hear it?"

    Belinda rose from the floor and said, "My mother told it to me when I was very young. I have always remembered it."

    Granny Nan just stared at her. "How old are you now?"

    "I have grandchildren."

    "Do you live here…at this house?"

    "Oh, no. I only come here when Miss Lavern asks me to. I care for children at an orphanage."

    "White children?"

    I did not know what Granny Nan meant.

    "White, yellow, black, red…we do not separate them by the color of their skin. We believe that all children are the same inside. They all like to play, to hear stories, to be loved."

    Again Granny Nan stared at her. "You are a good woman, Belinda. I can see by your eyes that you had a hard life as a child."

    "My family abandoned me when I was only a little older than Helmi. But another family—white settlers—took me in when they found me sleeping inside a hollow tree."

    "Where did that happen?" Granny Nan asked.

    "Michigan."

    Granny Nan walked over and put her hand on Belinda's shoulder.

    "Thank you for taking care of my grandchildren in the same way you would your own."

    I realized, years after, that the world was continually growing closer together. And I knew Granny Nan had done something incredibly difficult that day: she had overcome a horrific fear of the "red man."

    "Betsy! Where is Betsy?" I asked in a panic. I do not know what had prompted me to think about her.

    Granny Nan assured me she was fine. "One of the people who takes care of the outside property took her for a walk, and she is now tied to the railing around the veranda chewing on a big soup bone. In the shade."

    I was tired. It had been a big day for a nearly-four-year-old who had not had any naps. There had just been too much to look at, listen to, and do; I had not been willing to risk losing any of those precious minutes. But it had all caught up with me, and all I wanted now was to sleep. I yawned, and Granny Nan asked Belinda, "Is there a place where Helmi can take a nap?"

"Of course," Belinda said. She walked over to the changing table and pulled a folding cot out from behind it. "Will this do?"

"It certainly will, thank you," Granny Nan said. She helped Belinda unfold it and set it up. Then Belinda opened the cabinet under the changing table and removed two blankets and a small pillow. She handed one of the blankets to Granny Nan and spread the other one on the cot. Then she placed the pillow at one end. She motioned for me to come and lie down, and she took the other blanket from Granny Nan and covered me with it.

The pillow was stuffed with feathers! It was the softest thing I had ever felt. I put my head on it and instantly fell asleep.

❖❖❖

"Wake up, sleepy-head." Mama said softly. "It is time for supper."

I opened my eyes and looked around. "Is this our new house?"

"No, Helmi. We are at your Aunt Lavern and Uncle Julius's home. Remember?"

"Oh. I forgot." Then it all came rushing back to me. "Mama, I had cookies and lemonade, and Belinda told us a story about corn, and she changed Dora's and Bella's diapers on a tall table—right over there," I pointed. "And there is a giant bear, right there." Yosie was rubbing her eyes, sitting on the floor by the bear. "And I took a nap on this pillow." I picked it up and thrust it at her. "Feel how soft, Mama. Feathers!"

Her face had an expression on it that I had not seen before. It made me feel kind of sad, but I did not know why. Tears welled up in her eyes.

"You okay?" I asked.

"I am just fine." She picked me up off the cot and hugged me. "I am so glad you are mine," she said. "Now we need to go to supper. And there is a surprise for you." She put me down.

"Yuck!" I said. "I know the surprise. Belinda told me."

"You have never had a hot dog. How do you know you do not like it?"

"She called it lob… She said it is like a big crawdad. I do NOT want to eat crawdads."

Mama laughed, and the sound of little bells tinkled. "The grown-ups are having lobster. But you and Yosie get to have hot dogs."

"But I do not want to eat a dog, either," and I started to cry.

"They are not really dogs; they are just called that." Mama bent down and hugged me again. "I know you will like them. Just come and see. But first, we need to wash your hands.

I looked around.

"What are you looking for, Helmi?"

"The pump."

"Oh. Well, I have a surprise for you." She took me by the hand and led me to a tiny room with a white basin that had funny-looking handles sticking up out of it and a spigot under each one, but they were much smaller than the spigot on our kitchen pump. Mama reached up and turned one of the handles, and water instantly came out of it.

"No pumping?" I asked.

"No pumping."

I was fascinated; so fascinated, in fact, that I had not noticed the toilet sitting at the other end of the room. Then I saw it. "What is that?"

"It is called a toilet. *That* is where you do your business."

"No outhouse?"

"No. You do not have to go outside when you need to potty," she said. "Would you like to try it?"

I nodded, not too sure about the whole thing. There was water in it, and the hole in the seat was much bigger than I was used to. "Hold me, Mama." I did not want fall in.

She helped me, and then she said, "Now watch this."

There was a wooden box over our heads. Attached to the box was a pipe that ran all the way down to the toilet. There was a chain hanging from the box. Mama reached up and pulled the chain, and the water in the toilet began to swirl. It went round and round until it disappeared down a hole in the bottom.

I stood with my mouth open. I did not know what to think. *Am I still asleep and dreaming about all of this?*

"Now you must wash your hands," she said. "In the sink." She held me up, and I turned the handle—the water came splashing out really fast and went all over. Mama jumped back, and I squealed. She put me down and turned the faucet down to a trickle. She looked at me, and I thought I was about to get a scolding. But she broke out into a laugh (and the bells tinkled), so I laughed, too.

We managed to get my hands washed using a bar of sweet-smelling soap that sat in a white dish that was raised up on a tiny pedestal. The dish was made of what Mama called "milk glass." It had little bumps all over it, like bubbles. Then I dried my hands on a soft towel. I was beginning to like the things they had in Chicago.

"Will our new house have these things?" I asked Mama.

"I do not know, but they certainly are nice, are they not?"

"They certain are."

When we went into a room that Aunt Lavern called "the dining room," I saw two tables. There was a big one for the grown-ups and a little one just for Yosie and me. I had never eaten at my own table before. A large woman wearing a white apron was hurrying about, making trips back and forth between the kitchen and this room, putting food on the tables.

The hot dogs were great! I ate two of them and some corn. And I drank a big glass of milk. Then we had cake, even though it was no one's birthday. The cake was real soft, and it had sweet red raspberries on it. I was in Heaven, and I decided that was where I was supposed to be, because the cake was called "angel food." The woman who brought us our food asked me if I wanted another glass of milk. I looked at Mama, and she nodded and said, "half." I drank every last drop of it.

When everyone got up from the table, Uncle Julius came over to me and said, "You have a good appetite there, young lady. I don't see a single crumb on your plate." And he patted me on the head like I was a dog. I was not sure about him. The entire time we had been eating, he had been talking. Except for an occasional "Yes" or "No" or "Really?" no one else talked, only him. I did not pay much attention to what he was saying; most of it went over my head anyway. He took us into the sitting room. I sat down between Mama and Granny Nan.

The grown-ups chatted awhile about things I did not care about. Mama's hands were full trying to keep Yosie quiet and sitting still. The twins were on the floor, playing with some stuffed toys Belinda had given them right after supper. But she had disappeared. I was sorry I had not gotten to say good-bye to her. I really liked her.

Finally, Uncle Julius rose from his chair and picked up a box, bringing it over to Papa. "Cigar?" he opened the box and offered it to Papa, but Papa turned him down.

"They're Cuban…straight from the island," he said to Papa. Papa waved his hand and shook his head.

Uncle Julius straightened up and cleared his throat. "You don't know what you're missing, Heinrich." Then he lit his cigar, took a long drag on it, and blew out the smoke. It smelled terrible, and it made me cough. He walked over to the fireplace and leaned against the mantle. Then he took another drag on the cigar and looked up. There, on the wall, was a painting of the same photo he had sent to Papa, the one with the big ship between him and Aunt Lavern. "I trust you looked at the photo included in the letter Lavern last sent to Violet?"

"I did," Papa said.

Uncle Julius pointed to each word: *"The Chicago Iron Freight Company. Julius Gounaris."* The ship was named after him. "This is the epitome of my dedication to Chicago Iron Freight. I have poured my all into that company, and I have been rewarded." He sucked in and blew out another big load of smoke. "The ship is an ore freighter. She goes through the Great Lakes from Gary, Indiana, to Marquette, Michigan, traveling up Lake Michigan, through the Straits of Mackinac, up the Sainte Mary's River and through the locks at Sault Sainte Marie, then across the mighty Lake Superior to the docks at Marquette, queen of the iron industry, where she is loaded with taconite—raw iron ore. When her hold is full, she reverses the route back to Gary and unloads her prize, making it possible to provide steel, not only for our own country but for all of Europe as well. The steel industry is booming, Heinrich."

He puffed again on that awful-smelling cigar and walked to a wooden cabinet that had a fancy glass bottle and short little glasses sitting on it. He poured two glasses of what looked like iced tea, handed one of them to Papa, and said, "Ladies, would you excuse us? I have some business to take care of with Heinrich."

Without a beat, Papa said, "Yulius, the ladies may stay. I have no secrets from my family; my business is theirs. Vhatever you have to say, you can say it in front of them."

"But, but the children…" Uncle Julius stuttered.

"They vill stay," Papa said again.

Aunt Lavern had already stood in preparation to escort Mama, Granny Nan, me, Yosie, and the twins to another room. But none of us had budged. She looked at Uncle Julius with an expression of disbelief.

"Sit down, Lavern. I will conduct my business with an audience, just as Heinrich wishes." Aunt Lavern plopped back down in her chair, and he swallowed his glass of amber-colored liquid in one gulp. Papa set his glass, the liquid in it untouched, on the table beside him.

Uncle Julius clasped his hands behind his back and walked back and forth across the room twice. "Heinrich, I…" he turned toward Mama and said, "Excuse me if I do not address you personally, Violet, Nancy, children," his head moving from one of us to the next. Then he returned his attention to Papa. "I am creating a position in my company in Gary." He paused for affect. "I am prepared to offer that position to you, Heinrich." His pacing came to an abrupt halt. Then he spun around and faced Papa. "You could have all of this," he swept his arms around, "in time, if you work your way up the corporate ladder." He looked Papa square in the face, lowering his head and grabbing hold of his lapel.

Papa, too, lowered his head and pursed his lips. In typical Papa fashion, he sat there, thinking, for a full minute. The only sounds in the room were the babbles of Dora and Bella as they continued to play with the stuffed toys. Yosie said, "Ma..." but before she could utter the complete word, Mama had her hand over Yosie's mouth and uttered a pointed "Shh!"

Papa took a deep breath and blew it out slowly, making a hissing sound. Then he put his hands on the arms of the chair in which he was sitting and pushed himself up to a standing position at his full height; he was far taller than Uncle Julius. I did not know what Papa was going to do.

In a very low voice, Papa said, "Yulius, ve are farmers. Ve like farming. It vill never make us rich, but ve do not have to put fences around our house or lock our doors at night to keep people from stealing our possessions. Ve do not have to pay people to clean our house, cook our food, drive our truck, groom our yard, care for our children. Ve do not need to dress in fancy clothes and parade around town in order to be noticed. And ve vill never have a ship named after us. But ve vill be able to sleep at night vitout the fear of losing everything ve own if the bank closes. Ve need no vun to look after our money for us."

Papa put his head down for a few seconds, then he looked back up at Julius and said, "This country fought for freedom from England in the Revolutionary Var. Ve fought for freedom of the slaves in the Civil Var. And ve fought in the Great Var in order to help our allies, because Deutchland—my homeland—vas performing atrocities against this country. It broke my heart that so many American soldiers—fifty thousand of them—lost their lives in that var overseas. So today, I fight to show them how much I appreciate vhat they did for me and my family. I fight by vorking my fields, and I provide food for the American people to atone for vhat my homeland did to them." He stopped and cleared his throat.

"I may be of German heritage, but now I am an American, and I am proud of that. And if that pride means that I must vork the soil to earn it, I vill do it. I vill not be a part of some industry that cares more about making money than it does about supporting my..." he shook his head "...*our* freedom."

Julius stood motionless.

Papa reached down and picked up the glass of liquid, walked over to Julius, and put the glass in Julius's hand. "Thank you for your hospitality, but ve have a farm vaiting for us in Michigan. I think ve need to be on our vay."

Mama stood up and took Papa by the arm. She looked up at him with such respect, such regard for his character, that it made me proud, too—proud of Papa, proud of being a farmer, proud of knowing that living and working our farm offered us a sense of dignity that Uncle Julius and Aunt Lavern would never experience.

Granny Nan stood and stared at Lavern, then her eyes drifted to the man her firstborn had married, and I could see the sorrow there. She turned, picked up Dora, and walked out of the room. Mama walked over to Lavern and hugged her; not a word was exchanged. Mama picked up Bella and took Yosie by the hand and followed Granny Nan. Papa looked at me, and I went to him. I was so honored to take the hand of a man who had, in less than five minutes, made me aware of the unsung decency, the morality, of our simple life.

CABBAGE ROLLS AND MASHED POTATOES

With the help of Mama and the map, we managed to reach the southeastern outskirts of Chicago by nine p.m. For the first time since we had left our home in Oklahoma, we slept in a bed. I did not know anything about hotels or inns, but I quickly learned that they are much better than sleeping in the truck! The hotel where we stayed had indoor plumbing and electricity. I was beginning to like those amenities. However, it would be the only one we'd stay at throughout the whole trip because it cost a lot of money, and we did not have much of that.

Granny Nan said quietly to me, "The only reason we are staying here is because there is no place to park the truck where we are allowed to sleep in it."

Granny Nan had spent her late teenage years in Indiana. When we crossed the Illinois/Indiana border, her face lit up. "My heart will always be in Indiana, not Oklahoma," she had told me once. Her grandfather had moved his family from Massachusetts to the outskirts of Indianapolis when she was sixteen years old. She lived among some of the most elite citizens of that city, "But I loved it because there was so much open space around the city. I never tired of taking Sunday-after-church outings to remote areas on the outskirts of 'Indy' with my family and a picnic basket full of yummies. I think my father liked it, too, because that was when I saw him smile." She told me her grandfather had been a bit of a stick in the mud, but her father loved the outdoor life. Evidently, he was very athletic. "I remember my mother calling him her Olympian," she said, "though I did not know what that meant when I was young."

She did not talk about her early years very often, so I learned to listen carefully when she did; I wanted to commit every word of it to memory. I loved Granny Nan with all my heart, probably in part because she and I shared deep-rooted similarities. I would learn, too, that we shared many of the same genes, including the one that governed longevity.

We were not on a route toward Indianapolis, so Granny Nan

would not be seeing the city she loved. It did not matter to her. Though she had only lived in Indianapolis for a few years, it was special to her, and just being in the state sparked innumerable memories. There was a smile on her face and a glow in her eyes when the reminiscences began spilling over. I learned that she had been the belle of the ball when her grandfather allowed her to go to his company's annual dance. She had loved dancing and knew how to do every one that was popular in her day: the Grand March, all of the waltzes and polkas, the Schottische, the Virginia Reel.

"I never grew weary when dancing," she said. "Instead of becoming tired, I became more alive with each step, each twirl."

"Is that where you met..." I caught my tongue before finishing my question. I was going to ask about Buster, but I remembered that we did not talk about him.

"Yes," she said. "And he was dashing and debonair. And quite the dancer himself." But that was the only comment she volunteered about him.

"We wore long dresses with petticoats and big hoop skirts."

"What are those?"

"Petticoats are satin undergarments that make swishing noises when you walk or dance. A hoop skirt was something we tied around our waists to make our dresses stand out away from our legs. They made a dress take on the shape of a bell. They were made with circular channels that held whalebone, which stiffened them. The channels got bigger and bigger as they went from our waist to the floor. That is what made them flare out in a bell shape. They were quite fashionable, and they also kept us cool because they kept the fabric away from our lower body."

I loved Granny Nan's stories; I could listen to them all day. She told them in a way that made it easy for me to imagine what her life was like way back before I was born.

Before long, we were in Michigan City. I was so thrilled; I thought we were in Michigan. Papa said, "That is the craziest thing I have ever heard. A town in Indiana is called Michigan City. Who names these places?" But it was not long before we reached the Indiana/Michigan line. Papa had decided to go up to Benton Harbor, Michigan, and then cut a diagonal to Flint.

There was a lovely park in Benton Harbor, right on the lake's edge. Papa pulled into it, and for the first time, I took in the awe-inspiring view. I could not believe the size of Lake Michigan. And the color—it was blue and beautiful.

"It is like looking at the ocean," Mama said. "You cannot even see across it; there is no land visible on the other side."

I could smell a difference in the air, too. It certainly did not smell like the dusty air of Oklahoma. It was clean. And there was an aroma I could not identify. I am sure it must have been the trees. Having lived my whole life up to this point in a place where trees were few and far between, my olfactory sense was overloaded. I had to wrap my head around the fact that I was standing on the shore of one of the Great Lakes. Granny Nan laughed at me, standing there with my face turned upward, my nose in the air. But I was not the only one doing that; Betsy's nose was sniffing a-mile-a-minute. She was taking in as many of the wonderful smells as she could, and the clean air was a bonus.

We put blankets down on the sand and ate the best food I had ever tasted. It was the same old fare, but somehow it tasted so much better than it ever had before. Papa even said, "Vhy is this bologna so much better today than it vas a couple of days ago?"

We all agreed that the Michigan air would be good for us. "And for our crops and livestock, too," Papa added. Uncle Herrmann was not expecting us for a couple more days, so we stayed on the beach the rest of the day and slept in the truck that night with the sound of the waves lulling us to sleep.

It was no longer chilly—it was downright cold. But we snuggled together under our blankets and kept each other warm. It did not matter to me that it was cold. I had always tolerated the heat of Oklahoma, but I did not like it. It made me sweaty, and the dust always stuck to me. I could not imagine that happening here. I was finally in Michigan. This was where I was going to live for a long time, maybe the rest of my life. And I was okay with that.

Uncle Herrmann came bounding toward the truck to greet us. He was smiling and waving, shouting "Hello!" to us. He was the same height as Papa, but he was heftier. He sported a beard that was trimmed close around his chin, and a moustache curled up at the corners. He reminded me of the big stuffed bear at Aunt Lavern and Uncle Julius's house, and I loved him the minute I laid eyes on him.

Papa's eyes were overflowing with tears. He leapt from the truck and ran to meet his brother. They embraced and pounded each other on the back. It made me so happy. I climbed out of the back of the truck and was helping Yosie down when Uncle Herrmann grabbed us both around the waist and gave us big hugs. He kissed each of us on the top of the head, then he put us down and petted Betsy, who seemed to be barking for the sheer joy of being in the midst of so much happiness.

Papa was helping Mama and Granny Nan with the twins. Uncle Herrmann walked directly up to Mama, bowed, and then grabbed her by both shoulders; he looked her square in the eyes then kissed her on the cheek. "It is so good to see you, Violet. You look beautiful."

Next in line was Granny Nan. She yelped when Uncle Herrmann lifted her off her feet and spun her around. "You can keep your kisses," she said, laughing like a schoolgirl. "I am too old for such nonsense."

"One is never too old to be kissed," he said, and planted a kiss right on her lips. Granny Nan turned at least six different shades of red. Then he gently placed her feet back on the ground and picked up one of the twins off the front seat of the truck. He looked questioningly at Papa.

"Isabella—Bella," Papa said.

Uncle Herrmann gingerly handed her to Granny Nan. Then he picked up the other twin and said, "And you must be Isadora."

"Dora," I said.

He was so gentle with her. He cradled her in one big arm and said to us all, "We have so much to catch up on. And, of course, I have lots of news about your new home. Come. Let's go into the house and have some iced tea. I brewed some just this morning." He looked at Yosie and me, then he bent down and whispered to us, as if it were a secret, "And for you, I have root beer." I jumped up and down, clapping my hands with joy. I decided right then and there that, if this was any indication as to how wonderful Michigan was going to be, I would rather be here than in Heaven.

He lived in a modest frame house that was white with a dark green roof and green shutters. There were flowers along the base of the house; they were orange with dark spots and centers that stuck out past the petals, and they were on long stems poking out of lots of thin leaves that ran from the ground up and bent over until their tips were again touching the ground. There was a large flower bed on each side of the yard. The rest of the yard was covered in grass, green and lush. I had never seen such pretty grass, not even at Aunt Lavern and Uncle Julius's. I thought, *They have men who take care of their yard, but it does not look as pretty as Uncle Herrmann's.*

He opened the door for us, and we all traipsed in. There was no little room with statues and mirrors; we walked right into the living room. It was warm and friendly and cozy. I felt right at home. Papa and Mama and Granny Nan and Uncle Herrmann were all talking at once. "How was the trip?" "Your home is lovely." "The trip vas a long vun." "Yosie, stay here with me." "How old are the twins now?" "What a beautiful place you have here!" "Do not touch that, Yosie."

My mind was reeling, and I was giddy with joy, not just for myself, but for Papa and Mama and Granny Nan. I knew we had come to the right place; Michigan was exactly what I had hoped it would be.

Mama followed Uncle Herrmann into the kitchen. It was separated from the living room by an arched opening. There was a large pitcher of iced tea sitting next to a tray with four glasses on it. Mama poured the tea, all the while making conversation with Uncle Herrmann. Then Uncle Herrmann picked up the tray and brought it to the living room where he offered a glass to Granny Nan, Mama, and Papa. Then he headed back to the kitchen, turned and looked at me, and used his head to motion to me that he wanted me to come to the kitchen with him.

"If you open that icebox, you'll find a big bottle of root beer. I hope it's cold enough. It's been in there since last night." I had never seen root beer in a bottle. I had no idea it came that way. I pulled on the icebox door, but it didn't budge. "Pull harder," Uncle Herrmann said. "It sticks sometimes." I pulled hard, and it came open to reveal a big dark brown bottle. I recognized the words "Root Beer;" I had seen them many times at the ice cream parlor in Beaver City. I looked up at Uncle Herrmann. "Well, bring it over here," he said. It took both hands for me to lift it. I used my foot to close the icebox door.

"Wow! You even closed the door. You're quite a big girl. How old are you, now? Fifteen?" I stared at him like he was crazy. Then he laughed. And I did, too. He had a special tool that fit over the top of the bottle, and it made the lid pop right off. He got two more glasses and put them on the tray. Then he poured out the root beer, allowing it to foam up. He waited for some of the foam to disappear, then he poured more into one of the glasses. "That one's yours," he said. "I'm not going to fill Yosie's as full as yours. We don't want her to spill it."

Mama had sat down on a straight-backed chair, and Yosie was on the floor beside her. When Uncle Herrmann carried the tray toward her, Yosie tried to get up, but Mama pushed her down and made her stay. "Here you go," Uncle Herrmann said to her. Of course, she wanted the glass that had more in it, but Mama picked up the one with less in it and handed it to Yosie, whose lower lip began to pooch out. We had all been watching the whole thing take place, and it was Papa who laid down the law. "Josephina! Do vhat your Mama says." Yosie sat back down—hard—and folded her arms over her chest, lower lip still protruding.

Uncle Herrmann backed up and said, "Heinrich, I think a rooster could perch on that lip." Then without waiting for a reaction from Yosie, he turned and offered me the only other glass on the tray.

I noticed that Granny Nan was wearing a smile. I think she appreciated the way Uncle Herrmann had put Yosie in her place without reprimanding her. At any rate, Yosie quietly drank her root beer from her sitting position on the floor.

After some small talk, Uncle Herrmann invited us to go out back to the guest house. *A guest house!* He said, "I didn't know what I was going to do with it when I bought this place, but I found it to be really useful when people come into town on business. General Motors has a lot of visiting buyers and big wigs, and some of the other companies in Flint, even up the Saginaw way, need places to put visitors up, too. The word got out that I was willing to board them, so I use their payment as a little bit of added income."

"Ve vill be glad to…" But that's all the farther Papa got.

"You will NOT be paying me to let you stay there. The strangers who stay don't pay me directly; it's their companies that do. I won't even accept a tip from them, and I am certainly not going to accept any money from family. So put it right out of your head, Heinrich. Your money is no good here."

Papa was silent.

Mama changed the subject. "You do not have an accent anymore," she said to Uncle Herrmann.

"I've lived here long enough it's disappeared. And I've been among so many local people for so many years, their language rubbed off on me. In fact, they don't call me Herrmann (he exaggerated the rolling 'r'); they call me Herman."

"It suits you," Granny Nan said.

Uncle Herman's back yard was every bit as nice as the front, but instead of flowers, he had a huge vegetable garden. It was completely enclosed by an eight-foot-high fence. Papa took a look at it and asked, "Are you trying to keep something out or something in?"

"Deer," Uncle Herman said. "They outnumber us around here. Them and the rabbits."

"Ja, but so high?"

"The deer can jump over a six-foot fence, so I went on up to eight feet for better protection. And I also buried the fencing in the ground about a foot to keep the rabbits and other filchers out. So far, so good. Take a look at those cabbages. I'm kind of proud of them. They need to be cut, and I'm ready to cook up some cabbage rolls. How does that sound?" He looked at me and said, "Tomorrow morning, how about you and I come out here and gather them?"

My eyes got big, and I nodded.

"Then perhaps you ladies will give me a hand at wrapping the rolls," he said to Mama and Granny Nan, but he didn't give them time to answer. "I used most of the heads I harvested last year to make kraut. I canned it. Put up sixteen quarts."

"Oh my!" Mama said. She had never heard of anyone getting that much of *any* crop from the piddly gardens we had back in Oklahoma.

Granny Nan said, "Do you plan to use some of that kraut with the cabbage rolls?"

"Absolutely."

Papa said, "I have taught my two cooks vell, Herrmann. They know how to make a couple of German boys' bellies happy."

"I also have several hills of potatoes," Uncle Herman said. "Wilhelmina and I can dig up some of those tomorrow morning, too, and we can have mashed potatoes."

"Helmi," I said.

There was a moment of silence.

Mama explained, "Her nickname is Helmi. You do not need to waste so much breath by calling her Wilhelmina."

"Helmi it is, then," Uncle Herman said. "I like it."

He took us into the guest house. At first impression, it reminded me of our cabin back in Oklahoma, as there was one large room that contained a living space with a fireplace, a kitchen, and a dining table. But behind that area, down a hallway, were two bedrooms and a bathroom.

"Wander around a bit and make your sleeping arrangements. There's an extra bedroom in the house that I don't use. So that's available, too. And I'll expect you to use all three—the two here in the guest house and the one in the main house. When you figure it out, we'll get all the things you need out of the truck." He turned around and went back out on the porch, which was big enough to accommodate two rocking chairs. It also had a cover over it that followed the house's roof line.

Papa, Mama, and Granny Nan looked at each other. They did not move. What were they waiting for? I was ready to pick out the room I wanted to sleep in, but they just stood there with faces that appeared to be made of stone.

Without any warning, Mama grabbed Papa and hugged him. "He is such a gem," she whispered. "Thank you for bringing us here."

"I would hug you, too, Heinrich, if I could reach around your neck," Granny Nan said.

❖❖❖

I was awake earlier than usual. I wanted to lie in the bed a lot longer because it was so comfortable. But Uncle Herman had said we were going to cut cabbages this morning, and I was supposed to help him. Papa and I had been chosen to stay in the main house bedroom; Mama and Granny Nan could sleep with the twins and Yosie in the guest house.

I got up and tiptoed down the hall to go to the bathroom, being careful not to wake Uncle Herman, who slept in the bedroom on the other side of the bathroom. When I came out, Uncle Herman was standing at the end of the hallway, already dressed and drinking a cup of coffee. I waved at him, and he held his coffee cup out toward me. He whispered, "Want a cup?"

No one had ever offered me coffee before, so I was a bit taken back. I thought about it for a second or two, then I nodded. I went out to the kitchen and sat down at the table. Uncle Herman poured the steaming dark brown liquid into a small cup, then he poured some milk into it and added two spoonfuls of sugar and brought it to me, along with a spoon. "Give it a good stir," he said. He had buttered a piece of bread and sprinkled it with a mixture of cinnamon and sugar. He handed it to me on a plate. "Dunk that in your coffee. Makes a great breakfast." He was right. I loved it.

We sat there and talked—a real conversation. He talked to me like an adult. He told me about the school I would probably be going to in a couple of years, and I asked him about the Michigan winters and Mount Pleasant. He told me there was another town close to the place we would be living. "It's called Weidman. Depending on which farm your Mama and Papa decide to buy, you might live closer to it than Mount Pleasant."

"Vhat is this about Weidman?" (Papa pronounced it Viteman.) He was standing at the doorway to the hall. He was dressed and ready for the day. I, on the other hand, was sitting at the table in my underpants. Papa took one look at me and said, "I hope you did not cut cabbages dressed like that. It is a bit chilly for being outside in such a state of undress." He grinned, and I ran to him and hugged his leg.

"Papa, Uncle Herman says it snows here!"

"Ja, this is true. Ve vill have to get some vinter clothes soon."

"Pour yourself a cup of coffee, Heinrich. Milk and sugar are on the counter."

"I like mine hot and black," Papa said.

"You're easy to please." Uncle Herman smiled. "Violet must like that."

"A man who is easy to please also pleases easily." They both laughed. I did not understand why that was funny. They continued to talk and eat, so I went into the bedroom and put on my clothes. I only had a couple of outfits, and I did not want to get either of them dirty when it was time to cut cabbages and dig potatoes, so I made a mental note to be extra careful.

My mouth tasted bad. I wanted to brush my teeth, but the toothbrush and tooth powder were in a bag that Mama and Granny Nan had at the guest house. I went out to the kitchen and asked Papa if I could go over there.

"You might vake Yosie and the tvins. It vould be better to vait."

"We need to get out there and do our gardening anyway," Uncle Herman said. He gulped down the rest of his coffee and got up, stretching and grunting. "Take your time, Heinrich. Get yourself some more coffee. Your daughter and I have a date in the cabbage patch."

It was fun spending time with Uncle Herman. We cut all six heads of cabbage and dug up three hills of potatoes, and we talked about all kinds of stuff. He asked me about life on the farm in Oklahoma, the twister that hit us, and the livestock we had to sell. "Sometimes I miss the farm life," he said.

Mama and Granny Nan came out to the garden just as we were finishing. "Those will make fine cabbage rolls," Granny Nan said. "Violet, look at the size of those outer leaves."

"Where is Papa?" I asked.

Mama pointed toward the guest house. There he was, sitting on the porch in a rocking chair with one twin on each knee and Yosie picking at something in the dirt in front of him. He was smiling.

"Herrmann…"

"Please, Violet, call me Herman. It's much easier."

"All right. I have a favor to ask, Herman."

"And that would beeeee…?" Uncle Herman asked. I giggled. I thought he was the funniest person on the face of the earth.

"I have not been able to wash the twins' diapers in hot water since we started our trip. Oh, I was able to rinse them out occasionally and let them dry in the back of the truck, but I have not had the opportunity to use hot water."

"Say no more. Use my Thor." He grinned. "Well, that was poetic. She's kind of old, but she does the job. I'll have to wipe down the clothesline before you hang anything, though. The birds have been using it as a roost for a week or so. I only do my washing about twice a month. Seeing as how it's only me here, I don't have enough dirty clothes to make a full load more often than that."

Mama was caught off guard. "Your Thor?"

Uncle Herman nodded. "The first electric-powered washing machine. It was invented shortly after the turn of the century. Came from some company in Chicago. It has a galvanized tub and an electric motor," he said proudly.

"I have no idea how to use it," Mama said.

"Not to worry, my dear. I will show you how. Do you want to do it now?"

"Not necessarily. Or we could. I mean, anytime is fine. Whenever is convenient for you."

Granny Nan was already on her way to the guest house to gather up our dirty clothes. "I will get the ones out of the truck, too," she said over her shoulder. I think she was excited, not only that we were going to have clean clothes again, but also that she would get to use an electric washing machine. Our old wooden tub and washboard would be taking a back seat.

When the last of the laundry was hung on the line, Papa said, "Herrmann, ve need to get down to business soon about the new farm."

"You are absolutely right," Uncle Herman said. "How about I get the women started on the cabbage rolls, and you and I can go over the information I received from Abel."

"Goot," Papa said. "After I have seen vhat is available, ve can present it all to Violet and Nancy."

"And Helmi," Uncle Herman said.

"Vhat?"

"That girl is on top of everything. She wants to be a part of this, and I think she deserves to be. Granted, she's only four, but she has a mind that you don't often see in a child. In fact, I don't see that kind of intelligence in most of the GM representatives that come through here. And besides, she's your firstborn and will probably be responsible for all of it one day. I can guarantee you that, decades from now, she'll remember what we talk about today."

Papa rubbed his chin and thought about what Uncle Herman had said. "All right. I suppose it cannot hurt. She vill be quiet and pay goot attention, even though she may not understand much of vhat ve say. She knows nothing of mortgages, taxes, and so on."

"Doesn't matter. She'll have the opportunity to hear the words, at least, and one day it'll all make sense to her."

"I can see your point," Papa said.

"Helmi," Granny Nan called. "I need some help with the cabbage rolls."

I stopped what I was doing. "Me?"

"Yes, you."

"But I never cook," I said in amazement.

"This is a good time to start," she said. "Your mother is putting Yosie and the twins down for a nap in the guest house, so you and I should get things started. Cabbage rolls take a long time to make."

I shrugged my shoulders. "Okay."

"Uncle Herman has shown me where everything is, so we should not need to bother Papa and him while they are talking."

"It's about the new farm," I said, proud of myself for using a contraction for the first time, though I doubt Granny Nan noticed. "They said I should be there, too."

"You can be, but I know your Papa. It will take them at least half an hour before they get down to business. So come here. I will show you how to measure the rice and water." She took me by the hand and led me to the table, which was loaded with jars of this and that, along with bowls, spoons, measuring cups, cooking pots, a chopping board, and a big knife. "Get up on this chair," she said. "On your knees. You should be tall enough to work that way."

I did as she said.

"We need two cups of rice." She handed me the measuring cup and said, "The rice is in that bag. *One* cup is this mark." She pointed to a line on the small glass pitcher-like container. Then she handed it to me. "Fill it up to that line." She let me open the bag of rice and watched me pour some into the measuring cup. There was not quite enough to reach the line. I looked up at her with an inquisitive face.

"Not quite enough," she said. "You can use a spoon to finish." When I had exactly one cup, she smiled and said, "That is good, Helmi. Now pour it into that small pot." She pointed to the one she meant.

I poured it in, and it made a tinkling sound as it hit the bottom. I looked at her.

"We need *two* cups."

I looked at her again.

She looked back at me with an expression I knew; it meant, *figure it out.* "You already put *one* cup of rice in the pan. But we need *two* cups of rice. Do you know how to do that?"

I held up one finger. "This is one." Then I raised up another finger and said, "And this is two. So I put one cup in two times."

She smiled and nodded, then she watched as I added the second cup to the pot. "Now we need to add water. *Two* cups."

There was no water on the table. So…I got down off the chair and took the measuring cup to the sink. But I couldn't reach the faucet.

"You'll need to take the pot over there with you, too."

I went back to the table and got it. I carried it over to the sink and lifted it high up onto the counter being careful not to spill the rice.

Granny Nan came over and turned on the water. She lifted me up, and I filled the cup and poured it into the pot twice.

"That is exactly right!"

I had a good time talking to Granny Nan while we worked. She and Uncle Herman were a lot alike in that they talked to me as an adult. She told me about ice skating once when she was a child in Indianapolis. She said it got cold enough to keep the water frozen on the river that ran through town, and there were so many people skating on it, she didn't have to worry about falling down because they were packed in so tightly to one another.

"Will we skate here?" I asked.

"Probably," she said. "We are much farther north than Indianapolis. So if it froze there, it will definitely freeze here."

"We need skates," I said.

"All in good time," she said with a smile.

Mama came into the kitchen. "The girls are asleep—finally. It looks like you do not need me to help." She put her hands on her hips.

I was yawning. I had already had a big day. It had been a while since I was able to help Papa in the barn, so I wasn't used to being so busy.

"It looks to me like you need a nap, too, Helmi," Mama said. "You should go into the bedroom and let Granny Nan and me finish making the cabbage rolls."

"But, I need to be with Papa and Uncle Herman."

"They already discussed the fact that she should be in on the particulars," Granny Nan said to Mama. She may have winked at Mama, too, but I wasn't sure.

"Okay, be off then," Mama said.

I didn't argue.

❖❖❖

Supper was grand! I liked the cabbage rolls even better than I had liked the hot dogs at Aunt Lavern and Uncle Julius's. I had helped make the mashed potatoes, and I made it a point to tell everyone, "They are so good because I put in extra butter."

When we finished, Mama and Granny Nan gathered up the dishes to be washed, but Uncle Herman said, "Leave them. We can do them after we talk."

"But they..." Granny Nan started to say.

"No buts, Nancy," Uncle Herman said. "What we have to talk about is far more important than some dirty dishes. Now, come and sit. Heinrich already has all of the information in order."

Mama and Granny Nan just stood there.

"Come! Now!" Papa said.

I was sitting on Papa's lap. He put me down, so I started to leave. "No, Helmi. Do not leave. Ve are having a discussion that involves you, as vell. You should sit on that chair and listen to vhat ve are saying."

I couldn't believe my ears. *Papa wants me to stay. Has he gone mad?*

"Heinrich," Mama said. "Do you not think she is too young to understand…"

"She stays," Papa said. "She has a right to know vhat is going on. She may not understand it all, but she vill vun day." He looked at Herman, and they nodded to one another.

They talked about three different farms. Two of them already had existing out-buildings and a house, the third was land only. They threw around numbers to which I was oblivious, and they used words that I vaguely remembered from when Papa had talked to Mr. Setters about our Oklahoma farm. Words like mortgage, property tax, loans, interest, investment, profit and loss. I didn't understand, but I knew that someday I'd need to know about all of this, so I listened without allowing my mind to wander.

Uncle Herman pointed to photos and said to us, "These are the properties with the houses and out-buildings on them. I've made you an appointment to meet with the realtor tomorrow so you can see them in person. There aren't any photos of the inside of the houses, so you'll want to walk through them and decide if either of them is right for you, or if you think you should buy the empty property and build a place yourselves."

Papa added, "Herrmann says that lumber is getting more and more expensive vit each passing day, so if ve decide to build, ve must get started right avay. If ve vait, the cost could go beyond what ve vould be able to borrow."

I looked at the houses. One was small and very old; it looked like it might fall down any minute. The other one was very tall and kind of reminded me of a castle I had seen on the cover of one of Mama's books. The farm with the falling-down house had a new barn and several other buildings. There was a big machine sitting beside one of the buildings, but I didn't recognize it. It was kind of like a tractor but not like any tractor I had ever seen. Doc Weiser had a tractor, but his wasn't even close to being the size of this one. The castle-house farm had an older barn that was attached to a long, low building with another smaller building attached to that. The roof of the low building had holes in it. I was studying it and must have had a puzzled look on my face.

"What is it, Helmi?" Uncle Herman asked.

"What kind of barn?" I asked and pointed to it on the photo.

"Oh, that's a stanchion barn and milk house."

I was stumped.

"Your Papa wants to have a dairy farm. That means you'll be milking lots of cows instead of just one or two."

"And the cows come vit the farm," Papa said, "if ve vant them."

I asked, "What about chickens?"

Mama jumped in and answered. "We will definitely have chickens, Helmi, but we will start with just a few and let them multiply. We will not be selling eggs at first; they will only be for us. We will raise more chickens over time by allowing the eggs to be fertilized."

"And roosters?" I asked. I began to breathe hard.

"Do not vorry," Papa said. "Ve vill only have vun rooster, so he vill not be so mean. He vill not chase you around the barn lot."

"Whew!" I said. Everyone laughed.

They talked some more about the pros and cons of each farm until Papa said, "Ve cannot make a decision tonight. Ve need to see the places in person. So let us sleep on it, and tomorrow ve can look at them and come to a conclusion."

"You go, too, Uncle Herman?"

"No, Helmi. I have to go to work tomorrow."

"Where?"

"At the plant."

I didn't understand.

"...at General Motors where I measure things and draw pictures and talk to lots of people all day."

"I would rather look at farms and talk to cows," I said.

Papa threw his head back and laughed, and everyone else followed suit.

"She is definitely your daughter, Heinrich," Uncle Herman said. "She is farmer through and through."

The sky was turning amber, and I was outside playing with Betsy while Mama washed the supper dishes. Granny Nan, who had been on her feet most of the day cooking, was sitting on the sofa, reading to Yosie, Bella, and Dora from one of their storybooks. Papa and Uncle Herman sat on the guest house porch, rocking and talking. It had been a big day, but tomorrow promised to be even bigger.

MAKING A CHOICE

The first property we were scheduled to look at was on the east side of Mount Pleasant, closest to Flint. We met Mr. Zellers, the realtor, at the farm at nine-thirty a.m. He was a small man, not at all like Papa and Uncle Herman. He was very soft-spoken and moved without any noise. I couldn't imagine him having noisy children around, but he said he had four sons, one of whom was a dairy farmer. He had brought the son along to answer any questions we might have about starting a dairy farm. When Mr. Zellers introduced his son, I didn't quite catch the name. It sounded like Adding Some. *What a strange name*, I thought

"Farming is farming, but being responsible for a herd of dairy cows is something else again," the son said. "You'll be devoting an inordinate amount of time to them."

"I am avare of that," Papa said. "I am villing to make the sacrifice of my time in order to make goot money for my family. I vould also like to have a few head of beef cattle so ve have plenty of meat, and I vill keep some pigs. Oh, and chickens, of course. I plan to keep most of the land free from livestock so I can plant vheat for straw, and corn and alfalfa, maybe some clover, for feed."

Mr. Zellers said, "Well. All these farms have plenty of acreage for that. I am not a farmer, Mr. Schnier. That is why I brought Addison along; he can answer your questions. If you'd like, I can take the ladies and children through the house while you continue your discussion with my son."

"Goot," Papa said. "Violet, Nancy. You go vit Mr. Zellers. I vill join you later."

I took Yosie by the hand, and Mama and Granny Nan each carried one of the twins. We were about to enter the castle house. In a very quiet voice, I asked Mama, "Is this a castle?"

She looked up at it and paused. "Oh, I see why you think that. That round part on the corner is called a turret. Some castles have those, but this is only a house. It has a staircase that goes up through the turret. You will see when we go inside."

I had never been in an empty house before. Everything echoed, and it made noises all the time. I know now that it was because of expansion and contraction, but with nothing to soak up the noise, it was spooky. The floors were discolored, and some of the floorboards were either broken or missing. The kitchen had a pump at the galvanized sink, just like our Oklahoma cabin. The ceilings were cracked, and the walls were covered in old, faded, water-stained wallpaper. There was a single, small, round thing in the middle of the ceiling in each of the rooms with a wire running across the ceiling and down the wall to a button by the door. My eyes followed the wire from ceiling to doorway.

"This house was built before electric was commonly installed, so the lights were wired later," Mr. Zellers said. "Well. I know it is a bit unsightly, but it can be dressed up to look much better." Mama and Granny Nan said nothing.

The rooms each had a big hole in the floor that had been covered with a steel grating. "As you can see, this house uses what we refer to as a gravity heating system. Are you familiar with it?"

Mama and Granny Nan shook their heads.

"Well. There is a furnace in the basement. You feed coal into it, which burns slowly but very hot. Because heat rises, it goes up into the house. These are the grates where the air comes up." He pointed to one in the floor."

"Where do we get coal?" Granny Nan asked.

"There are a couple of fuel companies in the area who will deliver it to your home."

"Where do we keep it?"

"Well. There is a coal bin in the basement beside the furnace. There is a chute that runs directly from the coal truck to the coal bin. Then you shovel the coal into the furnace as needed."

"I do not see any fireplaces in this house," Mama said.

"Well. That is because you don't need them. You will have the furnace to keep you warm."

I thought the downstairs looked bad, but the upstairs was even worse. The stairs that went up through the turret creaked and groaned as we climbed. None of the doors could be closed because the house had settled, and the jambs were all crooked.

"What about plumbing?" Mama asked.

"Well. There is one bathroom. It was added onto the house in… let me see…" He shuffled through some papers. "…1912."

"May we see it?"

"Of course. Have you seen enough up here?"

"Quite enough," Granny Nan said and rolled her eyes as she

turned toward Mama and me; Mr. Zellers couldn't see her.

We went back down the staircase. Mama held my hand really tight, and I held onto Yosie's even tighter; I was scared we'd fall through the steps.

The bathroom was awful. It didn't have any windows, and according to Mr. Zellers, the electricity had been turned off since the previous owners had moved out—four years ago! There was a toilet and a sink, but both were so dirty they were almost black. And it smelled bad, too. I held my nose, and Yosie said, "Mama, stinky."

"Yes, it is. And very dirty." She turned to the realtor and said, "Mr. Zellers, we could never afford to fix up a house this size. And it would most assuredly take some fixing up before I could even think of moving my family into it. The final decision will, of course, depend upon Heinrich's opinion of the land and out-buildings, but I can guarantee you he will be most dissatisfied with the conditions inside this house."

"Yes, ma'am. I understand your concern. Well. Should we ask him to join us?"

"Please do," Mama said.

Mr. Zellers disappeared out the door.

"Good God in Heaven!" Granny Nan said in a loud whisper. "What will we do if Heinrich decides this is the place we should buy?"

"I have some say in the matter, as do you." She took hold of Granny Nan's arm. "We cannot let it happen."

Mr. Zellers, Addison, and Papa came into the house. Papa took one look around and said, "Gott im Himmel!" (God in Heaven!)

"Well. You must agree, Mr. Schnier, this is a perfect size for your family. And may I be so bold as to say, you and Mrs. Schnier are both young, so there is the possibility that your family will grow. Am I right?"

"Possibly," Papa said, distractedly, as he looked around at the disaster that was called a house. His lower jaw had dropped to an impossible distance from his upper jaw, and his eyes were glazed over. "I think ve need to see the next property."

"As you wish. Well. You may follow me in your truck. It is about three miles northwest of Mount Pleasant. It is the property without any improvements—land only."

We all piled into the truck and followed Mr. Zellers' Buick. It took a while to get through Mount Pleasant, but that was to be expected. The town was much bigger than Beaver City, but it didn't hold a candle to St. Louis or Chicago. Once on the other side of town, it didn't take long to reach the unimproved property. Papa got out and talked to Mr. Zellers, who said, "You realize, of course, that you will be getting this piece of land for a lot less since it doesn't have any buildings on it."

"Ja, of course. This has a stream running through it also, correct?"

"Yes, well. You should be able to see a portion of it right over there to the left. It loops around the property and runs across the road. We crossed over it on the way here."

"Ah, so that vas the stream that belongs to this piece of land."

"Yes. In fact, the property is divided by the road. You would own land on both sides. That could be a good thing."

"How vould that be goot?" Papa asked.

"Well. The previous owners had intended to use the land on this side of the road to build their house and keep their livestock. The larger portion of land on the other side of the road was intended to be used for agriculture."

"Vhy did they not stay here?" Papa asked.

"I…really…can't disclose the particulars." He put the back of his hand up beside his mouth and turned his head toward Papa, as if what he was about to say was a secret. "They had a problem with the bank. Basically, they had never farmed before, and when they discovered how much of their goods and property would be borrowed instead of owned, they decided farming was not for them."

"I see," Papa said. "I vould like to valk the property—both sides of the road."

"We can certainly do so, Mr. Schnier. Would you like Addison to come with us?"

"That vould be yust fine," Papa said. He turned toward the car. "Helmi?"

"Yes, Papa."

"Come vit us. Ve need to do some valking."

I climbed down out of the back of the truck and ran to Papa, happy to have something to do, and thrilled to be included in the decision-making process.

"Well. Hello there, young miss," Mr. Zellers said to me. "You going to walk with your father? It's a long way. Are you sure you can walk that far?"

"She is much more capable than I," said Papa, and he took off. I was used to his long strides, and Addison didn't seem to have much trouble keeping up, but Mr. Zellers was struggling.

Addison said, "Dad, why don't you stay in the car. I know pretty much where the property lines are, so you won't need to follow us. Besides, Mr. Schnier and I have a lot to talk about."

Mr. Zellers came to an instant halt. "That might be a good idea,

Addison." We hadn't gone more than about 100 yards, and Mr. Zellers was already huffing and panting. He turned around and moseyed back to his Buick.

Papa and Addison discussed the possibilities of the land on both sides of the road. I thought the idea of the stream running through both parts was a good idea. Of course, I had no idea how much it would cost to build a house, a barn, a stanchion barn, a milk house, and other buildings for the livestock.

Papa and Addison discussed everything from apples to zebras, but as it turned out, the land on which the buildings would be built was only a small fraction of the entire property. It might be too small a segment to keep livestock, especially a large herd of dairy cows. It wasn't ideal for us, but Papa said we could make it work.

We moved on to the last property. It was a lot farther away from Mount Pleasant and much closer to Weidman. The house, which had looked like it was old and falling down on the photo, was really only in need of new siding. The clapboards were dried out on the top part of the house and rotted out on the bottom. "Vhat made the rot happen?" Papa asked Mr. Zellers, who had recuperated from his earlier attempt at a hike.

"Well. We sometimes have a lot of snow here. When the snow piles up around the foundation and lays against the siding, no air circulates around it, and it mildews. Then rot becomes a problem. There are two options to keep that from happening. One is to continually keep the snow shoveled away from the building, and the other is to replace the bottom three feet with stone." I had seen several houses and other buildings with stone around the bottom, but I hadn't thought about any particular reason why. Now it made sense.

"We can go in and look around the house first, if that's all right with you," Mr. Zellers said.

Papa motioned to Mama and Granny Nan to come look around. Mama came, but Granny Nan stayed in the truck. Bella and Dora were both asleep, and Yosie had decided she was not going to go into another spooky house.

When we walked in, we were shocked. It looked almost new. The entrance was on the left side of the house, and there was a fireplace on the front wall with a stone chimney. Little windows decorated each side of the chimney above the mantle. The walls had been recently painted, and there were windows on the other two outside walls, so the sunshine brightened up the whole room. The floors were shiny hardwood—oak, Papa called it. There were no exposed electrical wires or light bulbs.

There were two doorways on the wall opposite the fireplace. The one on the left went to the bedrooms and bathroom. The other went to the kitchen and dinette; we went there first. There was a white sink with faucets, and there was a big stove/oven combination. Cabinets, which lined the whole wall above and below the sink, were made of the same wood as the floor in the living room. There was a space on one wall where an icebox had been, but the icebox itself was gone. A counter with cabinets underneath ran along half of that wall. The other end of the room was open. Mr. Zellers said that was the dinette, which was big enough to hold a table and chairs, but not big enough for a buffet and/or a hutch. I didn't know what either of those things was, but Mama said, "I have no reason to need a buffet; we do not entertain a lot of people. And as for dinnerware storage, I think we can make do with some of the space above or below the sink."

The bedrooms were next. There were only two, but one of them was big enough to hold a bed and a cradle or a crib. The other bedroom was small, but it still had plenty of room for a bed or bunks and a chest of drawers. Each of the bedrooms had a window that could be opened to let in fresh air. A bathroom was housed between the two bedrooms, and the space behind it left room for a closet in each room.

I looked at Mama and Papa, and they were both smiling.

Mr. Zellers asked Papa if he was ready to go out and see the other buildings and the land. Papa said he was, but he'd like for Granny Nan to come in and look at the house while they looked at the barn. Mr. Zellers agreed, and the two of them walked out. That left Mama and me in the house alone.

We looked at each other, and Mama whispered, "I think Papa likes this house." I nodded. I knew I did, and I was sure she did, too. Mama needed to take Granny Nan's place in the truck. Mama passed Granny Nan, who was just coming up to the door. She took one look at Mama and said, "You look like the cat that just swallowed the canary."

I took Granny Nan on the tour, and she, too, was impressed. She loved the stone fireplace. "Did you notice the chimney when we came up to the house? It looks real nice on the outside," she said. We talked about how our table would fit in the dinette, and she was thrilled to see so much counter space, which meant she and Mama wouldn't be taking up space on the table when they were preparing a meal. She liked my idea about bunks in the small bedroom, and she loved the big bedroom because it had enough room in it for Mama and Papa and the twins. And she was thrilled beyond belief with the closet space in each bedroom. "That is quite clever, the way they used the space behind the bathroom and divided it in half for two closets."

"Where will you sleep, Granny Nan?"

"Oh, we can figure something out," she said. I think she was going to vote for this property.

It had been a very long day, and Papa said we all needed to sleep on it before we had a discussion about who liked which and why. I was so tired, I fell asleep at the supper table! I remember looking up at Papa, who was carrying me into the bedroom. "Is it bedtime already?" I asked him as he put me into the bed.

"Ja, for big girls who did so much house-hunting today."

I don't think I answered; I was too tired. But I did wake up once long enough to hear all the grown-ups laughing. Uncle Herman had a big laugh that resounded throughout the whole house, and it made me love him even more. I hoped we would visit him often after we bought our own farm.

When I woke up, fresh air filled my lungs, as Papa had opened the window a crack. I could hear the birds outside as if they were right there in the bedroom with me, and I saw little slivers of sunshine dancing on the wall across from the window. I smelled sausage cooking! I jumped up and dressed, then I went to the kitchen. The grown-ups were all sitting around the table except for Uncle Herman, who was standing over the stove, frying up sausage patties. I crawled up onto Papa's lap.

"There she is!" Uncle Herman said, looking at me.

"Coffee, please," I said to him.

Mama's jaw dropped. "Helmi! Since when do you drink coffee?"

"I fixed her my special recipe," Uncle Herman said. "She knows how good a cook I am." He winked at me.

There was a big plate of hot cakes sitting on the table and a crock of butter beside them. A pan of maple syrup was warming up on the stove, and the sausages were sizzling and turning nice and brown in a big cast iron skillet. Hot cakes and sausage; we usually only had breakfast like that on special holidays.

"You have to go to work?" I asked Uncle Herman.

"Nope. It's Saturday."

I must have looked puzzled. The only day of the week that had mattered to us was Sunday, because we did things differently on that day, though we still had plenty of work to do, including tending the livestock. Not working every day of the week was foreign to me. I knew Uncle Herman had worked yesterday, so why not today, too?

He sensed my confusion. "General Motors only needs me Monday through Friday. That means I have Saturday and Sunday to do whatever *I* want to do. I go to town and run errands, or I stay at home to tend my gardens and clean my houses, or I go visit friends, or I cook breakfast for my family when they come to visit." He was all smiles, currently pouring my coffee.

"After ve fill our bellies," Papa said, "ve vill talk about property and houses and barns and streams, and…"

"Enough, Heinrich," Granny Nan said. "I, for one, cannot think about such things when the kitchen smells so good."

Uncle Herman put my cup of coffee down in front of me. "Don't forget to blow on it a little bit before you try to drink it. It's good and hot."

I felt so grown up.

After the breakfast dishes were washed and put away—Mama and Granny Nan insisted on doing them since Uncle Herman had worked so hard at making the meal—we "got down to brass tacks," as Granny Nan always said when there was something important to discuss. But before we could begin our discussion, Yosie told Mama she had to potty, and the twins, who had been crawling around on the floor and playing, began to fuss.

"I will help Mama change the twins' diapers," Granny Nan said to me. "You take Yosie to the bathroom."

Papa and Uncle Herman spread out some papers the realtor had given us. I could hear them through the door. "I need to apologize for Zellers," Uncle Herman said. "I thought Abel would be showing you around. You'd like him, Heinrich."

Papa chuckled. "Vell. Mr. Zellers is a goot salesman. Vell. His son, Addison, vas very helpful regarding the ins and outs of a dairy farm. Vell…vell."

Uncle Herman snorted a laugh. So did I.

We finally worked out the logistics around the table and began to discuss the properties we had seen the day before, all the pros and cons and how we could afford (or not afford) certain things about each of them. After about an hour and a half, we came to a decision.

"Ve all had our ideas about each of them," Papa said. "Vun had the best house, vun had the best barn, vun was a vaste of the time it took to look at it. But in the end, the best land for running a dairy farm is the vun vitout any buildings on it. Helmi vas right about the stream running through both sections. And I agree vit Addison that ve need to start fresh, not assume anyvun else's problems. As for the house, ve all liked the vun closest to Weidman, but ve vould need to add onto it anyvay, so vhy not build the vun ve need for our growing family.

"There vill be more to do than ve can imagine, I am sure. But hard vork has never stopped us before, right? The thing that vill be the hardest is trying to figure out vhat needs to come first: do ve build or do ve buy cows? If ve buy cows, ve vill be stuck in the cold vitout a place to live. If ve build a place to live, ve vill have to find a place to stay vhile ve are doing it, and ve von't have any cows to bring in milk money."

Uncle Herman was the first to speak. "We have a lot of Amish people who only recently moved into this area from Pennsylvania and Ohio. They're especially adept at building. I've seen them put up a barn in three days and a house in under two weeks with the help of some of the nearby farmers and people from one or more of the churches. They won't take any money for it, but you'd have to provide most of the tools, all of their food and water for as long as it takes to build, and the materials, of course. In turn, they'll expect you to purchase their wares every so often—baked goods, jams and preserves, vegetables they grow and pickle, furniture they make, and so forth."

"Is Amish a religion?" Mama asked.

"It's...it's more like a way of life. Seeing as how you're from Oklahoma, Amish ways are something you've probably not been exposed to." He ran his hand through his hair. "I'll try and explain." He paused in thought, just like Papa, before going on.

"Community is the center of the Amish way of life. Socializing with neighbors and relatives and having large families are the things that are most important to them. In fact, they believe that a large family is a blessing from God. The Amish that live around here usually have large families because they need sons to help with all the work around the farm; hard work is godly to them. They follow a special set of rules, an order that governs their lives. 'Ordnung' is their word for it. It covers religious duties, how they dress, how they interact with people outside their community, uses of machines. In fact, they reject machines thinking they'll give young farmhands too much free time."

"Machines...like vashing machines?" Papa asked.

"Yes sir. Automobiles, running water, and electricity, too."

"You said something about the way they dress," Mama said. "I saw a man in a horse and buggy on the road that runs through the property we are planning to buy. He was wearing a strange flat-brimmed hat. Could that have been one of the Amish?"

"No doubt," Uncle Herman said. He turned back to Papa. "If you want, I can do some asking around to see if there's a community who might be interested in helping you put up some buildings and a house before winter sets in."

"That vould be perfect. But do not give them any specifics. I must talk to the people at the bank first."

"Yes, that would normally be the first move. But it might be prudent to find out if some of the Amish are interested so you can tell the bank you won't need to borrow money for labor, only materials."

"Ah! I see vhere you are going vit this."

"Unfortunately, you'll have to wait a couple of days since the banks won't be open until Monday. I'd say, in the meantime, you should probably make some drawings that show what you want in the way of a barn, house, and any other out-buildings and where you want them on the property. You might also want to go to church tomorrow."

"Vhy is that?"

"Is there an M. E. Church in Mount Pleasant?" Granny Nan asked.

"Methodist Episcopal? Biggest one in the county," Uncle Herman said.

"Do you know what time the service is?"

"No, but we can take a little trip this afternoon and find out. I'd like to see where your prospective new place is, and at the same time I can show you around Mount Pleasant. We can also take a look at your neighbors-to-be," Uncle Herman said.

"Let us not get too far ahead of ourselves," Papa said. "Ve do not know yet if the bank vill allow all of our vishes to come true."

Mama said, "Mother, you go along with them. I will stay here with the children."

My heart sank. Although I loved Uncle Herman's place and wasn't wanting for things to do around there, I wanted, even more, to go with them.

Uncle Herman said, "We can take my Chevrolet, if you don't mind. It has a front seat *and* a back seat—plenty of room for the four of us."

"Three of us," Granny Nan said.

"No, four," Uncle Herman corrected her. "You, me, Heinrich, and Helmi."

❖❖❖

The church service was at ten a.m. Mama, Granny Nan, Papa, and the twins went; I stayed with Uncle Herman and Yosie. It seems that, somewhere along the line, Yosie had picked up a cold. She sneezed a lot, so I was constantly wiping her nose with one of Papa's big white handkerchiefs. She hadn't had a fever, so I figured she was going to be fine in a couple of days. She was cranky and was having trouble breathing. Mostly, she slept.

Uncle Herman said, "The service will probably last an hour to an hour-and-a-half, so that means they'll be home in time for an early supper. What say you and I make them a good meal, Helmi?"

"I helped Granny Nan make rice for the cabbage rolls."

"Well then, it sounds to me like you're an expert chef. I thought we'd make some chicken and dumplings. And you get to make the dumplings."

I looked at him with horror in my eyes. I had let my pride step in front of my ability. *I cannot make dumplings. I am only a little kid who has never cooked before. Food just sort of appears in front of me when it's time to eat. I have no idea where it comes from or how it's prepared.*

"Helmi? I won't make you do it by yourself. It's really quite easy, though. We make them out of flour, eggs, and water, add a little bit of salt and pepper, and drop spoonfuls onto the top of the broth. The lid goes on, and before you know it…chicken and dumplings. Sounds easy, right?"

I couldn't speak. I was overwhelmed. My heart was beating so hard I thought it was going to jump right out of my chest.

Uncle Herman walked over to me and picked me up. "I'm sorry, Helmi. I didn't mean to scare you. I never thought cooking could be scary. I guess I was wrong." He took me out to the front yard and carried me around, all the while distracting me with talk about the trees, the flowers, and the sky. "Have you ever looked for cloud figures?"

I shook my head. *At least I can answer questions, now, without being scared out of my shoes.*

"Look up at the clouds and tell me what you see."

I studied them for a moment, then I noticed one that looked like a big shaggy dog. "Betsy," I said and pointed to the one directly overhead.

"Well, I'll be. It *does* look like her. I think you need to stay out here for a while and look for other things in the clouds."

"All right," I said meekly.

He put me down and went back into the house. The cloud-watching made me forget cooking. It also made me forget Yosie.

Uncle Herman burst through the door with Yosie in his arms. He ran right up to me and asked, "Has she ever done this before?"

I looked at her and saw that her face was red and swollen—really swollen. "No," I said, touching her swollen lips. Her little heart-shaped mouth was puffed out and bright red. I felt her cheeks, and they were hot. "Fever," I said.

"What do we do, Helmi? I've never had children. I don't know what to do." It was Uncle Herman's turn to panic.

Yosie was breathing harder than she had been when I saw her last, about twenty minutes ago. "Cold cloth," I said. "Put it here." I pointed to her forehead.

"There's a washcloth in the bathroom. Let's get it, Helmi." He was carrying Yosie like a baby. Her little arms and legs bounced up and down as Uncle Herman ran with her. They had splotchy red patches on them.

I ran as fast as I could to the bathroom, Uncle Herman right on my heels. He turned on the faucet, and I held the cloth under the water. Then I tried to wring it out, but he grabbed it from me and wrung out most of the water with one hand. Then he put it on Yosie's forehead and began humming to her.

"Maybe on her lips," I suggested.

He got the washcloth wet again, wrung it out, and put it on her mouth and chin. She moaned.

"I'm going to get the dishpan and fill it with cold water, but I'll need to put her in the bed while I do that. Will you stay with her?"

I nodded.

He placed her on the bed, gently, as if she were a breakable china doll. I sat down beside her and felt something stick me in the leg. I looked down and saw that it was a twig with some leaves on it. *Where did that come from? And what kind of plant is it?*

Uncle Herman came running into the room with the dishpan full of water. It sloshed over the side when he stopped and made a wet spot on the bed. He plunged the washcloth into the cold water, wrung it out, and put it on her face.

"Look," I said. I held the twig up. "It was in the bed."

He looked at it. Then he looked at it closer. "Did you have poison ivy in Oklahoma?"

I shrugged. "I never saw it."

He muttered, "Yosie must be highly allergic to it. Which means you might be, too, Helmi. Put that down. Right now!"

I dropped it like it was going to burn a hole in my hand.

"Now go wash your hands and any place else it might have touched you—lots of soap and cold water. Go."

I did as he said, but I didn't understand. The more I thought about it, the more confused I became. How could a twig in the bed make Yosie swell up like that? I had to ask.

"Uncle Herman?"

"Yes." He sounded much more relaxed now.

"What is that poison twig?"

"It's called poison ivy. It vines around things like trees, fences, porch posts, other plants, or it just creeps along the ground. If you're sensitive to it, you have an allergic reaction that makes you break out with red, itchy bumps. They go away after a few days. But some people, like Yosie, are extra sensitive to it. Which means that, when they touch it, or if they put it in their mouths, which I'm sure Yosie did, it makes them break out in a fever, too."

"What do we do?"

"If you'll sit down here on the bed with her, I'll get the witch hazel from the bathroom."

"Get what?"

"Witch hazel. I'll put it on a clean handkerchief and hold it on her face where the redness is the worst. It'll make her feel better."

"Will she always be red like that?"

"No, it'll all go away, the redness, swelling, and the fever. The main thing is, we'll have to make sure she doesn't scratch, because that will open up the blisters and spread the poison." He got up from the bed and lifted me up to the place where he had been sitting. It was warm. I kept putting the washcloth in the cold water, wringing it out, and putting it on the red places—her face, arms, and legs.

Uncle Herman came back with a brown-colored bottle and a handkerchief, which he folded two times so it made a square. Then he held the bottle and handkerchief over the water and poured some of the witch stuff onto the handkerchief until it was completely wet.

"Uncle Herman?"

"Yes, Helmi."

"Is there a witch in that bottle?"

He chuckled. Then he laughed. Then he laughed even harder. "No, no, no, no. There's a plant called witch hazel. This liquid is made from that plant. It's good for healing poison ivy. You keep doing the cold cloths, and I'll keep doing the witch hazel until some of the redness goes away."

"I'm glad you had witch hazel."

"I'm glad you found that twig in the bed. Yosie must have been carrying it around with her for a while. And she must have put it in her mouth. She's had a pretty bad reaction."

"Will we still have chicken and dumplings?"

"No. We have to keep treating Yosie. Maybe we'll have bologna sandwiches."

I heard the Chevrolet drive up.

"You stay here," Uncle Herman said. "I'll go break the news to your Mama. I want to explain what poison ivy is before I bring her back here to see what it did to her daughter."

I heard him explaining it to Mama, and I also heard Granny Nan telling Mama that she reacted to it twice when she lived in Indiana. Nevertheless, Mama looked pretty scared when she came into the bedroom and saw Yosie. She pulled the covers back and saw Yosie's arms and legs, then I took the cloth off Yosie's face, and Mama lost it. She broke into tears and wailed, "Oh, my poor baby! Look at your face!"

That was all it took for Yosie to start screaming and bawling.

Somehow Granny Nan succeeded in getting both of them to calm down. Within a few minutes, the ordeal ended, and Mama and Granny Nan took over for Uncle Herman and me.

Yosie's swelling lasted another day; a few blisters hung on for a week. But it was difficult to keep Yosie from scratching.

Papa said to Uncle Herman, "From Oklahoma dust to Michigan poison ivy. I do not know vhich is vorse."

"I'll take the poison ivy," Uncle Herman said. "At least it goes away in a few days."

THE PROJECT BEGINS

Mid-October was upon us, and we had not yet begun to build our new house or other buildings. Papa had been in Mt. Pleasant every day since the last Monday in September. Sometimes he took Mama with him, but I had never been invited. I knew, somehow, that what he was doing was of no interest to a child, and I would only be in the way. That was okay with me. It wasn't like picking out our property or looking at houses; it was stuff that I had no business sticking my nose into.

Papa had drawn up some plans for a house that was big enough for our family to expand. He took some of the ideas from the two houses we had looked at and combined them, along with ideas of our own, to create a place where we'd all be happy. He was still dead set on having sons to help around the farm, even though he knew it would be years before they would be old enough to do much.

He had also come up with some plans for the use of the land we had bought. The small segment of land on the north side of the road would hold the stanchion barn and milk house, along with a small barn where we'd keep the dairy cattle, and there would be a silo attached to that barn for silage for them. That segment of land would also serve as pasture for the cows. It would have to be fenced in, of course, but we could start with a small fenced-in pasture and increase the size as our herd grew.

We would build our house on the large segment of land, close to the west edge of that part of the property. A large barn, which would have a hay mow on one end and one for straw on the other, as well as space for our equipment between the mows, would be built behind our house. In addition to the buildings, we would fence in a barn lot with a lean-to barn for beef cattle on one end and pigs on the other so they could get out of the weather. Close to the house would be a chicken coop and a large vegetable garden. The remainder of the larger portion of the property would be plowed and planted.

On October 18, Papa set us all down to talk about the plans. Uncle Herman was gone, so it was just Papa, Mama, Granny Nan, and me. He did not include Yosie and the twins. He began by saying, "Ve need to put our ducks in a row."

"We're getting ducks?" I asked excitedly.

Everyone laughed. "That is just a saying," Mama told me. "It means we have to decide what things come first." I didn't get it, but I didn't pursue it any further, either, though I still wanted ducks.

"I think it vould be best if ve proceed in this order…" he held up a piece of paper with a long list on it. "First, ve build our house. I imagine ve are vearing out our velcome here at Herrmann's. He has been a most gracious host, but it is time for us to move on. He vill not take a penny from us, but I know that caring for a family of seven does not come cheaply. I have offered to pay for at least our food and the gasoline he uses vhen ve go someplace in his Chevrolet, but he continues to refuse. It is time—past time—for us to be on our own."

"Agreed," Granny Nan said.

"So," Papa paused. "I vill go to the bank on Monday and get the money to buy the building materials needed for a house. The money is already there and vaiting for us. Some of it is from the sale of our cabin and livestock in Oklahoma; the remainder is in the form of a construction loan. Vhen the house is built, ve change from the construction loan to a mortgage."

"What is the difference?" Granny Nan asked.

"Interest rate," Papa said, and Granny Nan nodded.

I hadn't understood much of what Papa was saying, but I knew I would better understand the words someday when I was older and ready to build or buy my own house.

"Herrmann has taken care of the arrangements vit the Amish since he knows several of the families in their community around here. They vant to start building in three days—before it gets too cold. That gives us time to have the materials delivered to the property so they can start on October 21, Dienstag…uh, Tuesday." He looked at Mama. "Can you talk to the church people and see if any of them vould be available to help us raise the valls that afternoon?"

"Yes, I can ask tomorrow at church. I will talk to Reverend Burton; I am certain he will be able to steer me toward the most likely candidates."

"Then ve are ready, ja?"

"Yes," Granny Nan said.

"I think so," Mama agreed.

Papa looked at me. "Vhat do you have to say, Helmi?"

"Can we get some ducks?"

The exterior walls went up on Tuesday afternoon, as planned.

The weather cooperated, though there was a distinct chill in the air. Most of the leaves had begun to turn colors, something which I had never witnessed. A year ago Mama had shown me a post card Uncle Herman had sent us, and on the front were trees with leaves that were red, orange, and yellow. When Mama showed it to me, I thought it was fake. Now I was learning that it was not only real but also beautiful. And I was seeing it firsthand. I wondered what the people around Beaver City would think if they got to see it in real life…people like Doc Weiser and his family. I liked them, and I sort of missed them a little, probably because I knew Trot and Ham were living on their farm now. I hoped there hadn't been another twister and that their barn was still standing.

Betsy was barking at a squirrel that had taken up residence in one of Uncle Herman's maple trees. The squirrel—I had named her Nutty, because she ate the acorns that fell from the oak trees along the edge of Uncle Herman's property—had been working from sunup to sundown to make her winter nest and to gather and store the acorns. Nutty's tail was long and puffy, and it followed her like the waves that rolled up on the shore of Lake Michigan…the ones I remembered from Benton Harbor. Nutty would find an acorn that she liked, go to a perfect hiding place, dig a hole and put the acorn in it, then cover it up, patting it down with her little paws.

"Betsy! Be still!" Mama shouted from the front porch of the guest house.

I looked up, and she motioned for me to come. I ran as fast as I could to her. I grabbed her skirt and looked up at her. "What? What? What?" I asked in a funny, gravelly voice; I was beside myself with an overall feeling of happiness. I think it must have been the cool fresh air.

"I need the bag of baby stuff. I think I left it…"

"I'll get it. I know where it is." I was really getting the hang of using contractions now. I took off at a dead run, retrieved the bag, then ran it back to Mama.

"Thank you," she said and turned to go back into the guest house.

"Mama?"

She stopped and turned toward me. She said nothing, only looked at me.

"When will I go to school? I would like to meet some other kids."

She blinked a couple of times, then she said, "I will be right back."

While she was inside, I played with a fuzzy caterpillar that was crawling along one of the floorboards of the porch. It was orange on each end and black in the middle. It was soft, and I let it crawl from my hand clear up to my elbow before I took it in my other hand, but when I touched it, it curled up in a circle and didn't move. I held it very still in the open palm of my hand, hoping it would unwind. In only a few of my heartbeats, it straightened out and began to crawl again.

"It is looking for a place to go to sleep for the winter," Mama said. She was standing in the doorway.

I looked at it closely and pointed my finger at it. "You cannot sleep in my sleeve all winter," I scolded.

Mama mimicked me. "That is right, little fuzzy one." She came out and took it from me, putting it down in the grass. "Helmi has to have room for her arms in her coat, so you will just have to find another place to make a bed." It began to crawl away.

"I think it's happier now, Mama."

"How can you tell?"

"It's smiling," I said.

"Would you like to take a walk, Helmi?"

I clapped my hands and jumped up and down. "Yes, yes, yes!"

Mama went into the main house, then she and Granny Nan came out. Granny Nan waved at me then went into the guest house. I figured she was going to stay there in case Yosie or Bella or Dora wakened up from their naps before Mama and I got back. We had formed the habit of walking around the neighborhood once a day where Uncle Herman lived. There were some other houses, but none of them as pretty as Uncle Herman's. There was just something about the way his house glowed in the sunlight. I think that might be why I always wanted a white house with green shutters.

Some of Uncle Herman's neighbors' yards had a lot more trees in them, and they were turning colors, into what Mama called their "fall foliage." No one had ever explained the changing seasons to me; we only had changes in temperature in Oklahoma, not anything as noticeable as changing leaves or snow. I only knew that summer meant hot and winter meant cold. I was learning so much about this new place, and I only wanted to learn more.

"I think it is time you went to church with us every Sunday," Mama said. "They have Sunday School there, and you would meet some other children your age."

"Sunday School?"

"Yes."

"I didn't know there was school on Sunday," I said, highly interested in what she was telling me. "Is it inside the church or at a schoolhouse?"

"Inside the church," she said. "We can leave here a little earlier so all of us can go to our own Sunday School classes. Then when Sunday School is over, we will all go to the sanctuary and hear the reverend preach his sermon."

"Reverend Bryant?"

"No, he is still in Oklahoma. Here we have Reverend Burton."

"Does he read Bible stories?"

"Yes, he reads scripture, then he talks about what the scripture means, just like Reverend Bryant did."

"Who teaches Sunday School?"

"Different people teach different classes. Each class is for people of different ages, even grown-ups. Your teacher would be Mrs. Matsen."

"I would meet other kids? My age?"

"Yes. A few would be three years old, and the others would be four or five."

I was rapidly becoming interested. "Can I go Sunday next?"

"I think you should."

"Okay!" I was excited. I had never been to any kind of school before. I only knew it was a place where I could meet some other kids. I had no idea what was in store for me.

After our walk, I took a nap. The main house was quiet. Papa was at the new property, and Uncle Herman was at work. Granny Nan had been staying at the guest house with Mama, Yosie, Bella, and Dora. Betsy had given up barking at Nutty. The sun was shining brightly, warming up the inside of the house, and the leftover smells from breakfast still wafted through the air. I was contended and happy.

Granny Nan was fixing supper when I woke up. "You like to cook," I said to her, matter-of-factly.

"Yes, I do," she said. "I can think about anything I want when I am cooking."

"What you thinking about now?"

"About our new kitchen. Do you know, Helmi, that we will be cooking a Thanksgiving turkey there this year?"

That didn't thrill me much, maybe because I was sidetracked by the flowers either she or Mama had picked and put in a glass in the middle of the table.

"Chrysanthemums," Granny Nan said.

"What?"

"The flowers—they are chrysanthemums."

"Pretty," I said.

She laughed. "That was your first word."

I just looked at her.

"The first word you ever said was 'pretty.' You had been looking at some flowers then, too. I kept repeating the word 'pretty' over and over, and you finally said it back to me." I could see her eyes wander to someplace in her past. "I got married in October. Had chrysanthemums in my wedding bouquet," she said.

I didn't ask her anything about it; her mind was too far away to hear me.

STUMBLING BLOCKS

It had been almost two weeks since the walls of the house had been raised, and I had yet to see it. Papa was the only one who had been to the building site. But today, Sunday, we were all going to Sunday School and church, except for Uncle Herman; he didn't go to church—any church. Grandpa Wilhelm had made him go when he was a child, but he had a "bad experience" there and never went back. I don't know the particulars.

After church we were all going to see the new house in its current state. Papa had warned us that it did not have inside walls yet. We'd had some rain shortly before the roof was put on, so the subfloor had gotten wet, and it needed time to dry out before the interior walls could go up, which was supposed to be tomorrow, Monday. But the "vorking crew," as Papa called them, had built the lean-to and the small barn and silo while waiting for the house to dry out. "There is a long vay to go," Papa had said, "but ve are getting there."

This would be my third Sunday to attend church, and I was eager to go. Last Sunday had proven to be more fun than I could ever have imagined. I loved my Sunday School teacher, Mrs. Matsen, and I had met some children my age. We had made chains out of colored paper, the same colors as the fall leaves. Reverend Burton's wife, Ruth, had said they would all be put together and hung over the doorway that leads into the sanctuary. I couldn't wait to see them today.

There were wide steps up to the double front doors of the church, then the vestibule, then three more steps up to the sanctuary. Hanging over the entry into the sanctuary was the colorful paper chain we had made last Sunday, along with a sign someone had made that said: HAPPY AUTUMN. I was so thrilled to see my handiwork. I said, "Look! There it is!" and I pointed to the chain. Other people had gotten there at the same time as we had, and they all got a kick out of my excitement.

One woman, whom I didn't know, said to me, "That's beautiful. Did you help make it?"

"Yes. We all made little parts, then Mrs. Matsen put them all together, and Mrs. Burton said she would hang it, and there it is!" I pointed again. I think that was the longest set of clauses I had ever strung together; my answers were usually much shorter.

"Hello," Granny Nan said to the woman. "Our little Helmi, here, seems to like her Sunday School class. We have truly enjoyed your lessons the past couple of weeks, as well."

"Thank you," the woman said and turned to Mama. "Hello, Violet. I'm so glad you and Nancy are coming to my class." She had a wide face and, therefore, a big smile. She looked up at Papa and said, "My name is Rachel Neidhart. It's so nice to meet you." She offered her hand to Papa, who had not yet been to the church. "Is Helmi your daughter?"

"She is," he said proudly as he shook her hand. "I am Heinrich Schnier." He bowed. "You seem to have made my vife and her mother very happy the last two veeks. They have talked incessantly about your lessons."

"How kind of you to mention that, Mr. Schnier. Will you be joining us today?"

"Ja. I look forvard to it." He bowed again.

I learned a song that day in Sunday School. It was called, "Jesus Loves Me," and I sang it all the way to the new house after the service. I'm sure Mama, Papa, and Granny Nan were glad I was in the back of the truck. I was in the middle of the chorus, *"Yes, Jesus loves me. Yes, Jesus loves me..."* when I saw the house for the first time. I stopped dead, my mouth hanging open. It was so tall! Papa had said it was going to be big, but I never guessed it would be a two-story. I was astounded. Tears ran down my cheeks. "Papa…" I couldn't get anything else to come out.

I couldn't take my eyes off it, and I practically fell out of the truck trying to get down to look at it closer. I had the feeling that someone was carrying me toward the house, that I wasn't moving under my own power. But when I glanced down at my feet, they were on the ground. I walked right up to it and put both hands flat against the subsiding. It was real.

I wiped my eyes and turned back to see Mama and Granny Nan holding onto each other in silence. They, too, were obviously in awe.

Papa had come up behind us. He was smiling. "Now ve have to make it our home," he said quietly.

❖❖❖

Three more weeks passed, and the weather stayed nice. "Indian summer" Granny Nan called it. My birthday was coming up in a few days; I would finally turn four. We had moved out of Uncle Herman's place and were now "camping" in the new house. We all slept on the first floor near the fireplace. There were no amenities yet to speak of: we had no electricity and no running water. Papa had dug a hole away from the house and put a privy over it. We used the fireplace to cook, and we carried water from the stream, just like we had in Oklahoma. It was definitely a step backwards after what we had grown accustomed to at Uncle Herman's, but we all knew it would get better with time.

The building process went on and on and on… My birthday was uneventful. Thanksgiving came and went. Granny Nan hadn't gotten to fix a turkey in our own oven, but she did get to help Uncle Herman fix one in his, as he had invited us all over to his place for the holiday. "Maybe next year Thanksgiving will be at our house," she said.

On the last day of November, the gravity furnace was installed, and we were able to sleep upstairs for the first time. The heat rose up through the floor gratings, just as it was supposed to, and we stayed plenty warm under our red and black plaid buffalo-print wool blankets. I didn't much care for the smell of the burning coal, though.

In mid-December the Amish and some of the people from church raised our barn—the big one that would house our hay and straw and our equipment. Papa worked day-in and day-out to attach the stanchion barn to the milk house. We were ready to get some dairy cattle. Papa had located seventeen cows and eleven heifers. He had not found a bull that he could buy, but some of the men from church said they would be happy to loan him the use of one of theirs until he had one of his own.

Papa borrowed a Holstein bull from the Neidharts, Bill and Rachel, the same Rachel that taught the adult Sunday School class at church. Turns out, they were our closest neighbors. Since our properties butted up against each other, it was easy to get Bill's Holstein onto our property to perform his duty. The hard part was getting him to cross the stream. Papa wouldn't let me go out into the field when they were bringing him over to our side, and I was pouting. "Helmi, you vill stay away from that bull. He is not mean, but vhen he decides to move, there is no stopping him. You are just too small for him to see, and he could run right over you." Papa did, however, let me help him separate the Holstein heifers from the Jersey ones. He did not want any cross breeding. He would find a Jersey bull in a few days to take care of the Jersey heifers.

I knew cows were girls and bulls were boys, but I didn't understand the difference between cows and heifers, so I asked Papa. He said, "A heifer becomes a cow when she has a calf. She does not give any milk until then."

"How long till we have some calves?"

"A little longer than people—just over nine months."

"Why do we have two kinds?"

"Two kinds of vhat, Helmi?"

"Cows."

"Oh," Papa said. "Because Holsteins, the big black and vhite vuns, give much more milk than the Jerseys, but the Jerseys give much richer milk."

"Which is better?"

"Ve mix the milk from both kinds of cow together, and then ve have the best kind to sell," he explained. "Addison said ve could also keep some of the raw milk separated and sell the Jersey cream. But it takes a lot of Jerseys and a lot of milk to get enough cream to sell in bulk. So ve vill keep some of the cream for ourselves. Mama and your Granny vill be happy about that. I have not told them yet, so vill you help me keep it a secret?"

I nodded. "What is the milk house?"

"That is vhere ve keep the milk after ve get it from the cows. There vill be a big tub in the milk house called a 'bulk tank' that keeps the milk cold. If you let raw milk set vitout stirring it, the cream vill rise to the top, so the bulk tank stirs the milk ve put in it to keep the milk and the cream mixed together. There is a strainer in the top of the bulk tank that keeps any dirt from falling into it. The cows sometimes have dirt on their udders, and ve do not vant that in the milk, so vhen ve pour the milk through the strainer, it catches the dirt."

"How does the bulk tank keep the milk cold?"

"Electricity."

I didn't understand electricity, even though Papa had tried to explain it to me, but I knew it made lights come on when you pushed a button. "Will we push a button to turn it on?"

"Something like that," Papa said, and he smiled.

Addison had told Papa to let the cows and heifers come to the farm and get used to each other, as well as the stanchion barn, for a few days before attempting any breeding. Papa said, "According to Addison, ve vant happy cows; they give much more milk."

❖❖❖

On the second day of December, I woke up to a wonderland of white. What a sight to behold! The way it clung to everything sort of reminded me of the gray dust that used to cover our barn and house in Oklahoma after a dust storm, but the snow was pure white and beautiful, and there was no wind; it was falling silently. I could see the tiny shapes of some of the flakes when they lit on the windowsill. They looked so fragile, so delicate.

I was beyond excited. I forgot that it was cold. I went down the stairs as fast as I could and flung the front door open. I stepped outside, and my bare feet instantly turned ice cold. Papa had gotten up early, so he was in the kitchen. He had heard the door open and came running to see what was going on. I jumped back into the house and danced around trying to hold one foot, then the other. Papa realized what was going on, and he threw his head back and laughed. I must have looked like a wild animal jumping around the room. He picked me up and began to rub my feet to warm them.

"Snow is beautiful, but yust like anything vild, you must respect it," he said. "It can be fun to play in, but it can also be deadly."

I definitely had fun playing in it. Mama dressed me in two of my dresses, two pairs of socks, and one of Papa's long flannel shirts. She said, "Do not get down and roll around in the snow, Helmi. It is wet, and it is freezing cold." She really didn't need to remind me of that; I had already found out firsthand.

Granny Nan had knitted mittens for all of us except Papa; he needed gloves to work in. So she knitted him a pair of "choppers," gloves that exposed the fingers but also had the top part of a mitten that could be folded back to allow the hands to work freely or brought over the fingers to keep them warm. Since Granny Nan had lived in Indiana where it snowed, she was the only one of us who knew anything about living in the cold weather.

"Would you like to build a snowman?" she asked me.

"A man?"

"Yes, made of snow."

"Okay." I thought she had gone crazy, but she insisted it would look like a man. She dressed as warm as she could and followed me outside. She showed me how to roll up the bottom and middle balls and a head, making each one smaller. It took both of us to pick up the middle one and put it on the bottom one. And she had to lift the head up onto it because I couldn't reach that high.

"Now stay right here; I will be back in a minute." She disappeared around the side of the house and came back carrying something in a bucket. It was coal. She said, "He needs a face and some buttons." She began to push pieces of coal into the snowman's body in a row down the front; then she handed some to me. I finished them and stood back to admire our work. Then she put some pieces in the head: two eyes and a mouth. "You get the honor of giving him a nose." She handed me a piece of coal, picked me up, and I pushed the nose into the middle of his face.

"It's a man!" I said.

"But he has no arms," Granny Nan said. "We need to find a couple of twigs that look like they have hands." We scrounged around for a couple of minutes, found exactly what we needed, and each of us pushed one into the sides of the snowman's body.

"Much better," Granny Nan said.

Yosie had gotten up. Mama opened the door to show her the snowman. She took one look and backed away. Yosie and I were complete opposites; she always hated the snow and cold, but I have always loved it.

❖❖❖

On Christmas eve we had a blizzard. The temperature was in the low teens, and it was snowing. But this wasn't nice, soft snow; it was more like little ice balls. By noon the wind had picked up to around forty miles per hour. By late afternoon, it was blowing the snow around so hard that I was unable to see anything. Granny Nan called it a "whiteout."

I was kind of scared, and Mama could tell. "It is all right, Helmi. You do not need to worry. We are all warm and cozy in here. Snug as a bug in a rug."

"Will there be a twister?"

"No," Papa said. "The vind is just gusting, not like the vind ve had in Oklahoma."

I had no reason to doubt what they said, as they had never lied to me. Nevertheless, it was scary. The windows rattled, and there was a whistling sound coming down the chimney. Mama was sitting in the wedding rocker, and I crawled up on her lap. Yosie, of course, had to join me there.

We had a Christmas tree, albeit a small one, that Mama, Granny Nan, Yosie, and I had decorated. Mama and Granny Nan had attached candles to some of its branches. There were only a few decorations, but Granny Nan had helped us make a long paper chain like the one I had made in Sunday School. She cut the strips of paper, and we pasted them together using homemade paste, which consisted of flour and water. This paper chain was white, and when we hung it on the tree, it looked just like the snow drooping off the tree branches outside.

The tree was only lit once—on Christmas morning—and Papa stood by with a bucket of water, ready to douse the tree if it caught on fire. We all sang "O Come, All Ye Faithful" and "Hark, the Herald Angels Sing." Then we blew out the candles and opened our presents from Santa Claus. I got a pair of ice skates, the kind that attached to my shoes. I wanted to use them right away, of course, but the blizzard had left such huge drifts, we couldn't even get out the doors, front or back. Papa had pushed his way out the back door earlier in order to get to the livestock, but the wind had already filled in the space Papa had made.

People say our lives are remembered by the procession of holidays and special events. But I don't have any trouble recalling a lot of the everyday things that went on in my life, no matter how commonplace. I remember the feeling of going up and down the stairs in our big house. I know exactly how the furnace smelled when Papa removed the clinkers and shoveled in new coal. I can still hear the twins "talking" to each other just after Mama put them to bed. I know the sound of Granny Nan's soft breathing as she slept, and the feel of the blankets keeping me warm. Sometimes I think holidays and special events are overrated.

I realize, now, that our first winter was pretty typical for Isabella County. And there would be many more just like it. The change of seasons took some getting used to, but my favorite was always autumn. It made me think that everything was finally going to rest for a while. All the trees and flowers, the harvested fields, and maybe even us.

Spring came slowly at first, but then, almost without warning, everything was in bloom. Crocuses, jonquils, tulips, and a lot of other spring flowers, whose names I didn't know, poked their heads up through the soil, some even through the leftover snow. Flowering trees burst into bloom overnight. The Niedharts had a flowering crabapple tree in their yard, and when it bloomed, it looked like a pink cloud. But my two favorites were the flowering dogwood and the redbud trees. They grew in the woods, surrounded by all the non-flowering trees, which made them stand out. They flowered before they formed leaves. I learned that I could even eat the flowers of the redbud tree, though they didn't have much flavor, and I preferred merely to look at them.

Mama had always loved flowers. She learned to love them even more when we moved to Michigan. "One week it is winter, and the next week it is spring," she said. As soon as she could, she wanted to get outside and get her hands in the dirt. "It feels good to make pretty things grow," she told me. I think my love for flowers is one of the best things I inherited from her.

Granny Nan, on the other hand, loved vegetable gardening. She had planted every type of vegetable she could think of that would grow in each part of the country where she had lived. She and Uncle Herman had long discussions about what was best for the garden. Though she rarely mentioned it, the one thing that was a major stumbling block for her was how to keep the deer and rabbits out. At seventy-four years old, she was obviously not capable of building an eight-foot fence by herself. Papa could not take the time to do it for her. And she wouldn't think of asking Uncle Herman to do it. She was in a quandary.

On the first Saturday after Easter, early in the morning, we heard the sound of automobiles driving up to our house. We looked out, and there were a bunch of people from the church. They were taking shovels, rakes, and hoes out of their vehicles. One of the trucks had a two-blade plow on it, and another was loaded with rolled fencing and fence posts. Bill and Rachel Neidhart were coming across our field with their draught horse in tow. We were all standing on the porch, and Rachel came up to us.

"Good morning, Rachel," Mama greeted her. "I see you rounded up quite a crew."

"It's a great turnout," Rachel said. "Hello, Nancy, Helmi. Isn't it a beautiful morning?"

"Certainly is," Granny Nan said. "It is a pleasure to see you. What is going on here?"

"Well, a little birdie told me you want to have a vegetable garden. Am I right?"

Granny Nan looked dumbfounded.

"Do you have a place picked out for it?" Rachel asked. She was grinning from ear to ear.

Granny Nan could hardly talk. "Over...over there." She pointed to a wide-open space behind the house.

Rachel turned to the people who were busy loading up their arms with whatever tools they had brought and said, "Let's get started. We can't let this family starve!" She headed toward the rectangle Granny Nan had marked with stakes.

"This shouldn't take too long," the man with the plow said. "Let's hitch up that horse of yours, Bill."

Everyone talked as they worked. Granny Nan and Mama fixed fried bologna, potato salad, sugared corn, and boiled iced tea for everyone. I'd been assigned the job of laying down blankets for all the people to sit on as they ate. By noon, we had a garden plot—plowed, broken up, and raked—with an eight-foot high fence around it, complete with a gate, the latch of which was low enough even I could reach it.

When everyone had finished eating, Granny Nan stood up and said, "I have never been so pleasantly surprised. I look around and see the faces of people whom I have called 'church acquaintances.' But after today, I will be changing that to 'friends.'" Her voice quivered, and she paused and swallowed hard. I knew she was having a difficult time holding back tears. "Only last night, I prayed that somehow I would be able to find help in getting this garden ready for planting. And God answered my prayer. In fact, I was sure I would not have a fence around it, so I was prepared to keep the broom by the door to chase off the critters." Everyone laughed. "Now I can plant and grow and share the bounty with you, my friends. Thank you all, and God bless you." Then she cried.

That afternoon, Granny Nan took her hoe and made three rows for peas. She tied some twine—measured to the exact length of the garden—around two stakes. Then she pounded the stakes into the dirt, stretching the twine till it was taut, and hoed a little ditch right next to the twine. It was perfectly straight. "They really should have been in the ground before now. They will probably be all right if the sun does not get too hot for them. I hope it is not too late," she said. I hoped so, too. I loved fresh peas. Still do.

ANOTHER GIRL AND A ONE-ROOM SCHOOL

The next year-and-a-half went without a hitch. Our house was finished, all the outbuildings had been completed, and our dairy farm had begun making money. Our herd had grown from twenty-eight to thirty-five. In addition, we had a full chicken coop, and the hens were laying like crazy, so we had egg money, too. Mama was adamant about getting some sheep so she we could sell their wool. Papa said, "I vill still be paying for all of this from my coffin. But, by Gott, ve vill be living vell in the meantime." We didn't have money to waste, by any stretch of the imagination, but our debt was not keeping us from having the necessities.

We still didn't have any beef cattle; Papa said they would probably be purchased within the year. But we did have two pigs and the chicken coop full of laying hens, along with one rooster. I was scared of him when he first came to live with us, but I found out he was nothing like the big mean Rhode Island Red we'd had in Oklahoma. Instead, he was nice enough that I could even go into the pen with him when feeding time came around. I named him Mickey the Chickey.

Mama and Papa slept in one of the upstairs bedrooms, Bella and Dora had another one, and Yosie and I slept in another. Granny Nan occupied the big bedroom downstairs all by herself. With five bedrooms, we had plenty of space to cover any more babies that came along. And Mama was pregnant again, due in August; it was already May. Mama and Granny Nan were in the process of unpacking all the baby things and getting them in order.

"Hel-mi!" Mama called. I was swinging on a rope swing Papa had put up in the big tree that was on the other side of the road (now that I was five-and-a-half, I was deemed responsible enough to cross the road by myself). I wanted to pretend that I hadn't heard her, but I hollered back, "Com-ing!" I jumped out of the swing when it was in its highest position, so I went flying through the air and landed about ten feet from the swing.

As I was crossing the road, I saw the postal truck coming toward me. I stopped by the mailbox and waited. We were now an RFD customer, meaning we had rural free delivery, and we had our own address, not just general delivery that we had to pick up at the post office like we did in Oklahoma. There were so many great things about living in Michigan!

The postman pulled up beside me and stuck his hand out the window. He handed me a couple of items. "Here ya go. I saw you swingin'. You were really gettin' up there."

"I like to go really high."

"I remember doin' that when I was little," he said. Then he changed the subject. "Have you gotten any beef cows yet?"

"No. Papa says probably this year, though."

"Tell him George Franks has sixteen new Hereford calves, and he's looking for buyers."

"I'll tell him."

He saluted; he always did that instead of waving. So I saluted back and took the mail into the house. Granny Nan was cooking. "Mail's here," I said. "What does Mama want?"

"She needs help getting the cradle out of the barn. It has to be washed and possibly repainted."

"Okay," I said and went to the barn.

"It is right over there," Mama pointed. "I can take one end if you will take the other. We do not have to lift it, we can just drag it out into the open so I can wash all of the dust off it." We grunted and groaned, and between the two of us, we dragged it into the sunshine up by the back-porch steps.

"I can clean it up, Mama. You don't need to help." I went into the house and put some laundry powder in a bucket, then I added a little bit of water. I grabbed a couple of rags from a barrel in the "junk room" that was just off to the side of the back door. I dry-wiped the worst of the dirt off the cradle, then I washed off the rest. I dumped the dirty soapy water out of the bucket and rinsed it, then I put clean water in it. I used the clean rag to wipe the soap off the cradle. The sun dried it before I had a chance to rub it dry.

"Oh, thank you so much, Helmi. You are a life saver. Papa will carry it upstairs when he comes back from checking the fields." She was sitting on the porch steps, panting and holding her belly. "They were still pretty soggy two days ago. He is hoping the sun and this breeze will dry them up soon." We'd had a lot of rain throughout March and April.

"Do you need anything else, Mama?"

"No. You can go back to swinging. What were you singing?"

I always sang while I swung. "Nothing. Just made-up stuff."

"It sounded nice. God gave you a lovely voice."

I told Papa about Mr. Franks' Herefords.

"Vhere did you hear about them?"

"The mailman."

"Ah," Papa said. "He knows almost as much about everyvun around here as the local barber." He laughed, but I didn't get it. It didn't matter; I laughed along with him.

"Mama needs you to carry the cradle up to your bedroom," I told him.

"Already? She has three months to go. I suppose she is nesting," he said and shook his head. "I do not think it vill be tvins this time."

"Do you want a boy?" I asked him, although I knew the answer.

"It vould be nice to have a son to help me around the farm," he said. "Not that you do not do your fair share. You are a blessing to us, Helmi. You vork hard, but you need to concentrate on school, now. And I vould like you to be able to do other things. More girly things."

"I don't want to do girly things. Yosie does those things," I said.

"Ja, but you must not forget that you are a girl."

"I won't, Papa. I like being a girl, but I also like being outdoors and doing farm things."

"And you do them vell," he said and patted me on the shoulder. "But boys have bigger muscles and can do more of the heavy stuff. You should not do a lot of lifting and pulling. Girl muscles are not made for such. Now, go sving. I like hearing you sing vhile you do it."

His smile made me feel warm inside.

On August 6, 1926, Mama gave birth to Margaretta. She weighed ten pounds and fourteen ounces, and she looked like she was already six months old. Granny Nan handed her to Mama, who held her close and kissed her on the head. Then Mama said, "Let Helmi hold her." When Granny Nan handed her to me, I realized that I was holding a person who was less than two minutes old. I fell in love with her instantly. Retta, as she would be called, was destined to become my closest ally in my later years.

Retta created a lot of work for all of us, as new babies always do, but my first priority was getting ready for the first grade at the one-room school. One day Mama asked me, "Will you come with me, Helmi? I need to get out of the house, and Granny Nan said she will watch Yosie and all of the babies." She didn't have to ask me twice!

I wasn't paying a whole lot of attention to where we were going; I was much more interested in everything along the way. Birds were flitting around, probably gathering food for their second, or even third brood of the summer. Frogs jumped into the standing water in the ditches along the road as we approached. Grasshoppers leaped and flew all around us in the sunshine that was warming the gravel on the road. I heard a hawk scream overhead, but I couldn't see it because the sun was directly behind it.

A single automobile went past us, slowing down as it approached so as not to cover us in dust. It was Bob and Wanda Shields, people we knew from church. They waved as they passed. They lived a couple of miles to the northwest of us. I had been past their house a few times when we were going to Weidman. They had a fenced-in yard with a driveway that had pipes in the ground across the end of the driveway next to the road. It kept their cows from getting out. There was a space between each pipe that was big enough for a cow's foot to slip through, so the cows knew better than to try and cross them. I thought that was a very clever idea.

We turned off the road and began to walk up a long lane. I could see a little building up ahead. "Where are we, Mama? Does someone from church live here?"

"You will see," she said.

I continued to concentrate on the things around me, and I ran smack dab into the back of Mama; I didn't know she'd stopped. I looked up and asked her, "What is this place?"

"This is where you will be going to school."

"My school? I didn't know it was so close to our house!"

The building now captured my interest. It was on the same side of the road as our house, but it sat on a small rise that was back off the road about a quarter of a mile. There were trees on three sides of it; the front was exposed. It had a little bell tower on the roof above a bright red door, and a rope hung from the bell down to the top of the door. The siding had not been painted in who-knows-how-long, so the outside was dark gray secondary to the weather. There were two windows in the front, one on either side of the door.

Mama tried the door, but it was locked. "How about looking in the windows?" she suggested.

I ran right up to one of the windows on the front. The inside, including the ceiling, was finished with white paint. The floor had been shellacked, so it was shiny and well preserved. The back wall was covered with a slate chalk board; the bottom half was nearly white from chalk buildup for so many years. Even washing it couldn't revitalize the dark finish. It was divided into three sections, each of which went from about sixteen inches above the floor to about six feet high. There were three windows down each side of the building, which meant the sun would filter through the trees on one side in the morning and the other side in the afternoon. A pot-bellied stove sat in the back righthand corner with a pipe that went up through the ceiling, and there was a wood bin sitting beside it that extended from the back window to the middle one.

"Mama, look at the benches. Some of them are for people my size!"

"Come around here to the side windows. You can see them better," she said.

I ran around to the window she was looking in, and I put my hands up beside my face to shield my reflection. Each bench had a flat part that stuck out the back of it so the person in the seat behind had a place to write. This was beyond exciting!

But the best thing I saw was the bookshelves along the wall beneath the windows on the left side of the building. They were *full* of books. I could see all different kinds of them, some big, some thin, some so thick I wondered who had time to read them. There were musical instruments on the top of the bookcase, along with some animal skulls and a few funny-looking jars that were wide at the bottom and skinny at the top. An old upright piano sat on one side of the door, and the teacher's desk was on the other side. Boxes were piled up near the teacher's desk. Mama said they were probably supplies for all the students, and I might get some of them on my first day.

"When is my first day, Mama?"

"September tenth," she said.

"How many days away is that?"

"We will look on the calendar at home, and you can count them."

I was ready for September tenth to be tomorrow! "I can't wait," I said. "Will Mrs. Matsen be my teacher?"

"No. She teaches Sunday School. Your schoolteacher will be a woman we have not met. Her name is Miss Michaels. She does not live in Michigan during the summer, only during the school year."

I had so many questions, but I knew Mama was getting tired and needed to get back home. After all, she had just had a baby a month ago.

I thought September tenth would never arrive. On the evening of September ninth, Granny Nan said, "I will pack a sandwich for you. Do not forget to pick it up on your way out. I know you will be excited and possibly forgetful."

"Do you remember your teacher's name?" Mama asked.

"Miss Michaels."

"You already know your letters, and you can count…"

"...past one hundred." I said.

"Yes, and you know a lot of colors, too," Granny Nan said.

"Do not forget to say, 'Yes, Ma'am' and 'No, Ma'am,' and be very polite to everyone."

"I know," I said.

Mama added, "And when you get to the door, be sure to wipe your shoes on the mat before going inside, just like we make you do here at home."

"Tomorrow will be a big day," Granny Nan said, "so you may have to take a nap. Sometimes teachers have you do that. You put your head down on your desk. You might not fall asleep, but at least you will be resting."

"What if I fall asleep and don't wake up when it's time?"

"You need not worry about that, Helmi," Mama said. "If you fall asleep, you will hear Miss Michaels telling everyone to wake up. Now go brush your teeth. You can wash up in the morning before you get dressed."

"Speaking of that, I need to iron her dress," Granny Nan told Mama. "We do not want her to look like she slept in her clothes."

Morning came before I knew it, and it was pouring rain. *Not on my first day.* We did not own an umbrella, and Papa had taken the truck to do some business in Mount Pleasant, so he was not available to drive me to school. I kept looking out the window to see if the rain was letting up, but it continued to pour. Just before it was time for me to leave, a car pulled up in front of our house.

"Who could that be?" Granny Nan asked.

Mama went to the window and said, "I think it is Deidre Linley; it is hard to see through all this rain." She kept looking and finally said, "Yes, it is Deidre. She is coming to the door with an umbrella." Deidre was the daughter of George and Ruby Franks. A few years before, she had lost her husband secondary to a hunting accident. After a year, she found she was unable to keep their farm, so now she and her son, Duane, lived in a small house on the Franks' property. Duane was one year ahead of me in school.

"How nice to see you!" Granny Nan said as she opened the door and waved Deidre in out of the rain. "What brings you to our home so early of a morning?"

Deidre shook out her umbrella and put it down on the porch just outside the door. She stepped onto the rug inside. "Good morning to you both. I came to see if Helmi needs a ride to school on this soggy, sloppy morning."

"You could not be more of a blessing at this moment," Mama said. "Heinrich left early this morning on some business, so we have no vehicle to get Helmi there. She was going to have to walk. And it would be a shame for her to appear like a drowned rabbit on her first day of school."

"It surely would," Deidre said and smiled at me.

"But how did you know to stop by?" Granny Nan asked.

"Heinrich has been talking to Father about buying some of his Herefords, and somewhere in the midst of all the discussion, Heinrich must have mentioned that Helmi's starting school this year. So when the sky opened up, Father suggested I come by and see if Helmi needed a ride. I was taking Duane anyway, so it was no problem for me to stop by and pick up Helmi on our way."

"Thank you so much," Mama said.

When Mrs. Linley and I ran under the umbrella to her automobile, I recognized Duane from church. *So he is in the second grade, but he is much bigger than I am. I thought he was much older, too.*

"Duane, scoot over and let Helmi in," Mrs. Linley said as she pulled the automobile's door open. Duane did as she said.

As soon as I got in, he scooted over closer to his mother. "Your legs are all wet," he said to me.

"Duane! Is that any way to welcome our passenger?"

"Sorry." He hung his head and said to me, "Great weather, huh?"

"For ducks," I said. I had heard Papa say that when it rained.

Duane looked at me, smiled, then laughed. "You're funny."

It was the beginning of a great friendship.

School was even more than I had hoped it would be. Miss Michaels had an accent; she kind of dragged out her words. I would learn, over time, that she was from Tennessee, Chattanooga to be exact. Her family still lived there, and she went to live with them every summer. She liked talking about Chattanooga, and I found it interesting to listen to her stories, as well as her brogue. She was one of those people who absolutely adored every one of us in that little one-room school; she treated us like we were her own children, applauding us when we did well and dishing out the discipline when we needed it.

She had a knack for discovering our interests and encouraging us to expand on them. Within a week she knew I loved music, so she made sure I had every chance to put that interest to use. I got to sing solos and play musical instruments. Duane liked talking about the Civil War, and he was also good at drawing. So she asked him to make a Civil War mural that she could hang up in the classroom when we had our lesson about that war.

Miss Michaels was able to open our minds and fill them with knowledge. She simply loved educating young people. And she managed to make it fun.

I did well in school. Things came easily to me, and I was never in trouble. Miss Michaels liked me and gave me special attention that the other students seldom got. However…

One day, just as I was ready to go home, she gave me a letter to give to Mama and Papa. I was scared. *Have I done something bad? Am I going to have to stay after school? Is she going to ask them to send me to another school?* Whatever it was, I knew it couldn't be good. I walked extra slow on the way home that day; I didn't want to hand that letter to Mama and Papa.

I went straight to the rope swing. I needed time to think about how I was going to present that letter to them. I put my books down on the grass with the letter tucked between the pages of one of them. Then I started to swing; it always helped me think straight. I didn't sing, instead I thought about everything I had done over the last few days: *I helped one of the older girls clean the slate board. I did it just exactly like she told me to, so it can't be that. I made sure to throw my waxed-paper sandwich wrappers in the waste basket. I wiped my feet before I went inside—every time—so that's not it. I didn't fight with anybody when we had a recess. I didn't fall asleep during the lessons. I never spoke without raising my hand and being called on. I didn't write on my desk. Oh, what can it be?*

Finally, after at least ten minutes of swinging, I decided the moment had come. I would simply take my punishment, then I'd move on. I was prepared to apologize to someone if need be, even Miss Michaels herself, if I had inadvertently been out of line. I straightened up, held my head high, and crossed the road to the house. When I went inside, Mama and Granny Nan both greeted me, and Retta got excited to see me. She smiled, gurgled in her baby way, and waved her arms at me. Yosie ignored me. Bella and Dora looked up at me but continued to do whatever they were engrossed in.

"There you are," Mama said. "I was wondering when you would decide to grace us with your presence." *She saw me swinging.* "What is on your mind?" *Yep, she knows I have something going on in my head. I can't hide anything from her.*

I swallowed. "Miss Michaels asked me to give you this." I unbuckled my book strap and took the letter from inside one of my books. My hand was shaking; my heart was pounding; I could barely breathe.

"What do we have here?" She took the letter, opened it, and began reading.

My insides had turned to mush. *My doom is at hand.*

"Well, I will have to let Papa see this," she said.

Why doesn't she just tell me what I did.

Granny Nan was peeling and cutting up apples. She had a funny look on her face, as if she knew what I was going through. *Save me, Granny Nan. If you know what this is about, let me in on the secret, too.*

Mama refolded the letter, got up, and put it in her apron pocket. She walked to the door, then she turned to me and said, "Helmi, change your clothes and help Granny Nan with the apples." She walked out the door.

Maybe Papa isn't in the barn; maybe he's out in the fields. No, there's no reason for him to be in the fields at this time of day. The truck! I ran to the window and looked out. There it was, sitting beside the chicken coop where it always sat when no one was using it. *Rats! He must be here.* I saw Mama disappear into the barn, and I held my breath.

Both Mama and Papa appeared and came toward the house. *What am I going to do?* I put my head down, closed my eyes, and folded my hands in front of me. *God, please let my punishment be bearable.* Papa had always said, "If you get punished at school, you vill be doubly punished when you come home."

The door opened. "Helmi, ve need to talk."

God didn't hear me. He's doing more important things, not listening to the plea of some little kid. My stupid prayer wasn't worth listening to. "Okay, Papa," I said, my reply barely audible.

"Come, sit at the table. Your granny should hear this, too."

He appeared taller and bigger to me than he ever had, his voice more harsh. *Oh, just get it over with! I can't take this anymore.* By now I was numb. I pulled out a chair and sat down, my head hanging. I couldn't bear to look at anyone.

"It seems..." Papa looked at the letter again, dragging out the suspense, "...that you have done..."

Go on. Spit it out. Spit it out!

"...remarkably vell in your studies. Your teacher vants us to come to the school and discuss your progress tomorrow afternoon. She vould like to talk to me, Mama, and you altogether. So, tomorrow vhen school is over, Mama and I vill meet you at the schoolhouse."

That's it? I thought my bottom jaw was going to hit the floor. It was all good, not bad. I was so relieved, I nearly fell out of the chair, scrambling to see the letter Papa held. But before I could grab it, he refolded it and handed it to Mama, who returned it to her apron pocket.

Papa said, "Nancy, vill you mind vatching our other children while ve are avay tomorrow afternoon?"

"I would be more than happy to, Heinrich," she said and patted him on the arm.

I understood why I hadn't gotten a reply from God. He knew I wasn't going to be punished at all.

The next morning, Thursday, I told Miss Michaels my parents would be there when school was over. She said, "Good. I want you to know, Helmi, that we'll be discussing your future here at this school before your eventual transfer to the high school in Mount Pleasant."

"Yes ma'am."

The day crept by, but finally the last lesson was finished, and the other students were dismissed. When all of them had walked out the door, Mama and Papa walked in.

"Mr. and Mrs. Schnier," Miss Michaels greeted them, shaking their hands. "Come on over here and sit down." She motioned toward the larger desks where the older kids sat. "You too, Helmi." I loved the way she said my name—it sounded like "Hail-me."

I walked over to the big desks and climbed up onto one of the benches. I sat down, straightened my dress, and put my hands in my lap. Miss Michaels and Mama sat down, one on each side of me, and Papa sat down on the bench behind us.

Miss Michaels began. "I'll get right to the point. When I graduated from Michigan State Normal School in Ypsilanti, I thought I was ready to grab the world by the tail. I'd been taught how to handle every imaginable problem: how to reprimand and punish, how to deal with 'bad' students, even 'bad' parents. But I had no training in how to handle a student the caliber of Helmi, here. I have been struggling, to some degree, to figure out a way to…how should I put this? The only word I can think of is 'fix.' How to 'fix' this situation.

"Helmi is, by far, the most brilliant student I have ever encountered." She reached down and took my hand, then she reached over me and took Mama's hand. She looked squarely at Papa. "She has a brain that is like a sponge; she soaks up every bit of information she encounters." She let go our hands. "But that, in and of itself, does not make someone remarkably intelligent. What is a mark of high intelligence, however, is that she retains it and uses it in future endeavors. Am I presenting this in a way that makes sense to y'all?"

"I believe I am following," Mama said.

"Ja, so am I," Papa answered.

"Good. Now that we've established that this young lady is on the top of the heap," she looked down at me with the most genuine smile I had ever seen, "we need to figure out what to do to keep her interested in learning. You see, if we don't provide her with extra material, she'll become bored and lose interest in her studies."

"Ve certainly do not vant that," Papa said.

"No, we do not," Miss Michaels continued. "I have a bookcase full of all sorts of books," she indicated the bookcase along the east wall of the schoolroom, "but they are not what Helmi needs. Some of them are way beyond her comprehension, and some are far below her level of learning. There are but a few that are of interest to her at her age." She got up and took four books from the bookcase. "These are some she's already read." She handed two to Mama and two to Papa. "Bear in mind that she is only a first-grader."

She allowed Mama and Papa to look at the books for a few moments, then she turned to me and asked, "Helmi, do you remember what that one is about?" She pointed to the one Mama was currently holding.

I looked at it and said, "Yes. It's about a rabbit named Peter. He was always in trouble because he kept getting into a farmer's garden."

"Do you remember the farmer's name?"

"Mr. Mc…McGr…"

"McGregor," she said.

"Yes! I had trouble with that word and had to ask you what it was. McGregor. And Peter has three sisters: Flopsy, Mopsy, and Cottontail."

"You see? She is only six years old and is already reading things well beyond her years."

"That is goot, ja?" Papa asked.

"Yes, it is, but it'll soon become a problem if she isn't kept at a level that'll stimulate her mind. I have a possible solution, but I'll need your permission to go with it."

"What is your solution, Miss Michaels?" Mama asked.

"There's a public library in Mount Pleasant. Have either of you been there?"

"No, ve have not," Papa said.

"They have every book imaginable, and Helmi could use that resource to keep her mind active and her interest piqued. I know you're busy with the dairy farm and your other children, so I've devised a plan." She paused.

"Please go on," Mama said.

"I'd like to take Helmi to the library twice a week after school, each Monday and Thursday. Do you know how a library operates their lending service?"

Mama, Papa, and I all shook our heads.

"First of all, it costs nothing. Helmi can check out as many books as she can read in a few days' time and takes them home. Then she reads them and returns them to the library by the date they're due back. She just puts them up on the Book Return table there at the library, and she can check out more. The children's section at our Mount Pleasant library is excellent."

"You mean *you* vould take her there after school then bring her home?"

"Yes, if that's all right with the two of you."

Mama's mouth was hanging open. "But, it is three miles there, three miles back to our house, and then however many more miles to where you live. Why would you consider doing that for her? Perhaps we could work something out so you do not have to make the trips twice a week."

"Believe me, it would be my pleasure. I can guide Helmi in looking for books that would be related to the topics we'd be covering in the school lessons. She *needs* this, and I would be honored if you'd trust me to see to it that her education is as well rounded as possible and that she's stimulated to continue learning without losing interest. Bear in mind, also, that I will be giving her some extra school projects to work on. She may need extra guidance from you both, and from her grandmother, to complete some of them."

Mama and Papa sat there in silence. I could see that they were trying to digest everything Miss Michaels had just dished out. It was kind of awkward for me, so I sat very still and waited. Miss Michaels was right. I *had* read all the available books in the bookcase—some of them more than once—that had looked like they might be ones I'd understand. And I couldn't get enough. Going to a library sounded like a grand adventure. But getting to go with Miss Michaels was beyond my wildest dreams.

"I will allow it on one condition," Mama finally said.

Miss Michaels nodded.

"You must do us the honor of staying for supper each Monday and Thursday when you bring her home. I will not allow Helmi to do this unless you agree."

"And I second the motion," Papa said.

Miss Michaels looked at me with sincerity and genuine concern, took my hand, and said, "I won't do this unless I have your approval, too, Helmi. Does this sound like something you might want to do?"

Without hesitation I said, "I'd like that very much."

"Then we all agree. We'll go to the library every Monday and Thursday after school, starting next Monday. And I'll be more than happy to sup with y'all on those nights."

A GOOD DEED GONE BAD

Jim and Alice Chaney were a couple of the nicest people I ever knew as a child. They had no children, but they had a dachshund—Papa called it a sausage dog—named Tumbles. I think Papa liked that dog more than he liked Betsy, probably because dachshunds are a German breed. "Dachshunds vere used to hunt badgers. The vord 'dachshund' means 'badger dog' in Deutsch," he told us. "They have short legs so they can go right down into the badger tunnels, and their tails are extra heavy so you can pull them out vhen they get stuck!" I was sure Tumbles had never hunted badgers. He was friendly, and he did a special trick: when I sat on the floor or the ground and rolled a ball to him, he rolled it back to me with his nose.

Jim Chaney reminded me of Uncle Herman in that he was tall and portly with a well-trimmed beard and moustache, but his was red instead of brown like Uncle Herman's. He had lots of thick hair, and its color fascinated me. The twins had red hair, but theirs was more auburn than Mr. Chaney's; his was the color of carrots. He always had a funny story to tell.

Alice Chaney was a spitting image of Mama, but she had hair the color of wheat just before harvest. It was wavy and fell softly around her face, making her look like an angel. She spoke softly, but her laugh was deep and throaty, and it was contagious. She laughed at Jim's stories every time he told them, no matter how often she had heard them, and that made everyone else laugh, too.

My favorite story was the one about the buffalos:
Mrs. Buffalo gave birth to a bouncing baby boy buffalo, and they named him Bobby Boy. (I always laughed because Mr. Chaney puffed out his cheeks when he said words that began with the letters B or P.) *Mr. Buffalo was a mighty proud papa. He and Mrs. Buffalo raised that boy so that he was smart enough to go to college. The day finally arrived when Bobby Boy was ready to leave for an institution of higher education. Mr. and Mrs. Buffalo helped Bobby Boy pack the automobile, and Mr. Buffalo was going to drive him to college. As they drove away, Mrs. Buffalo waved, and what do*

you think she said to Bobby Boy? --- "Bison!"

One day I heard Mama and Granny Nan talking in low voices. "What are you talking about?" I asked as I entered the room. They looked at each other uncomfortably.

Granny Nan finally asked me, "Do you know what cancer is?"

"A disease. A bad one." *Please don't have it, either of you. Or Papa. Or Yosie or Retta or the twins. Or Uncle Herman.*

"Yes, it is," Mama said.

I was silent. I wished I hadn't asked about it. Just hearing the word was like having a knife stabbing me in the belly over and over. Granny Nan said, "Someone we know has it. Do you want to know who?"

Do I? If it's someone close to me, I know I'll cry. "I'm not sure. Is it someone in our family?"

"No."

Whew! "Okay, then who?"

"Mrs. Chaney," she said.

"She's going to die, isn't she?" I asked.

"I am afraid so," Mama said. "She went to see Doc Barrett, and he told her she only has about two more months to live."

Tears filled my eyes, but they didn't spill over. I was determined to be in control, but I didn't dare talk at that moment.

"There are lots of types of cancer," Mama said. "That is what Granny Nan and I were discussing when you came in. Mrs. Chaney has liver cancer, one of the worst, according to Doc Barrett."

"What will Mr. Chaney and Tumbles do when she dies?" I asked.

"I do not know. They will both be very sad," Mama said.

"Me too." I turned and left the room, afraid that I would break down in tears, and I was embarrassed by that, though I don't really know why.

Alice Chaney died six weeks after Christmas.

Granny Nan did not go to the funeral and graveside services; she stayed home with Yosie, the twins, and Retta. It was a bitter cold day in February. Luckily for the burial, it hadn't turned terribly cold before the grave had been dug. There are times during Michigan winters when it gets too cold to dig a grave; the ground freezes and occasionally doesn't thaw till spring, in which case the bodies are kept in cold storage in the morgue until interment. That wasn't necessary for Alice.

It was the first human death I had ever been a part of. Mama, Papa, and Granny Nan had all warned me that I would see Mrs. Chaney lying in her coffin at the funeral home. They explained how family and friends often felt the need to see the deceased person in order to believe he or she had truly passed. I was used to seeing dead animals; I had watched, and even participated in, their slaughter, but it was completely different when it was a person, someone I knew. It was a subject I had never dealt with. I didn't like it. Not one little bit.

Following the service at the funeral home, the coffin was taken to the cemetery. It arrived after all the rest of us had gotten there, and six men carried it from the hearse to the graveside. The minister—we didn't know him because he was from a church in Weidman—said a few words about life after death and recited the twenty-third Psalm. Then we all said the Lord's prayer while the six men who had carried the coffin lowered it into the ground using big, wide, long straps. When it reached the bottom, we all walked past it, and the adults threw either some dirt or flowers on it. Then everyone spent a little while talking to the family and other friends. I didn't talk to anyone until we got back into the truck and were driving home.

"Was Mrs. Chaney still in the coffin when they put it in the ground?"

"Yes," Mama said. "It was closed after we all left the funeral home."

"Did those men close it? The ones who carried it?"

"No, the people who work at the funeral home did that. The six men went to the cemetery at the same time as we did. They had already been chosen to carry Mrs. Chaney from the hearse to her final resting place."

"They are called pallbearers," Papa said.

"Were you ever a pole bear?"

"Pallbearer," Papa said. "Vunce."

"Who died?" I asked.

"My grandpapa's brother—my great uncle. It vas in Germany vhen I vas a teenager, yust before I came to America."

I waited for him to say more, but he didn't. And I didn't pursue it further. I had learned enough about death that day to last me a long time.

Three weeks after the funeral, Mr. Chaney came by our house. I saw him walking slowly to the door, so I opened it and invited him in. He said, "Thank you," removed his hat, and stepped onto the mat inside the door.

"Are you here to see Papa?"

"No. Actually, I'd like to see your mother."

"Okay. I'll get her. Please, have a seat."

"Thank you," he said again. "You are most polite."

Mama and Granny Nan had been upstairs changing the bed linens and were just coming down the steps when I started to go up. "Mr. Chaney is here," I said. "He wants to talk to you, Mama."

"Oh. All right." She came down and said hello to Mr. Chaney before taking her armful of linens to the kitchen, which was where Papa had hooked up Uncle Herman's old Thor. (He had given it to us when he bought a new Maytag.) Granny Nan said her salutations to Mr. Chaney and followed Mama with a bucket of dirty diapers.

Mama whispered to me, "Did he say why he is here?"

"No. Just that he wants to talk to you, not Papa."

"That is odd," Granny Nan whispered and began sorting the linens into piles.

Mama went into the front room. "What can I do for you, Mr. Chaney?"

I watched and listened from the bottom of the stairs.

He stood up when she entered the room and waited for her to sit down before he took a seat and spoke. "I have not said how happy I was to see you at Alice's funeral. She liked you, and I'm sure it made her happy knowing you were there." He paused.

"Is there something I can offer you, Mr. Chaney? Coffee, maybe?"

"Oh, no. I came to ask something of you."

"I would be happy to comply," Mama said.

"Well…it's like this…you see…I have…"

Granny Nan came into the living room with two coffee cups, a cream pitcher, a sugar bowl, and two spoons. "The pot is on to boil. We will have coffee in a few minutes. This is the kind of day when something nice and warm will make us all feel better." She set the items down and left.

"Please go on, Mr. Chaney," Mama said.

"Alice had a lot of nice clothes. She was unable to wear them after she got the cancer because she lost so much weight, so they hung in the closet for several months. I couldn't see them going to waste, so I thought…well, since you and Alice didn't go to the same places, like church or places in Weidman…no one will notice if you have on her clothes. You were both the same size, I mean before she…before she could no longer wear…" He broke down.

Mama jumped up and went to him, putting her arm around his shoulder until he recuperated enough to speak.

He was obviously embarrassed. "I'm so sorry. It's just…"

"No need to apologize. I cannot imagine what you have been going through," Mama comforted him. "It must be one of the hardest things you have ever had to do, sorting through her personal items. Every one of them sparked its own memory, I am sure."

"You are so understanding, Mrs. Schnier. That's why I wanted you to have her things. There is also some jewelry I thought you and your mother might like. Nothing of any value, but pretty, all the same."

"You are too kind," Mama said. "To think of us at your time of grief is one of the most selfless acts I have ever witnessed." She went back to the chair she had been sitting in.

"I'll go back out to the Buick and bring them in, if that would be all right."

"Of course it would, Mr. Chaney. May I help?"

"Oh, no. There are just a few boxes." He went out the door and made three trips to the front room with boxes of clothes and jewelry.

"I cannot tell you how much I appreciate this," Mama said. "I will wear them proudly, Mr. Chaney."

Granny Nan returned to the front room with the coffee pot and poured two cups full. Mr. Chaney added cream to his and stirred it. Mama added a spoonful of sugar and stirred hers. Granny Nan always drank hers black. I only liked coffee for breakfast; the idea of drinking it in the afternoon repulsed me.

Mr. Chaney sat back down. "Please feel free to give anything you don't want to someone else. I just hate to throw any of them away. Some of them are casual things she wore to her Bible study classes, some better ones to church, and even a couple of really nice ones she wore to the theater in Grand Rapids. She loved opera, so we attended one there every year. I never knew what she saw in it, all that foreign language. But it made me happy to see her enjoy something so much."

I could tell he was seeing her in his mind; his eyes were focused on some faraway place and time.

"How are things going on your farm?" Granny Nan asked.

"We didn't have much of a farm," he said. "We only raised enough livestock to feed ourselves. My parents died of cholera, but they left me with more than enough to care for a family for the remainder of my days. We ended up having no children, so Alice and I enjoyed some of the finer things that most people don't, or can't. I'm not bragging, mind you."

"Of course not, Mr. Chaney. Please be assured I was not thinking anything of the sort," Mama said.

"You are so kind, Mrs. Schnier." He finished his coffee in a single gulp and rose to leave.

Mama's gaze drifted to the boxes he'd brought in. "Thank you again, Mr. Chaney."

"No, no. Thank you, Mrs. Schnier. I can't think of another person I'd more like to have Alice's things." He and Mama walked to the door. He turned to say something else, but he couldn't speak. He merely raised his hand to Mama, then he turned and went to his automobile.

Mama stood in the doorway. I joined her, and we watched him drive away. She was crying. I didn't know what to say, so I took her hand. She looked down at me, hugged me to her, and led me back into the front room. We stood there, looking at the boxes.

"Is he gone?" Granny Nan asked.

Mama nodded, unable to speak.

"That was a nice gesture, but we will have to burn everything, you know," Granny Nan said matter-of-factly.

"What?" Mama was obviously confused by Granny Nan's statement.

"Well, the only way to get rid of all those cancer germs is to boil everything. And if the dresses are as nice as Jim says they are, then you can be assured they would not fare well after a good, long boiling. Some of them are probably made of silk or velvet, and those fabrics cannot be washed, let alone boiled."

"Mother, cancer is not contagious."

"We do not know that for certain," Granny Nan said. "I am putting my foot down on this subject, Violet. I will not allow you to wear those clothes. I will not even allow them to hang in your closet among your other things."

"But Mr. Chaney made the choice—the effort—to bring them to me. I cannot just burn them."

"Then give them away, but DO NOT handle them. I am telling you, this is how cancer spreads."

"Mother…"

"The subject is closed." And with that, Granny Nan got up, taking the coffee pot and her cup with her, and retired to the kitchen, where she sat down at the table with her back to the front room.

Mama knew better than to try and talk to her. When Granny Nan said the subject was closed, she was unmovable; her decision was not debatable.

"What will we do?" I whispered to Mama.

She whispered back, "I do not know yet. I will have to think about it."

The next morning, early, out behind the barn, Granny Nan set the boxes on fire.

DUCK FEATHERS

On a Wednesday in the late spring of 1927 I was walking home from school, ready to help Papa with anything he needed around the farm. I had been totally wrapped up in my schoolwork since Christmas and was enjoying my trips to the library with Miss Michaels two times a week. But I had already finished the books I'd checked out on Monday and had nothing pressing that day.

I reached a point on the road where I could see the house, and I noticed a strange-looking bundle lying on the ground by the truck. Whatever it was had been covered with a tarp. I wanted to go directly to it and look, but I knew I should go into the house and ask about it first.

"Helmi, is that you?" Mama called from upstairs.

"Yes," I called back. "I'll be up in a minute." Usually I had books, which I deposited on the kitchen table, but I was without any books that day, so I kicked off my shoes and went straight to the front door where I could inspect the tarp bundle from a closer vantage point. I still couldn't decide what it was.

Granny Nan came down the stairs. "Curious?"

She took me by surprise. "Yes. What is that, Granny Nan?"

She looked away and sighed. Then she did the strangest thing: she walked over to me and hugged me and said, "I am sorry."

I knew what was under the tarp. Betsy had not come running to greet me that afternoon as she did every day when she saw me walking up the road. My world went reeling, and I burst into tears. I went out the front door, ran to the bundle, and threw the tarp off. There she lay, lifeless.

Papa appeared out of nowhere and said, "Death is part of life, you know."

I nodded. I was now sobbing. "How did…"

"I do not know. Probably old age. Ve never knew how old she vas vhen ve found her." He came and kneeled beside me. "When I vent to the barn this morning, she vas lying there on some straw, wrapped around in a little circle vit her nose tucked under her tail, like alvays vhen she slept. She must have died in her sleep."

"I hope she was having a good dream."

"I think she vent in a very peaceful vay," he said. He reached into his back pocket, pulled out his handkerchief, and wiped his eyes. "Ve need to bury her, Helmi. Vhere do you think she vould be the happiest?"

I thought about it for a moment. "She always liked to lie in the shade under the tree with the swing. She stayed there the whole time when I was swinging." I looked up at him expectantly.

Papa hesitated. "I think that vould be a nice place, but…"

"But what, Papa?"

"Every time you go to your sving, you vould see her grave, and I am afraid it vould make you sad."

I thought about that. "It would. And I don't want to be sad every time I swing. Maybe we should bury her someplace else that she liked. Maybe beside the hen house. She guarded it. She was always watching out for foxes, and I think she liked doing that."

"Ja, she did seem to like that. She could be on guard for eternity. I think you came up vit a perfect solution."

So it was that Betsy kept our hens and roosters safe forevermore.

❖❖❖

I was depressed over Betsy's death for several days, but it became easier and easier with time. I stayed busy feeding the chickens and rooster every day, and Papa made sure he kept me busy with other things around the farm. As usual, I helped with the milking for an hour each morning before school and every evening except for Monday and Thursday when I went to the library with Miss Michaels.

Spring was calving time. We had a few heifers that we expected to drop calves any day, the Jerseys first and the Holsteins next. Jersey cows are smaller, and their gestation period is a little bit shorter than the big Holsteins, so we knew the Jersey calves would arrive first. They came without a hitch, but the Holsteins were a different story.

I had taken a liking to one Holstein in particular. I had taken care of her from the day she was born. She had a black patch on her left side that was shaped like a heart. I had named her Angel. I didn't tell Papa, though, because he said they were work animals, not pets, so they did not get names.

Angel and I, however, had a special relationship. It was almost as if she knew we could show affection to one another as long as Papa wasn't around. I would pet her and talk to her and sometimes handfeed her corn, but as soon as Papa appeared, she walked away from me, ignoring me as if I didn't even exist. It took a while for me to figure out that it wasn't because she didn't like me; it was because she knew she shouldn't be my "pet" when we were in Papa's presence. Cows are smart.

She wasn't a very big heifer, for a Holstein. She would be having her calf within the next few days, and I knew she was probably going to have twins. Her sides were bulged out so far that her back was almost flat. That reminded me of Ham, the Percheron we had to leave behind when we moved to Michigan.

Three days later, on a Sunday morning, Angel went into labor. Papa said, "I cannot go to Sunday school and church this morning. I need to be here for that heifer's delivery in case something should go wrong, and I vould like Helmi to be here, too."

I felt so special. I liked Sunday school, but I would forfeit it for Angel's sake, and I hoped God understood. And to think Papa had chosen me to help him! Birth was always a miracle, whether human or animal. I convinced myself it was spiritual, so I didn't need to go to Sunday school that day when I had the prospect of witnessing a miracle.

Cows usually spend up to two hours in labor. Angel had been in labor for almost four hours when Papa decided he should go get Dr. Pauley, our veterinarian. Unfortunately, Dr. Pauley was not home—probably at church. When Papa got back, he said, "Helmi, ve are going to be on our own. Ve must do vhatever is necessary to save our heifer."

I had watched lots of calves being born, and I was aware that sometimes a calf just wouldn't come out the way it was supposed to. If the heifer was having twins, their legs sometimes got intertwined, or one of them was backwards, which kept them from being in the right position to be born. Sometimes a calf's legs were tucked under the head and had to be straightened so they could come out first. All of those reasons required putting your hand and arm inside the cow. Or sometimes the calf was simply too big to come out on its own, which meant the vet had to put chains around its legs, and we all had to help pull it out. Angel was in that category.

Papa had tied Angel to one end of the stall. He tried to get his hand and arm inside her, but she was simply too small for his hand and arm to fit. "Helmi, you have smaller arms than I do. You vill have to check and see if there is vun or two calves."

"But Papa, I never..."

"There is a first time for everything, and this vill be your first time. I vill talk you through it. You are perfectly capable of doing this. You vill get blood on your shirt, though. Should you go put on an older vun?"

I looked down at what I was wearing. "This is the oldest one I have, Papa."

"Goot." He put my stepstool behind her and motioned for me to go ahead and check her.

I took a deep breath, stepped up on the stool, and put my hand inside. I didn't feel anything. I looked at Papa.

"You vill need to go deeper. You vill not feel anything until your whole arm is inside the cow."

I pushed my arm farther in, as far as it would go, clear up to my armpit. It was pleasantly warm inside her, very soft, and there was a lot of space. I could feel two hooves, but no more.

"I only feel one calf," I said.

"All right. Take vun of these chains." He handed one to me.

I pulled my arm out and took the chain. Then I started to put my arm and the chain back in, but she had a contraction right at that moment, and I couldn't get my hand back in. "She's tightening up, Papa."

"Give it few seconds and she vill relax."

I waited, and sure enough, she relaxed her muscles enough for me to insert my hand and arm, along with the chain.

"Now make a loop like this." He showed me how with the other chain. "You must be sure you have it looped correctly, or it vill cut into the calf's leg. Or vorse, it vill pull the hoof off vhen ve try to pull the calf out."

I tried to get it looped right, but I couldn't feel it well enough to know whether I had done it correctly. Evidently Papa could see that I was struggling. He held up the other chain with the end looped. "If it feels like this vun looks, you have done it properly," he said.

I closed my eyes and concentrated on the chain loop until I knew I had it right. Then I slipped it over one of the calf's hooves. "Its hooves are really big, Papa."

"Ja, I imagine so since it is not tvins. Now do the same vit this chain." He held the other chain up in front of me.

I took my hand out and grabbed the chain. Then I put my hand and arm back in and put the chain around the other hoof. "Okay, Papa."

"Now bring your hand out and help me pull. Be sure you keep tension on the chain."

I removed my hand, keeping the chain taut. I looked around for something to wipe my hand on, but there was nothing, so I wiped it on my shirt and pants. I looked up at Papa, who was holding the other chain taut.

"Here ve go," he said. And we pulled. And grunted. And pulled. The legs came out, but the head was stuck. "It is so big," Papa said wearily.

"Is Angel going to die?" Then I realized what I had said. *Oh, no!*

Dar Bagby

Now Papa knows I named one of the cows. He's going to be so angry with me.

"I do not know."

"I'm sorry. I know you don't like me to name the cows because..."

"Not now, Helmi. Ve have a calf to deliver. I do not know if the heifer *or* the calf vill live. Ve must keep vorking. It vould be the best if ve can save both the calf and its mother. Now pull vit all your might!"

I could see the calf's nose peeking out.

"It is coming!" Papa said. He grabbed hold of the rail of the stall with one hand and pulled the chain with the other. The head popped out, then the shoulders, and the calf came sliding out onto the straw.

"Ve did it!" he said.

"That's a huge calf!" I said.

Papa was panting. "Ja. A bull." He reached down and slapped the calf. It moved and took a breath. Then it raised its head. He untied Angel, and she immediately turned and instinctively began sniffing and licking her newborn.

I was not only thrilled but also enlightened. I loved seeing a new life come into the world, but even more, I loved the fact that I had participated in this one. I recognized that without my help it might not have happened; we might have lost the calf or Angel or both. I knew right then and there that I wanted to be a veterinarian. I couldn't wait to tell Mama and Granny Nan about the ordeal.

Papa loved "riddling" me. Riddles were one of his favorite things with which to torture me. He knew I would probably not understand the answer, even if he told me. One day we were in the milk house. He had run the first group of cows out and put the second group in the stanchions and attached the milkers to their udders. He stepped up to the sink where I was standing on my stepstool, washing a bucket, and asked me, "Vhich side do you get down from a horse?"

I rolled my eyes. *Another riddle. Why does he ask me these things?* "The left side," I said, certain of my answer.

He shook his head. "No. You do not get down from a horse. You get down from a duck." He laughed and walked back into the stanchion barn.

What? You can't ride a duck, so how can you get down from it? I was stumped. I also didn't understand that he was providing me with a hint at something that was going to thrill me beyond my wildest dreams.

We finished the milking and walked across the road. I started to go into the house, but Papa said, "Do not take off your shoes yet, Helmi. I have something to show you." He turned and walked toward the chicken coop. He opened the gate to the rooster pen. Earlier that week, I had put the rooster in with the chickens for a few days, so the pen was empty except for the low galvanized watering trough. The closer I got, however, the more I could hear soft peeping.

"Do we have new chicks?" I asked him. He did not answer.

Then I noticed a box sitting behind the trough. I went into the pen, and there, in the box, were four of the cutest little bundles of fluff I had ever seen. Ducks! Papa had gotten me some ducks. "Oh, Papa!" I picked one up and held it close to my ear. The peeping was more like a soft whistle, not like that of chicks. Papa scooped up the other three and set them down. They immediately began pecking at the dirt, as if something were there for them to eat.

"They are hungry. Had you better feed them?" he asked.

I was beside myself with joy. I had wanted ducks since I was three or four, but we never had a place for them. I picked up each one, petting it and speaking softly to it. There were two each of a different color; one kind had some dark spots on it, the other two were very pale yellow without any spots.

"The two plain vuns are Chinese Cresteds," Papa said, "and the two spotted vuns are Runners."

"They are so soft and cute," I said. "Thank you, Papa. Thank you so much."

"Their food is inside the hen house vit the chicken feed," he said.

I hurried and found the tin of feed and brought it out to the rooster pen.

"Only a tiny bit," Papa said.

I scattered some onto the ground, and the ducks pecked up the granules until they were gone.

"Now they must svim." Papa picked them up and set them in the watering trough. They floated, and their fluff didn't even get wet. "You vill have to keep them in the house at night until they are big enough to take care of themselves. In the meantime, you and I must build a pen for them. It vill only be temporary, though, because they vill need to be trained to stay around the barns and in the stream."

"I'll take good care of them, Papa," I said. "I'll train them, too. I'll take them to the stream to swim every day and only feed them in their pen so they know not to get too far away from their food."

"I know you vill be a good teacher, Helmi. You have a lot of patience."

I named the Runners Dash and Race. They were so fast that, after a few days of taking them from their pen to the stream, they learned the routine and passed me on the way, making sure they got to the stream before I did. And they did the same when I took them back to the pen for a treat.

The Chinese Cresteds had the funniest little tuft of feathers on the tops of their heads. Since they were Chinese, I decided they needed Chinese names. When I went to the library the first time after getting them, I found a book about China by Pearl S. Buck. It was called *The Good Earth*. It was much too long for me to read, and it had words that were too big for me to pronounce. But I found the names of two characters in the story and named my Chinese Cresteds after them: Wang and O-Lan.

I kept my word and trained the ducks to stay in our barnyard, except when they wanted to go swimming. Pretty soon they were on their own and came and went as they pleased between the stream and the barnyard. But when I came out the back door, they followed me wherever I went. I didn't know whether they were male or female, but I figured *they* knew, so it didn't matter much to me.

School was out for the summer, and the air was hot and sticky. I was miserable, especially at night. Leaving the windows open only made it more humid inside, especially upstairs. Papa said it was because heat rises. We had closed the floor vents that allowed the downstairs air to come upstairs, but that hadn't made much difference, at least not to me.

We had two more roosters, now, both hatched from the eggs of one of our laying hens. Both were Rhode Island Reds like Mickey the Chickey, and both were nice to me. Papa said it was because they understood that "it is not goot to bite the hand that feeds you."

Mama and Granny Nan divided up our eggs, giving some of them to an Amish family that didn't have chickens. The man, Jacob Miller, had been one of the people who helped us build our house and barns. He had been there throughout the building of each of the structures, and his sons, Eli and Samuel, had worked harder than anyone else.

I went out to the duck pen and found a single egg in the dirt. At least I knew now that one of my ducks was female. I took the egg inside and showed Mama and Granny Nan how big it was. "Jacob Miller and his family will love this," Granny Nan said. "I understand they are quite fond of duck eggs." We only got a few every month. Mama said she guessed only one of the ducks was a hen and the other three were drakes.

I played with the ducks every day, except when it was raining. But just like Papa said, they loved the rainy days. I sometimes went out on the front porch and watched them in the rain. They'd sit down on the grass and preen their feathers, leaving some of the loose ones behind when they got up and left. If the breeze didn't blow them away when the sun came out, I'd gather them up and keep them in a jar. I had that jar of duck feathers for many years; they filled me with fond memories when I looked at them.

One day in mid-summer I was in the garden helping Granny Nan and Mama pick snap beans. The temperature had risen into the nineties, and I couldn't stay bent over any longer. I stood up and said, "I need a drink of water."

Granny Nan took one look at me and said, "Heavens, child! You are red as a beet." I looked over at her and fainted dead away.

I finally came to, and it took me a minute to figure out where I was: I was lying on my back on the kitchen counter with my head in the sink. Mama was pouring cool water on my head, and Granny Nan had cool, damp towels wrapped around my arms and legs.

"We thought we had lost you," Granny Nan said to me when she saw that I was awake.

"You fainted from the heat," Mama said. "I never saw anyone turn as red as you did."

I tried to speak, but I had so little breath, I couldn't make anything come out.

"Do not try to talk," Granny Nan said. "Save your strength."

I closed my eyes. It felt so good to be cooling down. After a while, I told them I felt much better and would like to sit up. They helped me to a sitting position, and I reached up and felt my head. It was throbbing, and I had to blink several times before everything came into focus. "May I please have a glass of water?"

Granny Nan scurried around to pour me a glassful while Mama held onto me like I was going to try and run away. "I'm okay, now, Mama. You don't need to hold me so tight."

"I just do not want you to get dizzy and fall. We do not need you to crack your head open, now do we?"

I drank the whole glassful in one long drink and immediately felt better. "Another, please," I said. Granny Nan refilled the glass and handed it to me. I felt like I had not had anything to drink in days and days. "What do people drink in the desert?" I asked.

"I suppose they have to carry plenty of water with them," Mama said.

"I was in the desert," I said. "But I didn't have any water to drink. I must not have taken enough with me. Or maybe my camels drank it all."

Mama frowned and looked at Granny Nan. She said to me, "Well, you found an oasis, and now you have had some water to drink."

"You and Granny Nan are here," I said, puzzled. "Where are we?"

Obviously, I was delirious. Mama carried me upstairs and put me in my bed. Granny Nan pulled Yosie's bed up next to mine, sat down on it, and began to fan me with a newspaper. I don't remember anything until the following morning when I woke up and saw Granny Nan asleep in Yosie's bed. She awakened and sat up as soon as I stirred. "How do you feel?"

"I'm fine." I yawned.

"You gave us quite a scare," she said.

I had to think back on what had happened. Everything I remembered seemed out of sequence. "What did I do?"

"You passed out in the garden. It must have been heat stroke."

I sat there, blinking.

"You fell face-first into a row of snap beans. You were so red, I thought you were going to explode! So we took you into the kitchen, put your head under the running water, and covered you with cold cloths. Then you woke up and drank like a fish. Your mother carried you up here, put you in bed, and I have stayed with you, fanning you and keeping cool cloths on your forehead."

"I feel much better now, Granny Nan. Could I have some breakfast?"

"I am afraid you missed breakfast. And dinner. But I will be glad to fix you some leftovers."

Mama appeared at the door. "I thought I heard our little patient." She leaned against the door jamb.

"I guess I'm fine now," I told her. "I'm hungry."

"That is a good sign," she said.

Granny Nan pushed past Mama on her way to get me something to eat.

"I think you need to stay in bed for the rest of the afternoon," Mama said.

"But, Mama, I need to help Papa. I have to feed the chickens and the ducks. I haven't gathered eggs since two days ago, either!" I was frantic. I started to get out of bed.

Mama came to my bedside and took me by the shoulders. "No, you are staying right here. We have already taken care of your chores. You need to rest and build your strength back up." She gently pushed me back down on the bed, and I complied. I felt weak, "puny" Granny Nan would call it.

I spent the remainder of the day resting, slipping in and out of sleep. By the following morning, however, I was eager to get back to my usual schedule.

HIRED HELP AND OATMEAL PIE

The rest of the summer was uneventful. Miss Michaels had gone to Chattenooga to spend the summer with her family, so there were no weekly trips to the library. Our garden had done especially well, so there was a lot of picking and canning to do. Mama and Granny Nan were busier than usual with all of that, so I volunteered to take care of Yosie, Bella, Dora, and Retta when I wasn't doing my chores or helping Papa. The twins played well together, so I didn't have to do too much with them. I had been around babies enough to know how to care for Retta, so she was no problem. Then there was Yosie.

Yosie's "terrible twos" were still going strong, even though she was well into her "fours." She purposely did things that irritated me, and when I told her not to, she turned her back to me, bent over and put her hands on her knees, and wiggled her bottom at me. I hated that, and she knew it.

Papa said Yosie was "roly-poly," but I thought she was just plain fat—fatter than a tick. Her wrists and ankles had fat wrinkles, and her elbows and knees had deep dimples. But her beautiful round face, her dark pink heart-shaped mouth, button nose, and curly hair were eye-catchers that made most people overlook her chunky body. "That is baby fat," Mama said when I mentioned Yosie's condition. "She will grow out of it."

I guess I was worried that Yosie would become like one of the girls at school. The girl's name was Beulah. She was almost completely round from her feet to the top of her head, like a big ball, and the other kids called her Bouncing Beulah. She was very soft-spoken when Miss Michaels called on her in class, and she stayed to herself, so I didn't talk to her much.

When we had a recess, Beulah usually sat on a stump in the tree line that bordered the school. She had a little dolly that she brought to school each day, and she played with it by herself when we were outside. No one seemed to want to be her friend. I tried being friendly, but she was not interested in my effort. I didn't want Yosie to be the Bouncing Beulah of her class when she started to school.

Yosie's only interest seemed to be watching Mama and Granny Nan when they cooked. As a result, I didn't have to watch her very often. She sat on one of the kitchen chairs and never took her eyes off what they were doing. The funny part, to me, was that she didn't want to participate—only watch. Of course, Mama and Granny Nan always asked her to taste whatever they were making "to be sure it was okay."

Retta was the happiest baby I ever saw. She smiled, laughed, and babbled all the time. I only ever heard her cry when something scared her. Our back door was situated so that the wind often blew it shut. And when it closed, it closed with a bang. It often caught us all off guard, making us jump, but Retta was too little to understand what it was, so it scared her when it happened. Her little face would wrinkle up, her arms would flail in the air, and she'd cut loose with a screech that could make my hair stand on end. Luckily, all I had to do to calm her down was quietly sing her a little song. She especially liked my rendition of "Baa, Baa, Black Sheep." Her first words were "Baa, Baa."

There was so much to do around the farm, Papa was getting tired, and he looked it. He and Mama were discussing the situation one night in bed. I could hear them softly talking because their bedroom was right across the hall from mine. It being so hot and humid, we all left our doors open to try and improve the upstairs circulation. I couldn't hear every word they said, but I was able to put enough together to surmise what Papa wanted.

"Ve have so many cows now, I cannot keep up vit the rest of the farm. The fields are not being taken care of the vay they should be, so I need somevun who…"

I couldn't hear anymore, but I had heard enough. We were going to have help.

The subject didn't come up again until it was almost time for school to start in the fall. One morning I went to the milk house, and there stood a stranger. I stopped dead in my tracks and looked at him like he was an intruder.

"Hi, there!" he said in a booming voice. "I come to help you and your Pa. My name's Butch." He came toward me, extending his hand. I backed up a couple of steps, then I realized he was offering to shake hands, so I reached out and shook his, not able to speak. "Cat got your tongue?" he asked and laughed.

Papa appeared at the doorway between the milk house and the stanchion barn. "Helmi, say hello to our new farm hand."

"I think I scared her," Butch said.

"I didn't know anyone else was here," I said, sheepishly, but I recovered enough to say, "It's nice to meet you."

"Well, ain't you the polite one."

"She is the best farm hand anyvun could ask for, but she has to mind her studies so she can go to college. She cannot spend all of her spare time vit me in the barns or the fields," Papa said.

"College?" Butch said and looked down at me.

"I'd like to be a veterinarian."

"A ve…" He turned and looked at Papa. "Are you sure this is your daughter and not a son?"

"Ja, she is my daughter, and I am very proud of her. You vill have to vork extra hard, Butch, to match vhat she can do around here." I smiled up at Papa. He said, "Mr. Butcher—Butch—is a neighbor from Weidman. He is familiar vit all aspects of farming, even milking cows, but he has never milked them vit electric milkers like ve have. Vhould you like to show him how they vork?"

I nodded and walked over to the stanchion barn doorway to see if Papa had already brought in the first batch of cows. He had, so I motioned to Butch to follow me. I explained how each of the cows had her own stanchion and that they all knew which of the cows got milked first, so it was important to put the milkers on them in the same order every time. "It keeps them from getting nervous," I explained to him. "Papa says it makes them happy, and happy cows give more milk." Butch appeared to be listening to every word I said, so I figured he approved of being taught by a six-year-old.

We wiped off the cow's teats with a wet cloth, and then I told him we were ready to begin putting on the milkers. We had three sets of milkers, and we had enough stanchions for nine cows at a time, which meant we milked three-at-a-time and changed the milkers three times for each group that came into the barn. "I have trouble lifting the milkers—they're kind of heavy—so Papa holds them for me, and I put them on the teats." Butch picked up one of the milkers and held it under the cow's udder for me. "You do it like this." I showed him how to put them on. When the milkers were finished, I showed him how to take them off by releasing the suction with my finger.

"Then we have to take it into the milk house and pour it into the bulk tank." Butch picked up the full milker and dumped it into a bucket. Then we attached that milker to the next cow before going into the milk house. "You have to be sure there is a filter in this basket before you pour." I pointed at the filter cylinder. "Otherwise, it might con…cont…."

"Contaminate?" Butch suggested.

"Yes, contaminate the rest of the milk. Sometimes, even after washing the cow's teats, there might be some grass or dirt on them, and that could get into the bulk tank and ruin the whole batch."

"Heinrich, your daughter here sure knows her business," Butch said to Papa.

"Ja, she does," Papa said. I knew he was proud of me.

For the next couple of days, Papa stayed with Butch and me to be sure things went all right, but before long Butch and I were on our own. He brought the cows in and turned them out after being milked—Papa said I was too little to do that—and I did the same things for Butch that I had done for Papa, like keeping the buckets washed and changing the bulk tank filters. When I wasn't busy doing that, I was helping with the milkers. I also made sure there was silage in the trough in front of the cows when they came in so they could "munch" while being milked.

One of the Holsteins came in with some blood dripping from one of her teats. "Oh dear," I heard Butch say. "We better get your pa."

I looked at the teat and saw that it had a minor cut. "We don't need Papa," I said. "I know how to take care of it."

Butch looked at me like I was from outer space. "You do?"

"Uh-huh. You just wash it off as best you can, then you attach the milker to the other three teats and milk the cut one into a bucket by hand. But try not to touch the sore place. You might have to keep wiping it. Blood will probably drip into the bucket, so we won't be keeping that milk. We'll dump it out for the barn cats. When you're done, you put some of that salve on it." I pointed to a big tin of salve that sat on a shelf below one of the windows. Then I turned around and walked back into the milk house.

Later that day I heard Papa telling Mama and Granny Nan that Butch had said, "I learned how to milk a cow vit a cut on its teat. A future veterinarian taught me." I knew he meant me.

❖❖❖

On the day before school started, I went to the milk house expecting to see Butch, but instead there was a boy standing at the door between the stanchion barn and the milk house. I must have been very quiet when I entered, because he jumped when I said, "Hello."

I waited for a reply, but he only stared down at his shoes. Butch came up to the doorway and said, "Hey, Helmi. This here's my son, Jimmy." He looked down at Jimmy and said, "You gonna say Hi to her, or you just gonna stand there with a dopey look on your face?"

Jimmy mumbled something before looking up at me and saying, "Hi." He immediately looked back down at his shoes.

I proceeded to go about my business. Butch said, "I brought Jimmy along so he could see what it is that I do when I leave our house every mornin'. He starts school tomorrow mornin', too, just like you. He's in the fourth grade."

"Fifth," Jimmy said without looking up.

"Oh, yeah. He was in the fourth last year, and I ain't got used to saying 'fifth' yet."

"You go to Weidman?" I asked.

Jimmy nodded.

He isn't very talkative; sure doesn't take after his father, I thought. I went into the stanchion barn and filled the trough with little piles of silage for the first nine cows. Then I went back into the milk house while Butch brought the cows into the barn and tightened the stanchions around their necks. Jimmy hadn't moved.

"You might want to move so the cows don't see you standing there. They get nervous when they see a stranger, and it makes it hard to get them to come into the barn."

Jimmy looked up and saw the cows standing in the far doorway. He bent over and ducked his head down, covering it with his arms. But he still hadn't moved out of sight of the incoming cows. I could hear Butch shouting to the cows, "Hay-yup! Git in there! Hyah! Go on!"

"You need to move," I said to Jimmy.

He remained motionless. The first cow had seen him and stopped dead in her tracks. Butch hollered at her, but she wasn't paying any attention to him.

"MOVE!" I shouted to Jimmy.

He didn't change his stance. He scuffed his feet along the floor until he was out of sight of the incoming cows. They came in and went directly to their preferred stanchions. *Is this kid slow, or what?* I wondered.

Eventually Jimmy straightened up and went outside where he played with the ducks. I liked the fact that he was fond of them. I mean, anyone who likes ducks can't be all bad.

It was good that Papa had hired Butch. The fact that Butch was capable of milking the cows every morning meant that Papa had time to work the fields. Papa and I still milked at night, but not having to do the morning milking allowed Papa to care for the crops. He plowed under some of the old crops and fertilized the fields so they would be ready to disc and plant in the spring. Butch also fed and watered the beef cattle and pigs before he left each day. Sometimes he even stayed around and did repairs that Papa hadn't had time to do, or ones he needed help with because it took more hands than just his two, and sometimes more muscles than I had.

Butch's wife had died a few years back, so he had sold off most of his farm. It was only Jimmy and him now, living in a big farmhouse. They had hardly any livestock and very little land. I also learned that they didn't have enough money to buy electricity, and they still used an outhouse. I began to understand that Jimmy was shy, not slow.

School was even better for me than it had been the year before. I was a second grader now, so I was no longer the youngest. Duane helped me with some of my arithmetic—he was really good at it. Because I was learning so much faster than the other kids in my grade, I was doing things they couldn't yet understand. Miss Michaels and I returned to our library routine. She ate supper at our house every Monday and Thursday, just like last year, and this year Mama and Granny Nan invited her to our house for Christmas. She accepted without pause.

I'm not sure if it was because of all the time we spent together, or if we simply had been poured out of the same mold, but Miss Michaels and I got along splendidly. I loved learning and she loved teaching, so it was undoubtedly a good match. My family accepted her as one our own. It was almost like I had a big sister to depend on. At any rate, it worked, and I was most fortunate to have her around.

Miss Michaels had decided our school should perform a play in the spring. We all got to help with it in some way, and she even invited some of the kids from Mount Pleasant High School to come and help build the "sets," sew some of the costumes, and be the main characters in the play.

I knew nothing about plays, so Miss Michaels suggested I get some from the library and read them. She gave me the names of some she thought I'd be able to understand, and I asked the librarian to help me find them on the bookshelves. After reading a few of them, I became enthralled with the idea of reading what everyone *said* rather than reading mostly about what they *did*. Miss Michaels said that was the whole purpose of a play—to discover what was happening through dialogue rather than prose.

We did a play called *Peter Pan*, and I played one of the "lost boys" in Neverland. There weren't enough boys in our school to play them, so some of us girls had to be boys. It was great fun, and Granny Nan called me her lost boy for several weeks after the play was over.

In no time, it was 1928, and on May 20 Mama gave birth to yet another daughter, Marcelina (Celine). She was very tiny and very quiet, and she slept more than any of the other babies Mama had brought into the world. Mama had trouble getting her to eat and had to keep flicking the bottoms of Celine's feet to wake her up while she was breast feeding. Mama complained about how swollen and sore her breasts were because Celine wasn't emptying them. That made me skeptical about ever becoming a mother.

When Christmas rolled around, the weather was still tolerable.

We hadn't had any snow yet, though it was cold with frequent windy days. Christmas morning, however, was sunny and calm, and the temperature was above freezing. I was helping Papa with the morning milking; since it was Christmas day, he had given Butch the day off.

We had a Christmas tree that was so big it touched the ceiling. For the first time, it had strands of electric lights on it: red, blue, green, and yellow. There were presents under it, one for each of us kids from Santa, and ones that Mama and Papa and Granny Nan had made for each other.

Papa and I were standing behind the cows, waiting for the milkers to fill. I was a bit skeptical about Santa. "Papa, is Santa Claus real?"

He looked me square in the eyes. "Vhat do you think?"

"I'm not sure. Some of the kids at school say he isn't. They say their parents buy the gifts and just mark the tags with Santa's name. Is that how it is?"

He looked off into the distance, thinking before he spoke, Papa style. "Ja, Helmi, it is. Christmas is about the spirit of giving. It is celebrated as the day of Christ's birth, and that vas the greatest gift of all time. Children need Santa Claus, even though it is in name only, to remind them to keep that spirit in their hearts."

I nodded. "So when children get old enough to understand the true spirit of giving, we don't need Santa to remind us any longer."

"You are not only smart, Helmi, you are also vise—vise enough to understand such a concept. You vill go far in this vorld. And you vill live by both your head and your heart." He looked at me with an expression I'd never seen before, sort of a mixture of sadness and pride.

After the milking we all ate some breakfast and opened our gifts. The house already smelled of ham roasting in the oven, and there were all sorts of pots and pans on the stove. Mama and Granny Nan had been baking cookies the whole week before Christmas, and Granny Nan had baked her "famous" oatmeal pie (well, famous among all of us, anyway). She only made it at Christmas.

Mama and Papa were setting up two tables and extra chairs they had borrowed from the church, one of which was a "children's table." Instead of eating at the kitchen table, we were all going to eat in the front room. I counted the chairs and couldn't figure out why there were so many. "Who else besides Miss Michaels is coming for supper?" I asked Mama.

"Oh, just some friends," she said, smiling.

"Who?"

"It is a surprise," Granny Nan said.

Sometimes surprises were hard to wait for, but I knew better than to press the matter. I helped set the places; there were ten at the grown-up table and four at the children's table. No matter how many times I went over it in my head, I couldn't account for all of them.

There was a knock at the door. "I vill get it," Papa said. Miss Michaels came in with her arms full of presents. "Vhat have ve here?" Papa asked, taking some of the presents from her and putting them under the tree.

"Oh, just some little things I thought y'all might enjoy. And there's a loaf of cranberry bread and a loaf of hickory nut bread in the car," she said.

"I'll get it," I shouted. I ran past her and retrieved the loaves, bringing them in and putting them on the kitchen table with the cookies and the pie. They smelled wonderful!

Granny Nan took Miss Michaels' coat and hat and put them on the bed in her downstairs bedroom. Granny Nan had made her bed that morning using the cover her mother had crocheted back in 1865. It was one of the most beautiful things I had ever seen. Granny Nan had never used it before; she said it was too fragile. But today was going to be a special occasion, so she brought it out to share with everyone.

Another knock: Mama went to the door and welcomed Butch and Jimmy. I hadn't known they were coming, so that was a surprise, and it accounted for two more of the place settings. Butch and Jimmy were both wearing their usual clothes, but they had been washed and smelled of soap rather than cow manure! Jimmy had on a funny hat that made everyone laugh. It was pointy like a Santa hat and had a fuzzy ball glued to the very top. Jimmy had colored it red, blue, green and yellow, just like the lights on our Christmas tree.

"You match our Christmas tree lights," Granny Nan said. We all laughed and agreed. We made him stand in front of the tree. "Where is his head?" Granny Nan teased. "It disappeared!"

There was no place for everyone to sit except around the table, so we all just pulled a chair away from the table and sat down, but before we could start a decent conversation, we heard another car pull up. Papa looked out, then he spread his hands out and said, "Everyvun stay put. I vill get the door." He climbed over Butch and Jimmy, who were sitting closest to the door, and flung the door wide open. I saw a huge grin on his face, but from where I was sitting, I couldn't see who he was grinning at, nor could I see out the window to discover who had arrived.

Without words, Uncle Herman came barreling into the front room, arms around Papa in a bear hug, shoving him backwards until Papa was able to bring them both to a stop. Uncle Herman pushed

Papa away an arm's length and said, "Merry Christmas, you old farmer!"

"I vould rather be farming than scribing all day," Papa said. "How do you manage to get enough fresh air to keep your lungs clean?"

"I drive to and from the office with my head hanging out the window of the Buick." Uncle Herman stuck out his tongue, leaned his head sideways, and wiggled it like a dog with its head out of a car window. They both laughed as if the whole world were funny.

Uncle Herman's laughter came to a sudden halt, and he turned around. I had made my way to the window, and I saw two women coming toward the house. One of them was short and petite, and she wore a light blue velvet coat trimmed in white fur. On her head was a white fur hat, and she held a white muff. The other, much taller, had on a black wool skirt with shiny black buttons down the front, but off to one side. She wore a waist-length jacket that was red and black and dark green plaid, and her boots were black patent leather that caught the sun and flashed as she walked. She also wore fuzzy dark green earmuffs that exactly matched the green in her jacket, and she had on black gloves. Those two women were a sight to behold!

I eventually realized that Uncle Herman was talking to me. "…and you and Lizzy can get to know each other."

I ran to Uncle Herman and hugged him. "I didn't hear what you said, Uncle Herman. Merry Christmas."

"I got the feeling you were a bit engrossed in gawking at Mary and Lizzy," he said.

"Sorry. They just look so pretty. Who are they?" I asked.

He bent down and said in almost a whisper, "I'll let you know in just a moment." He turned and walked toward the two women, meeting them halfway across the yard. He took the young woman by her hand; he towered over her. And he opened his other arm to the taller woman, who ducked under it and stood up so Uncle Herman could put his arm around her shoulder. They came to the door. By then we were all looking at them either out the window or through the door. No one spoke.

Uncle Hermann and the two accompanying females stepped inside. Uncle Herman was smiling even bigger than usual. "I'd like you all to meet Mary Blodgett and her daughter, Elizabeth. You need to get to know them, as they will soon be family." It took a couple of beats for that to sink in; everyone just stood there for a few seconds before putting the pieces together.

Granny Nan was the first to speak. "You mean you…are the two of you…?"

"We are engaged to be married!" Uncle Herman said, proud as punch. He looked at Mary with such devotion—such admiration—my heart nearly burst.

"Oh, wow!" was all I could get to come out. I ran up to him and Mary and Lizzy and hugged them all at the same time. I had no problem accepting them, as I knew they would be the greatest people I'd ever met; Uncle Herman wouldn't allow anyone other than the best to be a part of this family.

"And this is Helmi," Uncle Herman said to Mary and Lizzy.

"Pleased to meet you both," I said, "and Merry Christmas." Everyone else came up to them, and they all talked at once.

I realized Lizzy wasn't as old I had first thought, and I asked her if I could take her coat, hat, and muff. She said, "Thank you, Helmi. Herman said you were polite, and he was right. He also told us 'Helmi' is your nickname, short for Wilhelmina. Lizzy's a nickname, too. It's short for Elizabeth. But Mommy didn't want to call me that all the time, so she began calling me Lizzy, and that's who I've been ever since."

Lizzy sure isn't afraid to talk!

I took her coat, hat, and muff, and I asked Mary if I could take her things. She handed me her earmuffs and gloves and thanked me. She also had a handbag, which I looked at, but she said, "I'll just keep this with me." She patted it and bent down to me and whispered, "A woman's never sure when she might need to powder her nose." Then she smiled and winked at me. I liked her already.

"Vell, this is qvite the Christmas present," Papa said after the chattering slowed down. "I could not be happier for you, Herrmann. You deserve some time to think about things other than vork."

Mary laughed; she almost sounded like Mama. "You say that with such joy and kinship in your voice, Heinrich. I can see why you have such a friendly, welcoming home."

"Vhat you see is vhat Violet and Nancy have done vit it. I only deal vit what is outside," Papa said. "And I am certain you have no interest in seeing barns full of cows and pigs and chickens."

"You might be surprised, Heinrich," Uncle Herman said. "Mary has a long history of farmers in her family, too."

"That's right," Mary said. "I can milk a cow and pluck a chicken with the best of them."

"You have goot taste!" Papa said to Uncle Herman and slapped him on the back.

While all of that was going on, Lizzy and I had been in Granny Nan's bedroom putting hers and Mary's coats and other accessories on the bed. "Herman says you're quite the student. He says you're learning much faster than the other kids in your grade and that you want to be a veterinarian when you grow up. Are you planning on going to college?"

"Yes, I have to go to college to be one. A veterinarian, I mean."

Lizzy said, "I figured as much. I'm finishing my last year in the junior high school, so I'll be going to high school next year. It's kind of scary, but Mommy says I'll have the other students with me that have been in my grade, so at least I won't be completely alone. Some of them are my good friends who will be going to the same high school."

I thought about that and asked, "Do you mean you have more than one high school you could go to?"

"Yes, we have three different ones, including the parochial school," she said.

"The what?"

"The parochial school. It's a religious school. I don't mean they only teach religion. I mean Catholic churches give money to them… I think. Anyway, I know some of the kids in my elementary are Catholic, and they're going to that high school. One of them is one of my best friends." She looked sad.

"Can you go the parochial school?"

"I asked Mommy about it, and she said I could, but we would have to *pay* for me to go there. Although, I don't think I'd go there just because one of my friends does. I don't want to become Catholic, and since I'm not Catholic, I wouldn't know what's going on most of the time, I guess." Lizzy had a funny little furrow between her eyebrows when she was trying to work things out in her head. I wondered if I did, too, when I was pondering something. I thought, *I might have to check that out in the mirror sometime.*

We went back into the front room and sat down. I began counting chairs again. Celine would be in the cradle, probably sleeping during supper, so I didn't have to include a chair for her. Yosie, Bella, Dora, and Retta would definitely be at the children's table, which accounted for those four chairs. The grown-up's table would accommodate Papa, Mama, Granny Nan, Uncle Herman, Mary, Miss Michaels, and Butch. But there were three more chairs and place settings at that table, which meant Jimmy, Lizzy, and I would get to sit with the grown-ups!

While Mama and Granny Nan, along with help from Miss Michaels and Mary, were doing the final preparations on the meal, I took Lizzy outside to see the ducks, and Jimmy tagged along.

"I didn't catch your name when everyone was introducing everyone else," Lizzy said to Jimmy.

He looked down at his shoes and mumbled his name.

"What is it? I didn't hear you," Lizzy said.

Jimmy looked up at her, and his cheeks turned red. "Jimmy," he said. "I help my dad 'round here when I ain't in school." He couldn't take his eyes off Lizzy.

"You a farmer, too?" she asked.

"Yeah. We don't got much of a farm no more, though, so Dad and me, we help out here."

"How galante of you!" Lizzy curtsied to him. I had never heard the word 'galante' before, and I had rarely seen anyone curtsy.

Jimmy turned even redder.

"Do you know how to milk cows?" she asked Jimmy.

He nodded, barely enough for Lizzy to see.

"Was that a 'yes'?" she asked.

I stepped up to the plate. "Jimmy's dad, Butch, which is short for Mr. Butcher, comes over to our place in the mornings to do the milking so Papa can get out into the fields and do other things that need to be done around here. When Jimmy isn't in school, he comes along to help."

Lizzy turned back to Jimmy and said, "Is that right? You must be very good at farming, then."

"Yeah, I guess so," Jimmy said. "I want a farm like this someday." He looked around at our farm. "I know I could make a go of it. Dad says ownin' land's what turns a boy into a man."

I had never heard Jimmy talk so much. I wondered if it took a pretty girl to bring out his voice.

He continued, "Helmi does the work mosta the time. She's *real* good with animals. She wants to be a vet. Wait'll you see how much the ducks like her."

The ducks had only just realized I was outside, and they came running up to me, quacking and uttering all other sorts of duck noises. Wang reached up and put his head in my hand like he always did when I greeted him. I petted him, and the other three began to peck at the dirt. "It's feeding time," I said. "If you want, you can come along to the hen house where the duck food is, but you'll want to be careful not to get your clothes dirty."

"I will," Lizzy said. She started to follow me, and Jimmy hurried up so he could walk beside her. "What are the funny little hats on the white ones?" Lizzy asked.

"Them ain't hats," Jimmy laughed. "Them's feathers." He was giggling.

"That breed is called Chinese Crested. I guess you can see why," I said to Lizzy.

"Yes, I can see." She and Jimmy waited outside the pen while I put some feed in a tin can.

"You want to feed them?" I asked her and handed her the can. But before she had a chance to answer, all four of the ducks began to peck at the can. That's when she made a bad mistake: she raised the can up over her head to keep the ducks from getting it. She had no idea those four critters would do anything to get to the food—even try to climb up her body after it. They began flapping and quacking and pecking as they did their best to climb up her nice, light blue coat.

"Just drop it!" I said to her. But she kept holding the can up in the air and, at the same time, trying to push the ducks away with her other hand. They were making flat-footed prints all over her coat, and there were now a couple of rips in the fabric from the ducks' toenails.

Jimmy ran up to Lizzy and grabbed the can out of her hand, throwing its contents on the ground. The ducks immediately followed the food, leaving Lizzy alone but tousled. Jimmy was the hero. To my surprise, Lizzy was laughing.

"Your coat!" I said. "It's ruined. I'm sorry, Lizzy. I didn't think about you not knowing how ornery they can be when it comes feeding time."

"I'm fine, Helmi," she said, still laughing. "Don't worry about the coat. This is probably the last time I was going to wear it anyway. I've outgrown it." She was brushing it off as best she could, and Jimmy was helping her, not paying any attention to where his hands were landing!

"Jimmy!" I hollered.

He stopped and turned toward me. He backed away, mouth hanging open.

"You'd catch flies if any were out-and-about this time of year," I said to him.

He simply stared at me, mouth still agape.

I opened my mouth extra wide, then, using the back of my hand, pushed my lower jaw back into place, making my teeth clack as they came together. He got the point and closed his own mouth.

"This was such fun," Lizzy said. "I can't remember laughing so hard." She chuckled all the way back to the house.

Supper was the best I ever tasted. Granny Nan's ham gravy was so good, I ate three helpings of mashed potatoes and gravy. I could barely get the oatmeal pie down because I was so full.

A WEDDING, A CAT, AND A RADIO

Herrmann Schnier and Mary Blodgett were married on April 8, 1930, at a huge church in Flint. I was nine, and I had never been to a wedding. I had no idea the extent of the celebratory occasion I was about to be a part of. Mary had asked me to be "in" her wedding, so I agreed. I figured I had been "in" a play, and that was nothing major. She wanted Lizzy and me to be "bridesmaids." I didn't really know what that job entailed, but I thought it would be a cakewalk. I couldn't have been more wrong.

Mary wanted Yosie to be her flower girl, seeing as how Yosie was the only relative at the right age to perform the mandatory dropping of rose petals as a prelude to the bride walking down the aisle. I was a bit on edge; Yosie was such a Mama's girl, I figured she'd cry and scream about having to walk down that long aisle all by herself. I couldn't have been more wrong.

Papa was to be Uncle Herman's "best man." I didn't know what that meant, either, but I guess Papa did. He seemed unconcerned. I couldn't have been more wrong.

Mary's best friend, Garnet, was the "matron of honor." I didn't know what kind of honor it would be. Would she get a medal? Or maybe have to make a speech? I asked Mama, and she told me it meant two things: first, Garnet was responsible to plan and hold a bridal shower, with the help of her bridesmaids; second, she would walk down the aisle just ahead of Mary and would be the one to hold Mary's bridal bouquet when Mary and Uncle Herman held hands during the ceremony. That certainly didn't sound too difficult. I couldn't have been more wrong.

At least I knew Uncle Herman would hold the entire thing together. He was always so jovial and knew how to make everything fun. No matter how nervous everyone else was, he'd be rock solid. I couldn't have been more wrong.

What is it about weddings that makes the impossible happen and the obvious unlikely?

❖❖❖

I was just putting the last tray of decorated cookies on the dining room table at the surprise bridal shower when Lizzy came up to me with tears brimming, ready to spill over. "What's wrong, Lizzy?"

She took me by my elbow and guided me into the kitchen. "Mommy was supposed to be here fifteen minutes ago. I *told* Garnet it was a bad idea to make this a surprise. Garnet has everything ready, but there's no bride. What if Mommy decided to stay longer?"

I knew Mary was going to be gone so we could make this a surprise, but I hadn't asked anyone where she'd be...until now. "Where is she?"

"At her final dress fitting. I'll bet the dress didn't fit right, so Mommy decided to stay until the seamstress made *all* of the alterations. It could take an hour or more. No, she wouldn't do that; she wouldn't leave Herman in the car for that long a time. Maybe Herman left her at the dress shop and went someplace else and lost track of the time. I hope they didn't have trouble with the Buick. Maybe Mommy convinced Herman to take her out to eat. No, that couldn't be, because Herman knew what was going on today. He'd have her back here at the right time. Oh, I just know something awful has happened." She was shaking. She broke down and cried—really cried.

I didn't know what to do. I was making a decision either to stay in the kitchen to console her or to go ask Mama what we could do, when we heard the front door open and everyone shout, "Surprise!"

"They're here!" Lizzy whispered. "And look at me. I'm so ashamed. I can't let Mommy see me like this. She'll know I've been crying the minute she sees me. I was supposed to warn Garnet when she was coming, and instead I was in here crying like a baby. I'm a complete failure." And she cried some more.

Jeepers! What have I gotten myself into? Is this what usually happens when two people are about to get married?

"Lizzy, you need to stop crying and start doing your job."

She stopped sobbing and looked at me. "You're absolutely right. What is wrong with me? I guess I'm just dead set on things going exactly right. I wanted everything to be perfect for Mommy. This will be her first wedding, and I want it to be everything it can possibly be."

"She and your father had a wedding, didn't they?"

"No, she was already pregnant with me, and Mommy said she'd have been too embarrassed. So they just went to a Justice of the Peace and got married."

I didn't understand. I'd have to ask Lizzy more about that, but this was neither the time nor the place. Right now, she just needed to calm down and go out to the front room with her mother. But we were in the kitchen, Lizzy in near hysterics, and her mother most likely wondering where her daughter was. I grabbed a kitchen towel and handed it to Lizzy. "Wipe you face and blow your nose."

"On a kitchen towel?"

"It's the only thing we've got. I'll put it in the wash when you're done. Where's the wash basket?"

"Down the hall, in the bathroom."

I waited for her to finish primping, then I shoved her through the door into the dining room. She was on her own. A few seconds later I slipped unnoticed through the door and down the hall to the bathroom. I put the towel in the wash basket and went to the front room. Lizzy was crying again, but she told Mary it was because she was so happy for her. I guess Mary bought it.

"Where were you?" Mama asked me.

"In the bathroom," I said. And I had been, so it wasn't a lie. I didn't have to tell Mama anything else. She didn't need to know about Lizzy being so nervous; that would be our little secret.

When we arrived at the church for the rehearsal and I saw the sanctuary, my nerves did a one-hundred-and-eighty-degree flip-flop. I was expected to walk down that aisle by myself, ahead of the bride, and not stumble, or worse, fall flat on my face? I could barely see the altar; it was so far in the distance. How could I, a dairy farmer's daughter who knew more about cows than weddings, perform such a feat? I was petrified. How was I supposed to know when to start walking? Was I supposed to follow or be the first one? How fast was I supposed to walk? What if I dropped the bouquet: should I stop and pick it up, or should I keep moving and just leave it lying in the middle of the aisle like a dead opossum in the road? Oh, what had I gotten myself into? I was a wreck.

Yosie was a completely different little girl. I wanted to ask Mama where she had hidden my real sister and where she'd found this wonderful child. Then it dawned on me: Yosie was the center of attention. She was eating it up. She listened to every word of her instructions and performed her job like she'd been doing it since she could walk. She stepped in time to the music. She looked around as if the church were full of people, and she smiled throughout her entire performance. She pretended to drop her rose petals along the way and was doing it as if *she* were the one getting married!

We all went through the motions twice, and then we all went to a hotel for a big meal. Papa told me, "It is the only part of the vedding I am interested in." Then he added, "but do not tell anyvun you heard me say that."

I was impressed with the amount and kinds of food we were

served. "Papa, is this free, like a church supper, or do we have to pay for it?"

"Your Uncle Herrmann is paying for all of this," he said. "Ve must be sure to thank him. It is qvite nice, ja?"

"The food is vunderbar!" I told him. He smiled and hugged me. "What do you have to do, Papa, I mean, as the best man?"

"I vill be making a speech at the vedding reception." He made a face. "I do not like to make speeches."

"What'll it be about?"

"I have been thinking about it for a long time, but I vill not tell you. You vill have to listen carefully tomorrow after the vedding." He drew in a long breath and slowly let it out through puffed-out cheeks. I could tell he was not looking forward to it.

During all the preparations, Uncle Herman had seemed distant. He wasn't his usual self. He hardly laughed at all, and he didn't make jokes like he always had.

The wedding was scheduled for Saturday afternoon. We had been staying at Uncle Herman's place since Thursday night. Butch and Jimmy were back home doing the milking for us, and Jimmy promised to feed the chickens, roosters, and ducks, and he also volunteered to feed our three pigs. Butch would feed all the cattle—dairy and beef. Papa seemed concerned about everything back home, though he confessed that he knew Butch and Jimmy would perform all the tasks without fail. Nevertheless...

The wedding was perfect, except that Yosie stole the show; the bride was supposed to get all the recognition. But Mary took it all in stride. I was watching from the front of the sanctuary and could see her laughing along with everyone else when Yosie made her grand entrance.

Mary was tall and thin and beautiful. She had chosen exactly the right dress. I watched her enter the aisle, but then I turned my attention to Uncle Herman. I figured he was almost as proud as Papa was when I was born, according to Granny Nan. I could see it in his face, and I could almost make out an aura of bright light around him as he stood there watching Mary come toward him.

When everything was over and we all retired to the church basement for the reception, I realized how nervous I had been the whole time. My neck was stiff, my feet ached, and I had been sweating. I decided right then and there that I would never put people through all of that just to marry someone. No sir. I figured it didn't make much sense to spend so much money on a single-afternoon affair. It didn't seem to me that all the hoopla made them more married than something a lot simpler would have.

It came time for Papa to get up and make his best man speech. He began by telling everyone a little bit about his and Uncle Herman's German heritage. Then he spoke about how proud he and Uncle Herman were when they became Americans. There was an occasional catch in his voice, and I knew he was feeling a bit emotional. A few times he had to stop and swallow, then go on.

But I'll never forget the last part of Papa's speech: "I am a lucky man to have a vife who is not afraid to let people know she is married to me." Everyone chuckled. "And I have a beautiful family, even though they are all females." That evoked more chuckles from the audience. "And I vant you all to know that my brother has taken a looong time to find the right voman. And I know she is the right vun, because I asked him, 'Herrmann, vhy do you vant to marry this voman?' And he lowered his head and thought about his answer—yust as our Papa always did vhen something vas important. Then he looked me in the eye and said, 'It is because she reminds me of all the goot things that have happened to me in my life.' If Herrmann has found somevun who can do that for him, then he has found the right vun."

He raised his glass, first to Uncle Herman and Mary, then to the crowd. We all clinked our glasses together and took a drink. Then Papa removed his handkerchief from his back pocket and wiped his eyes. Uncle Herman stood up, grabbed Papa's hand, shook it, then reached his big long arms around Papa and hugged him. They embraced each other for a long time. Mary was in tears, and the church basement was silent. Several seconds passed, then someone began clapping, and the place exploded with applause. Papa had made his speech, and it was a masterpiece.

Everyone danced, but they cleared the floor when Uncle Herman and Mary danced to their special song. Before the night was over, Yosie had danced with her feet on both Papa's and Uncle Herman's shoes, I had danced with Papa, Uncle Herman, Lizzy, Mary, Mama, Granny Nan, and just about every boy and girl who were close to my age. Granny Nan had danced with Papa and Uncle Herman, and when Mama and Papa weren't dancing with someone else, they danced together for most of the evening. It had been great fun.

Mary and Uncle Herman left the church at about 8:30 p.m. for a month-long honeymoon at Yellowstone National Park, and Lizzy was staying with a friend of hers because she had to go back to school. Our family was going to stay at Uncle Herman's for one more night, then we would be closing the place up and going back to our farm on Sunday.

When the sun came up, we were on the road.

Mama gave birth to Veronica on September 22, 1931. Once again, Papa had been adamant about naming a son. He had chosen the name Ronald, Ronny for short. According to Papa, however, "The Goot Lord is trying my patience," when Ronald turned out to be another girl. Papa said, "At least I can still call her Ronnie, but Mama insists on 'I-E' at the end instead of 'ypsilon'," (the German pronunciation of the letter 'Y').

Like Retta, Ronnie was a happy baby. She had lots of curls, like Yosie, but hers were blond—almost white—and Papa said she was a "towhead." I didn't know what that term meant, so I looked it up in our big dictionary at school and found out "tow" is the word for flax, which is a very light color (and it has German roots, so it made sense to me that Papa would use that word). Mama said Ronnie was "flaxen-haired" and said her hair would probably get darker as she grew up. Granny Nan told me that, when she first saw Ronnie, she thought Ronnie was an albino. That was another word I didn't know, so again I referenced the dictionary and learned that albinism results from a lack of melanin, the pigment which gives people the color of their skin, eyes, and hair. But when Granny Nan saw that Ronnie's eyes were not pink, she knew Ronnie simply had exceptionally pale blond hair.

For some reason, Yosie took to Ronnie like she was her own. I was so glad to see Yosie's interest branching out. Up till then she had been interested only in Mama, nothing else. But she talked to Ronnie and sang to her, and she stayed with her when Mama was busy. In typical Yosie style, however, she got angry when anyone else tried to play with Ronnie. Yosie was old enough to care for her new little sister, but her only interest in caring was superficial. She wanted nothing to do with changing Ronnie's diapers or feeding her. She only wanted to play with Ronnie like she was a doll. I was the one who had to do the dirty work. But I didn't mind; it was all part of being a family, and I was sure all families took care of one another.

Bella and Dora were in school, and they adored Miss Michaels, just as I did. Of course, they had become familiar with her while they were growing up since she was at our house twice a week for supper and on holidays. Bella was nearly a head taller than Dora. Unless people knew they were twins, they'd never have guessed. Both had beautiful auburn hair, and both were fair skinned, but people who didn't know them thought they were just sisters. Mama stopped dressing them alike when they started school. She said, "They are two separate people, so they need to dress like separate people." They were undeniably individuals, each with her own opinions about everything. Unlike some twins I'd heard about, Bella and Dora never finished each other's sentences, and they never knew what the other was thinking or doing at any given moment.

Dora's birthmark was a definite problem for the first couple of weeks of school. The other kids made fun of her, just as Mama had feared. They didn't want to play with her or even sit next to her in the classroom.

Miss Michaels was prepared for it, however. Only two weeks after the beginning of the school year, she did a lesson about characteristics that made people famous and made them stand out in a crowd. She never mentioned Dora's name, nor did she make any direct reference to Dora's birthmark, but she did cite other examples of famous people with birth defects. For instance, Joseph Merrick, known as "The Elephant Man," was born with proteus syndrome, a condition which causes huge lumps on the skin, and it also causes bones to thicken and deform. Merrick was intelligent and lived as normal a life as possible for someone who could not lie down to sleep because his head was too heavy. Miss Michaels showed a picture of him to all of us. In many respects, it was horrific for us to see, but it minimized Dora's birthmark, making it appear as nothing compared to what Merrick had to face on a daily basis.

Miss Michaels showed us a picture of Ludwig van Beethoven, a musician and composer who was deaf. He overcame his defect, however, and went on to write some of the most famous music in the western world. "Just because people look different doesn't mean they aren't normal. They can do the exact same things we all do. Sometimes they have to find a different way to do those things, and sometimes they simply look a little bit different from the rest of us. But they are all people, just like you and me, and we need to understand that so we don't hurt their feelings or make them uncomfortable when we're around them." She never even looked at Dora, yet she was able to get her point across.

The day after the lesson, the other students in our school began to overlook Dora's birthmark and treat her like any other person.

I had never thought about cats as pets. As far as I was concerned, they were wild animals that skulked around our farm catching and killing mice and other vermin that invaded our barns and the corn crib. At night, the cats' eyes glowed when a light was shined at them, just like the eyes of the foxes that persistently tried to invade our hen house. It was eerie.

In October, 1931, however, my poor opinion of cats came to a screeching halt. The road that separated our property into two parts had become much busier with automobile and truck traffic. We were on the main route between Mount Pleasant and Weidman, and we were on the route to Flint, as well, for people coming from the western part of the state. More people now owned automobiles and trucks, so there was bound to be a greater number of them using the most direct routes between cities. The days when we had only seen a few tractors or trucks and occasional automobiles on the road were long gone. Papa had to make sure the fences that kept our livestock off the road were reinforced, a tedious and ongoing project.

The number of barn cats around our property had, of course, increased over the years. Not only did they take shelter in our barns, they also had the privilege of receiving any unwanted milk that came from our cows. At times, they would even sneak into the stanchion barn when we weren't looking and steal any milk that leaked out of the cows' udders onto the barn floor beneath the cows. When we went back into the stanchion barn from the milk house, they'd scatter like roaches.

One day after school, Bella was in the tree swing when an automobile went by at a high rate of speed. It was full of teenagers, laughing and yelling and having a gay old time. At the same time, one of our barn cats decided to cross the road, and the car ran over it. I don't know if the kids in the automobile knew it had happened, as they never even slowed down.

I hadn't seen it happen, but Bella screamed, and I went running to the swing to see if she had gotten hurt. She was pointing toward the road. I thought she was pointing at the house, but I didn't see anything or anyone that would indicate the necessity of a scream. "What, Bella?"

"On the road," she said, sliding her feet in the dirt beneath the swing to slow herself down.

I still didn't see anything. Bella had stopped the swing and was running toward the road.

"Stop! Stay off the road! Look for automobiles before you cross!"

She stopped just before she reached the road. She knelt down and started to cry. I reached the road a split second later. There, just on the berm, lay a kitten, still breathing, eyes the size of saucers. It must have been in shock, because it allowed Bella to pet it.

"Be careful, Bella. That cat's wild. It could scratch or bite you."

"It's hurt bad," she said, crying. "Fix it, Helmi. Help it."

"It's just a cat," I said to her. "We should probably put it out of its misery."

"No! Mama! Granny Nan!" I looked across the road and saw them coming out of the house, Mama at a dead run, Granny Nan marching toward us as if she were on a mission.

"Bella!" Mama shouted, panic in her voice.

"She's okay, Mama," I called back. "It's a cat."

Mama stopped at the road's edge. "It is what?"

"A cat. One of the barn cats." I pointed to it on the ground

"It's a kitten," Bella cried. "It's hurt bad. Helmi can fix it."

"I can't..." But before I could say anything more, Mama had reached the kitten, which was now meowing at the top of its lungs.

"Help it, Helmi," Granny Nan said as she reached us. "At least pick it up and look at it."

I couldn't defy them, so I bent down and looked at it closely. I could see fear in its eyes. And it was in pain, too. So I got down on my knees next to it and picked it up. Its left rear leg dangled. I tried to stand it up, but it just fell over.

"Its back leg is definitely broken," I said. "And it's hard to tell if it has damage on the inside." I picked it back up and looked it right in face. It was cute. I couldn't believe how cute it really was. "It's real skinny, too, so I don't know if it has enough energy to heal itself."

Bella whimpered. "Can you fix its leg?"

I had seen the vet put a splint on a calf's leg, and in time, that calf was able to walk again. "I might," I said. It didn't have any blood anywhere, neither from the broken leg nor from its mouth or nose. I thought those were good signs. "Bella, Mama, I need a couple of sticks, but they have to be flat on one side. See if you can find any. Granny Nan, could you get me something to wrap around the leg and some adhesive tape to bind the sticks to the wrap?"

"I will see what I can find." She crossed back over to the house side of the road. "Oh, and a baby blanket, too," I shouted. She waved, acknowledging that she had heard me.

I sat there and held the kitten, talking softly to it. It wasn't such a despicable creature. I had never taken the opportunity to get close enough to one of them to find that out. Its body began to relax, and the fear vanished from its eyes. Bella came running up to me with some sticks she and Mama had found, and I looked them over, choosing two that held promise. Granny Nan was back in a flash with some gauze, a blanket, and the tape.

I felt the leg. The bones in the bottom of the leg were twisted at a funny angle, but the big bone in the top of it seemed fine. I was afraid its hip had been broken, though, because it cried when I moved the joint. But there was nothing I could do about that. I could only hope its upper leg was merely bruised, and that splinting its lower leg and making sure it got lots of rest would take care of anything else.

I wrapped some of the gauze around the bottom part of the leg, then I placed the two splint pieces, one on either side of it. "Mama, I need you to hold one of these while I get the tape started around them." She sat down on the ground beside me, and between the two of us, we managed to wrap the tape around the splint until it kept the bottom part of the kitten's leg from moving. Then I wrapped more gauze around it to cover the splint and taped that until it was secure.

Granny Nan handed me the blanket, and I put the kitten in the blanket, pulling the blanket tight around the kitten so it couldn't move anything except its head. "It's going to have to stay where we can keep an eye on it for a while," I said.

"I'll hold it," Bella said.

"That will be fine, Bella," Mama said, "but we will need to keep it in a box in the room off the kitchen when we cannot hold it. I will not have a cat—not even a kitten—running loose in my house."

Bella had a natural maternal instinct. She cuddled the kitten all afternoon and evening, and when bedtime came around, she asked Mama, "Can it stay in my room? I'll keep it in the box all night, I promise. It just needs me to be there so it won't be scared."

I must admit, Bella was pretty convincing. Mama agreed.

After a week, the kitten had grown to twice the size it had been when the accident happened. I had to change the splint to a larger one. The leg was still bent at a funny angle, but the kitten didn't cry when I tried to move it a little bit. Within the next week, the kitten walked on it. And after the third week, the splint was gone, and the kitten was getting around just fine. It had also gained weight.

Bella had named it Sparkle. "Its eyes sparkle every time it looks at me," she said. And it had a home in the room off the kitchen at night. During the day it was allowed to run in the yard, as long as someone watched it and kept it from crossing the road (easier said than done).

Somehow Sparkle lived a long, happy life.

❖❖❖

"Helmi, ve need to go to town."

I had a flashback to the days when Papa and I went to Beaver City. "Okay!"

"Ve must find a new radio. Our old vun has bit the dust," he chuckled. He always got a kick out of his own terminology, especially when it included an American idiom. Papa insisted that we have a radio so we could keep up with the latest news. The banks were having trouble, and lots of people had lost a lot of money because of it. The people on the radio called it a "depression," and Papa was insistent that we keep on top of it. I wasn't sure I understood it, but I knew it might have something to do with the security of our farm.

Dora wanted to go, too, so Papa told her it would be okay. We went on Saturday morning when we finished the milking. It was a rainy, chilly day, and the roads were wet and slippery. Papa had to drive really slow so the truck didn't slide off the road. Our road was still only dirt and gravel—mostly dirt—so we had to watch for places that might be washed out. Once we got close to Mount Pleasant, however, it turned to pavement, which was much nicer to ride on. There was even talk of our road between Mount Pleasant and Weidman being paved within a year's time.

Mama said, "That will be both good and bad. It will mean that the traffic will be able to go faster. And that worries me because of the children. But it will certainly cut down on the amount of dusting Granny Nan and I will have to do," She told Papa, "And as soon as that road is paved, the swing comes down."

Papa, Dora, and I went to a place called a pawn shop. Papa said they had used radios there, and we might be able to find a good one for a fraction of the price of a new one. He was right, but it needed new tubes. He paid for the radio, and then we went to the hardware store to find the tubes.

"What kind of tubes does a radio use?" I asked him. I had a mental picture of rubber tubes like the ones on our milkers, the part the milk flowed through.

"Do you know vhat a vacuum is, Helmi?"

I had to think for a few seconds before telling him I thought a vacuum was something where there was no air inside.

"That is right!" he said, apparently excited because I knew that. "The kind of tube ve need is a vacuum tube, the simplest vun that is made. It is called a *di*-ode because *di* means two. The tube has two parts, a cathode and an anode, and the electric current flows from the cathode to the anode."

At that point I tuned him out. I was not a scholar of electricity, and I didn't understand anything he was telling me, though I feigned interest just to please him. After a couple more minutes of "blah, blah, blah, blah…" he said, "and that is how ve can hear vhat the radio people are saying."

"Oh," I said. I hoped he wasn't planning on asking me any questions about what he had just told me. Luckily, we reached the hardware store at the precise moment he finished. While he looked around for the tubes, Dora and I looked at the seed packets that were on display. I thought it might be nice to get some for Mama since she loved working in her flower garden. And maybe we could even buy some vegetable seeds for Granny Nan. I knew they would last until planting time.

"I am so sorry," he said. "I only have enough money to buy the tubes. I alrcady spent most of vhat I had on the radio." He looked sad.

"It's all right, Papa. I understand."

He looked at me and sighed. "I vish I could buy you everything you vant. If your Mama had married a man like your Uncle Yulius, you vould have the vorld at your fingertips."

"But I wouldn't have you, Papa." I hugged him. And it was true; I'd much rather have him than Uncle Julius. If Uncle Julius were my father, I'd have to eat giant crawdads!

Papa was looking forward to putting the tubes in the radio and listening to the noon newscast when we got home, but Mama came out the door with a paper in her hand. Dora ran up to her and said, "We got it, Mama! We have a new…"

"Yes, that is nice, dear, but I need to talk to your father. Go upstairs." She walked right past Dora without even looking at her. "Helmi, go into the house," she said to me.

I knew better than to ask questions. Something serious was going on. I went inside, but I turned around and watched and listened at the door. I could make out a few words here and there, but mostly I could tell things were bad because Papa rubbed his forehead a lot. They came back into the house together, but the radio and tubes were still in the truck.

Mama and Papa sat down at the kitchen table with Granny Nan. "Ve cannot afford to make a trip there," Papa said. "Nancy, I know you vant to be vit your daughter at a time like this, but…"

"I have some money saved up for occasions just such as this," Granny Nan said. "But I will not travel alone. I would like to take Violet. She should be with her sister."

I couldn't remain quiet any longer. I crept into the kitchen. "What's wrong, Mama? Is Aunt Lavern sick?"

"No," Granny Nan said. She looked at Mama and Papa, and they looked at each other.

"Ve vill not keep a secret like this from you, Helmi." Papa sighed, then he took a deep breath and said, "It is not Lavern, it is Yulius."

"Uncle Julius is sick?"

Granny Nan turned toward me and said, "Uncle Julius is dead."

For some reason, I was unmoved. Normally a fact of that magnitude presented so blatantly would have knocked me to the floor. But I said, "*Was* he sick?"

"In a way, yes," Mama said. "He had a mental illness."

"I don't understand."

"Helmi," Papa motioned for me to come to him. I went to him and stood at his side. "Mental illness is a sickness in the brain," he explained. "He had…he and your Aunt La…" He looked at Mama. "I do not know how to tell her."

I looked at Mama, and she was crying now.

It was Granny Nan who came to my rescue. "You know that Uncle Julius had a lot of money, right?"

I nodded.

"He was what is called a *major shareholder* in his company. Most of the money he had came from the dividends he made from each of the shares." She sighed. "I know this is difficult for you to understand, Helmi, but I will try to make it as clear as I know how." She paused. "People buy shares of stock in a company. In other words, they purchase part of a company—one or more shares of it—hoping the company will grow and the value, or the worth, of the stock will rise. Are you able to understand that?"

"Yes."

"When the stock's value rises, the company pays a portion of the money it makes from that stock to its shareholders—the people who own parts of that company."

"I understand," I said. "And that means a *major* shareholder owns more than most of the other people who have bought shares."

"Ja!" Papa said. He smiled. "Go on, Nancy."

"The reason your Uncle Julius had so much money was that he…"

I finished her sentence for her, "…he owned lots of shares and made lots of money from them, from the dividends. I get it."

"I think you do," Granny Nan said. Then she changed her tactics.

"Have you been hearing about the depression on the radio?"

"Yes, but I don't really understand what that is."

"Basically," Papa said, "the value of most of the stocks has dvindled to nothing, vhich means…"

This time I finished Papa's sentence, "…which means Uncle Julius isn't getting his dividends, so he doesn't have any money now."

"That is right, Helmi," Granny Nan said. "And because he lost most of his money, he did not know how he was going to pay for everything he and Lavern owe money on. It would be the same as if we were unable to pay for our farm and were about to lose it. Luckily, we do not have that problem because people still need our milk and eggs."

"So…" I thought about all they had said. "…Uncle Julius had a mental illness because he was so worried about losing his house, automobile, servants, and everything else he owned."

"Yes, and the mental illness drove him to suicide," Granny Nan said.

"I'm not sure I know what that is," I told her. I was afraid I did, but I wasn't positive. I thought it meant that someone kills himself.

"It means that Uncle Julius took his own life," Granny Nan said.

I was right. I hated it, but I was right. Uncle Julius had killed himself. "How?" I asked.

"You mean, how did he kill himself?" Mama asked.

I nodded.

Papa said, "He leapt out of a vindow at the top of a very tall building."

Mama's crying became louder. I went to her and said, "I'm so sorry, Mama. I know how much it would hurt me if one of my sisters had a husband who did that."

She grabbed me, held on tight, and sobbed into my shoulder. I was crying now, too…big wet tears. I couldn't control them. The thing was, they weren't tears I was shedding for Uncle Julius or Aunt Lavern, but for Mama. Knowing and understanding her sorrow was one of the saddest things I had encountered in my nearly eleven years on this earth.

Granny Nan was stoic in her response. She rose from the chair, Aunt Lavern's letter in her hand, and walked to the window. She read the letter again, then she turned and faced Papa, Mama, and me. She had not shed a tear, even though it was her own daughter's husband who had committed such a heinous act.

"Violet, we must look into the bus and train schedules. You and I can make the trip by ourselves. Heinrich needs to stay here and tend the farm, and he needs Helmi to take care of the baby and the other children while we are gone. She can miss a little bit of school; she is smart enough to catch up when she goes back. It will only be for a few days. Train and bus fare is much less than it would cost to have Heinrich leave the farm and drive us to Chicago, and I know you would not want to leave Helmi alone without one of us remaining here with her. And it is *our* place to go, not Heinrich's. Do you agree?"

No one said anything.

"Then it is settled. We will check the schedules right away. Heinrich, can you drive me into town? We should go right now."

"Ja, I vill. I think you are right." He looked at Mama. "Violet?"

She nodded. Her eyes were swollen and red, and her nose was running. "I am just so thankful it was not you, Heinrich," she said in a thick voice.

"I could never leave you in that manner," he assured her. Then he picked up his hat and socked it on his head. He had not taken his coat off. He took Granny Nan's coat from the closet and helped her into it. He went to the truck and retrieved the radio and tubes and handed them to me. "You can put the tubes in and try it out vhile ve are gone," he said. They left immediately.

    Mama and I assembled the radio, plugged it in, and turned it on, but the only thing we could get was news, mostly about the effects of the depression. There wasn't even a weather report. Mama turned it off and went upstairs. I stood in the middle of the kitchen for a long time, trying to make sense of what had happened.

TWO-TONE AND A TELEPHONE

In two more months I'd be twelve years old. I was officially in the seventh grade, but Miss Michaels said I was studying some things on a tenth-grade level, especially English and history. I was good at arithmetic, but I didn't like it as much, so I didn't work as hard at it. My favorite thing, however, was science; I loved everything about it, but especially the part called biology. Miss Michaels said she would be taking me to the high school where they had microscopes so I could learn to use one. We would only be making our library trips on Mondays and going to the high school laboratory after school on Tuesdays.

"You'll get to see what different kinds of microscopes look like and how they operate," Miss Michaels told me, "and I'll be sure to ask the science teacher to leave some slides out for you."

"Slides?"

"The little glass things that go under the lenses of the microscope."

"Oh, yeah." I'd seen pictures of microscopes in a couple of the science books we had in our school room, and I remembered seeing the slides sitting in a box beside one of them.

"You also need to start using the biology section at the library. Those books will tell you all about what you can see under the microscope." I was excited.

One Monday before supper I was coming down from my room when I heard Mama and Granny Nan doing a bit of arguing with Miss Michaels. Evidently she thought she was taking advantage of us by eating supper at our house on the lab day in addition to the library day.

"It will be just the same as in the previous years," Mama said to Miss Michaels. "The only difference is, instead of it being on Monday and Thursday, it will be on Monday and Tuesday."

Miss Michaels said, "I can't tell you how much I appreciate what y'all have done for me over the last few years. It's awful to have to eat supper alone." She shook her head. "I feel like I belong to a family now, but…but sometimes I think I must be a burden to you and Nancy because I know I don't contribute much in the kitchen. I feel…"

"Do not be ridiculous," Granny Nan said, putting her hands on her hips. "It is the least we can do for you, seeing as how you cart Helmi to and from Mount Pleasant twice a week. And I can tell you another thing: that girl thinks the world of you and would be heartbroken if you decided not to sup with us twice a week."

"She is right," Mama added. "Helmi would think it was her fault if you were to walk out of her life even for one night's supper."

Miss Michaels took hold of Mama's hand and put her other hand on Granny Nan's shoulder. "Thank you, from the bottom of my heart. For Michiganders, you two have some of the best southern hospitality I've ever been exposed to." The three of them laughed.

Mama was right: I really would have thought it was my fault if Miss Michaels were to cease her bi-weekly visits. But I knew it would leave a void in Mama's and Granny Nan's lives, too. They had such fun figuring out what to cook on the nights when she was to be there. They even kept a list of what she didn't seem to care for. Even though she ate whatever was put in front of her, I could tell there were a couple of things she wasn't overly fond of. One of them was mutton. We didn't have sheep to butcher anymore, but Papa occasionally picked up some mutton at the butcher shop in Mount Pleasant; he said it was because he missed it. I never cared for it, either, because no matter how well it was cooked, it always left a lingering film of lanolin in my mouth. I'm not sure if that was a fact or just something I had "gotten stuck in my head," as Granny Nan would have said, but fact or fiction, I had never been, nor would I ever be, a mutton fan.

At any rate, Miss Michaels continued to eat at our house twice a week and on Christmas. The family of one of the other students at our school always invited her for Thanksgiving, and sometimes the families at her church had her over on Sundays. She lived close to the Mount Pleasant Indian Reservation, and she had told me she attended a little church just a few doors away from her home. I never knew, nor did I ask, the denomination of that church, but I knew it welcomed people from the reservation, because she sometimes mentioned the Native Americans when she and I were conversing on our way to or from Mount Pleasant.

The Chippewa River ran through the city and accounted for almost one square mile of its total seven-and-a-half square mile area. It wound around the southeast side, and we always saw people fishing from the shore. There were a couple of places where the Ojibway sold their fresh catch each day. Papa and I often stopped and bought some to take back to Mama and Granny Nan for supper. Fish (not crawdads) was always one of my favorite things, probably because we had so little of it in Oklahoma. In fact, we might not have had any when I lived there. My memory fails me on that point.

Retta was starting school that year. She and I had been close since the day she'd been born, and I had assured her I'd be watching out for her at school. I knew she was going to be a good student, because she could already read some of the children's books we had at home. And she was good at arithmetic—better than I had been at her age. She was able somehow to see things in her head. When I'd ask her something like, "How many is two puppies plus one puppy?" she could visualize the items in her mind, like two puppies and one puppy, and count them to come up with the right answer almost one-hundred percent of the time.

Now that Retta was starting school, we were a group of five marching down the road to the schoolhouse—me, Yosie, Bella, Dora, and Retta. Mama and Granny Nan made our lunches and packed them together in one sack, so each of us had to carry it one day a week. Even though the school was less than a quarter of a mile away, that sack got heavy. Poor little Retta; she struggled with it each time her day came around, but she wasn't about to let it get the upper hand, and she refused to let any of us carry it for her. But she did let one of us carry her books. Yosie, on the other hand, always begged someone else to carry the lunch sack on her day.

Just like me, Retta loved dogs. Between the two of us, we had pestered Papa long enough that he finally gave in and allowed us to get a puppy. She had black and white spots, one black ear and one white, and a little black mark over her upper lip that made her look like she had a moustache. Her tail was half white and half black with a white tip at the very end. We called her Two-Tone. She was the friendliest dog ever; she had no enemies. Though she'd bark when someone came to the house, she was only greeting them. She could actually grin, and she did it most of the time.

Two-Tone had great respect for Papa. She did whatever he said. If he told her to sit, she sat. If he told her to lie down, she did. She knew he was the one in charge—the alpha. I had read about wolves in one of the library books I'd checked out, and I understood that even family dogs (they were called "domesticated canines") still act like they are part of a wolf pack. Only one member of the pack could be in charge, and in Two-Tone's pack, that was Papa; it didn't matter that her pack consisted of humans.

She was a true farm dog, eating and sleeping in the big barn where we kept the hay and straw. Papa had given her a feed sack as a bed, and she had made an impression in some loose straw and carried her bed there, digging at it and moving it around with her nose, until it was exactly how she wanted it, wrinkles and all. The cold didn't seem to bother her. She followed Papa to the fields whenever he went, and she "supervised" the cows when they entered or left the stanchion barn, seeing to it that they didn't lollygag when it was time to move.

She walked with us to school every morning. As soon as we left the road and started up the lane to the schoolhouse, she'd turn around and hightail it back home, as if she knew she had completed her escort duty and now Papa needed her.

Though he didn't want to let on, I could tell he really liked that dog. I'd go out to the milk house every morning and find Papa sitting on an upside-down bucket, scratching her under the chin or behind the ears and talking softly to her. As soon as she saw me, she'd grin, then she'd get up and shake her body from her moustache to the white tip of her tail. My entrance was her cue to get busy. And if Papa sat there for more than a few seconds, she'd bark at him as if to say, "Hey! It's time to bring the cows in. What're you waiting for?"

Her only downfall was that she harassed the barn cats. Because of Sparkle's accident, I had learned that cats weren't all bad. And when Two-Tone barked at them and chased after them, it made me cringe. Sometimes I thought she might catch one and rip it apart. That was also the only time I heard her bark viciously. When Papa was there, he could yell, "HEY!" and she'd leave them alone. But when Butch or Jimmy or I yelled at her, she ignored us.

❖❖❖

Mama gave birth to Cynthianna (Anna) on February 26, 1933. She said it was the easiest birth she'd ever gone through. She was only in labor for about 2 hours. I missed the whole thing.

Anna was the first child Mama had been allowed to name. When Papa found out that Mama was pregnant again, he said, "I give up, Violet. You can name our next baby girl."

"How do you know it will not be a boy?"

"I do not know, but I am villing to play the odds," he said. "It does not matter anymore. By the time a boy gets big enough to help around here, I vill be dead."

"Heinrich! Do not say such a thing!" Mama scolded. But she told me she was secretly glad Papa had let her choose a name.

Anna was pink and plump and pretty. She had dark hair, like Yosie, and she made funny little grunting sounds when Papa tickled her feet. He played "This Little Piggy" on her toes, and she grunted even more. It made everyone laugh.

When spring arrived, Retta began going to the barn with Papa and me after school. I was glad to see her show an interest in what was going on. Up to that point, I'd been the only one who ever lifted a hand to help with the milking, or any other part of farming, for that matter, and I welcomed her company.

We'd had a very mild winter. There was no snow left on the ground, and the temperature was in the low-to-mid sixties—warm for that time of year. I was washing the supper dishes when Granny Nan said, "I hope the flowers and garden crops do not come up too soon and then get nipped if the temperature drops."

"I doubt the ground has thawed yet," Mama said.

"I hope you are right. Everything we canned last year is running low."

A voice at the back door said, "I can help with that."

We all turned at the same time to see Uncle Herman coming into the kitchen.

"How wonderful to see you!" Mama said. She rose and hugged him one-armed; she had Anna in the other arm.

I asked, "Did Lizzy come with you?"

"I'm glad to see you, too," he said, teasingly.

"I'm sorry, Uncle Herman. I really am glad to see you." I knew my face was red because it felt hot.

"Just teasing," he assured me. "No, I've been by myself all day. I just wanted to stop by and see all of you, and the newest addition." He took Anna from Mama and began making baby talk to her.

"What do you mean, 'stop by?' Where have you been?" Mama asked.

"East Lansing. Michigan State. Had some business with the financial big-wigs there. It seems they want to add automotive engineering to their program next year, and my boss at GM told them I was the man they needed to talk to."

"Would you be teaching there?" Mama asked.

"Don't know for sure. Mary and I've been discussing it. There'd be lots of logistics to work out, and the difference in pay's a major factor." He looked off into the distance, shook his head, and sighed. "And there's something I need to talk to Heinrich about. Is he across the road?"

"No, the milking is finished, but he had some other chores to complete in the big barn. He should be coming into the house any minute."

"How did you sneak up without Two-Tone letting us know?" I asked.

"Who?"

"The dog," Granny Nan said.

"Oh. Probably because I parked down by the schoolhouse and walked back. I've been in that car way too long today. Needed to give the old gams some exercise."

As if on cue, Two-Tone wailed a long howl and came running up to the back door. Uncle Herman handed Anna back to Mama and said, "She's another beauty, just like her mother." He added, "And grandmother." He started toward the door. It opened, and Papa walked in.

"Vell, look vhat the cat dragged in!" Papa and Uncle Herman shook hands. "To vhat do ve owe this pleasure?"

"On my way back home from East Lansing and thought I'd say Hi."

"He was at Michigan State," I said.

"Really? Big business?" Papa asked.

"Only the *possibility* of big business," Uncle Herman said. "They're looking into adding automotive engineering to their program next year."

"I see," Papa said and nodded. "A lot of things to vork out, ja?"

"You said it."

"Come and sit." Papa pulled out a chair. "Violet, have you offered our company anything to eat or drink?"

Uncle Herman said, "No, no. I don't want a thing, thanks. I do want to talk to you about something, though, Heinrich."

Papa said, "Let us go into the front room." The two of them left the kitchen.

"Dear me," Granny Nan said. "I wonder what this could be about."

"Probably just something to do with Buicks or trucks or farming versus a desk job," Mama answered. "The usual."

Bella, Dora, and Retta all came barreling down the stairs. "Who's here?"

"Uncle Herman," I said. "But he and Papa are discussing something important in the front room."

The three of them started to head that direction, but Mama squelched it. "Stay here! They do not need three young ladies interfering with their business."

"Aw, Mama," Retta said. Bella and Dora pretended to cry.

Granny Nan just shook her head.

"Is all of your schoolwork finished?" Mama asked.

"Yes," they answered in unison.

"Where is Yosie?"

"In her room. She says she doesn't want to talk to anyone else tonight," Dora said.

"Yeah, she says she's 'too worn out from talking to her friends all day'," Bella added, making a big deal of imitating Yosie.

"Bella, you know better than to make fun of your sister."

I thought Bella's eyes were going to disappear into the top of her head. "She's just so…"

"Ah-ah-ah!" Mama said, wagging her finger at Bella. "What did we talk about last night?"

Bella didn't answer; she pulled out a kitchen chair, plopped down on it, folded her arms across her chest, and stuck out her bottom lip.

"And who is supposed to be watching Celine?"

Dora threw her shoulders forward, groaned, and said "I am." She slowly began working her way back up the stairs. Then she turned around and said, "I want to say Hi to Uncle Herman."

"You can, but you have to wait until he and Papa are finished talking. I will call you when they finish their business and come back into the kitchen."

I don't know how Mama did it. She had all of us kids to keep in line, including a toddler and a new baby. In addition, she had to keep Papa happy, and she had to cater to Granny Nan's whims. I had more respect for that woman than I'd ever be able to convey to her.

After about half-an-hour Papa and Uncle Herman came back into the kitchen. "Bring everyvun in here, Violet. I have an announcement."

Mama started to get up, but Granny Nan rose and said, "I will get them." She slowly climbed the stairs. It seemed to be taking her longer and longer to get up or down the steps. I hoped nothing was wrong, but then I remembered that she was now going on 82 years old. Her mind was "as strong as a steel trap," according to Papa, but her body was showing some wear and tear. I hoped my mind would be as strong as hers when I was her age.

Bella turned to Uncle Herman and said, "I'm not supposed to interfere in your 'business' with Papa," she said.

Mama reminded her quietly, "Attitude, young lady."

Within seconds Dora and Retta came banging their way down the stairs. "Uncle Herman! Uncle Herman!" They were so glad to see him. He picked them both up and swung them around, one under each arm. "You are growing up so fast—too fast!"

Then he turned his attention to Retta. Uncle Herman had taught her a game when she was four. Uncle Herman started it: "Apple core."

"Baltimore."

"Who's your friend?"

"You are!" And with that, Retta would go running up to him, and he'd lift her up over his head. She'd giggle and hug him around the neck. He held her while we talked.

Papa began, "It seems…"

"Just a minute, Heinrich, I want Nancy in on this, too." He looked up the stairs and saw her coming down, Yosie in tow. Yosie was trying her best to get loose from Granny Nan's hand that was clamped around Yosie's arm. "Let go! Let go me!" Yosie was shouting as she struggled. Granny Nan made no comment, nor did she make any effort to placate Yosie.

"Hey, there's my favorite flower girl!" Uncle Herman had been calling her that since the wedding. She tried to stifle a smile, but it didn't work. She did, however, stop fighting Granny Nan's grasp and come down the steps ahead of her. She didn't run up to him, though. She put her feet together, clasped her hands in front of herself, and twisted back and forth…coyly. Then she looked up at him without lifting her head. The whites of her big eyes showed, and Uncle Herman melted.

YUCK! I thought to myself. *That is definitely not my style, but it sure seems to work for Yosie.*

"Celine is asleep," Granny Nan said when she reached the bottom of the stairs. "I thought it best not to wake her, Herman."

"That's quite all right, Nancy." He put Retta down, but she held onto his shirt sleeve. Then he looked at us all and said, "Your papa has decided to allow you to move into the twentieth century." He gestured to Papa to go ahead.

Papa cleared his throat and started again. "It seems…" he paused for effect, "…ve are going to get a telephone installed in our house."

Everyone was silent, waiting for more.

"That is all," Papa said.

I, for one, was ecstatic. Most of the other kids at school already had a telephone. They could talk to each other from their own houses; they didn't have to GO to someone's house just to discuss something. Bella and Dora did square dance swings, arms locked, and yipping like two fox kits. Retta pulled on Uncle Herman's sleeve, probably to ask him what a telephone was. Mama and Granny Nan were smiling from ear to ear. Yosie was pouting because no one was paying attention to her.

IT'S ALL A BLUR

The next few years all run together, maybe because I've tried to put most of the events out of my mind. I simply don't like thinking about them. But they were a major part of my life, and they deserve to be remembered, like it or not. It all began in June of 1933.

Celine had never been a healthy child. She slept a lot, and she couldn't do anything strenuous without running out of breath. She coughed all the time. Getting her to eat was like pulling teeth. Mama and Granny Nan did their best to put some meat on her bones, but to no avail. Her skin was pale, and she just looked sickly, "delicate" Granny Nan called it. She rarely played outside, and when she did, it was usually under the tree that had, for so long, supported our swing.

One hot, sticky morning in late August of 1933, when Celine was five years old, Mama said to her, "Granny Nan and I are going to mop the kitchen floor, and you need to go outside while it dries."

"No, Mama. I'll go upstairs."

Granny Nan spoke up. "You'll do no such thing. It is twenty degrees hotter up there than it is outside in the shade. You need some fresh air in your lungs. Now skedaddle!"

Celine hung her head and stood there, whimpering. "Mama, I don't…"

"You heard your granny. Now get outside and play. It will be a lot cooler under the swing tree. Just go there and sit on the nice cool grass. Watch for traffic before you cross the road."

"I don't wanna go," Celine whined.

Mama gave her "the look," and Celine knew she'd best do what she'd been told. We all grew up with "the look," and we all realized it was useless to try and argue with it. Celine disappeared out the door.

"I think we need to have Doc Barrett take a look at her," Granny Nan said. "She is so pale, and she has no energy. She is five years old but only the size of a two-year old. I think she has something wrong inside."

"She is just a small child by nature," Mama said, dunking the rag mop in the bucket of soapy water and sloshing it up and down.

"That persistent cough of hers bothers me, Violet."

Mama didn't answer.

"She sleeps way too much for a healthy child, and she has no interest in doing anything. That is simply not normal for a child her age," Granny Nan said. "Why not give the doctor a call and have her looked at. It would put our minds at ease, and you know it." Granny Nan went to the back door and hooked the screen so no one would come traipsing in unexpectedly with dirty shoes and leave footprints, or deposits, on the freshly mopped floor.

Mama was wringing out the mop. She stopped. After a few seconds, she turned to Granny Nan and said, "Maybe you are right. It is her lack of appetite that concerns me most. That and her cough."

"I think you have finally come to your senses, Violet. You should call Doc Barrett's office right after we finish the mopping. I will put the telephone in the front room." She picked it up and dragged the cord across the kitchen floor; the cord was just barely long enough to reach the front room.

Our kitchen was a big room because it had a dinette that held the table and chairs. It took at least forty-five minutes to clean the whole floor, including sweeping up all the crumbs and hand-scrubbing the sticky spots before mopping. I know, because I was often asked to help. Then it had to dry, and on a day like that one in August, it took what seemed like forever. Mama and Granny Nan took turns dipping, wringing, and mopping while the other moved the kitchen chairs just enough to reach the floorspace underneath each and under the table. At various intervals, Mama carried the mop bucket to the sink and dumped out the water, rinsing it and adding a bit of soap powder before refilling it.

Butch and I were finishing the milking. The heat had made me cranky, and even the cows seemed irritated because of it. Butch had done so much sweating, I thought he must have lost at least a gallon of liquid from his body, and it had all collected in his shirt and pants. He smelled bad, so I tried to stay upwind of him. Jimmy wasn't there that day; he was staying at his grandpa's place in Chesaning for a couple of weeks to learn how to make cheese.

Butch and I were standing behind the cows, waiting for the last of the milkers to fill up, and he was doing a lot of talking, as usual. Today his subject was Jimmy's future. "I know that boy wants to farm," he said, "but I just ain't got enough of the green stuff, meanin' money," he laughed nervously, "to invest in farmland. Jimmy's not gonna have enough, either, so he needs to have somethin' to fall back on. My wife's father—the one Jimmy's visitin' right now—owns a pretty lucrative cheese business, and I'm hopin' Jimmy takes to cheese-makin'. I'd sure feel better 'bout ever'thin' if I knew he could make a go of it after his grandpa dies…not that I'm lookin' forward to that happenin', mind ya. I'm just tryin' to plan ahead, ya know?"

I nodded.

"I wish the boy was a little smarter, like his ma was, but he seems to have took after me." He exaggeratedly shook his head from side to side. "It ain't unusual for a man to want his son to grow up just like him, but that ain't true in my case." He sighed. "You reckon your pa would want a son of his to farm…if he had a son, I mean?"

"Oh yeah," I said. "He's wanted sons ever since before Mama was pregnant with me, and he's proud of farming. I know he'd share your feelings about his own son, wanting him to be successful." I kicked at something on the floor and began moving it around with my toe. "Even though Papa still talks like a German, he's a true American, and he says. 'the heart of America beats in the fields of American farmers.' You know how he likes to make up his own way of saying things."

"Well, I'd say he's right 'bout the farms. I just wish I could provide somethin' uh…more uh…what's the word I'm lookin' for…more substantial, I guess, for Jimmy. He really is a hard worker, and it don't take a whole lotta brains to milk cows and till fields." His face went red, and he looked down at the floor. "I beg your pardon, Helmi. I didn't mean that as a slam to your pa."

"I know," I said. "I understand what you meant. Papa would never be happy doing anything else, smart enough or not. You just want the best for Jimmy."

Butch got up and checked the milkers on one of the cows. "Looks like she's given up as much as she's gonna. We better get back to work." He didn't say much the rest of the morning. The silence was kind of nice.

Papa was out in the cornfield checking for corn worms on the ears that had developed. Granny Nan had discovered some on her cucumber and cantaloupe plants. Luckily they had spared the cabbages, lima beans, and tomatoes, at least so far, but Papa knew he'd have to keep a close watch on the corn.

Corn worms, or corn earworms, infested nearly everything if not kept under control. Papa had sprayed a pesticide on the cornfield two weeks before, but he had used it sparingly, as it was expensive, and we didn't have a lot of what he referred to as "extra money to be throwing around." How he could consider pesticides as money to be thrown around was beyond my comprehension. The way I looked at it, if our crops failed, we would be destitute, and without pesticides, the crops *would* fail.

Butch and I were just coming out of the milk house and could see Papa going into the big barn across the road, Two-Tone at his heels. At the same time, Mama came out of the house carrying the mop bucket. She gave it a hefty heave-ho, flinging the water out over her flower bed. She had told me once that soapy water kept the bugs off her plants. She must have been right, because her flowers were untouched by aphids or other pests. I wondered if soapy water would kill corn earworms; I'd have to look that up at the library.

I waved at her, and she waved back. I guess Celine thought Mama was motioning for her to come back to the house, so she waved at Mama and took off across the road. At the same time, the milk tanker was coming up the road to empty our bulk tank.

I think we all saw it coming. The timing was exactly right for Celine and the tanker to be at the same place on the road at precisely the same moment. I suppose a five-year-old mind doesn't function on enough levels to encompass all of its surroundings at one time. Being five, Celine's brain was channeled toward Mama and was oblivious to the truck coming at her.

Everything went into slow motion for me. I saw Celine turn her head toward the truck only seconds before it hit her. I saw Mama's face as she watched the horror taking place before her eyes. I heard a scream, but I don't know if it came from Celine, Mama, or me. I must have either blinked, or intentionally closed my eyes, because I didn't see the truck make contact. Or maybe I did, but my brain blocked it out. I only remember hearing skidding tires.

Then everything went completely quiet. Granny Nan came running out of the house, Papa came running from the barn, and Butch went running around me. But none of them were making any noise. I have a vivid memory of watching the folds in Mama's skirt undulating with each step she took. The truck driver was out of his truck and kneeling in front of it before anyone else reached Celine. I couldn't move.

I watched Papa pull Celine's limp body from under the front end of the tanker. Mama was hysterical, though I could only see her actions, not hear her. Granny Nan had frozen with her hand over her heart. My sisters came out of the house, stopped short when they saw Celine, and began crying. All except for Retta; she was calm. Dear little Retta. She walked purposefully to Papa and Celine, put her ear down to Celine's mouth and nose, then looked up at Papa and shook her head. That's when Papa cried, and my hearing began to return, bit by bit.

I could hear Papa shouting, "NO! NO! NO! NO!" His face was pointed straight up at the sky, as if he were pleading with God to make it not so. The driver was talking and gesturing to Butch, who had his arm around the young man's shoulders. And through it all, I had been useless.

Later that afternoon, I cut down the tree swing.

At Celine's funeral, we all went through the motions without emotions; we were numb. In that dark room of the funeral home, I hated the tiny coffin sitting up on supports that were covered by heavy black velveteen fabric. Celine looked so pale against the light pink satin that lined her white sleeping box; it should have been sky blue, her favorite color. And it would have matched her eyes, had they been open for people to see.

The place was packed full of people, most of whom I didn't know. Miss Michaels told me, "A child's funeral always brings people out of the woodwork. Everyone feels extra sorry for the family of the deceased, and they want to offer kind words." She was right on that point; I don't think a single person in attendance passed us by without saying something nice to us. But no matter how nice they were, I knew that Celine couldn't hear them. I knew she was somewhere else, somewhere much more important.

We buried her in the church cemetery, which was about half-a-mile outside of Mount Pleasant. Mama and Papa had to buy the plots with a loan from the bank. Papa said the bank had told him he was "overextended," but they wouldn't let that stand in the way of burying a child. They gave Papa and Mama the loan but would only allow them to purchase four plots—one of them for Celine. The other three were probably for Granny Nan, Papa, and Mama, in time, as that would have been the natural progression of things.

After Reverend Burton finished the graveside service, I turned and walked away before everyone began talking. The old tradition of throwing dirt or flowers on the casket was no longer in vogue. In fact, they no longer lowered the casket in front of everyone. Instead, they waited until everyone had departed then did it without an audience.

Uncle Herman followed me. "How you holding up, kiddo?"

"I don't know," I shrugged. "I guess I haven't taken time to think about it. I just keep moving like an automaton." I had found that word in one of the books I'd checked out from the library, and I felt it described me perfectly at that exact moment.

"I understand," Uncle Herman said. "I haven't been able to get more than one or two words at a time from your mama and papa. Nancy, either."

"No one seems to know what to say about it anyway," I added. "Are you and Mary and Lizzy coming back to the house?"

"Yep."

"Good," I said with an exhale of relief. For some reason I felt better knowing they'd be there. I suppose it meant there would be familiar faces among the gangs of unfamiliar ones that were destined to invade our home. Mary and Lizzy were not only good at taking care of all the food everyone brought, but also at making people feel welcome, which pleased Mama and Granny Nan, as they were expected to ignore the kitchen and make small talk with the visitors.

Papa had Uncle Herman to lean on. Butch was by Papa's side most of the time, too; Jimmy was still in Chesaning. Mama and Granny Nan held each other up, almost literally. Most of the kids were outside playing; death didn't seem to dampen their spirits in the same way it did adults, probably because the adults were all thinking, "What if that had been my child?"

I stayed in the house, but I tried to make myself as inconspicuous as possible. I didn't feel like playing with the other kids, nor did I feel like being an adult. But those were my only two choices, so I opted for the adult route.

After about an hour, people began to leave, and the house began to seem like home again. For the past several days, I had experienced a strange feeling of not being a member of the family, not belonging in that house. Everything happened around me, and I hadn't been an integral part of any of it.

I hated death and everything associated with it, but I knew death was inevitable and that I'd probably have more practice at overcoming it throughout my life. I simply didn't know how to deal with the mental aspects of death. I also didn't know, at the time, that Mama was four months pregnant.

❖❖❖

Celine's death took a major toll on Mama. She appeared to have aged at least ten years. She was not interested in taking care of herself, either; her hair was usually uncombed, her skin was pale and dry and creased. The corners of her mouth turned down; I rarely saw her even attempt a smile. She held her back as she walked, bent over like a crippled old woman; she was only forty-two. She was extremely thin, which made her belly stick out more noticeably than usual. She couldn't pick up or carry Anna, so that poor child had very little bonding with her mother, and Mama seemed to ignore Ronnie, probably because she knew she couldn't care for a toddler in her current condition.

Granny Nan finally convinced Mama to stay in bed most of the time, on Doc Barrett's orders. He had told Mama, "Stop trying to be a martyr; you are in no condition for that. Your suffering needs to be done from a bed. The fact is, you cannot take care of anyone but yourself right now if you expect to give birth in a few more months."

By January of 1934, Mama was completely bed-ridden. Papa and Granny Nan had moved her to Granny Nan's downstairs bedroom to keep from having to run up and down the steps in the process of caring for her. When I wasn't helping Papa or doing my other chores or going to school, I was sitting with Mama.

Miss Michaels had stopped taking me to the high school on Tuesdays, though we still went to the library every Monday. She had suggested to Granny Nan that she not stay for supper each Monday, but Granny Nan was adamant about her being there. "I need an adult to talk to who is not in a separate room!" she told Miss Michaels. "And besides that, cooking is the only constant I have in my life right now." So Miss Michaels continued to sup with us on Mondays.

Bella was extremely good at caring for all my other sisters; her maternal instinct was strong, just like Mama's. Dora was old enough to take care of herself—most of the time—and Yosie surprised me by being more self-sufficient than usual. She helped Granny Nan and me take care of Mama, though she had little to do with Ronnie or Anna. Once the novelty of having Ronnie around as a new baby wore off, Yosie lost all interest in her.

I could tell Papa was worried; he rarely spoke. He seldom came to the milk house to talk to Butch and me, and he was silent during our meals. When he wasn't in the fields or barns, he was at Mama's side, holding her hand or watching her sleep. When he was with Mama, Yosie would retreat to our room.

I asked Yosie one night, "Why don't you want to be around Papa?"

"He doesn't understand me," she said.

"It might help if you'd at least try to be a human being around him," I told her. I knew it was mean to say that, but I couldn't help it.

I was rewarded with silence. She had never made an effort to overcome conflict, only to avoid it. Some of her friends had given her a tube of lipstick for her last birthday, and she smeared it on with one hand while holding up a hand mirror with the other. Then she'd make "kissy lips" at her reflection. She'd look at herself, act like she was kissing someone, then either giggle or emit a throaty laugh. She was eleven, going on thirty.

It began to snow on January 28, and it didn't stop until January 31. There was very little wind, so the snow just kept piling up. Before it was over, we had more than two feet on the level. And the temperature stayed below freezing, so there was no melt, only some settling when the sun poked out from behind the clouds on a few rare occasions.

Mama kept getting bigger and bigger, and she constantly complained of pain in her back. Doc Barrett came to the house twice during February to check on her, and both times he said he was pretty sure she would have twins. He could hear two heartbeats, but he said, "Sometimes the second heartbeat is just an echo of the mother's."

I was betting on twins.

I was sitting at the dinette table doing some schoolwork one evening. Granny Nan had fallen asleep in one of the kitchen chairs, her head hanging down on her chest. I heard Papa talking to Mama. He had decided he would like the twins to be named Alexandra and Adelina. I could barely hear Mama, but she must have made some reply that made Papa laugh. That made me happy; I hadn't even seen him smile for weeks.

On March 6 we had a blizzard. The temperature dropped almost forty degrees in fifteen minutes, and the wind howled continuously, not letting up. It raged for thirty-six hours. Everything turned to ice. And Mama went into labor.

She was having a hard time with the delivery, so Granny Nan decided to call Doc Barrett, but the telephone was not working; it was completely dead, and Papa said, "Probably the vires are down. You vill have to do the best you can. I have faith in you and Helmi."

I had never actually helped with a human birth, other than to assist Granny Nan when she told me to get something or to keep a cold cloth on Mama's forehead. This time, however, Granny Nan was worried. I could tell because she had that little furrow in her brow, just like the one Lizzy always got when she was worried or thinking very hard about something.

"This is not normal," Granny Nan told me quietly. Mama was sweating and panting. She screamed at the top of her lungs each time a contraction happened, and I was trying desperately to calm her down with the cool cloths. But she kept batting them away. She had a wild look on her face, as if she weren't in the same room with Granny Nan and me. She kept reaching for something out in midair and mumbling "…come back…" and "…do not let go…"

Papa was beside himself. He paced back and forth from the kitchen to the front room, and each time he passed the bedroom, he'd stop and look in. He kept asking God not to take her from him. That made both Granny Nan and me nervous—more nervous than we already were.

Mama was pushing now, and suddenly a huge amount of blood came rushing out. Granny Nan's face went white, and I uttered a surprised sounding "Oh!"

"We need more towels," Granny Nan said. I started to move, but she said, "Stay put! I need you here." She turned toward the door and hollered for Papa. "Heinrich! Bring us the towels in the kitchen drawer, bottom one to the right of the sink."

"How many?" he asked.

"All of them!" we both answered in unison.

He came to the door but wouldn't come inside the room. He held up the towels and looked at me. I ran over to him and snatched them out of his hands. Then I dumped them on the bed and went back to my station at Mama's head.

"Good God in Heaven!" Granny Nan muttered. There was blood gushing from between Mama's legs, and she had passed out.

"I need you here, Helmi." She was motioning for me to go to her, and I immediately went to her side. The sight of the blood didn't bother me. I had seen so much of it around the farm, it made no impact on me. Then it sunk in that it was coming from my mother, and my whole attitude changed. I swayed a bit, and Granny Nan said, "Oh no! You are not going to pass out on me." She looked back down at the pool of blood on the bed.

I followed her eyes. "We have to stop it, Granny Nan. She'll die if we don't. She's been so listless and pale, I think she's anemic."

"She is what?" Granny Nan asked me. She almost sounded angry.

"It means she doesn't have enough red blood cells. Look at how pink it is—it isn't bright red like it should be."

Granny Nan closed her eyes and went down on her knees. I thought she was on the verge of fainting, but I realized she was praying, instead. I stepped into Granny Nan's position and was beginning to soak up some of the blood when something appeared at the opening to Mama's birth canal. It was a head with blood-soaked hair. "It's coming!" I shouted.

Granny Nan rose from her knees and pushed me aside.

I moved out of the way, and within a couple of minutes, Granny Nan was holding something that resembled a baby, but it wasn't quite right. She looked at it, then she wrapped it in a towel—completely wrapped it; she didn't leave any part of it sticking out. From what I saw of it, I could tell it was deformed, and its skin was blue. It had obviously been stillborn.

Mama kept bleeding, and neither of us knew what to do to stop it, or if it could even be stopped. Mama's breathing was erratic and extremely shallow. I wanted to ask Granny Nan if Mama was going to die, but I was afraid to hear the answer. Then without warning, another head appeared, ready to be born. "Doc Barrett was right," Granny Nan said. "It is twins."

It took a long time for that baby to come out. I was afraid it, too, was going to be dead when it was born, but it cried when Granny Nan pulled its shoulders through the opening and into the air. It was a boy!

I laughed, partly as a means of relief, and partly because I found it humorous that Papa was so certain it would be twin girls, he had chosen female names. I was so happy. Papa had the son he'd always wanted. I went running to the door and shouted to him, but he was not within hearing range. I didn't know where he'd disappeared to. I didn't know whether it was more important to search for him or to stay there with Mama and Granny Nan. I got my answer when I turned back toward Mama and saw Granny Nan standing over her, holding her limp hand and crying.

I rushed to Mama's bedside, calling her name over and over and over. "Mama! Mama! Wake up, Mama! Mama! Come back! Do not let go!" Then I stopped shouting. I had just repeated the very words she had been mumbling less than an hour before.

Mama was gone.

One baby was gone.

Papa posthumously named the first baby Alexander. But another baby was still with us; Papa named him Aloysius. He was tiny with yellow eyes and skin, and he cried without stopping except when he slept.

Our normally happy household was now solemn and unsmiling. And twenty days later, on March 28, Aloysius stopped crying and joined his mother and brother.

❖❖❖

Following so many funerals in so little time—first Celine, then Mama and Alexander, then Aloysius—Granny Nan and I and all my sisters were depressed, though I didn't recognize it as that at the time. Granny Nan called it "melancholia." However, we all had each other to lean on.

Papa, on the other hand, suffered alone—deep hopelessness, forgetfulness, poor concentration, and even self-hatred. He blamed himself for Mama's death and withdrew from anything that involved interaction with people, including his own family. He was irritable and barely ate anything. He hardly slept and sometimes went to the barn hours before dawn where he simply sat and cried, which I discovered one morning when I heard him rustling around in the kitchen.

I went downstairs and found him standing over the sink, drinking cold coffee that had been made the previous day. According to the kitchen clock, it was just before 3:00 a.m. "Hi, Papa." He didn't answer. "How come you're up so early? Couldn't sleep?"

He was holding his head in his hand. "Headache," he said. He turned ever so slowly and walked toward the back door, shuffling his feet. He was barefoot.

"It's pretty chilly out this morning. You should probably put on some socks before you put on your boots."

"Oh, ja. I should vear socks." He just stood there, staring at his feet.

"I'll get you some," I said. I went upstairs and found a pair of freshly laundered socks lying on his bed among most of his other clean clothes, none of which he had put away in his chest of drawers. Then I heard the backdoor slam.

I hurried downstairs, and there, beside the door, sitting on the mat where we all deposited our boots, were his. I put on my own boots and slipped my coat on over my nightgown. Then I picked up his boots, yanked the door open, and raced to the barn. Papa was sitting on a bale of straw; he was barefooted, and tears were streaming down his face. Two-Tone was lying at his feet.

"Papa?" I didn't know what to do.

He didn't acknowledge me. He simply sat there, staring at nothing in particular, crying like a small child. He was bent slightly forward, his arms and hands resting on his thighs.

I petted Two-Tone and talked to her in low, soothing tones. Then I gently pushed her to one side, knelt, and put the socks and boots on Papa's ice-cold feet. He didn't object; he simply allowed me to go about it with no emotional response. I pulled up another bale of straw beside his and sat down. I didn't say anything; I merely sat there with him. I figured he'd talk when—and if—he wanted to. I don't know how long I sat there, silently waiting for him to speak.

"I killed her, Helmi. I killed your mama yust as sure as I am sitting here."

"Why do you think that, Papa?"

"She vas having my children. Do you not see that?"

"She had all of your other children, and she didn't die doing it. Her death was not because she was having your children, Papa. It happened because something went wrong inside her body. She must have been sick, and we didn't know it. Doc Barrett didn't even know it."

He seemed to be digesting what I'd said. "Do you think that could be it?"

"Of course that's it," I said. I scooted over closer to him and leaned against him. He offered no physical response; he just sat there, crying, for several more minutes.

"I have nothing," he said. "This farm is nothing. I have cows to feed and fields to plant and fertilize and pick, and it all takes money that I do not have. I owe more than I can pay, Helmi. Vhat am I going to do?"

"We'll figure it out, Papa. You and I and Granny Nan will talk about it and figure something out." I was grabbing at straws. I knew it. And he knew it.

"Violet vas my backbone; she held me up. Now I am spineless. She left me vitout a vord. Gott took her, but He did not think enough of me to let me say 'auf wiedersehen.' He must think very little of me." The tears, which had subsided, now gushed from his eyes.

"Do not turn your back on God, Papa. He is your spine now. He and I and Granny Nan. He wouldn't have taken Mama if He thought we couldn't manage without her. He needed Mama more than we do." I wasn't sure I truly believed that, but it was the only thing I could think to say.

He put his head in his hands and sobbed—long, deep sobs.

I was terrified. *Papa is sad, just like Uncle Julius, because he doesn't have enough money. What if he has a mental illness? What if he decides to jump off a building, or end his own life in some other way?*

I was angry with God. He had made Papa sad. No, it was worse than that. He had made Papa feel worthless, and that didn't sit well with me. I felt God had ignored Papa and Granny Nan and all my sisters and me. He had been so selfish, so uncaring. And now Papa was mentally sick, maybe sick enough to commit suicide. God wasn't good and kind like Mrs. Matsen and Reverend Bryant and Reverend Burton had all told me. God had taken Mama, and it had broken all the rest of us, especially Papa.

I stormed out of the barn, looked up into the early morning sky, waved my fist and screamed, "I don't trust You anymore!...Are You listening?...Are You even there?" My tirade was met with silence, and I felt nothing but complete emptiness inside. I knew I'd never put my faith in God again.

❖❖❖

The farm had been falling deeper and deeper into debt, and Papa fell deeper and deeper into depression. On May 8, 1934, I went to help Butch do the milking before school, as usual. Jimmy was there, too. He had changed over the last few years. He was almost as tall as Papa now, thin, and muscular. He was seventeen and had dropped out of school in order to work somewhere and make some money doing manual labor, seeing as how his grades were not going to propel him into a great career. Little Jimmy Butcher was now quite handsome. All I could think was, *His mother must have been a looker, because he sure didn't get his looks from his dad.*

I guess I was staring at him without realizing it, because Butch came up silently behind me and whispered, "Not too hard on the eyes, is he?"

I think I came three feet off the floor. I had thought I was alone in my musings. "Holy cow, Butch, you scared the bejeebies out of me!"

Butch didn't apologize, he just smiled, put his hands in his pockets, and walked away.

I was properly embarrassed. I didn't say much to either of them the rest of the morning, and I made sure I kept my eyes strictly on my work. I was glad when it came time for me to go to school.

Our walk to school was going to be a tough one this morning, as a front was coming from the east, unusual for our part of the state, and we'd be walking right into the wind. Just as we walked out the door, it began to spit freezing rain. Sometimes, when the weather was bad like that, Papa would take a break from whatever he was doing and pile us all into the truck. Then he'd drive us the short distance to school so we weren't wet and cold by the time we got there. But that day, Papa was nowhere to be seen.

Just before walking out the door, Granny Nan asked me if I had seen him that morning.

"No. He was already out and gone by the time I got up. His bedroom door was open, and there was no snoring coming from inside." We both laughed.

It was during dinnertime (we called it lunchtime at school) that the schoolroom went dead quiet. Miss Michaels rose from her desk. Granny Nan had opened the schoolhouse door and was standing there, wind-blown and shivering. "Nancy, how nice to see you! Please come in. Is everything all right?"

I knew immediately that everything was NOT all right. Granny Nan would never have appeared unexpectedly at my school unless something was decidedly wrong. My mind began to whirl. *Which one of my sisters is sick? Had something bad happened to one of them? Some sort of accident?* After Celine's death, I had become paranoid about them when I wasn't there. *I hate having to leave Granny Nan alone with them; she's getting old and can't always hurry if there's an emergency. And now, here she is at the schoolhouse door, which means she either had to leave them alone, or she had asked Papa to...*

As if she could read my thoughts, Granny Nan jerked her head and looked at me—looked straight at me—just as I had thought the word *Papa* in my mind. "Papa?" I asked aloud. Her eyes were boring holes in me. The air rushed from my lungs. I grabbed Granny Nan's hand and pulled her out the door. I didn't have to ask her anything; I knew I had to go home because there was something terribly wrong with Papa or she would not have shown up at the schoolhouse in the middle of the day.

I can't remember walking home. I don't remember if freezing rain was still falling or if the sun had come out. I was focused on one singular purpose: to get to Papa. *I'm coming, Papa! As fast as I can. I wish Granny Nan could walk faster.*

"What's wrong with Papa, Granny Nan?"

We had reached the house. Granny Nan was panting. I had hold of both of her hands, and she lifted her finger and pointed toward the big barn. I dropped her hands and ran to the small door that was built into the big sliding door on the front of the building. I stepped up and over the railing at the bottom of the doorway and looked around. "Papa?" There was no answer. "Papa?" I shouted louder.

Nothing.

The tractor was parked where it always sat, rear wheels toward the door, just as it had been run inside the barn, waiting to be backed out when it was needed next. Everything appeared calm and orderly. I could hear the ducks outside; they were excited that I was home so early.

I finally noticed Papa sitting on the floor at the front of the tractor, one leg sticking straight out and the other folded under him, the way he always sat when he was working on the tractor's engine. It was just a small tractor: a 1927 Fordson Model F. Because Papa was tall, he found it easier to work from a sitting position rather than bending over it. "What's wrong with the tractor, Papa?" He didn't answer, so I walked toward him.

Why had Granny Nan come to get me? Papa has never needed me to help him fix the tractor. That could certainly wait until I got home; it wasn't an emergency. And usually either Butch or Jimmy could help if Papa needed it right away or if the job took more than Papa's own two hands.

He appeared to be asleep; his head was down, his arms limp. He had been working with a wrench that now lay on the floor beside his open hand, as if he had allowed it to roll from his grasp when he drifted off to sleep. As I got closer, I saw that his eyes were open. I watched for him to blink or take a breath, but that didn't happen. His eyes only stared, and his chest was not moving. My heart stopped for a couple of beats.

No, this can't be. I won't accept it. He's playing a trick on me. That's what he's doing. I stood still, not making a sound, hearing my blood pumping in my ears.

Granny Nan appeared at my side. "I called him to come to dinner, but he did not answer. I thought he was maybe out behind the barn or across the road. When he did not show up for several more minutes I called again. He still did not answer me, so I went looking for him."

"And this is where you found him."

She turned and walked away.

I closed my eyes, hoping I'd awaken from this awful dream. But when I re-opened them, everything was the same.

Papa would no longer be there for us.

I was in shock. I went into the house and called Doc Barrett's office. "We're going to need him to come out and give us a death certificate," I told the woman who answered; I didn't know if she was a nurse or someone Doc had hired to take phone calls and make appointments.

"Oh, dear," she said. "Who is the deceased?"

"My father," I said, not thinking clearly. "Papa."

"And you are…?"

"Oh. Wilhelmina Schnier. My father is…was…is Heinrich Schnier."

"Do you know if the cause of his death was accidental? I'm sure the doctor will ask me," she said.

"It wasn't." That was all I said. I couldn't talk anymore. I didn't cry, I wasn't hysterical, I didn't even feel upset. I just couldn't talk. No more sound would come out. No more thoughts would form in my head; my brain was mush. I stood there with the telephone receiver hanging from my hand, and I could hear the operator telling me my party had disconnected. But it didn't matter. I closed my eyes. Nothing mattered. How long I stood there in my stupor was anyone's guess.

"There is no burial plot for Heinrich," Granny Nan said to me that night after everyone else was in bed. We were sitting alone in the front room. I had built a nice fire in the fireplace, and Granny Nan had made us each a cup of hot Postum. Between the two of us, we had called everyone we thought should know—Uncle Herman and Mary and Lizzy, Butch and Jimmy, Reverend and Mrs. Burton.

Miss Michaels had stopped by after school, bless her soul. We shared all the particulars. She told me to take a few days off school. Granny Nan had called the funeral home, and they had asked her where Papa was to be buried. She said she wasn't sure, but she'd call them back tomorrow.

"We can't afford a plot," I said. "We can't even afford a coffin. What are we going to do? How will we get Papa to his final resting place?" A single tear ran down my left cheek.

We had met Doc Barrett earlier when he'd arrived, and I had looked at the death certificate as he filled it out; under Cause of Death, he had entered *Grief*. He told us he would make arrangements with the people at the morgue to come and get Papa's body that night; they had arrived soon after he'd left. I didn't watch them load Papa into their truck. I only watched it drive away, taking my father away from our farm, the farm he had made for us. His home. Our home.

Granny Nan sat there, staring into her cup. I wasn't sure she had even heard me. I was about to repeat my questions when she looked up at the fire and began speaking to no one in particular. "My eldest granddaughter has been through more than any young woman should ever be made to endure. She has piled up more heartache in less time than the mothers of sons who go off to war and never come home. She is the strongest person I have ever known. Wilhelmina Schnier. (She pronounced my name exactly as Papa would have.)

"She has lived only fourteen years, but she is already a well seasoned woman because of her strength, her compassion, her intelligence, her competence. She has remained calm, without faltering. She has kept marching right through the battles, never flinching. I have the highest regard for her, not because she is my granddaughter, but because she has handled herself in a way that places her far above all others her age.

"Now, on the very night of the death of her father, her Papa, she sits placidly before a fire and drinks from a cup as calmly as if it were any other night of the week, willing to discuss the mundane and the abominable. To be so sound, so staid, so wise beyond her years is a significant insight into her character. I am proud to be her grandmother."

She had not blinked once throughout her soliloquy, nor had she ever once looked at me. I cannot explain how I felt; there were too many emotions all tangled together. We finished drinking our Postum in silence, then we went to bed. We would continue tomorrow, pick up where we'd left off. Everything that remained to be done would be. Like it or not, the earth was going to continue rotating.

TURNING THE PAGE

Two weeks had passed since Papa's death. It was time to make some decisions about the farm, college, family—those of us who remained. Papa had not left a will.

It was a Monday, and I was supposed to see a man at the bank in Mount Pleasant after school. It was a nice, sunny day, cold but pleasant in the sunshine, so Miss Michaels had insisted we all go outside to eat our lunch. She called me from the door of the schoolhouse; I went to see what she wanted.

"I talked to Nancy and told her I'd be taking you to the bank this afternoon instead of spending time at the library. I also have a surprise for you," she said, teasingly.

I sighed. "I don't know if I'm up to a surprise. I'm scared of what the banker's going to say; could be he'll have a whole bag full of surprises, none of which are the good kind."

"Helmi," she said, "you deserve so much better than what you've been dealt lately. Nancy, too. The two of you are working yourselves to death. I think a nice surprise is way past due." She was, without a doubt, one of the most sincerely kind human beings, other than Mama, that I'd ever met. "We'll leave right away when the last lesson is over, if that's all right with you."

"Sure. I don't have any reason to hurry home. I'll just have to tell Retta to let Granny Nan know that I'll be going with you."

Retta was taking after Papa and me. She was a very responsible little girl, and I loved her all the more for it. She was smart, too. Miss Michaels talked to her the same way she had talked to me when I was Retta's age. I could relate to that and appreciate it for Retta's sake. But Retta was more than that. She had a special talent. I called it her extra sense. It was almost as if she could read people's minds. Case in point: I went to her to ask her to tell Granny Nan that Miss Michaels and I were going to the bank right from school. "Retta, would you…"

But before I could finish my sentence, she said, "I'll tell Granny Nan you left right after school. Are you going to the library?"

"Only long enough to drop off a couple of books."

"Can you keep one longer?"

"I don't know. Which one?" I asked.

"The one about the middle of the earth."

"*Journey to the Center of the Earth.*"

"Yeah, that one."

"I'll check and see when it's due. I'll renew it for another two weeks if I can."

She nodded. "Thanks." And with that, she went back to eating her lunch. Short and sweet: that should have been Retta's byline.

At 3:30 that afternoon Miss Michaels told everyone to police the area around their desks. When she was happy with the way the room looked, she dismissed everyone. She and I walked out, and she locked the door behind us. We walked to her car, and I reached for the passenger door, but she stopped me. I looked at her like she was crazy.

"You're driving," she said. "Surprise!"

My jaw dropped open. "But I haven't…"

"You've driven the truck and the tractor—I've seen you do it. There's very little difference between driving those and driving this."

"But this is *your* automobile. What if I do something stupid and…"

"You won't," she said. "Now get in and drive, or we'll be late."

So it was that I had my first driving lesson in an automobile. I loved it! It was the epitome of freedom. I knew that if I could drive a motorcar, I would be able to go wherever I needed—or wanted—whenever. It was easy; Miss Michaels was right. Even when we got into town, I was able to "maneuver like a pro" according to her.

She told me I'd be able to get what was called a hardship license. "They are specifically for people who are between the ages of fourteen and sixteen, usually from farms, who have to be allowed to drive so they can take care of the family business."

We pulled up to the bank, and I went in, filled with fear of what might be in store. "I'm Wilhelmina Schnier," I said to the woman sitting at a desk just inside and to the right of the door. "I'm here to see Mr. Watkins."

"Is this about the job?" the woman asked.

"No."

"Then, what exactly is the nature of your visit?"

"I have an appointment," I told her.

"Oh, I'm sorry." She picked up a checklist that was lying beside the blotter on her desk. "Yes, I have you on my list. I'll tell him you've arrived. Please wait here." She rose and went through the door behind her. When she came back out, she smiled and said, "You may go right in."

"Thank you," I said. Then I took a deep breath and walked purposefully into Mr. Watkins' office. I had made up my mind to take the bull by the horns and not allow anything Mr. Watkins said to shoot down my positive attitude. I couldn't afford to let that happen.

He was a smallish man, not any taller than I, with tiny, perfectly manicured hands, which I noticed when he reached over his desk and shook mine. He had very little hair, and he wore round glasses. His dark gray suit was made of wool, and it had a nearly unnoticeable pattern that was obvious only by a subtle dark blue thread that ran through the fabric creating little squares. I couldn't see his shoes, but I was sure they were black and well shined. His desk was perfectly tidy with only one small stack of papers off to the side. "Please, have a seat," he said to me.

I sat, then he sat. "So, you are Heinrich Schnier's daughter. I understand you usually go by Helmi. Is that right?"

"Yessir," I said. I was surprised that my voice sounded so clear and strong; that wasn't how I felt inside.

"Let's get right to it, shall we, Helmi?"

Here we go. I don't know if I'm ready for this. I took another deep breath. "Of course," I answered.

Mr. Watkins pulled the pile of papers over in front of him and looked at the top one. Then he put it aside and glanced through the next page. "Uh-huh," he said, noncommittally. He nodded. He put that paper to the side with the first one and then read through the third. "Hmmm." He took a sharp breath through his nose and looked up at me.

I couldn't read his eyes or his facial expression. *This must be what Papa referred to as a "poker face."*

He looked back down at the paper in front of him and said, "I am not a farmer, Helmi, nor have I ever been exposed to farm life. But your father, may he rest in peace, was farmer through and through. He was proud of his farm right up to the end."

That wasn't what Papa had told me; he said the farm was nothing. Maybe he was letting his grief talk for him that day.

"He was a fine man, his word was as good as gold, and he did whatever he could to make his farm a place that his family would be proud of. Oh, he owed a lot of money, that's a fact. But he was good for it. At the end, however, he was a bit overextended."

"Yes, he told me that. That's why he could only borrow enough for four burial plots…"

"…which turned out to be one too few. I understand, and I am so sorry for all your losses. But we did end up loaning him enough for the extra one. We would not have disputed that, Helmi. We are not a firm without heart."

"And I thank you for that, Mr. Watkins. I plan…"

Again, he cut me off. "I know you plan to pay us back. I am certain that, in time, you will have the funds to do so. Have you considered how you might accomplish that?"

"Yessir, I have. We own four beef cattle, all ready for slaughter, and we have three pigs, two of which will be fattened up soon. I will sell those two pigs and all four of the cattle and use the money to repay a portion of our debts here at the bank."

"I see. What will you do about your own meat supply?"

"We will have the one remaining pig, and we have chickens, some of which are getting too old to lay. They will provide us with meat, and of course, we'll have eggs to eat and sell."

"What do you plan to do with the dairy?"

I sat there, stunned. I hadn't even thought about the dairy. It was our only means of steady income, and we depended on it as our livelihood.

"I don't understand, Mr. Watson. What do mean?"

"I mean, will you continue to milk cows?"

"Of course. That is our major source of income. We have continually been building up our herd in order to keep increasing our profits. I have no other plans for the dairy."

He looked at me over the top of his glasses, which had slid down his nose. Then he sat back in his chair and put his hands together, fingertip to fingertip. A smile began to develop. "Your father was right about you. You are perfectly capable of handling your situation. I assure you, we will not be taking the farm from you, as long as you continue to expand and make payments on your debts." He leaned forward, putting his elbows on his desk. "Have you thought about what will happen when you go to college?"

I moved around nervously in my seat. He had touched on a sore point. What *was* I going to do? I hadn't been able to see my way clear on that subject. I had pretty much decided college was out of the picture.

He reached for one of the papers he had set aside earlier. "I think I have at least a part of the solution to that problem. Do you know what a bank trust is, Helmi?"

"No sir."

"There is one in your name through this bank, and your father is to thank for it." His entire demeanor changed. His face now appeared much more pleasant, more personal, and he spoke to me more as a friend than a banker. He pushed the paper over in front of me and invited me to look at it. At the top it said: TESTAMENTARY CHILD'S TRUST.

"Let me explain," he said. "A trust is a common way for people to leave assets—cash, in your case—to their children. Your father was well aware that you want to become a veterinarian more than anything else, and he knew you need to go to college for that. Therefore, he designated our bank as his trustee. In other words, he allows us to manage the money he had been depositing in your trust account until you reach a certain age…um…" He turned the paper so he could read it, then he turned it back to me and pointed to the number seventeen… "that age for you is seventeen. When you reach age seventeen, you will be eligible to receive the money in this trust to be used for the purpose for which it was intended." He sat back and waited for what he'd said to sink in.

"You mean, Papa had been putting money into a special account for my college?"

"That is exactly right." He again pointed to a number.

I followed his finger and saw that he was pointing to $430. I blinked my eyes several times and looked at the number once more. It had not changed. "I'm not sure I understand. Is that the number that it would cost for me to go to college? That's way more than Papa made in a whole year, I'm sure."

"That number is how much your father was able to save for you to go to college. When you turn seventeen, that money will be yours, specifically for college. We, being the trustee, will take care of paying for your tuition, books, housing, and so forth, using the money in this account…the four-hundred and thirty dollars your father was able to put into your trust."

I had never claimed to be an overly emotional person, but that claim went right out the window when I was finally able to grasp the enormity of what Papa had done for me! I couldn't hold back the tears; they ran down my face like a waterfall. "I'm so sorry," I said. I was overjoyed, humbled, and embarrassed at the same time. I couldn't stop crying.

Mr. Watkins got up and left the office. I didn't know what I was supposed to do at that precise moment, but I took advantage of the opportunity to wipe my face with my hands, then on my sleeves, then I picked up the bottom of my skirt and wiped my face again. *Oh, Papa, wherever you are, you were the very best papa any girl could ever want!* I grabbed the paper and looked at it, reading the numbers over and over and was more excited every time I saw them. Without warning, a big "WAH-HOO" escaped my lips.

Then I remembered I was in a public place and should probably be more reserved. So I put the paper down on Mr. Watkins' desk, sat back in the chair, wiped my face one more time, and folded my hands in my lap, hoping no one had heard my ecstatic outburst. I waited patiently for Mr. Watkins' return.

The door opened behind me, and Mr. Watkins entered. "I trust you are pleased," he said.

"I apologize for my outburst, Mr. Watkins. I haven't had anything to be happy about for a long time. If Papa were here, he'd be telling me to act more like a grown-up and less like a child, I'm sure."

"You have every reason to be wah-hooing, Helmi." He grinned at me. "Your father did something that is nothing less than outstanding by providing you with the funds necessary for a college education. But there is one more thing we need to discuss."

I know my face must have drooped, because he said, "No, no, Helmi, this is nothing bad. It's just something I'm not sure you are aware of. Have any of your teachers mentioned the possibility of scholarships?"

"I've only ever had one teacher, Miss Michaels."

"Of course. You attend the one-room school just outside of town," he stated.

"Yessir."

"When will you be coming into town for high school?"

"I'll start in September."

"Good, good. Be sure and talk to Miss Michaels about scholarships. She should also be enrolling you in some college preparatory classes. You must understand that there will be very few women in those classes. It's not common for women to attend college. Not unheard of, mind you, but not common, either, especially when pursuing the career you've chosen. You'll have a difficult time convincing some people that a woman can do that job."

"Papa always said, 'Proving vun's self is based on methods, not mouths,' meaning…"

"…meaning, you gain credibility by *showing* people you're capable rather than merely *telling* them you are."

"Yes," I said. I was proud—and a little bit surprised—that he understood Papa's adage.

"We will mail you a letter explaining the trust procedure when you turn seventeen. Thank you so much for making my last appointment of the day a very special one, Helmi. Your father had every right to be proud of you."

I thanked him, probably more times than necessary, then I returned to Miss Michaels' automobile. She was not there, but I got into the passenger's side to wait for her. I knew I wouldn't be able to concentrate on driving. Then I realized the library was less than a block away, so I grabbed my two library books and walked there; it was a good way to use up some of my excess energy, thanks to Mr. Watkins.

Miss Michaels was just coming down the library's outside steps. "I'll be right back," I said as I passed her. "I need to renew one of these for Retta, then I have sooooooo much to tell you."

When I got into her automobile, my mouth started working and didn't stop until I went to bed that night. I didn't know if I dared to hope that, perhaps, events had begun to turn around.

For the next couple of days Granny Nan struggled with what she called "a case of the sniffles" after shoveling snow away from the front door. I had told her not to, but she insisted. "I will take my time. I just need to do something outside to get some fresh air. The house feels stuffy, and I need a change of pace."

To make things a little easier for her while she was under the weather, I even did some of the cooking. Well, it wasn't exactly cooking; I made sandwiches and boiled some eggs for our school lunches. But I was in the kitchen, so I figured that counted as cooking. I also did lots of house cleaning. Granny Nan's eyes weren't so sharp anymore, and there were some things that had escaped her, like the footprints that came into the kitchen from the back door, dust under the beds, and lots of crumbs around and under the kitchen table.

I had decided to begin doing more jobs inside the house before I went to school each morning. I dearly loved being in the stanchion barn and milk house, but Butch didn't really need me now that Jimmy was coming with him every day. And since I had talked to Mr. Watkins at the bank and found out we were not going to have unwanted pressure on us to pay back the money we owed, I figured we could pay Jimmy a little bit, in addition to what we paid his father, for the work he did.

We were expecting lots of calves, so there would be quite a few fresh cows to add back to the herd and some of last year's heifers that were expected to calve, as well. And of course, more cows meant more milk, and more milk meant more money. We still owed Leston Oakes part of the cost of the use of his bull, but that would be paid in full as soon as the size of our herd increased.

When I got home from school that day, Granny Nan met me at the door. "You are supposed to call Dr. Pauley's office," she said.

"Oh, no," I whined. "What's wrong? Please tell me it isn't something with the cows."

"It is not something with the cows."

"Thank you. What is it, then?"

"I do not know. I simply took a message from Mrs. Pauley when she called. I told her you would call her back when you got home from school."

I went to the phone and saw that Granny Nan had written Dr. Pauley's number on a piece of paper. I waited for the operator to ask me for the number, but she must have known it without my having to tell her because she said, "That number is busy. Do you want to wait?"

"Yes," I said. I figured it would take the operator a few tries before she got through. Dr. Pauley was the only vet within thirty miles, and he was always busy, which meant he might or might not be in his office.

"It's ringing now," the operator said.

"Thank you."

"Dr. Pauley's office. How may we be of help?"

"Hello, this is Helmi Schnier. I received a message that Dr. Pauley was trying to reach me."

"Who did you say you are?"

"Helmi Schnier."

"You must be Heinrich's daughter."

"Yes, I am."

"Hang on a moment. The doctor wants to talk to you right away." Their idea of "right away" differed from mine. It must have been three or four minutes before Dr. Pauley came on the line. "Helmi? Are you there?"

"Yes, Dr. Pauley. I understand…"

"I want to talk to you about coming to work for me."

Silence from my end of the line.

"Helmi? Did I lose you? Are you there?"

"Yes, yes. I'm here. I was just taken back by what you said."

"Well, you think about it and let me know."

"What do you mean, 'work for you'?" I asked.

"I mean help me with the animals. I know you want to be a vet, so I thought I'd give you a chance to learn and make some money at the same time."

"You do know I'm still in school, right?"

"Of course. That's why I'd only ask you to help me on the weekends, maybe a day or two after school. That sound reasonable? Don't answer right now. You need to take some time to think about it. But don't take too long. Spring is coming, and you know how busy that time of year is for us. Call me back with an answer."

I heard a click. "Dr. Pauley?"

The operator said, "Your party has disconnected."

I placed the receiver into its cradle on the phone. *What just hap-*

pened? Am I dreaming? I pinched my arm. "Ow!" I wasn't dreaming.

Yosie came up to me and said, "How much longer are you going to be? I have friends who are going to call me. They'll be ringing up anytime now."

I gave her a sideways glance. She was dressed in an extremely tight skirt—one I had never seen before—and a white V-necked blouse, the top two buttons undone and the collar turned up around her face. "Where'd you get that outfit?"

"From Georgina. She didn't like it on herself, but I think it looks divine on me. What do you think?"

What did I think? What *did* I think? What was I supposed to think? My little sister—my twelve-year-old sister—was dolled up like a Chicago call girl. I knew I was probably going to have to be the "bad guy" at some point in time and tell her she couldn't continue to dress like that, at least not in public. "Yosie, what do you suppose Mama or Papa would think?"

"They aren't here, now, are they?" she bent forward slightly and wiggled her rear end as she said it.

At that precise moment, Granny Nan had entered the room and had caught Yosie's little act. "You look like a slut," Granny Nan said. She always told it like it was.

I snorted.

"Do you think you are cute?" Granny Nan asked.

Yosie just stood there, staring at both of us. Then she flipped her head, which made her curls jiggle. "Doesn't matter what either of you say. You're not Mama or Papa. And since they aren't here, I can do whatever I want."

"Is that the way you think this works?" Granny Nan asked her.

"That's the way it works," Yosie said and wiggled out of the room.

Granny Nan and I looked at each other. Neither of us knew what to say. We both knew we had no control over her, and Yosie knew it, too. She was headed down the slippery slope, and we could only stand by and watch it happen, right before our eyes. She was way too headstrong for either of us to succeed in reprimanding her or even giving her any sound advice, which, I was sure, she wouldn't take from us anyway.

I almost felt sorry for her—almost. Wherever she'd end up was anybody's guess. Without Mama or Papa to put her in her place, she would probably come to no good end. She didn't care what anyone thought of her, as long as she was the center of attention.

The phone rang. I picked it up. "Hello?"

"Yosie?" an unfamiliar male voice came from the other end of the line.

"She's not here," I said. And I was right; she wasn't there. She was somewhere else in the house.

"Oh. I'll try her later." Click.

Yosie came running back into the room. "Was that for me?"

"Uh-huh," I said. "He didn't have time to wait for you to get to the phone, I guess. He hung up. Was it someone important?"

"None of your business," she pouted and left the room again.

"You are bad," Granny Nan whispered to me through a snide smile.

I got up off the chair, puckered my lips, twisted around, and wiggled my backside at her. "I don't care, because that's the way it works," I said, then I left the room, making sure I kept my legs tight together, putting one foot directly in front of the other so it would make my butt stick out. I could hear Granny Nan sniggering as I left.

I put on my heavy coat and went to the lean-to barn. Two-Tone met me on the way. She was confused. Papa wasn't there anymore, and I hadn't had a lot of time to spend with her. She desperately needed some attention. I'd only been inside the big barn a couple of times since Papa had died, but I knew I was going to have to get over the negative emotions it triggered. I kept telling myself that I should use that reminder as a way of recalling the good times, but that hadn't happened yet. It still made me sad.

I fed and watered the pigs, then I put new straw in the empty cattle stalls; I'd have to call them in real soon, or they'd be out all night, and I didn't know what to expect in the way of weather. If it got too bad, they might seek shelter under a tree instead of coming all the way to the barn. That wasn't anything to be too concerned about, but I knew how the weather could change in a heartbeat, and I didn't want them to be stranded in the middle of a blizzard.

When I saw the cattle making their way to the barn, I went to the coop and fed the chickens and ducks and watered them. Their watering trough had frozen solid, so I had to bust up the ice and refill it. My hands were freezing by the time I was finished. I gathered the eggs knowing my hands would warm up by putting them under the hens. Then I went to the big barn, sat down on a bale of straw, and thought about Dr. Pauley's offer, all the while petting Two-Tone.

There really wasn't much to think about; of course I wanted to work for him! It meant I'd make extra money, and I'd get a real hands-on education before starting vet school. On the downside, it meant Granny Nan would be strapped with way too much, so I decided to approach Bella and Dora about filling in for me when I was gone. They'd understand, and I knew I could depend on them. There were only two little ones left to be tended to—Ronnie and Anna. Ronnie was a little over three, and Anna would be two in a few weeks. Bella was already used to taking care of them both, so she'd be fine with it.

Dora, on the other hand, didn't like taking care of toddlers or babies, and she wasn't fond of doing things around the farm or in the house. She did it, but she always whined about it and pouted afterwards. I hoped she didn't start acting like Yosie. The one thing Dora had going for her was that she liked to cook. She was great at helping Granny Nan in the kitchen.

Retta was the farmhand. She was old enough now to tend the livestock, help with the field work, even bale hay and straw, which she seemed to enjoy, and help Granny Nan with the gardening, including planting, caring for, and picking and canning all the vegetables. During the summer before she had been born, Papa had planted six fruit trees down by the bridge that ran across the road. He knew the trees would have plenty of water and sunshine there. They were nothing more than twigs when he put them in the ground, but now they were big enough to produce fruit, and Retta couldn't wait to pick the apples and cherries. Unfortunately, the deer were good at picking them, too!

❖❖❖

Granny Nan, in all her wisdom, had told me once, "When we finish a chapter in a book, whether it is was funny, heart-warming, disturbing, or tragic, we always turn the page and go on to the next chapter hoping to find it better than the last."

The next morning I told Granny Nan about my plan, and she was thrilled. "Sounds like everyone will be helping, and you will be getting some extra money. Have you talked to Jimmy and Butch yet about Jimmy coming on to work steady?"

"No, I'll be doing that tomorrow." Tomorrow was Saturday, and I'd be free to talk to them without having to rush off to school after going to the milk house. I was really hoping Jimmy hadn't decided to move to his grandfather's place in Chesaning and become a cheese maker. "I'll also call Dr. Pauley back and tell him I'd like to take the job."

CUPID'S ARROW

Life moved on. I no longer went to the library every Monday, partly because there was a pretty good library at the high school. Miss Michaels still came to our house every Monday for supper. She and Granny Nan were great friends. They agreed on most issues, and when they didn't, they weren't afraid to disagree, be it politely. It made me so happy that Granny Nan had another adult to talk to. I know she must have been weary having no one around but us kids.

I worked for Dr. Pauley after school on Wednesdays and Fridays, all day on Saturdays, and after church on Sunday afternoons. Most of the time I went out on farm calls with Dr. Pauley, but sometimes I worked with him in the office seeing small animals, or I answered the phone and did chart filing with Mrs. Pauley. They were incredibly busy people, yet they seldom complained.

Dr. Pauley was a dig-in-and-do-it type of man; he didn't waste any time. He had a great rapport with his clients, and I realized he had a good sense of humor, once I got past his 'all work, no play' façade. He was a wonderful teacher, allowing me to do almost anything he did, except for castrating the beef cattle. "You need to add on a few more pounds and a few more inches before I'll allow you to take a chance with them," he told me. "You just aren't quite big enough to handle them yet."

I wasn't afraid of the bulls, but when the farmers ran them into the squeeze chute, it made them angry, and they kicked a lot. So I had the job of doing what Dr. Pauley called "tail-up," which squelched the kicking, so he could perform the castration and give injections when necessary. I had to climb up onto the outside of the chute, grab the bull's tail, and pull it straight up. That rendered the bull incapable of kicking, except when the tail slipped out of my hands as the bull moved around or jerked unexpectedly, or when I occasionally didn't get it up high enough—at which point Dr. Pauley would yell at me to "Get it up! Higher! Higher!"

I was also able to handle dogs, cats, chickens, rabbits, sheep, goats, and pigs, but I was uncomfortable around horses. And I didn't know why. I had never been afraid of Trot or Ham when I was little, probably because I knew Papa would never let anything hurt me. But now that I was older, I had developed an uneasiness around them. And they could sense it immediately. That tiny bit of hesitation I exhibited was all it took for them to show me what Dr. Pauley referred to as "equine attitude." He could walk right up to a horse, let it smell his hands and whatever he had in them, all the while talking nicely to it in a low, calming voice, and the horse immediately trusted him. (I would eventually learn to do the same thing, but it took me a long time to develop my own style.)

I had obtained a hardship driver's license from the Secretary of State's office. Miss Michaels said, "You probably don't really need it because the police don't seem to patrol the out-roads around Mount Pleasant. But you're better safe than sorry." Sure enough, on the way home that same day, a policeman stopped me just outside of town to make sure I had the right license for someone my age. He decided I was legal, and as soon as he had disappeared, Miss Michaels and I burst out laughing.

"Whew!" I said.

Miss Michaels responded with, "Doesn't that just beat all?"

Mid-summer of 1935 rolled around. Jimmy was turning out to be quite an asset to the farm. He not only helped Butch with the milking, he also did a lot of the field work. In addition to that, he even did repairs to the barns, some of which needed a roof patch or a piece of siding replaced, and he made sure to keep up with the necessary mechanical repairs on the equipment.

He also kept getting better looking! I occasionally found myself staring at him, remembering how "dumpy" he had been as a youngster and how different he appeared now. He was eighteen years old and had developed a distinct proclivity toward responsibility. And he had become a whole lot more verbal; he was adept at carrying on a decent conversation.

"Here's your pay for this week, Jimmy." I handed him some bills folded in half. He knew it included both his and his father's wages. "I added a little bit for you because you did that work on the tractor this week."

"You didn't need to do that, Helmi. I did it 'cause it needed to be fixed 'fore I could use it in the cornfield."

"You could have neglected doing both, but you didn't, and I appreciate that," I told him.

"Thank you most kindly," he said as he reached for the money.

I made a big deal of quickly drawing it back away from his extended hand. "Then again…" I teased, looking away and wrinkling my brow.

He stopped in mid-reach, then he realized I was not serious. He grabbed my hand, and a rush of warmth ran through me; it was like nothing I had ever felt before. I couldn't breathe. My mouth dropped open to let in more air, and I looked directly into his face. He smiled, and my knees went weak. *What is the matter with me?* He continued to hold my hand as he removed the bills from it with his other hand. Then he let go, but he kept looking into my eyes for another few seconds. I blinked. He looked down, turned, and went back to his chores.

I stood there like a bump on a log, not moving, barely breathing. Eventually I closed my mouth. My insides had melted—all except my heart, which was pounding as if I'd just completed a two-mile footrace. My muscles felt weak. My ears were hot; I reached up and put my hands over them, and sure enough, they were extra warm to the touch. I knew what it was, but I was not about to admit it.

I'm only fourteen. Well, fourteen-and-a-half. I can't let myself… Or maybe I can. What am I thinking? I have a farm to run, school to keep up with so I can get into college, a job with Dr. Pauley, and a family who depends on me. I have to keep my mind focused. But he's so nice and so… No, I can't allow myself to…

Up to that point I had made up my mind about not permitting myself to be smitten by some boy until after I finished college. After all, I had only just finished the ninth grade. I had gone to the Ice Cream Parlor with Duane Linley after school three times, and he had joined me several times at the Mount Pleasant Public Library, but he was just a friend. One of Duane's friends who, like Duane, was also a tenth-grader, had asked me out, but I had turned him down because I was too busy with other things.

❖❖❖

Summer was over in the blink of an eye, and I was now a high school sophomore. I was determined to be the top student in my class at graduation. I guess word had gotten around the high school that I was hard to get to know. I wasn't, and I knew that, but because I was so dedicated to my work, I came across as being standoffish.

I was not among the many cliques that existed at Mount Pleasant High. There had been some groups of girls who "hung" together at my one-room school, like the group Yosie led around, but that was nothing compared to the groups in the high school. Most of them were designated by year; tenth graders hung with tenth graders, eleventh graders with eleventh graders. Some cliques existed because of extra-curricular activities. The guys who participated in sports hung around together, and the "popular" girls had their own clique that was dominated by the goddesses who dated the god-like sportsmen.

Those of us who dedicated our high school years almost solely to learning were deemed unworthy to be in a clique. It didn't bother me at all. I was bound and determined to become a veterinarian, and I wasn't going to let something so trivial as being in a clique stand in my way. I did, however, join the high school chorus. We probably could have formed our own clique, but most of us had other interests and didn't have time to hang around together much.

I had never been taught to read music, so I had my work cut out for me in the chorus. One day, just after I had eaten my lunch, I heard someone playing the piano in the music room. I looked in and saw that it was Sandra, the girl who accompanied our chorus. She was in in the eleventh grade. I stood outside the door, mesmerized by her music. I waited for her to come out of the room. "Sandra?"

She stopped and turned to me. "Oh, hi."

"I was listening to you play. It was beautiful," I said.

"Thank you. You're Helmi, aren't you?" she asked.

"Uh-huh. I'm in the chorus."

"Alto, right?"

"Yeah. But I have a little problem. I can't read music, so I just listen to what the other girls sing and then try to remember it. Could you teach me?"

"Wow! That's a big undertaking."

"But most of the other altos don't play any instrument, and they seem to know how to read it," I said.

She thought for a moment. "You're right. It's not like you're asking me to teach you how to play the piano. C'mere." She went back into the music room, motioning for me to follow. She looked at the clock on the wall above the door and said, "We only have a few minutes, but maybe I can get you started." She sat down on one end of the piano bench and patted the other end. I sat down beside her. "I want you to draw the keyboard," she said, pointing at some of the piano keys. "Just from here to here," indicating which section of the keyboard she wanted me to draw. "Tomorrow, meet me here at noon. We'll eat our lunch while we work." Then she got up and walked out.

I quickly took out a piece of paper and rough-sketched the part of the keyboard she wanted me to draw. That afternoon I went to the school library and finished a proper drawing of the white and black keys as they appeared on the piano. Obviously, the keyboard wasn't music, so I was a bit skeptical. I couldn't imagine what that was supposed to do for me, but I had to trust Sandra, as she was the only person I knew who might be able to teach me what I needed to learn.

The next day, I met her at noon. She was pleased to see my drawing and told me it was "perfect." I thanked her for the compliment. "But how is this going to teach me to read music?" I asked.

"You'll learn to make the connection between the notes and where they appear on the keyboard. Then you'll be able to see the keys in your head when you see the notes written on the page. I think it's the easiest way to learn."

"Whatever you say." I still didn't get the connection, but I was willing to let her explain further.

She took out a piece of music and set it up on the piano's music rest in front of me. It was notes on lined paper that looked like the music I had been singing. "Now, I want you to write the names of the notes on your drawing." She pointed to one of the piano keys and said, "This is called 'F.' It's the note you'll find in the first space on your music. If you notice, there are five lines on a staff, which makes four spaces in between them." She pointed to the music and counted the four spaces. "Each of the spaces represents one note, and from the bottom up, they spell the word FACE." She pointed to each space and said, "F-A-C-E."

"That's easy enough," I said and pointed to the bottom space. "And F is this note on the keyboard," I said and pointed to it with my other hand.

"That's right. Now you can write F on your keyboard." She played the F note a few times while I wrote 'F' on my drawing. I went on writing the names of the notes on the keyboard I had drawn and matching them with the spaces on the music. Then Sandra played the notes in order on the real keyboard. "Sing them with me while we say their names," she said. We did, and I was beginning to understand. "Take this music with you and practice singing the notes in the spaces. Tomorrow we'll do the lines."

I was fascinated with matching the notes to the lines and spaces on what Sandra had called a staff. And the idea of them all being represented on the keyboard made me aware of where they fell within a whole piece of music. An entirely new world was opening up for me. I couldn't wait to go to chorus each day and see how many of those notes were in the alto part of the pieces we were singing.

Over the next three weeks, I met with Sandra every day in the music room at lunchtime. I picked up the idea of following the notes up and down within the music we sang. I even conquered flats, sharps, and naturals, and I knew about octaves and clefs and pianissimo and fortissimo. I learned about meter and tempo and the differences in quarter notes, eighth notes, half notes, whole notes, and rests. For the first time, I understood the range relationships among sopranos, altos, tenors, and bases.

Sandra was good at helping me understand what she taught me. I found out years later that, after she graduated, she went to a special music school in Michigan and became a famous pianist who traveled all over the world performing with major orchestras.

Miss Michaels had never taught us to read music; I'm not sure she even knew how herself. We did lots of singing, but she didn't use the piano that was in our one-room school, nor did we have music books. Everything we sang was either what we already knew or something she taught us from her memory. Once in a while some of the kids sat down at the piano and "played," but nothing that resembled actual written music.

The main thing Miss Michaels said was, "Don't bang on the keys!" Someone once asked her to play something, but she said she didn't know how. I remember the piano in the one-room school sounding a lot different from the one in the high school. I learned it was because that piano had never been tuned.

I asked Sandra who could teach me to play piano. She referred me to her teacher, Lillian Andrews. I took lessons for the remainder of my high school years, practicing in the music room each day at lunchtime. Sometimes Sandra was there to help me, too. I loved being able to turn those little black blotches on the page into something beautiful. Well, maybe not beautiful, but at least good enough to be recognized as music.

Bella and Dora were growing up so fast I hardly recognized them from one day to the next. Retta was going to be nine in August, and without her, I fear the farm might not have survived as well as it did after Papa died; she was a true blessing. Ronnie was three, but she was a whiner; nothing was ever right—food, living arrangements, her sisters. Granny Nan said she was "a difficult child."

Anna, too, was difficult, but not because of attitude. Her difficulty was physical. She didn't want to learn to walk. She had turned two in February, and now it was late May, and she still had no desire to go anywhere unassisted. She didn't even like to sit and play; she wanted to lie down all the time. When Granny Nan or Bella sat her up, she bent over forward and put her hands in front of her, propping herself up. After sitting in that position for only a short amount of time, she began to cry and rolled over into the fetal position.

Granny Nan talked to Bella and me about it, and we decided it was time to take her to see Doc Barrett. He took one look at her and said, "She has scoliosis. She needs therapy." He gave us a paper that showed how we should "bend" her in various positions. We tried our best, but after only a minute of Anna screaming in pain, we couldn't take it any longer.

We took her to Flint to see a spine specialist, and he said we were doing exactly what needed to be done. "Dr. Barrett's right. You'll just have to tune out the crying and screaming and keep it up. She has no chance of getting better if you don't."

I felt so sorry for Anna, but I knew that sometimes we have to do things that make us uneasy. Or in Anna's case, things that make us cringe.

Granny Nan agreed that no child could be more difficult, however, than Yosie. She had turned thirteen in April of that year. When someone talks about how challenging it is to care for a thirteen-year-old, they have no clue as to the challenge that girl was. The tantrums, the obstinance, the moodiness, and the downright disrespect were beyond maddening for all of us. I can remember one instance in particular: Granny Nan was making sandwiches for us for school, and Yosie came down the stairs. She was still in her nightgown.

"Good morning, glory," Granny Nan said to her. "How does your dew drop?"

Yosie looked at her with pure disgust in her eyes. "That is so stupid. Why do you say that?"

"Just trying to cheer you up."

Yosie rolled her eyes.

Granny Nan continued making the sandwiches. "You are a little late coming down for breakfast this morning. And you are usually dressed when you come down."

"I'm not going to school today."

"Are you sick?" Granny Nan asked.

"No."

"Is there some other reason behind your decision not to go?"

"Just don't want to," Yosie plopped down on one of the kitchen chairs.

Granny Nan stopped making the sandwiches and asked, "Why do you not want to go?"

Yosie said through a yawn, "Just don't."

"Well then," Granny said and disappeared into the front room.

After a few minutes, Yosie appeared at the front room archway. "Are you going to fix my breakfast?"

"No," Granny Nan said, nonchalantly.

"Why not?"

"Just don't want to," Granny Nan said.

Yosie obviously got the message. She whipped around, returned to the kitchen, and picked up one of the sandwiches Granny Nan had made. She sat back down at the table and ate it, dropping crumbs all over the floor and leaving the bread crusts on the table. Then she went back upstairs. Granny Nan returned to the kitchen and finished making the sandwiches. She put three of them, not four, in a lunch sack, and mine remained on the table, as usual.

I had finished my chores, including feeding the chickens and ducks and saying hello to Butch and Jimmy. I came back into the house and found my sandwich, wrapped in waxed paper. I always carried a cloth bag with me to school; it held necessities, and I slid my sandwich into that bag. Then I went upstairs to finish getting ready for school. When I came down, I went into the front room to say goodbye to Granny Nan. She had a smirk on her face.

"What are you smirking about?" I asked her.

"Oh, nothing. What was Yosie doing upstairs?"

"I guess she was getting ready for school. Why?"

"Just curious. She said she was not going to go today, but I have a feeling she will change her mind."

Yosie stomped down the stairs and flew past Granny Nan and me, picking up the bag of sandwiches as she passed. She flounced out the back door, letting the door slam (or making certain it did, I wasn't sure which) with not so much as a look at either of us.

"I cannot wait until lunchtime," Granny Nan said.

"What?"

"Oh, nothing." Granny Nan went back to the kitchen and began cleaning up the mess Yosie had left on and around the table.

I wondered what Granny Nan had up her sleeve, but I couldn't pursue it, or I'd be late for school. I usually dropped the girls off, then I went on to the high school. Bella, Dora, and Retta all came bounding out to the truck. Yosie was sitting in the passenger seat, pouting. Retta said she was going to walk because it was such a pretty morning, and Bella and Dora decided they would, too. Yosie, of course, didn't budge.

I dropped her off at the end of the lane that went to the one-room school and said, "Tell Miss Michaels I said hello."

I got no response. Yosie got out of the truck and turned to leave. "Wait, Yosie! The sandwiches."

She snatched the bag from me and turned back toward the school. I couldn't help myself; I said, "You look really pretty. I hope you have a nice day." Again, no response, but I could almost feel her eyes rolling into the top of her head. I went on to Mount Pleasant.

That afternoon, when I got home, I found Granny Nan and Yosie in the middle of a heated discussion, Yosie creating the majority of the heat. "I had to ask the other kids for something to eat. Do you know how embarrassing that was?" She was shouting at Granny Nan.

Granny Nan was staring right through her, not saying a word.

"What's the problem?" I asked.

Yosie pointed at Granny Nan. "The problem is sitting right there!"

"And Granny Nan is a problem because…?" I asked.

"Because she didn't make me any lunch."

Granny Nan calmly said, "You ate your lunch sandwich for breakfast, and you told me you were not going to school today. Why would I make you another one?"

If the glare Yosie gave Granny Nan had been only a tad stronger, it would have stopped time. "I wasn't going to go to school until I realized I'd have to spend the day with YOU. I HATE YOU!" She whirled around to go upstairs, but I stepped in front of her.

"Take it back."

"NO!"

"Yosie, apologize to Granny Nan."

"I won't, and you can't make me!"

Granny Nan calmly said, "She does not have to apologize. I have been told I was hated by *far* more important people than Yosie."

That must have really gotten Yosie's goat. She sputtered unrelated syllables, trying desperately to form a sentence, but failed. So she looked straight up at the ceiling and screamed at the top of her lungs—a long, exasperated scream—then crumpled down onto her knees, sobbing and breathing heavily, as if she were about to die.

Without another word, Granny Nan got up and left the room, and I headed upstairs, both of us doing our best to ignore Yosie's tantrum. Later, I came downstairs, and Yosie was still lying on the floor where she had collapsed. *She's really good at this*, I thought. But it didn't matter; I wasn't going to acknowledge her cry for attention. I walked toward her, and she started to get up, probably thinking I was going to offer some sort of commiseration. Instead, I made a point of stepping over her on my way outside.

When I came back in, quite a while later, Yosie was no longer occupying the floor. She didn't come down to supper that night, either. I suspected she was getting pretty hungry, considering she had only eaten the paltry bits she could sponge from the other kids at school. And it had been a long time since her breakfast sandwich. I wasn't sure whether her absence from the supper table was self-inflicted or a direct order from Granny Nan.

❖❖❖

September, 1936, arrived. I was entering my junior year of high school. I would be sixteen in two months. I had taken a growth spurt during the summer. I figured I was destined to be tall, like Papa. Unfortunately, none of my clothes fit me anymore. I was going to have to use part of my wages from Dr. Pauley to buy some new "duds." I thought I might ask one of my friends from the chorus to go with me to help me find things that were more in vogue than what I was used to wearing. We set a date for the next Thursday. Granny Nan even said, "I will be happy to watch the 'young ones' by myself if it means you can get yourself spiffed up at bit."

"Are you saying I've been looking less than spiffy in the recent past?" I asked her, teasingly.

"Not for doing your chores."

Wow! Maybe I am overdue for an update, I thought. "I didn't know you were such a fan of fashion."

"I go to church and other places once in a while, and I can recognize the difference between spiffy and dowdy."

My dedication to our farm had become a major concern for me. I was facing the daunting task of deciding what to do about it when the time arrived for me to go to college. And it was coming up fast. I knew it would be a topic for discussion with Granny Nan, Butch, and Jimmy. I thought we should probably include Retta, too, since she would be filling my shoes around the farm.

Butch's age was beginning to show; he was moving much slower, he groaned a lot when he stooped or lifted, and he fell asleep at the drop of a hat. In fact, he told Jimmy he'd found himself on the floor of the stanchion barn one morning when he drifted off while waiting for the last batch of cows to finish milking. Seems he'd gone to sleep sitting on the bucket and wound up falling over sideways. He told Jimmy he didn't even wake up when he hit the floor.

Butch and his wife had been up in years when they had married, and Jimmy, it turns out, was a change-of-life-baby, meaning he was born just around the time his mother was experiencing the onset of menopause. She didn't even know she was going to have a baby until the fourth month of her pregnancy. And her death, I'd come to find out, was partly due to her inability to recuperate after Jimmy's birth. All of that information accounted for why Butch seemed to be deteriorating so rapidly. Jimmy's parents were the age of most kids' grandparents.

I'd finally learned to be around Jimmy without having trouble breathing. He had become a pleasant source of conversation. He talked about regular life as if it were something special. He was a hopeless romantic and wore his emotions on his sleeve. I realized he had been extremely shy when he was young. What I had originally perceived as being "slow" was, instead, a result of his shyness. I had learned that he was becoming more and more decisive as he grew older. He wouldn't put one foot in front of the other before determining whether that was the right place to put it.

He was not very well informed about the world outside of our little part of Michigan, so our conversations were limited to some degree. I tried to talk about worldly things, but he was simply not equipped to do so. Neither he nor his father ever listened to any radio shows except Jack Benny, Fred Allen, and "Your Hit Parade." They only heard the news if a news flash interrupted or followed a program they normally listened to.

Jimmy was intelligent, however, be it on a different plane than mine. He did a lot of thinking; he simply couldn't communicate it well. I could almost see the wheels turning in his brain, but the road didn't usually lead to his mouth; he was often unable to express his thoughts in words.

I understood why he hadn't been a good student and why he chose to quit school and do what he did best—farming. He knew just about everything there was to know on that subject. He made a point of going to the local feed store and talking to the other farmers who frequented it. He was a good friend of the county extension agent for Isabella County and recognized him as a prime source for information in all matters related to farming.

"Dad's gonna have to quit," Jimmy said to me one day, out of the blue.

"Why? What's the problem?" I asked, immediately thinking the worst.

"He's just too old and tired to keep going."

I had known this day would come. "Do you know someone who could step in for him?" I asked, my insides churning. "We have to have more help around here. I wouldn't think of asking you to take over all the work; it would just be too much. It'd have to be someone who knows how to handle cows and could be here every morning and evening for the milking. Maybe…"

"Wait, wait, wait!" Jimmy grabbed me by the shoulders, and that feeling of warmth came over me. "Let's not jump off the bridge just yet," he said matter-of-factly.

He was right. I'd gone ballistic without legitimate instigation. But in my own defense, he had hit a nerve, and I was truly scared about what would happen to our farm if I lost the man in whom I had total confidence to run the dairy. I took a deep breath and looked up at Jimmy. He didn't say anything else, he just held me by my shoulders and looked back at me.

"Sorry," I said, looking down and breaking the gaze between us. I closed my eyes and took another deep breath. I looked back up at him, and without warning, he kissed me. His lips were soft, moist, warm, and wonderful! I didn't struggle against him; I *allowed* him to kiss me. When the kiss ended, he smiled down at me, his head still cocked sideways. Then he let go my shoulders and backed away a couple of steps.

I was completely befuddled. I was panting. I looked at him and said, breathlessly, "Cheese and crackers!"

Jimmy laughed, quietly at first, then louder, then he broke into a full-on guffaw. "That's the first time I ever got that reaction," he said.

"Just how many reactions have you gotten?" I asked.

"I've kissed my fair share of the ladies."

And why wouldn't he? He was gorgeous, and I was sure the ladies hadn't fought him off. Probably all he had to do was indicate the least bit of interest, and they'd fall all over him.

"I have to gather eggs." I turned and left.

THE ARTIST AND THE SKUNK

It was Sunday afternoon. Everyone else had come home from church, and I was getting ready to go to work at Dr. Pauley's. Granny Nan and Dora were in the kitchen fixing our lunch. We had become so accustomed to calling the mid-day meal "lunch," now, that we rarely used the word "dinner" anymore. I could smell it upstairs where I was gathering up dirty clothes that would need to be washed for the upcoming week. I knew we were going to have leftovers, which was fine by me. I was never one to mind eating something twice within a few days; I had come to realize that we were lucky enough to have food to feed all of us three times a day every day, and I was thankful for that.

I went into the room where Dora and Yosie slept, and there, lying on Dora's bed was a big pad of paper, not the usual writing paper like we used in school. This was much larger. I had never seen paper that big, so I was curious. I lifted the cover, and to my surprise, there was a drawing of Yosie sitting at the window with her back to me. Her dark curls were fluffy and shiny; I could almost make out each individual hair. She was looking into a hand mirror, which reflected her face. Her expression was provocative, restless, lascivious, as if she knew someone were watching and she purposefully wanted to project a wanton appearance.

I leafed through the pages and gazed at drawing after drawing of the animals and buildings around our farm, our old dilapidated truck, people from the one-room school—some of whom I recognized and younger ones I didn't—and each of us in the family, even Papa. *Where did Dora get this?*

Then the truth of the matter hit me like a bolt out of the blue—those were *her* drawings! She was the artist! I had no idea she possessed such a talent. I closed the pad and scooted back away from it as if it were alive and might bite me. I knew I had snooped into something I had no business seeing. Not that it contained anything I shouldn't see, but because Dora had not seen fit to show it to me. I went back to gathering dirty clothes, most of which were strewn on the floor instead of in the downstairs laundry basket.

I went back downstairs and separated the dirty clothes into loads, making sure the load of whites didn't include something of another color that would bleed. I put that load into the washer, added soap powder, and turned on the hot water, all the while thinking about the quality of Dora's drawings—the moods she had captured, and the detail. I felt so guilty about having invaded her privacy, as if I had innocently walked into a room and caught people in the middle of an intimate moment. It was gnawing at me, but I knew I'd have to keep it a secret until Dora decided it was the right time to reveal what she had created.

Everyone finished lunch and went back to the things that occupied them on a normal Sunday afternoon. "You certainly are quiet today," Granny Nan said to me. "Something you want to talk about?" She had taken Mama's place at perceiving my usually well-hidden emotional diversity.

"No. I just need some time to think through something," I told her. "Thanks for asking, though."

"I will be here when you are ready to talk about whatever it is."

I smiled at her. I loved her so much, and I cherished her reciprocation of that feeling. "I need to get going, or I'll be late for work."

"Thank you for putting the load of laundry in for me," she said.

"Wish I could be here to take it out and hang it for you, too."

"Do not be concerned about that. I would not know what to do with myself if I had five minutes without a pressing duty."

"I know how you feel, Granny Nan. Sometimes I wonder what a life of luxury would be like. But then I think of poor Uncle Julius and realize his life was no better than ours, even though he paid people to do the things we work at every day."

She sighed. Her face became long and sad. "I got a letter from an asylum in Chicago. Lavern is there. She has developed brain fever and does not recognize anyone."

"Oh, Granny Nan! How long ago did the letter come?"

"Just last week. I cannot make a trip to see her. My bones are too brittle."

Her daughter, her eldest, her only remaining child, was wasting away in an asylum in a city filled with too many people. I had no idea how many friends Aunt Lavern had, but I knew she didn't have any family to comfort her. And I didn't know exactly what Granny Nan meant by "brain fever."

I couldn't speak; there was a huge lump in my throat. I put my hand on her arm and wanted so desperately to say something that would ease her pain. I hoped the touch between us would convey that feeling.

"Go, now," she said. "You must not be late."

We both rose from our chairs and proceeded to do whatever needed to be done. That was the way of our lives—we did whatever needed to be done. Day in and day out. Over and over.

Dr. Pauley was waiting for me in the clinic parking lot. He was pacing beside his truck and looking at his pocket watch when I pulled in. "Hurry!" he shouted. "We have an emergency!"

I parked next to his truck and got out. He handed me the key to the clinic door and said, "Put on your coveralls and get your boots. We have what sounds like an LDA at Jacob Miller's place."

I hurried to the back entrance where we all kept our coats, coveralls, and boots.

"Be sure you lock the door on your way out. And hurry!"

I slipped into my coveralls and picked up my boots, figuring I could put them on in transit since Dr. Pauley was in such a hurry. I started out to his truck then remembered I hadn't locked the door. I turned and went back. I fumbled trying to put the key in the lock, I was in such a rush. I finally managed to lock it just as I heard Dr. Pauley shout, "Come on! Come on! We don't have much time."

I ran to his truck. He had already gotten in and started it, and before I could get all the way in, he had the truck in gear and was pulling away. I hung on for dear life, struggling to close my door. I finally managed and let out a "Whew!" I looked over at him, and he was concentrating on the road in front of us; his face was wrinkled with tension. "OK, what's an LDA?" I asked.

"Left displaced abomasum," he said. I waited for more, but that was all he said.

I waited a few seconds longer. Nothing. *Should I ask? Is he going to tell me?* More seconds passed. "I realize that's what the acronym stands for, but I don't know what the condition is."

"I thought you'd know," he teased, and he looked over at me, smiling.

I closed my eyes and shook my head. "I need more information if I'm going to help you," I told him.

"Good. I'm glad you had enough intestinal fortitude to ask. Cows have more than one stomach. You know that, right?"

"Yes, and I think one of them is called the abomasum."

"You are absolutely right. Sometimes it acts like a balloon and floats up out of place. We have to put it back where it belongs and tie it there so it doesn't float away again."

I said, "So...the cow's abomasum floats out of place and has to be put back and tied. How do you do that?"

"We roll her over onto her back."

I blinked a few times. *Roll her over? Did he really mean that?* "Will she be standing up when we get there?"

"Maybe. Maybe not. Hopefully not, which will eliminate the step of getting her to lie down."

I was eager to see how all of this was going to be accomplished. "And what do you tie it with?"

"A big-bore needle and very large suture."

This could be pretty exciting. I can't wait!

When we arrived, Dr. Pauley shouted, "Jacob!"

The Amish man appeared in the doorway of a large barn and waved. Dr. Pauley waved back in response then went to the back of the truck and opened the tailgate. He pulled things out, handing them to me, then we went to the barn.

"Jacob." Dr. Pauley shook the man's hand. "Good to see you. Where is the cow?"

"Right over here," Jacob said and led the way into the dark barn. I recognized the man as one of the Amish people who had helped build our barns and house.

A big Holstein was standing up in a straw-covered stall; she was tied to the front of the enclosure. Jacob Miller turned toward me. I said, "Hello, Mr. Miller. I'm Helmi Schnier. You and your sons helped build our house and out-buildings several years back."

"You have grown up," he said. "How is your father?"

"I'm afraid he passed away sometime back."

"I'm so sorry," he said.

"Are your sons around?" Dr. Pauley asked him.

Jacob Miller nodded.

"We'll need them," Dr. Pauley said. "We have to roll this cow onto her back, and you and I and Helmi aren't going to be able to do that by ourselves." He looked over at me and pointed. "Helmi's a strong girl, but we're going to need more muscle to roll this cow."

Mr. Miller turned and left.

Dr. Pauley said, "Jacob is a man of few words, as I'm sure you gathered."

I nodded. "He and his sons sure made short work of putting up our buildings when we moved here."

"They are hard workers, that's for sure." Dr. Pauley untied the cow and led her to the open part of the barn. "Get some straw and scatter it around over there. It'll take three or four bales to cushion her when she goes down."

By the time I had the straw down, Jacob and his two sons had returned. Dr. Pauley had tied the cow to the outside of the nearest stall and was listening to her side through his stethoscope. At the same time, he was flicking her side with his thumb and middle finger. "It makes a pinging sound, like an inflated ball. Here, listen." He handed me the stethoscope. I inserted the earpieces, and he flicked the cow's side. He was right. It sounded exactly as he had described.

As if on cue, the cow lay down on the straw. "Well, there's a piece of luck," Dr. Pauley said. "Okay. Each of you position yourselves at one of her legs. Why don't you big guys," he motioned toward Jacob's sons, "get on the back legs. Be careful, she'll probably want to kick. Jacob, you take her left front leg, and Helmi, you push up on her right front as she begins to roll." I handed the stethoscope back to him.

Everyone got into position. "Ready? One, two, THREE!" Samuel, the bigger of the two sons, and Jacob pulled the cow toward them. Surprisingly, she didn't put up much of an argument, and I was able to push her front leg until she was lying there on her back, all four feet straight up in the air. Once again, Dr. Pauley listened to her, but this time he was pinging her belly. "And there it is," he said. He moved to my position and handed me the stethoscope. "Flick it and listen."

I did.

"Do you hear it? Move the stethoscope around and listen to the difference in sound in various places."

I was amazed at how clearly I could tell exactly where the abomasum was. "And it just floated back to where it's supposed to be when we rolled her?"

"Yep. Her rumen, the largest stomach, was most likely empty, or close to being empty. It's usually full and holds the abomasum in place. But when a cow doesn't eat, the rumen gets empty and shrinks up, so it can't hold the abomasum down."

"So that's why you're going to tie it in place," I said. "I get it."

"Come back over here and hold this leg," he said. Then he took out the big curved needle and thick suture material. He stuck the needle into the cow's belly, pushing it hard to penetrate the thick hide, and it came back up a few inches away. He pulled it through and tied a knot in the suture, making a loop. Then he repeated the procedure.

"OK, let's get her up. Roll her back over toward me."

We rolled her, and she immediately stood back up.

Dr. Pauley talked to Jacob about what he was feeding her. Jacob told Dr. Pauley he was dry feeding her. Turns out, she had just had twin calves, which left a lot of extra space in her abdomen. The dry feed wasn't filling her rumen the way it should have; it was allowing the rumen to remain small enough to let the abomasum float around it, and the increased amount of space following the birth of the twin calves made that even more possible. That's why it had to be tied in place.

While Dr. Pauley and Jacob conversed more about the changes that needed to be made in his cows' feeding regimen, I took the supplies back to the truck. When the men all came out of the barn, I waved and shouted, "Nice to see you all again." Then I got into the truck, and they talked for a few more minutes.

When Dr. Pauley and I were on our way back to the vet clinic. I said, "I guess people just lost their cows before there were phones to call the vet. Am I right?"

"Or they came looking for me if they didn't know how to fix the problem themselves," he said. He sounded much calmer than he had at our initial greeting that day. "Usually by the time I got there, the cow was already dead. Telephones have certainly made life more pleasant for the farmers and their cows, but they sure have created more work for us."

"I don't mind the work," I said. "I just like that 'feel good' reaction when it's over. Makes it all seem worthwhile."

"Well, you have to realize that sometimes that 'feel good' reaction doesn't happen. It can be the opposite, you know."

Yes, I knew…more than I wanted to admit.

We went back to the clinic, and the phone rang within a few minutes after going inside. I had just removed my boots and hung my coveralls on their hook. I answered it and spoke to a woman who was in hysterics; it was difficult to understand exactly what she was saying. "Just a minute, I'll talk to the doctor."

I put the receiver down on the desk and found Dr. Pauley in his office. "There's a woman on the phone, a Mrs. Anderson, I think, who says her dog was attacked by a coyote. She's really upset and wants to bring it in. What should I tell her?"

He forced a stream of air through his nose. "Damn that woman! She knows there are coyotes around her farm, yet she insists on allowing her precious little mutt to roam free after I've told her time and again, 'Either confine it while it's out, or walk it on a leash.'"

I was taken back for a moment. I had never heard him talk about a client before. But I realized he was right. I was about to have my first lesson in dealing with a pet owner who either wasn't smart enough to figure out why the dog had gotten mauled, or too obstinate to pay heed to what a professional had suggested to her numerous times.

"Tell her to bring it in. But she needs to know she'll be paying for an after-hours call."

I went back to the phone and gently coaxed her into calming down enough to give me the necessary information. I also informed her about the additional charge. She didn't seem to have any problem with that. She told me she'd be right in. I pulled her chart and found out she lived about twelve miles from the clinic, so I knew she'd arrive in less than half an hour.

One hour and ten minutes later she pulled into the parking lot. I watched as she calmly got out of her car, went around to the other side, and picked up her little dog, which looked like a small terrier mix. She wrapped it in a blanket and came leisurely up to the door. I waited until she rang the bell, then I unlocked the door to let her in. As I opened the door, I saw her face make an immediate change from placid to frantic.

"Is the doctor here? I called his wife, and she said he'd be here. I'm so worried. Oh, please help my poor little baby." She began to cry.

I was getting mixed emotions. *Am I supposed to feel sorry for her? Her little dog doesn't appear to be in pain—it's not shaking, panting, or whining. It doesn't even seem to be in shock. I swear this woman just turned the tears on to convince me that her dog is in far worse shape than I'm guessing it is. I wonder if she has some ulterior motive.*

I started toward Dr. Pauley's office to let him know she was there, but he met me halfway to the exam room. "Bring her in," he said.

I asked Mrs. Anderson to follow me, but she shoved me aside and wailed, "Oh, Dr. Pauley, my poor little baby is nearly torn to shreds. You have to help her." She went into the exam room and gingerly laid her "poor little baby" on the table, all the while making sobbing noises and putting on quite a show. I had to give her credit for her performance.

"Mrs. Anderson, what did I tell you about not letting Wiggles out by herself?" He looked pointedly at her.

"I forgot. And when I heard scratching at the door, I looked out, and there she was, limping and crying. I knew immediately what had happened. But I knew you'd be able to fix her. You're such a good doctor."

Oh, brother! How can he legitimately deal with people like this?

"Let's take a look at the damage." He unwrapped the dog, Wiggles, and did a once-over. "I think she was lucky. She may have a bruised paw. Nothing's broken, though, and I don't even see any broken skin. Was she bleeding when she came to your door?"

"I don't know. I was afraid to look. I just can't stand the sight of blood." She leaned over the table and kissed Wiggles from head to tail, crying all the while.

I was standing by the door. Dr. Pauley looked over at me with an expression I had never before encountered, neither on *his* face nor anyone else's. When the doggie kissing stopped, Mrs. Anderson reached for Dr. Pauley's hand, but before she could make contact, he turned to the counter behind him and picked up the instrument used for looking into eyes and ears. "Come and hold Wiggles," he said to me. "Mrs. Anderson, you'll have to step aside."

She moved about six inches to her right. I stepped up to the table and not-so-gently moved her over another foot or so.

"Why don't you take a seat, Mrs. Anderson," Dr. Pauley said to the woman. "I want to make sure I haven't missed anything." My back was to Mrs. Anderson, and I looked up at Dr. Pauley, forcing myself to remain professional when what I really wanted to do was turn around and smack the woman to bring her out of her false display of hysteria.

Dr. Pauley listened, poked, probed, bent, twisted, and did everything possible to check that little dog. There was nothing wrong with it, not even a bruised paw.

"I think you and Wiggles were lucky this time. I can't find anything wrong with her."

"I'm soooooooo relieved," she pretended to be close to fainting, fanning her face with one hand and placing the other hand over her heart. She came to a sudden halt. "Oh, thank you, Dr. Pauley. I knew you'd do whatever would be best for my little Wiggles. You are so kind." She started toward him, but he dodged her maneuver by moving around the back side of the table, putting me between her and himself.

"Helmi, here, will take care of your bill. She informed you there would be an after-hours charge?" He handed Wiggles to me, and I passed the dog along to Mrs. Anderson.

"Yes, but since you didn't find anything wrong, I don't see why I need to pay extra."

"You aren't paying for what was wrong or not wrong with your dog, Mrs. Anderson. You are paying for the time that your visit took us away from our families and homes on a day when the clinic is not normally open. You can understand that, I'm sure. I trust you'll have a much better evening now that you know Wiggles is without injuries. Good day, Mrs. Anderson." He left the room and went back down the hall to his office.

I went to the front desk, followed by Mrs. Anderson and Wiggles, who was now living up to her name, wiggling to get down. Mrs. Anderson put the dog on the floor where it immediately squatted and left a puddle on the floor of the waiting room. The woman watched the ordeal but offered no apologies. She simply turned to me and asked, "How much?"

I gave her the figure, and she handed me a twenty-dollar bill. "I don't have change for that, Mrs. Anderson. Do you happen to have anything smaller?"

"Why no. I guess you'll just have to send me an invoice," she said in a syrupy voice, a smirk on her face.

"I have change," Dr. Pauley said. He was standing at the hallway door.

"Oh, Dr. Pauley," Mrs. Anderson said, an air of surprise in her voice. "Why, let me look again. I...I *might* have something smaller tucked away in my wallet." She put the twenty-dollar bill back in her handbag and said, "Here you go," giving me the exact amount due.

I wrote up a receipt, tore it out of the book, and gave it to her. She didn't say a word to me, but she smiled at Dr. Pauley and said, "Sometimes these big handbags tend to hide their contents." She bent down and picked up the dog, stepping in the urine on the floor. "Thank you again, Dr. Pauley. Please give your wife my regards. She's such a nice lady. You are lucky to have her."

Without a reply, Dr. Pauley opened the door for her, closed it behind her, then made a point of acting like he was kicking it shut. "And that, my dear Helmi, is one of the darker sides of the veterinary business."

I mopped up the dog's urine and the footprints Mrs. Anderson had left behind when she walked to the door. When I was finished, I opened Wiggles' chart and wrote down what had taken place. Dr. Pauley and his wife had both told me, "If it isn't written down, it didn't happen." Usually, Dr. Pauley wrote the stuff down himself, but because I was there, he knew I'd take care of it. And I think he was probably afraid he'd write something in the file that he'd regret later.

❖❖❖

I got home around five-thirty. Granny Nan and Dora were both scurrying around putting supper on the table. I picked up the silverware, but Dora snatched it from my hand and said, "Oh, no you don't! You go wash up and change your clothes. You stink!"

I hadn't thought about that, but she was probably right. I went to the junk room by the back door. I could smell myself, and it wasn't pleasant. I began to undress. The smell seemed to be getting stronger, but it didn't smell like anything I had encountered during my afternoon affairs; it was much more pungent. I wondered if there was something outside that might be wafting in, so I went to the door. There was Two-Tone, wagging and grinning at me like she always did when I came home. The aroma almost knocked me off my feet. It dawned on me that she hadn't come running up to greet me when I had first arrived.

"What is that awful smell?" I heard Yosie shout from the stairwell. She was just coming down for supper. She hadn't helped with any of it. *Imagine that!* And she had her nose pinched between her thumb and index finger.

"A skunk!" Granny Nan shouted, her voice breaking as she gagged. I looked out past Two-Tone and caught a glimpse of black and white fur disappearing behind the big barn. That's why she didn't greet me. I closed the door on her and said, "Sorry, but you'll have to wait until some of that stench disappears before anyone will be petting you." I felt sorry for her, but I was going to throw up if the smell became any stronger.

"We will have to leave that entrance closed for a while," Granny Nan said. "The dog will have left some of the oil from that skunk on the stoop, and if we walk in it, we will drag it right into the house." She came back to where I was standing in my underwear, reached up and clicked the lock, and put her hand over her nose and mouth. "Did you touch her?" she asked me, the words muffled behind her hand.

"No, thank goodness," I said. "I saw the skunk just in time to realize what happened. Brother! Does that ever stink!"

No one seemed too interested in supper that night; more than half of it was left for another meal.

FOUR EYES

I squinted, blinked, and rubbed my eyes, but the print didn't get any clearer in the book I was reading. I closed the book and turned off the light beside my bed. Retta was already asleep; she was always able to fall asleep immediately, even when I was up late doing homework. Sometimes I'd try to carry on a conversation with her, but as soon as her head hit the pillow, she was out.

No one in my family had ever had eye problems, so it was difficult for me to accept that I was unfortunate enough to be the first. Since there was no ophthalmologist in Mount Pleasant, I was going to have go to Flint for an eye exam. I had never driven in Flint before, so I was nervous. I had called Uncle Herman and asked him to take me, but he couldn't because he'd still be at work, and Lizzy was away at college. I really hoped Mary would be able to go with me, but she had a conflicting appointment. I was on my own.

I had suggested to Granny Nan that she might want to make an appointment at the same time as mine, but she had taken it as a personal affront and said, "I can see perfectly! Why would I need to go to an eye doctor?"

I thought she probably needed to see the eye doctor more than I did, but I said, "I guess I was just hoping for some company."

"You will do fine by yourself. Consider it a vacation from all of us," she said and giggled. "And you will be eating supper with Herman and Mary after your appointment, so you will be in good company. I need to stay here to fix supper for your sisters. You just be careful driving after dark."

"I will."

I had to take an appointment during school, so I was excused from my last three classes of the day, one of which was chorus; I hated to miss that. The others were English and geometry; I didn't mind missing them. English was no problem whatsoever, but I knew I'd need help to get the geometry homework done if I didn't hear and see it being done on the blackboard in class. Hopefully I'd be able to get help during my one study hall, second period of the day. I knew there were a couple of kids in there who were also in my geometry class, and I was sure one of them would show me any new material they'd covered during my absence.

It was odd leaving school in the early afternoon; I felt like I was doing something sinister, committing some sort of crime. But as soon as I got on the road, I forgot all about that feeling and began getting jittery about driving through Flint. The woman who had made my appointment over the telephone had given me explicit directions to the office, and it sounded easy. I had also confirmed the directions with Uncle Herman, and he'd said, "It's easy, kiddo. You'll find it without any trouble, I guarantee it. Just go four blocks past our street, turn left onto the main drag, and the office is in that block on the right. The parking lot's behind the building, so turn right on the other side of the building, park, and use the rear entrance." I knew it must be easy; Uncle Herman wouldn't steer me in the wrong direction.

I did fine, just like Uncle Herman said I would. When I walked into the building, there was a sign listing all the businesses within. Dr. Cecil Allen, Ophthalmology, was on the second floor.

I climbed the stairway beside the entrance. When I reached the second floor, I looked around and saw three separate doors. I located the one that had his name painted on the glass and went into his office. It was plain, and when I went up to the counter, my footsteps echoed. The woman behind it asked for my name; her voice also echoed. I filled out a couple of papers and then sat down.

After only a few minutes, a small young woman with blond hair came to a side door and called my name. I rose and followed her down a hallway with rooms on either side, all of them dark. She took me into one and sat me down in a special chair in the back of the room. She asked me some questions then said, "Dr. Allen will be with you shortly," and left me alone.

I was fascinated with what was all around me. I had never seen any ocular equipment before, so it was all strange. Dr. Allen came in and greeted me with a big smile. He was as tall as Papa had been, maybe even taller. He made me feel calm and comfortable. He proceeded to examine my vision and determined that I did, indeed, need glasses.

"You will only have to wear these for reading and studying. Your distance vision is still good," he said. "I suggest you get a cord that goes around your neck and holds the glasses when you aren't using them. That way you won't have to keep looking for them all the time. Most people who use reading glasses put them down someplace, then they promptly forget where they used them last and have to retrace their steps to find them the next time they need them."

I nodded and asked him, "What exactly is my visual condition called?"

He stopped writing in my chart and looked up at me with a startled expression. "You are considered to be farsighted," he said.

"Yes, I understand that, but what is the medical term for it?"

He let a few seconds go by, then he said, "Hyperopia. Why are you interested, if I may be so bold as to ask?"

"I'll be going to veterinary school when I graduate, and I'm just interested in learning medical terminology whenever possible," I explained.

He laughed. "You won't be checking animals for hyperopia or any other optical problems."

"I know. I just like being informed."

His attitude changed, and he began to describe some of the other problems he frequently diagnosed: myopia, presbyopia, amblyopia, cataracts, glaucoma. "It's highly unusual for someone of your age and gender to take an interest in the medical field. I'm impressed. Have you chosen a college yet?"

"I have applied to several, but I'm hoping to go to The Ohio State University. They appear to have a highly respected veterinary school, and I want the best education possible," I told him.

"You are an ambitious young woman, and I can see that you're serious about your education. My son is a student there."

"A vet student?" I asked.

"No, no. He's studying foreign languages. He wants to be an interpreter, but he isn't sure which language should be his primary target. He's thinking probably either German or French. Maybe Italian. He says there is talk of a war igniting in Europe, and he thinks he can be of help."

I had been hearing talk of that, myself, on the news broadcasts over our radio. And I was taking a current events class in school; the teacher had been talking about the same thing happening. It seemed to me that Europe was on the brink of exploding into a major fracas.

Dr. Allen and I talked about college and war and the need for medical people in all branches of the field. Then he looked up at the clock on the wall behind me and said, "It looks like I need to move on to my next client before Bonnie comes in here and scolds me. It's been a real pleasure talking to you. I wish you the very best in your endeavors." Then he shook my hand and left the room.

Bonnie, the small blond woman, came in and explained the procedure for choosing the type of frame I wanted for my glasses, how long it would take for the lenses to be made and placed in the frame, and how the payments would be set up. I thanked her and left the office.

The sun was already going down by the time I got to Uncle Herman and Mary's. Mary had the table set and was stirring something on the stove when I knocked on the back door. Uncle Herman opened it and greeted me with a big hug, as usual.

We talked while we ate. Uncle Herman tried to convince me to go to Michigan State University, but I had done my homework comparing colleges, and I had made up my mind that OSU was the place for me. I only hoped I'd be accepted there.

"But it's so far away," Mary said.

"It's only one state away," I said with a smile. "Straight down route 23."

"But, won't you feel like you're in another country?" she asked.

"Oklahoma was another country."

Uncle Herman laughed. "You got that right," he said. "I always felt, how should I put this…out of touch with the rest of the United States…when I lived there. I have no desire to go back, even though I realize there's a lot more to that state than just the panhandle." He took a bite of beef stew and looked at Mary. "Best you ever made, my sweet."

It was good, and I told her so.

She blushed. "I may not be the brightest biscuit in the batch, but I can cook."

"No doubt about that," I said. I would never tell her that Mama's beef stew had been far superior to hers. Mary had made custard pie for dessert, and that, however, rivaled even the best of Granny Nan's.

We finished the meal with coffee and conversation, and Uncle Herman smoked a cigarette while he drank his cup of the dark brew. I still drank mine with milk and sugar, as did Mary, and Uncle Herman teased us both about drinking "baby formula."

When I looked at the clock, it was already past seven. "I need to go," I said and stood up to leave. "Thank you so much for supper. It's been a long day for me, and I need to get home and do my homework."

"You are so conscientious," Mary said. "I certainly would hate to think about doing homework late at night."

"I'd hate to think about doing it at all," Uncle Herman said.

After hugs, direct orders to tell Granny Nan and "the girls" hello for them, and promises that I'd drive carefully, Uncle Herman and Mary finally allowed me to leave.

I looked up at the sky before getting into the old truck. There was no moon, so it was quite dark. The stars filled the clear sky, but they shed very little light. At least the weather had cooperated. I slid into the seat behind the steering wheel of the old truck and started the engine. It took several tries before it came to life, but I felt confident it would get me home safe and sound. I pulled out the knob that turned on the headlights and backed out of the driveway. It would take three hours to get home from Uncle Herman and Mary's house, so I decided simply to relax and enjoy the drive.

Before long I could see the lights of Flint disappearing in the rearview mirror. I sang the alto part to all the songs we were rehearsing in chorus, then I sang some of my favorite old songs, ones Papa and I used to sing when we were either going to or coming from Beaver City. Uncle Herman was right: the Oklahoma panhandle did seem like a world away.

I came to Mount Pleasant at precisely ten o'clock. It only took a few minutes to get through town, and I was glad to be on the last leg of the journey. I was only two miles from home when the truck coughed, slowed down, and then came to a complete stop. I knew what the problem was: I had forgotten to fill the gas tank before leaving Flint. I knew I'd never have enough fuel to get there and back, but because of all the events of the afternoon and evening, the responsibility of refueling had slipped my mind. Now I was going to pay for my negligence. I closed my eyes and sighed.

I gathered up all my papers from the ophthalmologist's office, took the truck keys out of the ignition, and slipped my handbag over my wrist. Then I got out and began walking. It was really quite pleasant out, so I knew I'd enjoy the late-night stroll. I did lots of thinking as I walked—about OSU, the farm, Granny Nan and my sisters, Uncle Herman and Mary and Lizzy, things I needed to do for school tomorrow. It was nice to be alone with my thoughts. That is, until I heard a car pull up behind me and slow down.

I could see my own shadow in front of me, the car's headlights lighting me from behind. *What was I thinking? I shouldn't be out here at this time of night. By myself. Walking along the road, completely oblivious to what could happen to a young woman by herself.* I hunkered my shoulders down, as if that would somehow cause me to disappear, and I sped up my pace. The car matched my speed. *I won't turn around. I will NOT be a victim of some horrible crime committed by a sex-crazed maniac just driving up and down the backroads, looking for a female in distress.*

"Helmi? Is that you?" someone shouted.

It's a man. I just knew it. But he knows my name. This could be even worse. If he does something to me, I'll have to keep it a secret for the rest of my life and not...

"Helmi, stop. I saw the truck parked at the side of the road a ways back. Did it break down? Helmi! Stop!"

I stopped, but I didn't turn around. My heart was ready to jump right out of my chest. *How could I be so stupid? Why hadn't I remembered to fill the gas tank before I left Flint? Maybe he'll just kill me, and I won't have to be concerned about running into him and keeping his actions a secret for the rest of my...*

The car stopped behind me. I could hear the driver getting out. I was ready for anything. I whirled around, preparing myself for a fight. *If I'm going to have to undergo whatever befalls me, I'll at least go out knowing I put up a good fight.*

The figure coming toward me was silhouetted against the car's headlights. I backed up a couple of steps. I had planned on facing my attacker with fire in my eyes, but that wasn't working out quite the way I had it pictured in my mind.

"Hey, it's me," he said.

My brain went through a microsecond of processing the available information and selecting possible matches for the voice I was hearing. Then it locked onto the voice's identity. "Jimmy?"

"Yeah, What're you doin' out here at this time of night? Don't you realize how dangerous…"

All I heard from that point on was "…blah, blah, blah." My body and brain were trying desperately to recover from the adrenaline that had shot through my system and clouded my ability to listen to the reprimand I was getting from a man I knew and trusted. I hadn't breathed for the last minute-and-a-half, so I was gasping for air by the time he reached me.

"I'm sorry," was all I could mutter.

"What's wrong? Is everybody okay at the farm?"

"Yes. Yes. I just forgot to get gas."

"Where you comin' from at this ungodly hour?"

"Flint," I said.

"Flint?"

"I was there for a doctor's appointment, and…"

"Doctor? Are you okay? What kinda doctor?" he asked. He sounded like he was nearly in a panic. He took me by the arm and led me back to his car.

"I'm fine. It was just an eye doctor. I have to get reading glasses."

We reached his car, and he stopped me, turned me around, and looked down at me with an expression I had only ever seen in Papa's eyes. It was one of concern, relief, and tenderness, all wrapped up together. Papa had looked at me that way when we were in Beaver City and he had just gotten the letter and photo from Uncle Julius and was so angry, he had inadvertently dragged me a short distance down the boardwalk.

I melted into Jimmy's chest, and he put his arms around me and hugged me to him, kissing me on the top of my head. I took a big breath, then I began to cry.

"It's all right now," he said, holding me close with one arm and stoking my hair with his other hand. "Shh, shh, shh."

I was so embarrassed. I didn't think I'd ever be able to face him again. I just stood there and let him take command of the situation. He gently turned me around and helped me into the passenger seat of his car. I was still crying when he settled into the driver's seat.

"I'm sorry," I said again.

"For what?" he asked.

"I don't know," I said, blubbering like a two-year-old.

"You musta had a late appointment if you're only now comin' home."

"I ate supper at Uncle Herman and Mary's after my appointment, and I didn't leave there until after seven," I told him, keeping my head down, allowing the tears to fall into my lap.

Jimmy reached into his pocket and pulled out a clean, white handkerchief. He shook it out and handed it to me. "It's fresh off the line."

I took the handkerchief and wiped my eyes, then I blew my nose on it.

"Well, it *was* fresh," he said, jokingly.

I laughed. "I guess I'm recovering." I had stopped crying and was now feeling ashamed. "It was just that I thought you were, well, going to attack me."

"Are you disappointed?"

I jerked my head toward him. He was grinning. I started to laugh.

"That's better," he said. "Now there's the Helmi I know and love."

What did he just say to me? I know I heard the word 'love,' but I'm sure he just meant it in a familiar kind of way. He didn't mean he loves me. That would be way too presumptuous on my part. Friends do love each other. That must have been what he meant.

He reached across me and took my right hand, the one without the handkerchief in it. "Let's get you home. You need some rest in a nice soft bed."

I held onto his hand like I'd fall off a cliff if I let go.

"I need that," he said.

I looked at him. "Need what?" I asked.

"My hand. I can't drive without it."

It's a good thing we were in the dark, because my face was crimson—I knew because I could feel the heat rising up my neck. My brain kept telling me to let go his hand, but my fingers wouldn't release their grip. I slid across the seat so that I was sitting right next to him, the left side of my body touching him from my shoulder to my knee. It was heavenly, the warmth of his body and mine, mingling together there in the dark.

Without letting go my hand, he raised his arm up and put it around me, pulling me closer. "You know how to shift, so that'll be your job."

I dropped the handkerchief in my lap and reached up with my left hand, putting it on the gearshift. He stepped on the clutch and revved up the engine. I put the car in first gear, he eased out on the clutch, and we began to roll forward. He depressed the clutch two more times, and I shifted at the precise moment until we were moving at a somewhat lively speed, so lively that I was home way too soon.

"We need to do this more often, and under better circumstances," he said. He let go my hand and turned off the engine.

I didn't want to move. I felt so secure in his embrace. "I'd like that," I said. *It must be because I'm so tired. I had a stressful day, and now I'm simply letting myself unwind and… No, that isn't the case at all. It has nothing to do with any of that. It's a simple case of being wrapped up in the spell of this tall, handsome, funny, loveable man sitting so close to me.*

"Kiss me," I whispered.

Jimmy had become our fulltime employee. He worked as if he owned our farm. Butch came only for the morning milking. Jimmy did the evening milking and everything else associated with keeping things running smoothly. Retta helped him with everything, and I helped whenever I could.

He and I occasionally went out to various places around Mount Pleasant—the movie theatre, the ice cream parlor, the restaurant, and to the park for picnics, which I loved. He took me fishing and even took me to Flint a couple of times. We had so much fun together. I didn't date anyone else. Some of the girls at school suggested we were "going steady," but Jimmy wasn't in school, so that sounded juvenile to me. He was, after all, almost four years older than I.

We had so little time to spend together, it seems amazing that we accomplished all we did. He was dedicated to the farm, and I was dedicated to school and work with Dr. Pauley. I knew, however, that it was all going to come to an end very soon, as I was graduating in a month and would soon be heading off to Columbus, Ohio, and a new life.

My plan to graduate first in my high school class had panned out—I was the 1938 Mount Pleasant High School valedictorian. I would proudly accept my diploma as a straight-A student. I invited Granny Nan, Uncle Herman, Mary, and Jimmy to the baccalaureate service, and all of my sisters, Miss Michaels, and Butch were added to the list for the actual graduation ceremony. It was held on June 12; it was so hot that day, I thought I'd melt sitting there in my cap and gown. The mercury rose to eighty-seven, and the sun shown as bright as if it were about to burn a hole in the sky. The school passed out cardboard fans to everyone as they entered the auditorium, and I doubt that there was a single one of them that wasn't in use.

Because I was the valedictorian, I had to give a little speech. But the guest speaker, A. B. Graham, talked about helping the youth of our country with some practical, hands-on learning experiences outside the classroom. He was responsible for starting the 4-H program in the United States in 1902 in Springfield Township, Clark County, Ohio, and he developed the Cooperative Extension System in 1914. He eventually went on to become the Federal Extension Director of the United States Department of Agriculture. I agreed totally with his ideas.

Most of Mr. Graham's speech to us, however, emphasized becoming something outside of our individual realm of comfort. I wasn't sure I agreed with him on that point, as I was pretty comfortable with the prospect of becoming a veterinarian, and I couldn't imagine being something outside that realm. But it was a good speech, and his voice was pleasant to listen to. He made it a point to come up to me and offer his congratulations on being the class valedictorian.

"Thank you," I said as I shook his hand.

"I understand you are headed for Columbus come August."

"Yes, I've been accepted at the OSU School of Veterinary Medicine."

"You want to be a veterinarian?"

I nodded.

"That's mighty ambitious. Will you be on a scholarship?"

"Yes, partly," I told him. "My scholarship will cover the first three years, and my father saved money in a bank trust for me before he died. So with the scholarship, I'll have enough money to get through all five years without taking out a loan."

"I wish my daughter had been as good a student. She was not a scholarship recipient, so I'll probably be paying for her schooling until doomsday." He laughed.

"Where is your daughter going to school?"

"University of Dayton in southwest Ohio," he said. "It's a great school. She chose it because of its school of nursing. It's closely associated with three big hospitals in Dayton. She's wanted to be a nurse since she was still in diapers."

We chatted a bit more until one of my classmates came up to me and said the photographer was ready to take our class picture, which would be framed and hung on the wall inside the school for future generations to walk past on a daily basis, probably never noticing the individuals whose faces stared out at them. I excused myself and went with the girl to the photo site.

When the photo shoot had been completed, Jimmy came running up to me, lifted me off my feet and spun me around. "I saw you talking to Mr. Graham," he said. "Do you have any idea how famous that guy is, and more importantly, are you two on a first-name basis now?"

"Yes and no. I *do* know how famous he is, but I will continue to refer to him as Mr. Graham. And I have a question for you."

"Okay," he said as he put me down.

"What does A. B. stand for?"

He looked at me with a total lack of awareness written all over his face.

"A. B. Graham—his name. What do the initials stand for?"

"Oh. I think the A is for Albert. But the B? Your guess is as good as mine."

I made a mental note to look it up, not for any particular reason other than to quell my curiosity.

"Everybody's goin' back into the school for the big party," Jimmy said. "They're gonna have cake and punch. Are we goin'?"

"We'd better, considering I'm someone important," I said, making a point of emphasizing the word 'important.' "But we don't need to stick around for very long; just long enough for me to do some hand-shaking and offering my personal thanks to the people who donated money to the scholarship fund."

"You already thanked 'em in your speech," he said.

"But I need to thank them *in person*."

"Oh, yeah, I guess that would be the right thing to do. Then can we leave?"

"I guess so. We'll need to take Granny Nan and my sisters home. They won't all fit into Uncle Herman's Cadillac."

"Are you kiddin' me? He could fit an army in there!"

"Well, I can't just abandon them. After all, they came to my graduation, which I'm sure was terribly boring for them."

"Okay. But after you do your duty, can we go somewhere else?"

"Sure. I guess there's nothing pressing before milking time," I said as I began taking off my gown. "Why is it so hot today? I'm about to melt."

"You and everybody else who agreed to be here," he said, wiping the sweat from his brow.

"Where do you propose we go?"

He looked at me with a funny expression and didn't say anything for several beats. "Well, I thought I'd take you someplace special for supper tonight."

"And just what do you consider 'special'? We only have one restaurant here in town. And we can't go all the way to Flint. There's nothing but a little diner in Weidman, and it's closed on Sundays."

He was silent, and he appeared to be interested in a stick on the ground; he was moving it around with his foot. "It's a surprise," he finally said.

"Good. I need a surprise." I realized he was struggling with the whole subject, so I thought I'd better let it lie. "In the meantime, let's go to the party and then gather up the group and go home."

I ate my piece of cake and gave the right people my obligatory thanks, then Jimmy and I went around the room, gathering up the family and taking them to our vehicles.

Uncle Herman came up to me and said, "You don't need to take anyone back to the house. I can get them all in the Caddy. It'll be kind of fun, seeing how many people will fit. And besides, Jimmy wants to take you someplace special. So go with him. We'll be fine."

"But..."

"We'll be fine." He turned me around and pushed me toward Jimmy, who was just coming up to us.

Jimmy looked past me and smiled at Uncle Herman. Then he gave him a little nod of his head, as if to say "Thank you" without actually doing it verbally.

I looked back over my shoulder at Uncle Herman, but he was already walking away, whistling, hands in his pockets, just like Papa used to do when he was up to no good.

"What's going on here?" I asked Jimmy.

"What? Nothin'. Nothin'. Just...let's go." He turned and walked toward his car, leaving me standing there alone. I got the feeling I was about to be the recipient of some enormous prank. I went to the car and got in. Jimmy was silent.

"Okay, what's up?"

"I told you, nothin'. I just wanted us to have some time alone on your very special day."

"Yeah, right," I said. "I don't believe a word of it."

He offered no more discussion on the subject. He merely started the car and began to drive in the opposite direction from home. He took route 127 out of town and finally stopped at a nice little park in

St. Louis (not to be confused with the St. Louis in Missouri).

"What are we doing here?" I asked.

He was already getting out of the car. "Havin' a picnic," he answered. He got out of the car and reached into the back seat, pulling out a picnic basket and a cold chest. He set them on the ground, then he came around to my side of the car and opened my door. He reached down and took me by both hands, pulling me up and out of the seat. It was a perfect setup to hold me close to him, and I raised my arms to reach around his neck, but he moved to my side before I could close the distance between us. *That's not like him; he usually jumps at the chance to make bodily contact. Something strange is definitely going on here.*

"Can you grab that blanket from behind your seat?" he asked.

"Sure," I said, reaching into the back seat and grabbing the blanket. He went to the other side of the car and picked up the basket and chest and walked purposefully to a spot away from all the usual places people sat. There were a lot of people around, but none of them seemed to be in a hurry to claim the place Jimmy was heading toward. "Come on," he called.

I saw him disappear behind a stand of trees with brush around their bases. When I reached the opposite side, I realized Jimmy had found a place with both shade and privacy. I was even more convinced that something was up.

He took the blanket from me and spread it on the ground in the shade. I moved the basket and cold chest over onto the blanket's edge, and we both sat down, Indian-legged. He removed his coat and tie and said, "Now, isn't this better than bein' in the house where the temperature's prob'ly just about at the boilin' point?"

"It certainly is. This is really quite nice. And I like being alone instead of among the crowded masses."

He smiled, but it wasn't his usual smile. He appeared to be nervous.

"Come on, Jimmy. You have to tell me what's on your mind. You aren't acting like yourself."

He looked at me, then he looked away, far into the distance, but he said nothing. He took a deep breath.

Well, two can play this game. I sat there, silent as a church mouse, and waited. And waited. And waited. Then I began thinking about what was happening. He hadn't made any advances, and his silence was worrisome. *He's going to break up with me!* I'd been concerned that this would happen. *He knows I'm going away to school in two months, and he's going to tell me he wants to stop seeing me. He doesn't want to sit around Mount Pleasant just waiting for me to come* home. He wants me to tell him he can see anyone he wants and do anything he wants with whomever he wants. If I grant him his freedom, he won't have to feel bad if he slips up and gets "familiar" with some other girl while I'm away at school.

I'd figured it out. I took the cover off the picnic basket and began removing the food. He opened the cold chest and withdrew two bottles of root beer. He knew I loved it. *He probably figures that'll soften the blow.* I wasn't about to say anything. I was going to be sure he was forced to make the first move.

We each filled our plates with fried chicken, which greatly resembled the kind that Granny Nan made, pickled cucumbers for which Dora was famous, and huge biscuits that I would have bet came from the little bakery in Mount Pleasant. There was a jar of freshly churned butter and some apple butter. We ate in silence. It was so good.

Then Jimmy pulled an oatmeal pie out of the cold chest. *But it isn't Christmas, and we only have that after we open our presents.*

Before I could say anything about it, Jimmy said, "I know we don't eat oatmeal pie till after we open our presents, so I brought one for you." He reached into his pocket and produced a small blue velvet box tied with silver ribbon.

I think my heart stopped beating. My throat was dry, my hands shook, and I felt like I'd been swept up and transported to another planet. I was seeing myself from a distance, as if I'd died and my soul had left my body and was now looking down on me. I knew of only one thing that came in a box like that.

I looked up at Jimmy and confirmed that this was not an out-of-body experience; I was sitting right there on a blanket in a park in St. Louis, Michigan, across from the only person, other than family, with whom I'd ever been one-hundred percent comfortable.

Jimmy was beaming, his face lit up so bright it rivaled the sun itself. "Miss Wilhelmina Schnier, will you do me the honor of becoming my wife?"

Had he really asked me that, or was I only imagining it? I was afraid to answer because I wasn't sure he'd said the words out loud, and I didn't want to appear a fool. I sat there, my hands out, half-reaching for the box, my mouth hanging open, staring into his irresistible dark eyes.

Then I chanced it: "I will."

I took the box from his hand and opened it. Staring back at me was a beautiful diamond ring, one single diamond on a thin silver band. He took it from the box and placed it on the ring finger of my left hand. I looked down at it, then back up at Jimmy, the man I had just agreed to marry, and saw the face I would spend the rest of my life looking at every morning when I awakened and every night before I went to sleep.

"Cheese and crackers."

BIG DECISIONS

"We can't get married yet, Jimmy. We've only been engaged for two weeks!"

"I don't understand why you're makin' such a big deal of this. You're gonna go off to college in...um," he was struggling to count up the time, "...um... six or seven weeks, and I'm gonna be left here without you." He sidled up to me, an inviting expression on his face. And usually it worked; I'd give in without a fight. But this time I was adamant about how I felt concerning our plans for the future.

"Come on," he coaxed. "You know you can't resist my charm. And my good looks."

I backed away. "We aren't discussing your charm or your good looks, both of which are irresis...usually *irresistible*. We're discussing getting married before I head off to the netherworld of Columbus, Ohio."

We were in the hen lot. I had let the big Rhode Island Red rooster in, and he was getting agitated because of our louder-than-normal discussion. He charged Jimmy, who jumped back and shouted, "Hey, you ornery old bird!"

I laughed, looked at the rooster, and said, "Thank you."

Jimmy appeared exasperated. He raised his arms in the air and shook his head in a "what-am-I-supposed-to-do?" gesture.

I grinned at him. "Look, Jimmy, I know you feel like I'm a fallen tree across the road in front of you right now, but there are way too many things to be considered before we just up and get married." I turned and went into the henhouse. "What would people think?"

"That never used to enter into your decision-making," he said, following me.

He had me there. I stopped dead, my hand under one of the hens. She cackled, looked up at me, and pecked my arm, as if to say, "Get it done and move on." I jerked my arm back.

It was Jimmy's turn to laugh. He looked at the hen and said, "Thank you."

"Let's talk to Granny Nan and your dad," I said. "They might shed some light on this topic, maybe bring up some points we haven't considered. What about that?"

He sighed and said, "As usual, you're right. We need some other input."

"And I'd like to talk to Retta, too. She's got a lot invested in our decision."

"What? How?"

"She does an unsung amount of the work around here, doesn't she? She's always working out here when she isn't in school. She helps you and your dad with the milking, works in the fields, takes care of the pigs and chickens and cattle and…"

"Okay! Okay, okay," he said. "I'd never be able to do everything around here if it wasn't for her. She's a Godsend."

I'd never heard him use that word before. In fact, I'd never heard him talk about God at all. I knew he didn't go to church, but I didn't know where he stood on the whole subject of religion. "Do you believe in God?"

His mouth dropped open as if he were going to say something, but he only stared at me, mouth agape.

"You trying to catch flies?" I asked him.

He closed his mouth, and it made a funny popping noise. I tried not to laugh, but I couldn't help it. He was completely befuddled, poor guy. Our discussion had gone from marriage to the farm to Retta to religious beliefs in only a matter of minutes. I knew he must have felt overwhelmed. The look on his face was enough to garner empathy from the Devil himself. I sighed and walked up to him, taking his hands in mine. "I really think we need to table this whole discussion until we have some other opinions. How 'bout that?"

He nodded. "When?"

"As soon as possible," I said. "You're right that we don't have much time before I leave." I stopped and blinked; those last three words sounded so final. I looked up at the man I loved and saw on his face and in his eyes such concern, such devotion, such confusion. I wanted to spend every minute of every day with Jimmy, but I also wanted to become a vet, and I knew I couldn't do both at the same time. I had to find a way to make this work, but I would have to convince him somehow that getting married immediately wasn't the obvious solution to the problem.

"No hanky-panky in the henhouse," I heard Retta's voice and saw her coming through the henhouse door.

"What's up?" I asked.

"I need to borrow your fiancé," she said. She was wearing a pair of boy's bib overalls with the hems rolled up in big cuffs and one of

Yosie's sleeveless, faded, cotton hand-me-down blouses. She was clomping along in a pair of muck-covered swampers, and her hair was in pigtails, loose wisps of it sticking out around her face. She could have been the poster child for "Tomboys of America."

Jimmy visibly shifted mental gears. "You still workin' on that bad stanchion?"

"Yeah, but I'm gonna need some help when you can get to it." She turned to leave.

"Be right there," Jimmy said. He turned and looked back at me.

"Go on," I said. "I think our conversation has reached an impasse anyway."

"Does that mean we've discussed everything we're goin' to?"

"It does. And besides, we were getting close to hanky-panky, and Retta said none of that's allowed in the henhouse."

"I am not sure why you think I might be able to offer any suggestions," Granny Nan said after we'd finished washing the supper dishes. I had told her of Jimmy's and my idea about getting more input from her and Butch regarding our marriage plans. "Have you forgotten how my marriage turned out?"

We were sitting at the kitchen table. All my sisters were upstairs, and Jimmy had left before we ate. Granny Nan had packed enough for his and Butch's supper, but Jimmy wasn't going to take it, using the excuse that Butch probably already had something going on the stove. Granny Nan told him, "You will take it anyway. If not tonight, you can eat it tomorrow night." Jimmy knew better than to argue with her.

"Quite frankly, Granny Nan, I don't know anything about your marriage except that it's something we were never allowed to talk about."

She sat motionless, staring straight ahead at nothing. She closed her eyes and lowered her head. "I can come up with no reason why I should try to keep it a secret anymore. Buster is long gone. And so is that part of my life. Funny, but I remember it as if it belonged to someone else, not me."

She raised her head but kept looking into the distance. "We started out as a happy couple. We had big plans for our life." The corners of her mouth turned up ever so slightly. "He was so handsome, and he made all the girls swoon. I had no idea he had his eye on me. He had the kindest smile I ever saw on a man." She paused, obviously picturing him in her mind.

"He was the best dancer I ever partnered with. When he held me, I did not have to think about where my feet were supposed to go; he cast a spell over me, and all I had to do was look into his eyes, and my feet were not even a part of my body. He was that good.

"Years passed, and we moved to Oklahoma. Buster became a womanizer, if ever there was one. I do not know if he grew weary of having so much responsibility around our home or if he grew weary of me, but one afternoon he left without a word—just took off on his horse and did not tell me where he was headed. I supposed he was going to town for something he needed to fix the wagon or some odd thing. Suppertime came and went, and he had not returned. I knew, deep in my heart, that he was not coming back. I do not know how I knew, but I knew all the same."

She sighed, and her face sagged. "Later that night—it was almost midnight—a man came to our door, banging on it with his fist, and he was shouting for someone to answer." She put one hand on her face, as if she were reliving the whole thing. I could tell she was scared.

"I did not know whether to answer it. Violet was just a baby, and the banging wakened her. She began crying, a frightened, lonesome sort of cry. I picked her up out of the cradle and held her tight, trying to decide if I should answer the door. He kept banging and shouting, banging and shouting. And Violet kept crying that strange cry. Lavern came up to me and whispered, 'Mother, I will take Violet. You answer the door.'

"I handed Violet to her and motioned for her to get away from the door. I did not know who was there, nor did I know what he wanted at that time of night. I kept wondering 'Why is he here? Why our house?' And still he banged and shouted." She put both hands on her head, one on each side of her skull, as if she were trying to keep her head from exploding.

Eventually she lowered her hands and continued. "I pulled the pin from the hasp and threw open the door. The man stumbled inside. I did not recognize him. I was frightened of him. He smelled of liquor and sweat and smoke. He straightened himself up to his full height, though he leaned to one side, as if one of his legs was shorter than the other. He looked me up and down. He had a bushy beard the color of Oklahoma dust.

"Buttons were missing from his filthy shirt, and I was eye-level with his exposed chest, hairy and dark; I could not guess if his skin was dark because of the sun or if it was just plain filth. I turned my face from him." She turned away, just as she described the moment. "I could stand neither the stench nor the sight of him."

She was talking faster now, and her breathing had become more rapid. I wanted to stop her—comfort her—but I was glued to the chair and could not move.

"He asked me if I was Buster Deacon's wife. His voice was thick, and he slurred his words. I asked him who he was. He said, 'My name don't matter. You his wife, er ain't ya?' I remember nodding, still not looking directly at him. 'Well, he's dead. Killed a whore and shot a man in a bar fight. Then he put the barrel of his pistol in his mouth and pulled the trigger. Fell dead right in front of me. The whole back of his head was gone, splattered all over the front wall.' Those were his exact words."

She closed her eyes. "With no further explanation, he turned and left. I stood there for a long time—minutes, I guess—then I closed the door, returned the pin to its position in the hasp, and went to the other end of the room where Lavern was holding Violet, swinging her from side to side, back and forth, whispering to her to try and keep her quiet. To calm her. But Violet still cried, her little face red and wrinkled with some emotion I could not identify."

Granny Nan paused and opened her eyes. Then she said, "Violet knew. Somehow, she knew."

And then she was no longer in the room with me, even though her body was right there, sitting at the table across from me. She was spent. Her face was gray, and she seemed tiny and helpless at that moment. I wanted to wrap her up in my arms and tell her it would all be fine. That it would all go away. I swallowed hard, but my throat was dry; I stifled a cough. I could not interrupt her silence. I would not allow my presence to invade her memory.

I understood why she had not wanted to talk about it. I knew the original act had hurt her deeply, but her memory of it was even more distressful, malicious. I could not imagine how she had managed to keep it hidden in her heart for so many years. My heart was breaking...for her. I had just been a secondhand witness to a terrifying moment in her history, and I was momentarily paralyzed by it. I did not move until I was sure her consciousness had allowed her to re-enter the present.

Finally, she took in a long, cleansing breath. Then, without even looking at me, she got up, went into her room, and closed the door. I put my head down on the table until I could find the strength to carry myself upstairs.

❖❖❖

I was up early the next morning. Truth be told, I never really slept at all that night. I tossed and turned for a couple of hours until Retta said, groggily, "Why don't you just get up and do something. But do it somewhere other than in this room."

I took her suggestion to heart. I grabbed the OSU Bulletin that had been sent to me by the University Admissions Office, and I went downstairs to the front room to peruse it. I learned a lot about what they offered and about what I'd be taking my first year. I would have to take what they called General Education Requirements. Those were courses in addition to a student's major, unless the student was majoring in one of those fields.

OSU's schoolyear was divided into quarters. As a student of veterinary medicine, I would have to take three quarters of basic English, three quarters of American history, and three quarters of two different electives, from which I could choose a foreign language, one of the social studies, psychology, or political science. My major would include mathematics, several of the sciences, and business courses, so those were not included on my list of the possible General Education Requirements.

I had talked to Miss Michaels about it earlier. She said her college curriculum was different because the entire school was dedicated to training teachers and nothing else. Of course, they had to learn ALL the subjects in order to teach them. The only difference in the courses for her major depended on whether she had chosen to teach the first eight grades or high school.

I knew I was going to have to report to OSU two weeks before the quarter actually started because I'd have to talk to a counsellor, who would help me decide which courses to take, and I'd also have to complete some entrance exams. If I did well on those, I might be excused from taking one or more of the courses everyone must take. I had never struggled with test-taking, so I was hoping I'd do well and not have to sit through some of those classes.

I was prepared to carry as many credit hours as possible during my first year in order to get the necessities out of the way and be able to concentrate solely on my major in my second, third, and fourth years. My fifth year would be dedicated completely to hands-on learning, or what the bulletin referred to as the "in-the-field" portion of my education.

I talked to Lizzy a lot, and she said the people she knew who were smart enough to be able to skip some of the freshman classes were rewarded by being able to do that. She was way past that, currently working on her master's degree in pharmacology at University of Michigan in Ann Arbor. She acted like she wasn't smart, but I knew better. Mary and Uncle Herman were so proud of her; she was the gist of most of our conversations.

At four a.m. I snuck back upstairs and got dressed. I went out to the milking barn, Two-Tone at my heels, and filled the spaces in front of each stanchion with silage. I turned on the paddle in the bulk tank so it would stir the milk and cream together, ready for the tanker truck that would arrive around five a.m. to siphon out yesterday's yield. After that, one of us would wash out the bulk tank so it was ready for today's yield. At six o'clock Jimmy showed up, and about two minutes later Retta made her appearance. The cows were eager to come in; they were already at the door to the barn, mooing to let us know they wanted to empty their chock-full udders.

None of us spoke. We operated without having to think, each of us doing exactly what we did twice every day. When one of us wasn't there, someone else filled in without any argument. It had to be done, and we did it. Usually Jimmy ran the cows in and out of the stanchion barn. He manned the full milkers, dumping them into the buckets, and either Retta or I or both of us carried the buckets to the bulk tank where we emptied them. Then we carried them back into the stanchion barn so Jimmy could fill them again. I tended to any of the cows' medical needs, and Retta changed the filters. And so on. Over and over.

At some point either Retta or I would walk over to the lean-to barn and feed the pigs and beef cattle, then we'd feed the chickens and roosters and ducks. As soon as the milking was done, we went about the other chores as they arose. One of us always made sure to fill Two-Tone's food bowl from the bag in the junk room inside the back door. Some days there was field work, some days I worked at Dr. Pauley's, some days there was gardening to tend to, but somehow it all got done without a time-clock to punch and without someone telling us how to do our jobs. That was a big part of why I liked farming.

That day was no different except that Jimmy smiled more than usual. "Why so happy?" I asked him.

"I just like workin' with ya. It makes me feel good," he said.

"Did you happen to mention to your dad that we'd like to talk to him about our prospective plans?"

"No, he was really tired when I got home." He paused, then he said, "The way I see it, we aren't kids anymore. We should be able to figure it out ourselves. It's our problem, and the solution should be ours, too."

A smile began to creep onto my lips, and by the time it was complete, it had turned into a full-blown grin. I truly loved that man. He may not have been incredibly intelligent, but he was wise. And in my book, that made him more desirable than anyone else I could name. "I like the way you think," I said to him.

"C'mere, beautiful," he said to me.

I jokingly turned around and looked behind me, like I expected to see some gorgeous woman there.

"I'm talkin' to YOU." He pointed at me.

"Me? Li'l ol' me?"

"You betcha!"

I think it was due, in part, to the fact that Jimmy had decided we should make the decision ours and ours alone that I strayed from my usual 'by the book' tendencies and told him, "I want to marry you on July 14."

"Of this year?"

"Yessir."

"Why, Miss Schnier, what will people think?" he mocked me.

I gave him a well-deserved punch in the arm and then told him I liked that date…no special reason, it just sounded like a good day to be married. "It's on a Thursday, so the Justice of the Peace's Office will be open."

He feigned a swoon and said, "You mean you don't wanna have a big wedding?" Then he came back to earth and said, "I never knew a woman who didn't. Are you okay? There's not somethin' wrong with you that I should know 'bout, is there?"

"You want a punch in the other arm?" I asked him. Then I turned as if I were going to walk away, but he grabbed me around the waist and lifted me off the ground, my back against his front. I was struggling and giggling like a crazed schoolgirl. "Put me down!"

"No."

"Jimmy, put me down!"

"No."

"Please?"

"No."

I went completely limp, like I'd fainted. I waited for a response, but none came. It was a standoff now; who'd give in first? He didn't move, he just kept holding me. I didn't move, I just kept hanging there. We must have remained there in the big barn in that position for a full two minutes.

"Am I interrupting something obscene?" Retta asked as she appeared in the doorway.

"Not at all," Jimmy said. "Your sister just thinks she can get away with punchin' me in the arm any time she likes. So I'm teachin' her a lesson."

Retta shrugged her shoulders. "Okay," she said, unconcerned. She walked past us and grabbed a pitchfork that had been stuck into a bale of straw and proceeded to carry it toward the doorway.

I asked her, emoting like a character from *Of Thee I Sing*, "Do you have no sympathy for your own flesh and blood? Your poor, poor sister is being ravaged by this ogre, and you simply…"

Dar Bagby

With that, Jimmy dropped me like a hot potato. I landed on all fours.

Retta burst out laughing. "You two were made for each other," she said and left, pitchfork in hand.

Jimmy watched me get up, offering no assistance.

"Aren't you even going to help me?" I whined.

"Not until you promise you won't punch me again."

"Okay, I won't again … today."

"I can live with that," he said.

I said, "Now that we've set a wedding date, don't you think we should seal it with a kiss?"

"I think you know how to make me happy," he said and kissed me long and sensuously. I went limp again in his arms, but this time it was because my legs wouldn't hold me up.

And on July 14, 1938, in the office of the Mount Pleasant Justice of the Peace, with Granny Nan and Butch as witnesses, Jimmy and I each said two little words and became Mr. and Mrs. James Butcher.

222.7 CUBIC INCHES

My head was spinning; there were so many things to take care of with so little time remaining before I started college. Jimmy and I knew we'd have to take Granny Nan to town to approve and witness the addition of his name on the deed to the farm, and my last name would have to be changed to Butcher. We decided to take care of that on Tuesday next, and I could also take care of the particulars regarding name-change and so on with my bank trust. I had called the bank, and they said I wouldn't need an appointment; any one of the available loan officers could take care of that for me; that meant we could kill two birds on the same day.

I'd mailed a letter to the OSU Admissions Office, along with a copy to the Bursar's Office on Friday, the day after our "wedding," with the information for changing my name on all the paperwork before I arrived on Admissions Day. I hoped they'd have everything taken care of before I got there, or it would be a disaster trying to get it all straight on that first day. I had actually written the letter before we got married, so all I had to do was put it in the mailbox on July 15.

Uncle Herman invited all of us to his home in Flint on July 16, the Saturday after Jimmy and I had gotten married. "You didn't get an actual reception after your wedding, and you deserve one. Mary and I would like to provide that for you," he had said to me on the telephone. Granny Nan was insistent that she be allowed to bring something, so Mary asked her to bring some home-churned butter; that suited Granny Nan to a T.

I had to ask Dr. Pauley if I could take Saturday off. He was so excited for me that he told me I didn't have to come into work on Sunday, either, if I needed an extra day. But I told him there really wasn't anything pressing, so if it was all right with him, I'd come in anyway, and he agreed. In truth, we needed the money. The old truck had reached a point of requiring weekly—sometimes even daily—repairs, and Jimmy was wearing himself out trying to keep up with the truck, his old Chevrolet, the farm, and his Dad's place. We needed a reliable vehicle to get me to Columbus, too, (though I wouldn't be keeping it there, since freshman weren't allowed to have one on campus), and he would need a good car to take my sisters and Granny Nan wherever they needed to go, mainly school, church, and to town for groceries, etc. while I was away. So we were in the market for a new car. Every time we went anywhere, Jimmy kept his eye peeled for one that had a FOR SALE sign on it. So far, our luck had not been so good.

Saturday arrived, and we finished the milking and other chores, then we all got cleaned up to go to Uncle Herman's. There were ten of us: Granny Nan, Butch, Jimmy, me, Yosie, Bella, Dora, Retta, Ronnie, and Anna. We took Jimmy's Chevy and our old Ford truck, since the truck couldn't hold all of us without people having to ride in the bed, and if we took only Jimmy's Chevy, some of us would have to sit on others' laps. Neither of those options was suitable for a three-hour ride.

So I drove the truck and took Bella and Dora with me, and Jimmy took everyone else in his Chevy. The only one who had to sit on someone's lap was Anna. She was five, and she really liked Butch, so he sat by a window and held her, the two of them discussing everything under the sun the whole way there, except for the last twenty-five minutes when she fell asleep; Butch and Granny Nan let her lie across their laps.

It was a beautiful morning when we left Mount Pleasant; the temperature was a balmy seventy-two degrees with a slight breeze. I hoped it was the same in Flint. I led the way; Jimmy said he wanted to keep an eye on me. I wasn't sure if that was because he was watching out for the truck and possible breakdowns, or if he wasn't totally sure how to get to Uncle Herman's house and just didn't want to admit it.

When we turned onto the street where Uncle Herman and Mary lived, we could see the top of a yellow-and-white-striped tent. I wondered if that was for us, but I didn't say anything. It was Bella who leaned forward and said, "Hey, look! I think we're going to have your reception in a tent." She was right. When we pulled up to the house, we could see that the tent had been set up in the back yard between the main house and the guest house. Nothing could have erased the smile from my face.

There were three cars in the driveway: Uncle Herman's Cadillac, another that I suspected was Lizzy's, and a third one I didn't recognize. I was guessing it belonged to someone who was occupying the guest house for the weekend.

Before I could get the door open, Uncle Herman was at the truck window. "Well, if it isn't Mrs. Butcher!" He bent down and gave me a big smooch on the cheek. Then he whispered to me, "Herzlichen

Glückwunsch zu euer Hochzeit!" (Congratulations on your marriage!)

That was the first time I had ever heard him speak German. It took me by surprise; I had actually forgotten that he was just as German as Papa had been. I smiled up at him.

"That's the kind of smile I like to see," he said as he opened my door and helped me out of the truck.

Granny Nan was already out of Jimmy's car and making her way toward us. "This certainly is festive," she said.

"Only the best for the best family any man could ask for," Uncle Herman said. He reached around Granny Nan's shoulders and squeezed her to him. She, too, was smiling like I hadn't seen her do in a long time.

Mary and Lizzy came out the front door of the house. "Greetings, all!" Mary called to us.

Lizzy made a beeline toward me, and I went running to her. We slammed into each other, hugging and giggling.

She grabbed my left hand. "Let me see your new jewelry," she said. "Oh, Helmi, how lovely! It's so tastefully simple. Don't you just love it? Of course, you do. What am I thinking? I'm just so glad to see you. It's been eons since we've had a chance to talk face-to-face." Then she leaned down close to my ear and whispered, "And I can't wait to see your better half. Mary says he's grown into the handsomest man she ever laid eyes on."

"And she's right," I said.

Jimmy appeared out of nowhere. "Hi. You look familiar," he said to Lizzy.

She blushed. "Hi, Jimmy." She shook his hand. "I'm Lizzy. We met years ago. I think you were also at Herman and my mother's marriage announcement, but I'm not sure."

"I remember you now. You were the one who tried to fight with the ducks. We were all a lot younger then, weren't we?"

"Yes, but we're all much prettier and more handsome now!" Lizzy said, then laughed. Her laugh was infectious, and Jimmy and I couldn't help but laugh, too.

Everyone had finally come out of the vehicles, and Uncle Herman had made it a point to say something to each and every one of us. He was such a schmoozer. But then, that was part of his job. Whoever had hired him at General Motors did well in choosing him to fill the position. "Come on back to the tent," he held his hand up and motioned for us to follow him. He reminded me of a cowboy in charge of a cattle drive, getting ready to move the herd out, just like I'd seen in one of the movies Jimmy had taken me to.

The tent was open on the long side next to the house, and the other three sides were enclosed. It was decorated with rows of crepe paper that draped across the tent from side to side. Every few feet green, yellow, and white balloons hung down from the top; there must have been a hundred of them. And on the back wall of the tent was a great big banner that said:

CONGRATULATIONS!
MR. & MRS. BUTCHER
JULY 14, 1938

Decorated tables were set up on one end of the tent, each with two vases of cut flowers from Uncle Herman's flower beds, and there was a long table that I was certain would hold the food for a buffet luncheon. A raised wooden platform took up the other end. In one corner of it was a drum set with three chairs in front of it; there were going to be musicians who would play for us to dance to! But the best part was that all the decorations were yellow, green, and white. The day we got married I had worn a yellow and white dress and carried a small bouquet of daisies, and Jimmy had worn dark pants with a light green shirt. Mary and Lizzy must have talked to Granny Nan in order to coordinate the colors.

"Pretty nice digs," Jimmy said to me, quietly.

"And how! Leave it to Uncle Herman to come up with something like this," I said low enough that no one could hear. "I feel like royalty."

Mary came up to us to offer her congratulations. "You two are just perfect together," she said.

"Thank you so much for doing this for us," Jimmy said.

"I second that motion," I said, not able to take my eyes off the banner.

"Everyone take a seat," Uncle Herman shouted. "All but the guests of honor," he said, waving for Jimmy and me to come up to where he was standing on the wooden platform. He waited until everyone had found their places, then he went to one side of the tent and picked up two chairs, which he placed side-by-side in the middle of the platform. He motioned for us to sit. We did.

He walked back and forth in front of us. Then he stopped and faced the audience. He began by rubbing his chin and pursing his lips. He finally spoke. "Back in the olden days, it was common for people to perform what they called a 'shivaree' for a newly married couple." Granny Nan and Butch giggled. Everyone else looked at them.

Uncle Herman went on. "The act involved making as much noise as possible outside the newlyweds' bedroom. People beat on pots and pans, they sang loud and raucous songs, and they even did such things as tying bells under the couple's mattress; then when the bells rang, they knew it was time to interrupt the bedroom follies and keep the couple awake all night, not permitting them to…uh…let's see. I need to put this discreetly…uh…consummate their marriage."

Granny Nan had her hand over her face. She obviously knew exactly what Uncle Herman was describing.

"As fun as it may have seemed to the ones performing it, it was equally *dis*tasteful to the recipients. That tradition has gone on for more than seven-hundred years."

I was beginning to get a little nervous. *What does he have planned for us?* I looked over at Jimmy, who was staring at his dad. Butch was grinning from ear to ear, watching the two of us squirm.

"Today, we have something special planned for the Butchers." He turned and looked back at us. Then he faced front again and asked, "Do we dare do a shivaree here?"

He got no response, so he repeated his question. "I ask you, do we dare perform a shivaree for Helmi and Jimmy?"

"Why not?" Butch was the first to answer, and that was all it took to start the room buzzing. The kids found it fun to be included in Uncle Herman's ploy, and they were all yelling. "Yes!" "Shivaree!" "Do it!"

Retta stood up and began chanting, "Shi-va-ree! Shi-va-ree!" and in no time, she was joined by the rest of my sisters. Of course, most of them didn't have a clue as to what it meant to "consummate a marriage." They were simply taken up in the excitement, loving that they could be a part of the shenanigans the grown-ups had concocted.

The next thing we knew, two men came into the tent with a makeshift bed: it was an old Army cot that had been covered with a big quilt. They placed it on the platform directly behind us. Two other men each carried out a long piece of grosgrain ribbon with jingle bells sewn onto them. They proceeded to tie them around our ankles, one on Jimmy and one on me.

"Now, I'd like the two of you to stand, please," Uncle Herman said to us. We stood. "Helmi, will you do us the pleasure of walking to the front of the platform?" I did, and the bells jingled with every step of my right foot. Uncle Herman motioned to Jimmy to do the same. He did, jingling just as I had.

Uncle Herman turned back to the crowd and slowly grinned, then he emitted a sinister laugh. Everyone laughed with him. "Your duty, my fellow shivaree-ers, is to keep the bells jingling until mealtime. Whenever there is no sound of jingle bells, the silent partner must be dragged to the bed and placed upon it." He turned to us, again, and said, "and you, my dear bride and groom, must do your best to avoid the nuptial throne." He motioned to the bed.

"Does everyone understand his or her part in this?" There was no response. "I'll make it much simpler…KEEP THEM DANCING!" And with that, the four men who had brought out the bed and the ankle bells came sweeping back into the tent with their instruments, playing lively music.

Lizzy came up to Jimmy, grabbed him by the hand, and started to hop around like she had St. Vida's dance! "You'd better start making some noise," she shouted at Jimmy, "or you're going to the bed!" Jimmy stamped his foot, and the jingling began.

Uncle Herman grabbed me around the waist and said, "Let's polka!"

I had no idea how to polka, but I followed his lead, and my bells jingled loud and clear. "This is fun!" I said. "I didn't even know I could polka."

While we all danced with each other—and the bells kept jingling—a crew of ladies brought out bowl after bowl and platter after platter of food, placing it all on the long table. I danced with Mary and Retta, and Jimmy was taking turns going around the floor with first Bella, then Ronnie, then Dora. Granny Nan kept her foot tapping while sitting with Anna. Butch clapped his hands and sang; he appeared to know most of the songs the band was playing.

Yosie sat by herself, checking and rechecking her lipstick in a little mirror she always carried in her handbag. Jimmy couldn't leave well enough alone. He jingled up behind her, lifted her up, and dragged her to the dancefloor. She stood motionless while Jimmy tried his best to get her to dance. I could tell she was thinking this whole thing was "stupid," her favorite adjective. But Jimmy didn't give up. He pestered her until she finally gave in and moved her feet from side-to-side, swinging her hips and looking sour.

I was standing there, motionless, watching the two of them when, out of nowhere, Uncle Herman came up to me and lifted me up, carrying me baby-style to the bed. "You weren't jingling," he said. "You have to spend some time on the bed."

When everyone noticed what was happening, they laughed and pointed at me, then they began chiding Jimmy, asking him if he was abandoning me and shaming him for leaving me alone in the bed. All the youngsters thought it was great fun, so they dragged him to the bed and pushed him down with me. I couldn't believe that I was blushing. Then I looked at Jimmy, and his cheeks were far more red than mine. I pointed to his face and sniggered.

"It's from all of the dancin'," he said.

"No it isn't. You're embarrassed because everyone sees us in this bed and has ideas about what we do here."

"Well then, let's show them they're right," he said.

"Wh…?" But before I could finish the word, he covered my mouth with his and kissed me—I mean, really kissed me—right there in front of everyone!

I heard a few hands clapping, then the entire tent exploded with applause. And shouting. And whistling. And the band stopped playing, all except the drummer, who made as much noise as he possibly could.

When we finally came up for air, Jimmy stood up and bowed. The crowd…our family…loved it.

We ate and ate and ate some more until I felt like a tick ready to pop. It was delicious. The band took a break while we ate, then they came back and began playing slow music. Everyone, including Granny Nan and Butch, danced. Uncle Herman told Jimmy and me we could take the bells off our ankles, but we agreed that we kind of liked them, so we left them on.

Yosie actually got up and danced, albeit by herself, to a couple of the slow songs that she liked. She appeared to have transcended into another dimension, writhing and swaying, her eyes closed and her facial expression limp.

Jimmy and I were dancing as close as we could in the presence of other people. I said to him, "Look at Yosie. If I didn't know better, I'd think she's drunk."

He watched her for a few measures, then he said to me. "She isn't drunk, Helmi. I think she's on some kind of drug. She acts like she's doped up."

I frowned, but as I watched her, I began to think that Jimmy may have been right. *Her recent attitude, her moodiness; could it really be the product of some sort of drug? And if it is, how did she get it? Where did she get it? She hasn't been to a doctor, so it's not something prescribed. Or maybe it is liquor. Maybe she found some in Uncle Herman's house.* My feeling of lightheartedness disappeared in the blink of an eye. The party had instantaneously become less than fun. I was genuinely worried about Yosie.

"Hey? You in there?" Jimmy was tapping my forehead with his index finger.

"Oh…yeah. Sorry. I just…" I couldn't finish my sentence; the words wouldn't form in my head.

Jimmy stopped dancing and backed away from me a little. "You have to remember who we're talkin' 'bout here. Your sister's from another planet."

I laughed half-heartedly. "Yeah, she's always been unlike anyone else I've ever known. I'm probably making way too much of it."

"We'll keep an eye on her. It's probably nothin' at all—just a typical Yosie-ism."

"I like that description," I said. "Yosie-isms. That describes her actions perfectly." I let the subject drop. After all, this whole affair had been set up for us in honor of our happiness. I couldn't let Yosie stand in my way of enjoying what Uncle Herman and Mary had done for us.

It was about two o'clock in the afternoon when the band quit playing, and Uncle Herman took the stage again. He introduced the band members and thanked them, then he brought out the caterers and thanked them. We all applauded for everyone, then Jimmy got up and took a place beside Uncle Herman. I was stunned at the sight. *What is he doing? I hope he doesn't embarrass himself, or me, or us. I would never have predicted this.*

Jimmy held his hands up to quiet everyone, then he turned to Uncle Herman and said, "Herman, I wanna thank ya. You've gone way above the call of duty here; this has been like a dream come true for me and Helmi. I'm real proud to be a part of this family. I've known mosta you for a lotta years. I grew up around ya, and I always felt I belonged with all of ya." He stopped for a moment but soon went on. "I think this means at least as much to Helmi, if not more, because she couldn't share it with her parents."

My heart stopped.

"Her mother woulda loved to see her daughter get married, even it was only to me." He chuckled nervously. "And her father…well, he was a man I always looked up to, but he meant the world to Helmi. Herman, you somehow lessened the blow of his passin' by bein' like a father to Helmi. And for that, I'm most grateful. I hope you can eventually look at me and see me as a son."

Herman hung his head, then he reached up with one hand and wiped his eyes. He put his other hand on Jimmy's shoulder.

My heart was beating again, but my mouth was hanging open. I inhaled a quick breath. I had no idea that my husband was capable of sharing his feelings with my family, now *his* family, on such a public level. I was proud beyond words. Then I realized I was crying.

There was not a sound in that tent at that moment. Jimmy reached out and shook Herman's hand. No words were exchanged—they weren't necessary. Then Jimmy came back to me, reached down and lifted my chin until my mouth closed. He bent down and whispered in my ear, "You tryin' to catch flies?"

I snorted, and everyone knew he'd said something funny to me in order to lighten the mood. At that moment, I felt like there was no one else in the tent—only Jimmy and me.

Herman composed himself and said, "I know you all have to get on the road real soon. Those cows aren't going to be too happy if they have to wait past their normal milking time. So I believe the time's ripe for making a presentation to the happy couple. Helmi, as we all know, will be heading south in another month, and it's no news flash that the old Ford truck Heinrich bought when you all moved here has just about reached the end of its road. But then that's a Ford for you." The adults all laughed.

"If you'll all come outside with me, I'll let Helmi and Jimmy in on the secret." He stepped down off the platform and took one of Jimmy's hands in one of his and one of my hands in the other. He led the way to the front of the house and over to the unfamiliar car that was parked in his driveway. He stopped, and he handed each of us a key. He didn't say a word. He knew we understood.

Jimmy and I looked at each other with awe in our eyes, then we both hugged him.

"It isn't just from me," Uncle Herman said. "Nancy, Butch, Mary, Lizzy, and all of your sisters gave whatever they could to help buy it for you. It isn't new, it's used, but it only has sixteen-hundred miles on it. It's a 1937 Pontiac six-cylinder with 222.7 cubic inches…"

But I didn't hear anymore, though Uncle Herman went on to tell Jimmy all about it. I turned around and looked at my family standing there, all of them wearing smiles, and thought about how lucky I was. My mind flashed through everything that had happened to me in nearly eighteen years, and I was overwhelmed with the love that had seen me through it all.

One of the band members lived in St. Louis (the town where Jimmy had proposed to me), so he drove the truck to his place and told Jimmy and me that we could pick it up whenever we had the chance. Butch drove Jimmy's old Chevrolet, and Jimmy drove the new burgundy-colored Pontiac. There was plenty of room for everyone, but I got to ride right beside my husband.

He talked about the party and the new car all the way home—a full three hours' worth—and I was more in love with him than I had ever been.

DORA'S ART AND A MISSING SISTER

Two days before I was to leave for OSU Dora came to me and said, "When you can, I'd like for you to come up to my room. There's something I want to show you."

"Okay. As soon as I finish hanging this load of washing, I'll be up."

The sleeping arrangements had changed again. Since I was now married, Jimmy and I slept in the room that used to be Mama and Papa's. Retta's and my room now housed Retta and Bella, Dora and Yosie still shared a room (though Yosie had requested her own room, but that was out of the question), and Ronnie and Anna were old enough to share a room by themselves. Granny Nan was in the downstairs bedroom as usual.

Jimmy had decided to stay at his own house with his dad when I was away at college. He'd said, "Dad needs me there. And besides, at your house it's pretty hard to get into the bathroom with seven females all trying to get in there at the same time."

"It's not *my* house, it's *ours*," I had reminded him.

I pushed a clothespin onto the last pair of wet socks and gathered up the clothespin bag and the laundry basket and went inside. I deposited them on a table beside the old Thor and went upstairs to Dora and Yosie's room. Dora was sitting on her bed with the big pad of paper I had looked through earlier in the summer. I still felt bad about having invaded her privacy.

"Where's Yosie?" I asked as I sat down on Yosie's bed.

She shrugged. "Don't know. Don't care."

I had never heard Dora respond in that manner. Her replies were usually pretty noncommittal, but they were rarely that succinct. And I could detect a bit of attitude that was unbecoming to Dora. I wondered if she had started mimicking Yosie; after all, they'd been sharing a room for quite some time. But I let it drop and asked, "What's on your mind?"

"There's something I want to show you," she said quietly. She pulled the big pad of paper up onto her lap and opened it to the first page. I expected to see one of the drawings I had looked at previously, but this one had not been included in the pad of paper I had looked through. This was a portrait of Jimmy and me sitting at the table at our wedding reception at Uncle Herman's. My mouth dropped open.

"Do you like it?" she asked timidly.

"Like it? I LOVE it! Where did you get it? Who drew that? It's absolutely perfect. Look how happy we are!"

She smiled and said, "I drew it. I was hoping you'd like it. I want to frame it for you, but I was afraid you might not want to display it. Thought maybe you'd think it wasn't good enough for that."

"Dora! How long have you been working on it? It's incredible! So professional. I had no idea you knew how to draw like that."

She was blushing. "I've been drawing ever since I could hold a pencil," she said. "I especially like to draw people. Faces tell so much about us. I like capturing moods. And I think this one says a lot about how you and Jimmy feel toward each other." She was looking me square in the face.

"It says exactly how I feel, Dora." I was looking at Jimmy, seeing the love in his eyes. I could recall my feelings from that exact moment in time. *How does she do it? I didn't see her drawing while we were there.*

"Thanks. That's what I wanted you to say." She was smiling from ear to ear.

"Dora, you have a very special talent. Does Miss Michaels know you can draw portraits like this?"

"Uh-huh. She's the one who told me I should do one for you guys," she said, almost with embarrassment.

"Do you have others? Drawings of other people, I mean?" I knew the answer, but I didn't know if she wanted to share them.

She nodded.

"I'd sure like to see some of them, that is, if you want to show them to me."

She smiled, stood, then got down on her hands and knees and pulled three more large pads and seven or eight small ones from under her bed.

My mouth dropped open again. I couldn't believe how much time the drawings must have taken her—I guessed most of her life. She grabbed one of the small pads and came over to Yosie's bed and sat down beside me.

"These are just quick sketches, but they give me ideas for my larger portraits." She lifted the cover and there, looking back at me, was Papa. His face showed the age lines that had appeared right after Uncle Julius committed suicide. That's when I knew Papa was beginning to go downhill, as Granny Nan had mentioned to me once.

"I can't believe how alive that is," I told Dora, "like Papa is still here, looking at me."

She turned the page to reveal Granny Nan standing at the kitchen sink, her back mostly to me, but I could see part of one side of her profile. Her shoulders were bent over her work, her elbows out at an angle. The back of her long dress was raised to the middle of her calves as she bent over, and the hem was permanently darkened from dragging in the dirt; some of the fabric had begun to wear thin leaving broken threads visible along the very bottom. The soles of her shoes were unevenly worn, indicating that she walked with one foot turned slightly over on its side. Her apron showed fingerprints by the side pocket where she had either put something in or taken something out with dirty hands. Her hair was tied back, tendrils of it sticking out every which direction. The sunlight coming through the window was lighting them up and making them glow.

I reached over and touched the drawing, as if I could feel the portrayal in three dimensions. The detail Dora had captured was so obvious, yet none of it detracted from the overall depiction. I looked up at Dora, and she seemed to know that I wanted to see more. So she slowly turned the pages, and I continued to be in awe.

One of the sketches was a close-up of Yosie's reflection in a hand mirror. I was sure that was the one she had used in the large drawing of Yosie that I'd seen before. "Your proportions are perfect. Not just of the faces, but of everything around the people. I'm at a loss to express how proud I am of you," I told her. "I had no idea I was related to an artist, let alone one of your caliber."

We spent the next hour looking at her renditions of nearly everyone we knew. Everyone, that is, except for Mama. I kept expecting to see Mama appear on the next page each time Dora revealed one, but Mama's face never showed up.

"You're looking for Mama, aren't you?" Dora asked me.

"How did you know?"

She shrugged. "I could never get her right. It's as if she was transparent, ethereal. I could never nail down the exact nature of her face; it always eluded me. I can see her in my mind's eye, but I can't get it to transfer to the paper. I've tried and tried, but she just won't allow herself to be drawn."

I thought about that for a moment, then I said, "You know, that doesn't surprise me. I think she wants to be remembered as always being in motion. And until you learn to make drawings that move, she's going to remain elusive."

"I like that," Dora said. "I feel better about it already."

She had done a portrait of Lizzy, her mouth open and her hands flailing in the air, just like they do when Lizzy talks. I was in the illustrated company of all of my sisters, Granny Nan, Uncle Herman, Mary, Miss Michaels, some of the kids Dora knew at school, and even Two-Tone; there was a bundle of expression on that dog's face, and I had never even taken the time to notice it.

"Tell me you're considering going to art school," I said to Dora when she had finally finished revealing her likenesses.

"It's something I've had in the back of my mind, but I still have a long way to go before I graduate from high school, and I don't want to put the cart before the horse," she said. "Besides, I don't want to go far away like you. I want to stay close to home...at least I do right now. Maybe after I get older I'll think otherwise."

"You're being quite mature about this," I told her. "Why haven't I ever seen this side of you before?"

Dora got up off Yosie's bed, gathered up her sketch books and large pads, and slid them all back under her bed. "I don't wear my emotions on my sleeve like Yosie does." She sat back down on her own bed. "I don't pay much attention to her anymore. She has to make such a big deal out of every little thing." She sighed. "She's really getting on my nerves. I try not to spend much time around her. Don't want her to rub off on me. I know that's not nice to say, but I sure wish she'd learn that the world doesn't revolve around her."

"That'll never happen, I'm afraid," I said. "She's been like that since the day she was born." *I think Mama had a lot to do with that, but, according to Granny Nan, it's not nice to speak ill of the dead.* "I think she's going to have a hard time when she has to light out on her own."

"If she ever does," Dora added.

"Huh...I never thought about that," I said. "Maybe she'll just stick around and become a lonely old spinster."

Dora laughed. "You're probably right. No one will ever live up to her expectations. You should hear the things she says about people," Dora went on, imitating Yosie: "'So-and-so doesn't know a thing about fashion.' 'That girl thinks she's so smart.' 'He's a complete waste of ...'" She stopped short, looked at me, and her face turned red.

It was apparent that Yosie had been talking about Jimmy when she had said that, and I knew the quote had simply rolled out of Dora's mouth without any thought behind it. I immediately said, "Yeah, Yosie has some pretty major bad opinions about people, most of which are unfounded."

But I could tell Dora felt the damage had been done; I knew she hadn't wanted to insult Jimmy or me, and she probably felt she had done that very thing to both of us. "You're smart not to want her to rub off on you," I said. "Just ignore it and move on as best you can. That's what I've always done." I hoped I'd covered up Dora's little faux pas without making it seem too obvious.

I was just finishing up my chores and heading to the milk house when I heard Granny Nan call us all to supper. I saw Jimmy and Retta coming toward me; he had her in a headlock, obviously kidding her about something, and she was laughing and struggling to release herself from his clutches. I loved the way the two of them got on together.

We all washed up and sat down, waiting for Granny Nan and Dora to put the food on the table. Bella asked, "Where's Yosie?"

We all remained silent until Dora finally spoke up. "Early this morning she got into a car I never saw before. I think it was some boy driving, but I'm not sure."

"How early?" I asked. Jimmy, Retta, and I had all been doing the milking, so I thought we should have heard the car. But then I realized that, with the milkers going and us being on the other side of the road, we didn't always hear cars coming or going.

"You mean she did not tell you where she was going?" Granny Nan asked.

"Or with whom?" I added.

"Not a word," Dora said. "But that's not unusual. She hardly ever tells me what she's doing."

I took in a big breath and looked over at Granny Nan; her eyes met mine.

"What kind of car?" Jimmy asked.

"A black one," Dora said.

Jimmy rolled his eyes. "Black's a color, not a kind. What'd it look like?"

"I don't know!" Dora said, apparently exasperated. "It was old, not like your new Pontiac. It was more like Uncle Herman's old Buick."

"And you did not recognize the driver?" Granny Nan asked.

"No. I already said it looked like a boy, but I'm not sure. It might have been a girl with really short hair."

I put my elbows on the table, dropped my head in my hands, and exhaled. I had a bad feeling about this.

Jimmy scooted his seat back at the same time as Granny Nan attempted to reach between him and me to set a big bowl of hot green beans and potatoes on the table. He recklessly backed right into Granny Nan, and the bowl flipped backwards, spilling all over her and the floor.

"Dammit!" he shouted. "I'm sorry, Nancy. I had no idea you were there. Are you okay? Did it burn ya bad?"

"No, it was not that hot. It did not feel good, mind you, but I do not have any burns that will need to be treated," Granny Nan told him as she was on her way to the sink to get a towel, Jimmy right on her heels. "That girl causes trouble even when she is not here!" Granny Nan said.

"Should I go looking for her?" Jimmy asked as he was wiping the mess up off the floor.

"What good would that do?" Retta asked. "She's never where you figure she'll be anyway. You'd be wasting your time."

"She's right," Bella said. "Half the time she's not even in school when she's supposed to be."

Silence.

"What?" I finally uttered.

"She goes to school and makes an appearance, then she ducks out and goes someplace else. God only knows where," Bella said.

"And why am I just finding this out? How long has it been going on?" I asked.

"According to the kids I know, since she started high school," Bella answered.

Dora turned to me. "You were always busy with your classes, so you were never able to pay any attention to what was going on with her."

"Not that you could have made any difference," Retta said.

"And you were doing exactly as you should have," Jimmy said, looking up at me from his position on his hands and knees.

"But…" I began.

"No buts," Granny Nan said. "He is absolutely right. You are not responsible for Yosie. Though I do wish we had known about this before now."

"It wouldn't make a bit of difference," Dora said. "She has a mind of her own, and not one of us knows what goes on inside that unglued brain of hers."

"What're we gonna do?" Ronnie asked.

"What *can* we do?" Jimmy said. "She's sixteen, old enough to think for herself and make her own decisions."

Poor Anna just sat there, her little head turning from one of us to the other as we each spoke, tears welling up in her eyes. "Is Yosie coming back?" Her face scrunched up and she began to cry.

Bella, who was sitting next to her, said "Oh, Anna, honey, don't cry." She put her arm around the youngest member of our family, then she picked up Anna's napkin, and began to wipe the tears from the poor little girl's face and eyes.

"We'll find her." Bella looked up at me with an expression of complete confidence in my ability to find Yosie and bring her home.

But she was wrong. I had no idea where to begin looking for her. "I think we just need to eat our supper…"

"What's left of it, thanks to me," Jimmy said under his breath.

"…and wait for her to come home. I'm sure she won't be gone much longer," I finished, but I was less than certain that was true.

By the time we went to bed that night, Yosie was still missing. The next morning I helped with the milking, then Jimmy and I took Dora to Mount Pleasant to look for a black Buick, probably around ten years old. It was hopeless; we must have seen fifteen or more black Buicks from the late 1920s.

After circling around town for the third time, Dora said, "They all look like possibilities. I've seen too many. It's confusing. I can't identify the exact one."

I could tell she was frustrated, so we went to the police station and reported Yosie missing. I asked the officer at the desk if he would call our house and make sure she had not returned while we'd been gone. He did, but Granny Nan said Yosie had not shown up.

"There isn't much we can do except put out a bulletin to some of the surrounding stations. We can radio the information you gave us about her to each dispatcher, but that's about it. Without a definite description of the car and the driver, our hands are pretty much tied." We thanked him and left.

I took hold of Jimmy's arm and said, "I'd be willing to bet she's nowhere near here. She's always had big city lights in her eyes. It wouldn't surprise me to find out she went to a place with a whole lot more people than Mount Pleasant, or even Flint."

"Yeah, I'm inclined to agree," Jimmy said.

Dora remained silent. I could tell she was feeling defeated, and she probably felt like she hadn't been of any help. So I said to her, "Dora, thanks for coming with us. I know trying to find the car was like trying to find a needle in a haystack."

She looked off into the distance. I don't know where she disappeared to at that moment, but she certainly wasn't with us. "Chicago," she eventually said.

"Chicago?" I said, completely befuddled.

"She talked about it all the time. She said she wanted a house like Aunt Lavern and Uncle Julius's. She talked about the Indian woman who let her pet the bear."

"The bear? How long ago was that?" Jimmy asked.

Then it came to me. "It was when we were moving from Oklahoma." I said. "We stopped at Aunt Lavern and Uncle Julius's house on the way here. Their house was huge. It had an entryway the size of our entire cabin in Oklahoma. Yosie loved the big stuffed bear in the nursery and wanted to pet it," I said. "Yeah, the nursery. We had cookies and lemonade. Yosie must have eaten four or five of those cookies. That Indian woman, Belinda, let Yosie fall asleep on the bear's leg. The rest of the house was like a mansion with great big rooms, lots of fancy furniture and rugs and drapes at the windows. I remember watching Yosie; when she wasn't busy stuffing cookies into her mouth, she was mesmerized by it all."

"I guess we'd better check the bus station, huh?" Dora said.

Jimmy drove us to the bus station. I got out and said, "I'll see if she bought a ticket and to where."

Dora was right; Yosie had purchased a bus ticket to Grand Rapids and had most likely gotten on a train, probably Chicago-bound. I wondered if she would find out that Aunt Lavern was in a home for people with dementia—Granny Nan had called it "brain fever." I don't think Granny Nan had ever told anyone but me, and I definitely hadn't told Yosie, Bella, or Dora. I got back into the car.

"Well?" Dora asked.

"She bought a ticket to Grand Rapids."

"That's not too far away," Jimmy said. "We could probably ask the police to check for her there."

"I have a feeling she won't be there—at least not for very long. I'm betting she either transferred to another bus or took a train to Chicago thinking she'd stay with Aunt Lavern."

"Then all we have to do is call Aunt Lavern and find out if she's there," Dora said. She was excited.

"No, she won't be there," I said.

Jimmy said, "You just said she'd probably be staying..."

"I said she's probably *thinking* she'll stay with Aunt Lavern. What she doesn't know is that Aunt Lavern doesn't live there anymore."

"She moved?" Dora asked.

"Kind of..."

"What's that s'posed to mean?" Jimmy asked.

I didn't want to betray Granny Nan's trust, but I knew I had to explain the situation to Jimmy and Dora. "A while back, Granny Nan got a letter saying Aunt Lavern's not well. She has dementia and is in a home for people who need twenty-four-hour care."

"Did she sell the house?"

"I don't know. I only know that Yosie isn't going to find her there if she goes to the Gounaris house."

"We're not going to find her, are we?" Dora asked, on the verge of tears.

"She'll call. I know she will. She'll run out of money at some point and need us to send some to her," I said.

"I think we need to go back to the police station and tell 'em what we've learned. It's only fair to them," Jimmy said.

"Yeah, you're right," I said.

The drive back to the station was silent. I was going over the details in my head, and I was pretty sure Dora and Jimmy were doing the same.

We all went into the police station again, but there was a different man at the front desk. He wrote down everything we told him and said he'd do his best to see to it that every possible scenario was checked out. We thanked him and went back to the car.

"I'm sorry I didn't tell you about Aunt Lavern," I said to Dora. "But Granny…"

"It's okay," she said. "If Granny Nan told you in confidence, you were right not to say anything to the rest of us."

"And how was anybody s'posed to know Yosie would do somethin' so moronic?" Jimmy added.

"We aren't sure she has," I said. "But I'd give my right arm to be sure she's safe." I couldn't hold back the tears now. Granted, Yosie left a lot to be desired in a young girl her age, but she was, after all, my sister. And like it or not, she was family, and families stuck together, stuck up for one another. My mind began wandering back to when she was born; the episodes that had dictated our lives since that April morning in 1922 went racing through my head. It was a quiet ride back home.

When we pulled into the driveway, I asked Jimmy and Dora to let me tell Granny Nan about what we'd found out, especially since I needed to apologize for telling the two of them about Aunt Lavern. I was sure she'd understand, considering the consequences, but I knew it should come from me. I told Dora she should tell Bella and Retta, and we all agreed not to say anything to Ronnie and Anna quite yet, unless one of them asked. "We'll cross that bridge when we come to it," I said, and they thought that sounded like a good idea. I knew Jimmy would tell his dad if and when he thought it was necessary to do so.

Granny Nan took the news exactly as I had expected. I could see the concern in her eyes, but she had shown very little sympathy for Yosie. As I imagined, she understood why I had to spill the beans about Aunt Lavern, and she thanked me for keeping it confidential until the time was necessary to bring it out into the open. Even though the times had changed, and those kinds of things were openly discussed among most people, Granny Nan was from an era where that sort of topic was considered very private, and I respected that.

She asked me about letting the others know, and I told her about our plan to tell Bella and Retta but to keep it from Ronnie and Anna as long as possible. She nodded and issued a sigh of relief. "What are we going to do about bringing Yosie back?" she asked.

"What do you propose?"

"I will have to think about it. I suppose I will have some time to do that considering we do not really know the whole truth yet," she said.

"You're right. We need to hear from the police—or a hospital somewhere, God forbid—before we move on." I knew the conversation was over, as Granny Nan had that faraway look. I could only imagine what was going through her head.

I went back outside to find Jimmy leaning against the car, his arms crossed over his chest and his head down. He was studying the ground as if there were something interesting in the gravel at his feet.

"Didn't know what you were getting yourself into, did you?" I asked as I joined him.

He put one arm around me and said, "I knew exactly what I was gettin' myself into. That's why it bothers me so much."

"What bothers you?" I asked.

"That she left without tellin' anybody. Not a word."

He was thinking about Yosie. He barely knew her, but his insights were keen enough to allow his feelings to be hurt by her actions. He was truly part of our family. I was both proud and amazed at his reaction to her disappearance. "I love you, but you know that," I said.

"I knew it long before you did."

CHECKING IN

I said my goodbyes to the family, then Jimmy and I left for Columbus. Butch and Retta had agreed to cover both the morning and evening milkings for the next two days, and I knew Retta was perfectly capable of tending the livestock by herself for that amount of time. Dora said she'd feed the chickens and ducks and gather the eggs, "… but it better not be for more than two days."

The Ohio State University was three-hundred and twenty-plus miles from Mount Pleasant, so it would be an all-day trip one way. Jimmy and I would have to stay overnight someplace in Columbus so that I could be on campus first thing in the morning, then he would make the trip back home after dropping me off. Granny Nan had packed plenty for us in the cold chest and picnic basket, and that included meals for Jimmy on the way back.

The directions that came in a packet from OSU were right on the mark, and we found the "Freshmen Orientation" parking lot without a hitch. But saying goodbye to Jimmy was a different story. I'd gotten away from home without shedding any tears, but I was sure I'd have a far more difficult time when I saw Jimmy drive away. I was right, but I was also among like company, as many of the new students were shedding tears when they and their parents, aunts, uncles, brothers, sisters, or friends parted ways.

After wiping my eyes, blowing my nose, and taking a deep breath, I proceeded to the building wherein I was to meet my counselor. I entered and found that the place was a madhouse, a crazy-farm full of animalistic humans all searching desperately to find one person or another, one table or another, or even a sign that might guide them in the right direction. And I was one of those animals.

More than two-thousand people were beginning their education that year at OSU, and about twenty-five percent of them were enrolling in biological sciences, which included the School of Veterinary Medicine. My first task was to find the vet school table. Luckily, the title of every major had been assigned to a table and arranged alphabetically, and I had entered the building at the end of the alphabet, so

'V' was right in front of me. My luck was holding up, and I was off to a good start.

There was a line of prospective students waiting to sign in, so I stepped up to the end of the queue to wait my turn. When I finally reached the table, I was met with a military-like barrage of questions: "What is your major? Do you have a counselor? Name?" And that's where my luck ended. Even though I was certain I had covered my tracks by sending the letters to the Admissions and the Bursar's offices explaining my name change after I had been accepted and enrolled, the people at the Vet School table had no record of me as Wilhelmina Butcher, only Wilhelmina Schnier. *So much for my good run of luck.* I was headed for a discouraging next step.

I had been assigned a dorm room and a counselor. I was given a campus map with the dormitory and the counselor's building both circled in red pencil. I was to report to the dorm by six p.m. and was to meet with my counselor the next day at eight-thirty a.m. I appreciated the map, but I was unable to locate the building I was currently in, so creating a heading to find my dorm and the other building was impossible. I tried asking some of the other freshmen, but they were as flummoxed as I and were of no help.

I looked around at the confusion and decided I was not going to allow myself to be overcome by all that chaos. I went back to the 'V' table, stepped up to the end of it, and said to the man sitting there, "I can't locate the building on the map where…"

"You'll have to go to the end of the line."

"I've already been through the line and was given this…"

"Please! Go to the end of the line!"

Well, at least the man had said, "Please." I understood that the people who were working there were as exasperated as I, so I again took my place at the end of the queue. Within what I figured was about twenty minutes, I reached the table and was greeted with: "What is your major?"

I interrupted the inquisition and said, "I've already been through this once, I just have a question. I was given…"

"I'm sorry. All questions need to be discussed with your counselor. I'm assuming you have one?"

I stood up straight, inhaled, and looked at the man; I'm certain my eyes were shooting daggers at him. His facial expression changed from one of authority to one of submission. I had gotten my foot in the door. "I can't very well discuss ANYTHING with my counselor if I can't locate my counselor's whereabouts. Would you please point out my current location on this map?"

"It's circled in blue."

"There are two buildings circled in red." I bent over and gently placed the map in front of him, pointing to each. "This one indicates my dorm, and this one indicates my counselor's building," I said with pointed enunciation. "No blue. My problem is that I cannot determine the building in which I am standing at this moment." I stood back up.

"Yes, I see the dorm and the other building. You are currently right…right…" He moved his finger over the map and said, "Oh, my. This map doesn't include this portion of the university, only the School of Veterinary Medicine." He picked up the map and said, "I'll be right back." Then he disappeared. I could hear the people in the line behind me complaining.

I wondered, *Is this how the rest of my college education is going to go? I don't know if I can stand five years of this disorganization. But the school's been in business since 1870, so it must be doing something right. I hope today is no indication of the days to come.*

Minutes passed, and finally the man returned. "You were given the wrong map. No, excuse me, *we* were given the wrong map. I apologize." He handed me another map which included the entire campus, and he had circled our current location in blue. "I hope this makes things easier for you. Again, my apologies."

I took the map, thanked him for clearing up my problem, and lit out to find my dormitory. It was only two doors down from the building I was currently in! *What a stroke of luck!* I walked to the dorm and stood in another line for what seemed like an eternity but was probably about three quarters of an hour. *What is taking so long? How can it be so difficult to get everyone situated?*

My suitcase was getting heavier by the minute. I kept setting it down and picking it up then setting it down and picking it up each time the line inched along. By the time I reached the front steps, it had begun to rain. I was in no mood to be drenched, so I stepped out of line and slipped sideways past everyone into the building's lobby. I didn't care if I had to wait until I was the last person to check in; I simply did not want to be soaking wet when that finally happened.

A couple who appeared to be my age came rushing in right behind me. They smiled at me, so I said, quietly, "Hi. Welcome to OSU—Ohio State Unorganized."

They laughed. The man reached out and took my hand, shaking it as he said, "Richard McConkey. This is my wife, Ivy."

I shook her hand, as well, and gave them my name.

"Where's your husband?" Ivy asked.

How does she know I'm married? I'm not wearing my rings. I instinctively reached my left thumb over to my ring finger to make sure the rings were not there. *I left them at home so they wouldn't get lost, and besides, the instructions I received specifically said, "For sanitary purposes, students enrolled in the School of Veterinary Medicine must refrain from wearing any jewelry."*

I must have frowned, because she said, "You are married, right?"

"Yes, but how did you know that?"

"This is the married dorm," Ivy said.

"The what?"

"The married dorm," Richard repeated. "Only married couples live here."

Scheist! "My husband is not a student here. I'm attending without him," I said. "We own a dairy farm in Michigan, and he's taking care of the farm while I go to college."

"Uh-oh...looks like somebody missed that little fact," Ivy said.

Richard confirmed it with a nod of his head.

I sighed, but I really wanted to cry. "I guess I'll have to work that out with the people at the desk over there. If I ever get a chance to talk to one of them, that is." The line had not seemed to grow any longer, but the people who had opted against coming inside were appearing more and more agitated as the inclement weather increased.

"Hey! You folks!" We all looked across the room at a young man, most likely an upper-class student, standing up on his tiptoes on the other side of the line, and he was waving at us. He began moving toward us, weaving in and out of the people who were lingering in the lobby. When he reached us, he said, "I saw you come in. There's something to be said for those who are smart enough to come in out of the rain. I have a little bit of pull around here...just give me a minute."

There were both an elderly man and a younger woman sitting at the table, and he walked up to the elderly man and said something to him. The elderly man looked over at us, then he said something to the young man with "pull." The young man motioned for us to come over to the table, so we all picked up our suitcases and ventured over. The young man smiled at us and, without a word, turned and walked away.

"I understand you are here to register for housing," the elderly man at the table said to us.

"Yessir," we all said.

He looked up at me. "Okay, I'll start with you."

"Thank you. My name is Helmi, I mean, Wilhelmina Butcher."

He looked through his lists. Then he started over and looked again. "I'm sorry. What is your last name?"

"Butcher."

He looked a third time. "I don't have anyone by that name on my list."

"Try Schnier."

He turned to the last page and said, "Ah! Here it is."

"I just got married in July, and my last name became Butcher. I had already been accepted here as Wilhelmina Schnier, but I sent letters to the proper offices immediately after my marriage, and they *assured* me the name change would not cause any problems today."

"Hmmmm. So much for assurances," he said. "What is your husband's name?"

"James, but I don't see why that matters; he's not a student here, nor is he applying to be enrolled."

"Is he paying to live with you here in the dorm?"

I shook my head. "We own a dairy farm in Michigan, which he's currently returning to after dropping me off here. He will not be staying with me. I'm staying by myself. Alone. Just me."

He looked at me as if I were speaking a foreign language. "You can't do that."

Now I looked at him as if he were the foreigner.

There was a long pause, during which my mouth hung open.

He finally said, "I can't admit a single person. Our rooms are reserved for married couples only. Who told you to come here to this dorm?"

I closed my gaping maw and said nothing. I produced the map I'd been given, placing it on the table in front of him. By this point, I was afraid I might bite someone if I opened my mouth again.

He studied the map, carefully noting the red and blue circles, then he scratched his head. "Did the people in the building two doors down give you a deadline for checking in at your dorm?"

"Six p.m."

He looked at his watch. I glanced at it, as well, and saw that it was now two-twenty p.m. In a tiny, unfamiliar voice I asked, "What am I to do?"

"That, my fine young woman, is a good question." I could almost see the wheels turning in his brain as he tried to figure out a way to resolve this problem. Eventually he said, "I'll take care of everything." He turned to Richard and Ivy and said, "The woman beside me will be checking you in next." He then turned to the woman, explained that the McConkey's were next in line, and that he would be helping me.

"But…but…what…" she stammered.

"Just handle it, Dorothea," he said to her, then he turned back to me and said, "Come with me."

I looked back at the McConkeys and waved, then I shrugged my shoulders and followed the elderly man who, surprisingly, moved at an extremely rapid pace; it took everything I had just to keep up. I blamed it on the fact that I was carrying the suitcase.

He led me into a small office that obviously belonged to a woman. It was decorated with a lace curtain at the tiny single window, probably to offer a bit of shade when the sun came up each morning. There were pots of house plants on a table beneath it and two enlarged photographs on the wall opposite the desk, both of which depicted the elderly man, the woman he'd spoken to at the table, and three children, the oldest probably near high school age, and two younger boys, maybe ten or twelve years old. There was a floor-to-ceiling bookcase on the wall just inside the door to the right; it was filled with books about plants, trees, and gardening, and there was an entire shelf devoted to *Poor Richard's Almanacs*, some of which looked extremely old.

"Please, have a seat," the man said and gestured to one of the two chairs under the photographs. "I'll be back as soon as I straighten this out. We won't make you sleep on the street tonight."

"Thank you." I was glad to be able to sit for a few minutes. Up to that point, I hadn't noticed how tired I was. *I'm sure it's because of the situation. I'm exhausted, and I shouldn't be; I'm used to a lot of physical labor.*

The wall behind the desk revealed a small chalkboard on the left. An easel stood on the right, and on it was a large hand-made calendar, the month of August currently visible, the other months rolled behind the giant pad of paper. There was a large red border drawn around the current week. I was too far away to read anything that had been written in any of the daily squares.

I blinked several times and realized my eyelids were having a tough time retracting after closing. Then it dawned on me that I had not had anything to eat or drink throughout the day. I'd been too nervous to eat breakfast, and I hadn't taken any time to get so much as a sip of water since starting the enrollment process. I was hungry and dehydrated. No wonder I felt so sluggish.

I have no idea how long I sat there, dozing and then jerking awake at every little sound. I finally stood up and stretched my arms up over my head. Then I bent over and touched the floor in front of me. Someone behind me cleared his or her throat. I bolted back up to a standing position and whirled around to see the young man who had been so kind to the McConkeys and me in the lobby. I instantly blushed.

"You possess extraordinary agility," he said.

"I just…I…I was just…I needed to…"

He said nothing. He simply stood there looking at me, allowing me to wallow in my own embarrassment. I looked him square in the face and said, "My name's Helmi. Thank you so much for your kindness in the lobby."

"Link," he said.

"Link," I repeated dumbfoundedly.

"It's my name."

"Oh!" I was digging myself in deeper, and I didn't even have a shovel. "My name's not really Helmi; that's just a nickname. My full name's Wilhelmina Schnier. Er…Butcher."

"Okay, Wilhelmina Schnier Er Butcher. It's nice to meet you."

"Likewise," I said. We stared at each other for a couple of seconds, then we both snorted a laugh. "It's been a long day. I'm not usually so addle-brained."

He sat down in the chair behind the desk.

"Is this your office?" I asked.

His eyes wandered around the room. "Does it look like an office I would choose to work in?"

"That's a loaded question," I said. "I have no idea what kind of décor you favor, so I could possibly get myself into deep water with my answer."

"I knew you were smart. I could tell by the way you took command of yourself when you first came into the building. This is my wife's office. She was the woman at the table in the lobby. The man you followed in here is her father."

I turned and studied the photographs again. I recognized the woman as Dorothea, who was his wife, so the children were probably hers and his. "Your family?"

He nodded.

"And Link is short for…?"

"Lincoln," he said. "D.K. Lincoln. Are you planning on majoring in the field of veterinary medicine?"

"I will graduate as a veterinarian, and I will be at the top of my class," I announced to him.

"You are a woman of purpose."

I didn't answer. Instead, I took the opportunity to take a good look at him. He was probably in his late twenties, maybe early thirties. He had thick dark hair, a well-shaped face that was devoid of beard or mustache and tanned from the sun, big blue eyes, a prominent nose, and a nice smile. He was muscular, as if he worked at a job that required him to perform physical labor.

His eyes drifted up to the photos behind me. A far-away look crossed his face for a fraction of a second. "Dorothea is my second wife. My first died of pneumonia. And I don't have the slightest idea why I'm telling you that or why I'd think you might be interested."

He continued to stare at the photos.

I was speechless, but I decided it was probably best that I had nothing to say.

The elderly man came through the door. "Wilhelmina, you will sleep in a bed this night. A female student has already withdrawn from school, so you'll be taking her place in a dormitory on the east side of the Olentangy. You're lucky, because it's actually closer to the main campus where you'll be taking your General Education Requirement classes. On the downside, it's further from the School of Veterinary Medicine, so you'll have a fair hike to get to the classes in your major."

Thoughts raced through my head. *I'll be talking to my counselor tomorrow morning, and I have to be certain to ask about taking the exams to see if I'm able to get credit for some of the General Ed Requirements without having to sit through the classes. I need to explain to her that I've been working with a veterinarian and would like to start taking medical classes as soon as possible. I probably should also mention that I'm on a scholarship and will be using my trust for the last portion of my education. I'm sure I'll find out about the books I need. I need to have her mark the bookstore on my map. MY MAP! Where did I leave it?*

The elderly man said, "I've marked the dormitory on your map."

Oh, yeah. That's where I left it.

He placed it on Dorothea's desk and showed me where I would be staying; 'Wilmington Hall' had been hand-written on the map with an arrow pointing to one of the buildings.

I took the map from him and said, "Thank you. It was nice to meet you, Mr…"

"Aldridge. And it's *Doctor*. I'm afraid you're going to be seeing more of me than you may want to. I'm actually a professor emeritus, but I have nothing better to do than substitute teach some of the classes and bother the other professors by attending their classes when I'm bored."

"What type of doctor?" I asked.

"Veterinarian," he said. "Link, here, took over my business when I retired. He's not only a good teacher, he's also a top-notch vet. He'll be teaching some of your classes." His brow furrowed, and he scratched his chin. "If memory serves, animal husbandry is one of the first ones you'll be taking, and Link teaches it."

I looked at Link and said, "I'll be looking forward to it, Professor Lincoln."

He mimicked a man tipping his hat and disappeared through the office door.

"I appreciate your effort in taking care of my dilemma, Dr.

Aldridge. I think I'll make my way across the river and find my new temporary home."

"It's still pouring rain out there."

"I don't seem to mind that so much now," I said. I picked up my suitcase and my map and left, feeling much better than I had a few minutes earlier.

Wilmington Hall was about as far to the southeast as one could go on campus. But it was easy to find, and the rain had stopped by the time I reached it. There was no line, and a female was sitting at a beautiful oak rolltop desk in the lobby. She saw me come in and came over to me. "Can I help you with your suitcase?" she asked.

"Thanks, but I can manage. I just need to find out where my room is."

"I can tell you in a jiffy if you'll give me your name."

Here we go again. "My name's Wilhelmina Butcher, but you probably…"

"So you're our fill-in for the girl who withdrew. Went from Schnier to Butcher, right?"

"Uh-huh." I was totally bewildered. *How had Dr. Aldridge taken care of everything so fast?*

"Dr. Aldridge told me I'd better be nice to you. I'm Olivia, by the way, but you can call me Liv."

"I'm Wilhelmina, but you can call me Helmi," I said and smiled at her.

"I'm the oldest person in this dorm, so that qualifies me as the dorm adviser. Whatever you need, you come to me for it. You'll also have a floor monitor to keep things running by the rules. You know: no guys on the floors—only in the lobby, no cooking in the rooms, no loud noise after ten p.m. I'm sure you received the dorm booklet in your admissions packet."

"I didn't get an admissions packet. Was it supposed to be delivered to my house by post?"

"No, everyone receives one when they check in on orientation day."

"Well, not everyone. I got nothing except a paper with my counselor's name and time of my appointment and a map showing me where he or she's located on campus."

Liv hung her head and shook it back and forth slowly. "I'll get one for you after we get you settled in. You'll be on the third floor, room thirty-six. It's the biggest room in the dorm, and you'll be sharing it with three others. Follow me."

She set a folded card on the top of the desk; it said, "Be Right

Back…Please Wait Here." Then she started up the stairs, and I followed, toting the suitcase up the two flights to the third floor and panting by the time I got there. There were numbered doors off each side of the hall—the numbers painted on—and at the end of the hall was number 36. Liv knocked on the door, and a girl whose head barely reached my shoulders opened it slightly.

"Got a new roommate for you," Liv said.

The girl flung the door open and said, "Hi. Come on in. You're the last to arrive. You must be Elsie Wexler."

"No," Liv said, "she's not. Elsie Wexler withdrew from school. This is Helmi Butcher." Liv introduced the other three girls to me.

"Thanks, Liv," I said to her as she turned to leave. Then I looked at the other three girls and said, "Just point me in the direction of my bed. After what I've been through today, I'm ready to collapse."

GLAD TO BE HOME

My first quarter exams were finished on Friday, December 9. I was eager to see the headlights of our Pontiac coming toward me to take me home for the holidays. But I was more eager to see Jimmy, my knight in shining armor who would whisk me away from this prison and take me to our castle in Mount Pleasant. Well…sort of.

Being December, it was already dark. Jimmy would have driven all day to get there, so we'd have to find a place to stay overnight, then we'd drive back home the next day. I had spoken to him on the telephone once a week, as each of us in the dorm was allowed to make a long-distance call to our family one day of every week, unless there was an emergency, of course. My day had been Sunday, and I lived for that day each week. Just hearing the voices of the people I loved carried me through the next week.

My first question was always about Yosie. But there had been no word from the police, no phone calls from Yosie herself, and no one from town had come forth with any information. She simply seemed to have vanished. She was always in the back of my mind; everything I saw or heard, and even things I thought about, reminded me of her. But I kept telling myself she was probably all right as long as we didn't hear anything bad about her. That was all there was for me to hang onto.

I'd passed my entrance examinations for General Education Requirements and was able to skip all the first-year English classes and basic mathematics courses. In their place, I had taken a second-year American History class. I had to study extra hard; I'd never learned much about our country's past and the people who were responsible for forming our nation other than some facts about the most recognizable names like George Washington, Benjamin Franklin, Thomas Jefferson, and Abraham Lincoln.

The professor liked hearing and reading his students' ideas regarding certain historical events, so he made us do a lot of writing. One of the second-year students in that class told me, "A large portion of getting a good grade in any class is based on learning exactly what the professor wants." I took that to heart and figured out early on that this professor wanted our opinions more than facts, so that's what I gave him in my writings, and I'd gotten an 'A' on every paper I'd turned in.

The second quarter of that class was going to cover the wars and people who were prominent in defending the United States, so I figured I'd bone-up on that subject by using the resources at the Mount Pleasant Public Library during my Christmas break. I also jotted down a lot of notes regarding things Papa had said about being a German in the United States, but also his pride in being an American citizen. I was counting on Papa's ideas being of great interest to the professor.

My three roommates were Wanda, Eileen, and Hannah. We were all freshmen; I found out the university always placed same-year students together in dorm rooms. They thought it was more conducive to studying. I wasn't sure how much sense that made since all of us were enrolled in different majors, but I guessed there was obviously more to the idea than I was aware of or could even imagine.

Wanda was majoring in nursing, Eileen's major was Home Economics, and Hannah wanted to be a horticulturist. I was pleasantly surprised to find out that one of Hannah's instructors was Dorothea Lincoln, Link's wife. That explained all the books about flowers and trees I had seen in Dorothea's office. I'd asked Hannah about the *Poor Richard's Almanacs*, but she said she had only been in the office once and didn't remember seeing them. I figured I might have to look into that someday, purely for the sake of feeding my ever-present curiosity.

I was looking out the window, daydreaming, when I heard Liv outside the dorm room door. "Helmi?"

She knocked, and I came back to the present. "Yes! Just a minute," I called to her. I rushed to the door and opened it.

"Your ride is here," she said calmly.

"Wah-Hoo!" I shouted. I grabbed my suitcase—much lighter from a wardrobe standpoint than when I had arrived. I was leaving a lot of my clothes, but I did have to take enough of them home to have something decent to wear for the holidays. The suitcase was, however, packed with books, so it was even heavier than when I'd arrived on Orientation Day.

"Thanks, Liv." I bounded past her and flew down the stairs. I ran through the lobby, but before I reached the door, a voice shouted, "Hey!" I stopped, turned around, and there, by the fireplace, stood Jimmy. *How could he have become so much more handsome in three months?*

I dropped my suitcase. Tears of joy filled my eyes. I couldn't speak. I didn't know, until that very instant, how much I had missed him. I don't remember whether I went to him or he came to me or whether we met in the middle, but it was the sweetest reunion I could remember. We held each other for countless seconds. I felt as if I were already home—it didn't matter that I wasn't at the farm. Jimmy was all I needed. His embrace was wonderful, and it made me feel secure.

I glanced up at Liv standing at the bottom of the stairwell. Her hand was over her heart, and her expression was one of sadness. I had learned that she'd been engaged to a professor from the OSU School of Medicine. He'd taken a job at a hospital in Philadelphia over the summer and had told her he'd send for her as soon as he found a place for them to live. Instead, he'd found a place for him and his new lover, and he'd sent Liv a "Dear John" letter. I knew her heart had been broken, and I knew that seeing Jimmy and me together brought back feelings she so desperately cherished and missed.

Jimmy finally released his hold on me, and I momentarily closed my eyes. I felt so sorry for Liv, but I was so happy for me, and I couldn't hide it. I thought about going to Liv and trying to say something reassuring, but I figured it would only make things worse for her, so I merely gave her a little wave, and Jimmy and I walked out the door.

We stayed in a small motor lodge north of Columbus in a little place called Worthington. We ate the supper that Granny Nan had packed for us—it was pure ecstasy to taste homemade food again. I usually ate in the cafeteria in the student union, and it was pretty good, for the most part, but there's nothing like a home-cooked meal. We sat on the bed together, cross-legged, like we were having a picnic. There was so much to tell Jimmy. I'm not sure I ever let him get a word in edgewise. My mouth kept going and going; I couldn't turn it off.

When I was talking through a bite of Granny Nan's raisin pie, I realized Jimmy was yawning. "I'm so sorry. I haven't shut up since we left the dorm, have I?"

He smiled at me and said, "That's okay. You don't get a chance to tell me much durin' our short phone calls, and I really do wanna hear all about it. But I've had a long day, and it seems to be catchin' up with me."

"Of course it is! And you have another long day of driving tomorrow. I can help drive, you know."

He nodded. "I'm countin' on it. But right now, I need to get some shut-eye."

I had been looking at him the entire time I'd been rattling on about everything at school, but I hadn't noticed how tired he looked. *How could I have been so selfish?* "I don't know why I didn't see how tired you are. I..."

"Hey, hey. Not to worry. You're excited, and I really do wanna hear all about it, but I'm 'fraid I'll miss some of what you have to say if I don't sleep for a while." He yawned again, then he stood up and said, "I'm gonna go brush my teeth. Maybe that'll wake me up enough to help you put all of this away." He looked at the wrappers and such on the bed and sighed.

I said, "You just go. I'll take care of cleaning this up." I immediately jumped up and started wadding up the waxed paper and rewrapping the food and putting the leftovers back in the picnic basket. Jimmy hadn't moved. I stopped and looked up at him.

He met my gaze with eyes that were saying, "I want you." I set everything on the floor and pulled down the bedspread. "The toothbrushin's gonna have to wait," he said and took me in his arms. Then he picked me up and gently put me down on the bed. I never even thought about returning the perishables to the cold chest.

We took turns driving on the way back home. I made it a point not to monopolize the conversation. I asked him about everyone and everything at the farm and about his dad.

"Dad's really movin' slow these days. He says he wants to do more at the farm. Says it'll keep him goin', but I'm not sure that's the best idea. He's gettin' kinda frail."

"I understand. Granny Nan was slowing down some before I left for school, and I'm sure she hasn't been running any races while I've been gone," I said.

"How old is she now?" Jimmy asked.

"Well, let me think. She was born in 1850. September tenth, to be exact. So that makes her..." I did the ciphering in my head, "...88." The significance of that number hit me like a ton of bricks. All the blood rushed from my face for a moment. I hadn't thought about her age until that very moment. It's as if she had always been a constant in my life—a staple—and I never really thought about her age or the fact that she would one day be gone.

"You okay?" Jimmy asked. "You're kinda pale, and you're frownin'."

I glanced over at him and said, "Yeah, I just..."

"You never thought about her age, did you? She's just always been there. You could depend on the fact that she was gonna be there no matter what."

I sucked in some air and swallowed. *How could he have known what I was thinking.* "Have you been learning to read minds while I've been gone?"

"I never had to learn how to read yours. That's what makes it so

Dar Bagby

much fun to be with ya. I can almost always tell what's on your mind. We have a special connection, Helmi. Have you not been aware of that?"

I didn't know if I had been aware of that or not. *Have I? All this time, Jimmy's been tuned in to my thoughts, and I was unaware that it was even happening.* I looked over at him with a puzzled look on my face. "You are one special man, James Butcher."

He started to speak, but I cut him off. "You were going to say, 'I know I am,' weren't you?"

He laughed. "I guess I was. So now you think you can read my mind, too."

"Of course I can, most of the time. Sometimes. Once in a while. Okay, maybe only when I get lucky every now and then."

He had that little smirk on his face that I absolutely adored. It always left me wondering just exactly what was going on inside that handsome head of his. And it was one of the little things I loved most about him.

We got home around nine-thirty p.m., and everyone was there to greet me—even Butch. I think the happiest one to see me, though, was Two-Tone; she jumped around and barked and whined and, after she calmed down, she glued herself to my legs and wouldn't leave me alone. I'm sure she could feel how much I had missed her, too. It's funny how attached we become to an animal, and vice versa. I guess that's part of what pushed me toward becoming a vet.

Retta, too, seemed a bit clingy. I think it was mostly because she didn't have anyone else who loved doing the work around the farm like I did. I'm sure she missed having a partner in crime there at home. I felt sorry for her, in a way, because of all the responsibility she'd been dealt, and I could identify with that. She was more like me than any of my other sisters, and because of that, we shared a common bond.

Everyone had stories to tell, and I, of course, had plenty to talk about. We rambled on until almost eleven o'clock, then Granny Nan said, "It is time to break up this party and get some sleep. We have church tomorrow, and I, for one, do not want to look like I have been on a three-day toot when I show up."

On Sunday morning after the milking was done, Jimmy dropped Granny Nan, Bella, Dora, Ronnie, and Anna off at the church in Mount Pleasant. Retta and I stayed home and tended the livestock, including the chickens and ducks. There were only two of the ducks left there at the farm: Wang and Dash. Retta told me she had found some feathers down by the creek one morning shortly after I'd left for school. "There were prints, too," she said. "Looked to me like coyote. They were too big for fox." She said she and Jimmy followed the prints for a ways, but the winter wheat was too high to follow them very far. I was sad, but I knew that was one of the risks of life on the farm.

Jimmy was home in no time, so he and Retta and I sat down at the kitchen table and talked about nothing in particular. It felt so good to be back home where life was on a day-to-day schedule instead of hour-to-hour as it had been for me at OSU. Home was slower than I had been exposed to for the last three months, and I realized how much I'd missed it.

Jimmy had begun calling Retta "Squirt," and I think she kind of liked it, though she acted like she didn't. Jimmy had been her go-to person while I was gone. She didn't care much about dressing up, like Bella and Dora always had, and she treated school quite matter-of-factly. She said, "Miss Michaels asks after you a lot."

"What do you tell her?" I asked.

"Not much to tell. I only know what you talk about when you call, and the biggest portion of that I get from Jimmy, since he's the one you talk to most. She said you sent her a couple of letters, and she was *really* happy about that."

"She's been a pretty important person in my life," I said. "Does she still come every Monday for supper?"

"Yep. Says she wouldn't know what to do with herself if she didn't have Granny Nan to talk to."

Jimmy added, "She's one nice lady. I never had a teacher like her at Weidman. I went through six different teachers while I was in the one-room."

"Really? I didn't know that," I said. "I guess there's a lot I still have to learn about you."

"And I'm gonna be happy to tell you when you get a chance to be home for longer than just a few weeks." He reached over and put his hand on mine. "And I'll have a lifetime to do it."

"Ick!" Retta said. "If you two are gonna get all lovey-dovey, I'm gonna go outside."

Jimmy leaned over toward me and made loud kissing sounds, and Retta tried to stifle a laugh but couldn't. She giggled, and it made me giggle, too.

"You two need to grow up," Jimmy said. He got up and headed toward the back door. "Hey, Squirt. Did you wash our bed sheets? I laid 'em out yesterday before I left."

Retta's face went red. "I'll get 'em done before the two of you retire to your little love nest."

I was truly enjoying the show. It was obvious that two of my favorite people loved each other like brother and sister. I had missed being around that while I'd been away. Thing after thing was reminding me how much I missed home. And when the time rolled around for me to go back, I was sure it would be extra hard to leave.

Christmas was only three days away, and I was busy making presents for everyone. I'd been so involved around the farm and at the library and visiting with Miss Michaels and talking to Granny Nan and all of my sisters, it had slipped my mind. Miss Michaels, Uncle Herman, Mary, and Butch were all coming over to our house on Christmas day, but not Lizzy. She was staying in Ann Arbor because her new beau had asked her to meet his parents on Christmas eve. I was excited for her, but I sure would miss her bubbly personality.

Granny Nan and Dora had been busy in the kitchen for a week baking and preparing everything they could for a huge Christmas dinner. Granny Nan said she was making some special stuff this year. I had no idea what "special stuff" meant, but I had no doubt that it would be as yummy as everything else she always made.

I finished my gift-making, so I went outside to join Butch and Jimmy in the milk house. I figured they were probably finished milking by now and would most likely be sitting on a couple of buckets and shooting the bull. It was a bleak, cold day. The wind was blowing, and before I reached the milk house, freezing rain started to fall. It was coming from the north, so it pelted me right in the face. I put my hands up and covered my face as best I could, running the last few yards to the door. But when I reached the little stoop at the milk house, I misjudged the step, caught my toe on it, and plowed face-first into the door, scraping my knees on the concrete and catching myself with my hands as I fell.

I heard a muffled voice from inside say, "What was that?"

"Sounded like somethin' hit the door," another voice answered.

The door came open, and there was Jimmy, looking down at me. Blood was seeping from my nose, and I could tell my right eye was swelling up. I knew my knees had gotten skinned because I looked down, and sure enough, my pants were torn over both knees.

"WHAT THE…!" Jimmy shouted. "HELMI!"

I looked up at him, and he saw the blood. "What kind of a crackpot move did you pull?" he asked.

The blood loss from my nose was increasing by the second, and my right eye was nearly swollen shut. Jimmy had me in a bear hug, both his arms under my armpits, and he was lifting me up and into the milk house. Butch, his face white and looking like a lost puppy, was standing behind Jimmy. "Get her a bucket to set her on," Jimmy said.

Butch was so flustered, he evidently couldn't think straight. "Where?" he asked Jimmy.

"Right behind you. The one you were just sittin' on. Scoot it over here so I can set her down on it."

Time had slowed for me by that point, and for some odd reason, I found the entire scenario humorous. I started laughing, and it got louder and louder until Jimmy finally stopped and looked down at me. I was nearly hysterical, and he couldn't help but laugh with me. "Helmi, stop it!" But by the time he got me down on the bucket and was kneeling beside me, we were both laughing like we were insane.

Butch's mouth was hanging open, and he was staring at us. "Have you lost your minds?"

We managed to stop guffawing enough to be able to size up the situation. I intended to explain what had happened, but every time I tried to talk, my nose bled worse. "I thick by dose is broke-ed," I said, sounding like I had the king of all head colds. "Add I cad odly see you with wudd eye."

Jimmy was peeking through my pants legs to see how badly I had skinned my knees, but I knew those wounds there were only superficial. "Well, it looks like you'll be able to walk, but you're gonna have a helluva time blowin' your nose."

I looked at him with my one good eye.

"It's so crooked," he said, "you won't be able to line up either side to empty it."

"Add besides that," I said, lifting my left arm, "I odly have wudd hadd to blow it with." My left hand was dangling at an odd angle. I knew my wrist was broken.

"Jesus, Helmi!"

I spent the next several hours at the Mount Pleasant Medical Facility, then Jimmy had to take me to the hospital in Flint where they were better equipped to cast my broken wrist. Retta and Granny Nan insisted on going along, and I can't say I wasn't glad to have them there. By the time we reached the Flint Hospital, my wrist was hurting bad enough that they had to give me laudanum to ease the pain.

The result of my clumsiness only put a small dent in Christmas. I felt like an invalid, everyone waiting on me. But I can honestly say I was glad to have the help. Granny Nan's "special stuff" turned out to be a roast goose. We had never had one before, so she'd had Jimmy pick one up at a nearby farm that raised geese specifically for Christmas dinners; he picked out the one he wanted, and they dressed it on the spot. She also fixed a new dish called scalloped potatoes. They were sliced real thin and baked in a creamy white buttery sauce. I loved them, almost as much as mashed potatoes.

It wasn't much fun having to eat with only one hand, but I was thankful it was my left wrist that had been broken and not my right, since I was right-handed. I had another week to let the healing process continue before I'd have to go back to OSU. *As if it won't be difficult enough to leave again, I'll be going knowing that I have this to contend with.*

Jimmy wouldn't leave my side except to do the milking and any odd jobs that crept up. Granny Nan tried to get me to sleep in her downstairs bedroom, but after I began to explain that Jimmy and I had so little time together, she held her hand up and stopped me and said, "That is enough! I do not need, nor do I *want* to hear anything more regarding that topic."

Jimmy and I continued to sleep in the upstairs bedroom.

We always talked a lot when we went to bed. It just seemed natural since the day's work was done and we could finally relax. Mama and Papa always talked a lot when they went to bed, so I assumed it was what all couples did. It was a great time to solve problems that we hadn't had time to clear up during the day. Jimmy and I would lie there like spoons, each of our curves fitting up next to one another, and if time had permitted, I think we could have figured out a way to end all the problems of the world.

ROOMMATES AND THE TRUTH

I was going to have to leave the cast on my arm for several weeks, which meant I'd be returning to OSU with it in place. When I got to the dorm, everyone did their best to help me. There was nearly a fight over who was going to carry my suitcase up to my room.

After explaining how I came to be wearing the cast, I thanked them all abundantly and said, "I can't tell you how wonderful it is to feel so welcome and so loved by everyone. But I don't think it's going to be too much of a problem since it's my left wrist and not, thank goodness, the one I need for almost everything." I still had a piece of tape across the bridge of my nose. My black eye now showed only little speckles of blue under the skin in a few places, and my knees were fine.

Nevertheless, Wanda, Eileen, and Hannah were absolute angels and pampered me at every turn. Liv checked on me three or four times a day, every day, for the first two weeks of the quarter; after that, she was convinced I'd go to her for anything I needed, so she cut back to checking in on me only morning and bedtime.

My Biology Lecture class was difficult to sit through, as there were nearly one-hundred students in a huge classroom. The professor, a man from Bolivia, was not easy for me to understand because of his accent, and he spoke so quietly that, if I didn't find a seat within the first three rows, I could not hear most of what he said. And because of the size of the class, in-class questions were not allowed. If anyone had a question, it was to be taken up with the professor in his office during his office hours. Luckily, he taught strictly from the book we were using, so I was able to garner most of the important things directly from the written pages.

On the other hand, Biology Lab was wonderful! It was taught by a woman who had dual degrees, one in entomology and one in laboratory science. She was very dynamic and made the class not only fun but also thoroughly educational. Since Miss Michaels had taken me to Mount Pleasant High School to use their microscopes, I already had a leg-up on using the dissecting microscope in Bio Lab.

Professor Lincoln—Link—was an excellent teacher. His first-quarter animal husbandry class had been one of the only things that had helped me maintain my sanity, and that didn't change during second quarter. He often talked to me after class and occasionally invited me to come to his office so he could give me extra reading material and simply chat with someone who was, as he put it, "smarter than a box of rocks."

It was during one of our office chats that Dorothea came through his office door with an armful of *Poor Richard's Almanacs*. Link jumped up and helped her with the load of magazines. "What are you doing with all of these?"

"I need more space on my bookshelves, and I figured you wouldn't mind using a little bit of space in your nearly-empty closet to store them." She looked up and saw me. "Oh, hi Helmi! I didn't see you sitting there. How's your wrist?"

"Doing fine, thanks."

"As you can see, I collect these," she said. "I have three copies of the very first one ever published, but I don't keep them here. They're locked up at home, safe and sound."

That sated part of my curiosity about them, but I still wanted to know why. "That's an unusual thing to collect. Your reason?"

"I use them in my classroom to show my students how they can predict the weather patterns, temperature ranges, and other factors that govern the success of whatever they want to grow."

I had never thought about that. "Of course…it makes perfect sense. Since we know that certain patterns in nature repeat themselves over various time periods, people who grow plants could estimate what the conditions might be in any given year. That has to be what the almanacs do. But by purchasing them, farmers and other growers don't have to do the tracking themselves; 'Poor Richard' does it for them. That's really interesting," I said.

Dorothea was blinking at me and had a blank look on her face. She turned to Link and said, "Did you tell her about that premise?"

Link shook his head and grinned. "Can you see, now, why it's so much fun to talk to her? She gets it." He looked over at me, then back at Dorothea. "She always gets it, no matter what we're talking about."

Dorothea turned back to me and put her hand up to her mouth, shielding it from Link. Then she spoke in an exaggerated whisper, "Be careful. He'll be using *your* brain power to dictate what he says in the classroom and taking credit for it himself. You might want to copyright your thoughts before you verbalize them."

We all laughed. I really enjoyed spending time with those two. Dorothea asked when I'd be getting the cast off, and I told her I wasn't sure, but it seemed to be getting better. "It itches like crazy, but at least it doesn't hurt nearly so much now." Then I quickly added, "And I'm NOT on laudanum. I guess I'm going to have to find a doctor close to the campus to take a look at it in another week, though. The doctor who originally set and casted it for me suggested it be checked after three weeks."

"You don't need to find an off-campus doctor," Link said. "Since you're a student, you can see an intern at the School of Medicine for free."

I was blinking, and I think I now had that blank look on my face, the same one Dorothea had when I told her my idea about the almanacs. "Do I need to make an appointment?"

"Yes," Dorothea said. "Come to my office, and I'll give you the number."

She and I left Link's office and went downstairs to hers. We chatted about trivial subjects, and she looked through her mechanical file and wrote down the number I needed.

"Thanks so much," I said. "This is a real lifesaver. I didn't know where I was going to start if I'd had to find my own doctor."

"The nice thing about seeing one of the interns on campus is that you can specify which type of physician you need to see. In your case, you'll want to ask for an orthopod."

"What kind of pod?"

"Orthopod. An orthopaedic specialist."

I was blinking, and my face was evolving into that blank look again.

"A bone doctor."

"Got it," I said and grabbed a pencil from the cup on her desk that held all manner of writing utensils and other things unidentifiable. I wrote ORTHOPOD on the paper with the number.

"Oh dear," Dorothea said. "I'm sorry to have to shoo you out, but I have an appointment with one of my doctoral students in a couple of minutes, and I need to find something to…"

"I'm outta here," I said as I turned to leave. "Thanks again for the number."

One week later I saw an orthopod, and he suggested taking off the current cast and applying another. "Since all the swelling has gone down in your arm, wrist, and hand, the cast you're currently wearing is too loose. We should put another one on that's a little bit tighter in order to keep the range of motion at a minimum until those bones have a chance to set completely."

"Whatever you think is best," I told him. "You're the expert."

When he finished, his cast was much more professional-looking than the one I'd been wearing. And I told him so.

"I've practiced a lot; put casts on every shape and size of anything that resembled a body part. I've casted firewood, drain pipes, broken stair balusters, even people!" he said, jokingly.

"Let it be known that your patients—at least this one—are highly impressed with your work. *And* your bedside manner," I told him, holding my left arm up and turning it in every direction I could, inspecting the workmanship. "I really appreciate the application of lotion to my skin before you covered it up. That was the best it's felt since…well, since day one."

"It appears to be healing nicely. I don't think you'll have any problem with it once it finishes growing back together like it's supposed to." He wrote something down on a paper attached to a clip board. "What are you majoring in?"

"Veterinary Medicine."

"Third year? Fourth?" he asked.

"No, I'm only a freshman."

"Can't be."

"Can and am," I said.

"Wow! You make the beginning student population look good."

"Thank you," I said humbly.

"I'm serious," he said. "I remember when I enrolled as a freshman. Most of the enrollees were…how can I say this nicely? They were less than mature and far less than intellectual."

"I have it on good authority that I'm smarter than a box of rocks."

He burst out laughing. "I'll have to remember that one." He chuckled again. "I'd like to see you back in three weeks. Probably at that time, if all goes as well, as I figure it will, you can get that cast off permanently."

"I look forward to that day."

"On your way out of the office, just before you reach the door, there's a woman who'll set you up with an appointment. You can either set up your next appointment now, or you can get the number from her and give us a call after you've checked your calendar for an appointment time that won't interfere with midterms or whatever."

"I'd better settle for the second option," I told him. "Thanks again. And good luck in your career."

"Same to you," he said. Then he shook my hand and left the room.

I repeated his name several times in my mind so I could ask for him on my return appointment: "T. Avalon. T. Avalon." I didn't know it was simply going to be luck of the draw when I called to make the follow-up appointment.

❖❖❖

The cast came off, my wrist looked good, and I was able to use it—a little bit. T. Avalon was not the doctor who removed the cast, but the man I did see was quite pleasant. He had another man with him, and both of them were using medical terminology I wasn't yet familiar with. The intern left the room, and the other man gave me a list of exercises I needed to perform every day, at least twice—more if possible—to help me regain full use of my wrist. He helped me do all the exercises and showed me exactly the right positions to get the best results.

"Are you also an orthopod?" I asked the man.

"No, I'm a physical therapist. My main job is to help treat the athletes here at the university."

"I never knew there was such a thing as a physical therapist," I told him. "I'm going to be a veterinarian, and I don't think the veterinary field has that kind of specialty."

"Not yet, at least," he said. "Give it time, though. We're working our way into a lot of different fields, and veterinary medicine is one that's on the horizon."

I was fascinated, and I'd have to talk to Link about what the man had said.

❖❖❖

I got straight A's in all my classes during second quarter. My favorite class, hands down, was animal husbandry. And it wasn't only because Link taught it. I found it so fascinating, probably because I had been involved in animal husbandry my entire life and hadn't even realized it.

I was discussing that class with Eileen and Wanda one day, and I told them, "It's a branch of agriculture concerned with raising animals for meat, milk, eggs, even fiber, like wool. It includes raising fish, mollusks, and crustaceans as food—that's called aquaculture—and even raising insects for food! Some places in the world where people eat llamas, rabbits, and guinea pigs, they raise as livestock, as well."

Eileen asked me why it was called animal "husbandry." I explained that it stems from the original meaning of the verb *to husband*, meaning *to manage carefully*. "Clear back in the fourteenth century," I told her "it referred to the care and ownership of a household or a farm."

"I never heard of it until I met you," Eileen said. "I thought you were crazy when you said you were taking that course. I couldn't figure out why someone would marry an animal."

In a deep, throaty voice, Wanda said, "I can think of a couple of reasons. I know a couple of ponies who could make any girl VERY happy!"

We all giggled like thirteen-year-olds. That was the point at which I realized no one had ever explained sex to me. I had always seen our farm animals performing the act, and I somehow understood what was happening. I knew that was how they got pregnant. I just didn't realize how pleasurable sex could be until I married Jimmy.

I looked off into the distance, reminiscing about our lovemaking. It was a pleasant thing to think about. He had been gentle and considerate of my feelings our first time. I'd been a little bit worried, knowing that I had never been with a man before, but he had put me entirely at ease. Maybe it was because we were such good friends, or maybe he'd had enough experience with other women to know how to make me completely comfortable. No matter; it always brought us closer together.

"Helmi? Come back, Helmi. Yoo-hoo," Wanda was saying.

"Oh, sorry. I was, um…"

"Yeah, we can imagine. All anyone has to do is take one look at that hunk you're married to, and everything else goes out the window," Wanda said. "You're already married, but I'd like to know how many of the women enrolled here at OSU are in pursuit of a special degree called an M.R.S. I can name several who are in my nursing program."

Eileen frowned. "What's an M.R.S?"

"Are you sure you aren't retarded?" Wanda asked her. "Think about it. M.R.S. What does that spell?"

I could see Eileen thinking about it, but she appeared to be coming up empty-handed. "It doesn't spell anything, does it?"

I took over. "When a woman gets married, she becomes a missus. And how do you abbreviate missus?"

The light came on in Eileen's head. "Oh, missus. M.R.S. I get it."

Wow! I'm in the presence of a box of rocks! Then I asked Wanda, "Why would they enroll in Nursing if they want to find a husband? That's probably the least likely major to include males."

"Only for a couple of years, then you start working with doctors."

"Ohhhhh, I see. And doctors end up making the big dollar signs, so that makes them highly popular."

"On the nose," Wanda said and tapped the end of her nose a couple of times with her index finger.

"I don't even know if I want to get married," Eileen said. "It all seems so intimidating."

I frowned, and Wanda pursued it. "What do mean, intimidating?"

"Oh, you know. The man always wants something, and the wife has to take care of it for him or he…well, he…he makes sure he gets it, no matter what it takes."

"Wait a minute, Eileen. Is that what you think marriage is all about? The man takes, takes, takes, and the woman gives, gives, gives?"

"Well, isn't it? I mean, that's the way things worked between my mother and father. And Mommy said that's always the way it is. She says every man's the same."

Without thinking, I said, "She's wrong!" Then I regretted my outburst. I put my hand over my mouth, as if that would erase what I'd said. "I'm sorry, Eileen. I didn't mean to dispute what your mother said. I was out of line. I apologize."

Wanda looked at Eileen and said, "No, Eileen, Helmi's not out of line. It doesn't have to be at all like your mother said. At least not all the time. My parents weren't like that. They did their best to make each other happy."

"Mine, too," I said. "And Jimmy is one of the kindest, most attentive and loving people I've ever met. My papa was the same way. He cherished my mama. The grief over her death is what killed him." I had never said that out loud.

By then, Eileen was crying. Wanda and I both got down on the floor where Eileen was sitting, and we all hugged each other, our heads together and our arms around each other.

After a little while, Wanda snorted and said, "I'll bet we look like a squad on the synchronized swim team." That made us all laugh, even Eileen; though to be honest, I'm not sure Eileen knew what that was.

❖❖❖

I went home for spring break, which only lasted a week, then Jimmy made the trek once again taking me back. I felt really sorry for him. "I hate making you do this all the time."

"Do what?" he asked.

"Run me back and forth to Columbus."

"It doesn't bother me in the least," he said. "I just want you to live your dream. And besides, you'll be makin' good money when you become a vet."

"Does it bother you that I'll probably make more than you will with the farm?"

"Bother me? Why, my dear, I don't give a damn how much money you make as long as you remain happy. If you're happy, I'm happy."

I couldn't help but think about the afternoon when Eileen said men take and women give. I wished she could have heard what Jimmy had just said.

By the end of May, I had completed my first year of college, and my grades were right on track. I was determined to graduate Magna Cum Laude, and following that year's finals, I was elated to know that my determination was paying off. Link and Dorothea both congratulated me on my good academic work.

"Will you be putting in time at the vet's office back home?" Link asked. "If you ever decide not to go back home over the summer, I'd be happy to have you come work with me."

"Oh right—like that's gonna happen," Dorothea said. "She has a husband, you know."

"I know!" Link said and looked at me. "But if he ever leaves the picture, you've got a place to stay."

"Thanks, but I couldn't possibly think of leaving the farm under any circumstances," I said. "I'm as married to it as I am to Jimmy."

We said our good-byes and offered our best wishes to each other and parted company. I did the same with my roommates. I wouldn't be staying in that dorm next year; I would be living on the other side of the Olentangy River where the School of Veterinary Medicine housed its students.

Jimmy and I had left earlier than usual so we could get back to the farm while it was still daylight. Home looked better than ever. Everything was green and glowing in the bright sunset. Granny Nan was sitting on a chair in the front yard when we pulled up. She waved, and I noticed she was having a little more trouble than usual getting out of the chair to come and meet us.

Two-tone did her normal barking and whining, and she even let loose a howl, which I'd never heard her do. Retta slammed into me like she wanted to run me over, but I held my ground and remained upright, hugging her as tightly as I could without crushing her. Bella and Dora each offered hugs, as did Ronnie. I got down on my knees and hugged Anna, who was five now, and I gave her a big kiss on the top of the head. She looked so different, so much older than when I'd seen her three months ago. She told me she was "really extra happy" because I was going to be home for the whole summer. Poor thing; she was bent over so far, I didn't know how she could even see where she was going.

Butch wasn't there. He'd been having some trouble with swelling in his legs, so he stayed home with his feet up. I told Jimmy I'd like to go over to his house tomorrow morning and see if there was anything we could help with after we finished the milking.

It felt good to be among my family, but there was one person missing. I silently said, *If you were here, Yosie, I'd hug you, too. I miss you, even though you've been a thorn in my side most of my life.*

I had only been home for three-and-a-half weeks when Granny Nan got a letter from the home where Aunt Lavern had been staying. It said she appeared to be going downhill rapidly. She could no longer talk, could not use her arms or legs, and she was losing weight because she was unable to swallow; they had put her on intravenous feedings.

They suggested that Granny Nan come to Chicago as soon as she could arrange to do so. The letter also said the doctor, under whose care Lavern had been for several months, would call shortly after the letter had had time to reach Granny Nan.

The next morning, Granny Nan answered a phone call, and the voice on the other end of the line offered condolences, as Lavern had passed away during the night. The person told Granny Nan that it happened much sooner than they had anticipated. I was sure that hadn't made Granny Nan feel any better about her daughter's death.

"We can make the trip together," I told Granny Nan.

"For what? She is already dead," Granny Nan said. "We just need to make sure the arrangements to get her buried are in order. I know she has a plot next to Julius in some cemetery there in Chicago. It will all be in writing; they never did anything without an attorney's approval, and I know the attorney was smart enough to get plenty of money from them for drawing up a will."

She spoke of Lavern as if she had only been an acquaintance instead of her daughter, and I didn't understand that response from Granny Nan. So I took my chances and asked her, "Why do you not want to go, Granny Nan? She was your only living daughter. Don't you feel it's necessary to be there when she's buried?"

Granny Nan pursed her lips and said, "Sit down, Helmi." We were alone in the kitchen, so I sat down at the table, and she came over and placed her hands on it, leaning over slightly as she talked. "I know you will not fully understand this because you are fortunate enough to have loved ones around you, and that has been the case for your entire life. But you see, Lavern was not like us. She was not interested in family, at least not ours." She raised up and moved around to a chair on the side opposite me.

She folded her hands in front of her and said, quite matter-of-factly, "Your mother was my daughter. Lavern was not." She paused to let that sink in.

My mouth came open, and I started to speak, but Granny Nan held her hand up to silence me. I let her go on without interruption.

"Buster had an affair with a woman right after we were married.

She was a whore, well-known around Indianapolis, and she got pregnant. I do not know if it was Buster's child. One morning an Irish woman came knocking at our door. She was carrying a bundle that contained a baby. In her Irish accent she said, 'Your husband agreed to take this here child, whether it be his or nay. The mother wants it not.' She thrust the bundle toward me. I stood stark still, not offering to accept the bundle, but the woman thrust it at me again and again until the baby was wailing at the top of its lungs. I could not turn it away.

"When Buster got home that night, I told him what had happened, and he immediately took the baby from me and cooed at it and rocked it and smiled at it. If it was not his by birthright, it was his by choice. He named it Lavern, after his own mother, and he left it to me to raise it."

She put her head in her hands and sighed. Then she raised herself up off the chair. She walked to the window and stared out at that beautiful summer morning. I thought she had finished the story, but then she told me more.

"Out of shame, Buster and I moved to Oklahoma. We rarely spoke, but there was no choice for us but to remain married because of Lavern; we had taken her in, and it was our responsibility to care for her as if she were our own. But Buster had become a slave to liquor, and he was always full of anger, a mean drunk. He came at me one night with a pitchfork, threatening to kill me if I did not lie with him. The sight of him sickened me, but for Lavern's sake, I did not want to die.

"The result was your mother; she was not a product of love, Helmi. She was the result of an angry, drunken moment on her father's part. After I knew I was with child, I went to every woman I thought I could trust to find out if there was a way to abort that baby inside me. But no one offered any suggestions. Oh, one of my so-called friends said to me, 'You made your bed, now you have to lie in it.' That woman died six months later, and I was glad, God forgive me.

"Less than two weeks after Violet was born, Buster left. I did not know where he went until I got the message from that awful man who came to our house later that night. I told you that story."

I nodded.

"So I raised Violet alone; Lavern was no help. She blamed me for Buster leaving and shooting himself. She was fifteen, and she hated me, though she could not hate Violet, who was the most beautiful child I ever saw. However, when Violet was almost two years old, Lavern disappeared.

"The following year I received a letter from her saying she had gotten married and was on her way to becoming one the wealthiest women in Chicago. I threw the letter into the fireplace and watched the ashes rise up the chimney. I did not want to know her husband's name nor their address. I wanted nothing to do with her or the man she married. But she kept sending me letters. After a while I decided not to open them. When your mother was the same age as Lavern had been when she left, she asked me if she could open the letters and read them to me. I agreed, for her sake, though I did not even want to touch them.

"Lavern spoke to me in the letters as if she actually cared about me and Violet and our whereabouts. But I knew it was nothing but a means to get me to come to her. And I knew that, if I went, my poor opinion of her and her husband could only be confirmed. Or made worse. Your father knew that, too, and that is why he never wanted to go there or see them. The only reason we stopped at their house on our way here to Mount Pleasant was because Violet said she wanted to see her sister. She said she did not care about what had happened in the past; she wanted to make things right and start over with Lavern.

We talked about it night after night when you and your sisters were asleep. Finally your father and I gave in to your mother's wish, though we knew nothing good would come of it."

She turned from the window and said, to me, "I must tell you, Helmi, I was never more proud of your father than when he stood up to Julius and put him in his place that day." She smiled, remembering. "I loved your father like he was my own son."

I knew Papa had always been kind to Granny Nan, and I expected it was because he knew she loved him as much as she loved Mama. Now I knew I'd been right. I also had my answer regarding a trip to Chicago. Granny Nan was no longer a part of Aunt Lavern's life, and she had no intentions of making it seem as if she were.

I called the rest home in Chicago the next day and told them to proceed with the burial as outlined in Lavern's will. I apologized for Granny Nan, saying she was unable to contact them or make the trip to Chicago for the funeral. I used her age as the excuse, and Granny Nan had no problem with that.

SUMMER ENDS, LIFE GOES ON

Granny Nan could usually be found inside the house, not venturing outdoors often. The radio was her constant companion. Bad things were brewing in Europe, and she was right on top of it, listening to the reports all day. Dora, and sometimes Bella, had begun helping more and more with the cooking because Granny Nan couldn't stand up for long periods of time like she used to.

"These old brittle bones just will not cooperate," she said. She'd sit down and rub them a lot. "It is a shame we do not have a horse anymore," she told me one day. "I need some horse liniment for these old gams."

"You want to walk around smelling like Ham or Trot used to?" I asked her.

"It would be better than not being able to walk around at all," she said.

"My guess is, there's probably some sort of medication for sore legs that doesn't smell quite so bad," I told her. "I'll take a look at the drug store when I go to Mount Pleasant later today." I had planned on going into town to buy some lined paper for school; I knew it would be cheaper in town than at the university bookstore.

I was certain I'd never convince Granny Nan to go to the doctor about the leg pain she was having. If Mama had still been there, she'd have *made* Granny Nan go, but I didn't have the same powers over her that Mama did, so I put myself in charge of doctoring her at home as much as I could.

I told Jimmy I was going to town and asked him if he needed anything. "You goin' to the pharmacy?" he asked.

"Yes, I have to get something for Granny Nan's legs. What do you need?"

He rubbed his face and said, "I was there a couple weeks ago, and they had this new aftershave lotion called 'Old Spice.' It smelled pretty good to me. Why don't you take a sniff of it, and if you like it, you can bring me a bottle."

"I can do that, but I'll need a little bit more money. Can I take it out of your billfold?"

"Sure," he said.

"Is it on the dresser?"

He felt his back pocket. "Must be."

I got the money, gave him a peck on the cheek, told him goodbye, and went to the drug store in Mount Pleasant where I found a parking place right in front. I got my notebook paper, which was on sale, liniment for Granny Nan's legs, and the Old Spice aftershave for Jimmy. I was feeling good about my shopping luck.

I put the bag on the back seat and slid behind the steering wheel. I noticed a paper stuck under the windshield wiper. *Oh, no! I forgot about the parking meter.* Mount Pleasant's politicians didn't normally concern me much, so I didn't make a concerted effort to follow their opinions or their decisions regarding the town. I sort of blindly went my own way and was just thankful that we lived close enough to be able to get whatever we needed, whenever we needed it, without having to drive very far. It was truly a matter of convenience for me, nothing more. Politics had never been a major concern of mine. I'm sure Papa was spinning in his grave over my lack of interest.

The parking meters had just been installed at the beginning of that summer, and I was not used to paying attention to them when I parked; my mind was more concerned with what I had to buy than with the "meter maids" who patrolled the streets looking for parking offenders. I remember Butch saying something about how Mount Pleasant was proud of the fact that they were one of the first cities in Michigan to install them, seeing as how the meters had only been perfected in 1938, one year ago. Now we had to put coins in them every time we parked, unless we were lucky enough to find one that had time left on it from the previous "parker."

"Scheist!" I swore. My luck had run out. I sat there for a moment, allowing myself to cool down before getting out to retrieve the ticket. Now I'd have to go to City Hall and pay the fee, but because this was Saturday, they would not be open, so I'd have to return the following week. I got out and looked at the ticket; I'd never gotten one before. It was a simple piece of paper that said I owed the city three dollars. *Three dollars!* It may as well have been three hundred dollars in my eyes. *That's highway robbery.*

I went home, mad as a wet hen, and stomped into the house. I threw the bag on the table and plopped down in one of the kitchen chairs, putting my head in my hands. "Damn! Damn! Dammit!"

"Nice language," Jimmy said.

His voice startled me. I hadn't seen him when I came in. I looked up and saw him getting up off the floor under the kitchen sink. It had been leaking a little bit lately, so he must have figured it was time to fix it.

"I don't care!" I shouted.

"And should I ask why, or should I quietly leave the room and pretend I didn't hear you cussin' 'bout somethin' that obviously hasn't made you happy?"

I looked at him and said through gritted teeth, "I got a parking ticket."

"Ohhhh, I see. So Mount Pleasant's a few dollars richer because of your negligence, huh?" He was smiling, and that made me even more angry.

"Well I, for one, don't see the humor in it." I slapped my hand on the table.

Granny Nan came limping into the kitchen. "What is all the hubbub about?"

Jimmy said, "Helmi got a parkin' ticket."

"A what?" Granny Nan asked.

"I forgot to put a nickel in the parking meter. When I came out of the drug store, there was a ticket on the car."

"I had forgotten they put those meters in a couple of months back," she said as she struggled to sit down, Jimmy doing his best to help her as she grunted and groaned. "Seems to me, it is a good way for the city to make some extra money, and I am all for that. It is your responsibility as a driver to pay attention and feed the thing when you pull up to it. I like the fact that Mount Pleasant can use the money to keep the roads repaired."

"Well they never had meters when we all drove horses," I said, angry and getting angrier by the second. "And that mode of transportation left deposits all over the streets, but no one paid any extra to have that picked up and done away with, did they?"

Jimmy and Granny Nan both looked at me with blank faces. Jimmy finally said, "Are you done grousin'?"

"I don't know. I guess I am until I think of something else to grouse about." I looked away, embarrassed. My good mood had gone out the window with my good luck.

"When's it say you have to have it paid by?" Jimmy asked.

I looked at the slip and said, "August 24."

"Do you want me to take you there?"

"No, I can go by myself."

"Don't forget to feed the meter when ya park," he said, grinning from ear to ear.

Granny Nan snorted.

On September 1, 1939, Hitler's Germany invaded Poland. Two days later, Britain and France declared war on Germany. Granny Nan was sure the United States would eventually become involved, as well. It's unfortunate that she was right.

Jimmy took me back to Columbus on Labor Day. Classes would begin on Wednesday. He had made arrangements with his dad and Retta to cover the farm for three days so he could take an extra day to stay with me while I moved into my new dorm. He would then stay overnight at the motor lodge in Worthington (where we always stayed when traveling back and forth) before returning to Mount Pleasant.

I had taken care of all the "red tape" (lining up the new dorm, getting my class schedule, etc.) through the mail, and I had a room confirmation in my hand when I entered Pickerington House, only a stone's throw from the buildings where I would be attending most of my classes. I still had to take a couple of prerequisite courses, but they were at least on the road to vet med. One of them was a chemistry class, which I was really looking forward to. I had only dabbled in chemistry when I was in high school, but it piqued my interest, so I had done as much extra studying about it as I could manage.

I was the first one in the dorm room, so I got to choose which bed and desk I wanted. This was a two-bed room, so I naturally chose the one closest to the window. After about twenty minutes, my roommate showed up. I was preparing to take Jimmy on a tour of the campus when a female came barreling into the room, arms loaded with bags, and kicking a suitcase in front of her as she walked. She was panting and grumbling under her breath.

She was a large girl, dressed in lots of clothes; she was wearing a long canvas skirt with a shorter one over it that was made of a gauzy material. Tucked into the skirts was a long-sleeved pink cotton blouse, and over that was another see-through shirt with flowers printed on it. There was a scarf around her neck, and she had one side of her dark brown hair pulled back with a barrette, and there was a real pink carnation behind her ear. Covering her feet was a pair of boots like I used on the farm in winter.

She looked up and saw me. "Oh, hi. I'm Millie." Then she noticed Jimmy and did a double-take. "Have we gone co-ed?"

"Not that I'm aware of, but I'd be happy if we had. I'm Helmi, and this is my husband, Jimmy."

"Rats!" she said in a rapid, clipped fashion, almost chewing her words. "I was hopin' he was up for grabs. I'm Millie. Oh, I already told you that, didn't I? Well, it's nice to meet you, Helmi. But it's especially nice to meet you, Jimmy."

I couldn't believe it...Jimmy was blushing! "Hello, Millie." He nodded at her and stepped toward her, relieving her of a couple of the bags she was toting.

"Manners, too," Millie said. Then she looked at me. "He's a keeper!"

"That's my plan," I said.

She put the rest of the bags on the bed opposite mine, since mine was already piled high with things from home: my suitcase, books, and a special comforter Granny Nan had made and given to me at Christmas last year. It contained squares of fabric from everyone's old clothes…hers, mine, all of my sisters, and even Mama and Papa. She called it a "memory quilt," and I cherished it.

"Thanks, I'll take those," Millie said to Jimmy, reaching for the bags he was holding. She tossed them toward the bed, then she turned and left the room.

Jimmy and I looked at each other. In a low voice, he asked, "What sorta whirlwind just went through?"

"Reminds me of an Oklahoma twister," I said, softly. "I lived through several of those, but I'm not sure I'll survive this one."

There was a ruckus in the stairwell, so Jimmy and I both headed to the door to see what was making the commotion. Millie was walking up the stairs backwards, hefting up a rocking chair, and another girl was on the downside, pushing it up toward her. Millie was talking a-mile-a-minute. *What have I gotten myself into?* I thought. *I hope she doesn't talk like that ALL the time. I'll have to find someplace else to study.*

I nudged Jimmy with my elbow, and he turned toward me, a deer-in-the-headlights look on his face. I whispered, "Go help her."

"Are you kidding me? I'm not about to get in the middle of that!"

I couldn't help but smile.

When they reached the top, and the chair was on level ground, Jimmy walked out, picked it up, and brought it into the room, Millie watching his muscles flex as he moved. She said to the other girl, "You and Helmi, here, can argue about where you're gonna put that." She looked at me and said, "It is Helmi. Did I get that right?"

"You did," I said.

"I'm usually pretty good with names, and I saw yours on the roster and room assignment sheet. I pooped out at figuring what Helmi's short for, if it's a nickname, that is. Is it short for something?"

"Wilhelmina," I said.

"Whoa! I'd be wantin' to ditch that mouthful, too."

The other girl was standing in the doorway. She was tall and thin as a rail; she couldn't have weighed more than ninety pounds. *No wonder she needed help getting that chair up the stairs.* She had straight, pitch-black hair. Her skin was a golden color, different than any I'd ever seen, and smooth as silk. Her eyebrows were thick and black, like her hair, and her nose was long and flat. Her eyes were almond-shaped with eyelids that came right down to the lash line. Her lips were thin, the color of Michigan clay.

I walked over to her, offered her my hand, and said, "Hello. I guess you know my name, so you're one up on me." She didn't take my hand. She put her hands together, prayer style, then bent at the waist and bowed to me! I didn't know what to do, so I bowed back. She bowed again. Then she said, "I please to meet you. My name Shinju."

"Shinju," I repeated. "What a lovely name. Are you from Japan?"

"Mother Japanese. She name me. Shinju mean pearl. What Helmi mean?"

"Helmi is just my nickname. My full name is Wilhelmina. But I like Helmi better."

"I too," she said and smiled. Then she shook my hand. We had exchanged our first bit of personal information, two different people from across three-quarters of a country and an entire ocean.

I was about to introduce Jimmy when Millie reappeared. "You two gettin' to know each other?"

"Yes, we are." I turned to Shinju and was going to ask her which room she would be staying in, but it dawned on me that Millie had said Shinju and I could argue over where to put the rocking chair. "Are you going to be my roommate?" I asked instead.

She smiled and nodded.

I smiled back and breathed a sigh of relief.

"Okay, then," Millie said. "You two need to know that you can come to me *anytime* with *anything* you have on your mind. I'm usually not at that silly desk they keep in the lobby. Feel like I'm a banker or somethin' when I'm sittin' there. I'm on the first floor, though. Only room with a door. Just knock."

"So, you're the dorm adviser?" I asked.

"Adviser, listener, problem solver, monitor, mother, mentor, and whatever else crops up," she said. "Oh, that reminds me." She snapped her fingers, then she went out the door, and as she left she was muttering something about somebody needing a pillow.

I looked at Jimmy, and we both looked at Shinju, and we all had a good laugh on Millie's behalf.

❖❖❖

After the campus tour, Jimmy and I went to a little café that was just off campus. We hadn't eaten out together for a long time. It was only about 4:30 p.m., but we'd missed lunch, so we were both extremely hungry. And we had beaten the supper crowd.

We were sitting at a little table for two—nothing fancy, just a round, laminated, wooden top on a metal pedestal. Jimmy said, "Do you realize how lucky we are that you got that scholarship and the money your dad saved up for you?"

"I think about it all the time. I feel so sorry for the students who'll have to pay back the money they've been forced to borrow. I can't imagine being under that big of a financial burden."

"Me neither," he said. "Dad and I never had much, but at least we don't owe anybody." He sighed and continued, "We only used the downstairs part of our farmhouse the whole time I was growin' up. After Mom died, there just wasn't any reason to heat the upstairs, so Dad nailed some barn siding to the upstairs door to keep it sealed. At least, that's why he said he was doin' it. I've wondered, now that I'm older, if that was the real reason, or if he just did it so he couldn't get back up there where all the memories were."

"Wow, that's rough," I said. "Is it still nailed shut?"

"Yep. I haven't been up there since I was about three years old. Mom died when I was two."

"Your father did a fantastic job of raising you by himself. And I'm betting that wasn't easy." I grinned.

"What? You think I was a difficult child?"

"I didn't say that. I think you were a difficult teenager."

Then he grinned, but he didn't say anything.

"I'm waiting," I said.

"For what?"

"For a response."

"None offered, none necessary," he said through his grin. "I had the sense to remain sober and single until I got my foot tangled up in your wiles."

"A terrible fate," I said as I shook my head and offered several tsk, tsk, tsk's. "Or maybe not. Seems to me you were stumbling around until I put my spell on you."

"You did work some magic," he said. "That's why I'm always at your beck and call."

"As well you should be," I teased, sitting back and flipping my hair, just as the waitress brought us our dinner.

We walked back to the dorm, and I knew the hardest part of being in college was about to rear its ugly head again; I was going to have to say good-bye to Jimmy for another three months. We went into the lobby, and I said, "Wait right here. I'll check with Millie to find out if the one-call-a-week rule is enforced in this dorm." I went to the only room with a door and knocked, just as she'd said to do.

No answer. I knocked again. Still no answer. I put my ear to the door to see if I could hear any rustlings within.

"Lookin' for me?" Millie's voice behind me made me jump.

"Holy cow!" I said, my heart threatening to jump out of my chest.

"Yes. How often can I make long distance calls to my husband?"

"Well, now, there's a question I've never been asked before," Millie said. She put her index finger over her upper lip as if in deep thought. "Hmmmm... Does he have the dorm number?"

"Of course," I answered.

"How's he feel about payin' for the long-distance charges? That once-a-week-call is only for outgoing calls. As far as I'm concerned, he can call you as often as he wants."

My face lit up. "But, doesn't the phone only ring here in the lobby?"

"Yeah. Is that a problem?"

"Well, who usually answers it?"

"Anybody who's here. This isn't a freshman dorm. We operate like a family, not a military barracks. You're right at the top of the stairs, so if Jimmy calls, someone'll answer it and yell up the stairs for you to come down and take the call. You won't have a whole lot of privacy, but at least you can hear your honey's voice." She looked over at Jimmy on the other side of the room and gave him an exaggerated wink.

It didn't seem to faze him. I figured he'd considered the source and was no longer taking Millie too seriously.

"If you think it's all right, I'll ask him to call me whenever he gets lonely and..."

"Now wait a minute. You have to keep your grades up, which means you'll be spendin' most of your time studyin', right?"

I snorted a laugh. "Okay, I'll tell him it's alright to call me a couple of times a week, and I'll call him once a week. How's that sound?"

"Hmph. Sounds like you're gonna be doin' some husband-rationing." She sucked in a big breath and blew it out slowly. "Oh, the perils of being married and livin' in a women's residence. Tell him to call you *at least* three times a week. It's gotta be hard to run a marriage from such a distance, especially if you can't communicate."

I was beyond ecstatic. I hugged her; couldn't help myself. "Millie, I think you and I are in for a great relationship."

"Well, one of us has to save your marriage, so it might as well be me." She motioned me out of the way, so I moved over, and she entered her room, closing the door behind herself.

I slowly walked over to Jimmy, my hands behind my back. He straightened up and looked down his nose at me. "And the verdict is...?" he asked.

"You are required to call me three times a week...AT LEAST...and I'll be calling you once a week. Can you live with that?"

"I don't know. It might interfere with my social life while you're..."

I punched him in the arm.

"Ow!" He rubbed his arm. "Okay, AT LEAST three times a week. From the sounds of things, I can call you on whatever days are best and at whatever times are best to catch you before or after classes."

"You have to remember that classes start at seven-thirty a.m., so you'll probably still be milking. Your best bet will be to call after my classes. Probably after supper. I left a copy of my schedule taped to the kitchen door, and I also left one on our nightstand. I know you're going to be staying at your Dad's house again, so you'll have to grab your copy after you do the milking tomorrow."

"Got it," he said. "Will you still be calling home on Sunday?"

"That sounds good. We'll keep it at the same time as it was last year. That way I'll catch everybody at home when I call. Unless I find out otherwise," I said. "Oh, and I won't be answering the phone most of the time when you call, so just ask for me, and I'll come running." I leaned up against him and looked up into his face. "There's one more place I'd like to take you before you leave."

"I thought men weren't allowed in the dorm rooms," he said.

"That's unfortunate, I agree. But the place I'm taking you is a pretty good second choice."

There was a spot on the OSU campus that lovers frequented. It was close to the student union and was called Mirror Lake. It always offered a pretty view of the evening sky when the weather cooperated. I hoped it would remind Jimmy of the place he proposed to me in St. Louis.

We walked south, hand-in-hand, crossing the foot bridge across the Olentangy from the north parking lot to the little lake. There were several couples milling around, but I didn't pay any attention to them, and I don't think Jimmy did, either.

"And just how did you manage to find out how nice of a place this is for lovers?" he asked.

His inference went right over my head. "I saw it for the first time one evening after eating supper at the cafeteria. There was a temporary warm spell in February, so I decided to go for a walk. I hadn't ever seen the lake in person before, only on my campus map. So I made it a point to seek it out. I sat down on one of the benches and looked up: the moon was full, and the stars were only barely visible because of the moon's bright light. I was, of course, thinking about my husband

and missing him terribly, so I thought, 'Helmi, the next time you come here you should be with Jimmy.' And here we are."

"And it's great," he said. "But only because you're with me." He kissed me, and then we walked all the way around the lake, talking about things that needed to be done on the farm and what classes I was going to be taking and my new roommate and all sorts of other odds and ends. Just before we came back around to our starting point, Jimmy said, "This kinda reminds me of the park in St. Louis where I proposed to ya."

SADNESS ON THE HOMEFRONT

I wouldn't say Jimmy was worried, but he was definitely concerned. "Dad's not doin' so good," he said after we'd finished the milking one June morning in 1941. "I think he's a lot worse than he lets on."

"His face is red as a beet," I said, "And not just when he exerts any effort. It's that way all the time. His blood pressure must be off the scale. I'm worried about his heart."

Jimmy had a look on his face that was completely foreign to me. "I can't get him to go to a doctor. Says he's afraid a doctor would put him in bed, and he doesn't wanna miss work. It's not like he can't afford to miss; he just doesn't want to."

"The only socialization he gets is when he's here with us. He likes being here. I think it makes him feel comfortable."

"Yeah," Jimmy said, "he seems more at home here than at his own place. I wish we could convince him to sell the old house and stay here at the farm."

"Why won't he?" I asked.

"Thinks he'd be in the way."

"He told you that?"

"Not in so many words. But I've been able to pick up on it by some of the stuff he says every now and then. He's from a different time, Helmi. People didn't encroach on other people's families back them. You lived your own life in your own house and took whatever cards were dealt to ya."

"Granny Nan's of the same opinion," I said. "She's laid up in that house," I gestured toward our farmhouse, "and refuses to go to the hospital like the doctor told her she should. They need to be running tests on her all the time to see if her medication's right and to monitor the swelling in her legs. But do you think she'd go of her own free will?"

In March of that year I had insisted that she go to see a doctor. He immediately placed her on a blood thinner and gave her leg wraps and support hose to wear. I hadn't discovered how bad her legs had become until she finally got to the point where she could no longer bend over to rub the "liniment" on them. So she asked me to do it for her. I was flabbergasted when I saw them for the first time.

She always wore thick hose held up with garters that she kept rolled around her lower legs, just below her knees. The doctor said it was the absolute worst thing she could possibly have done, as it cut off the circulation she desperately needed to keep her legs from swelling and looking so horrible.

Now she was paying the price for her obstinance; she was confined to a hospital bed that we'd moved into the house so she could keep her legs elevated. One of us girls gave her a bath in bed every other day or so. She was only allowed to get up to go to the bathroom and to get dressed and undressed. That meant she had to stay in one of the upstairs bedrooms because there was no bathroom downstairs, and she could not climb the steps anymore. That's the way most houses were built back then.

Bella was the best at doing things for her. Care and nurturing seemed to come naturally to Bella, and she had decided to become a nurse. I knew she'd make a good one.

"You got any ideas about how to get your dad to change his mind?" I asked Jimmy.

"Not a one," he answered dejectedly. "Sometimes I think people get blindsided when they get older. It's like they can't think past the moment. They forget about the ones around 'em who care so much about 'em; they don't seem to understand how important they are to us, and that we only want what's best for them."

"I understand how you feel," I said. "But there's another side to that story."

He looked at me with a furrowed brow.

I went to him and ran my fingers across his forehead, hoping to smooth away some of the worry hiding in those wrinkles. "I learned something in school that might be useful here. It's just like with pets. Sometimes we love them so much, we can't conceive living without them, so we put them through things that we shouldn't in order to make them hang around longer than what's best for them."

His face changed, and I could see that he was working that out in his head. "You're right. You're absolutely right. I never thought about it like that. I don't wanna lose Dad, so in order to keep him around, I impose my own feelings on 'im and forget to consider his. Maybe he's tryin' to tell me he's ready to go, but I'm tryin' to stop him. That's really selfish, isn't it?"

I didn't answer; I didn't have to. That concept had hit him like a bolt out of the blue. He put his arms around me and hugged me to him.

"You are every bit as wise as your papa."

He couldn't have said anything that would have made me happier.

❖❖❖

On August 9 of that year, Jimmy and Retta and I were finishing up with the last batch of cows. Butch had been sitting on a bucket, like usual, when he suddenly grabbed his chest, tried to stand up, but fell backwards, hitting his head hard on the concrete floor of the stanchion barn.

We all ran to him at the same time. Jimmy kept hollering, "Dad! Dad! Dad!" and I saw Retta's face turn the color of the lime we sprinkled on the floor to keep the odor and the flies at bay. There was no movement of Butch's chest, and all expression had disappeared from his eyes; it had taken less than a minute for the entire scenario to play out.

Jimmy was kneeling beside Butch and had his hand on his father's chest. I knelt beside my husband and placed my hand on his back. He reached over and took my hand. Retta came around to the same side and put one hand on Jimmy's shoulder and the other hand on mine. We were all connected by touch, and three of us cried, silently, for the fourth.

A few days after Butch's burial, Jimmy and I were sitting on the C-spring metal rocking chairs in the back yard after the evening milking. Jimmy said, "Is there any reason why you think we should keep Dad's farmhouse and land?"

I was almost afraid to answer, knowing I could possibly say the wrong thing and hurt his feelings, so I countered with, "What do *you* want to do with it?"

"I shouldn't have much trouble gettin' rid of it. There's a man in Weidman who buys up land and uses it to grow money crops. Our fields have been layin' fallow for years, so they should be pretty temptin' to the guy. He won't want the house, but it's prob'ly not even worth tryin' to sell by itself; he'll likely tear it down if he buys the property. He won't give me what I'd earn off the whole thing if I sold it outright, but at least I'll get out from under it, and we can get on with our life here. If you think that's a good idea."

"I think you need to make the decision," I said.

He shook his head. "I want your opinion, too, Helmi. We're in this together."

I loved that man so much. "In that case, I agree with you. Let's sell it to that guy and take what we can get out of it. No telling how long it might sit there if it goes on the market. And from the sounds of things, the guy you're talking about isn't gonna be interested in paying realtor fees. I'm not greedy. I don't need top dollar for it."

He nodded in agreement. "I'll go talk to him tomorrow mornin' after the milkin's done."

And it was settled. By the following month, Jimmy no longer owned a farm in Weidman. But he had dickered with the man and ended up with more than what I thought he'd get for it. We immediately put the money into our savings account.

"I want the two of you to take my name off the deed to this farm," Granny Nan said to Jimmy and me. We were sitting with her in the upstairs bedroom that had once been Dora and Yosie's, as it was closest to the bathroom. Jimmy and I slept in Mama and Papa's old room, Retta, Bella, and Dora shared a room, and Ronnie and Anna slept in the fourth.

"What's your reasoning, Nancy?" Jimmy asked her.

"When I die, there is no need for it all to have to go through that thing the lawyers came up with…what is it called? It puts everything on hold for months."

"Probate," I said.

"Yes, probate," she said. "I want the two of you to be the sole owners of this place. We should be able to make it out like it is a gift from me."

"But, Nancy, you…"

"No, I will not take any guff from anyone. The matter is closed. I have made up my mind."

Jimmy had found a used wheelchair for sale in Mount Pleasant. It wasn't very pretty, but it served the purpose. We had used it to take Granny Nan to Butch's funeral, and now we would use it to take her along with us to City Hall to get her name removed from the deed to the farm. She was all smiles when she signed the papers agreeing to "give" the farm to us.

We got her back home and upstairs. Jimmy was able to carry her up and down the steps with very little effort; she had lost a tremendous amount of weight and was nothing but a "bag of bones," as she called herself. I wondered what else was going on inside her to make that happen, but I was not going to find out because, as usual, she refused to go to the doctor. "I am too old to be concerned about my health anymore," she told me. "My time is coming, and I am ready to meet my maker. I have atoned for any sins I may have committed during my life—you know some of them, so you know they were humdingers." She laughed, though it was only a hint of the snorting she and I used to do when she had been a healthy woman. It made me sad to see her in such a state, but I knew she was content having completed all the plans she'd made regarding her unstoppable future.

"Now I can relax and wait for the Good Lord to call me home," she said. Some of the people from church visited her occasionally, and the minister came by our house at least once every week. Granny Nan always wanted to look nice for him and his wife, if she came along, so Bella made sure her hair was combed, her teeth were brushed, and she was wearing a nice bed jacket.

The radio stayed on nearly twenty-four hours a day on her bedside table, only ceasing occasionally at night; Bella or Dora would creep into her room and shut it off when they were certain she had fallen asleep.

Uncle Herman and Mary came to visit two weekends before I was to go back to OSU for my fourth year. I was finally going to be starting my clinical work, though it would be limited until I became an intern and was doing both clinic and field work nearly every day. I had not been working with Dr. Pauley; there had simply been too much for me to take care of at the farm during the three months I spent at home in the summer and the three or four weeks over Christmas.

One week before I was to be back at school, Jimmy said, "Hey, there's somethin' I need to talk to you 'bout."

"Okay," I said. "What's on your mind?"

"I think you need a vehicle down in Columbus. Would you consider takin' the car?"

"Geez!" That had really slapped me in the face. "Let me think about it a minute or two." I hadn't been ready for such a suggestion.

"I'll help you make a decision," he said. "We need a truck. Dad's old clunker isn't holdin' up, and I'm afraid it's time to bury it, too."

I knew he wouldn't suggest such a large purchase if it weren't truly necessary. "Okay. We'll get a truck. But if I take the car, that would leave you with *only* the truck. What happens when my sisters want to go to church? Or to town? Or anyplace else, and they leave you without a vehicle? Or if you need it and they want to take it someplace? You can't be a dairy farmer and a chauffeur," I said.

"Yeah, I understand that. It'd leave us short-handed without the second means of gettin' someplace."

"I appreciate the offer, but it's much more important for you to have two vehicles that'll be used constantly than for me to have one that'll probably sit in a parking lot most of the time." I paused and asked, "Are you wanting me to take the car to school so you don't have to drive me there and back all the time?"

"No, Helmi," he said, almost like he was hurt that I'd think such a thing. "I don't mind one bit takin' you there and back. I've told you that before. I'm just tryin' to make things work the best way."

"And you are, but I had to ask. I know going back and forth to Columbus so many times is a chore, no matter how much you tell me it isn't."

"It's 'bout our only opportunity to spend time by ourselves," he said. "Do you realize we never had a honeymoon? And if it hadn't been for Herman and Mary, we wouldn't even have had a wedding reception. I just feel like I've let you down."

"Oh, Jimmy, you can put that thought right out of your head. Now let's get down to brass tacks here. You need the truck for the farm, and the girls can use the car. Let's go find you a truck."

"We don't need to go find one. I think I already have one lined up. I can get a used one from a guy I talk to all the time at the feed store. He doesn't need a truck. His son's gonna be startin' high school this year, and he's talkin' 'bout tradin' it in 'cause he wants to get a new car so the boy has somethin' dependable to drive. I asked him what he'd want for it instead of usin' it as a trade-in, and he gave me a good price. So I thought maybe…"

"No," I said.

Jimmy looked at me like I was crazy. "You just said we should get a truck."

"Yes, I did. And yes, we should. But we are not going to get a used one. We are going to buy a new one. We have all that money in the bank from the sale of your dad's property. We can afford a new truck so *you* have a dependable vehicle. And we can probably pay cash for it so we won't have another monthly payment to be concerned about. Plus, you've always taken good care of our car. It's only four years old, so I feel confident about Bella or Dora taking it out."

He looked down at the ground. "You're makin' a lotta sense." He paused. "Did you know that GM employees get a discount on GM products?"

"You've been talking to Uncle Herman."

He kept his head down, but he looked up at me, the whites of his eyes showing.

"You set me up!"

"I just wanted to find out your real thoughts 'bout the matter. All I have to do is say the word, and Herman'll put our name on a 1941 Chevy Truck, sky blue—prettiest thing you ever laid eyes on."

I jumped up and threw my arms around his neck. He raised me up off the ground and twirled me in a circle. We were gonna have a new truck.

❖❖❖

We took our new truck to Columbus on Labor Day. "I hope we don't have a break-down," Jimmy said. "There won't be any repair places open."

"It's new. What's gonna happen?" I asked.

"Well, ya never know. It's not broke in yet."

He was right, but I wasn't going to let something worry me that was probably ninety-nine percent unfounded. I was enjoying the ride, windows open, my hair flowing in the breeze. It was a warm day, but there was rain on the horizon, so I was making the most of the sunshine while it lasted.

We reached our little motor lodge in Worthington at about ten p.m. and checked in. There was a new person at the front desk, so we asked after the couple who were usually there to greet us, and he said they were on vacation. He was their grandson. We'd stopped to eat supper at a restaurant along the way, something we had never done before. The rain had started just before we crossed the Michigan/Ohio state line, and it hadn't let up since.

The next day we arrived on campus at about eight a.m. Millie was there to greet us, and she said, "You have a new roommate coming in."

"What happened to Shinju?" I asked.

"Don't know. I just got the roster and room assignment sheets, and she's not on there. You know a Penelope Wall?"

"No."

"I think she's a horticulture major. She won't be here till tomorrow, though, so you have the room to yourself for tonight." She looked at Jimmy and said, "I'd offer to let you stay, but my butt would be kicked all over this campus if word ever got out. And it *would* get out."

"Understood," Jimmy said. "If I didn't have nearly two hundred cows to milk twice a day, a granny to take care of, and five girls to keep track of, I might try and sneak in anyway. But I need to be headin' back. I should be on the road right now, but it keeps getting' harder and harder to leave every time I drop that woman off." He looked over at me and smiled.

I went into meltdown, the tears welling up. I was usually able to control myself and not cry till after he left, but on that day, I was an emotional wreck. Jimmy came over and held me, stroking my hair. He didn't say anything; he just understood. I let him hold me for a bit, then I backed away, sniffed, and wiped my face. I looked up at him, and I could see how much it hurt him to have to leave, too. He was biting his lip.

Millie said, "I'll let you two have your moment," then she turned and left the room.

"Why's it so hard this time?" I asked.

"First separation after a difficult summer, I guess," he said. "We've never before had the responsibility of bein' the sole owners of a dairy farm, lost a parent, had a granny go bed-ridden…"

I put my hand over his mouth. "I get it." I sighed. "I keep thinking of the difference in what we're about to face, too. Here I am looking at an exciting time in my future, and there you are with the weight of way too much on your shoulders. I wish I could be there to help."

"Thank God we have Retta," he said.

"But you know, she's reaching the age where things other than the farm are going to begin interrupting her life."

"Don't say that; it sounds too final. Too real. I can't think about that right now. I'll think about that tomorrow."

In unison we said, "After all, tomorrow is another day." It was a famous line from *Gone with the Wind*. We both smiled. We had seen the movie at the Mount Pleasant Drive-In that summer. We hadn't been able to catch it at the theater the year it came out, so we had taken advantage of it being on the second-run bill at the drive-in. Problem was, we missed some of it because of the mosquitos! We couldn't get the driver's side window of the car rolled up tightly because of the speaker hanging on it. But we swatted and smashed while still listening and watching as best we could.

We kissed each other especially long before Jimmy turned and walked away without a word. I couldn't speak, and I thought maybe he was suffering the same fate. But I knew I'd be able to talk to him several times a week, so that helped ease some of the pain of separation.

❖❖❖

I had a week and a half to go before Christmas break. I happened to be going through the lobby of my dorm on the way to my room when the phone rang. I stopped and looked around. It appeared that I was the only one in there at the time, so I answered it. A voice I recognized said, "This is James Butcher. I'd like to speak to my wife, Helmi."

I lowered my voice about an octave and said, "Well, hello, James. How 'bout talking to me instead. I'm lonely and could use some sweet talk about now."

There was a momentary pause on the other end of the line. Finally James quietly said, "Helmi?"

"Of course it's me. You expect someone else to answer like that, you big, wonderful hunk of maleness?"

"This is serious, Helmi."

It took me a couple of beats to realize he wasn't kidding. "How serious?"

"Come-home serious."

Oh no! My breathing became irregular, and my knees were weak. *I need to sit down.* I fell into the chair behind the big desk.

"Who?" I asked, afraid to hear the answer.

"Nancy," he said. "I'm gonna leave to come get you first thing after I finish the milkin' tomorrow mornin'."

"Okay. Hurry, but be careful. I'd rather you take your time than not show up at all."

"See you tomorrow. I love you," he said and hung up.

I sat there wondering if what I'd just heard was real, hoping I'd figure out that it wasn't. But that was not going to happen.

I had to gather my thoughts together. I didn't know how long I'd be gone, so I would need to make arrangements to take my quarterly finals when I got back after Christmas, which meant I'd have to talk to all of my professors. Talking to the ones whose classes I'd have tomorrow was no problem, but the ones who taught the classes I took on alternate days might be difficult to catch.

Then it hit me—Link. I could talk to him and see if he'd be able to contact the other profs for me if I was unable to reach them. With only a week and a half before the break, I figured missing a couple of clinical sessions wouldn't be a problem. At least I hoped not. All the prof's offices were closed by now, but they'd open up at seven a.m., and I figured I'd hit Link's first. He might have some better ideas about how to handle things, anyway. Surely other students had gone through something similar.

I staggered up to my room; it was empty. *Penny's either at supper or out with friends, or maybe she...why am I trying to figure out where she is? That's totally irrelevant. I should get everything packed tonight.*

I began taking things out of my closet. Then I realized I could call Link's office just in case he might be there. I went back downstairs and dialed his office extension. No answer. I tried Dorothea's office, and she answered on the first ring.

"Hi Dorothea. This is Helmi. I need some help from either you or Link."

"Sure, Helmi. What's on your mind?"

"I just got a call from Jimmy. He's coming to get me tomorrow because my grandmother is evidently very sick. When I asked him how serious it was, he said it's 'come home serious.' So I have to go, which means I won't be able to..."

"Calm down, Helmi. You aren't the first student this has happened to. You're lucky it's nearly the end of the quarter. You won't have to make up any classes. Do you have any idea if you'll be back right after the Christmas break?"

I hadn't thought that far ahead. "Oh, gosh, I don't know. I guess it'll depend on how bad she is." My brain shifted into "what if" mode, and I didn't hear what Dorothea said next.

"I'm sorry. What did you say?"

"It doesn't matter. Can you come to my office tomorrow morning at seven?"

"I'll be there."

"Good. See you then. And try to get some sleep."

"Wasted words," I said. "But thanks."

We both hung up.

I was sitting there in a trance when Millie came in. "Helmi! My favorite married resident! How's things?"

I looked at her like she was a stranger; my mind was three-hundred-and-twenty-plus miles north. "Oh, hi." My voice didn't sound like my own.

"Are you okay? Helmi, honey, tell me what's wrong." She bustled up to me, pulled up a chair, sat down, and put one arm around me.

"I have to leave tomorrow. Jimmy just called and said my Granny Nan is really sick. He said it's 'come home serious.' I have to go. I have to go," I repeated.

"Of course you do. You don't need to worry about a thing. It'll all work out just fine. I'll do anything I can to help you. Do you need to call any of your professors?"

"I'm going to meet Dorothea Lincoln tomorrow morning at seven a.m. in her office. I already talked to her. She and Link should be able to talk to any of them who I won't see tomorrow. She said this has happened to other students." I started to sob, big hiccupping sobs.

"Breathe, Helmi," Millie said. She took a deep breath and I followed. Before long I was back to being myself.

"My mind is racing," I said. "I need to go up to my room and take a few minutes to put my thoughts in order."

"If that's what it takes, then you go right ahead. I'll be here for the rest of the night; I'm not going out again. You let me know whatever you need, and I'll take care of it." She took me by the shoulders and looked square at me. "I don't give a damn if it's only a glass of water. You got that?"

"I do," I said. I stood up and climbed the stairs like a normal person instead of an insane maniac. I reached my room and quietly closed the door. I sat down on my bed, closed my eyes, and said, "Granny Nan, I'm coming. Don't you go anywhere until I get there. You hear me?"

The next morning at six-thirty I left my suitcase and books behind the big desk in the lobby. Millie was up and assured me she would

Dar Bagby

not leave them unattended until I got back. I explained to her that Jimmy would not be there until that evening, but I wanted to make sure I could simply run in and grab them if he got there before I finished my last class.

"I told him to drive carefully, but I don't know whether he'll make more than a couple of stops for gas and Mother Nature's call. I don't want him to get here and not find me. I know he's going to want to turn around and leave immediately. If we have to, we'll stop for a couple of hours along the road and sleep, then we'll get right back at it."

"You just go to your classes and talk to whoever you need to, and I'll see to it that your stuff is here, untouched."

"Thank you, Millie." I hugged her and walked out, knowing that I could be at Dorothea's office in about five minutes.

Link and Dorothea were both there; they met me at the door to the building. Link took my hand and led me to Dorothea's office, as if I'd never been there before. He gently helped me into one of the chairs under the photographs, and said, "I'm really sorry to hear about all of this, Helmi. But I want you to know that you will not have any problems with any of your professors. We all know what it's like to be faced with something from home when home is far away."

"We will take care of everything for you, Helmi," Dorothea said.

"Link and I talked about it until late last night, and we think you should forget about trying to attend classes today. You should go back to the dorm and try to get some sleep so you can help Jimmy with the driving. At least one of you will be awake to get you both safely home."

"My bet is that you didn't sleep a wink last night," Link said.

"I didn't. You're right. I kept thinking about what life will be like when Granny Nan's gone. It was only a couple of years ago that I began to accept the fact that she won't be here forever. When she dies, everyone who was an adult when I was growing up will be gone except for my uncle in Flint." *I'll need to call him and Mary right away when we get home if Jimmy hasn't already done that, I thought. I wish I knew where Yosie is. She doesn't have the slightest idea about Granny Nan...if she even cares.*

"Helmi? Did you hear?" Dorothea asked.

"I'm sorry. Hear what?"

"Link wants to walk you back to the dorm. I have a class to teach in ten minutes, and I don't want to have to hurry to get you there and make it back in time for my class. Link doesn't have a class until 8:00 this morning."

"That's fine. I appreciate it. Really I do." Everything I said sounded far away, like someone else was saying what I was thinking.

"Come on," Link said. "Let's take the long way back." He helped me up out of the chair as if I were an old woman, like Granny Nan. But I didn't care; I didn't try to be brave. I'd done enough of that for Celine and Mama and Papa and Yosie and Butch. I couldn't do it anymore. I swayed a bit, but I steadied myself on the arm of the chair. We left Dorothea's office.

Link talked to me about all manner of things unrelated to either school or Granny Nan. We discussed Jimmy's and my new truck. We talked about the war in Europe. Link told me about his son, who was going to be starting college next fall. For the first time, he explained to me that all three boys were his and his first wife's, and he had married Dorothea when the youngest was only a little over a year old. It dawned on me that other families have problems just like ours, and Link wanted me to know that he understood what I'd gone through during my life.

By the time we reached my dorm, I was ready to sleep. I felt much calmer, and I had Dorothea and Link to thank for that. Link made sure he gave me their home phone number so I could let them know what was happening since the school offices would be closed over the holidays. I would be eternally grateful to them.

I told Millie what was happening, and she thanked Link for walking me back. "I was afraid she was gonna try and sprout wings so she could fly back to Michigan," Millie told him.

I went up to the room, fell on the bed, and immediately slept. I don't remember dreaming. I only remember Jimmy waking me.

"What are you doing up here?" I asked him when I remembered where I was. "You'll get me in…"

"I'm right here, too," I heard Millie's voice. "I thought it might do you good if that handsome face of his was the first thing you saw when you woke up."

I sat up. "What time is it?"

"Six-thirty," Jimmy said. He was holding my hand with both of his.

"In the morning?"

"No, in the evening. Are you prepared to leave right now?"

"Oh. My stuff's all downstairs at the desk," I said, still half asleep.

"It's already in the truck," he said. "Millie and I loaded it before we came up here to wake you."

"Is Granny Nan…" I couldn't say it.

"She's hangin' in there," Jimmy assured me. "But we should try to get back as soon as possible. Bella and Ronnie have been absolutely glued to 'er side for two days. And Retta and Dora have taken care of everything else."

"How's Anna taking it?"

"She's unsure about everything, but she's not afraid to ask questions. She's such a little trooper," Jimmy said as he smiled.

Okay, Helmi. Pull yourself together and get for home!

We were there before daybreak. I had driven the last two hundred miles while Jimmy slept. I knew it would take me a couple of days to get my sleep pattern back on track, but that didn't matter.

At a little after five-thirty a.m. I heard the radio come on upstairs. Jimmy and I had been sitting in the kitchen. I hadn't wanted to wake Granny Nan, or anyone else, when we got home, so we had kept ourselves quietly entertained until milking time arrived.

I stretched and yawned and made my way upstairs to the room where Granny Nan had been staying. She looked like a ghost lying there. My dear, wonderful Granny Nan was on death's door. As I approached the bed, I saw her eyes open, so I went to her side and touched her lightly on the shoulder. She slowly turned her head and looked up at me.

I couldn't hold back the tears. I said, "Hi, Granny Nan. I'm home from school. I came home for Christmas."

She blinked a few times, then she lifted her hand to me. I took it in mine; I couldn't believe how cold and dry it felt.

Her voice crackled, but I could make out my name.

"Yes, it's me," I said to her. I didn't know what else to say, and I couldn't see through my tears.

Bella appeared and said, "Two of my favorite people, right here in this room." She put her arm around me and looked down at Granny Nan. "You want some breakfast, Granny Nan? I fixed scrambled eggs, and I put a little bit of bacon in them."

Granny Nan hadn't stopped looking at me. "Helmi will get some," she said, her voice barely audible.

"I'll get some for you and for me. We'll eat them together. How's that sound?" I asked her, my voice thick from crying.

"Yes," Granny Nan said.

I didn't want to let go her hand. I didn't want to leave her side, not for an instant. And somehow Bella knew that. She said, "I'll get them, Helmi. You stay here with her. You two haven't seen each other for almost three months. I'll bet you have a lot to talk about."

I didn't say anything, couldn't say anything. I just stood there, holding Granny Nan's hand and crying. And she just kept looking up at me, the corners of her mouth turned up ever so slightly in a smile.

I was so glad to be there, and I knew Granny Nan was glad I was there, too. We didn't have to talk to each other to know that; it was evident without words.

I didn't want to leave her for even short periods of time. I was so afraid she'd go when I wasn't there. I rushed to dress, to wash, to brush my teeth. I was on a death vigil. I knew she was going to die, and I was not going to be away from her when she did. I even slept in her room every night.

On the morning of December 7, she didn't want to wake up. I kept talking to her, trying to get her to respond, but she only opened her eyes a little bit for a few seconds. Then I heard that awful sound, the one people called "the death rattle." Everyone had always said, "Once you hear it, you won't forget it." And they were right. I can still hear it in my nightmares.

Later that afternoon, the radio told us Japan had attacked our naval base at Pearl Harbor in Hawaii, and the U.S. was officially in the war. And that evening, Granny Nan slipped away.

NOW WHAT?

With Butch and Granny Nan gone, we needed help. Jimmy was tending to the farm almost single-handedly. Retta could only help with the milking for a little while on weekday mornings before having to leave for school. I could only stay until Christmas break was over. It was time to come to grips with all that had happened.

"We need to look closely at our budget," I said to Jimmy while we were lying in bed two nights after burying Granny Nan. "We're going to have to hire some help."

"I sat down and studied things the week b'fore you came home 'cause I knew this was gonna be in the works," Jimmy said. "I think it's only right that Bella, Dora, and Retta are in on the process of makin' some decisions."

"I agree. But before we have a discussion, don't you think we should come up with some suggestions?"

"Yes, I do," he said. "Unfortunately, I've come up short in that department. I mean, other than hirin' help for the milkin', whadda we gonna do 'bout all the cookin' and cleanin'? We can't make Bella and Dora do all of it. It's just not fair to them."

I sighed. I was remembering when I was their age. "Bella and Dora just turned eighteen a couple of days ago, and we didn't do anything for them. I feel bad about that."

"Don't be concerned," Jimmy said. "They weren't expectin' anything with all the confusion goin' on around here."

I said, "They'll both graduate, come June. Then they'll head off to college. Retta's fifteen and wants to participate in some of the extracurricular activities at school. Plus, she's beginning to show an interest in boys. Ronnie's so quiet; she hardly ever even speaks to us, let alone to anyone else. She spends most of her time in her room, reading and listening to Granny Nan's radio. She has absolutely no desire to do farm work."

"Yeah, I know," Jimmy said. "She hates it to the point of cryin' when I ask her to help with any of the chores, includin' somethin' as simple as feedin' the chickens and gatherin' eggs."

"She's deathly afraid of the animals. All of them." I said. I had no idea where that fear had come from. No one in our family had ever had a fear of animals.

Jimmy continued, "And then there's little Anna. I was hopin' I wouldn't have to say anything about it, but she's havin' a really hard time at school. She comes home two or three days a week cryin' and not wantin' to go back the next day."

"Why?"

"The kids. Because of the way she's hunkered over, they call her 'Anna Banana.'"

I sat straight up in the bed. "What? That's awful! Doesn't Miss Michaels take care of that?"

"Miss Michaels didn't come back this year. She sent word sayin' that she had to stay in Tennessee because of family matters, so there's a new teacher. Both Ronnie and Anna hate her," Jimmy said. "Now lie back down here, Helmi. If this is gonna upset you, we should just go to sleep and talk about it tomorrow."

I lay back down and stared up at the ceiling. I was on the verge of tears myself. "We have to talk about this now; I won't be able to sleep until we come up with some possible solutions."

But my mind wandered. A new elementary school was being built in Mount Pleasant, so this would be the last year for the one-room school. I knew I might never see Miss Michaels again. I hadn't informed her about Granny Nan's passing; I'd have to write a letter to her. That wasn't a chore I was looking forward to.

"I think the first priority is to get you some help," I said to Jimmy.

"I can get along without…"

"No, Jimmy. You need help more than any of us. Bella and Dora can do whatever needs to be done around the house, even if it's only the bare minimum," I said.

"But, Helmi…"

"No buts," I said. "We have to think of our income first. Without it, we won't have a farm. And no farm means no place to live."

Jimmy was silent. I looked over at him and could tell he was doing some serious thinking; his eyes didn't move, he only blinked occasionally. Finally, he said, "I have to get my brain settled down. It's bouncin' around from one thing to the next and not lettin' me stop on any one situation." He rolled away from me.

I knew it would be best to let him think and not bombard him with anything else. I closed my eyes, and the next thing I knew, it was dawn. Jimmy was already up and out of the bedroom, probably outside getting ready to do the milking.

I could hear Bella and Retta in the kitchen. They were having a conversation, but it didn't sound pleasant. I jumped up and stepped partway into the hall so I could hear them better.

"It's too far for her to walk! What if it's raining? It'll ruin her books, and then we'll have to pay for them," Retta said. "Dora and I and Ronnie would be okay, but Dora will probably have her sketch books with her. You wouldn't want her to ruin those, would you?"

"I can't help it, Retta. I *have* to be there right after school or I'll miss the interview. You can get a ride home with someone else; I know you can."

"What you know and what really is, are two different things, Bella. I can't name anybody in my classes who drives to school. Their parents or brothers or sisters drive them and pick them up. And Dora won't ask anybody. You know her; she'd feel like she was imposing. It's only six miles, Bella. It doesn't take that long. They'll understand at the theater," Retta said.

"You'll just have to stay after school until I can come back and get you," Bella said.

The conversation ended, and Retta came stomping up the stairs. She went into her room and slammed the door.

Should I interfere, or should I let sleeping dogs lie? I have to help Retta. She's so good about doing everything around here, I can't leave her in a lurch. And if no one can drive Anna, that throws the entire thing into a different realm.

I crossed the hall and knocked on Retta's door.

"What?" She sounded angry.

"It's Helmi. Can I come in?"

She paused then said, "Sure."

I opened the door a crack. Retta was sitting on her bed, her arms folded across her chest. I entered, closing the door behind me, and said, "If you need a ride home from school, I'll be glad to pick up you and Dora and stop for Ronnie and Anna at the one-room."

"Thanks, but that's not the point. Bella's trying to get an after-school job at the theater in Mount Pleasant."

"I gathered that," I said. "I couldn't help overhearing."

"The problem is, if she does, it means she'll have to be there every day right after school and won't have time to drive the rest of us home. Anna can't walk home from the one-room. Bella always picks her up on the way by. I don't really care about the rest of us; we can handle it if we have to, but not Anna."

"Why can't Dora bring you all home?" I asked, assuming that was the easy solution.

"She won't learn how to drive. She's afraid," Retta said.

I looked at Retta and saw myself sitting there. We were every bit as much twins as Bella and Dora; it's just that we were six years apart instead of a few minutes. I nodded and said, "Undeniably a problem. Let's work it out."

"Some problems can't be fixed," Retta said. "Without Butch and Granny Nan, this place is doomed. That's why Bella wants to get a job. I originally thought she wanted to work so she could earn some money for college, but that's not it. I had no right to get angry downstairs; she's doing her best to make a go of things around here, and I made it out like she was only thinking of herself. I feel like a heel."

Wow! That's more than I've ever heard Retta say at one time.

"So…you're angry at yourself instead of her?"

She nodded. Then she picked up her pillow and threw it across the room, growling as she did it. I knew it was time to let her in on the fact that Jimmy and I were working on some solutions and that Jimmy and I had decided she and Bella and Dora would be included in our discussions from here on out.

"You really think you're gonna be able to clear things up? Do you know how bad things *really* are around here? I mean, we don't have enough food. We don't use the electricity unless we have to; most of it's used for the milking, and I've been out there when we don't even turn on the lights. Jimmy and I use a couple of lanterns to light up the stanchion barn and the milk house. I don't do anything after school because we can't afford to buy enough clothes for me to participate in sports. Dora can't buy sketch pads. We all need to go to the doctor once in a while, but we just hope we get over whatever we have because we can't afford the doctor OR medicine. And Anna." She threw her hands in the air and said, "I don't think there are any answers to making things better here, Helmi. I know you want to help, but you're so far away, you aren't aware of what's going on."

I stood there, looking at Retta, my mind in a whirl. She was right; I didn't have any idea that things were so bad. They were living like paupers, and I hadn't taken the time to notice. *Why hasn't Jimmy told me?* But I knew why. He didn't want me to worry. He always mentioned how important it was for me to finish school so I could get a good job as a veterinarian and make enough money to keep the place afloat. *How long has this been going on? How could I not have seen it? Have I been so wrapped up in myself that I was oblivious to it all? Or was I subconsciously ignoring it?*

"Sit down, Helmi," Retta said. She got up off the bed and pulled Mama's wedding rocker over to me and pushed me—actually pushed me—into it. I plopped down and stared off into space. Retta sat back down on her bed and hung her head.

"I've been in another world," I said. "I don't mean that as an excuse. I'm saying, I've really, honestly been in another world. OSU is so far removed from what actual life is like. Normal people don't live in dorms and take classes and strive to make straight A's in real life. I've abandoned my family." I ceased staring into nothingness and looked at Retta. "I'm so sorry. So sorry, Retta. I'm…I…I don't…"

I broke into tears. I cried. I sobbed. I wished, at that moment, that I could just disappear.

Retta said quietly, "You can't blame yourself, and I didn't mean to make you feel like you should. I'm so frustrated and completely at a loss to know what to do about it."

I bent forward, reached out, and took her hand. "Oh, Retta. I know you, inside and out. You and I are so much alike. I can feel you hurting. You're lost and can't find your way back home."

Not only her face, but her whole demeanor changed. "That's exactly it!" she said. "I couldn't think of a way to put it, but that's it. I can't find my way back home. And home is where I want to be more than anywhere else." She reached into her pocket and extracted a handkerchief, one of Jimmy's. I looked at her questioningly. She lowered her head and said, "I always keep one for myself when I help fold the laundry. So far, Jimmy hasn't said he's missed any. Sometimes I need one when I lie here and cry."

I was so sad for her. "How often does that happen?"

"Only when it's dark. Or when I'm by myself. Or when I'm doing my chores. Or…"

"I get it," I said. "You don't happen to have another handkerchief in here, do you?"

"Nope. You're on your own."

I used my sleeve to wipe my eyes and face. I sniffed, long and deep, and did it several times. I looked at Retta, and she was trying to stifle a grin.

I held up my sleeve. "That's the best I can do," I said, and we both laughed. "I still want us all to get together and talk about things. I want to get all of this out in the open. What time do you think we can get Ronnie and Anna to go to sleep? They don't need to hear all of the bad stuff."

"Too late," Retta said. "They live it, so they already know about it."

"You're right. I think maybe they should be included in our discussions. What do you think?"

"I know they aren't very old, and they might not understand all of it, but they deserve to be a part of the solution, not just the problem."

I thought back on how many times I had been included in decision-making processes when I was young—much younger than Ronnie and Anna—and I knew Retta was right.

We were all in the front room, and Jimmy had built a fire in the fireplace. It was cozy and homey, and it should have felt comfortable, but I could tell everyone was on edge. We had never had a major, possibly life-changing discussion without Papa or Granny Nan being in charge. Now it was up to Jimmy and me, and I passed the gavel to him.

"We all know why we're gathered together here," Jimmy said, "So let's get right to it. What can we do to make things better around here?"

"Rob a bank?" Dora asked.

"Sorry," Jimmy answered and looked at me. "We aren't Bonnie and Clyde."

But Dora's suggestion wasn't nearly so funny as it should have been...no one laughed.

"Let's get some things down on paper," he said. "Helmi, would you be our secretary?"

"Sure will." I was holding a piece of notebook paper and a pencil, so I raised them up for everyone to see.

"Problem number one..." Jimmy said.

"Lack of funds," I said. Everyone agreed, so I wrote it down.

"Problem number two..." he said, and so it continued until I had written no less than fourteen items on the notebook page.

We tackled them one by one, and it took us nearly two hours to come up with possible ways of making things work better, more efficiently, and less expensively. Two of the items, however, remained unanswered.

"Let's all try and think of a way to use a little less gasoline," Jimmy said. "It's somethin' we seem to have taken for granted."

As I looked around the room, I saw yawning, fidgeting, and general lack of attention. "I, for one, think we all need to get some rest and not rack our brains anymore tonight," I said. "We can resume our meeting tomorrow night."

"I can't be here," Bella said, "at least not until about 10:30."

We all looked at her.

"I got the job at the theater."

"Good for you, Bella!" "Yea, Bella!" "I'm so glad!" "Congratulations!" "Wah-hoo!"

Bella, Dora, Retta, and Ronnie rose and went upstairs to get ready for bed. Anna stood at the bottom of the stairway and waited for one of us to carry her up. Jimmy started toward her, but I intervened, looking at Jimmy with an "I really want to do this" look on my face. He backed away, smiled and winked at me, and I scooped up Anna, carrying her to her room. I helped her get her nightgown on and took her by the hand; we slowly made our way to the bathroom. She jabbered the whole time about Two-Tone and the cows and how Jimmy had taken her to the stanchion barn a couple of times, and she loved watching the milk go through the filter into the bulk tank and seeing the big paddle stir it.

At last it was her turn to brush her teeth; everyone else had finished and gone to their respective rooms, so we had the bathroom to ourselves. "Tell me about school," I said.

She clammed up, and her attitude seemed to go into reverse.

"Anna? How's school?"

"Don't wanna talk about it."

"Why not? Don't you have fun with all the other kids?"

"No."

"No? What seems to be the problem?" I hoped she couldn't see through my ploy; I was blatantly pumping her for information.

"They don't like me."

"How could someone not like you? You're kind and funny and pretty, and I know you're a good student. What could it be about you that they don't like?"

"They call me…a name."

"What name?"

She didn't answer.

"Is it something bad?" I asked.

She nodded.

"Is it something you don't want to say?"

"It's not bad words. Just a bad name."

"I see. Do only a few of the other kids call you that name?"

She shook her head. "Everybody."

"What does your teacher do when they call you that name?"

"Nothing."

"What do you think she should do?"

"Tell them to stop," Anna said, her lower lip starting to extend and tremble.

I bent down and hugged her and patted her on the back. She put her head on my shoulder and began to cry. I was sorry I had ever started the conversation with her. "What is your teacher's name, Anna. I forget."

"Miss Welch," she said.

"Do you want me to talk to Miss Welch? Maybe she doesn't know the other kids are calling you a bad name."

"She knows. Sometimes she even smiles when they do it."

I was horrified. I would definitely be making a trip to the one-room school the next day.

I walked to school with Anna and Ronnie on Monday morning. All of the kids were outside playing until the bell rang. I followed them to the door. Miss Welch did a double-take and sighed, noticeably. She came over to the door and said, "Well, either come in or out. It's December, you know, and we don't need to try and heat up the outdoors." She spoke to me as if I were a student rather than an adult.

I was immediately put off by it. "I'd like to speak to you in private, and that means we may have to go outside." I did not give her a chance to respond. "I'll wait for you on the stoop." I turned, leaving the door standing open, just for spite.

She grabbed an old knitted shawl off the back of her chair and joined me. "What is it? I have a school full of children who are here for the purpose of learning, not to get into mischief while I converse with someone I don't even know."

"I am Helmi Butcher, Anna Schnier's sister. I understand she is the brunt of everyone's joke."

"I am at a loss, here, Miss Butcher," she said, drawing the shawl closely around herself. "I do not know of what you speak."

"Mrs."

"I beg your pardon," she said, a wrinkle appearing in her brow.

"Mrs.," I repeated. "*Mrs.* Butcher. And I think you are well aware of the subject about which I speak."

"Oh, you must mean the name-calling." She backed down a little bit, and I jumped on it.

"Of course that's what I mean. How can you allow such an altercation and not respond to it with authority? Instead, you idly let it pass, and I understand that you may also share in the frivolity indicated by the other school children's use of the name."

I could tell she was taken back by my accusation. Her face became strained, and her eyes closed to slits. Her lips nearly disappeared as they formed a tight, straight line on her face. "I don't know where you are getting your information, but I can assure you I have had no active part in reinforcing what the other children do. Name-calling is a normal part of a child growing up among other like-aged children. It cannot be…"

"I beg your pardon, Miss Welch, but Anna is my informant. She has told me how often she has been embarrassed, belittled, and intimidated, and her demeanor changes dramatically when asked about her school experience. She loves learning, as should be evident by her eagerness to please you, but she has lost her initiative and her confidence because of your lack of discipline of the other students when they blatantly call her 'Anna Banana.' Are you so callous that you cannot see the discomfiture she displays at being the recipient of such an injurious episode?" I rose to my full height, towering over her, and looked down my nose at her. I could see her squirming, and I loved it.

After a few seconds, she rearranged her shawl and said, "Perhaps I have been a bit lax regarding my recognition of her response to the incident. I must make it a point to be more observant in the future."

"You must make it a point to admonish the other children's behavior regarding their use of the slanderous attack on my sister. If I hear from Anna that she continues to be called 'Anna Banana' without you making an assertive effort to correct it, I will take this matter to a higher authority. Good. Day." I turned and walked home.

On Friday of that week, Anna came to me—all smiles—and said, "Miss Welch paddled two boys today, right in front of the whole school, because they called me 'Anna Banana.'"

MAJOR CHANGES

By Christmas eve, we had begun to get used to doing things differently. For instance, we never cooked one meal at a time; we only cooked extra-large quantities of whatever we made, and once the oven got hot, we could make lots of things at the same time so we didn't have to wait for it to heat up so often. We only had to use enough electricity to reheat things.

We all decided to go to bed a lot earlier and not sit up using the lights for so many hours; homework was done immediately after school instead of before bed. Retta had suggested using less silage and putting hay in the troughs in the stanchion barn. The cows weren't real happy about it to begin with, but they got used to it.

Several years back, we had gotten a Frigidaire to replace our old ice box, so we made it a point not to open it so often. We didn't leave the water running while we washed dishes or brushed our teeth so the pump didn't run as much. And we decided to keep the house a little bit cooler so the fans didn't have to come on so often to push the warm air up from the furnace. We were conscientious about how long we held the exterior doors open so as to keep the cold outside instead of allowing it to creep in.

All-in-all, we had made big changes in how we lived. But on Christmas eve, we let the lights burn on the tree most of the evening. We had all made a pact not to buy any gifts for anyone, but there were still multiple packages under the tree on Christmas morning, the majority of them wrapped in old newspapers or brown paper bags from the grocery. Everyone had made things for everyone else.

I had helped Anna draw pictures and paste sequins on them; she had found an old brooch in Granny Nan's things, and it had been decorated with sequins. Since none of us would ever wear it, I told Anna she could use the sequins to decorate her drawings. She was ecstatic, to say the least.

Bella had learned to crochet, so she used Granny Nan's leftover yarn and made various things for each of us, including a hat for Jimmy. When he tried it on, we all oooo'd and ahhhh'd over it, though it was a bit too small and barely covered the top of his head.

Ronnie had used straw to weave tiny little baskets, only big enough to hold a ring or some other trinket, and Retta made necklaces for all of us girls out of braided fabric. She cut strips from a bunch of old dresses that had belonged to Granny Nan, braided them together, and hung a piece of Granny Nan's jewelry on each. She made one without the jewelry for Jimmy and said, "Now you won't have to keep coming back into the house for the key to the truck. You can keep it with you around your neck."

"I wouldn't have to do that if someone would sew up the holes in my pockets, RETTA!" he said. That made her laugh.

I had found an old map of the United States in the junk drawer, so I ironed it flat, pasted it to a board I found in the back of the big barn, and outlined our travels from Oklahoma to Michigan using string that I wrapped around little nails I'd pounded into the board to notate our stops. I wrote notes about our experiences on little pieces of paper and pasted them next to the places where they'd happened. Everyone spent a long time studying it, Bella and Dora and I recalling some of the memories and embellishing the notes. Everyone else was mesmerized by our stories, many of which included Yosie.

Jimmy had a special surprise for us, but he said it would have to wait till after we ate supper. We tried and tried to guess what it might be, but he refused to give us any hints.

The most extraordinary gifts, however, came from Dora. There was one for each person, except for Jimmy and me; we had one labeled, "To the Lovers."

She gave everyone a pencil-sketched portrait. Jimmy's and mine was the one she had shown me earlier of the two of us at our wedding reception.

I was still in awe of it, but Jimmy was mesmerized. He couldn't keep from staring at it. He'd look at me, then he'd look back at the portrait and shake his head. "Dora, you have a talent beyond your years. I've seen professional portraits that don't capture what you see in people. This is, far and away, the most impressive thing I've ever seen." And he was serious. But the one thing that impressed us all, in addition to the art, was that each of them was framed in beautifully finished wood. The frames had tightly fitted mitered corners and were coated with shellac, making them shiny.

"Did you make the frames?" Jimmy asked.

"No, a friend did."

"You have a friend?" Retta asked, kiddingly. We all chuckled.

"He's very special," she said.

"Uh-oh!" Bella said. "This could be serious."

"I mean, he has a very special talent. He does fine carpentry. His father taught him."

I recognized the workmanship. "Is he Amish?" I asked.

"Well, sort of," Dora said.

"How can you be sort of Amish?" Retta asked.

"He's going through Rumspringa," she said as if we should all understand. Instead, we all just sat there and stared at her.

"Explanation?" Retta said.

"Each Amish boy goes through it, if they want to, and so do some of the girls."

"Like puberty?" Bella asked.

"NO!" Dora said, rolling her eyes. "When they turn fourteen or fifteen, they go out on their own and do things that are basically against the Amish rules. If they like doing them, they can leave the Amish community. Most of them choose to be baptized within the Amish church and stay, but some decide to remain in non-Amish society."

"How bad of things can they do?" Retta asked.

"Anything and everything," Dora said. "Do you know what the *Ordnung* is?" I had heard that word before, but I couldn't remember where. "It's the laws and customs that are laid down by the Amish community, but adolescents haven't yet become adult members of the church, so they aren't bound by the *Ordnung*."

"Now I remember," I said. "Uncle Herman told us about the Amish when I was little, and he used that word."

"I was really shocked when Isaac, my friend, told me he was Amish. I asked him why he wasn't wearing the usual clothes the Amish wear, and he said that was part of being in the Rumspringa. He said he was allowed to 'dress English,' as he called it. He can drive a car and even drink alcohol. He doesn't even have to attend home prayer."

"How long does this Rumspringa last?" Retta asked.

"I think it can go until he's twenty-one. But most of the guys make a decision about being baptized before then."

"Has Isaac decided yet?" I asked.

"He says he wants to be a member of the non-Amish world."

"But he could change his mind?" Jimmy asked.

"Not after he's baptized. But he only just started his Rumspringa, so he has lots of time left to make a final decision."

"Well, he sure does nice work," Jimmy said, running his hand over the frame on our portrait. "Almost as nice as your drawing."

Dora smiled shyly.

I was so proud of her.

We finished supper and were preparing to wash the dishes when Jimmy said, "No dishwashing yet. I have to give everyone my gift."

We all started back to the front room, but Jimmy stopped us. "Everybody sit back down at the table." He came over to me and whispered in my ear, "Give everybody a bowl and spoon while I'm gone." He disappeared out the back door.

When he came back in, he was carrying a large container. "Merry Christmas! Now dig in—it melts fast!" He uncovered the container; it was filled with snow ice cream!

"Did you make this yourself?" I asked.

"Yep. Just followed Dad's—well, originally Mom's—recipe. It's real easy."

"You have to teach us how," Ronnie said.

"Yeah, teach us," Anna said.

"Eat up, and I'll give each of you a copy of the recipe. You can keep it forever and think of me when ya make it," he said.

"What a wonderful surprise! I didn't even know you were going to have a gift for us," I said.

"Gotta keep ya guessin'."

That was probably the most memorable Christmas I ever had. I missed Mama, Papa, Granny Nan, Butch, Celine, and Yosie, but we all knew we had each other, so we were happy to be together.

That night, just as we were getting ready to go to bed, I saw Dora standing at the top of the staircase. She motioned for me to go downstairs with her. I followed her into the kitchen. She said, "Stay right here for a minute."

I did as she had ordered, and she came back with another package, which she handed to me. I took it and asked, "What's this?"

"Just open it," she said.

I tore the paper off it and there, looking at me, was Yosie's reflection in the hand mirror. This drawing was not framed with an Amish-made wooden frame; instead, it was glued to the oval mirror from Yosie's vanity. Dora had painted Yosie's lips dark, damask pink; that was the only color on the portrait.

"I know you miss her. I thought you'd like to have this so you can see her whenever you want."

I was overwhelmed with emotions, and I couldn't put a finger on any particular one; they all ran together. Some were a result of Dora's ability, some were a direct result of Yosie's disappearance, some were because Mama and Papa were gone...

"I don't know what to say."

"Then don't say anything." Dora put her arms around me and held me close. "I know you like it. Recognizing emotions is one of the things I do best."

It certainly was.

On the day after Christmas Jimmy went into Mount Pleasant to pick up a part he had ordered for the tractor. When he came home, he was practically jumping out of his skin with happiness.

"What on earth is wrong with you?" Retta asked him. "Are they selling happy pills at the repair shop? If they are, you over-dosed."

"Something almost as good," he said. "Come with me. We gotta find Helmi."

"You won't have to look too hard. She's in the hen house."

Jimmy came bounding up the steps and into the coop. He grabbed me around the waist and swung me around, one-armed. "We're gonna have help. I just got word from Jacob Miller."

"The Amish guy who built our barns and house?"

"Yes ma'am."

Retta entered the hen house and said, "Watch him, Helmi. He's way too happy. I think he swallowed too many happy pills."

"There's no such thing as too many," Jimmy said. "It's impossible to over-dose on 'em."

"I'm not so sure," I said. "What's this about help? And Jacob Miller?"

"Isaac, his youngest son, has agreed to work for us. He doesn't want a lot of money, and he can be here all morning because he doesn't go to public school. He's agreed to help us do the evening milking, too. All we have to do is feed him supper and pay him five dollars a week, which is less than minimum wage. He's really interested in working at a dairy farm. He says he wants to learn to use the electric milkers."

"How old is he?"

"Seventeen."

"Wait a minute. Is this the Isaac that made the frames for the drawings Dora gave us?"

"One and the same. He's a really great kid. Seems to have his head on straight," Jimmy said.

"You mean," Retta asked, "I won't have to break my neck trying to do *everything*?"

"Whadda ya mean 'do everything?' I don't just sit and twiddle my thumbs," Jimmy said to her.

"Yeah, it's real tough sitting on a bucket then turning it over and dumping milk into it every few minutes." She grinned.

"You lookin' for a fight?" Jimmy started toward her. She gave a fake scream and jumped down out of the hen house. "*I've* got work to do," she said. She turned around to walk away, and Jimmy jumped down, grabbed her by the hair, and bellowed like a caveman, thumping his chest with his other hand.

She screamed again, this time for real.

Jimmy let go her hair, and she made a beeline for the house, laughing the whole way. He came back up the steps. "She's gonna make some guy a great wife someday," he said.

"What makes you think that?" I asked, picking up a couple of exposed eggs and gently putting them into the basket.

"'Cause she's just like you."

I smiled, turned to him, and planted a kiss on his cheek. "I think Retta's right: you did have too many happy pills."

He pulled me closer and gazed into my eyes. He had that little smirk on his face, and he was breathing heavily.

"You got any more of those pills?" I asked. "I like you this way."

❖❖❖

Jimmy took me back to OSU on December 31; my classes didn't start until January 2, but Jimmy and I wanted to watch the fireworks in Columbus on New Year's Eve and be awake at midnight to welcome in 1942. Then Jimmy would go home on New Year's day, and I would prepare for the exams I'd have to make up from the previous quarter.

Jimmy'd had almost a week to teach Isaac how to use the milkers, and he knew he could trust Retta to take care of anything else Isaac needed to know. He felt confident about leaving Isaac alone. "He learns so fast," Jimmy had told me. "Sometimes he even surprises me with his knowledge of cows. He told me he was used to being around them on his father's farm, except there weren't nearly as many, and he wasn't worried 'bout anything to do with the milkin'. He's a natural at it, Helmi. He just needed a place to use his abilities, and he found us!"

"I've been meaning to ask you. How *did* he find out about us?"

"He never said. He just came up to me at the repair shop and introduced himself. Then he said, 'I understand you own a dairy farm. Could you use some help?' I jumped on it like a duck on a June bug. I figured if he was capable of doin' the kind of work he did for Dora, he'd be more than capable of milkin' cows."

"I think Dora might have been the little birdie who informed Isaac of our need."

"When I get back home, I'll be sure and listen to see if I hear her chirpin'."

We ran into a group of the vet med kids from one of my classes, and I drank my first champagne that night. It was so bubbly, and it tickled all the way down. I liked it. A lot.

"Watch her," one of the guys told Jimmy. "She'll become a lush if you let her have too much."

"I think she can handle it," Jimmy said. "She's got a pretty strong constitution."

"I'm betting it's not her constitution you're trying to make tipsy," the guy said.

"Tipsy?" I said. "Tipsy won't cut the mustard. I'd have to be completely sloshed before my constitution would collapse."

"And she's shy, too," Jimmy said and laughed.

"I can see that. You two...close?"

Jimmy held up his left hand. The guy saw the wedding ring and immediately backed off. "Sorry, buddy. I didn't mean to insult your wife."

"You didn't," Jimmy said. "Like I said, she's got..."

"Yeah, a strong constitution," the guy said. Then he tipped his hat and returned to his friends.

Jimmy said, "You realize that guy was flirtin' with you right under my nose?"

"Uh-huh."

"How often does that happen when I'm not here?" he asked. I think he was seriously concerned.

"Every day," I told him. "But don't worry. I have a very strong constitution." At that moment sirens sounded, bells rang, and it was suddenly 1942.

"Here's to a much better year," Jimmy said.

"When I'm with you, every year gets better," I told him. We kissed long and sensuously.

"Are you sure you don't want to come back to the motel for the night?" he asked me, pressing himself against me and slowly wiggling back and forth.

"God, it's tempting," I said. "But I *have* to study for my make-up exams tomorrow, and you *have* to leave early to go back home. It's already past midnight, so we should go our separate ways and do the right thing."

Jimmy sighed, backed away, cleared his throat, and said in a husky voice, "I hate strong constitutions."

He took me back to the dorm, kissed me one more time, then turned and left without a word. Words weren't necessary. We both knew how important it was to be responsible at that moment, and we handled it like the adults we were. But when the truck disappeared around the corner of the parking lot, I cried like a baby.

A GRADUATION SURPRISE

From New Year's Day, 1942, to my graduation from OSU in May, 1943, the days, weeks, and months went by, for the most part, without any outstanding situations. I can't say I was disappointed. It was as if my life needed a break, so I was granted one.

Bella and Dora graduated from high school. Bella went to Ann Arbor to begin her studies toward a nursing degree at University of Michigan. She had been given a small scholarship because of her good grades. She had gotten high scores on her college entrance exams, so she was approved for a government student loan, based on both her scores and personal need, that could be used at any state-affiliated university. Luckily, she had a friend, Minnie (Minerva), who was also going there to nursing school, so Minnie's parents drove the two of them.

Dora, on the other hand, had decided not to go to college. She was happy doing her portraits and working at home, doing all the gardening, including picking and canning. She had taken an interest in a young artist named Stephen Spicer, whose works she had seen in an art magazine. He was fairly well known along the east coast. His specialty was portraiture, which he did using a new and unusual technique. Dora found it extremely intriguing. He was going to be in Flint as one of the stops on his upcoming exhibition tour.

On July 3, 1942, Dora came running up to me while I was peeling potatoes for potato salad. "Helmi, just look at what he does!" She pushed the magazine under my nose.

"That's really interesting. I like the way he uses color."

"So do I. I'd love to see his works in person and actually talk to him. Do you think maybe Uncle Herman and Mary would put me up for a couple of days so I could meet him?"

I paused. "I hate to ask, because I know this is obviously very special to you, but how much..."

"It's only a dollar-fifty to get in. I have that much saved up. Please, please, please say I can go." Dora wasn't usually so demonstrative, and she rarely asked for favors, so I knew she had her heart set on meeting this guy.

"Give Uncle Herman a call and see what his plans are for those dates," I told her. She was, after all, eighteen years old and was quite old enough to make her own decisions about things. But because we were such a close-knit family, she had the courtesy to ask, knowing that we would have to add her usual work to our own.

"Oh, Helmi! I love you! Thank you so much!" She ran to the phone and immediately placed a call to Flint. She and Uncle Herman arranged for him to pick her up on the night before the show and bring her back on the day after. She'd be staying at his and Mary's house for two nights.

Uncle Herman had taken a job teaching mechanical drafting at Michigan State University in East Lansing. He only worked there two days a week during the summer term. He had retired from his job at General Motors and said he was bored, so he went to East Lansing every Thursday, taught a night class, and stayed overnight on campus. Then he taught a doctoral class on Friday morning, after which he drove home. Sometimes he stopped at the farm to say hello and visit with us. I was always thrilled to see him.

He told Dora he would pick her up on his way home on Friday before the Saturday art show, and he and Mary would bring her home on Sunday and visit with us, "...if that's okay with Helmi...," he added. Of course it was okay with me! And Dora was probably the most excited girl in all of Michigan, or at least Mount Pleasant.

So...on that Sunday in early August, when Uncle Herman and Mary brought Dora back, we all sat down together for a nice supper. It was such fun seeing Uncle Herman and Mary. Mary gave me the scoop on what Lizzy was up to. She said, "Now don't give me away if you happen to talk to her. I'm not supposed to tell anyone, but I'm going to burst if I keep it a secret any longer." She looked at me expectantly, waiting for me to ask her to spill the beans.

"Well?" I asked.

"Lizzy's pregnant! She and Walter are expecting a bundle of joy in January of next year."

"How exciting for them!" I said.

"She wants a boy, but Walter wants a girl. Isn't that funny? It's usually the other way around."

The phone rang before I could say anything else. It was Dr. Pauley's office. I'd been working for him during the summer, getting prepared to do my internship at OSU when I went back at the end of the month.

"I'm so sorry," I announced to everyone. "I have to go. There's an emergency that's gonna take two people."

"Oh no!" Mary said. "I hope it turns out all right. I hate to think of some poor animal in distress."

I was already grabbing the key to the car and was on my way out of the house. "The roast is in the oven. Everything else is in the Frigidaire. Oh, and there's a pie on the counter. Go ahead and eat. Don't know when I'll be back," I shouted as I ran out.

Jimmy was just coming up to the back door with Uncle Herman. "Uh-oh. Looks like our visit's gonna be cut a little short today," Uncle Herman said.

"Emergency. Dog with a pyometra, and Dr. Pauley needs help for the surgery. That's what I get for being on call on a Sunday."

I hugged Uncle Herman and gave Jimmy a quick kiss on the cheek. "I'll be back just as soon as I can." I was already getting into the car. "You know what they say: 'You never sleep on a pyometra.' Bye. Love you both!" And I took off, leaving Jimmy and Uncle Herman standing there, watching me drive away.

As I was en route to the clinic in Weidman, I was thinking about how much I loved what I would be spending the next portion of my life doing. I was going to be a veterinarian, the thing I'd wanted to be ever since my childhood. There was something exhilarating about having to leave at a moment's notice and hopefully save an animal's life. *I never know what kind of animal it'll be: a horse, a dog, a pig. It doesn't matter. My purpose is to save lives, if at all possible. That makes me feel so good inside.* I knew it sometimes inconvenienced the people around me, but they understood how happy it made me, and I couldn't ask for more.

I got back to the house about three and a half hours later. I was starved, so I immediately went to the Frigidaire and pulled out some leftovers. I didn't bother to reheat anything, I just stood at the counter next to the "fridge" and ate everything cold.

"You just missed Uncle Herman and Mary," Dora said. "How's the dog?"

"She's gonna pull through. I waited around for a while after she came out from under the anesthesia, just to make sure she was up and drinking some water. Dr. Pauley said he'd check her again tonight. It was a big one!"

"The dog? What kind?" Retta said as she came into the kitchen, followed by Bella.

"No, I meant the pyometra. The dog's a beagle."

Bella said, "I know what a pyometra is from my medical terms class. *Pyo* means pus, and *metra* means uterus. Obviously, the dog had an infected uterus. Am I right?"

"On the nose," I said. "I love medical terminology. Isn't it fun to know that almost every condition is made up of Latin terms that fit together to describe it?"

"You two are crazy boring," Retta said. "I can't believe I'm living with two med heads. I'm never gonna understand what you're talking about."

Bella and I looked at each other and said, in unison, "Med heads?"

Retta didn't expound on it. She merely grabbed a bite of the cold roast I'd been nibbling on and popped it into her mouth. Then she turned and left.

"Is Jimmy doing the milking?" I asked Bella.

"Yeah. He should be just getting started."

"Okay. I'll go help him. I'm guessing that's where Retta was on her way to." I put the roast back in the fridge and made my way to the milk house.

❖❖❖

Dora had been in constant contact with Stephen Spicer. He had taken a look at her portraits after his show in Flint, and he was, Dora said, "Flabbergasted."

"I'm assuming that was the good kind of flabbergasted and not the bad kind," I said.

She blushed. "Yes, it was the good kind. He said he was surprised to find out how good my stuff is. He said usually people who want him to look at their work are pure amateurs with junk. According to him, mine was on a level way above the norm. And he wants me to come to one of his shows in Detroit. It's going to be much bigger, and it's not just his stuff on exhibit. A lot of portrait artists' works are going to be displayed, and he says he wants me to see how many different ways there are to draw and enhance the same things. He says if I'm willing to branch out, I can have my stuff in an exhibit within another year."

"Detroit, huh?"

"Yes, but don't worry. He's willing to come and pick me up and bring me back home. Can you believe it?"

"How well do you know this guy, Dora?"

She smiled. "You don't need to be concerned, Helmi. He isn't some masher who's out to rape every girl he sees."

"I didn't mean…"

"In fact," she interrupted me, "he said if I can go with him, he'll even bring some friends along when he comes to Mount Pleasant to pick me up. One of them is a woman artist, like me. I met her and one of the others at the show in Flint. They're all very nice people. Most of them have families like ours."

"I just care about you, Dora, and I don't want anything bad to happen to you."

"Well, if you think about it, I have a much slimmer chance of that happening than you do."

I frowned.

"I'm talking about meeting up with a few people who all share the same love of art. You're at a university where thousands of people all congregate in a small area and probably include more than a hundred sex offenders."

"Hmmm. I never thought about it like that. You're right."

Dora had grown up without me noticing. She was a responsible young woman who was aware of what was going on around her, and I had missed that happening.

"When does the Detroit exhibit happen?" I asked.

"There are two of them, one in December and one in March, and I think I'd be best off going to the one in March. It lasts for three days, so I'd be gone for five. I'd be staying in the same room with the other woman, and we'd split the hotel bill. They assured me it wouldn't cost much. Of course, I'd have to offer to help pay for the gas, since they'd be driving all the way up here and back twice."

"And you have enough money to do that?"

"Almost. Stephen says I should try and sell a couple of my portraits before the show so I can earn enough money to pay for the trip, including some spending money. I told him no one in Mount Pleasant is interested in my kind of art, but he says I'm wrong. He told me that if one person gets a look at what I'm capable of doing, I might even get some commissions."

I was standing there with my mouth hanging open. "I think he's probably right. Dora, your work is outstanding, though I'm not an art critic. But if you would be willing to hang a couple of your portraits in the right places and put our phone number on them, you could probably either sell them or at least find out if other people would be interested. I'd say, give it a chance!"

"I've already talked to a lady who works at the library, and she's agreed to it. I have an appointment with the man who owns the theater, thanks to Bella. He seems interested, too."

"Well, aren't you the entrepreneur extraordinaire!" I was so happy that she had finally decided to step out of her secure little box and show the world what she was made of, albeit the small world of Mount Pleasant. But everyone has to start someplace. "You have my blessing. I hope it all pays off."

"Thanks, Helmi. You're opinion means a lot to me."

That night I was telling Jimmy about Dora's intentions, and he, too, was a bit apprehensive at first, but after I explained the whole thing, he was in favor of it, as well. "She's got some real drive under that 'little girl' act she puts on," I said.

"She's no little girl," Jimmy said. "You need to stand back and take a good look at your twin sisters. Retta, too. She's more grown up at sixteen than I was at twenty."

"Girls always grow up faster than guys," I said.

"Well, if that's the case, then Retta's provin' it to be true. She's a looker, too, Helmi. And I think she has her eye on Isaac. I know he's sweet on her."

"I thought Dora was sweet on him."

"Nope, they're just friends. But Isaac and Retta share the same love of workin' hard for a living. Neither one of 'em is afraid to get their hands dirty. Haven't you seen 'em talkin' in the barn and the milk house? Once in a while they appear to be havin' some pretty long conversations. Mosta the time they just tease each other, but every now and then I see 'em with some real serious expressions on their faces when they're talkin'."

"Well, I'll be," I said. "Kinda sounds like two other people I know."

"I keep tellin' ya, Retta's your twin even though she's a lot younger.

"I like Isaac. I guess it could be a lot worse."

The end of August arrived way too soon, and I went back to Columbus for my last year of college. I would be doing my internship, and I was lucky to be one of the ones who was chosen to do it at the OSU School of Veterinary Medicine rather than having to go to a nearby clinic, which would mean I'd need my own transportation. I was inclined to believe that Link might have had some say in the matter.

Since I was more interested in the treatment of large animals than small ones, I would be working mostly with cattle, horses, pigs, sheep, and goats four days of the week and with small animals, like dogs, cats, rabbits, etc. another two. I would have one day off, but I would be on call every other week on my day off. That meant I'd have two days out of every month completely to myself. I would also have to work during either the first week of Christmas break or all of spring break. I wouldn't know which of those was going to be available for me until after the first week of my internship. I was hoping it would be the first week of Christmas break. I knew that by the time spring break rolled around, I'd be seriously wanting to spend time with Jimmy.

After the first week of the quarter, I was beat. I had no idea it would be that difficult to keep up the pace of being on twenty-four-hour call. I felt like I could probably sleep standing up.

Link was my mentor. He encouraged me to keep pushing. "I know you feel like you can't move another step sometimes, but it really does get easier," he said to me.

"It has to," I said through a yawn. "My eyes are at half-mast most of the time. And I can't remember when I ate last. Come to think of it, I've never seen a fat veterinarian. Now I know why."

Link laughed. "Just keep plugging away. Give it time."

I got my wish; I would work through the first week of Christmas break and then have a week off for spring break, which meant I'd get to be home for the entire week.

The only actual classwork I did was learning to draft letters to prospective veterinary hospitals asking for a job, learning to write letters to various universities to secure positions on staff, writing letters of recommendation for employees, and other such necessary communications.

I passed all my final exams, most of which were orals and "performance" exams where several of the professors witnessed me doing various procedures ranging from simple examinations and blood work to some fairly complex surgeries. And I would graduate Magna Cum Laude.

❖❖❖

I had decided to forego attending "The Ohio State University School of Veterinary Medicine Graduation Ceremony, Class of 1943." I had learned that we would not receive our actual degree at the ceremony, only the folder that would hold it after it was mailed to us. There was no way I was going to put any of my family through the long, hot, unnecessary rituals, especially since the keynote speaker was someone no one knew; I didn't care how good his speech might be.

When Jimmy showed up on my last day there, I was chomping at the bit to get home. I was not responsible for making any speeches as a Magna Cum Laude graduate; they would only mention that accomplishment when they called my name. I knew I wouldn't be sorry that I'd forfeited crossing the stage and shaking the university president's hand. I wanted only to be in my honey's arms. I sat as close to him as I could on the way home.

"I can't believe you aren't goin' to your own graduation," he said, "though I'm not gonna complain about it."

"Can you imagine how long that ceremony would take?" I asked. "It couldn't help but be torture, not only for the graduates, but also for everyone else who attends. And since I won't be getting my degree at that time anyway, what's the point? Besides, I have much more important stuff to celebrate when I get home."

"Such as…?"

"Just… things," I said. "Think about it: you won't have to make these awful trips anymore, I can be at home with my family knowing that I won't have to leave them for nine months out of the year, I can use my spare time to help you and Isaac and Retta…"

"Nope, not Retta," he said.

"What's that mean?"

"She's not helping with the milking anymore. She's got a job."

"Where?"

"The pet store in town. She's a real whiz kid when it comes to sellin' little critters to people. I think it's 'cause people see how good she is with 'em, and they wanna get the same results."

"Why didn't anyone tell me this before now?" I asked.

"Maybe 'cause it was next to impossible to reach you mosta the time. When one of us did, you were like some sort of walkin' dead person who kept askin' us to repeat what we'd said."

"I was that out of touch?"

"You were barely in touch at all. Don't you remember how you did nothin' but eat and sleep when you came home in late March?"

"Oh, yeah. I seem to remember something about spring break, but I'm not sure exactly what? Wait a minute, it's coming back to me. I *do* remember *something*."

"And what would that be?"

"I'll tell you about it later. Right now I just want to put my head on your shoulder and have you wake me up when we pull in the driveway."

And that's pretty much what happened.

The following week I received my degree, my name hand-lettered in a beautiful script, and beside my name was a round, gold sticker that had MAGNA CUM LAUDE on it. I was lucky enough to get the mail that day, so no one knew I had received my degree. I decided to have a private ceremony that night after supper. It was a Thursday night, and neither Bella nor Retta had to work.

We finished the dishes, and I told everyone I'd like to have them gather in the living room. Grumbles and whines met my request.

"What are we gonna discuss now?" Bella asked. "We can't be having another 'how to save money' meeting, can we?" She had a look of disbelief on her face.

I offered no explanations. I merely waited for them all to sit down. When they had each claimed a seat, I looked around at them:

Dar Bagby

Bella, Dora, Retta, Ronnie, Anna, Jimmy. My family.

I started to speak, but my emotions caused me to have to wait a few seconds and then start again. "I owe every one of you my most sincere gratitude. I can only imagine how difficult life has been for all of you in my absence, because as a family, we all depend on each other every single day. And I wasn't here to offer any help. But things are going to be different now." There was a huge lump in my throat, and I was having trouble talking around it. Everyone sat quietly while I recuperated enough to speak.

"I received something important in the mail today, though it's only symbolic. It's a mere representation of everything I worked for the last five years, and without your help, I wouldn't have it in my possession tonight."

I reached behind the clock on the mantle and brought out my degree folder. I briefly hugged it to my chest and closed my eyes. Then I opened the folder and held it out in front of me, showing them all my actual degree. To my surprise, Retta started to clap. Then Dora joined her, and everyone in the room was suddenly applauding. For me. For what I had done over the last five years. And for what I would be doing in the foreseeable future.

The tears flowed down my cheeks. Jimmy came up to me and took me in his arms. At that moment, everyone else in the room seemed to fade away; it felt like there was no one but him and me.

Eventually I turned to everyone and said, "Thank you for coming to my graduation. This ceremony has been far more important to me than any ceremony that went on at OSU. And I have a very important announcement to make."

"You got a job and you're gonna start working to make some money for us?" Retta asked. Everyone laughed, including me.

"Well, not yet," I said. "But the most important announcement is this: in December of this year, you'll all have a new niece or nephew."

Dead silence.

Then it sunk in, first to Retta, who jumped to her feet and shouted "Yippee!" at the top of her lungs. Then everyone else caught on. The entire room went wild with shouts of joy, whistles, and applause.

I looked up at Jimmy. He was looking back at me with an expression on his face that I'd never seen before. It was intimate, happy, and proud. And he was crying.

I stood on my tiptoes and whispered to him, "Congratulations, Daddy."

WHERE DO WE GO FROM HERE?

With Link's help, I had been able to send letters to many places in Michigan requesting job applications. According to Link, my Magna Cum Laude graduation from The Ohio State University School of Veterinary Medicine made me a much sought-after commodity. Most of the return communications, however, came from small animal clinics, which were rising in popularity at that time. Large animal medicine jobs, as opposed to the care of only dogs, cats, and other small animals were, it seemed, few and far between.

There was one offer, however, that appealed to both Jimmy and me. Its description was exactly what I had hoped for. There was a possible downside, however; it was in a remote farm area in Michigan's eastern upper peninsula. Neither Jimmy nor I had ever been there.

We went to the Mount Pleasant Public Library—I hadn't been there since high school. It was completely changed; not only was it much bigger, having a whole new addition to the building, but it also contained far more books and a huge reference section. We were trying to find where we would be if I decided to take that job.

We knew Michigan consisted of two peninsulas, the lower peninsula (the L.P.) and the upper peninsula (the U.P.), divided by the five-mile-wide Straits of Mackinac (pronounced Mackinaw). The only means of getting from one to the other was via car ferry across the straits from Mackinac City in the L.P. to St. Ignace in the U.P. There were, at that time, very few cities in the U.P. that could boast a population as big as Mount Pleasant. The eastern portion of the U.P. was covered in either forests or farms, and one of its most densely populated cities was Sault Sainte Marie. Just a few miles to the southwest was the village called Rudyard, a stopover for the railroad and a growing farm community, and the place where the large-animal vet job I was interested in was located. We liked what we read and saw.

With the baby now due in two months, we decided to plan a trip to the U.P. in the following spring. We had five head of Herefords, three cows, a bull, and a steer. We were prepared to sell our Hereford bull, which would give us some extra cash, part of which we could use to travel. We would have the steer butchered in late November for our own supply of beef, and we'd keep it in cold storage. We'd butchered a hog in early June, and for a small fee, the butcher shop in Mount Pleasant was keeping the meat frozen for us; we picked up parts of it from the shop whenever we needed it. They would do the same with the steer, but we would pay them to do the butchering, and they would keep it in their freezer for us at no extra cost.

I made a long-distance call to Doctor Tom Bell, the veterinarian in Rudyard. He said he was ready to retire and needed another vet to help the man who was his current partner and who would be taking over in January. I told him our plans to visit in April of next year, and we settled on a temporary date.

"My partner's name is Aune Halvorsen. Right after I got your letter and credentials, I spoke with him about the possibility of having a woman as a partner, and he said, 'I don't care if you hire a moose, as long as it's one who's knowledgeable and dependable and strong enough to pull a calf.' He's a no-nonsense kind of guy who swears that what he does for the farmers is more important than any other job out there."

"Sounds like he and I agree on that count," I said. "Can you send me a map so I know how get to your place in Rudyard?"

There was silence on his end of the line, followed by some chuckling. "It's entirely evident that you aren't from around here," he said. "Pardon me for laughing, but there are only a few main roads up here, and most of those are only gravel. They aren't even labeled." He chuckled again. "Your best bet's to stay in a cabin. I have a friend in Brimley, which is not far from here, who rents them by the week. I can contact him and see if he'll have one available during the time you plan to visit us, then I can let you know. Somebody'll give you the directions to my office when you get up here. Well, it'll be Aune's office by then."

"All right, Dr. Bell," I said. "I'll wait to hear from you about the cabin. Oh, and I understand it's a lot colder up there in the spring than it is down here in Mount Pleasant. Should we pack for chilly weather?"

"At the end of April, it's still winter up here," he said. I could tell he was grinning by the way his voice sounded. "I just hope most of the *big* snow drifts are gone by then."

I wasn't sure if he was serious.

We traded pleasantries and hung up.

"Well?" Jimmy asked.

"Looks like we're in for a wild ride."

December 13 started out with snow coming down so thick I couldn't see the lean-to barn from the house, let alone the stanchion barn and milk house across the road. Our baby was due any day, and I had felt some "twinges" just before dawn. I hadn't said anything to Jimmy about it; I hadn't wanted him to worry about hurrying to get the milking done. Besides, twinges were nothing to be concerned about. But those twinges soon turned into pains, and before Jimmy came in from the barn, my water broke.

Luckily, Bella was there on her Christmas break from U. of M. She had already had some maternity training, and she said, "We'd better get you to the hospital." She was very calm, which I appreciated greatly. She called to Retta and asked her to go to the barn and tell Jimmy it was time.

"It's time? Now? You mean Helmi's gonna...? Oh my gosh! I'll get Jimmy. Should I get Jimmy? Oh, yeah. That's what you..." She took off on a dead run, out the door, no coat, no boots.

Bella and I looked at each other and snorted a laugh.

It was only a matter of seconds before she came back in, shivering and stomping her feet. She was frantic. "I can't even see out there. I'd better put on my coat. Do I have time to...?"

"Retta," I said calmly, "just stop. Stop right there." She had one arm in her coat. She didn't move. "Take your time. I have a while before anything happens. I just need you to put on your boots and coat and tell Jimmy he should come directly to the house when he's finished and not sit there talking to Isaac, like he usually does."

"But he might still have another two or three..." she began to argue.

"It's okay. He can come to the house as soon as he *finishes*. Bella and I will have everything ready. He just needs to drive me to the hospital."

This would be the first baby in our family to be born in a hospital. All the rest of us had been born at home. There was never a need for hurrying; everything we needed was right there. But I couldn't help wondering if Mama and Papa would still be alive had Mama given birth to the boys in a hospital. That's something I'd wonder about for the rest of my life.

When Retta returned, Jimmy was with her.

"Did she drag you away from the rest of the milking?" I asked.

"Didn't have to. I was done. Isaac and I were just talkin'." He was calm as a cucumber. "Are you ready to go, or do I have time to change my clothes?"

"Go ahead and change. Be sure and dress warm, though; with this weather, it's gonna be a long trip, even though it's only three miles," I said.

"Actually, I think it's lettin' up a little. I could *almost* see the house from across the road." He turned to go upstairs.

Retta was halfway up, looking back at us. She wore a funny expression: part excitement, part disbelief, part wonder, and part sympathy. The sympathy part seemed to take precedence when she asked me, "Will they give you something so it doesn't hurt so bad?"

"Only if I ask for it," I answered.

"Please ask. Please!" she begged.

"I'll have to play it by ear," I said. "I won't let it get so bad that I can't stand it."

"Promise?"

"Promise," I answered.

"Swear on FDR's eyeballs," she said.

"Retta!" Bella chided. "What a terrible thing to say!"

I ignored it. "I swear."

"Okay, then," Retta said. "You better not be lyin' to me."

"No lie," I assured her. I could see her rubbing her thumb and middle finger together on her left hand, something she'd unconsciously done whenever she became frightened; she'd done it ever since she was just a tiny little thing. Jimmy gave her hand a squeeze as he passed her on the stairs. She took a deep breath, and her expression changed back to excitement, disbelief, and wonder with only a hint of sympathy. I thought, *How would Dora see Retta's face right now? I'd sure like to see her interpretation.* Funny how the mind wanders, even when we're in the midst of something as important as having a baby.

Just before midnight that night, a new life came into the world. Not only would it be under the parental guidance of Jimmy and me, it would also be under the influence of five proud aunts.

Jimmy and I had decided not to pick out a name until after our baby was born. Unlike Papa, neither of us was inclined to hope for a specific gender; we'd be happy with whichever we got. And we had not decided on a name for either a boy or a girl. We had discussed the fact that certain names were not appropriate for all babies. Some babies, after being born, simply didn't look like the name their parents had pre-chosen for them.

After a brief discussion following the birth, Jimmy and I both agreed that our son would be called Herman Lloyd Butcher, after Uncle Herman, of course, and Jimmy's Grampa Lloyd. But to make things easier during family get-togethers, we'd call him Lloyd. And to us, he looked like a Lloyd.

Every couple of hours the nurses brought him to me so I could feed him, and he was always hungry. The nurses said he hadn't cried hardly at all. I missed not having Jimmy there with me; that was one disappointment about having a baby in the hospital. Lloyd and I had to stay for three days before we were allowed to go home.

The day for our discharge couldn't have been sweeter. I was so proud when I got into the car and the nurse handed our son to me. Jimmy was all smiles. He slid into the car behind the wheel, pulled the door shut, and sat there. I looked over at him.

He said, "I wanna remember this moment for the rest of my life. Just me, my wife, and our son makin' our first trip home as a family."

Tears of happiness ran down my cheeks. I'm sure part of it was due to the post-partum emotional spikes I knew I'd have for a while, but that didn't matter. I was as happy as I'd ever been. I remember thinking, *Every time one of these moments happens, I think it's the best that's ever been. I just hope the best keeps happening.*

Jimmy reached across the seat and gently touched Lloyd's head. Then he looked up at me, grinned, and said, "Cheese and crackers!"

❖❖❖

On February 12, Lincoln's birthday, we had a mid-winter thaw. The snow melted, the temperature reached into the low fifties, and the sun shown more brilliantly than it had for several days, which definitely made me happy. There was a mild breeze that reminded me of spring. The house seemed so bright, and everyone and everything seemed more alive than usual.

Lloyd and I had an appointment at the obstetrician's office, so I bundled him up and took him outside in the sunlight to wait for Jimmy, who was washing up, shaving, and putting on clean clothes. Lloyd was making all sorts of noises, most of which I recognized as the same happy sounds that accompanied the sunlight that shone through our bedroom window. Isaac had built us a crib (at Jimmy's request), and when Lloyd wasn't sleeping in the bassinette, I'd put him down in the crib and watch him try to touch the rays of light suspended above him. He was just as handsome as his daddy: dark hair, eyes with beautiful long lashes, and a smile that sometimes became a smirk when he thought he was being cute. I knew he'd be a real catch for some lucky woman one day.

Jimmy emerged from the house and came up to us. He gently took Lloyd from me so I could get into the car. He talked to Lloyd like he'd talk to another man; he didn't make baby talk. Lloyd always stopped whatever he was doing and looked up at Jimmy's face, and I could almost see Lloyd's thoughts, as if they would manifest themselves as something tangible. I relished the way the two of them communicated.

At the doctor's office I went into the exam room by myself so the doctor could check my condition. He was happy with everything and told the nurse to bring in the baby and the father.

"Both?" I asked.

"Absolutely. I want your husband to be as involved in taking care of your son as you are."

I was so glad to hear that. I knew Papa had always been involved in my life and my sisters' lives as much as Mama or Granny Nan, so nothing could have made me happier. I was sure Lloyd would grow up to appreciate his daddy more if Jimmy was as responsible for parenting as I was.

Lloyd passed his first physical exam with flying colors.

We decided to take a little walk around town since the weather was so nice. The schools were closed for the holiday, but most of the businesses in town were open. We took turns carrying Lloyd, but after about twenty minutes he began to fuss a bit. "He's hungry," I said.

"Guess we'd better go back to the car," Jimmy said. We were angle-parked on the main street running through the center of town. I began to unbutton the front of my dress, and Jimmy asked, "What are you doing?"

"I'm going to feed him," I said matter-of-factly.

"Not right here in plain sight."

It had always been completely natural to see Mama nursing one of my sisters. The thought of doing it at any time, no matter where I was, only made sense to me. "Are you afraid it'll embarrass me if someone sees?" I asked, smiling.

"It's not you who'd be embarrassed," he said. "It'd be everybody who walks by and sees you doin' it."

I thought about what he'd said. Then I looked around at all the people milling about and said, "Maybe you're right."

"I know I'm right. If anybody reports us to the police, they'd get you for indecent exposure."

I began to realize how sheltered I'd been. *I went all the way to Columbus, Ohio, for five years of college; I'm an educated woman. But I've never been exposed to the outside world. Public opinion is completely foreign to me.*

By that time Lloyd was crying, his little face red and wrinkled and his fists balled and waving in the air. He was just plain mad because I hadn't accommodated his need in what he considered a timely manner.

Jimmy started the car, put it in reverse, and backed out of the parking space. He drove farther down the main street, then he turned right and stopped in a secluded place by the river. "Now you can nurse him. I don't think anybody's gonna come close enough to the car to have a reason to complain."

I was still in shock over my lack of "worldliness" as I fed Lloyd. Jimmy slouched down in the seat and took a nap. After burping Lloyd over my shoulder, he went right to sleep. I didn't want to wake Jimmy; there was nothing at home demanding our immediate return. So, I put Lloyd down on the seat between Jimmy and me and put my head back, falling asleep instantly. The three of us slept for half an hour as the sun continued to rise higher in the sky. It was some of the sweetest sleep I'd had since we'd become a family of three.

Jimmy drove slowly on the way home. When we reached the lane that led to the old one-room schoolhouse, we saw smoke rising behind our house. Neither of us spoke, but Jimmy's foot pressed harder on the accelerator. The closer we got, the more we could tell that it was coming from the lean-to barn. Then we saw the flames.

"Oh, God, no!" Jimmy said. He turned into the driveway going much faster than he should have, causing the car to sway to the passenger's side. Gravel crunched and sprayed into the yard as we skidded to a stop. It scared me.

I realized I was clutching Lloyd so tightly against me that he must have been unable to breathe. His muffled scream jolted my brain, and I loosened my grip. He was wailing at the top of his lungs.

Jimmy didn't even turn off the ignition. He had managed to put the car in neutral before jumping out, leaving the door standing open. Dora came running around the house, her face bright red and her lavender blouse darkened in spots from the smoke.

"Hurry, Jimmy! The animals can't get out!"

I had gotten out of the car and went racing toward Dora. "Here," I handed Lloyd to her and ran back to the car. I reached across the driver's seat and turned the key to shut off the engine.

Flames shot up higher than the roof of our house. Everyone was yelling in the direction of the barn, and I remember thinking how odd that was. Then it came to me: they aren't yelling at the building, they're yelling at someone in the building. I took a quick look around and made a head count: Jimmy, Lloyd, Ronnie, Bella was in Ann Arbor, Dora was holding Lloyd, Anna was on the stoop at the back door…

Retta! Without another thought, I bolted through the opening of the lean-to barn and saw her trying desperately to open the gate to the pen that held our pigs. A ring of heavy wire had been slipped tightly over the corner post of the pen and the frame of the gate to keep it closed. The fire had reached the straw that was directly under the gate and was rapidly working its way into the pen.

The wire closer was burning Retta's hands; through the smoke I could see them blackened and bleeding as she struggled to free the squealing animals. I put one hand in front of my face and stepped toward her, shouting over the roar of the fire, "Retta! Get out! Leave the pigs! You're getting burned!"

She refused to budge. The determination on her face reminded me that I would have done the same thing. The heat from the fire was so intense I could not reach her. I turned toward the stall where we kept our Hereford cows and the steer, but the gate was open; they'd been turned out, as had the bull in the adjacent pen.

Then I heard Jimmy yelling. I couldn't make out what he was saying, but I saw Dora run to the house with Lloyd.

For a mere instant, I panicked. *My baby!* But I gathered my wits about me and told myself he would be fine with her.

I glanced back toward Retta and caught sight of her running out of the barn, the pigs around her feet, racing to reach the doorway before her.

"Get out of there! Helmi! Get out!"

I ran for all I was worth, but my feet and legs were burning. It was then that I realized the hem of my dress was on fire, and the flames were shooting upward. I stopped and tried to beat out the fire that was steadily climbing up my body, eating up my dress. Jimmy appeared and swept me up in his arms. He took me outside, put me on the ground, and covered me with his body, snuffing out the flames.

Without a word, he got up and ran toward the big barn but stopped dead. The tractor was blackened, and the tires were melted. For the first time since we'd gotten home, I saw the charred remains of the barn siding. The smell of the burning hay became apparent as it crept its way into my nostrils.

Then it hit me: the fire had started in the big barn and then jumped to the lean-to barn. There had only been a slight breeze, but it had been enough to help the fire leap from one building to the next. I looked up and could see blue sky through what used to be the barn roof. I heard the sound of creaking lumber, and the next thing I knew I was screaming at everyone, "GET AWAY FROM THE BARN! IT'S COMING DOWN!

Jimmy stood stark still, obviously not aware that he was in danger of being crushed by the falling timbers. Before I could get my feet to move, Isaac appeared out of nowhere and grabbed Jimmy, pulling him to safety as the big barn collapsed in on itself, pieces of siding and roofing flying wildly in all directions. Sparks shooting out. Ash floating upward. Hissing and high whistling noises filling my ears.

I gained enough composure to get my feet working, and I ran to

Jimmy. Isaac had already taken off in the direction of the house. I slammed into Jimmy, throwing my arms around him, squeezing him. I could see little particles of light flitting around, as if I were in a jar with the lightning bugs I used to catch as a child.

Jimmy turned, and his body went limp. I dared to look up at his face. He wore a strange expression that I could not read, not even recognize. He was looking at the house, and the reflection of fire danced in his eyes. I followed his gaze, and I saw it: the house was engulfed in flames. My hair was blowing in the draft created by the heat. Once again, I looked around and counted: Dora, who was holding Lloyd, Retta, her hands limp and bleeding, Isaac, his arms around Retta from behind, and Ronnie, holding Anna's hand, all watching the hungry flames devouring our home.

Two-Tone, thin and gray from age, shivering, not knowing what was happening, came to my side, sat down, and whimpered. I let my hand fall onto her head, and I patted her out of habit, barely aware of doing it.

We all watched silently as our lives disintegrated. Sirens in the distance didn't even divert my attention from the blaze destroying everything that had been a part of us for so many years. And I thought about the portraits that Dora had drawn: the one of Jimmy and me at our wedding reception and the one of Yosie's reflection in the mirror.

I would never see those faces again. I would never again sit in Mama's wedding rocker or look at Granny Nan's beautiful dishes that had traveled, unharmed, all the way from Indiana to Oklahoma and then to Michigan. And I thought of Papa. He was lucky to have missed all of this. He'd worked so hard to create it, and this…he didn't deserve to see this.

Then I cried. I cried for my sisters, those who were with me and those who were not. I cried for Mama and Granny Nan and Butch. I cried for the buildings and all the memories they'd kept hidden in their cracks and crevices. I cried for the animals that were now without shelter and for Two-Tone, who didn't understand any of what had happened. I took a deep, hiccupping breath and cried for Jimmy and Lloyd and me. But mostly, I cried for Papa.

THE JIGSAW PUZZLE

I hadn't been the only one who cried. Tears had cut pale, thin lines through the soot on all our faces, even Jimmy's and Isaac's. I couldn't imagine what was going through each person's mind that day as we had stared at all we'd ever known disappearing before our eyes in the ravenous flames. The happiness that had come with that bright sunny morning was carried upward with the smoke, dissipating without a trace.

I was sitting on the ground, my legs in a wide V before me, my hands resting on my thighs. I was numb. My brain was completely inactive at that moment, no thoughts disturbing its respite.

Dora came over and handed Lloyd down to me. He was sound asleep. Even he had remnants of soot staining his tiny features. "He never cried," Dora said. Then she turned and walked away.

I paid no attention to which direction she went; I simply said, in a mechanical voice, "Thank you for watching him." I didn't know if she heard me.

I was aware of someone standing behind me. I raised my head and tilted it backwards, looking up. Jimmy was there. His usual tall stature had been reduced to that of an old man. His shoulders were slumped, his chest was heaving. He dropped to his knees and sat back on his calves, then he put one hand on my shoulder and the other on the blanket that was wrapped around Lloyd's feet. Neither of us spoke.

Anna managed to come over to us, and it was she who jolted me out of my catatonic state. "What're we gonna do, Helmi?"

With those few words she reminded me that I was now the matriarchal figure in my family's lives. At that moment, I would have given my right arm to be little again, to be dependent on Mama and Papa and Granny Nan. But when I looked at Anna, that small, round, flawless face caused a surge of energy to run through me. I didn't know where it had come from, but I was able to fix both my thoughts and my eyes on a whole new level.

I sat up straight, took in a good-sized breath, and said, "We're going to go on. We're going to pick up the pieces that are left and fit them all together, just like a jigsaw puzzle."

She sat down beside us, and I pulled her close. She was almost eleven years old now, but I knew she felt like a much smaller little girl at that moment; I did, too. Or at least I wanted to.

Dora, Ronnie, Isaac, and Retta were all sitting together on the lawn at the other end of the house. No, it was the other end of the foundation of what used to be our house. Our home. Our lives.

The crackling fire had ceased. But despite their efforts, the firemen had been unsuccessful at saving even a miniscule portion of what Papa had built. It reminded me of our barn in Oklahoma after the twister. There was nothing left of either of them but a memory.

"There aren't any pieces," Anna said.

"What?"

"You said we'd pick up the pieces, but there aren't any."

"Not so," Jimmy said to her. He pulled her back beside him. "We all have lots of pieces right here." He tapped her on the head. "And here." Then he tapped her on the chest, over her heart.

She reached up, tightened her fingers around his, and nodded her head. "I get it," she said. "If we all have pieces, it's gonna be a *big* jigsaw puzzle."

"As big as our family," Jimmy said.

The people who had arrived in the ambulance were worried about Retta's hands. "She has some third-degree burns. They're the worst," the man who had examined them said.

"But they don't hurt," Retta said.

"That's why they're the worst," the man told her. "The fire was so hot it burned most of the nerve endings in your hands, which means you don't feel much pain. It's really important to get them dressed and keep them treated around the clock until they begin to heal. Because there's been so much damage, they'll be highly susceptible to infection." He looked at Jimmy and me and said, "She should go with us to the hospital."

"I'll go with her," Jimmy said. "I won't be of any use around here. I'll follow the ambulance there and bring her back home after her wounds are dressed."

I started to say something, but Jimmy stopped me. "You have to stay here. You're the foundation that keeps this family from fallin' apart."

I touched his cheek and looked as deeply into his eyes as I ever had. I was overwhelmed by what I saw in them; it was respect for me. I nodded my head and watched him walk toward the car. I waved as he backed out of the driveway. He waved back with a hint of a smile on his tear-stained face.

Our closest neighbors, Bill and Rachel Neidhart, had seen the fire and made the call to the fire department. They were now sitting in their car on the side of the road about a quarter of a mile west of our property. I had not seen them since I'd been away at college for five years, and I hadn't attended church since Papa had died.

As soon as the firetrucks and the ambulance were gone, the Neidharts pulled into the driveway. Rachel got out and immediately came over to me. "Oh, Helmi! I'm so sorry. What can we do to help?"

It took me a minute to recognize her; she looked much older than I remembered. I stood up to greet her. "Mrs. Neidhart! How thoughtful of you to come by." She hugged me, but I backed away saying, "I'm covered in soot. You'll get it all over you."

"No matter. That's unimportant. What is important is that all of you are taken care of. I saw the ambulance taking one of your sisters away. How badly was she hurt?"

"Retta. Her hands were burned. She refused to let the pigs die in the lean-to. She kept working and working on the wire that kept the pen closed, and the straw was burning right underneath her hands. It was so hot I couldn't even reach out to her, but she wouldn't stop until they were safe and out..." I stopped. I'd been "rattling on," as Granny Nan would have called it.

"I know you must be devastated," Rachel said as she put her arm around me. "I often wonder how anyone could possibly handle a fire. It happens all too often on farms like ours. It's a frightening thing to think about, let alone to be a part of. Let's go sit under that tree on the other side of the road. The smell might not be so bad over there." She waved to everyone to come and join us. Everyone made their way to the old swing tree. She and Bill put down some heavy blankets. The ground was damp from the melting snow, and it seeped through the cloth, but not one of us seemed to care.

"I have a box full of food in the car."

Bill went back to their car, opened the trunk, and carried a large box over to us. I looked up at him. "Hi, Mr. Neidhart. Thank you for..."

"No need for thanks," he said, setting the box down in front of Rachel.

Rachel said, "I imagine food is one of the last things on your minds right now, but we all know how much better you'll feel when your stomachs are full."

Bill was headed to the milk house with two pitchers. "Bill's going to get you something to drink. Oh, shoot. I'll be right back with paper plates and some silverware and glasses." Normally I would have gotten up to help her, but I could not make my legs move. She went to the car and came back with all the eating utensils. Bill returned with the two pitchers, one filled with water and one with milk.

I sat there like a bump on a log, watching her do all the work. "I should help," I said as I reached for the plates.

"No, no," she said softly. "You just sit there. You don't need to bother doing anything. Bill and I will take care of it."

Lloyd began to cry, and I knew I needed to feed him, so I turned my back to everyone and let him nurse. Besides, I didn't feel the least bit hungry. By the time Lloyd had gotten his fill, everyone was eating bologna sandwiches with butter, Miracle Whip, and lettuce on Rachel's homemade bread, and they were all talking about the fire. I think it was great therapy. I took a sandwich and ate it without even tasting it.

While Rachel picked up everyone's plates, glasses, and silverware, Bill came to me and helped me up off the ground. "I want to talk to you in private," he said quietly. I carried Lloyd with me; he was sleeping again. We walked into the milk house. I sat down on an upturned bucket, and Bill leaned against the bulk tank.

"We'd like you to live at our house until you can find a more permanent place. It's not very big, so you'll have to double up, or more, to have enough beds, but at least you'll know you have a place to put your heads at night. And Rachel loves to cook, so she'll be pleased as punch to have all of you there so she can make her favorite things for you. With our kids gone, it gets kind of lonely for both of us. And, thank God, the fire didn't take your livelihood. The cows and barns on this side of the road are untouched. By stayin' with us, your husband'll be close to work each morning and evening." He studied my face, waiting for a response.

How can I say no? We have nowhere to go, and here are these wonderful, kind, thoughtful people opening their home to us. I started to cry. *Damn these emotions! I never used to be like this.* "Mr. Neidhart, I cannot possibly repay you for your kindness, but I have no alternatives at my fingertips right now. I would be more than happy to accept your offer, but only until we find another place to stay."

"Done!" he said, clapping his palms together. "Let's go tell Rachel and the others."

Rachel ooo'd and ahhh'd over the baby. We discussed finding clothes for everyone to wear and diapers for Lloyd. The girls would not be attending school for a few days since they had nothing to wear. And, of course, Retta wouldn't be working at the pet store for a while. Bill said he'd help Isaac and Jimmy build a shelter for the animals, even if it was only temporary and could get them through the rest of the winter. We told them we had pork and beef in the freezer at the butcher shop and would share that with them.

It was going to be a challenge, but we'd find a way to make everything work. For the first time since I'd watched Jimmy leave, following the ambulance with Retta, I felt positive. People have asked me how I managed to overcome that awful tragedy, but I've never had an answer to that question. I don't know if I'm simply incapable of expressing how we all went about the process, or if it's such a profound thing to overcome that there are no words to describe it. At any rate, we all found the right pieces in our hearts and minds in order to make each one fit into that big jigsaw puzzle.

GETTING BACK ON OUR FEET

We never found out exactly what had caused the fire, though the inspectors speculated that it was spontaneous combustion of the hay stored in the big barn. When it's tightly packed, hay sometimes gets so hot that it catches fire of its own accord. The dairy portion of our property had survived the fire untouched; neither the cows nor the dairy-related buildings had received any damage, and the fields that produced the hay and straw necessary to maintain our herd were intact.

The majority of losses regarding our livelihood were: 1) the destruction of our tractor, which we could replace with the help of our insurance coverage, 2) the loss of our small lean-to barn that housed our pigs and beef cattle, also covered by our insurance, and 3) the loss of the big barn where we stored hay and straw, only a portion of which would be covered by insurance.

It seems that, when Papa had taken out the insurance policy on the big barn, there was a clause stating that, because of the nature of the use of said building(s)—meaning, in our case, the storage of highly flammable material—premiums would be in relationship to the amount of coverage desired. Papa had chosen the least expensive monthly premium, effectually gambling that he would never have to replace it due to a major loss. *So much for that train of thought.*

When Jimmy and I took over the farm, we had simply changed the name on the policy and continued paying the premium for the amount of coverage Papa had initially chosen. It never occurred to us to check it out first, and our insurance agent had failed to suggest that we should. Needless to say, we were not too happy about that, and as a result, we discussed changing to a different insurance company. However, the possibility of moving and selling the dairy farm left us wondering if an insurance change was actually necessary, or even wise, at that time.

We had been up-in-the-air about what to do with the farm, seeing as how I might be required to take a veterinary job elsewhere. It depended partly on what other jobs were available, and there was the ever-present matter of possible sexual discrimination to contend with; we were both aware of the hesitancy of many well established vets to hire a female veterinarian. That's why the offer of at least an interview in the U.P. was on the top of our list. Unfortunately, all the information about the place in Rudyard had been destroyed in the fire, along with my tangible college degree, all of my books, notes, and other reference materials I'd gathered while at OSU. All the letters I had received from small-animal vet offices were gone, and the phone numbers of everyone we frequently called were now nothing more than traces of numbers we were incapable of remembering. And obviously, we had lost our actual telephone.

Using the phone at the Neidharts' place, I'd been able to call Information and get most of the numbers we needed, and I'd contacted everyone I could think of in order to give them our temporary number. We'd been there for eleven days, and so far I had not heard back from Dr. Tom Bell; I was getting nervous about it, as we were depending on him to let us know if there would be a place for us to stay in Brimley while there. We still planned to go at the end of April.

We had also begun to look into possible places for Jimmy to work if we needed to make the final decision to move there. The Selective Service Act, also known as The Draft, had been passed in 1940, and Jimmy had registered, but he had not served because of his occupation as the owner and operator of a dairy farm. The government deemed that our farm's milk production was more important to the nation than Jimmy's active service in the military, so he was deferred, or exempt, and carried a card indicating that he was Class II-C (Deferred in Occupation).

Despite his deferment, he would be eligible to get a government job if he changed his classification. We knew that Rudyard and Brimley were both fairly close to Sault Sainte Marie (around twenty miles), so he might be a candidate for a job with the Army Corps of Engineers. They were responsible for building, operating, and maintaining the locks in Sault Sainte Marie.

The purpose of the locks was to bypass the unnavigable rapids that drop twenty-one feet from Lake Superior down to the level of the Sainte Mary's River at a spot between Sault Sainte Marie, Michigan, and Sault Sainte Marie, Ontario, Canada. The Corps of Engineers also hired civilians, but Jimmy didn't have any experience at the jobs described in the reference books, so it might be best not to depend on being employed by them, even though the war meant lots of jobs were available that might not otherwise be accepting men of his age and employment history.

There were a lot of mining jobs available for both iron ore and copper, but most of those were much farther west, so that was out of the question. Jimmy also had the prospect of finding a job at one of the dairy farms that were, apparently, quite common in the eastern U.P. From the information we had gathered at the library, dairy cows, beef cattle, and horses made up the largest percentage of farm animals raised in that part of the state. The deciding factor might be the difference in wages earned at one job or the other. Of course, Jimmy said he'd feel much more comfortable working on a farm. He was truly a man after my own heart in that regard, and I supported him without question.

The civilian war effort on the home front had been spreading throughout the United States, and Mount Pleasant had not been left out. Military posters promoting active participation in the effort appeared in the windows of nearly every business in town. Propaganda of all sorts—movies, cartoons, comic books, etc.—played an enormous role in boosting the morale of American citizens, including my sister Bella. She decided to serve in the Cadet Nurse Corps (CNC).

By making that decision, she was able to receive her education for free. She applied for and received a government subsidy that covered not only her tuition, but also her books and uniforms, and she received a stipend, which came along with her pledge to serve actively in federal government and essential civilian services for the duration of World War II. Her education would be compressed into thirty months instead of the usual thirty-six.

The program was targeted mainly at high school students, but college women were also recruited, and Bella was pleased as punch to take part. She was so proud, in fact, that she made it point to sing "The Cadet Hymn" to me, and I had to admit, the words were certainly moving:

> *Faithful ever to my country.*
> *To the Corps, my sacred trust.*
> *Grant that I may follow wisely,*
> *All the guidance offered me.*
> *Give me kindness, Grant me patience,*
> *That I may not fail this noble challenge,*
> *Here to heal the suffering ones.*

I think our family's pride in her rivaled her own.

Dora, Retta, Ronnie, and Anna showed their patriotism by collecting scrap. They even got the Neidharts involved. All of them were bent on saving tin, newspaper, and kitchen waste fat (a raw material used to make explosives).

Anna had told us to be sure and bring her all the rubber bands we could find. We didn't know why she wanted those, specifically, but we were enlightened when she came to breakfast one morning with a large bundle wrapped up in a feed sack under one arm—a major feat for her.

"Whatcha got there?" Bill asked her.

"Is everyone here?" she asked, unable to straighten up enough to see everyone around the big table.

"I am," Retta said.

"Me, too," Dora and Ronnie both said.

"So am I," I told her. "And Lloyd."

"We're both here," Rachel said, referring to herself and Bill.

Anna struggled to put the bundle down on the floor and uncover it, but when she did, she backed away from it, spread her arms, and said, "Ta-da!" It was a ball the size of a small musk melon, and it looked like it was made of rubber bands.

We all looked at it, but not one of us said anything until Retta finally asked, "What is that thing?"

"Yeah," Bill said, "And what's it do?"

Anna laughed and said, "It's a rubber band ball. I've been collecting rubber bands for the war effort."

"So that's why you wanted them," Retta said. "I figured maybe you and Dora were making some artsy-fartsy thing out of them."

"Well, it is kind of intriguing," Dora said, "in an 'artsy-fartsy' sort of way." She rolled her eyes and stuck her tongue out at Retta.

"I meant that as a compliment, Anna," Retta defended herself. She retaliated by sticking her tongue out at Dora.

"Well…" Bill said, scratching his head symbolically, "I think it's the best lookin' rubber band ball I've ever seen, and it's probably the best lookin' one in all of Mount Pleasant. You want me to take you into town after school so you can turn it in at the donation building?"

"No," Anna said. "not today. I'd like to keep working on it a while longer. I want it to be the biggest one they get."

"Where were you keeping it that it didn't get burnt up in the fire?" I asked her.

"I hid it in the dairy barn. I figured the cows wouldn't mind," she giggled. "Isaac helped me keep it a secret."

"Well, if that isn't the most unique thing I ever saw," Rachel said. "You have every right to be proud of it, Anna."

Anna beamed.

Retta always took Anna and Ronnie to school, and she'd bring them home after school and then go back into town to go to work. Her work schedule came pretty close to coinciding with the school schedule, and she was such a good employee, her boss gave her a bit of leeway in order to make the trips. Dora had graduated, of course, but she didn't drive. She helped Rachel in the kitchen, and she did most of the laundry.

Retta's hands were getting better, but we had to change the bandages three times every day: when she got up, when she brought the girls home after school, and before she went to bed. But there would only be three more days of that; the doctor said she'd only have to change them once a day in the third week, then he wanted to see her again.

I helped Rachel by doing all the house cleaning. Thank goodness Lloyd was such a good baby. He seldom made any fuss except for when he got hungry or when he needed to be changed. He'd sometimes get a little bit cranky when he was extra tired, but that didn't happen often.

Bill retired to the living room with yesterday's newspaper. I bundled the rubber band ball up in the feed sack and put it back in the room where Anna, Ronnie, Retta, and Dora were all sleeping. Dora was stripping the beds, getting ready to wash the linens. "What would you think about me taking Lloyd for a walk?" she asked.

I thought for a moment. I'd already fed him, and he was making little grunting sounds and cooing while playing with the mobile we'd hung from the top of his crib. "I guess that'd be okay. It's kind of cold, though. I'll have to really bundle him up. Are you sure you want to carry him on a walk? He's pretty heavy when he's dressed in his winter duds?"

"I don't plan to carry him," she said.

"Well you can't drag him," I teased.

"No, but I *can* push him." She walked to the closet, opened the door, and pulled out a baby buggy. "I saw it in the garage and asked Rachel about it. She said it belonged to their daughter, but she and her husband moved away after their kids got bigger, and they didn't have a place to keep it at their new house, so she brought it here and left it. She told Rachel she couldn't part with it, so Rachel gave in and said it'd be all right to leave it here. I cleaned it up, and I think it looks pretty good."

"By all means, take your nephew for a walk!" I said. I got Lloyd all bundled up and took him downstairs. I handed him off to Rachel, who seemed to love having him around. Then I went back up and helped Dora bring down the baby buggy. It took all three of us to get him strapped into the contraption. I think Dora and Lloyd were both happy to get out of the house.

"He is a joy to have around," Rachel said. She sighed. "I'll be lonely when you all leave."

"And speaking of that…" I said.

"I didn't mean to imply anything by that!" Rachel apologized.

"I didn't mean to make you think you did," I said.

In unison, we both said, "I'm sorry." Then we laughed. It was fun being with her, almost like being with Granny Nan or Mama again. It dawned on me that Lloyd wouldn't have the pleasure of sharing his life with any living grandparents.

"What's wrong?" Rachel asked.

I looked at her questioningly.

"You suddenly looked very sad," she said. "Your whole face changed. Your body even sagged. I can certainly understand that, though, with what all you've been through lately."

I told her about the thought that had crossed my mind, and she sat back down at the table, patting the seat beside her. I obliged and sat down.

"Helmi, Bill and I have been wanting an opportunity to talk to you about something, but the time has never been right. I think the time's right now, though." She called to Bill, and he came into the kitchen and sat down across from us; he obviously knew what was about to take place.

Rachel put her hand on my arm. "Please don't think that we're meddling old people who want to poke their noses into places where they don't belong, but we're really fond of you and your family."

I smiled at her. "Thank you, Rachel."

She smiled lovingly back at me. "We don't know your exact plans for the near future, but we know you're trying to get a job as a veterinarian, and we know it's going to be extremely difficult for you to find one in this area. So we were wondering, are you and Jimmy planning on selling the dairy and moving away?"

Bill jumped in. "We only ask because we know someone who might be interested in buying it."

I can't believe I'm hearing this. Jimmy and I have gone round and round about it, and we knew it wouldn't be easy to find a buyer. I tried my best to react calmly and in an adult manner when, in fact, I wanted to jump around the room and shout "Wah-hoo!" at the top of my lungs.

"That's interesting," I said, "because we've been discussing the matter a lot here of late."

"I wish we coulda found a time to bring it up when Jimmy was here, too," Bill said. "But things just haven't worked out that way. We didn't wanna bring it up in front of your sisters 'cause we didn't know if you'd discussed it with them."

"Thank you for that," I said to Bill. "We have not, so you were wise to keep it strictly between us for now. May I be so bold as to ask who the interested buyer is?"

"Our nephew," Rachel said. "He's been working at a dairy farm in Kentucky for several years. It's somewhere around Lexington. He lives just outside of the city and drives about three-quarters-of-an-hour to get there. He says the place has been paying him good wages, and he's been saving up for a long time. He's not married and has no children, and he wants to move back here to his hometown, but there hasn't been any work that's interested him until I mentioned that you might be wanting to move and sell your dairy business. I hope you don't mind that I told him without consulting you and Jimmy first."

"Mind? Mind?" I said. "I can't believe how serendipitous this is!" *Where did that word come from?* "Would it be possible for us to get together and discuss this as soon as Jimmy comes back from milking?"

"I can't think of anyplace I have to be," Bill said, looking at Rachel.

"I don't have any plans until Bible study tonight," Rachel said.

"Good. It's a date!"

It couldn't have been more than three or four minutes before Jimmy walked in. "Brrrrr!" he said. "It's downright cold." He looked around. "Where's my boy?" he asked.

"Dora took him for a walk."

"I hope you bundled him up," he said.

"Not to worry, my dear. I put enough clothes on him to go through a blizzard and still sweat."

Jimmy leaned down and gave me a peck on the cheek. We filled him in about our desire to talk about some things. "I need to go up and change my clothes," he said. "I'm sure you don't want me sittin' around smellin' like cow manure. I'll be right back down."

In the meantime, Dora and Lloyd came back in. "I think it might snow soon. The sky's getting dark over to the west, and it just feels like snow. You know?" she said.

"Yeah," Bill said. "I usually know when weather's movin' in, too. My joints tell me."

"You're old," Rachel said. "All old people know when weather's moving in."

Dora said she'd like to go upstairs and do some drawing. She'd taken to using some of my old lined paper instead of sketching paper; all of her sketch pads were gone secondary to the fire. I felt bad for her because we didn't have the funds to buy her one. And I felt worse because the money she had saved up had been destroyed, as well. But she had appeased me by saying, "We're all making sacrifices right now. Don't think twice about it."

After more than two hours of discussions, we came to some agreements. Bill and Rachel's house was large, not huge, but it certainly had more room than the two of them needed. So Dora, Retta, Ronnie, and Anna were to live with them. Permanently! And they wanted Jimmy and me to stay as long as we needed to. "We don't want you to rush into anything 'cause you feel pressured to move outta here," Bill said. "We want you to know you're more than welcome to stay as long as it takes for the two of you to be certain of your future."

Jimmy and I couldn't wait to tell the girls the news.

I was ready to call Dr. Aune Halvorsen. I hadn't heard from his office since two days after the fire when I'd let them know my new phone number. Bill said, "Callin' him's probably a good idea. He'll know you're serious. I can tell you from experience that I was always more willin' to interview prospective employees when they took the initiative to contact me about a job opening."

"I just called a little more than a week ago to explain about the fire," I said. "I don't want to bother him too much."

"If he's worth his salt, he won't misconstrue your interest as bein' a bother."

"I hope you're right," I said as I dialed the phone. Because of my job-hunting and Bella being at U. of M. and our weekly communication with Uncle Herman and Mary, I had insisted that we pay for every long-distance call we made.

"You just went through a traumatic house fire where you lost everything," Rachel had said. "Long distance calls are something you shouldn't have to worry about." But I wouldn't hear of it. I made sure they showed me their long-distance bill from the phone company each month so I'd know we were paying them for *every* call that was ours.

I made the call, and the woman on the other end of the line said, "Dr. Halvorsen is out right now, but I'll be happy to leave him a message. I'm sure he'll want to talk to you. Don't say anything to him, but I just checked his calendar, and he has your number written on Wednesday. That usually means he intends to call whoever is at that number on that day."

"Thank you so much," I said, hoping I didn't sound overly eager. "And I didn't catch your name."

"I'm Shirley, the receptionist, office manager, vet assistant on twenty-four-hour call, *and* chief cook and bottle washer."

I laughed.

"Don't be too surprised if Doc doesn't call you until after 9:00 p.m. Is that too late?"

"Are you kidding?" I said. "I have four sisters, a husband, and a new baby to take care of, and I'm living in someone else's house right now. I rarely make it to bed by eleven."

"Got it," Shirley said. "I wish you luck."

"Thanks again." I hung up and mentally crossed my fingers.

Shirley had been right. The phone rang at nine-thirty-seven on Wednesday night. Dr. Halvorsen didn't mince any words, he proceeded to tell me that Dr. Bell's friend, Andy Atkinson, had a cabin that would be available the whole month of April, so we had our pick of the dates. He gave me Atkinson's phone number and said, "You'll probably get his wife when you call. She's Finnish, so she's a little bit hard to understand if you aren't used to hearing that accent. But she's used to people not understanding her, so don't be shy about asking her to repeat things."

I explained that, because of the fire, I may not have any degree or tangible credentials to bring with me. I said, "I called Ohio State, and they're going to send me…"

"Oh, don't be concerned about that. Do you have a person who can vouch for you? I don't want a letter; I want to talk person-to-person."

I gave him Link's number, and Dr. Halvorsen repeated it back to me. I told him, "It's his office number at OSU, so you might have to try more than once. I don't know his schedule this year."

"You're right on top of things, I can tell," Dr. Halvorsen said. "I like that. Looking forward to seeing you. Let me know when you have definite dates, and we'll set up a meeting." He hung up.

I must have looked befuddled because Jimmy asked me if I was okay.

"More than okay. Dr. Bell's friend in Brimley has a cabin we can rent anytime during April. All we have to do is call. And Dr. Halvorsen wants to talk to Link in person."

"Link isn't gonna share our cabin, is he?" Jimmy asked.

"He wants to talk to Link on the phone. And he…" Then I realized Jimmy was teasing me, so I punched him in the arm.

"You gotta quit that," he said, rubbing the point of contact. "The guys at the athletic club are gonna start wonderin' why I'm always black and blue."

"Just tell them you get kicked by a lot of cows. And since when do you go to an athletic club?"

He looked at me sideways with that sly smirk.

"You don't need an athletic club," I said in my sexiest voice. "You're already an Adonis without it."

He grabbed me and pulled me into his body. It was solid and muscular, and the strength in his arms was obvious by the way he held me.

Retta walked up to the door. "Am I interrupting something?"

"Yes," Jimmy said. "Leave."

"No!" I said, struggling to escape Jimmy's grasp. "What do you need?"

"Help with my bandage change. Dora's in the middle of a drawing, the other girls are already in bed, and Lloyd turned me down when I asked him to help."

Jimmy snorted a laugh. "You're all wet," his way of letting her know she was all right in his eyes. "Come on, I'll help you tonight." I could hear him teasing Retta on the way down the hall. "Do we need some butter to put on those burns? Or maybe some motor oil?"

I walked over to the crib. Lloyd was sound asleep, one of his hands opening and closing, probably trying to grasp some special toy in the midst of a dream. I was so in love with that little boy, just as I was still so much in love with his father.

FAREWELLS AND HOW-DO-YOU-DO'S

It was final: I'd be the new kid at the "Chippewa County Farm Vets" office in Rudyard, and my name—W. Butcher, DVM—would be painted on the sign beside the office door along with Dr. Halvorsen's. Jimmy and I had fallen in love with the U.P. the first time we drove off the ferry in St. Ignace that late April. As we kept going north, the houses became fewer and farther between, the number of farms increased, and the road became less and less traveled. Just like Dr. Bell had said, there was still a lot of snow on the road, though the drifts he'd predicted were gone.

Now it was the third week of May, and all of the ice was gone from the straits when we crossed. Some of the trees were beginning to show a few buds. The branches hung over the road, making it seem like we were driving through a living tunnel. Just off the side of the road, however, there were still patches of snow, but that didn't matter to us. We were breathing the freshest air we'd ever inhaled. Lloyd was enjoying his newest toy; we'd gotten it at the ferry dock in Mackinac City. While the cars wait there in the lines for the ferry, vendors walk around selling things to eat and toys to entertain the kids.

We'd been on the road for most of the day, but we were determined to reach Brimley before dark. It had been dark when we'd left the Neidharts' that morning. I was to start working on the first Monday in June. Dr. Halvorsen wanted to make sure we had time to settle into our new home before I had to be on the job. And that would also give us a few days for Jimmy to look for work and for us to find a person to watch Lloyd during the day.

We had taken the truck and left the car with my sisters. Retta said she wanted to buy it from us, so we sold it to her for one dollar. She paid us in full the day we signed it over at the Secretary of State's office in Mount Pleasant! The trip reminded me of when I had traveled from Oklahoma to Michigan in the back of Papa's truck. On this trip, however, the back of our truck carried only a couple of suitcases filled with some clothes and baby things, Jimmy and I had next to nothing in the back; we owned next to nothing since the fire. We'd be starting over, "Just like newlyweds," Jimmy had said. I took his comparison to heart and treated the whole thing exactly like that.

The sun was already down when we saw the sign that pointed left and had the faded word "Brimley" written on it. We looked at each other and grinned. We were almost home. The little house we had found was on Waiskai Bay, an Indian name, and was less than a mile from the eastern edge of the reservation. A tribe of Chippewa Indians, also known as the Ojibwa, lived there.

When Jimmy and Lloyd and I had come up to Brimley in April, we had taken a ride through the reservation. I wondered how they endured the U.P. winters living in their tar-paper-covered shacks that were passed off as houses. If the winters were as bad as everyone talked about, the natives must have been a hardy people. I began to understand how badly they had been treated throughout the history of the United States, and I knew we had a lot to learn about the native people who would be our neighbors.

When push came to shove, however, our place probably wasn't a whole lot better. We had bought it without getting to see it inside. It had been used as a rental cabin for a couple of years before the owners had been killed in a boating accident, and no one had done anything with it since then. It was a two-room log cabin with an outhouse. It didn't have electricity or running water; there was a spring just down the hill, so we'd be carrying water for cooking and washing.

But we knew it would only be temporary. And we had gotten it for a song. As soon as we became acclimated to the area, we'd find a permanent place to build, or if we were lucky, we'd find one already built that had a few more amenities.

Our truck bounced into the driveway just before dark. Jimmy shut off the ignition, and we sat there, looking at our home. As diminutive as it was, it was ours, and we were proud to have it. Lloyd had been sound asleep on the seat between us despite the bumpy roads, but he awakened when the car engine stopped. He made a couple of "waking up" noises and rubbed his eyes. I picked him up and sat him on my lap so he could see where we were.

"Hey there, sleepyhead," Jimmy said to him. "We're home."

"This is gonna be your new house," I said. "Let's go in and see what's waiting for us."

Jimmy came around to my side of the truck, and Lloyd reached for him. Jimmy took him from me, and I got out and inhaled deeply. The air was clean and fresh with the dominant aroma of pine. I took another breath. I couldn't get enough of it.

We went into our house. Hanging just inside the door on the left was a kerosene lantern, which would be our sole source of light. Jimmy checked it, but the kerosene well was empty, the wick dry. "Looks like we're gonna be in the dark tonight," he said. "Unless you have some kerosene packed away someplace."

"Fresh out," I said.

To the right of the door and sitting against the wall under a window was a small table with three chairs. A wood-burning stove sat in the corner, and next to that, on the front wall, was a bin that held firewood, or it would when we'd be able to get some. There was a wall cabinet with two doors that hung above a makeshift countertop over the wood bin. There was no stovetop or oven; food would be cooked on the top of the wood-burning stove, and that included baking things in a Dutch oven. I'd be learning how to cook all over again.

Beside the wall cabinet was a window that looked out over Waiskai Bay. But because it was nearly dark, we weren't able to see the view. On the other side of the room was a single overstuffed chair; the upholstery was in surprisingly good condition, at least in the little bit of light that filtered into the room. There was a dressing table with a mirror attached to the back, and in front of it sat the fourth chair from the kitchen dining set. On the back wall of that room was a washstand, but there was no basin. There was also a door that led to the bedroom.

"So far I can see that we'll have to invest in kerosene, a highchair, and a wash basin," I said. "Let's take a look at the bedroom."

Jutting out from the right wall was a bedframe. There was no mattress or bedding.

"Guess we need to add a mattress to that list, huh?" Jimmy said.

"Guess we'll be sleeping in the truck tonight," I said.

Behind the bed was another window, the same size as the one in the main room. Across the wall opposite the window hung an iron bar that was suspended from the ceiling by ropes on each end; that was our "closet." There were three empty hangers dangling from the bar.

I couldn't wipe the grin off my face.

"You really like it here, don't you?"

"Yes, I do. This is just the prelude to everything I've been dreaming about since I was a kid. I know it's nothing to brag about right now, but it's ours, and I have a new job waiting for me, and we have our whole lives to make the U.P. our home. The fact that we're starting with nothing only makes it seem like every little thing we do to improve it will put us closer to the life we want for our family."

He smiled at me and said to Lloyd, "I think your mom looks at this poor little shack and sees a castle."

We spent the next day in Sault Sainte Marie, better known to the locals as "the Soo." We had taken inventory that morning and realized we needed more than we had originally thought. But we had come prepared to buy a lot of necessities, and we had enough cash to do so, thanks to the Neidharts' nephew.

Bill and Rachel's nephew had come to take a look at our farm and said he'd buy it on the spot. He talked about replacing the milkers with the newest in-line system that pumped the milk directly from the cow to the bulk tank. The suction cups that fit over the cows' teats were attached to the pump and piping system, so there was no need to fill and empty buckets over and over. He showed us a photograph of the actual working system in the dairy farm where he'd been helping, and I tried to imagine what our cows would think of it. I also wondered if Isaac would continue to work for him. *But that's no longer of any concern to me*, I thought.

Bill and Rachel had plenty of money in a savings account in the bank, so they gave us cash for the farm—a very fair price, I might add. Their nephew would pay them back, with interest (at his insistence), so they wouldn't be out anything on the deal. We'd keep half of the money and divide up the other half into five parts for my sisters. Each of them was responsible for keeping their potion in an individual savings account that had been opened for them before we left Mount Pleasant.

When we had broached the subject of sending money to Bill and Rachel on a monthly basis to help cover the cost of food and extra utility usage, they said, "We're adopting your sisters without signing any adoption papers, so it'll be our responsibility, not yours." We couldn't convince them otherwise.

We had not bought a new tractor, nor had we hired anyone to rebuild our barns or house, so we were able to cash in our insurance policies and get a bit of extra money from those. One of our first stops in the Soo was at the bank, where we opened an account and deposited the checks we had brought with us from the Mount Pleasant bank and the insurance company. We also opened our first personal checking account; up to that point, we had only dealt in cash.

We spent most of the day shopping for the things we had on our list—a long list—and ate a big meal at one of the downtown restaurants. Lloyd's eyes were as big as saucers when the waitress brought him his own plate full of macaroni and cheese. Jimmy and I had fresh whitefish, the first we'd ever eaten, and it was scrumptious.

When we had finished all our shopping and the back of the truck was full, we got some ice cream and a block of ice to put into the ice box we'd found at a metal shop. The guy who sold us the ice box said he goes through a lot of them because most of the people who own and rent cabins around there didn't install electricity in them. "Dey like to keep dem places low-cost, doncha know? It's easier on de budget, eh?"

I loved the way he talked. I understood that one of the major populations who had settled in the U.P. was Scandinavian based. I remembered that Dr. Halvorsen had told me Andy Atkinson's wife was Finnish, and he'd said I'd probably have a bit of trouble understanding her—I did.

We had fun putting all our things into the cabin, but we made sure to stop before dark and take advantage of the view at sunset. It was more beautiful than I could have imagined. The water was calm, and the reflection was indescribable. The colors ranged from pink to purple and from gold to bright orange. We stood with our arms around each other and didn't speak a word. Except for Lloyd; he seemed to have a lot to say in his own language.

As the sun disappeared behind the horizon, the temperature dropped. "It's gonna be a cold one tonight, I think," Jimmy said.

"Scheist! Especially since we forgot about getting wood for the stove. And I won't have any way to fix us a hot breakfast tomorrow, either."

"We have a new bed to sleep in, plenty of blankets, and each other to keep us warm. We won't be cold. And as for breakfast, I'll take care of it," Jimmy said.

I had no idea what he had in mind, but I was willing to wait to find out. I was completely bushed and just wanted to snuggle with Lloyd and Jimmy and take a trip to Dreamland. I knew I'd remember this night, the first in our new home.

We were all toasty warm, and I was about to drift off when I heard a noise outside. I lifted my head and turned it in the direction of the noise. "Did you hear that?"

No response.

"Jimmy!" I whispered.

Still no response, so I reached across Lloyd and shook Jimmy's shoulder.

"Hmpf. What?"

"Did you hear that?"

"No, and neither did you. Go to sleep."

"Jimmy, there's something out there!" I got up and walked toward the window, but my socks weren't enough to keep the cold floor from stinging my feet. "Come here! Look at this!" I whispered as I shifted from one foot to the other.

Jimmy sighed. Then he rose and came to the window with me. His eyes got big, and he was instantly wide awake. About five feet from the window was a black bear. It was working at rolling an old bucket over to inspect the interior. "Holy…"

"We won't dare leave Lloyd alone out there to play," I said. "I had no idea those things came right up into the yard. I thought they'd be afraid to come around people."

Jimmy didn't answer; he was looking off to the left. I followed his eyes and saw two cubs. I always thought they were cute, but now that they were a possible threat to Lloyd, I failed to see any cuteness whatsoever.

"They aren't gonna try to get in," Jimmy said. "Let's go back to bed. We'll talk about it in the mornin'."

"You really expect me to sleep? After that?"

He didn't answer. He simply crawled under the covers, rolled onto his side with his back to Lloyd, and went to sleep. I, on the other hand, sat up half the night, occasionally going to the window to see if our visitors had left. I finally fell asleep sitting up in the bed.

I awoke to the smell of smoke. I panicked. *It can't be! We just went through this!* I checked to see if Lloyd was still asleep, but he was gone. I flew out of the bed and into the main room. Neither Jimmy nor Lloyd was there. I looked out both windows, but they were not in sight. I flung the back door open, and there they were, Jimmy sitting on an upturned log, Lloyd on his knee. They were watching a fire burn in the middle of a ring of stones.

"What…" I started to ask.

But Jimmy saw me and said, "Good mornin', Glory. How does your dew drop?"

Granny Nan used to say that, I thought. "What are you doing?"

"Fixin' breakfast. Want some coffee? I even have milk and sugar for ya."

I blinked several times before my brain engaged and I was able to come to grips with the fact that I was, indeed, awake and this was really happening.

"The bears?"

Jimmy laughed. "They're long gone. They don't stick around in the daytime when people are out. They only come around at night. And I can guarantee you, if we woulda opened the window or the door and made some noise, they woulda high-tailed it last night, too."

"I don't believe you," I said.

"Have I ever lied to ya?"

"Well…I have to think about that." I looked around, my feet feeling like two blocks of ice at the end of my legs. Without a word, I went back into the house, put on some clothes, extra socks, and shoes, and I wrapped myself up in one of the blankets off the bed. Then I went out to the fire. Jimmy had upended a log for me to sit on. He poured me a cup of coffee, adding milk and sugar and sticking the sugar spoon in my cup. It smelled wonderful. And that wasn't all that smelled good. There was bacon in a cast iron skillet that was balanced between a couple of the rocks beside the fire.

"Are you sure the bears won't smell the bacon and come to investigate?" I kept looking around, anxiously.

"Do you honestly think I'd have Lloyd out here if I thought there was any danger?"

I looked at him.

"Well, do ya?" he insisted on an answer.

"No, I guess not." I couldn't help but take one more look around to make sure the creatures were not in sight. "Where did all of this come from?" I gestured toward the fire.

"I have my sources," he teased.

I knew I wasn't going to get a straight answer, so I let it go.

"I need to gather wood today," he said. "Lloyd and I took a walk through part of the woods on our property b'tween here and the main road, and there's plenty to be had. Just need to pick it up. There's a lotta *big* deadfall, too, so I can cut that up as soon as I get a good crosscut saw and bring it back here to the cabin. We can use most of it for the wood-burnin' stove inside, and we'll keep some of it out here for fires."

Lloyd reached up for me to take him, so I wrapped him up inside the blanket with me. Jimmy threaded two slices of bread onto a long, straight stick and held it over the fire until it was toasted exactly right, nice and brown without being burned. He took one of the slices off the stick, picked up two pieces of bacon, and folded the toast around them. Then he handed it to me.

"I didn't know you knew how to do this outdoorsy stuff," I said with my mouth full.

"Pay attention, woman. There's a lot you don't know 'bout me."

And I have a lifetime to find out, I thought. He gave me that smirk I was so fond of, and my insides melted.

❖❖❖

We had eight more days before I would start my job. Jimmy said he'd like to use the truck to go do some job hunting, and I told him Lloyd and I would be fine. I wanted to wash the windows and do some major cleaning. I also wanted to wash the sheets and get them hung out before it got too late for them to dry.

A fire was already going in the wood stove, so I put a couple of pots of water on to heat, and I retrieved the new galvanized tub from the shed out back. I put some soap into it and carried it to the back door. By that time, the water was hot, so I poured it into the tub and added the sheets. I put another pot of water on the wood stove. I scrubbed the sheets together on themselves and wrung them out as best I could. Then I dumped the soapy water out and put a couple of buckets of cold water into the tub. I used it to rinse the sheets, and again I wrung them out. My hands got tired really fast, and I knew I needed to get back in shape for doing what I'd have to do at my new job. Being a vet was synonymous with a lot of physical labor.

I went back into the cabin and took the pot of water off the stove, carried it outside and dumped it into one of the buckets we used to carry water from the spring. Then I carried the bucket and a rag to the front of the cabin where we had hung a clothesline between two trees a few days before. I dipped the rag in the warm water and ran it along the clothesline to wipe off any dirt that had accumulated. Then I fetched the washed sheets (and my new bag of clothespins) and hung them in the breeze to dry, being sure to stand the clothesline prop up so it would keep the line high enough to avoid letting my clean sheets touch the ground. All the while, Lloyd was playing with some stones he'd found in a patch of sand at the end of the cabin. I had to keep telling him to get them out of his mouth; he was determined to chew on them.

It was such a pretty day, I hated to go back inside to do the cleaning, so I decided to wash the windows. I needed to fetch more water, so I put Lloyd in the wagon we had bought. It had removable wooden sides. We figured we could use it to haul the buckets of water and keep Lloyd happy by allowing him to ride in it when we went down to the spring. We also knew he'd have fun with it when he got big enough to play by himself. I put the three empty buckets and Lloyd into the wagon. He laughed and squealed and wiggled.

"You have to sit still now. We're going to the spring."

He calmed down and held onto the sides of the wagon. I pulled him down the hill, and he laughed all the way. I filled each of the buckets, then I put them into the wagon and turned to pick up Lloyd, but he was gone.

Don't panic, Helmi. I knew he was too little to have gotten very far, but I also had those bears in the back of my mind. I did my best to remain calm. I looked around and called his name. The spring was in a small clearing, but the woods around it was pretty dense with the dried ferns and other underbrush from last summer.

Okay, so much for being calm. Your son is missing, and you need to do something—fast. I couldn't see past the edge of the clearing from where I was standing, so I ran around the perimeter calling his name into the woods. He was nowhere to be seen. I stepped into the woods, into the underbrush; it grabbed at my ankles. I took another step and fell flat on my face, my arms scraping against the brittle stems that stuck up through the surface. I could feel the sharp points of last year's growth scratching my face.

All I could think about was bears. I stood up and called to Lloyd again. *Was that a response?* I whirled around, and there he was, sitting in front of the wagon, playing in the dirt and making typical Lloyd faces.

He had been hidden from my sight where I was standing at the back of the wagon, concentrating on filling the buckets. He had crawled up to the front of the wagon when I was distracted and had found something interesting. He was now looking at me like I was mentally deranged.

I emerged from the woods, scratched and bleeding, and went to him. I picked him up and said, "You little imp. Did you hide from your mom?" I lifted him up over my head and rolled him from side to side. He giggled, and it was a delightful sound.

I took a big breath, savoring my relief at knowing he was safe, and settled him on my hip. I grabbed the wagon's handle, then I pulled the water-filled buckets back to the cabin where I put mercurochrome on the worst of my scratches. I finally washed the windows, keeping my eye on Lloyd.

When Jimmy came home later that afternoon, I was sitting on a blanket in the front yard, watching the water. Lloyd was asleep beside me. Jimmy walked up to us, bent down and kissed me on the top of my head, and I put my finger to my lips in a "be quiet" gesture. He sat down beside me and put his arm around me.

"How was your day?" I asked in a whisper.

"I have a job," he whispered back.

My eyes got big, and I whispered, "Yes! Yes! Yes! Where?"

"Right here in Brimley. Do we have to keep whisperin'?" he asked.

"Right here?"

"Well, we could go somewhere else to whisper if you want," he said.

"I mean the job."

He switched to a low voice as opposed to the whispering. "Yep, right here. Just down the road."

I followed suit and said, quietly, "That's great! What are you gonna be doing?"

Lloyd stirred but didn't wake up.

"You're lookin' at the new caretaker of Andy Atkinson's rentals."

It took me by surprise, and my mouth dropped open. I would

never have guessed that Jimmy'd be happy doing something like that.

"You mean, where we stayed in April? That Andy Atkinson?"

"One and the same. I stopped at the hardware store up there at the top of the hill on my way home from the Soo—can't remember the name of it. It's a guy who lives here in town and owns a lot of the businesses."

"Get to the point," I prodded him.

"Well, Andy was there, and I overheard him sayin' that he was gettin' to the age where he was gonna either have to pay somebody to take care of the cabins and the grounds, or he was gonna have to sell 'em off." He looked at me with a funny expression. "What happened to your face?"

"It's not just my face," I said, holding out my arms. I had pinkish orange slashes all over myself from the mercurochrome. "Lloyd and I played hide-n-seek."

"I didn't know that was a contact sport," Jimmy said.

"You don't know how to play by *our* rules. Anyway, tell me more." By now we were talking at our normal volume, and Lloyd was still sleeping.

"Well, I walked up to him, introduced myself, and he recognized me. I told him I'd overheard what he was sayin' and asked him if he was serious. He told me he was, and I said, 'I'd be interested.' I told him we're just livin' down the road, and he asked me when I could start. I told him tomorrow, and he asked me if I'd be willin' to work for minimum wage, which is thirty cents an hour. I said, 'Okay.' He said, 'See ya in the mornin' at seven.'"

"We're gonna have to find someone to take care of Lloyd real fast. I start in a week," I said.

"I think *you're* gonna have to find someone to take care of Lloyd real fast. I'm gonna be at work."

"Are you working five days a week? Three? Six?"

Jimmy winced. "Don't know. We didn't discuss that."

"Okay, I'll try to find someone tomorrow. Maybe I'll have as much good luck as you."

"It can't be just anybody, ya know," Jimmy said, looking concerned.

I looked back at him with an expression that oozed disbelief. "Do you really think I'd just walk up to someone we don't know and ask them to take care of our son?"

His face went red. "I guess that was kinda stupid."

"No comment," I said. "Can I have the truck tomorrow?"

"Sure. I'll be *walkin'* to work."

❖❖❖

That night, as I lay in bed before going to sleep, I began thinking about all that had taken place since Lloyd's birth. When I finally got to the night before we left Mount Pleasant, I broke into tears. I turned my back to Lloyd and Jimmy so I wouldn't wake them, and I went through every good-bye:

Dora wanted to give us another sketch, but I told her I didn't know if we'd have a place to hang it right away. "I don't want it to get ruined. I already lost two, and I'm afraid to take another one without knowing it'll be safe." I asked her to keep it for us until we come back for our first visit. I had hoped she understood, but the thought of that not being the case made me cry even harder.

Ronnie asked me if we were ever coming back. I told her, "Of course we will. We'll come for Christmas sometimes, and we'll be here for other special occasions. And you'll get to come and visit us sometimes." That didn't seem to satisfy her, however, so I asked her if that was what she meant. "No. I mean, will you ever *move* back here? This is your home." That had hurt; I was already thinking of the U.P. as our home. I cried some more.

Anna was mad. She didn't want to talk to me. I asked her why she was angry, and she said, "You don't care about us anymore." Wow! That one came out of left field. "Anna, Anna, Anna." I had bent down and pulled her up close to me. "You have it all wrong. It's because I do care about you that I'm moving to the U.P. Someone has to take care of this family, and I'm the oldest now, so I have to do it. When Jimmy and I have made enough money, we'll have all of you come to our new place, and we'll take care of you again, just like the old days." She was crying, which made me cry even more. "Do you understand?" I asked her. She paused, then she said, "Maybe I'll be able to stand up by then." I had no further words to console her.

But far and away, Retta had been the hardest to say good-bye to.

She was more a part of me than any of my other sisters. We looked at each other, tears filling our eyes, and then we grabbed each other and hugged. We didn't exchange any words; the contact said it all.

I fell asleep crying after rehashing all the good-byes. In the morning it was raining out, and our little cabin felt cold when I woke up. Jimmy had gone to his first day at work. Lloyd was still sleeping. So I went into the main room, and there, lying on the table was an envelope with my name on it…in Retta's handwriting. Beside it was a note from Jimmy that said: *I was instructed to give this to you when we got settled in. I think we have reached that point.*

I put on a pot of coffee. When it was done perking, I poured myself a cup, added my milk and sugar, and sat down at the table. I drank half of it before I could bring myself to pick up the note.

Dear Helmi,

I am so proud of you. After Papa died, I thought we'd never have anyone strong enough to keep the family going. But you proved me wrong.

When you and Jimmy got married, I thought I had lost you. And when you went away to college, I missed you more than you'll ever know. I thought I had lost you again, but Jimmy was there to pester me and keep my mind off being so sad, and I learned that he was not only your husband, he was actually a part of you. I hadn't lost you; there was part of you right there with me all the time you were gone.

Then you came back home after your graduation and announced that you were going to have a baby, and once again I thought I was going to lose you. But you made us all feel so important, so much a part of your life, and Lloyd never took anyone's place; he only made it more apparent that you not only loved us but also needed us.

Then the day came when you announced that you were moving. And that was when I realized, for the first time, that I would never lose you. Even though you are far away, I know you're always here for us...for me.

So visit us when you can, because we need to share some more hugs. They do a lot to keep me from going insane.

I love you with all my heart. And I love that crazy man you married. And I know I could love your cute little man just as much if I had the chance to get to know him.

Your Retta

AT HOME IN THE U.P.

I had noticed a house out on the main road with a sign in the yard that said, "Hair Styling by Betty," so I decided to take a chance that she might have time to cut my hair in the next day or two. I'd been wanting a "bob" for quite some time, especially since I was about to start working and didn't want my hair to get in the way. So after Jimmy went to work, I cleaned Lloyd up, put on a nice dress, and drove to her house.

She had a separate salon entrance on the side of the house. There were windows on three sides of the room, but I didn't see anyone inside. There were no vehicles parked close to the house, so I wasn't sure if anyone was there. But I went up to the door and turned the knob—it opened. I called, "Hello?" and a voice from within the house said, "Be right there!"

It was a nice room with a sink and chair in one half for washing and cutting, and two chairs with big half-circular hair driers attached to them in the other half. I thought it had probably been a screened-in porch at one point and had been converted to the salon.

A small, well groomed woman came through a door from the main part of the house. "May I help you?" she asked.

"Hi, my name's Helmi Butcher. Are you Betty?"

"Guilty," she said.

I smiled. "I'm new in the area. I saw your place a few days ago and thought I'd stop by and see about getting a haircut."

"Do you want a wash and set?"

"No, just a cut. I'll be starting a new job in a few days, and I don't want all of this dangling in the mess." I grabbed hold of my long ponytail and whipped it around in front of me.

"Would you like me to do it now?"

"Can you?"

"I don't have another appointment until later this afternoon."

"That would be great," I said. "I have my son in the truck. Is it all right to bring him in?"

"It's better than all right. I can't wait to meet him."

"Thanks. I'll be right back." I went to the truck, picked up Lloyd, who was trying to catch the dust that was floating in the sunshine coming through the windshield, and went back up the steps. Betty opened the door for us.

"Well, look at you!" she said to Lloyd. "Aren't you the handsome little man."

"Thank you," I said. "I thought maybe I was the only one who thinks he's handsome. His name's Lloyd."

He smiled at Betty. "Kids and dogs—they all like me," she said. "Come on over here and put him in the playpen."

I hadn't noticed it sitting beneath the front window. There were all sorts of toys inside it, and there was a stuffed chair-back in one corner. "I never saw one of these," I said, leaning Lloyd in the corner and placing some of the toys within his reach. "I might have to get one."

"The chair-back?" she asked.

"Well, that too, but I meant the playpen."

"Best thing ever invented for mothers," she said. "It keeps little ones where you want 'em and gives 'em a place to play. I never had one for my kids, either, but I wouldn't be without one now. Have a seat." She went to the chair and turned it toward me. I sat down, and she swiveled it around so I was facing the mirror. I felt like a princess.

"A bob, huh?"

"I think so. I've been seeing a lot of women my age with them, and I think I'd look okay with mine cut like that."

"You'll look better than most women who get one. You have nice thick hair, and your face is shaped just right for one. That cut doesn't look real good on women with round faces. It accentuates the roundness, makes them look heavy. But you have a nice oval-shaped face, perfect for that style."

"Really? I never even thought about all of that." I said.

She leaned down close to my ear and whispered, "That's why I get paid to do this."

I laughed, and she grinned. Lloyd must have thought it was funny, too. He laughed and waved a tiny stuffed pig that he'd found in the playpen. He seemed to be having the time of his life.

"What a good baby," Betty said. "Is he like this all the time?"

"Pretty much. He doesn't seem to mind playing by himself."

"Wish my kids had been like that. Every one of mine was a holy terror. I swear it had nothing to do with their mother!"

"How many did you have?" I asked.

"Six. Three and three."

"How far apart?"

"Two years between each. Had three boys and thought I was finished. Then I had three girls. I finally figured out what caused it, though." She threw her head back and laughed. Her laugh was contagious, and I laughed right out loud with her.

We had a splendid time talking and laughing, and I gladly paid her the seventy-five cents, plus a ten-cent tip. It was worth every penny.

When Jimmy came home, I met him at the door. He stopped dead, backed up, and looked at the outside of the cabin.

I frowned. "What are you doing?"

"I had to make sure I had the right place," he said. "Where's my wife, and who let this bomb-shell in?" He came toward me, arms extended.

"I have no idea where your wife is. I just let myself in and liked it, so I decided to stay."

He held me out at arm's length. "You look…you look… gorgeous! I'm gonna have to chain you to my leg when we go out, or every man who sees you is gonna try and steal you from me."

I smiled shyly and put on a southern belle accent. "Why, Mr. Butcher, you do go on."

He just kept staring at me. "I can't get over it. You look, well, beyond words."

At that point Lloyd squealed to remind his daddy that he was there, too. Jimmy grabbed me by the hand and pulled me over to where Lloyd was playing on the rug I'd bought a couple of days ago. "Is this your mother?" he asked Lloyd, pointing at me.

Lloyd giggled and waved his arms to be picked up.

"I'm sorry, miss, but I have a son who wants some attention from his dad." He let go my hand and scooped Lloyd up with one arm, then lifted Lloyd's shirt and blew a raspberry on his bare belly. Lloyd laughed like a wild man.

"And how was your day?" I asked Jimmy.

"Nothin' special. I worked on fixin' some steps that go down to the water in front of one of Andy's cabins. How'd the rest of your day go? I'm figurin' the haircut went just fine."

"The whole day was fun; first totally fun day I've had in a while," I said. "I wanted to get my hair cut short so it doesn't drag in all of the blood and guts and muck and…"

"I get it," Jimmy said. "You don't need to be quite so graphic."

"Sorry. I'm used to being around other vets when I talk about the stuff. It doesn't bother any of us. We can talk about S-H-I-T and eat lunch at the same time. And I have other good news."

"And that would be…"

"Betty—she's the hairdresser—said her oldest daughter, who lives in Rudyard, does what she called 'day-sitting' for two other kids, along with her own two, so she gave me her address and said I should go there and check it out. She asked me what I was going to do with Lloyd when I was at work, so I told her I didn't know yet but would have to find someone pretty quick. That's when she told me about her daughter. I can't believe she's right in Rudyard. I wanted to wait until we could both go and look at the place and talk to her. Her name's Sheila Benjamin, and she keeps the other kids all five days of the week. I told Betty we'd need her for that, too, but I wasn't sure how long you're going to be working at Andy's. I mean, will he keep you on during the winter, or should you be looking..."

"Whoa!" Jimmy said. "Take a breath."

I stopped and, as Jimmy had suggested, took a deep breath. "I'm just so excited," I said. "I think we need to go see her as soon as possible. Tonight. Betty said she'd call her since we don't have a phone, and I told her to set us up for tonight, but I couldn't tell her what time for sure. She said that shouldn't matter. Sheila's home most of the time and rarely goes out after having the kids all day. Can we go?"

Jimmy had sat down with Lloyd on his lap. He said to me, "Did you say something?"

"You're just begging for a punch in the arm, aren't you?"

"Of course we can go," he said. "Sounds like a good idea. After supper?"

"Great! I've got soup in the Dutch oven; it's been simmering all afternoon."

"Sure smells good. Makin' me hungry," he said, as he jiggled Lloyd on his knee. "And I can't take my eyes off the cook."

❖❖❖

Sheila Benjamin was a carbon copy of her mother, and Jimmy and I both liked her a lot. Her house was cozy; nothing fancy, but clean and orderly. And that's a tall order to fill when you take care of not only your own kids but someone else's, too, for eight hours or more five days of the week.

She charged one dollar and ten cents per day for youngsters in diapers, but it went down to eighty-five cents per day after they're potty trained. It included a lunch and an afternoon snack, and she would add ten cents for every part of an hour after the first eight each day; she said, "It keeps people from leaving their kids for an extra fifteen minutes or so and expecting the extra time to be free." I told her that shouldn't be a problem for us. She understood the arrangements when I told her I was a vet in Rudyard.

"Will you be working with Dr. Bell?"

"He just retired. Dr. Halvorsen is the vet now. Oh, and me."

"I didn't know Dr. Bell had retired. He's been there so long, I guess I just thought he'd never leave. Are you excited about getting started?"

"More than you can imagine," I told her.

"Well I, for one, think it's about time our work force has finally begun including women in what have traditionally been men's jobs. But I think the war has had something to do with that."

"I think you're right," I said. "With all the factories that have begun hiring women, it has probably placed a bit of pressure on some of the other businesses. I just hope Dr. Bell's and Dr. Halvorsen's clients are open-minded enough to realize that my degree is as good as any man's."

"Well, if any of them give you trouble, you just tell my mom. She'll be all over them. Believe me, she can handle the worst of them. She might be small, but she's big on seeing to it that people get the respect they deserve."

When Jimmy and I left, I felt much more at ease.

"You sure you don't have any problem leavin' Lloyd with a stranger?" Jimmy asked.

"You saw her and talked to her the same as me. Is it a problem for you?"

"Not at all. I just know that sometimes mothers have trouble trustin' someone else with their kids," he said.

"I think you're forgetting where we are, Jimmy. People up here *have* to help each other. There are barely enough people to go around to fill all the niches that need to be filled, so everyone just seems to jump in and do their level best to make life easier for 'the other guy'."

Jimmy said, "You are an amazin' woman, Mrs. Butcher."

"I know."

He punched me in the arm.

The next several years rolled by uneventfully. Brimley became our true home, even more than Mount Pleasant had ever been. We loved the community, and we loved the weather and the changing seasons. After my first two months on the job, we built a new house. It wasn't big, but it had three bedrooms—Jimmy said that was "just in case." Our view of Waiskai Bay never grew old. We also bought a used car for me to drive, which made life much easier for our busy schedules.

At the end of that first summer, I came across a dairy farm that needed someone for the morning milkings only. I told Jimmy about it, and he jumped at the chance to take it. He still helped Andy now and then when a big job arose, but he'd explained that he would only be able to help him after he finished with the milking job each day, and Andy was okay with that.

The milking job was, obviously, right up Jimmy's alley. It was on a farm between Rudyard and Pickford, only about four miles west of Rudyard. Jimmy didn't seem to mind the distance, and it left him free for the rest of the day. That meant Lloyd only spent a few hours a day at Sheila's. But when Lloyd turned four, Jimmy and I decided he was old enough to accompany Jimmy to the farm each morning. Like the Schnier/Butcher offspring he was, Lloyd took to the farm like a duck to water.

I had my share of incidents with stubborn animals and stubborn farmers, but nothing that created more than a mere bump in the road now and then. I also received my share of kicks and bites and head-butts and being stepped on, but that went with the territory. The great majority of the farmers accepted me without question after they saw what I was capable of. In fact, some of them even asked for me specifically when they called the clinic.

Dr. Halvorsen had decided to begin caring for small animals in the clinic two days a week. I fulfilled that duty one day each week, and he covered the other day. Both of us also juggled emergency cases for small animals whenever they occurred. Neither of us *preferred* caring for small animals, but neither of us minded it. Some days, especially in the dead of winter when there was a blizzard or when the temperature dropped to double digits below zero, it was a blessing not to have to venture out to fix a prolapsed rectum or relieve a case of choke or float a horse's teeth or correct an LDA in a thousand-pound cow.

We had removed the word "Farm" from the clinic's name and changed the word "Vets" to "Veterinarians," making us "Chippewa County Veterinarians, Large and Small Animal Care." The reason for removing "Farm" from our name was obvious when we began advertising our choice to treat small animals as well. But the word "Vets" had to be changed because new people in the area began asking us if we were war veterans!

Except for Bella (and Yosie, of course), my sisters had all been to visit us a time or two. Uncle Herman and Mary had been there the first spring after we'd built the new house, and Retta had made the trip more often than any of the others, each time with a different girl, none of whom we knew, but all of whom were quite nice; that was to be expected, seeing as how they were Retta's friends. It was always great to see the family, but Jimmy and I had more fun with Retta than any of the others.

In the spring of 1950, however, Retta's "friend" turned out to be the man who owned the pet store where she worked in Mount Pleasant; they surprised us by announcing their engagement. They were to be married in late August. Of course, Uncle Herman had insisted that he and Mary have a reception at their house the week after the wedding.

But Retta wasn't the only one with a surprise. I was pregnant, and the baby was due in early September. I knew it would be a difficult trip when I was eight-plus months along in the pregnancy, but I wasn't about to miss it. There was another stumbling block, too. Neither Jimmy nor I could take more than a week off work, so Retta was going to have to make the choice as to whether she wanted us at the wedding or the reception.

She chose the reception. "I want us all to be as happy and have as much fun as we did at yours," she told Jimmy and me. Her fiancé, Wil Devers, offered to let us stay at his place in Mount Pleasant, and we agreed.

"You know we'll have Lloyd with us," I said.

"I certainly hope so," Wil said. "I have plenty of space, so he'll probably have a room to himself. I don't have a large family like you, so there won't be a lot of rooms taken up by my relatives."

"That's mighty kind of you," Jimmy said. "But if you find that it becomes necessary, Lloyd won't mind sleepin' in the same room as us." He looked at Lloyd. "You won't mind, will ya?" But I was sure Lloyd's mind had been wandering while the grown-ups talked, and Jimmy had to get his attention. "Hey! Lloyd! You here with us?"

Lloyd looked over at Jimmy with an expression that was ripe with both embarrassment and confusion. "Uh-huh," he said. The four of us grown-ups laughed. Poor Lloyd.

"What did I miss?" he asked. He was six and was going to start first grade the day after Labor Day; we'd be coming back home on Monday or Tuesday of the week before, which gave us just enough time to get him some school clothes and supplies in the Soo.

Retta asked Lloyd, "Have you been to see your school yet?"

"Uh-huh. I know which room I'll be in, and I know that my teacher's name is Mrs. Coffman."

"We all went to a first-grade orientation," I told Retta. "They gave us a list of what Lloyd's going to need, and they took us around to each classroom and into the gymnasium and cafeteria."

"Gee! We sure didn't get anything like that," Retta said.

"You only had one room to see," Jimmy said. "I doubt an orientation was necessary for most of the kids. But *you* might have needed to be shown around so you didn't get lost."

Retta was sitting across the room from us, so she said to me, "Give him a shot in the arm for me, will ya?"

"Nope," I said. "I'm not a hit man. You gotta do your own dirty work."

"I would if I weren't so fat from eating that great meal you cooked."

"Thank you," I said.

Wil said, "I didn't recognize the meat that was in your stew. What was that?"

"Venison," Jimmy and I both answered.

Wil just sat there, but I could see the blood draining from his face; he got whiter and whiter.

"It's not like you were eating Bambi," Retta said to him.

"Jimmy and some of his friends go deer hunting every November," I said, "and last year each of them got a nice-sized buck, so we have plenty in the freezer at the meat market right here in Brimley. They keep it for us, just like the butcher shop did in Mount Pleasant."

Wil didn't say a word. He just sat there, white-faced, staring into space.

"Are you all right?" Retta asked him.

He finally blinked and looked at Retta. "I could never shoot anything the size of a deer. I guess I could kill an animal if I had to, but I could never do it just for sport."

"I couldn't either," Jimmy said. "We count ourselves among the lucky ones who get to dine on such fine cuisine once in a while. And it makes great chili soup when it's ground up." He turned to Retta. "I'm sure Helmi'd give you her recipe if you asked her real nice."

Retta looked from Wil to Jimmy and back to Wil. "I have a feeling that's not gonna be at the top of Wil's ten favorite foods list."

Wil swallowed as if he had something lodged in his throat.

"You aren't gonna puke, are you?" Retta asked him.

QUESTIONS AND ANSWERS

Retta and Wil's wedding reception was fun, as Retta had hoped it would be, despite several of our sisters' absences. Bella had been working at a hospital in New York City, but she had been able to make it to the wedding, so at least Retta had gotten to see her.

Dora was now living in a little town in Ohio called Yellow Springs. It catered to a part of society that favored art above all else. She was living with a woman she had met on one of her treks to art exhibitions with Stephen Spicer. The woman, Trina McAlister, was not an artist but an art critic, and she had a standing column in several newspapers across the Midwest. One of her favorite art subjects was portraiture, and she had critiqued Dora's work, giving it nothing but the highest praise.

It seems that Dora's birthmark had turned her life around. Now, instead of it being the brunt of people's jokes, it had become Dora's personal signature. Everyone who was in the know around the Midwest's artistic crowd knew her as "The Marked Artist." And because of it, Dora was becoming famous. She was, however, unable to travel to Flint because she was between commissions and didn't have enough money to get there. Uncle Herman had offered to pay her way, but she told him she did not want to feel obligated to him, so she'd rather not make the trip, and Retta didn't seem to be too upset over it.

According to Mary, Ronnie had been struggling with muscle pain and weakness and was unable to attend the reception. I found out from Mary that Ronnie had been seeing a specialist who was putting her through multiple tests for a disease called amyotrophic lateral sclerosis (ALS), also known as Lou Gehrig's disease. Mary said, "Poor thing. She trips all the time when she walks, and I have a difficult time understanding her because she slurs her words." She told me that Ronnie couldn't seem to hold onto things because her grip was too weak.

That was the first I had heard about her symptoms, so I was worried. "Have they said when they'll make a definite diagnosis?" I asked Mary.

"Probably within a month or so." She was on the verge of tears when she grabbed my arm and said, "If it's at all possible, it would be so nice of you and Jimmy and Lloyd to stop by the Neidharts' place and see her on your way back home. She's really down in the dumps, and I think seeing you would cheer her up tremendously. Please don't tell her I told you anything about her condition." She hung her head. "She wants to keep it a secret as long as possible. They're already talking about a wheelchair."

I was beside myself with worry. Of course Jimmy and I would go to see her, even if we could only stay a short time. She hadn't been fond of being on the farm; her interests lay elsewhere. Now she might not be able to pursue any of those interests.

Anna was her jovial self. She was even more bent over than she had been when I saw her last, but she took it all in stride. She said she was waiting for the day that she could stand up and look everyone in the face. "I know that day's coming," she said to me. "I just have to wait for it to get here." What a positive attitude!

Just as Uncle Herman and Mary had done for Jimmy and me, they rented a tent and hired musicians to provide live music. Music had changed significantly from when Jimmy and I had gotten married. The popular trend was now "Rock and Roll," and it took some getting used to. I asked Jimmy if we were getting old, and he responded with, "Only if you can't dance. Let's give it a whirl." So we joined the kids on the dance floor and did our best to imitate what we saw. Most of the guests at the party were Retta's friends, and they really showed us up. Even Lloyd was doing a good job at making some impressive moves.

I was more than eight months pregnant, and Uncle Herman came up to us and asked me, "Are you sure you should be doing that?"

"It's easier than trying to castrate an Angus bull while in this condition!" I said.

The only dances Jimmy and I would truly have felt comfortable doing were the slow ones, but since I looked like I'd swallowed a watermelon, we couldn't get close together without a struggle. We finally gave up and sat down at the table with Anna and Mary. I gasped and grabbed my belly.

"What's up?" Jimmy said.

Mary was holding onto the edge of the table with both hands and had a worried look on her face.

Anna asked, "What? What happened?"

"Not to worry," I said, trying to sound as if it had been nothing. "The baby just kicked me really hard."

"Probably protestin' your poor attempt at dancin'," Jimmy said.

"I wasn't alone out there, you know. I didn't see you doing any better," I retaliated.

But I wasn't convinced it had been a kick I'd felt. I excused myself and went into the house to the bathroom. When I turned to close the door, Jimmy was right on my heels.

"You're a lousy liar," he said.

"Was it that obvious?"

"Totally transparent. I'll bet your water breaks b'fore you've had dessert." He came into the room with me and sat down on the edge of the bathtub, closing the door behind us.

"Well…damn." I said. "Today's supposed to be about Retta and Wil, not me." I leaned against the sink and rubbed my distended midsection. We talked for a while and decided we should make our departure, using our stop at the Niedharts' place as an excuse.

I told Mary and Uncle Herman that we should get going so we could stop and see Ronnie. "I'm sure the Neidharts will put us up overnight. Then we can get back on the road first thing in the…" Another contraction hit me at that precise moment. I winced and closed my eyes.

"Sit down and relax," Mary said to me. Then she said to Jimmy, "Come on. Let's get all your stuff packed up and into the car."

Jimmy got Lloyd's attention and motioned for him to leave the dance floor and come over to the house.

"Do we *have* to leave?" Lloyd asked, obviously disappointed.

"I need you to pack all your stuff and get it into the back of the truck. I think you're about to have a little brother or sister."

Lloyd's expression changed to a wide grin, and he didn't hesitate. He raced off into the house and came back with his suitcase in less than three minutes.

We didn't have time to get to the Neidharts' place. My contractions were happening much more rapidly than I remembered from when Lloyd was born. We went straight to the hospital in Flint. They finally had to break my water, and after being admitted, another baby boy joined our family. Papa would have been proud. And probably a little bit jealous.

We made it a point to include Lloyd in the naming process. Jimmy and I liked the name Craig, and Lloyd said he liked the name Wendell; he had a really good friend named Wendell at the dairy farm where he and Jimmy went every morning, so our new son became Craig Wendell Butcher. We liked the sound of that, and Craig looked just like his name.

Retta and Wil stopped by the hospital on their way to Niagara Falls for a honeymoon. Retta immediately asked if she could hold Craig, and the nurse looked at me questioningly. "Of course," I said.

"Every newborn should have an aunt as wonderful as this one." Retta smiled, took Craig from the nurse, and began to tell him all about what he and she would do in the future.

Wil kept his distance; his only remarks were made in reply to our questions. I truly did not understand what Retta saw in him. But that was none of my business.

Craig and I only had to stay at the hospital for two days. Everything was just as it should have been when we left to go visit Ronnie and the Neidharts. But our joy at having a new son was squelched when we got there.

Mary's description of Ronnie's condition was nowhere near the actual sight we beheld. Ronnie was sitting in an overstuffed chair, slumped to one side, her hands lying limply in her lap. Her head was tilting to her left, and drool was running out of the corner of her mouth. I decided it would be best not to react negatively, so I walked right up to her and said, "You have a new nephew. Meet Craig Wendell Butcher," and I held him up in front of her. She looked at him and tried to smile—I could see her lips working—but the corners of her mouth wouldn't turn up. Tears ran down my cheeks, unchecked.

Jimmy took Craig from me, and I got down on my knees in front of Ronnie. "Oh, Ronnie," I said. "I wish I'd have known what you've been going through. I had no intentions of abandoning you, but I didn't know."

"So-kay," Ronnie said slowly, with apparent difficulty when forming her words. "I knew you…you'd…come when…when you cou…" Her breathing was labored and shallow. She was a stick figure sitting there in front of me. I couldn't stop the tears.

Rachel said, "She wouldn't let me write you about it."

"I'm glad you honored her wish," I said, lying through my teeth.

Jimmy had turned away and was moving around the room making a big deal of trying to get Craig to go to sleep. I knew it was just a ploy to keep from having to look at Ronnie. But I looked at her and said, "I need to know about everything that's been going on, but I don't want you to have to talk. Would it be okay if Rachel sat down here with us so she and I can talk about it? That way you can hear what we say and add anything you need to."

Ronnie tried to nod. It was dreadful seeing her like this, heartbreakingly pitiful, painful to watch. We discussed the next steps, just as the doctors had suggested: Ronnie was going to die of respiratory failure, and there was nothing anyone could do about it. "How can I possibly leave you in this condition?" I asked Ronnie.

Somehow Rachel made sense of it all. "Helmi, you have your own responsibilities with your husband, your home, your job, and your two sons, one of whom is only two days old. Lives come to an end—all of them. Sometimes much sooner and in much worse conditions than any of us want to witness. It's just the way life and death are, and we have to accept that. But life also goes on with new beginnings and new joys." She looked at Lloyd and at Jimmy, who was lovingly carrying that new life in his arms.

Then she looked back at me, and I saw, in her eyes, the same expression I had seen in Granny Nan's eyes when she had held Mama's lifeless hand on that awful day that Alexander and Aloysius had been born. "Ronnie understands that she cannot be a part of our lives as long as she would like." She turned toward Ronnie with the most sincerely sympathetic look I'd ever seen on anyone's face and said to Ronnie, "Don't you?"

It was then that I realized Rachel had not mentioned God. Though I knew her strength came from her belief in Him, she did not try to console me with what she knew I didn't believe, and I had the utmost respect for her at that moment.

I looked over at Ronnie; her eyes were closed, and her breathing had become more regular, though still shallow. And I knew, the next time I saw her, she would be lying in a casket. I was saddened beyond words.

Only last week, when Jimmy and I had gone to bed, we'd discussed the idea of an afterlife. I had explained my take on the whole matter to Jimmy. "I don't believe in a deity or an archfiend. I don't believe there's a Heaven or a Hell. But I do believe in an afterlife.

"In college I learned that energy can neither be created nor destroyed. My body's full of energy: it makes my heart pump, my brain think, my muscles move, and it governs all the systems that cause me to be me. But when my body can't put that energy to use any longer, my flesh and blood and bones and organs will die, but my energy will spread throughout the entire universe, filling the voids that are created by everything that dies—plants, animals, even planets and stars. Think of all the places that require energy for the sole purpose of maintaining the delicate balance that is life." I looked at Jimmy. "Are you with me so far?" I asked.

"Go on," he said.

"I want to be cremated, to be reduced to my most basic chemical compounds. And I want my ashes spread at the base of a big red pine and covered with pine needles. Over time, the roots of that red pine will absorb my ashes—my chemicals—and it'll grow tall and strong, in part because I'm there.

"And maybe one day a pair of hawks or ospreys or even eagles will build a nest in that red pine's branches. They'll rear their chicks, and those chicks will raise their own, and so on into perpetuity. With a little bit of luck, future human generations might momentarily gaze at those birds in awe, just as I did when I was living, and in each of those brief moments, I'll continue to live. That will be my afterlife."

"How long you been thinkin' 'bout that, Helmi?" he asked, his voice and the expression on his face as serious as I'd ever heard or seen.

"Ever since Papa died."

"I guess I'd better do some thinkin' of my own."

SURPRISE CALLS

Lloyd loved his first day of school. The school was at the top of the hill that went into Brimley, so he was able to walk there and back. We had practiced the walk several times during the summer; either Jimmy or I would walk with him and make sure he knew which door he was supposed to use. He'd play for a while on the playground equipment, then we'd walk back down the hill, making sure to look for cars when we crossed the road.

When he came home that first day, he was such a chatterbox; he had to tell Jimmy and me every single thing that had gone on. I was so glad to see that he was caught up in it. I had loved school, too, so I was hoping his opinion of our educational process was as positive as mine had always been.

"They have big boxes of crayons—every color you can think of!" He was so excited. "Look." He produced a picture he'd colored that had been torn from a coloring book. He had folded it multiple times and stuffed it into his back pocket.

"Wow! I guess they do have lots of colors," I said, taking the picture from him and trying to smooth out the wrinkles. "Did you do arithmetic and writing and reading, too?"

"Uh-huh. I like arithmetic. It's not so hard, Dad. You said it was your hardest thing, but I think it's easy. Here." He produced another paper from his other back pocket that had the numbers from one to ten written on it, and there were lines underneath where Lloyd had copied them. Quite frankly, he had done a pretty good job in my estimation. It wasn't exactly arithmetic, but I figured learning to write the numbers was a good start. "Looks like you can write your numbers just like the examples," I said.

"Mrs. Coffman told me I did a good job, too."

"Do you like Mrs. Coffman?" Jimmy asked.

"Oh, yeah! She's real nice, and she smells real good."

"Now, that's important," Jimmy said. "There's nothin' worse than havin' a stinky teacher comin' 'round your desk all the time." He pinched his nose and said, "P-U."

Lloyd mimicked him, and we all laughed.

I had taken the afternoon off so I could be home with Jimmy when Lloyd got there after school. Aune (Dr. Halvorsen) was really good about making sure I had time to spend with my family. And I always made it a point to fill in for him when he wanted some time off. It was difficult, especially for Shirley, when only one of us was on the job, mainly because of the emergencies that came up. But since most of our clients were farmers, they understood if we had to juggle appointments in order to accommodate everyone.

Lloyd hurried to see his new baby brother. Craig was asleep. "Can I hold him?" Lloyd asked me in a whisper.

"As soon as he wakes up," I whispered back.

"How long will he be tiny like that?" Lloyd asked.

"Not long enough," I said and sighed.

"What?"

"Babies grow really fast, and moms always wish they could stay little for a long time."

Lloyd wrinkled his forehead. "Why?"

"We know they're going to leave us one day when they're grown."

"I'll never leave," Lloyd said. "I like it here."

I smiled at him and pulled him close to me. We stood there together and watched Craig sleep.

❖❖❖

Shortly after supper the phone rang. I answered it. "Hello?"

The operator said, "I have a long-distance call from Josephina Schnier. She has requested a reverse of the charges. Will you accept?"

My heart stopped. *Is it really her, or is this someone who's playing an awful prank on me?*

The operator asked, "Are you still on the line?"

"Yes, yes. I'll accept."

"Go ahead," the operator said to the other party.

"…Helmi?"

"Yes."

"Um…this is…this is…it's…"

"Is it really you?"

"Yeah."

"Oh my God!" My heart was now pumping so fast I could hardly speak. I had to hold myself up by putting my hand on the back of the chair we kept by the phone. "Where are you?"

"Um…Chicago."

"How long have you been there?"

"Since I left home. I need help, Helmi."

"What kind of help? Are you hurt? Are you in trouble?"

"I...I need money."

"How have you been living so long without...I mean, what are you doing? What have you been doing for money? Do you have a job? Where are you living?" I was so overwhelmed with emotions I couldn't pull my thoughts together to make sense of the call.

"I have a job...had a job...a good one. But the place closed, and I need some money to buy...stuff."

"What was the name of the place where you worked?"

"It was a nightclub. I was a...a performer. I made good money, but now I don't have any, and I can't find another job."

"Do you live alone? Have you been alone all this time?"

"No. I've been living with...um...friends."

"Yosie, I..."

I looked at Jimmy. He rose and came to me, then he put his ear to the receiver so he could hear what she was saying, too.

"My name's Jo-Jo now. No one calls me Yosie. That's a stupid name."

I couldn't be sure, but she sounded drunk to me. Jimmy's mouth was hanging open.

"Okay, Yosie..."

"Jo-Jo. My pro...prof...professional name."

"Jo-Jo," I said. "Please tell me where you are."

"I told you...Chicago." She sounded agitated.

"But *where* in Chicago. It's a big city, I need..."

"Oh, sure. You don't *need* anything. You never *needed* anything."

"Yos...I mean, Jo-Jo, you haven't been in contact for so many years. How did you find me?"

"I called you in Mount Pleasant, but they didn't have your number. Then I sent a letter, but it came back saying there was no...um...um..."

"...forwarding address," I said.

She coughed, a raspy, wet cough. "I...I got Uncle Herman's number, and he said you moved to...to um...someplace else. He gave me your number." I heard her fumbling around for something. "Here it is."

"Did you tell him why you wanted to get hold of me?"

"Huh-uh."

"Yosie, I need..."

"DON'T CALL ME THAT! I HATE IT!"

"I'm sorry. It's just that it's going to take me a little bit of time to get used to calling you Jo-Jo. You were Yosie to me for so many years."

"Can we just cut the chatter, here, and get to the point?" She coughed again. "I nee moey." She was really slurring her words.

I couldn't come to grips with the fact that it really was her on the line. *Why hasn't she called all these years? What does she mean by "a performer?" What has her life really been like?*

"How much?" I asked.

"Well…I nee…um…foo n clothes n... S'almost winner. I don't have…I nee ta buy…"

Then silence.

"Yos…Jo-Jo? Are you there?" She didn't answer. "Talk to me!"

I heard a lot of noise, like she had dropped the phone and was trying to get it back up to her ear. Finally she said, "I used to live with…with um…Charlie. He got tired of me." She began to cry. "He pushed me out the door. Wouldn't let me back in." She was crying harder. "I slept in the hallway, but he came out. He kicked me and said, 'Get away from me, whore.' And then he… he…" She broke down, sobbing.

"All right. Let's think about what to do. What is his last name? Charlie who?"

"I don't…I can't…I…I'm not…I think maybe…yeah… Be… Becham?"

"Wait a minute. You said you were living with him. How could not remember his name?"

"Things are different here, Helmi." Her voice was rising. "I don't live on a GODDAMNED FARM."

I didn't know how to respond. I tried to calm down, but that just wasn't in the program. I asked her, "Do you have enough money to come to Michigan?"

"Enough? Enough? I don't have ANY. Don't you get it, Helmi? I have NOTHING!" She cried some more, then she whimpered, "I don't know what to do?"

I could barely make out what she'd said, but I knew she needed my help. "Are you at a pay phone?"

"Yes. Helmi, I…" Her response was barely audible and unrecognizable.

"Say it again. I couldn't make out what you said."

"…need help…money…please…please…"

I had to think, but my thoughts would not cooperate. They simply rolled around inside my head; I was unable to organize them. They were like grains of sand being tossed over and over in the waves, creating no obvious patterns. There was no rhyme nor reason to what she had said.

I tried my best to decipher what I was hearing. *I can't imagine the conditions under which she's been living, and for how long. Has it been this way since she first arrived in Chicago, or is this the result of some horrendous mistake she's made? Her judgment never was the best, but she's been gone for all these years, and this is the first contact she's made, so she must have been doing something right. Until now. I have to give her the benefit of the doubt; she was never witless, only unwilling to fit into the life she was exposed to as a child. Although, she wasn't very capable of fitting into society. Oh, Mama, why did you spoil her so? No, it's not fair to put all the blame on Mama. I have to figure out how to help her. But I don't know how. I don't even know for sure if money is the answer.*

I heard a distinct click. "Jo-Jo? Yosie? Are you there?... Yosie? Yosie…?"

Nothing.

Jimmy pulled the phone away from my ear and put it down. He was staring off into the distance. I had no idea what was running through his mind. "What do I do?" I asked him.

He continued to stare straight ahead.

"Jimmy? Jimmy!"

He finally blinked, then he turned away from me and walked toward the kitchen. I watched him go to the cupboard where we kept a bottle of whiskey on the very top shelf. He brought it down. Then he placed two glasses on the counter and poured a little bit of the whiskey into each. He put the top back on the bottle and returned it to its place in the cupboard and closed the cupboard door. He stood there, leaning on the counter for nearly a full minute, staring down at the countertop.

Without turning around to face me, he said, "I suppose you think we should help her."

I wanted to react to that, but I was at a total loss. "What can we do? We can't reach her."

Jimmy suggested, "The operator might be able to give you the number where she was callin' from, and the police might be able to track her down."

"All they can do is tell us where the pay phone's located. How is that going to help us find her?" I started to cry. "We don't know whether she'll stay in that area or if she'll walk away. To another part of the city. She's my sister, Jimmy. I love her."

He picked up the two glasses, sat down at the table, and motioned for me to join him. "Drink this. You need to calm your nerves and clear your head."

I sat down and drank the whiskey in one gulp. It burned all the way down, but I was too wrought up to respond to the fire that scorched a path from my mouth to my stomach.

We were both silent…for a long time.

Lloyd came into the kitchen. "Whatcha doin'?"

I was so deep in thought, it took me a few beats before I realized he'd asked us a question. "Uh…just trying to figure out some things," I said, trying my best to sound normal. But he saw the streaks on my face where the tears had left their marks.

"Are you okay, Mom?"

I looked at him and knew I couldn't lie. "Not right at the moment," I said. "But Dad and I are trying to figure something out. So why don't you…"

"Is it something bad? Why are you crying? Mom, what's wrong?"

I could see the fear on his face, and I heard the concern in his voice. I thought, *It's only childhood fear and concern, incapable of grasping the scope of what his mom and dad were discussing, but it's as real to him as it was to us and just as difficult for him to harness.*

Jimmy said, "Come over here, partner." That's what he always called Lloyd when he was going to talk about something unfamiliar. "Have you ever heard us talking about Yosie?"

Lloyd nodded. "One of Mom's sisters. But we don't know where she is," he said. There was a steadiness and a concerned regard in his voice that was beyond his years.

"That's right. We just got a phone call from her, and it's pretty hard for your mom to understand why it's taken her so long to contact us," Jimmy explained.

"Did she say where she is?" Lloyd asked.

"Chicago," I said. "Do you know where that is?"

Lloyd shook his head.

"It's in the state of Illinois, way down at the bottom of Lake Michigan. You know which one of the Great Lakes that is," I said. "We've looked at all of the Great Lakes on the map."

"Yeah, I know which one," he said. He held his left hand up in front of him, palm facing away. Then he pointed to the little-finger side of his hand. "It's this one."

"That's exactly right," Jimmy said. He put up his own hand in the same position and pointed to the place where his wrist and arm met. "Chicago's clear down here."

"Oh," Lloyd said. "Is she coming to visit us?"

"I don't think so," I said. "At least not very soon."

He accepted what we'd said and asked, "Can I stay after school tomorrow and play with Malcolm on the playground?"

Jimmy and I looked at each other. Jimmy said, "I think that'd be okay. How about I walk up to the school when it's time for you to come home? Then we can walk home together."

"Okay," Lloyd said, matter-of-factly, then he got up and went to his room.

Jimmy and I looked at each other and managed to smile through our confusion. "I need some of that boy's stability right now," I said. "Seems I've left mine someplace and can't remember where."

My head was still swimming at bedtime, and my sleep was fitful that night. When morning came, I was glad to see the sun shining; somehow, it made coping with everything a lot easier. Jimmy and I didn't talk about Yosie; we simply ate breakfast. Jimmy left. I cleaned up the breakfast dishes. Lloyd set out for school. I left with Craig and dropped him off at Sheila's.

I had trouble keeping my mind centered on the tasks at hand that day. Luckily, I was on call for farm emergencies, and Aune was taking care of the small animals' needs. We hadn't gotten any calls, so I was catching up on some of my paperwork and helping Shirley with the filing. I figured she was the perfect person to spend time with because I knew she'd have plenty to talk about, and that would keep me from brooding over Yosie's plea for help.

Shirley took a call from one of our clients in Pickford. A mare kicked out a piece of the barn siding from inside her stall and ripped open a big section above her hock. She was limping a little and bleeding badly. I gathered up a few things I thought I might need that weren't already in the clinic truck and took off toward Pickford, passing by the farm where Jimmy worked. I wondered how he was faring after last night's call.

Because it was necessary for me to be in veterinarian mode, my thoughts were more aligned than they had been since the previous evening. I was able to do some clear and meaningful thinking. I decided to call Uncle Herman; maybe I'd find out something from him about Yosie that I hadn't been able to discern from my own conversation with her.

I reached the farm and found the mare still in the barn. Her leg was bleeding profusely. The only one who was there at the time was a boy, maybe ten or eleven years old, probably the farmer's son. "How long's she been bleeding like this?" I asked him.

"Coupla hours," he said. "She kicked out one of the boards on the barn. Musta got her foot stuck or somethin' and cut it bad."

I walked up to the horse and said, "Whoa, girl." I reached out and touched her on the right side of her face, the same side as the leg wound. She saw my hand coming and knickered, but she didn't move.

With my hand, I followed her body back to her leg and ran it down to the wound. She turned her head enough to be able to see me. I could tell she was hurting. Her skin vibrated when I touched the wound. It was pretty bad.

"She's lost a lot of blood," I said to the kid and stood up. "I'm Dr. Butcher." I extended my hand. He reached out and shook it. I bent over and lifted up the skin flap that was sticking out away from the leg. "Looks like it's a pretty clean cut," I said. "It definitely cut through a major blood vessel, though. But I think we can fix her up."

The kid smiled.

"Is she yours?"

He nodded. "Is she gonna be able to run again?"

"I think you can pretty much count on it. May take a few weeks, but when it heals, you'll hardly know it was there," I said.

I went back to the truck and gathered up three syringes and needles. Then I took a vial of mild sedative, one of a local anesthesia, and one of antibiotics from the medicine box. I also picked up a couple of large curved needles and suture, scissors, sponges, and a box of rolled cotton and two rolls of bandages and tape. I put all of them in a bucket along with a tin of antiseptic ointment and went back to the barn. I removed everything from the bucket and asked the kid to fill the bucket with water.

He ran off at a trot, so I used the moment to inspect the wound a little closer. It had not injured the muscle or bone, and it was fresh enough that no granulation tissue had built up, so I wouldn't need to trim the wound before sewing it. All I was going to have to do was stop the bleeding and clean the wound before stitching it closed. Then I'd bandage it, and the next step was for the kid to keep an eye on it for a few days. If I didn't hear anything bad from him, I'd come back out and re-dress the wound, making sure it was healing okay.

All went well, and just as I was finishing up, a man, whom I assumed was the kid's dad, came in from one of the fields on his tractor. He pulled up next to the barn and shut the tractor off. I saw him looking toward the clinic truck, then he came in.

I introduced myself and offered my hand, but he didn't shake it. Instead, he turned to his son and said, "How long's she been here?"

"I don't know," the kid shrugged his shoulders. "Not very."

"When did this happen?" He pointed at the horse's leg.

"Just after you went back out," the boy said. "She kicked the back of the stall. Kicked off one of the boards, and she musta…"

The man turned to me and asked, "Did he call you?"

"I don't know who called. My office manager took the call, and I came right out."

"Where's the real doctor?" he asked me.

That hit a nerve. "I beg your pardon, sir, but I am a real doctor." I was not in the mood for this.

"I don't need you traipsin' out here thinkin' you're gonna get paid for doin' somethin' I coulda taken care of myself." He turned to the kid and backhanded him right across the face! The kid stumbled backwards and fell.

My mouth dropped open as I gasped, and I immediately went to the kid and helped him up. "You okay?" I asked the boy.

He didn't acknowledge my question. He only stared at the ground.

"Did you make that call?" the man asked the kid.

The kid nodded.

"Why, I oughta…" and he raised his hand again.

The kid cowered and covered his face. I moved between the boy and the man. Then I gathered up my equipment and loaded it all into the bucket. I walked up to the boy and showed him a bottle of oral antibiotics. "Do you have any of these?" I asked. "Your horse is going to need to take them for the next two weeks, twice a day."

He glanced at the bottle, then he looked up at the man.

I couldn't hold my tongue. "This boy did exactly the right thing by calling. That horse could have bled out, and if the wound hadn't been treated, she might have had to be put down either because of sepsis or because she couldn't walk. A horse with only three good legs is a dead horse." I was furious.

"Don't you be preachin' at me," the man said. "I don't take no lip from any woman."

No one had ever talked to me like that, and I was brutally insulted by that moron's actions. I looked at the boy, who was now obviously scared to death that he was going to be the recipient of the man's anger, whatever form it took. I was torn between saying something to the boy or leaving it all behind me as I walked away. If I said or did anything, I knew either the boy or I would be the recipient of the man's actions, both physically and vocally. But I was the professional in the crowd, and I was representing the Chippewa County Veterinarians, so the only smart choice was to walk away, even though I seriously wanted to deck the guy—to give *him* a backhand across the face just like he'd given that boy.

I restrained myself, biting my tongue to keep from saying something I'd regret, and walked away, hoping I was wrong about the boy receiving unwarranted punishment for doing the right thing. I tuned them out completely. I didn't even want to hear the man's voice…ever again. I made a mental note to explain the situation to Aune and let him decide what the next step should be.

The drive back to the clinic gave me time to do some serious thinking. When I returned to the clinic, Aune was sitting behind the desk. He looked up at me and said, "Holy whah! You look like the Devil himself has been ribbing you. Tell me I'm wrong."

"You hit the nail on the head." I slammed the keys down and threw myself into a chair. "Grrrragggghhhh!"

"You want to talk about it?"

"Yes, I do! I have never, ever, in all my life been so insulted and so angry. I can't believe the vindictive thoughts that have been running through my mind for the last twenty minutes. Ohhhh, the things I'd like to do to that man." My fists and my teeth were clenched.

Aune leaned back in his chair. "I take it Mr. Martin was unhappy with you showing up at his farm."

"Unhappy? He made me feel about this big." I held my hand up with index finger and thumb about a quarter of an inch apart.

Then Aune smiled. "I'm glad you took the call. I'm assuming it wasn't him who called, but his son?"

"If his son is ten or eleven, then yes, it was his son who called." I came to the front of the chair I was sitting in and asked Aune, "Do you have any idea what he did to that boy? All because the kid took action to save his horse?"

"I've seen him in action. I feel sorry for the boy, but there's nothing we can do to stop it. It's his affair, not ours." He stood up and turned to walk away.

"Wait a minute. I'm not finished. I want you to know that I *will* be going back out there in a week to check that horse's leg. Me." I tapped my chest with my index finger." I'm going, not you. I want to show that S.O.B. what I'm made of."

"Now wait a minute," Aune said and turned back toward me. "I think you're on the right track, but I'm not going to let you go alone. We'll both go..." I started to say something, but Aune put his hand up, squelching me. "We'll both go, but I'll stay in the truck and make it clear that you're the one who's going to handle the situation. Martin will know I'm there, but I won't take an active part."

"We can't both go. That'll leave the clinic without a doctor," I said.

"We'll just close the clinic for a couple of hours and go together. Shirley can handle whatever comes up," Aune said. "There's a principle riding on the line here, and you're right; you need to prove to him that you're more than capable of handling it, both medically and professionally. I'm only going to be there for backup. It's your case, and you need to show him that he can't scare you away that easy." He looked me square in the face. "If, however, he raises a finger toward you, I'll flatten the S.O.B. before he has a chance to do any damage. I don't handle one-ton animals because I'm weak."

I earned a whole new respect for Aune. Up to that point, I'd only thought of him as my boss. Now he was my partner. "You promise to stay out of it unless he makes a move?"

"You got my word on it."

I planned to call Uncle Herman as soon as I got home that evening, but when I pulled up to the house, Jimmy came out the door with a severely serious look on his face.

"What's the problem?" I asked him.

"How'd you know there's…nevermind. Yes, there's a problem. It's Yosie."

I started to get out of the car in a rush.

"Take it easy," Jimmy said, helping me stand up. "Herman called. He…"

"Is Yosie all right?" I asked, panicking.

"Just hear me out," Jimmy said, taking me by the arm and keeping me from rushing into the house. "Herman said that, when she called him, she sounded like she was high on somethin'—booze, drugs—he couldn't tell. He said he was gonna call ya right away to warn ya, but he didn't 'cause he was afraid Yosie would be tryin' to call ya at the same time, and he didn't want ya to miss her call."

"That sounds like him. He's always so tuned-in to everyone's feelings."

"He wants us to call the Chicago Police Department. He said they can find out from the phone company which pay phone Yosie made the call from; we just have to tell them our number and the approximate time of the call. He says he knows they can trace it. He says the cops can then maybe check around that neighborhood and find out if anyone saw her or knows her. It might be worth a try, Helmi."

I sighed. I know I was frowning, and I know I must have looked like I'd been beaten with a stick. *Why is it that the worst things happen all at once?*

Jimmy put his arms around me. "You look so tired. I'm sorry I threw this whole thing at ya b'fore ya even had a chance to come inside. Let's go sit down and think about all of this for a few minutes b'fore we make any decisions."

Thinking. Making decisions. I didn't know if I was capable of doing either, let alone both. I let Jimmy lead, and I simply went along. He took me into the front room and sat down beside me on the davenport. Lloyd came through the room on his way to the kitchen and said, "Hi, Mom" as he went by. *Oh, to be young again like Lloyd. I wouldn't have to deal with any of this on an adult level.*

Jimmy said, "After you sit here for a few minutes, you need to go change your clothes and get some supper. I made us a casserole."

"I smelled something good when we came in. I thought it was still lingering from last night."

"Nope. It's made with macaroni, tomatoes, beef, and lots of spices. It's called 'goulash.' Dad used to make it for us after Mom died. He said it was her mother's recipe. It's so easy, even I could do it." He was smiling.

I wanted to smile, too, but I was having a hard time accomplishing even that simple task. I just looked at him. I hoped he could see the love and the appreciation in my eyes.

"Now go change. I'll put supper on the table and remind Lloyd to wash up before he sits down." He stood and took me by both hands, pulling me up. He hugged me to him and kissed me on the top of my head.

"I need to check on Craig," I said.

"He'll be happy to see ya."

"And call Uncle Herman."

"And you will," Jimmy said, "right after supper."

A SPECIAL GIFT FROM SANTA

I called Uncle Herman and thanked him for helping us make a decision regarding the procedure to find Yosie. I explained that I had very little hope about the Chicago police being able to turn anything up, but I was going to keep my fingers crossed. He said he would, too.

One week after the ordeal with Mr. Martin's son's horse, Aune and I returned to their farm. Aune stayed in the truck, as he had promised, and I went to the barn to see if anyone was there. Sure enough, the boy was mucking out one of the horse stalls.

"Hi there!" I called.

The boy looked up. It must have taken a few seconds for him to recognize me, but when he did, he was all smiles. "Oh, hi!" he said, leaning the pitchfork up against the wheelbarrow and coming toward me with hand extended.

I shook it and asked after the horse.

"She's doin' great! There ain't been any more bleedin', at least none I been able to see. I was gonna call you at your office today to see if I needed to change the dressing."

"That's what I'm here to do," I told him. "Is you father around?"

"Nope," he said, still smiling.

"I never even asked you your name," I said.

"Ben. Ben Martin. Pa ain't gonna be around for a while," he said.

"Oh. Is he out of town?" I asked.

"You could say that," Ben said.

I looked at him with an expression that must have conveyed my eagerness for him to go on.

"He's in jail in the Soo."

I thought for a second that I'd misunderstood what Ben had said. "He's where?" I asked.

"In jail. He and Ma got into a real knock-down-drag-out, and he punched Ma in the face a few times. I decided it was my place to step up and put an end to it, so I called the cops. They showed up just in time to hear Ma and Pa yellin' at each other, but neither of 'em would open the door. So I did, and right at that very minute, Pa swatted Ma, and she fell backwards over a chair. That was all the cops needed to see. They hauled Pa's ass...oh, pardon me." He put his hand over his mouth, and his face went red, but he went on. "Ma's got a broken collar bone. She's still in the hospital, but she's s'posed to be comin' home tomorrow."

"How old are you, Ben?"

"Turned twelve three days ago." He was still all smiles.

"Well, you are certainly doing a good job of taking care of things around here." I made it a point to look around the barn and nod. "Where's the mare?" I asked, hoping to be able to digest all he'd said and still appear as a responsible veterinarian when, in fact, I had been completely awestruck by the entire story.

"She's just outside. It was too purdy a day for her to have to stay here in the barn." He turned to go get her, then he stopped and turned back to me. "You want me to bring her in?"

"Not necessary," I said. "I'll take a look at her outside. There's more light out there."

We walked together to the double doors that opened into the barn lot. Ben lifted the latch, and pushed one of the doors open. We walked out. The mare was standing at the other side of the area, so Ben whistled, and she came walking toward us; it didn't seem to bother her in the least that I was standing there. "She's a really well socialized animal," I said.

Ben looked up at me.

"I mean she isn't afraid of other people. How's she act around other horses?"

"Like they ain't even there," he said proudly. "I wanna be able to enter her in some races. Just local ones at first, then maybe some farther away."

"Well I'll be," I said. "Sounds to me like you've been thinking about this for a while."

"Ever since I can remember," he said. "I wanna be a stable boy in Kentucky where all the well bred racehorses are, but I have to start out slow and work my way up. That's what Ma says."

I watched the mare walk toward us. She had no limp. She stopped in front of Ben and lowered her head to him. He reached in his pocket and produced a carrot. I understood why she had come to him immediately when he whistled.

"She seems to be walking fine," I said, then I patted her on the neck and went back to the bandaged wound. "You been giving her the antibiotics?"

"I did, but I ran out yesterday. I didn't have enough for two weeks."

"I'll give you another bottle. It's really important to keep her on them until we're certain there's no more chance of infection." I went back to the truck, grinning at Aune.

"Martin must not be here. You look like you just scored," Aune said.

"I did better than that. I'll tell you about it after I redress that wound." I gathered up what I needed and picked up another bottle of the antibiotics and took everything back to the barn lot. Ben and I discussed all sorts of things while I tended to the horse's leg, which was nearly healed. Then I reiterated to Ben about how important it was to continue the antibiotics, even though the wound looked fine, and I returned to the truck, replacing the equipment I'd used, and sliding into the seat beside Aune. "Thanks for coming along. It's a shame I didn't really need you."

"So fill me in," he said.

I told him the story, and he laughed right out loud when I got to the part about Mr. Martin being in jail.

"Mo-om!" Lloyd shouted at the top of his lungs.

I was only in the next room. "Stop shouting like that!" I scolded. "I could've heard you from the other side of the county."

He handed me the phone. "Hello," I said.

"Mrs. Wilhelmina Butcher?" an unfamiliar voice asked.

"Yes."

"This is Sergeant Avery Dickerson with the Chicago Police."

My heart leaped inside my chest.

"I understand you called regarding one Josephina, aka Yosie, aka Jo-Jo Schnier. Is that correct?"

I paused long enough to let all of that sink in. "I did, yes."

"Your relationship to her?" he asked.

"I am her sister."

"Do you happen to know her date of birth?"

"I do. It's April 18, 1922." It took every ounce of restraint I had in me to keep from asking if they'd found her.

"Just making sure we've reached the correct party," he said. "Unfortunately…"

Oh no! Unfortunately. Unfortunately. That could mean so many things.

"…we have not been able to locate her to date."

I stood there like a bump on a log. *What am I supposed to say? How am I supposed to react?*

He continued, "But that doesn't mean we have given up the search."

I hadn't realized I'd been holding my breath until that moment. I exhaled, but I didn't know whether it was because there was still a glimmer of hope or simply because my lungs couldn't stand another second without exchanging air.

He said, "There are still some possible leads to her whereabouts. I only wish we had a photograph to show people in the area. To find out if they recognize her. But I know that's not possible."

"No, it isn't. Wait. Would a drawing help? My sister is a portrait artist, and she might be able to send you one."

"A rendering would be a great help."

"Thank you, Sergeant. I'm…well, I'm…"

"No need to thank me, Mrs. Butcher. Just doing my job. I'd like to be able to call you soon with more news…good news."

"I hope that's the case," I said. I got the necessary information from him so I could pass it along to Dora. I didn't know what else to say.

"Don't let your hopes get too high, but don't give up all hope just yet. This could go either way. I'll talk to you again soon."

I started to say good-bye, but he had already hung up.

I immediately called Dora, told her the whole story, and asked her to send a "rendering" to the sergeant. She sounded excited and said she'd do a sketch as soon as we hung up. "I'll put it in the mail tomorrow," she said without asking any questions. I think she knew how important it was to me and didn't want to prolong the process.

I fell into the chair that sat beside the phone. I blinked, several times, not sure if I had interpreted Sgt. Dickerson's call correctly. I was to keep hoping but not allow myself to hope too much. *Where does that leave me? That wasn't a call that provided me with any news one way or another. I guess no news is good news, though; that's what everyone always says.*

Lloyd came up to me and said, "I think Craig needs to be changed. He smells like poop." That brought me back to reality.

"Okay. Thank you for letting me know. Where's your Dad?"

"Down by the water. He said he was gonna clean up the beach after the storm last night."

We only had about ten feet of what we referred to as "beach." It was actually ten feet of clay from the bank to the edge of the water and was covered in a few inches of sparse sand and pebbles. But it provided plenty of room for Lloyd to play on warm summer days. This being late fall, it was far from warm, and we had just undergone a November gale. When that happens, anything that has been drifting on the water ends up on the shoreline and requires removal, that is, if one wants to maintain a nice "beach." Obviously, Jimmy had taken it to heart.

"You want me to get him?" Lloyd asked.

"No. If he's busy cleaning up the waterfront, let's leave him alone."

Lloyd went to his room. I changed Craig.

I had Sunday off, so I put a pot roast in the oven to bake with potatoes and carrots. I had half a head of cabbage that was going to go bad if I didn't use it, so I shredded it and made refrigerator slaw, the kind Granny Nan made with shredded carrots and minced green peppers and onions. The dressing consisted of vinegar, sugar, salt, pepper, and salad oil. We all liked it, especially Lloyd. I had become a pretty good cook, and I liked cooking.

Baking, on the other hand, was not my forte. I had attempted to bake bread and rolls, but the result always reflected some sort of malady: flat, sticky, full of air holes, tough, overly brown. Cookies weren't easy with a baby to tend to; I'd usually end up burning at least one batch because I had to turn my attention to Craig. Cakes often shared some of the same conditions as my bread, or in the process of icing the things, there tended to be more cake crumbs in the icing than in the cake. Pies were usually okay; I used Granny Nan's recipe for making crust, and her little secret of using extra cold water when mixing the dough usually did the trick. But overall, I didn't care much for baking, to my family's regret.

On that particular Sunday, following the removal of the roast from the oven, I again attempted to bake some cookies for dessert.

The phone rang. "Hello," I answered.

"Helmi?"

"Yes."

"This is Rachel."

Oh no. Ronnie must be really bad. Rachel wouldn't call for just any reason. "Hi, Rachel. It's good to hear your voice."

"I have some bad news."

I braced myself, ready to hear the awful message I knew I was about to receive. "It's Ronnie, isn't it?"

"No, Helmi. It's Bill. He's in the hospital." I could hear a waver in her voice.

"Oh no! What happened?" I asked.

"He fell and broke his hip. They have him in traction. It's awful. He looks so helpless lying there with that horrible contraption they have him in." She had been crying; I could hear it in her voice.

"Is he hurting really bad?" I asked.

"I don't know. He's so full of medicine he hardly knows whether it's day or night."

"I'm so sorry, Rachel."

"My problem is that I need to be there for him, but I can't leave Ronnie alone. Anna just isn't up to…"

"Of course Anna can't take care of Ronnie," I said. "And your place is with your husband."

"I'm so glad you understand. What I'm wondering is, do you know of anyone in our area who is familiar with your family and could possibly come and sit with Ronnie while I'm at the hospital? We have racked our brains and can't think of anyone who Ronnie would be familiar with."

I immediately thought of Mary. "I might, Rachel. I'll call her and get right back to you."

I hung up and immediately called Mary. Uncle Herman answered. "This is Herman," he said.

"Hi, Uncle Herman. It's Helmi."

He broke into the popular song by Hank Williams, "Hey good lookin'! Whatcha got cookin'?"

At least he'd made me smile. "Well, I need to talk to Mary, but I enjoyed the entertainment."

"I love a woman who's able to appreciate great talent. I'll get Mary for you."

Mary came on the line. "Helmi! Hi. It's so good to hear from you. What's on your mind?"

"A favor," I said.

"You doing one or asking for one?"

"The latter, I'm afraid."

"Just name it." She sounded so jovial, I hated to throw the bad news at her.

"You know Bill and Rachel Neidhart, right?"

"The couple who sort of adopted your sisters after the fire."

"Yes. Well, Bill fell and broke his hip and is in the hospital, and Rachel needs to be there with him, but Ronnie…"

Before I could finish, Mary said, "Ronnie needs someone to take care of her until Bill comes back home."

"That's exactly right. Is there ANY way you could stay at the Neidhart's place for a few days and nights? Just till Rachel can take over again? Ronnie knows you and would feel comfortable if you were there."

"I'd be more than happy to help. When should I plan on being there? I'll have Herman drop me off."

"I know this is sudden, but Rachel needs you as soon as possible."

"Consider it done. Give me her number and I'll call her myself so we can work out the details. You needn't be concerned about it at all. How are you and yours?"

"We're all fine. I can't tell you how much I appreciate this, Mary." We talked a few more minutes, and I gave her Rachel's number before hanging up. I couldn't help but think how easily that disastrous problem had been solved.

Then I smelled the smoke. I ran to the kitchen and saw black smoke billowing out of the oven. All I could think about was that awful day when fire destroyed our lives as we had known them.

I grabbed a towel and put it over my face. Then I attempted to open the oven door, but the smoke was so thick I was having trouble getting close enough to reach the handle. By then, Lloyd had arrived on the scene, and Jimmy appeared out of nowhere. Lloyd started coughing, and Jimmy was feeling his way through the smoke-filled room as if he were blind. Our hands both reached the oven door at the same time, throwing it open and fanning the smoke away.

Jimmy snatched the towel from me, using it to pull the cookie sheet out. He dropped both it and the towel in the sink. The combination of smoke and clattering noise must have scared Craig, who was in the next room, and he let loose a wail, the likes of which should only have been emitted by a banshee. Jimmy and I both ran to the window; he opened it, and we and sucked in as much non-smoke-filled air as our lungs would hold.

"You okay?" I asked Jimmy, breathlessly.

He nodded. "You?"

"Been better," I said between chokes and coughs.

Then we started to laugh, one of those inappropriate laughing fits that seems to escape someone when laughing is undoubtedly the least likely response to a dire situation. We were nearly hysterical, laughing till we cried. Lloyd stared at us like we were from outer space—aliens who didn't understand the seriousness of the situation. We were holding onto each other as if it were necessary in order to keep ourselves upright.

Eventually our hysteria began to wane. Between irregular bursts of laughter, our chests heaved in great attempts to replace the foul air in our lungs with the cold, fresh air coming through the window. We both leaned against the counter, but our bodies slid to the floor, as if melting, where we sat splay-legged, still uttering an occasional giggle.

"I don't understand grown-ups," Lloyd said, shaking his head.

We looked at each other, sputtered, snorted, and laughed some more. I finally rose and went to the sink, picked up a round, flat, black object about the size of a Mason jar lid, held it up, and said to Jimmy, "Cookie?" I thought we'd never regain our composure.

After about an hour, we had the kitchen back in order and had washed most of the smoke film from the cabinets, counter, cooking utensils, and backsplash. The ceiling would have to wait till another day. And dinner would end without dessert.

I did my best to keep in touch with Mary and Rachel regarding both Bill and Ronnie—not an easy accomplishment while trying to balance work, a first-grader, a baby, a husband, and a home. I learned there is no such thing as equal time for family and career.

That winter was a tough one, more cold than snow. Sub-zero temperatures went on for days without any help from the sun; our furnace ran almost continually, and the fireplace was kept burning when we were at home. We couldn't let Lloyd walk to school, so I dropped him off every day before I took Craig to Sheila's and then went on to work.

It also meant that Lloyd couldn't spend much time playing outside, so we had to invent things to keep him occupied indoors and use up some of his excess energy.

No one had ever explained parenting to me, and I had never thought about it being something other than a duty that came naturally to parents. But I had never been around boys when growing up, so I had a whole lot to learn. And none of it was easy.

Betty, my hairdresser friend, invited us all over to her place for Thanksgiving. Luckily, she didn't ask me to bring cookies! Betty's husband, Gene, was one of the fellows who went to deer camp every year with Jimmy. They had just gotten back home a few days before the holiday, and both of them had gotten a nice-sized deer. Gene's was a ten-point buck—a real beauty. Jimmy's was nothing to brag about, but it would provide some good meat for us over the winter.

I spoke almost daily with Mary. She said she was getting along fine with Ronnie, and she also said she loved talking to both Rachel and Anna. "Don't tell your Uncle Herman, but I find it quite refreshing to talk to females." I asked her about Lizzy, and she said, "I hear from her about once a week." Lizzy and Walter and their daughter, Melody, lived in California where Walter was an executive with an insurance company that catered to corporations.

"I don't know how you do it," Mary said to me. "I cannot imagine being away from my home and children every day. It just seems odd to me that a woman would want to have a job when she has children to care for."

"I have Jimmy," I said. "He's as involved in raising our children as I am. In fact, he probably spends more time with them than I do, not that I don't often wish I could be there more. It seems that our relationship works *because* of our schedules, not in spite of them."

"What would you ever do if anything happened to Jimmy, perish the thought?" Mary asked.

"We'd just have to cross that bridge when we'd come to it," I said.

Christmas was special for us in 1950. Retta came to visit, without Wil. She had been to visit us several times since we'd moved to the U.P., so she refused to let Jimmy come and get her, though he offered. She had said, "Are you kidding? I'm a big girl, now, Jimmy. I can get around on my own. Wil doesn't want to close the store until five o'clock on Christmas eve, but I want to be at your place for Christmas morning to see the look on Lloyd's face when he sees the gifts Santa left for him." There was no talking her out of it (not that we tried very hard).

I was convinced that she and Wil were not getting along very well. Jimmy and I had talked about the fact that she didn't seem concerned about not spending their first Christmas together. She arrived at our house in the afternoon two days before Christmas. We were both home, and Lloyd was there, too, since he was out of school for Christmas break. We were all happy to see her and greeted her with smiles and hugs. Even Craig smiled at her.

"Should you call Wil and tell him you arrived safely?" I asked.

"Not necessary. He's busy, I'm sure, with last-minute customers," Retta said. Then she started a conversation with Lloyd that took them into his room where he had "tons of stuff" to show her.

Jimmy and I looked at each other. We didn't need to exchange words; our expressions said it all. We knew their marriage was doomed, and we were sure it would only be a matter of time before Retta was ready to talk about it. The time arrived that night after Lloyd went to bed.

Retta and Jimmy and I were sitting around the kitchen table, drinking some eggnog I'd found a recipe for in a *Better Homes and Gardens* magazine. "You probably already figured out that things aren't real great between Wil and me," Retta said.

Neither of us replied. I only sighed.

"We're getting an annulment."

"I don't know what that is," I said.

"Neither do I," Jimmy said.

"It means we don't actually file for divorce. We just end our marriage. We figure out who gets what and make a list that we give to our lawyer—we only need to hire one lawyer, not two. Then we sign a paper that says we agree to that list. Thirty days later we go to court, and when the judge asks us if the agreement still stands, we tell him it does, and he basically says, 'Okay, you're not married anymore.' And that's that."

Jimmy and I were both silent. I had mixed emotions; I wasn't sorry to see it happen, but I wasn't glad about it, either. I knew Retta was perfectly capable of making her own decisions, and I also knew she wasn't the kind of woman who would put up with someone who didn't make her happy just to keep up appearances.

Retta was strong-minded and strong-willed, and Wil was not. He'd made that quite evident when we met him the first time. I never knew why she had chosen him in the first place; there had to be something there that I hadn't seen, possibly wasn't even capable of seeing. But whatever it was had disappeared, and Retta was determined that her life was not going to be forever broken by something she could fix. That's why I loved her so.

Jimmy had changed the subject. He was telling her about deer camp. "Mostly we drink beer and play cards, but once in a while we stumble out into the woods and shoot a buck." He had Retta laughing so hard she was snorting. It was just the medicine she needed.

On Christmas morning Lloyd was ecstatic when he saw the bicycle Santa had brought him. He had written a letter to Santa asking for the bike, but he had been sure to include a sentence saying that he understood he couldn't ride it until the snow melted, which might be in the spring. And he promised Santa he wouldn't ride it in the house.

We all had fun exchanging our gifts, but there was one package under the tree that none of us recognized. Retta swore she hadn't brought it. Jimmy was adamant about not being the one who had put it under the tree. And I was completely baffled by its presence. The tag on it said, "To: Helmi and Jimmy." There was no "From:" on it.

Lloyd was on the floor playing with the Lincoln Logs Retta had given him. "Lloyd, do you know anything about that present under the tree?" Jimmy asked him.

Lloyd looked over at the present and said, "Yeah. It's for you and Mom."

"We know that; the tag says so," I said. "But do you know who put it there?"

"Me," he said, matter-of-factly.

"It's from you?" Jimmy asked.

"No."

"Then who?" I asked him.

"You'll know when you open it." He continued to play with the

Lincoln Logs. But the corners of his mouth had turned up ever so slightly.

Retta got up and retrieved it from its place under the tree. She handed it to me. "You better come over here and join her," she said to Jimmy.

"Aha, so you DID bring it!" I said.

"No, I didn't. Seriously. I have no idea where it came from. I swear on Truman's eyeballs." She sat back down.

Jimmy studied her face. "She's tellin' the truth," he said.

"Open it," Lloyd said. Then he abandoned the log cabin he had been building, crossed his legs Indian style, and rested his hands on his knees.

"So you did put it under the tree," Jimmy said.

"But it's not from me."

"Well, I for one, have played detective long enough. I'm gonna open it," I said. I untied the ribbon and tore the paper from it, revealing a plain, unmarked, corrugated cardboard box. "Your turn," I said to Jimmy and handed it to him.

He held it up to his ear and said, "I don't hear any breathin', so it prob'ly isn't alive."

Lloyd and Retta both giggled.

Jimmy whipped out his new pocketknife, which I had given him, and cut through the tape that held the box closed. Then we both lifted the flaps to reveal the contents. Jimmy's mouth fell open; it took my breath away.

Retta said, "Hey, cut the drama. I wanna know what's so special." She came around behind me, but she didn't utter a sound at what she saw.

There, framed with beautifully finished oak, was a portrait done in charcoal of Jimmy and me. It was in a vignette style, showing only our profiles. We were facing each other, our foreheads touching. My eyes were down, nearly closed, but Jimmy's were looking at me, every thick, dark lash evident. There was a hint of a smile on Jimmy's face, and my lips were colored in deep damask-rose pink, just as Yosie's had been so many years back.

Jimmy raised the portrait from the box, and under it was a paper which I lifted out. It had elegantly written calligraphy on it:

Lady, when I behold the roses sprouting,
Which, clad in damask mantles, deck the arbors,
And then behold your lips where sweet love harbors,
My eyes present me with a double doubting.
For, viewing both alike, hardly my mind supposes
Whether the roses be your lips, or your lips the roses.

All my love, Dora

The room was completely silent; not even Craig was making any sounds.

Finally, I asked Lloyd, "Where did this come from?"

"Santa," he said. "He delivered it with a message to put it under the tree. So I did."

1951

I was mopping the kitchen floor the day of New Year's Eve, 1950, when the phone rang. It was Dora. She proceeded to thank me for the Thank-You note I had sent her for the portrait she made for Jimmy and me.

"I still can't believe you got that past us. How did you manage?" I asked.

"I called Lloyd's school and explained my plan to the secretary. She's a real sweetheart, by the way. I sent it to the school, and she gave it to Lloyd with instructions to keep it hidden till Christmas morning. Then he could put it under the tree when you and Jimmy were busy doing something and wouldn't see him putting it there. And he wasn't allowed to say who it was from—just Santa."

"As usual," I said, "you outdid yourself. It's absolutely gorgeous, Dora. We will cherish it forever."

"Just don't burn it up, okay?"

"I'll do my best to keep the fires at a minimum," I assured her. We talked for nearly half an hour.

That night when I got into bed, Jimmy was already lying there with his hands behind his head, staring up at the ceiling. A full moon was shining through the window. I turned onto my side toward him and studied his profile. The light reflected off his eyelashes each time he blinked.

"Where are you?" I asked.

"Back at Dad's house." He didn't say anything for a couple more minutes, but I knew he'd eventually tell me what he was thinking. "I can't remember Mom's face. I've tried and tried, but it's just not there. I'd give anything to be able to remember her face, the texture of her skin. I used to tangle my hand up in her hair as a baby; I know it was light-colored, but I don't know if it was 'cause it was naturally light or 'cause it had turned gray."

He took one hand from behind his head and put his arm under my head. Then he went on. "I have one memory of her and Dad sittin' across the table from me. Mom was leanin' over with her arms on the table. Dad leaned over and put his arms on the table, same as her, then he reached over and took hold of her right hand with his left; I can see that clear as day, but I can't make out Mom's face. I was on my knees on the chair across from 'em, and I slid down and crawled under the table, then I popped up between 'em. I guess it was funny 'cause I remember us all laughin'. Why can I remember all the details except her face?"

"Maybe because you were only two?"

He sighed. "I don't think age makes a difference. It's like there's somethin' in my head that blocks me from bein' able to picture her."

I studied the shadows of the trees on our bedroom wall. I felt sorry for Jimmy; I could remember every detail of both Mama's and Papa's faces, and I could conjure up Granny Nan's face at the blink of an eye.

Jimmy asked, "Do you think we're born knowin' how to love, or are we taught how?"

"Neither. I think we learn it by example. I watched the love Mama and Papa shared with each other and all of my sisters and Granny Nan, and that's how I understood what it is to love."

"I know Dad really loved Mom, but I don't remember ever thinkin' 'bout it. After Mom died, he never seemed to have any interest in another woman. He was sad most of the time, especially when somethin' reminded him of her. I know he missed her somethin' fierce."

I said, "That's the way Papa was after Mama died. He was never the same."

"Don't leave me, Helmi."

That caught me off guard. "If I ever do, you can be sure it won't be by choice. I love you way too much, and I have too big a debt to pay to you; I owe you my life."

He rolled over toward me and put his arm across my chest. It was just past midnight, and 1951 had arrived unannounced. We both fell asleep as the moonlight carried the shadows up the wall.

❖❖❖

Three days into 1951 the phone rang shortly after supper. Jimmy was in Lloyd's room helping him with something he had to make for school, and Craig was playing in his playpen. "Scheist!" I said, rinsing the dishwater soap off my hands and grabbing a towel to dry them. I was expecting it to be a veterinary emergency, as I was on call that night. I grabbed the receiver and said, "Hello, this is Dr. Butcher."

The voice I heard was not that of some frantic farmer whose prize cow was down with milk fever. Instead, it was vaguely familiar and very business-like. "Is this Wilhelmina Butcher?"

"Yes. Who is this?"

"Sergeant Avery Dickerson, Chicago PD."

"Oh yes, Sergeant. I remember speaking with you recently." I didn't ask him anything about Yosie; I was wary of the answer he might give me.

"I'm afraid I have some bad news."

The room began to spin. All sound was distorted. My entire body went into meltdown. I couldn't speak or think or function. I was momentarily paralyzed, suspended in time.

He continued, but his voice sounded as if he were talking underwater. "Thanks to the rendering we received from your sister, we think we have located Josephina. We found a body that matches the description."

"A...a body?"

"Yes ma'am."

"Meaning, it's not a live body."

"I'm afraid so. But we need positive identification."

"Could you hold the line for a moment?" I asked and covered the mouthpiece with my hand. I felt like I was going to scream.

"Certainly," I heard the sergeant's faint voice through the earpiece.

I had to tell my lungs to breathe and my heart to beat. I leaned against the wall. Then I called to Jimmy, my voice barely audible. I called again.

Jimmy came out of Lloyd's room. "Is it for me?"

I held out my free hand to him. He frowned, then he came rushing toward me, catching me as I passed out. I hadn't even known I was fainting. It lasted only a few seconds. "Yosie," I said, over and over. "Yosie. Yosie."

Jimmy took the receiver, prying my clutching fingers from the mouthpiece. "Yosie?...Oh, sorry. I'm her husband, James Butcher... Yes...I see...We'll have to make some arrangements...All right. Just a second." He grabbed the pencil and pad of paper from the little cubby hole under the shelf that held the phone. "Okay, go ahead." He wrote something on the paper, then he repeated a phone number back to the sergeant. "And this is a direct line to your office?...I understand...Yessir. We'll be in touch real soon."

I looked up at Jimmy and reached for him, afraid he would slip away.

❖❖❖

I hadn't told any of my sisters other than Dora about my conversation with Yosie or about Sgt. Dickerson's previous calls. The only other ones who knew were Uncle Herman and Mary. I thought it best to wait until I had enough information to assure them that Yosie was all right…or not.

Now it was time to let Bella in on the secret. Following the completion of her work with the CNC in New York City, she had taken a nursing/teaching job at University of Chicago Medicine. The hospital was in the process of adding a children's hospital to their facility, and Bella wanted in on the ground floor.

When I was finally capable of speaking coherently, I called her, reiterating the entire situation from the day Yosie had called Uncle Herman and then me until yesterday, when the police sergeant called with the news of finding a body that might be Yosie. It was difficult for me to talk about it. "So what it boils down to," I said, "is that I need you to identify the body. I'd do it, but…"

"…but since you and Jimmy both have jobs and two kids, one in school and the other practically a newborn, to say nothing of the fact that you're almost in another country up there, and since I'm in Chicago, you're asking me to do it."

"In a nutshell," I said. She got it. She understood. "Would you?"

"Of course I will. I'm not going to like it, but I'm going to do it."

"What can I ever do to repay you for this?"

"Well, let's see…how about you just keep being my big sister and including me in your life."

I gave her all the information: names, phone numbers, etc., and she took it like a real trooper. I asked her to give us a day so we could notify Sgt. Dickerson regarding our plans before she called him.

Maybe it was because she was used to seeing bodies and death and living in a big city, but she had no obvious qualms about doing what I considered a next-to-impossible task. Even if that were true, I still felt like I was passing the buck. In my mind, dead human bodies were WAY different from dead animal bodies, and the fact that it was probably my own sister who was lying in that Chicago morgue, made it unbearable for me to consider.

Bella agreed with Jimmy's and my choice to keep it from all our other sisters until we knew for sure. I explained to her that it might take a while after the identification before we could actually bury Yosie, or cremate her, or whatever we ended up doing with her body, because, according to Sgt. Dickerson, the whole thing had to go through Homicide before the body could be "released to the family for disposal." Whenever a body was found, the possibility of foul play had to be eliminated. Our only sliver of hope was that it wasn't Yosie, but the chances of that seemed slim-to-none. Even if it wasn't her, I felt bad because, in all likelihood, someone, somewhere, would mourn the loss of whomever it might be.

I spoke with Sgt. Dickerson and gave him all the necessary information about Bella. I explained that she would be in contact with him and would, at my request, be doing the body identification. I thanked him for his part in leading us to Yosie, assuming it was really her body they'd found.

From day to day I functioned as if I were inside some sort of box that paralleled my world, but it wasn't the one I normally lived in. Everything was familiar, but none of it was comforting; none of it felt safe. I clung to Jimmy and Lloyd and Craig, feeling that, if I let them out of my sight, they might disappear.

One final call from Sgt. Dickerson sent me back into the real world. Yosie had died on New Year's Eve of an overdose of heroine combined with alcohol consumption. Her body had not been found until three days later in an apartment in a bad part of town. We had no idea who had found her or whether she had been alone or with "friends" on that night, and we hadn't a clue as to how she obtained the drugs and alcohol. Even though the outcome was not what we'd hoped it would be, at least we had been granted relief from the constant underlying concern regarding Yosie's whereabouts.

After three-and-a-half weeks, it all came to an end. She was cremated, and her cremains were sent to us. We decided to scatter them over the graves of Mama, Papa, Granny Nan, Celine, Alexander, and Aloysius in the Mount Pleasant Cemetery the next time we visited there. She would also have a marker, just like everyone else, but she would not be put in the ground. The Yosie we knew could not stand to be kept in one place. After all she'd been through, she needed to be—maybe even *deserved* to be—where the wind could carry her away at will.

❖❖❖

Winter lingered until almost Memorial Day. But the first two weeks of June warmed up and melted most of the snow. The spring flowers sprang from the ground as if they'd been catapulted. One day the trees had barely any buds on their branches, and the next they were fully leafed out.

School was over for the year, so Lloyd went to work with Jimmy each morning. The farm where Jimmy worked had expanded and installed the new automated milking system the Neidharts' nephew had shown us. Jimmy had been promoted and was now the overseer of the entire dairy farm, so he did very little actual physical work. And with his promotion came a raise—a pretty substantial one, at that—since he was now putting his mathematical abilities to use with bookkeeping and dealing with distributors and their pricing.

Just before the fourth of July, we bought our first television set. After having Gene help put the antenna on the roof, we got three channels, one of which came from Canada and was in French! We were mesmerized. Lloyd had seen a lot of television at his friends' houses, so it wasn't a big deal to him. But Jimmy and I watched it every chance we got. We could get the latest news and weather, and there were a couple of variety shows on every week; we became familiar with the faces whose entertainment we had only heard on the radio up to that point. To put it in Jimmy's words, "It was a true marvel of modern-day mechanical and electrical engineering."

The summer flew by. My schedule at work kept getting longer and longer, and Aune and Shirley and I had decided we could no longer handle everything without some more help. So we hired not only another vet, but also a vet tech who could do all of the blood work and x-rays and medicine inventory, among other necessary jobs around the clinic that Shirley wasn't certified to do.

Dr. John Napoleon, DVM, was in his mid-thirties and had been a vet for about twelve years. His specialty had been small animal care, so he was a blessing for Aune and me. Billie White, the vet tech, had graduated from a vet school in Colorado three years before and had a job with the DNR, but she decided she wanted to get away from the mountains. "There aren't a lot of farms out there," she had told Aune, "just lots of bears and bison and elk and mule deer, and most of them don't need to see the vet very often." She was tall and muscular with broad shoulders, large hands, and a husky voice. And she liked to hunt.

I was more at ease than I had been for quite some time, once we hired the extra help at Chippewa County Veterinarians. Jimmy and I had been discussing a day trip to see the lighthouse at Whitefish Point and visit Tahquamenon Falls. I had the day off on a Saturday in early August, so we packed a lunch and took off. The road to the town of Paradise, which is on the shores of Whitefish Bay, was paved for only a short distance; the remainder went from gravel to a two-track. It took a little over two hours to get to there, but it was worth it.

The wind was blowing at a pretty good clip, and the waves rolling in were magnificent. There were five-to-six-foot swells that produced monstrous breakers. The sound they made pounding on the beach was something I'd never been exposed to before. The wind roared, and we put on every bit of clothing we'd taken with us in order to battle the cold. It was exhilarating, to say the least.

The Whitefish Point Light, which is the oldest lighthouse on Lake Superior, sits on the south shore of Lake Superior at the entrance to Whitefish Bay, the point all ships have to pass when leaving or entering Lake Superior, either heading toward or coming from the Soo

Locks. The area is treacherous and has claimed more ships and crew members than any of the other lakes, so many in fact, it's known as the "Graveyard of the Great Lakes." The steel structure of the lighthouse was built in 1861 and was designed to relieve stress caused by high winds. It didn't take much to imagine how bad the wind could be during a gale. We were standing on the shore, watching the waves break over the sand and stones, when Jimmy shouted, "It's like looking out over the ocean, isn't it?"

"I remember looking out over Lake Michigan when we first got to Benton Harbor," I shouted back, "and that's the exact thing we thought then, too. But we didn't have to yell at each other to be heard. What a wind!"

But the day was only half over when we returned to the car, so we ate our picnic lunch then went back into Paradise and turned right on route M-123 to get to the falls. There are two sets of falls, the upper falls and the lower falls. They are about four miles apart on the Tahquamenon River, which eventually dumps into Lake Superior. We went to the upper Tahquamenon Falls, which is the third largest waterfall in volume east of the Mississippi—only Niagara and Cohoes Falls, both in New York State, are larger. We had to walk pretty far to get to the overlook.

We could hear the water long before we saw it. Jimmy and I took turns carrying Craig; his poor little legs were worn out from running along the beach at Whitefish Point, and they just couldn't make the trek to the falls. Jimmy finally put him up on his shoulders, allowing Craig to straddle his neck like riding a horse. Craig was giggling nonstop.

When the falls appeared, Lloyd said, "It looks like root beer." There was a wooden-framed box with a poster inside it. Glass covered the front of the box. The poster explained why the water was root-beer-colored. Jimmy read it to Lloyd and me, but just like the waves at Whitefish Point, the falls were so loud, he had to shout. "The Tahquamenon River drains the surrounding cedar swamps. Tannic acid leaches out of cedar roots and colors the water brown, making it look like root beer."

We stood there for a long time, watching the fast-running water tumble over the forty-eight-foot drop. Then we made our way down to the river, just above the falls. We had to keep telling Lloyd to stay back from the river's edge; he seemed determined to get close enough to put his hand in the water. Jimmy finally gave Craig to me and grabbed Lloyd by the arm, giving him a good wallop on the backside!

We finished our picnic when we got back to the car. The sun was getting close to the horizon, so we headed back home. Both boys slept the whole way, but Jimmy and I were wound up like a couple of tops.

We talked and watched for deer and bears. We didn't see any bears, but we did see four deer, a fox, a flock of wild turkeys, and a coyote. What a wonderful day!

❖❖❖

Before we knew it, September was upon us. Lloyd was back in school, and Craig had turned one year old. The temperature dropped, indicating the onset of autumn, my favorite time of year in the U.P. The fall colors usually reach their peak somewhere around the tenth of October each year. There is nothing capable of doing justice to the spectacle of that season without seeing it in person. Yellow, red, and orange leaves blanket the forest, and deep green pines offer cool contrast against the palette of warm colors. Where the tree branches bow over the roads, it's like driving through a golden tunnel with splashes of crimson and bittersweet on the ceiling. The air is crisp and clear. The water even seems to be more alive, as if it wants to have one last romp before turning to ice. The deer's coats turn from summer tan to winter gray, and the bears do their best to fatten up on everything edible before they retire to their dens for a long nap. It's the time of year when I come to life.

Within a few days, the leaves vacated the trees and covered the ground, leaving their hosts standing naked in the cold. The forest went from loud colors to muted ones, and it slept. The fifteenth of November marked the opening of deer season, and Jimmy was preparing to go to deer camp out in the western portion of the U.P. He and Gene were going to meet three other men, one from Ishpeming and two from Negaunee, and the five of them would travel to their deer camp close to Lake Michigamme. It was something all the hunters looked forward to every year. In fact, it was such an important event, the schools were even closed on the opening day of deer season. November 15 in the U.P. was "Deer Day."

On the morning of my birthday, two days before Jimmy was scheduled to leave, he asked me out to dinner. "Is this a date?" I asked.

"Call it whatever you want, but I'm 'bout to leave my best girl for a coupla weeks, and I wanna make sure she knows how important she is to me 'fore I go."

"What'll we do with the boys?"

"Already taken care of," he said, and he flashed me that little smirk I so loved. "Your only job is to be ready for a night on the town. I'll pick you up at six. And don't be late!"

I was ready at six on the dot. We dropped Lloyd and Craig off at Gene and Betty's on the way to the Soo where we ate a nice dinner at the restaurant in the Ojibway Hotel. Then we bundled up for the cold and walked among the trees in the locks park. We stayed to watch a ship go through; it was the Wilfred Sykes. I couldn't help but think of Uncle Julius every time I looked at the name on a ship. It made me sad to think that his life was over so soon and that all the money he'd acquired meant nothing now. But the night was not meant for sadness; it was for relaxing and just enjoying each other's company.

We walked through the only souvenir shop that was still open—the rest of them had all closed immediately after Labor Day when the tourist season ended. We couldn't help but laugh at all the hokey things the tourists seemed to love. There were miniature birchbark canoes and jewelry boxes made of cedar with pictures of the locks or the rapids or the freighters painted on them or burnt into the wood. There were kid-sized bows and arrows, rubber tomahawks, and Indian drums. There was also all manner of jewelry made from local agates that had been polished to a high sheen and some pieces made of turquoise and silver, neither of which was abundant in our part of the country, but because they were suggestive of the natives, the tourists bought them up like crazy.

When we finally decided it was time to go back home, we walked hand-in-hand to the car. I'd had a glass of wine at the restaurant, and it was working its magic on me; I was feeling mellow. Jimmy opened the car door for me and closed it after I'd gotten in. Then he slid in behind the steering wheel and closed his door. We both sat there enjoying the quiet. It was a cold night, but I didn't care. I was daydreaming about how wonderful our life was when I realized Jimmy was holding something in front of me. I looked down, and it was a little blue velvet box tied up with silver ribbon, exactly like the one my engagement ring had been in. I looked over at him and smiled.

"Open it," he whispered.

I took it from him and untied the silver bow. I opened the box. Staring up at me was a ring with four small stones arranged in a diamond shape: a sapphire, a citrine, a peridot, and a diamond. They were surrounding a larger ruby. I studied it for a few seconds before realizing the four small stones represented the months in which we had each been born: Jimmy in April (the diamond), Craig in August (the peridot), me in November (the citrine), and Lloyd in December (the sapphire). The ruby had me stumped for a moment, then it dawned on me—we were married in July. "I don't know what to say."

"Tell me you like it."

"Jimmy, I love it." I just kept staring at it. I couldn't take my eyes off it. It was the most beautiful thing I'd ever seen.

"Are you just gonna sit there and look at it, or are you gonna put it on?"

I removed it from the box and handed it to Jimmy. "You have to put it on me, just like you did my engagement ring."

He slipped it onto the ring finger of my right hand, then he took hold of my fingers on that hand and pulled my hand toward himself. He looked at the ring, then he looked up at me and said, "I wanted to do something to show you how much I love our family and our life, but I couldn't fit all of that on a ring, so I had to improvise."

"Well then, it's just perfect," I said. "Improvisation has always been our strong suit."

Two days later Jimmy left for deer camp. We had worked out all the details for me to get the kids to and from school and day-sitting, and I had been cleared at the clinic for no on-call duty till Jimmy got back home in two weeks. Billie was going hunting, as well, but she was only going one county away for three days, so we had all agreed to cover for her. Besides, the need for a vet always slowed down during deer season because most of the farmers were out hunting and didn't call us for much.

I was hoping Jimmy would have some luck and bring home a prize-winning buck. I wanted to have it taxidermized for either Christmas or his birthday, depending on how busy the taxidermist was. In addition, a good-sized deer would mean we'd have more meat in the freezer.

The two weeks passed, and I was looking for Jimmy to be home that evening. By eleven p.m. he still hadn't arrived, so I reluctantly went to bed. At a little after two a.m. the phone rang. It took a few rings before I realized what I was hearing. I leaped out of bed and made it to the phone in about four strides.

"Hello?"

"Mrs. Butcher?"

"Yes." I was panting.

"I'm calling about James Butcher."

"Oh, no." *I can't take anymore. I've had all the bad news I can handle. Please be someone calling about car trouble.*

"I'm afraid there's been an accident. I'm calling from Marquette Hospital. James has been hurt."

"How bad?" The panting had led to panic, and I was now gulping for air.

"It's pretty bad, I'm afraid. He had to undergo emergency surgery. He's in recovery right now."

"I'll be there by morning." I looked at the clock on the kitchen wall. "It's already morning, isn't it?" I sucked in a big breath. *I don't have any idea why my brain prodded me to do that.* "I'll be there just as soon as I can. I live in Brimley, and I have two small children."

"Please be careful, Mrs. Butcher. I understand the roads are pretty treacherous right now."

I hung up. *Now what? I can't be calling anyone this time of the morning. But it's an emergency, and I know either Betty or Shirley would understand. I can't call Shirley; she has to be at work first thing. I'll call Betty; she can keep Craig and still work. What'll I do about Lloyd? He has school. He'll just have to miss it for a day or two until Jimmy can come home.* My brain had never raced so fast.

I finally decided my first step was to get everything packed up that I'd need for a couple of days, then I could make the necessary calls. That's when Lloyd came wandering out of his room, rubbing his eyes. "What's up, Mom?"

"We're going to make a trip to Marquette. Your dad has been in an accident and is in the hospital, so we need to go and bring him home."

"What kind of accident?" he asked.

Was it an automobile accident? Had the nurse, or whoever it was that called, said it was an automobile accident? I don't think she said. Maybe he's been shot! "I don't know."

I took a deep breath. "We'll get your stuff packed up first, then I'll take care of my things. I won't need much, just some clothes and... why am I telling you this? Let's go to your room. The first thing you need to do is get dressed."

I was frantic. I grabbed things from his closet and chest of drawers and threw them on his bed. *Warm clothes...they need to be warm clothes. Underpants, undershirts, socks. Two pairs of pants plus the ones he'll be wearing. Three shirts and the one he wears; he might spill stuff on one, so he needs an extra to change into.* "Where is your suitcase?"

Lloyd bent down and reached under his bed and drew out his suitcase. He stood there holding it with one hand, yawning and rubbing his eyes with his free hand. I snatched the suitcase from him and stuffed his clothes inside. "Close that," I ordered him. I was already on my way out the door to get stuff from the bathroom. "And get dressed," I said over my shoulder.

"What should I wear?"

"The same thing you'd wear to school," I told him. "And a flannel shirt. And your long underwear."

I grabbed everything I could think of that we'd need in the way of toiletries and carried them into our bedroom. I looked under the bed for a suitcase, but there wasn't one. *Oh, it's on the closet floor behind Jimmy's hunting boots. No, his hunting boots won't be there; he has them with him. I hope they were warm enough to keep his feet from freezing. But the suitcase will still be there; he never takes that hunting, only a duffel bag.* My thoughts were disjointed and inappropriate.

I took another deep breath. By now I could hear Craig crying in his crib. I went back into Lloyd and Craig's room.

"I tried to be quiet, Mom, but he…" Lloyd started to say.

"It's okay. He needs to get up anyway." Craig was standing up in his crib, so I lifted him out, shushing him and telling him we were going to go for a ride. "It's all good," I said to him, which was my usual way of calming him down and stopping his crying. But I think my demeanor and the general electricity in the room belied the fact; he could sense that things were not "all good."

Lloyd was dressed, so I asked him to take his suitcase to the door. "Put your coat on; it's very cold outside, and I don't want you to catch your death."

I dressed Craig and told Lloyd to put Craig's coat on him. Then I dressed myself and packed a few things in my own suitcase. I went back to the boys' bedroom and packed some of Craig's things into a pillowcase. *I'm rolling now. I just need to make the phone calls.*

"Mom, can we go outside? I'm hot."

"Get in the car. I don't want you playing outside at this time of night. Bears!"

"Okay. We'll go right to the car." Lloyd sounded so grown up. I knew I could trust him to get Craig into the car and keep him occupied.

I went to the phone, picking up a few of Craig's toys on the way and adding them to the pillowcase.

The phone was ringing at Betty's. Then it hit me: *Gene was at deer camp with Jimmy. They were both in Gene's car. Oh my gosh!* I hung up immediately. *If Jimmy was hurt, what shape is Gene in? I have to think this through a little better. I'll just have to take Craig along, too. I can work something out when I get there.*

I checked to make sure there were no active coals in the fireplace, and I turned the furnace down. I went into the bathroom and opened the cold-water faucet enough to allow it to drip so the pipes wouldn't freeze. I knew I'd need the Michigan map; it was usually in the car unless Jimmy had taken it with him. I took my suitcase and the pillowcase out to the car, threw them into the back seat, and asked Lloyd to check for a map—he was riding shotgun, so he could easily look for it in the glove compartment. "It's here." He held it up and shook it.

"Good. Just keep it out." I decided, on the spot, that I wouldn't

Dar Bagby

call Aune until the sun came up, even if I needed to use a pay phone to do it. I went back into the house and turned off all the lights. Then I took the keys from their hook beside the door and locked the house. *I hope I covered everything.*

It took me till I reached M-28, the main road running east and west, to calm myself down enough to drive safely. I wanted to speed, but I knew that was the worst thing I could do under the circumstances. I had our two children to think about, and it was more important to keep them and myself safe than to have an accident of my own.

THE HOSPITAL

We didn't reach Marquette until nearly nine a.m. The weather in the western portion of the U.P. had already taken on the feel of winter. The roads were icy in places, and the sky in the west remained dark as we traveled toward it, even though the sun had risen behind us. I followed the map and the road signs to the hospital and parked in the hospital parking lot. I made sure the boys were bundled up, then we walked to the entrance. A big sign hung beside the door; the visiting hours were printed on the sign, and in big, bold letters it said: NO VISITORS ARE ALLOWED IN PATIENTS' ROOMS AT ANY TIME OTHER THAN THOSE DESIGNATED. I took one look at that and said, under my breath, "Just watch me."

I went up to the information desk, but no one was there, so I rang the little dome-shaped bell that was sitting on it. A woman with gray hair and half-glasses looked out of the room behind the desk. She took a good look at us, realized we were some patient's family, and said, "Sorry. Visiting hours don't start till two."

"I received a call at two this morning saying that my husband had been in an accident and had to have emergency surgery. We live in Brimley, and I just got here. Is there someone I can talk to about his condition?"

"Oh, dear," she said and disappeared back into the room. She emerged wearing a white lab coat, which she had obviously donned just before coming out. Her name tag revealed that she was Essie, Volunteer, and her glasses were now hanging from a fancy ribbon around her neck. "What is the name of the patient?" she asked.

"James Butcher." *Jimmy must have been conscious and given them his name and our phone number. That's good. Or maybe they had to go through his things to find it. Or maybe Gene is okay and just told them the information. But he wouldn't know our number by heart. Of course, if Gene told them we live in Brimley, they could have called and gotten our number from Information.*

"You can talk to the nurse on his floor." Essie picked up the phone, dialed two numbers, and waited. Finally, I heard a voice but couldn't make out what the person was saying. Essie said, "This is Essie at the front desk. I have the family of James Butcher here. They just arrived from Brimley and would like to know Mr. Butcher's condition." There was more talk from the other end of the line. "Thank you. I'll inform Mrs. Butcher." She hung up.

I started to ask her what the next step would be, but she interrupted me. "Just one moment," she said and picked the receiver back up. "I'll contact an aide." She dialed two different numbers and waited. There was an answer, then she said, "Please send someone to escort Mrs. Butcher to the waiting room on the surgery floor." More talk from the other end. "No, she'll be walking. Thank you." And she hung up the receiver again and turned to me. "Someone will be here shortly to take you upstairs to a waiting room. The nurse on duty will come in and give you the details. It may take a few minutes, depending on how busy she is and how soon she can reach the doctor."

"Why does she need to reach the doctor?" I asked.

"He will go over Mr. Butcher's chart with her and make sure she knows all the details so she can fill you in about everything."

"That's all well and good, Essie, but I want to see my husband."

"Of course you do, dear. But you need to be filled in about everything first. We find that works best in cases like this."

"Cases like this? What does that mean?" I was ready to push the panic button any second.

"It means Mr. Butcher went directly from the ER to surgery, and the staff members on duty at that time have gone home, so this shift was not here when the patient came out of recovery. They need to be informed directly from the doctor regarding the protocol for allowing anyone into his room."

"Will I get to talk to the doctor personally?"

"There's a good chance that you might. He normally makes his rounds right before visiting hours, so you will probably catch him. The nurse on duty knows how important it is for you to talk to him, so she will do her best to make that happen."

I was just beginning to grasp all that she had said when she continued. "I will need to take the children to the playroom. They are not allowed on the surgical floor."

Holy whah! "It's not bad enough that I'm beside myself with worry. Now I have to leave my children with people I don't know." *Calm down, Helmi. This is a hospital, and I'm sure they handle this type of situation all the time. They are just doing their jobs.*

Essie ignored my comment, took me by my arm, and led me to a chair. "Please have a seat, won't you, Mrs. Butcher?"

"I thought an aide was coming right down to get me."

"It may take a few minutes." She turned and disappeared into the office behind the desk.

I'd like to say, *"And my husband is lying in a damned hospital bed in who knows what condition with no familiar faces in sight. But the aides are too busy to..."*

Essie emerged pulling a wagon behind her—a red wagon just like the one we had at home for Lloyd and Craig to play with. She bent down to Lloyd and asked, "What is your name, young man? You appear to be in charge here."

"I'm Lloyd. This is my brother Craig. Can we see our dad?" He was looking at the wagon, and Craig was already trying to climb into it.

"You'll see him in time, I'm sure, but first your mother needs to find out whether he's awake. We don't want to wake him up if he's sleeping. In the meantime, how about a ride to the playroom?" She helped Craig over the edge of the wagon and said, "Lloyd, would you like to ride and hold onto Craig so he doesn't fall out?"

"Sure," Lloyd said, seating himself behind Craig and putting his arms around his brother.

"Here we go," Essie said as she began to pull them away. Neither of them appeared to be the least bit concerned about leaving me behind. My opinion of the hospital took a giant leap forward, and I sat down to wait for the aide, feeling somewhat ashamed for my less than appropriate behavior and my rather acidic words. I could only hope that Essie was used to that kind of reaction and would take it with a grain of salt.

Less than three minutes later a young man came up to me and asked if I was Mrs. Butcher, then he asked me to follow him. He took me to the elevator and punched the "UP" button. It turned green. When the elevator arrived, there was a loud "Ding!" I jumped, and the doors opened. I had ridden elevators at OSU, but none of them were this big, and none of them made such loud dinging noises. I appeased my embarrassment of jumping by telling myself it was because I was so nervous about my upcoming conversation with the nurse and, hopefully, the surgeon.

Surgery was on the second floor. We exited the elevator, and the young man walked with me to a room containing two davenports, each with a chair across from it. I assumed the chairs were for the nurses or doctors. There was a coffee table between the davenport and chair in each location. On one wall was a small table that held a Thermos and some heavy paper cups, the kind with handles that were wrapped around them and unfolded when someone was ready to drink. There was a cream pitcher and sugar bowl on the table, as well as a glass jar holding several spoons. A pile of small cocktail napkins sat beside the spoon jar.

I was eyeing the Thermos when the young man said, "Please feel free to help yourself to a cup of coffee. I just made it a few minutes ago."

"I sure could use one," I said, and dropped my pocketbook on one of the davenports.

"There's a coat rack right over there," he pointed to one standing beside the door. "I'd be happy to hang your coat." I hadn't noticed it when I came into the room.

"Thank you," I said, handing my coat to him.

"My pleasure," he said. "Is there anything else I can get for you?"

I breathed out a sigh of relief. "Only an assurance of good news about my husband," I said.

"I'll do my best." He left the room.

I poured some cream—and it was real cream, not milk—into one of the cups and added two sugar cubes. Then I reassessed the situation and added two more cubes before opening the Thermos and filling my cup. I put a spoon into the cup and took a napkin. I turned and put my cup down on the coffee table and sat down on the couch, bending forward to stir the wonderful-smelling brew. That's when I recognized my exhaustion. I had been operating on adrenaline since the two a.m. phone call.

The coffee tasted wonderful, but I was only able to take one sip before a nurse entered the room. "Mrs. Butcher?" she asked.

I nodded, barely able to keep my eyes open.

"I'm sure the past several hours have been terrible for you."

"Almost seven of them," I said.

"I'm Catherine. I wasn't here during your husband's surgery, nor was I on duty yet when he was brought out of the recovery room. I have, however, talked to both of the surgeons, the one who performed the amputation and…"

"Wait…wait. What?" Adrenaline shot through me again, and the enormity of what she had just said pierced my foggy consciousness.

"I'm so sorry. I thought you knew."

"I don't know anything. I got a call at two a.m. saying my husband had been in an accident. There were no details, only a request that I come to the hospital as soon as I could. Is my husband still alive?"

"Oh, yes. Please be assured that he is in a room being well taken care of, Mrs. Butcher. I was under the impression that the nurse on duty at that time had informed you of his condition on arrival."

My voice was rising in both volume and pitch. "Your impression was wrong, Catherine. I don't know why you thought that, but..." I stopped and regrouped. "Excuse my bad manners. I'm under some duress here. I would just like to know what happened from the moment he arrived here until now. And don't be afraid to tell me in medical terminology. I'm in the medical field, too."

"That will make things easier," she said. "And again, I'm sorry that I was misinformed about how much you had been told." She opened Jimmy's chart. "He was involved in an automobile accident. We don't have the police report, but one of the officers on the scene told our ambulance crew..."

I hadn't even thought about Jimmy having to be brought here in an ambulance.

"...that Mr. Butcher—may I refer to him as James?"

"Jimmy," I said. "And please do."

"Jimmy's left leg had been pinned under the vehicle for quite some time before the ambulance arrived on the scene. It took four policemen, the ambulance crew of three, and the ambulance driver to lift the car enough to pull him free of the vehicle. His femoral artery was crushed. There were multiple fractures of the femur, and the knee joint was demolished." She stopped and sighed. "Are you okay?" she asked me. "Why don't you drink a little more coffee before I go on."

I did as she said, then I told her, "I'm ready to hear more."

"You're awfully pale. Why don't we wait just a little longer so you have some time to let this all sink in."

"I think I'm pale because my adrenaline has been pumping on and off and my poor body doesn't know what's happening to it."

"You're probably right," she said. "If you're ready, then I'll go on."

"Please. So the knee joint was beyond repair..."

"Yes, and the lower leg was shattered, so there was nothing they could do about it except keep it immobilized. When Jimmy got here, the doctor immediately did x-rays and saw the extent of the damage. He and the radiologists all determined that the leg could not be saved."

I heaved a giant sigh and made some sort of noise I didn't even recognize. I mechanically drank what was left of my coffee, ignoring the fact that it burned all the way down.

Nurse Catherine sat back in the chair and studied the chart. I could tell from the look on her face that there was more to come. I closed my eyes. "Go on."

"His right arm was broken in thirteen places."

"Thirteen breaks? Does he still have it?"

"Yes," Catherine said. "The breaks were all clean, and his elbow is intact, so the doctor wrapped it until the swelling decreases somewhat. Then Jimmy will need surgery to put it back together."

"What about infection?" I asked.

"There is always the chance of infection, as you well know, so he will need to remain in the hospital for as long as it takes to make sure infection does not set in. That includes both the amputation site and the future surgical sites on his arm. If there is any sign of infection, he will be treated accordingly. We currently have him on preventive IV antibiotics."

I was watching her eyes. She averted them momentarily, a sure indication that she was still not finished telling me the extent of his injuries. "I know there's more," I said quietly.

"We are also keeping him highly sedated. The pain would be unbearable if he were awake. He will not acknowledge your presence when I take you to his room."

"I understand. Can we go there now? Have you told me the worst of it?"

"Yes. He does have multiple abrasions on his face and body, and there is a large hematoma on his chest, just below his left clavicle. But in his case, those are minor. You understand that he will be on a catheter for quite some time, and he will only be nourished via hyperalimentation."

"I'm a veterinarian. I'm not familiar with that term."

"It's a type of intravenous feeding. The doctor makes an incision in the chest, inserts a large-lumen tube into the subclavian vein, and sutures it directly to the skin. Unfortunately, it usually has to be changed more frequently than we'd like because it is so susceptible to infection."

"I see. Please take me to him, Catherine. I need to see him so I can swallow all of what you've told me and confirm it all with a visual interpretation."

"Right this way." She stood and moved toward a door on the side opposite the room from where I had entered. I picked up my pocketbook and started toward the door. Then I realized I'd left my coffee cup on the coffee table and turned to pick it up.

"No, no. We'll take care of that." She retrieved my coat from the rack, which I had also forgotten about, and passed by me on the way to open the door through which my whole life would change.

I followed her, watching each numbered room go by as we walked down the hall. When we came to number 241, Catherine stopped. She turned to me and handed me my coat. She let me enter the room first.

It was difficult to make my feet move. I wanted nothing more than to see him, but my body was rebelling. I forced myself to enter the room, and I hesitated before peeking around a curtain that was pulled part-way closed.

"Is that him?" I asked Catherine. I thought she had made a terrible mistake and had led me into the wrong room. That couldn't be Jimmy lying there. It looked nothing like him. The man in the bed was completely uncovered except for a sheet that had been folded and draped across his mid-section. *At least they're taking his modesty into consideration.*

I crept closer to the bed. I was horrified at a large white bundle lying beside him; for a moment my mind told me they had wrapped his missing leg and laid it there. Then I came back to reality and recognized it as the wrapping around his broken arm.

There were tubes and wires and hoses and all manner of other paraphernalia coming out of his body and attached to his body and lying beside his body; it was overwhelming, even to me. I had never been in the company of an animal with that much going on at the same time, and I reckoned I probably never would be. There just wasn't that much to be done for a sick animal.

I worked myself up to looking directly at the man's face. It was swollen and marked with crisscrossed abrasions. Bandages were taped to several places, one over his left eye. I looked at the other eye, and I recognized Jimmy's dark lashes.

"Oh, Jimmy. My Jimmy," I cried. I wanted to embrace him, to console him, to make all the bad go away. But I was helpless.

Catherine came to the bedside and took one of my hands. "You are here now. He'll know that somehow. They always do."

Uncontrollable tears were streaming down my face, and my bottom lip quivered of its own accord. The thought of losing Jimmy passed over me like a wisp of smoke—there and gone in a flash.

I was looking out the window but seeing nothing on the other side of the glass. All the death my family had dealt with came hurtling back to me. I could see each one I'd lost as clearly as if they were standing before me. But I was not about to let Old Man Death score again. Not with the man who was part of me, part of our children. "I hear you knocking at Jimmy's door, Old Man, but no one's going to answer."

SOMETIMES LIFE GETS EASIER, THEN…

Five long weeks passed before Jimmy was transferred to War Memorial Hospital in Sault Sainte Marie via ambulance (he was not able to ride in a car). I had made four more trips between Marquette and Brimley. At the end of the five weeks, I swore I'd never go back to that city again.

I forced myself not to think about the future each time I drove back and forth from west to east and east to west, often during the worst weather the U.P. could throw at me. I played mind games and sang every song I knew. I even tried, in my mind, to play some of the pieces I'd learned on the piano when I was in high school, picking out first the lefthand part, then the righthand part, then putting them together. I could hear them in my head. I conjured up the memories of Jimmy and Lloyd and me when we had moved to the U.P. and started over. I did, basically, anything that would keep me from thinking about what was to come. I knew the time for starting over *again* would arrive all too soon.

I had been granted a leave of absence from work, thanks to John Napoleon, the newly hired doctor covering the small animal portion of the business. Of course, that meant Aune had to do all the field work, but he never complained, at least not that I was aware of. He was a bachelor, so he didn't have to deal with a family in addition to work. And his concern about both Jimmy and me was genuine; he called at least twice a week to check on us, and every time he'd make it a point to tell me not to worry about work. "Your job will be waiting for you when you can come back."

When I did go back to work, Lloyd stayed at Betty and Gene's place for several weeks while Jimmy was undergoing physical therapy. Betty took Lloyd to and from school every day. Craig, on the other hand, slept at home and stayed at Sheila's during the day; Betty came and got him each morning after she dropped Lloyd off. In the afternoon she picked Craig up at Sheila's and dropped him off at home before getting Lloyd at school and taking him back to her place. I can't imagine the traumatic effect it must have had on the boys, being so young and having their lives turned completely upside down for such a long period of time. I was going to be forever grateful to Betty.

I think Betty and Gene felt obligated, but they never said that in so many words. It turned out that Gene, who had been driving, was thrown from the car when the accident happened; aside from three broken fingers, his wounds were mostly superficial, though no one knew how. The car had left the road when it hit a patch of ice and rolled over several times down an embankment, with Jimmy inside.

By the time mid-1952 came around, Jimmy was able to sit in a chair for almost an hour at a time. He could talk, but unbeknownst to the doctors immediately following the accident, he had suffered some head trauma that left him unable to speak clearly. His comprehension was unaffected; he simply had trouble forming words—his mouth wouldn't cooperate—and it frustrated him, especially when I had to ask him to repeat things, often more than once.

He occasionally complained of blurred vision, too. I remembered seeing one of his eyes covered with a bandage when I went into his hospital room that first day. I had asked the doctor about it, and he had told me, "It appears that one eye is a bit lazy. It's called amblyopia, or lazy eye. We initially covered it so it didn't have to work so hard. He needed to center all of his concentration on other things. It will probably correct itself as he continues to improve." But every once in a while, I'd see Jimmy blinking hard or squinting. I hoped it wouldn't become worse as time wore on.

Since Jimmy was right-handed, he had to do a lot of practice using a pencil after the thirteen fractures in his arm bones healed from the surgery. He underwent daily therapy for his arm, his leg, and his speech. It was tough to handle for a man who had worked at a physical job his whole life; now he was confined to a wheelchair except when he slept or sat in a regular chair. He was building up strength in his right leg, and he was learning how to balance on that one leg, but it would never be the same as standing on two.

The boys took it all in stride, and of course, Jimmy spent as much time as he could with them; he was such a great father. He explained to them everything that had happened—as best as he could with his newly acquired speech impediment—and he was adamant about allowing them to help in his recovery, even though the physical therapists sometimes disapproved. Jimmy said, "It hurts, and I want my sons to know that their father feels pain, just like they do sometimes. I'm not above cryin' out now and then, and I want them to know it's okay to do that. Men don't have to pretend that they're unbreakable."

Whenever I was away from him or was someplace where I could

see him but not allow myself to be seen, I cried. I cried for him, for the boys, and for me. I didn't know how we'd ever become a normal family again, but I relied on the fact that, with our previous track record, we'd work it out somehow. And it seemed that, for every bit of determination I had, Jimmy had double that, or more.

It was another year before things began to feel somewhat "normal" again. Jimmy had learned to walk with a special crutch with a ring around his left upper arm, and it had a handle that he used to support his left side. He was even able to go back to work at the farm. His speech returned to normal, too.

True to form, Uncle Herman came to the rescue by getting us a big discount on a Chevrolet Powerglide; it shifted gears without the use of a clutch! That meant Jimmy could drive himself with only his right leg. It was the first car we ever owned with an automatic transmission, and it was a lifesaver for Jimmy. Once he was able to drive again, he became a new man. We were all amazed at how much his attitude improved when he was finally able to get behind the wheel. The only drawback was that he had to wear glasses to drive. When he took his driver's test to renew his license, which had expired while he was recuperating, he was unable to pass the vision test. But after he was fitted with glasses to compensate for his amblyopia, he passed without a hitch.

It came as no surprise that we lost Ronnie in early September of 1953. She hung on longer than any of her doctors had predicted. They tried putting her on all sorts of different medications and breathing machines, but most of them did little to mask her discomfort. When she finally stopped breathing, she was nothing but twisted skin and bones. We made sure the casket was closed for the funeral.

The Neidharts were determined to take care of all the doctor bills and the funeral and burial arrangements. Ronnie had become Bill and Rachel's adopted daughter. Bill even referred to her as "our Ronnie." I think Mama and Papa would have approved.

It was difficult for Jimmy to make the trip to Mount Pleasant for Ronnie's burial, but under no circumstances was he willing to stay home. "I'm just as much a part of this family as you," he told me. "So I'm gonna be there when they lay Ronnie to rest. Besides, I haven't seen much of the family for a long time, and I miss 'em."

Three of my sisters had settled in places outside of Mount Pleasant: Bella was in Chicago and Dora was in Ohio. Retta had moved to a little town on Lake Michigan called Frankfort. She had enjoyed working at the pet store in Mount Pleasant, where she'd done everything associated with the business, so she talked to one of the local banks in Benzie County, and they ended up loaning her enough money to start a pet store of her own. She called it "Fur, Feather, & Fin of Frankfort." The only sister left in Mount Pleasant was Anna, who still lived with the Neidharts.

All of them managed to come to Ronnie's funeral. I think part of the reason they wanted to be there was that we were going to spread Yosie's ashes on the graves after Ronnie was buried. The minister who would perform the graveside service for Ronnie had agreed to mention Yosie at the same time. It was destined to be a sad morning, but we made it as positive as we could, and I think all of us left the cemetery a little happier than we'd been when we arrived. Well, maybe not happier, but at least more at peace.

The hardest part of the trip was having to drive past our old farm. The Neidharts' nephew was not living on the property, so no house had been built. But he had built a new barn, not as big as our old one, but in the same place where it had stood. The old stanchion barn and milk house on the opposite side of the road were gone, too; however, a large new milking facility had taken its place. It looked like something from a science fiction movie. Bill and Rachel said he was now milking over two hundred and sixty cows and had a herd of nearly three hundred and forty, counting the calves and fresh cows and heifers. It was big business.

We said our good-byes and left for home. Jimmy wanted to get home so he could rest up the next day before going back to work at the dairy farm he managed in Pickford. Lloyd and Craig had worn themselves out at the cemetery playing hide-n-seek around the tombstones…not necessarily appropriate, but at least it kept them occupied while we were engaged in the grown-up tasks we had to perform.

"Would you mind drivin'?" Jimmy asked me. "I'd kind of like to sit in the back seat with Craig. He and I haven't spent much time together over the past few days."

"Fine by me," I said.

"Yay! I get to ride shotgun," Lloyd shouted. "Can I get a toy at the ferry?"

"We'll see," I said.

We stopped for some lunch in Gaylord, and Lloyd and Craig both got little trinkets at the ferry dock in Mackinac City, though we didn't have to wait very long before boarding the big car ferry. We managed to get home just after dark. The dropping temperature was cold enough to chill me to the bone. The first thing I did was build a fire in the fireplace. Jimmy tucked the boys in, and he and I sat down in front of the fire, each with a cup of hot chocolate I'd made for us. Without thinking, I reached over to put my hand on his leg, but it wasn't there.

Jimmy smiled.

"I don't know if I'll ever get used to it," I said, obviously embarrassed.

"Don't be embarrassed." He knew me so well. "I sometimes forget about it bein' gone, too. It still hurts now and then, even though it isn't there. What's that called?"

"Phantom pain."

"Oh yeah." He assumed a funny-sounding voice. "I am the Phantom. Beware!" and he grabbed me around the waist, allowing his hand to slide up to one of my breasts, which he immediately began fondling.

"Shhh! The boys probably aren't asleep yet. They'll hear you and come wandering out."

"They're dead to the world," Jimmy said. "I think we need to revive some of our old tricks in bed. I sure could use some lovin'." We hadn't tried to make love since the amputation.

"Are you sure you're up to it?" I asked him.

"I may be missin' *one* of my legs, but the third one's still fully intact and ready for some exercise."

I looked over at him and saw that smirk. "Looks like we'd better do a trial run," I said quietly.

"And then some."

The years went by without any unusual or outstanding instances. Everyone remained healthy, and our lives finally assumed a normalcy of sorts. Jimmy and I worked, Craig started school, and Lloyd was turning out to be a big kid, tall and muscular like his father, and he made good grades, not straight A's, but good enough to make us proud.

He also became obsessed with trains. We supported his interest and took him to various train yards and stations around the U.P. and often parked beside the tracks at crossings we knew would be busy at certain times of the day or night. One of Lloyd's favorite places to watch the trains was at the west end of the locks. There was a swing bridge between the two locks closest to the road. The bridge rested in an east/west position when not in use, but when a train traveled between the Michigan Soo and the Canadian Soo, that portion of the bridge swung around ninety degrees to a north/south direction, blocking the freighters traveling through the locks so the train could pass across them.

Neither Jimmy nor I were train aficionados by any stretch of the imagination, but we definitely shared Lloyd's excitement when watching that bridge. One day in 1956 we were sitting in the car watching it turn slowly when Jimmy asked Lloyd, "How does it turn? I don't see anybody makin' it move."

"It sits on a pivot mechanism in the middle, and there's a motor there that turns it. It's operated by someone in one of those little buildings." He pointed to some of the small structures that had been erected on either side of the locks. "It's so well balanced, it only takes one person to flip a switch or hold a button down, or something like that, to get it to move."

"Okay," I said, "I get that. But how does it keep from tipping when those heavy trains cross it? It looks like one end or the other would sink down when the weight of the locomotive reaches it."

He explained, gesticulating with his hands to show me how the mobile tracks and the stationary ones joined. I was impressed by his knowledge.

"Did anybody ever tell you how smart you are?" Jimmy asked.

"They don't have to. I already know," Lloyd said.

Jimmy punched him in the arm.

Jimmy was helping Craig with some first-grade arithmetic in a workbook. Craig had been home for a few days with the measles; there had been an outbreak at the school. Craig was zooming through the addition and subtraction problems.

"Hey, slow down there, Slick (Jimmy's pet name for Craig). You gotta take your time and make sure your answers are right."

Craig looked at Jimmy like he was an imbecile. "Dad, they're only the 'ones.' They're the easiest."

"The ones? What's that s'posed to mean?"

"You know, one plus one, one plus two, one plus six. All you have to do is look at the other number, not the one, and make it the next number higher. See, one plus eight would be nine, which is one number higher than eight. Get it?"

"Ohhhhh. Yeah, I get it. So tell me how you do the subtraction problems," Jimmy said.

Craig sighed an agitated sigh. "Da-ad! It's just like adding 'cept you take away one from the big number instead of adding it. Here, look." He turned the workbook toward Jimmy and pointed to a problem. "Seven minus one. You just take one away from seven and that leaves…?" He looked expectantly at Jimmy, who was just sitting there, staring at the problem. "And that leaves…?" Craig repeated.

"Oh! Oh! I got it. That leaves six."

"Yep, you got it." Craig continued to complete the page in less than a minute.

"Helmi," Jimmy said to me in an exaggerated voice, "we have some very talented children, here. Why, I 'spect they'll both go on to be famous thinkers. Don't you agree?"

"Certainly could happen," I said. I could see a smug expression on Craig's face.

❖❖❖

It was during that year that Jimmy got his new leg. We made trip after trip to University of Michigan where he was fitted for a prosthesis. After months of physical therapy in Ann Arbor, Jimmy was approved to continue his PT at War Memorial Hospital's Rehab Unit in the Soo.

One night after the boys had gone to bed, Jimmy and I were sipping some wine in front of a nice crackling fire in the fireplace, and Jimmy said, "Helmi, I'm whole again. I know my leg isn't permanently attached, but I feel like…like…I'm back. I'm me again. I haven't been able to put it into words until now. I feel like I've been somewhere else for the past few years, and I'd drop into our home every once in a while, just to visit. Does that make sense?" He didn't wait for a response. "Even though I have to buckle it on every morning and take it off every night, it's a part of me, no different than puttin' my glasses on and takin' 'em off. I'm finally me, now that I can walk without that damned crutch. Everything's gonna be fine in our lives for a while."

He reached over and took my hand, then he looked into the fire with an expression I hadn't ever seen on his face. It was as if he were looking into the future and could see our lives passing before him. I watched him smile briefly. Then his smile got bigger. And at one point, he even laughed a single sniff. Then he closed his eyes, squeezed my hand, and took another sip of wine.

I leaned my head against his arm. I knew it had been difficult for him to come to grips with what had happened all those years ago on that horrible night. I, too, had had a hard time putting everything into perspective. But I knew that tonight was his crowning victory: he had ultimately realized that our lives weren't over, only altered.

"I know you've been somewhere else since the accident," I said. "Sort of in Limbo."

"That's exactly it. I've been stuck somewhere between a theory and reality. Is that even feasible?"

"It most certainly is. I've been there several times myself. Sometimes I wonder if it's been detrimental or beneficial for us. But the boys just seem to have taken it all in stride. And that amazes me. We should consider that an important life lesson and try to be more like them."

"Do you s'pose other people in our position think about it in the same way?" Jimmy asked.

"I think everyone has their own way of coping, and ours is, luckily, the ability to talk about it."

"You always seem to be able to say the right thing. I used to think it was 'cause you went to college and were extra smart when it came to explainin' things. But I know now that college had nothin' to do with it. It's just 'cause of who you are."

"And I'm who I am because of my own life experiences and exposures."

"Well, you sure aren't lackin' in that department. I think 'bout your family and all the people you've associated with your whole life, and I'm almost jealous."

"What? Why?"

"Well, think about it. You had a big family, and I only had Dad."

"But..."

He interrupted me, "No, I mean it. I was pretty much on my own most of my life until I met your dad."

"Yeah, and look where that got you!"

"It got me into the best possible life a man could ever hope for."

The fire was fading. Without words, we rose and, still holding hands, went into our bedroom and slept peacefully in each other's arms.

In February of 1959 we underwent twelve continual days of sub-zero temperatures. It was one thing for the temperature to be below freezing for a few days in a row, but being below zero for that period of time was extra hard on the animals, as well as the farmers who continually had to break up ice in the water troughs and refill them with liquid water. And they had to bump up the amount of straw in stalls so the animals were insulated against the cold. Most of the farmers provided some sort of shelter, even if it was only a lean-to that allowed their livestock to get out of the prevailing winds. But our vet clinic still got calls on a daily basis about some of the critters getting frostbitten ears or an occasional animal that was down and couldn't get back up. Most of our work during those times consisted of telling people how to correct their problems right over the phone without having to make a trip to their farms.

I was surprised when Shirley told me there was a caller who had specifically asked for me.

"Must be someone who's calling with a followup," I said.

Shirley gave me an "I don't have the slightest idea" shrug and handed me the receiver.

"This is Dr. Butcher."

"Dr. Butcher, this is Ben Martin. Remember me?"

I did a quick inventory in my head, and sure enough, it rang a bell. "Ben! How nice to hear from you. It's been a long time." I was trying to calculate how old he'd be now.

"I hate to bother you at work, but that's the only number I have for you."

"What is it you need?" I asked him.

"Don't need a thing. I'm just callin' to tell you that I've been workin' at a stable in Kentucky. Been here since last summer."

"You made it!" I said. "Congratulations!"

"Thank you. I was hopin' you'd be pleasantly surprised." He sounded so grown up. "I pretty much quit growin' after I turned twelve, so I'm the right size to be a jockey."

"NO! That's incredible, Ben. Have you done any prestigious races?"

"Not yet. Mostly I do my ridin' here at the stable for the mornin' and evenin' exercises. But I have jockeyed in some of the local races, and I do a lot of jockeyin' for the trainers. I've got some wins under my belt, in addition to a lot of places and shows. The people here all say I'm good enough with the horses to move up pretty fast. The hard part's bein' good enough in the owners' eyes to land jobs." He laughed.

"I have to keep stackin' up wins in the local races 'fore I'll even be considered for some of the big-name ones."

"I'm so happy for you. Do you ever get back up here?"

"Once in a while. Ma's still there at the farm, but she's raisin' sheep and goats now. There isn't much call for goat jockeys."

I laughed and said, "Well, the next time you make it back up, please stop by and see me. Maybe we can work out a way to spend some time together. I'd love for my husband to meet you."

"I'd like that. I'll give you a call when I come to visit Ma."

"Let me give you my home number so you can call me there." We exchanged numbers, then we said good-bye. I hung up the phone and just sat there, going over our conversation in my head. There must have been an obvious smile on my face.

"Some long-lost lover?" Shirley asked.

"Not hardly. Do you remember the incident I had with a guy named Martin?"

"The one who beat up his wife and ended up in the hoosegow?"

"That's the one. I helped his son, Ben, fix up his horse's lacerated leg. Ben had just turned twelve and wanted to be a stable boy in Kentucky horse country. Well, he made it, and he wanted me to know."

"Awww! That's one of the perks of being a vet," she said. "People of all ages look up to you when you do a good job and treat them right."

"Ain't it the truth?" I answered.

I was telling Jimmy about the call right after supper that night when the phone rang. Jimmy answered it. I watched his expression change from pleasant to horrified.

"I can't believe it," he said to the voice in the phone. "He didn't appear to have a problem in the world the last time we were together. How could somethin' like this happen so unexpectedly."

Now he really had my attention.

"Do you want me to come and help? I'll be glad to," Jimmy said.

I caught his attention and silently mouthed, "Who is it?"

He turned away from me and put his index finger in the air, essentially telling me to wait a minute. "Okay. Let us know as soon as you have some things figured out. We'll be there in the blink of an eye." He hung up. It was a few seconds before he turned around to face me. When he did, his face appeared twice as long as normal. "It's Herman."

"Oh no! What's wrong with him? Is he in the hospital?"

Jimmy shook his head slowly from side to side. "Heart attack. He's gone, Helmi."

I thought the floor had fallen out from under me. "No. He can't be. I won't let it be true!" I couldn't accept the notion that Uncle Herman wasn't going to be there to talk to, to depend on, to make me laugh. To remind me of Papa.

Jimmy put his arms around me and held me as I sobbed.

The cold had invaded lower Michigan as well as the U.P., so Uncle Herman had to wait until the ground thawed in order to be buried. Retta ignored Mary's orders not to go to their home in Flint. She left the pet store in the hands of her manager, who was a little older than Retta and had worked in a retail store of some kind since she'd been Retta's age. So she knew the ins and outs of running a business, and Retta trusted her to keep things on an even keel while she was gone.

I was talking to Retta just before she left for Mount Pleasant. "Just take your time and stay warm."

"Yes, Mama," Retta teased.

"I can't help it. I've been a mother long enough, it just comes out of my mouth without thinking," I said. "But seriously, you could freeze to death if you have car trouble and don't have enough clothes to keep you warm."

"I'm not in the U.P., remember?"

"I wish you were," I said.

"I'm happy, Helmi."

"I know. And I couldn't ask for more than that. But I want to be there with you. I want to be there for Mary and Lizzy, too. Just think about all the times they and Uncle Herman came to our rescue. I know it's out of the question, but I can't help wishing it."

"If wishes were horses…" she said.

"…then beggars would ride," I finished the old maxim.

Retta said, "I'll let you know just as soon as Mary has some order in her life. You know how hard it is to make sense of everything when someone dies."

"Unfortunately, I do. Give her my love. And call me when you get to their house. I want to know you're safe," I said.

"I will. I promise. Unless I forget."

My eyes disappeared into the top of my skull, and I shook my head. "You're a pip."

I NEED THE SUN

Uncle Herman was buried in mid-March. The weather had taken a warm turn, and it appeared that spring was on a direct path to the lower peninsula. Retta and I were walking around the cemetery. Retta said, "When Mary and I were talking about the burial plans for Uncle Herman, I discussed the possibility of cremation for him, especially since it might be several weeks before he could be buried, but Mary said she wanted to visit his grave knowing his body was there, lying in peace, and she could talk to him. I said to her, 'To each his own, but it's only gonna be bones you'll be talking to. Isn't his soul supposed to be all around you all the time, not just in that grave? Isn't that what you believe? Couldn't you talk to him anytime, anywhere?' But Mary told me she believes his soul went to Heaven." Retta stopped. "I don't get it," she said. "Who's she going to talk to if Uncle Herman's in Heaven?" She threw her hands into the air. "It's all so confusing."

I smiled. Many years ago I had emotionally worked my way through the same thing that Retta was now trying to make sense of. I never tried to impress my beliefs on anyone, Retta included. But I felt she needed a cohort at the moment. "I can relate. I didn't used to get it, either. Truth be known, I still don't. That's why it's not my belief. I've never told you my take on an afterlife, have I?"

"Huh-uh. But I'd like to hear it."

I told her about what I wanted after I die, and she was quite intrigued.

"I'm gonna have to consider what you just told me," she said. "It sounds a lot like what I've been thinking about, too. I mean, when we die, our bodies just deteriorate anyway, so why spend all that money on a vault and a casket and all those flowers? The person's just gonna end up being nothing but a little pile of chemicals anyway. Why not speed up the process and create the remains in the first place? After a certain amount of time, all the graves in this world are gonna take up so much space, there won't be enough places for the living to inhabit. And the living people who were so concerned about talking to their dead relatives will all be dead themselves in time."

I said, "You think about it and let me know what you come up with. Just in case you end up dying before I do, I need to know what you want done with that long, gangly, shapeless body."

"Hey! Don't forget that this long, gangly, shapeless body is related to you, so you carry the same genes as I do."

"Yeah, I also know those genes arranged themselves in a more desirable pattern in *this* package." I turned sideways, put my hand on my hip, and stuck my chest out.

"All matronly women have curves."

"Matronly? Matronly?" I said, with mock indignity. I turned on the southern brogue. "Why, Miss Retta, that's blasphemous." But she was right. I had middle-age spread. "Big Daddy likes his woman with a little meat on her bones."

"You just keep telling yourself that," she said. "And you'd make a lousy southern belle. Can you imagine having to explain to Big Daddy why the apple of his eye is a veterinarian?"

"Oh, my!" I put my hand over my heart. "Somethin' tells me Big Daddy would have a coronary over that, wouldn't he?" I ditched the southern belle act and said, "Good thing we moved north!"

"I second that," Retta said. "How'd you ever survive in Oklahoma? From what I've heard about it, I don't think I could stand it."

"I know I couldn't anymore."

We walked back to the house and made small talk with everyone and ate all sorts of finger food brought to Mary's house by Uncle Herman's co-workers from General Motors and Michigan State, the church Mary attended, neighbors, and other friends.

"There is one thing I can tell you," I said to Retta. "My philosophy makes it much easier to handle things like this," I spread my arms, indicating all the people who were there to pay their respects.

"How's that?" she asked, shoving some kind of hors d'oeuvre into her mouth.

"When I die, I will no longer have to be concerned about making sure the napkins match the plates."

"Now that's really worth considering," Retta said sarcastically and snorted a laugh.

"It's a grown-up thing," I said. "You wouldn't understand."

She punched me in the arm.

Jimmy came up to us. He looked at Retta and said, "I saw that." Then he turned to me and asked, "Did you deserve it?"

"Without a doubt," I answered.

We had left the boys in Brimley and made arrangements to take an extra day to go to Frankfort and see Retta's shop since we were already in the L.P. She didn't have room enough to put us up in her apartment, but she had made reservations for us at a little inn just across the bay in a tiny town called Elberta. We loved it.

And we loved Retta's shop. Since it was a Sunday, the shop wasn't open, so we got an uninterrupted tour. The fish tanks, in which she displayed her assortment of tropical fish, were spotless and decorated with porcelain mermaids, corals, and sunken ships, and she had added pretty plants, some fake and some real. The cages for the small animals—she called them "pocket pets"—had cedar shavings on the bottoms, and they were all clean and had no nasty smell. The birds, mostly parakeets and finches, along with a couple of cockatiels, were chirping and begging for her attention. She had shelves all around the outside walls that held every kind of pet food imaginable, and she had lots of displays on free-standing pegboard uprights in the middle of the floor; they included everything I could ever imagine would be necessary for raising small animals.

"Where's the puppies and kittens?" Jimmy asked.

"I don't deal with them," Retta said. "There's too much involved in getting their shots, worming them, keeping them washed and brushed and presentable. I leave all of that up to the breeders. I know several good ones in the area, so when someone comes in wanting a dog or cat, I can send them to the breeders. I worked out a deal where I give the interested party a card that allows them to get a discount from the breeder, and the breeder gives me a gratuity for the referral."

Jimmy and I both just stood there with our mouths open.

"You'd catch flies if there were any in my store," Retta said.

We both closed our mouths in unison.

"You've really got yourself a good thing going on here," I said.

Jimmy added "Yeah. Where'd you get the brains to figure all of this out, Einstein?"

"Certainly not from you!" Retta kidded him.

"Hey! It's not nice to pick on a cripple," Jimmy said.

Retta and I both looked at him with horror on our faces.

"I'm allowed to say that about myself," he said. "Just don't think for one minute that *you* can get away with it."

❖❖❖

The Lincolns, Link and Dorothea, had kept in contact with me over the years. Link had retired from being a veterinarian and only taught a few classes at OSU, much like his father-in-law had done. Dorothea was fighting cancer. A letter came from them on the Monday after we got back from Frankfort. Lloyd and Craig were outside shoveling the last of the snow off the walk, and Jimmy was napping. I was extremely tired from the trip and my day's work at the vet's office and the emotional drain of losing Uncle Herman, so I grabbed a root beer out of the refrigerator and sat down to read the letter. I needed a lift. I was always brightened by Link's ever-optimistic attitude:

Dear Helmi,

It is with great sadness that I send this letter. My darling Dorothea lost her battle with cancer three weeks ago. She put up a tremendous fight, having suffered through it for more than a year. I cannot put into words the loss I feel, but knowing your numerous personal brushes with death, I think you probably understand my heartache better than anyone else I know.

I have her ashes in an urn, at which I cannot stop staring. Her absence—the lack of her constant companionship—haunts me day and night, and I find myself talking to the urn, as if she can hear me from inside it. I have never felt such grief, such loneliness, such despair.

Tell me it will become easier, Helmi. I know I can believe what you say, as you have endured much more agony than I, and still you persevere with an upward outlook.

With friendly affection,

Link

I covered my mouth and said, aloud, through my fingers, "Oh no!"

"Oh no what?" Jimmy said through a yawn as he came out of the bedroom. He bent over and kissed me on the top of the head. "Is that the letter from the Lincolns?"

I nodded, unable to speak.

"Uh-oh. Doesn't look good," he said. "You usually smile when you read letters from them."

"It's not good. Dorothea died. The cancer finally took her."

"I'm really sorry, Helmi. I know how much she meant to you."

"That's only the half of it," I said, handing him the letter.

He started to read it aloud, "Dear Helmi, It is with great sadness that I send…" His voice trailed off. When he finished reading, his arm dropped, and he sighed. "How much more can you take? People seem to think you're made of iron. But he's right, you do continue to persevere…how'd he put it?" He looked back at the letter. "Oh yeah…with an upward outlook."

I was at a loss. My ability to persevere was dwindling even as I stood there, thinking about those wonderful people who had helped me through everything I'd undergone while at OSU. And now Link was looking to me for solace. I couldn't ignore my duty—my desire—to reciprocate. Link was depending on me every bit as much as I had depended on him among a smattering of school-related incidents when

Dar Bagby

Granny Nan died. "How am I going to offer him the help he deserves?" I asked Jimmy.

"Now's not the time to think about it," Jimmy said. "You're tired and weary and in need of rest. Isn't that from some poem or book or movie?"

But I was far away, back at Dorothea's office with the family pictures above the chairs and the bookcase full of *Poor Richard's Almanacs*, and the handmade calendar that always stood beside her desk, and the plants under the windows, growing toward the sunlight. The sunlight. That's what I needed. There hadn't been any sun for days, not down at the cemetery where Uncle Herman was buried, not in Frankford where Retta's store stood, and definitely not here at home.

"I need the sun," I said.

"You can't just summon it when you need it," Jimmy said. "This is the U.P. It only shines when Mother Nature's mood improves and she allows it to peek through the clouds."

"Then I need to have a discussion with Mother Nature."

"She's a strong woman, Helmi. Maybe the only other woman I know who's as strong as you."

"Then I need to use some of that strength to answer Link's letter."

I took the letter from Jimmy and walked to the kitchen. I leaned against the sink and read it again and again, and still I had no supportive words to offer, only sympathy, and that wasn't what Link needed; I was sure he'd received plenty of that from everyone else. No, I couldn't just offer my condolences. Link was in need of something constructive, something he could grab onto to pull himself out of the mire in which he was wallowing. I'd been there many more times than I wanted to recall, and each time something had plucked me out of that hole. What was it? And how could I offer it to Link?

I laid the letter off to one side and went to the bedroom to change my clothes, and I was thinking, *I just want to live in a world where nothing bad happens. Where everyone wears a smile. Where no one dies. I only want the impossible.* I put my dirty clothes in the hamper and turned around, bumping into Jimmy.

"I'd like to offer you a suggestion," he said.

"I'm open to that."

"How about havin' a picnic tonight?"

I frowned. "Have you been into the goof juice?"

"We're fresh out. But I think the boys would *like* it as much as you *need* it."

"Jimmy, it's still freezing outside, and the boys are going to be tired when they come in. How long have they been out there shoveling?"

"They've been out there 'bout an hour, but as for how long they've been shovelin', that's a different matter. I'm not talkin' 'bout an outdoor picnic; I'm talkin' 'bout an indoor one."

The light began to dawn in my head, and I smiled. "Good idea. I'll put together some sandwiches, and we can spread a blanket on the floor in front of the television set and…"

"No television. This is gonna have to be just like an outdoor picnic."

"…but without bugs!" I said. I was already feeling better, heading for the refrigerator and thinking about what to have for dessert.

"Oh, yeah," Jimmy said, "on my way home from work, I picked up some of those little paper cups of ice cream that you eat with a wooden spoon. The ones from the Brimley State Park store. Thought that'd be fun."

How did he know what I was thinking?

It took me two days to respond to Link's letter. I could only hope it would work some magic on him and make him feel less alone. I made it a point to tell him, at least in my case, I'd learned that time had been my friend. "When Old Man Death reared his ugly head, time allowed me to overcome the deepest grief and eventually accept it—not like it—but function in spite of it." I figured if it had been possible for me to come to grips with Papa's death, then it had to be possible for someone with as strong a constitution as I knew Link possessed.

❖❖❖

We were well into May when Dr. Napoleon said to me, "You need a vacation."

"What?"

"You heard me. You need some time off. Not for hospitals and rehabs and burials and what not. You need to go enjoy yourself for no reason other than just because."

"John, I've taken so much time off in the past couple of years, I almost feel like I'm a stranger here. Besides, Aune's been filling in for me WAY more than I've been able to repay."

"It's his idea."

I looked at him like he was crazy.

"I swear it. He said to me just the other day, 'That woman is working on borrowed time. She's gonna blow a gasket one of these days.' I kid you not, he said those exact words."

"Blow a gasket?"

"Yep. That's what he said. I just thought I'd let you in on it before he demands that you take time off for some fun."

I was stunned. I hadn't really communicated much with John,

not because I didn't want to, but because he worked in the office all the time while I was out seeing to farm calls.

I couldn't help but wonder what I'd done to make Aune think I needed time off. And how bad it could have been for him to talk to John about it before coming to me directly. I decided to take the bull by the horns, so I went to Aune the next morning while we were all having our first cup of coffee of the day. "Aune, I'd like to take some time off to regroup. I know I've had a lot of time off in the recent past, but not one day of it was for relaxation. I need to get my mind off everything. I've been dealing with…with…*stuff* for the past year or so, and I desperately need some rest. And Lloyd is going to be sixteen this year, so he's not going to be interested in taking a vacation with his parents for many more years."

He blinked a couple of times, then he rubbed his chin, then he smiled. But before he answered me, he put on a solemn face. "Well, you'd be missed. But I guess you might be right about having one helluva year or more. You probably deserve to get everything off your mind except for some pleasure. I suppose we could arrange it."

The proverbial door was open, and I was gonna walk in. "Don't get me wrong. I'll understand if you don't want me to take the time. I know how busy it is around here, and I know you'll get the brunt of it by me not being here. You'll have to cover for me. So just think it over, then give me a yay or a nay. If you're agreeable to it, however, I'd like to be assured I'll have a job when I get back."

His shoulders drooped, and he rolled his eyes. "Helmi, you do more in the time you're here than I can accomplish in two days. I wouldn't think of giving your job to someone else, not that anyone else would want it. I don't know how you handle it and a family, too." He shook his head. "Now go on and check that stallion of Red Nicolet's. Sounds like it has choke. You can get back with me when you have some dates picked out." He refilled his coffee cup and disappeared.

I looked over at John, who had been feigning the study of some animal's chart. But his eyes followed Aune out of the room. Then he looked up at me, grinned, and quietly said, "Well played!"

On July twentieth, the Butcher family took off for Copper Harbor. We stayed at Munising the first night and went on the Pictured Rocks boat tour the following day. The next morning we got up early and went to Houghton and Hancock where we were able to see an actual working copper mine. We finally made it up to Copper Harbor; the temperature was only forty-six degrees the night we arrived, and the following morning, it was in the mid-thirties.

"I can't believe there's really a place in this state that's colder than Brimley is in July," Helmi said.

We stayed at a lodge just a few miles south of the actual town of Copper Harbor. It was decorated with old-style furnishings; the place looked like it had been dropped right out of the early nineteen hundreds. Lloyd and Craig thought it was funny that their parents knew what most of the items on display had been used for.

"Let's play a game," Jimmy said. "You ask us what somethin' did or what it was used for, and if we can't tell ya, we'll give ya a dime."

"Yeah!" Craig said.

"Wait a minute," Lloyd said. "How are we gonna know you're tellin' us the truth? You could just make somethin' up, and we wouldn't know the difference."

"Are you insinuatin' that we'd lie to ya?" Jimmy asked.

I decided to stay out of their conversation.

"It's just that...well," Lloyd skirted around the question. "If we don't believe you, can we ask someone who works here?"

"Of course. But don't bank on the fact that they'll know. Most of 'em don't look much older'n you," Jimmy said, looking around. "I'll bet most of the workers are college kids doin' this for a summer job so they can earn some spendin' money."

I looked around, too, and I think Jimmy was probably right. I knew that a lot of college students worked on Mackinac Island during the summer months for just that reason, so why wouldn't the kids up here do the same at a place closer to home?

Craig grabbed his brother's arm and hung from it. "Come on, Lloyd. Let's play. I bet we can get rich 'cause Mom and Dad aren't gonna know what *everything* is. Please? I want some dimes."

I decided to interject my opinion regarding the game. "You have to take turns. You can only pick out one item at a time."

"Me first! Me first!" Craig said, jumping up and down.

We played the game for about five minutes before both boys became bored...they were losing. When the game ended, neither one had earned a single cent, but Jimmy said, "Well, ya tried pretty hard to stump us, so how 'bout I give each of you a dollar? You can spend it on whatever ya want."

"You mean really GIVE us each a dollar?" Craig asked.

"We don't have to earn it by doin' somethin'?" Lloyd asked, stunned.

"Are ya deaf? That's what I said," Jimmy told them. He reached into his back pocket and pulled out his billfold. He opened it up and said, "Aw, shucks, guys. Looks like I ran out of money."

"Da-ad!" they both said.

Jimmy and I both laughed, and Jimmy handed them their dollar each. "Now be careful what you choose. Don't waste your money on some little trinket that you'll play with for ten minutes and then abandon for the rest of your life. Spend it on somethin' that…"

I put my hand on Jimmy's arm, and he stopped mid-sentence. I looked at the boys and said, "You can get whatever you want—that was the deal, right Dad?"

Jimmy smiled and said, "Your mom's right. Get whatever you want." But he couldn't leave well enough alone. "It just has to be somethin' you can keep. You can't buy ice cream."

"I think that's fair. Whadda ya say, guys?" I asked.

"Yeah, I think that's good," Lloyd admitted. "When we want ice cream, you'll buy it for us anyway, 'cause you'll want some, too!" He giggled.

We went into town the following morning and looked around in some of the souvenir shops. There was one shop where a real Indian was on site, making things out of birch bark, and not just little canoes or other things we had seen back in the Soo. He was crafting baskets and furniture and other items that were beautiful…and very expensive.

Then we drove up to Brockway Mountain. The road was treacherous in places, dropping off at a nearly straight-down angle at some of the turns. The good thing about it was, there was one road going up, and another coming down, so we never had to worry about meeting any oncoming traffic. The view was amazing when we reached the top.

Everyone in Copper Harbor had told us to be sure and go up there for the sunset. We reached the summit just before the sun disappeared below the horizon. I can honestly say I had never before nor ever since seen any sunset to compare with that one. And as soon as the light disappeared, the temperature dropped at least ten degrees.

The next morning I awakened before anyone else. The room was exceptionally light, even with the curtains pulled shut. I opened one a little bit and was rewarded with the brightest sunshine I'd seen in what seemed like ages. I sat down facing the window, closed my eyes, and soaked up its warm, therapeutic rays.

As with all good things, our vacation came to an end way too soon. But the away time had served its purpose, and I felt much more at ease when I returned to work. I actually looked forward to each day and what it held…a fact that probably surprised me more than anyone else. I was enjoying not only the work associated with my job, but I was eager to communicate with the clients who were in need of my knowledge.

I surprised a man whose horse was down and wouldn't get back up. I explained that we needed to move it enough for it be able to see the horizon. For some reason, a horse will stay down if there are trees or buildings or other things in the way. We rolled the mare onto a tarp and spun her around so she could see the sun coming up, and the next day she was wandering around the pasture as if nothing had ever happened.

I was called to Ben Martin's house by his mother. One of her goats was acting funny. I did a quick examination and told her it had polio. She had no idea that polio is a somewhat common malady in goats. I couldn't promise that the poor creature would come out of it, but Mrs. Martin was willing to do her best to treat it. Luckily, we had caught the polio early enough that the goat turned around and was back to normal within a few weeks. In addition, we had a good time discussing Ben's current situation.

Of course, some of the problems weren't so easily solved, nor was the outcome what we hoped for. I saw a batch of newborn calves so badly infested with worms that I wasn't the least bit optimistic about their survival. Several of them ended up dying even though the owner treated them extensively with de-wormers. That was a case of too little too late.

But the most heart-wrenching case was a donkey named Bullet that Mason Pomranky had obtained for his seven-year-old daughter. The family also owned a horse that was nearly thirty years old, and they counted on the donkey taking the horse's place when it died. Mr. Pomranky was unaware that donkeys form strong bonds with other animals, especially horses. I did my best to inform him of that fact, urging him and his daughter to provide Bullet with the necessary socialization he would require when the horse was no longer around.

Donkeys exhibit a lot of character. They can be fun for children to ride and play with, but their demeanor requires lots of tolerance, meaning that they're not as easy to train as horses, and they require a lot more attention physically, mentally, and socially than a horse normally requires.

Bullet was a jack (a male). The original owner had not castrated him, and the new owner was not well informed regarding the care of the animal. As a result, Bullet became overly aggressive toward the young girl, kicking and biting at her, and she abandoned him. At about the same time, the horse, who had been Bullet's constant companion for more than a year, died, leaving Bullet alone in the small pasture. He became lethargic, lame, anorexic, and given to coughing. But everyone in the family ignored the symptoms, thinking that was simply how a normal donkey acted.

Because donkeys are much less prone to showing fear than horses, their lack of fear is often mistaken for stubbornness. In Bullet's case, his emotional instability, along with what the Pomrankys perceived as stubbornness, led to him eventually being completely ignored by the man and his daughter. Poor Bullet needed much more attention than he was getting. He needed to be castrated, his hooves were in terrible shape due to laminitis, he was showing signs of respiratory disease, and I wasn't at all sure he didn't suffer from hyperlipemia, a disease of the liver.

At any rate, he was in terrible condition when I first saw him. I had never treated a donkey for so many problems at once, so I took some blood and a fecal sample back to the clinic to check for internal parasites and other obvious disorders. I wanted to talk to Aune before I did anything in the way of treatment.

I did, however, discuss with Mr. Pomranky the necessity of Bullet needing immediate attention to his hooves. "I'm not a farrier," I told him, "but I can give you the name of one who works all over the eastern U.P. He's well acquainted with the hoof work necessary for donkeys, as their feet are much different from those of horses."

But Mason Pomranky made it quite clear to me that he was unwilling to spend much money on the beast, and unfortunately, before Aune and I could put together a medicine regimen based on the results of the blood work, Bullet died.

Mason Pomranky called our office and insisted that he talk to the senior veterinarian on staff, not, as he put it, "that woman who calls herself a doctor and who allowed my animal to die while she did a bunch of unnecessary tests."

Thank goodness Aune had worked with me on the case, so he was aware of the multiple problems that existed. However, nothing Aune said could placate the pompous, irate man. We could all hear Pomranky shouting on the other end of the line, as Aune was holding the phone several inches away from his ear.

"You're a fool for hiring someone who knows so little about being a vet. No woman is capable of learning what needs to be known about the care of farm animals. She should be in the kitchen where she belongs. And I will see to it that your business is closed unless you find someone who is more educated and can tell me what's wrong with my animals before they die. I'm up for election to the county board of directors next month, and I can promise you that when I take my seat on the board, you'll be out of business before the blink of an eye if you continue to allow her to work for you."

Aune calmly put the receiver to his mouth and quietly said,

"Well, Mr. Pomranky, I think I should point out that you have succeeded in alienating me and my staff, so you can be certain you have lost our votes, and we will be certain to spread the word that you are not a fit candidate to be running for office. Good day." And Aune hung up.

"Holy whah!" I said.

"Holy double whah," Shirley said.

John was doubled over laughing, and Billie was standing there with her mouth gaping open.

Aune stood up and said in his best U.P. accent, "And dat dere's how ya handle irate politicians in de U.P, doncha know, eh?" And with that, he took a bow.

We all applauded. We never heard from Mason Pomranky again, and when the election results were posted in the newspaper, we saw that he had received less than one percent of the votes in the county—eleven to be exact.

A CHRISTMAS STAR

Lloyd turned sixteen on December 13, 1959, and three days after his birthday Jimmy took him to get his learner's permit so he could drive—legally. Of course, Jimmy had been letting Lloyd drive the backwoods two-tracks since he could reach the pedals and see over the steering wheel (or through it). In typical Lloyd fashion, he had been studying the driver's manual for a month, so he knew he'd pass the written test without a hitch. He also knew he was not permitted to drive without a licensed driver in the vehicle with him, a point which we reiterated quite often.

When they got home, Lloyd came galumphing into the house, waving his permit over his head. He had taken a growth spurt between August and December. He was now at eye level with Jimmy. His feet had grown three sizes! Every step he took was accentuated, as he hadn't learned to place his feet quietly on any surface. But then, I'd never had to learn that trick, so maybe it was an impossibility for a boy with feet his size. His arms and legs had extended, too, but he hadn't gained more than about ten or twelve pounds, so he was decidedly gangly.

"Mom! I got it! Mom!"

I was coming out of the living room and he was dead set on a course into the living room; we collided under the archway. "Geez, Lloyd! Slow down!" I said.

"He wasn't running," Jimmy said. "That's just his normal gait." He was grinning.

"Well, normal gait or not, he's gonna have to learn to take it easy."

"He's excited, Helmi."

"I know." I rearranged myself and said to Lloyd, "Let me see." I reached for the permit, but he held it just out of my reach.

"You're gonna give it back, right?" he asked.

I emitted an exasperated sigh and said, "Of course. I just want to see it. I never saw one before."

"You mean you never had one? How'd you get to drive?"

"I had a special license for people who had to drive when they were fourteen because there weren't any adults around to do it."

"Wait a minute," Lloyd said. "You mean I could have had a license at fourteen instead of waiting till now?"

"No, Lloyd," Jimmy said. He reached up and snatched the permit out of Lloyd's hand and gave it to me. "You don't live on a farm."

"Yeah, but..."

"Water under the bridge," I said.

Lloyd looked down at his feet. "I didn't miss any on the test."

"I knew you wouldn't. You're a good student when you put your mind to it." I handed the permit back to him.

He stood there looking at it, admiring it. "When can I get a truck?"

"Let's not put the cart before the horse," Jimmy said.

"What's that supposed to mean?" Lloyd asked.

I rolled my eyes, and Jimmy just stared at Lloyd.

"Really, what's it mean?" he asked Jimmy.

"Look it up," Jimmy said and sat down to watch the noonday news on television.

Lloyd shrugged and went through the room toward his and Craig's bedroom. He stopped and turned back to us. "How much longer do I have to stay in the same room as Craig?"

I hadn't thought about it. I looked at Jimmy, but he was staring at the television, oblivious to what else was going on around him.

I made an executive decision. "I think we could make arrangements for you to have your own room. We'll just have to clear the stuff out of the spare room. With your help, of course."

"Gee, thanks Mom!" He was grinning from ear to ear.

I think I really surprised him by agreeing so readily. He and Craig had shared a room since 1952. But the way I looked at it, a sixteen-year-old and a nine-year-old shouldn't spend too much time together. A sixteen-year-old needs his own space to do his own things, and that doesn't include babysitting his little brother. On the flipside of the coin, a nine-year-old shouldn't have to put up with the verbal and mental abuse an older brother is capable of inflicting.

"Tomorrow?" Lloyd asked.

I thought for a moment about what was going on tomorrow. I wasn't on call, so I figured it would be a good time for him to make the move. "Tomorrow after I get home from work. We'll start, but I don't know if we'll be able to finish moving everything in one night."

"That's okay. I'll start organizin' my stuff tonight and finish when I get home from school tomorrow." He smiled at me, and I knew it meant "You're a great mom." At least that's what I told myself it meant.

"That was easy," Jimmy said from his position on the sofa.

"I didn't know you were listening. It looked to me like you were zoned in on the news."

"I can do two things at once."

"Since when?" I teased.

"Since I could concentrate on milkin' the cows at your farm and watch every move your cute little behind made at the same time." He didn't look up at me. He just kept his eyes on the television and grinned.

Craig appeared and asked, "Why does Lloyd get a new room?"

"Because he's older than you," Jimmy said, still not looking up.

Craig turned and left.

"Talk about easy," I said. "How'd you manage to do that without resultant whining?"

"Because I am alpha!" He beat his chest like a gorilla, then he howled like a wolf.

I just shook my head. I was beginning to think there was way too much testosterone in that house.

The phone rang, and it was Retta asking if she could join us for Christmas.

"Oh, please, please do," I begged.

"Sounds like you need some female companionship," she said.

"You couldn't be more right."

"How about if I bring someone along who'd like to see you?"

"Who?"

"Anna."

"I'd love to see her, too! Can she make the trip?" I asked.

"She'll do it if it kills her," Retta said. "She's been to see some specialists about having surgery to correct her ky… ky…"

"…kyphosis."

"That's it!" Retta said. "She'd like to talk to you about it, but she doesn't want to do it over the phone. She wants to talk to you in person."

"I don't know a lot about it, but I'll do some research so I can be more prepared to talk to her about the current methods of correction."

"We'd like to come up a few days before Christmas. We understand that you and Jimmy will be working, so we'd like to stay at a nearby hotel."

"You'll do no such thing!" I told her. "You'll stay here, or I won't let you come up at all."

"I knew you'd say that. The problem is, Anna needs to sleep by herself; we can't share a bed."

"Can you stand sleeping on a cot for a few nights?"

"I can sleep on the floor if need be," Retta said. "I just want to see you guys, and I want Anna to be able to talk to someone she trusts. She's unsure about whether she should undergo the surgery they're talking about."

"Has she actually talked to surgeons who do that kind of surgery?" I asked.

"No. Not yet. The doctors that she's seen so far want her to go to the Mayo Clinic in Minnesota and talk to the surgeons there."

"Have any of her doctors suggested U. of M.? It's a whole lot closer."

"I don't think so. All she's talked to me about is Mayo."

"Okay. Like I said, I'll do some research and see what I can find. One way or another, we'll get her standing upright. I'm so glad she finally decided to do something about it."

"I guess it hasn't been the deciding as much as having the money to do it," Retta said.

"Where's the money coming from?"

"Some group that Bella heard about. We'll tell you more when we come."

We set the dates, and in only a couple of days we were going to have house guests. Then it dawned on me what I'd just done. I went to Lloyd and Craig's room, knocked, and opened the door. Lloyd was lying on his back holding his new learner's permit over his head and staring at it. Craig was on the floor playing with something I didn't recognize. I asked him, "What is that?"

He didn't look up, he simply said, "My rock collection."

I looked a little closer and saw that he had five rocks lying in a line, and he was holding a couple of others. "Have you ever looked them up in a book to see what they are?"

"Nope."

"Do you even care what kind they are?"

"Not really. I just like them because of their colors."

I abandoned that conversation and said, "I have some good news and some bad news. Which do you want to hear first?"

Lloyd said, "Bad," and Craig said, "Good."

I ignored the opposition. "Aunt Retta is coming to visit us for Christmas."

"I hope that's the good news," Lloyd said.

"That's part of the good news," I said.

They both looked at me. "The rest of the good news is that Aunt Anna is coming along, too."

Lloyd sat up. "Is she gonna be able to ride all the way here from Mount Pleasant?"

"Retta says she is. Aunt Anna wants to talk about maybe having surgery on her back."

"Will it make her so she can stand up straight?" Craig asked.

"We hope so. I'm going to the library in the Soo and check out the latest information about it."

"So what's the bad news?" Craig asked, his attention back on the rocks.

"Lloyd's going to have to stay in this room while they're here."

"That's okay," Lloyd said. "I'll still help you clear the stuff out of the spare room. That'll make it easier for me to move in when Aunt Retta and Aunt Anna leave."

For a moment I thought I'd been hit in the face with a baseball bat. I shook my head to bring myself back to reality. "That's really nice of you, Lloyd."

He didn't acknowledge my compliment, he just asked, "Mom, when I move into that room, will I sleep in the double bed, or are you gonna move it in here and move my bed in there?"

"We aren't going to be moving any beds. You'll sleep in the double."

He smiled, and I caught the slightest resemblance to his father's smirk. "Copacetic!"

I went to the library on Saturday morning and found some interesting information about congenital kyphosis, as I knew Anna's condition had been determined to be a problem since birth. None of what I saw, however, was very promising, not because it couldn't fix the problem, but because the current methods to correct it required more than a year of wearing braces following the surgery, along with extensive life-long physical therapy. I was certain that newer methods must be available, but they hadn't been added to the information that was available at the library. Needless to say, I wasn't very enlightened. It appeared that Anna would definitely be making some trips to the Mayo Clinic to learn if her dream of standing up straight would ever come to fruition.

I picked up a couple of books I thought I might like to read. But then I realized I'd be busy throughout the holidays, so I put them back on the shelves and went home. Jimmy and Lloyd had cleaned out the spare room, and Lloyd was vacuuming the floor.

"Holy whah! Would you look at this!" I entered the room, put my arms straight out from my sides, and twirled around like I was on a dance floor. They had stripped the bed and put the sheets in the washer, as well.

"I got the blankets hangin' over the line outside to air 'em out,"

Jimmy said from behind me, shouting so I could hear him over the vacuum.

I twirled my way right up to him and threw my arms around him, kissing him as I stood up on my tiptoes. "You and your son have made my day!" I stepped back to see how clean everything looked. The mirror above the old chest of drawers had been washed, and there was a faint aroma of furniture polish in the air. I ran my finger across the top of the headboard on the bed—it came up without any dust on it.

Jimmy locked his thumbs into make-believe suspenders and said, "I may take my newfound talents on the road. Ya think I could make any money as a maid?"

Before I could answer, Lloyd turned off the vacuum. "Hi, Mom. Should I move my chair into this room so Aunt Anna has a place to sit?"

"I think that's a very smart idea. You can use your bed as a chair for few days, can't you?"

He nodded as he moved past me on his way to retrieve the chair.

I whispered to Jimmy, "What did you use to bribe him with?"

Jimmy turned his head in the direction Lloyd had gone, and when he was sure Lloyd was out of earshot, he whispered back, "It was his idea. Can you believe it?"

Retta and Anna arrived on Sunday evening just before suppertime. It was only the second time Anna had ever been to the U.P. and it was the first time she'd been to this house. She wanted to see our view, but because of the snow we'd gotten two days before, we couldn't get out to the waterfront. I started to tell her she'd have to settle for seeing it through the windows from inside the house, but I caught myself before actually saying it; she'd never be able to get her head up high enough to see the water from there.

"How'd you like the bridge?" I asked. The Mackinac Bridge had beenbuilt between May, 1954, and November, 1957, which eliminated the need for car ferry service across the straits, and most people were happy about it.

"Better than the ferry," Anna said. "No waiting in those awful lines."

"I agree," Retta said.

"Us, too," I added. "But I think Craig's a little disappointed that he doesn't get a toy each time we cross the straits now." I looked over at him, and he blushed. "Of course, he's getting too old for that now anyway." I rolled my eyes at Retta.

"You haven't decorated for Christmas yet?" Retta asked.

"We decided to wait for you." That wasn't really the truth; we just hadn't had time to get that done with everything else we'd been doing, and I'd been on call every night but two and both weekends for the last two weeks.

"Let's get supper on the table. I'm starving," Retta said.

"If you put all the dishes and silverware in a pile on the table, I'll set it," Anna said.

I had forgotten how upbeat Anna always was.

"You two just finished a long drive. Why don't you go sit down in the living room and…

"We've been sitting for the past six hours. We're ready to do something that requires standing," Anna said.

"Hey! Speak for yourself!" Retta teased.

"I'm gonna ignore you," I said to Retta. "The tableware and glasses are in the cupboard closest to the archway. There are napkins in the pantry, and the silverware's in that last drawer on the left."

The phone rang.

"I'll get it," Lloyd shouted.

I heard a muffled "Hullo?" then silence. He came into the kitchen and looked at me. "It's for you."

I closed my eyes for a moment, took a deep breath, then went to the phone. "This is Dr. Butcher."

"Helmi, it's Link."

"Oh my gosh! Hi! How are you?"

"I'm pleased to say that I'm actually pretty good, thanks to your wise words about letting time work its magic."

"I'm so glad I was able to help."

"I'm calling because I'd like to come up there and see where you do whatever it is that you do in the U.P. of Michigan. I'll be teaching my last class at OSU right after the next graduation ceremony. I'll be a free man from then on, and I was hoping we could find a time when I can come up and visit. I'd like to see Jimmy again, and I've never met your boys. Two, aren't there?"

"Yes, Lloyd and Craig."

"I've gotten really bad at remembering names. Thank you for reminding me."

"It's so good to hear your voice. When would you like to come up?"

"Sometime during the summer. I don't want to gamble with the weather."

I sniffed a laugh. "You can't count on that at any point in time up here."

"I'll be perfectly happy to stay in a motel once I get there. I'd like to take my time and see the area, considering that I've never been there before. And I don't want to be a bother."

"You could never be a bother, Link. Let me look at the boys' school calendar and my work schedule, and I'll get back to you soon after Christmas. How's that sound?"

"Sounds like a winner to me. I'm going to be dancing around like a fart in a skillet until I hear from you."

I laughed. "I'll be looking forward to it, too, though my dancing days are over."

He laughed. "Merry Christmas, Helmi."

"You, too, Link." I hung up and just stood there. In only a matter of seconds my mind had conjured up long-lost memories of OSU and Link and Dorothea and her father. They were happy memories, and that's just what I needed to help me through the tough times I'd have to face over the next few days with Anna and her decisions about surgery.

"Who was that?" Jimmy appeared out of nowhere.

"I thought you were outside."

"I was in the shower."

"That's pretty obvious. You smell wonderful, almost edible."

"Geez!" Retta said as she stepped up behind me. "Why is it that I always get in on the mushy stuff?"

"Just good timing, I guess," Jimmy said.

"Where am I gonna be sleeping? I wanna get our stuff out of the car, and I need to know where to deposit everything."

"I can handle that," Jimmy said. "You just stay put in the kitchen with your sisters. And you'll be sleeping in the same room as Anna, but you'll be on the folding cot. Anna gets the bed."

"S'okay with me," Retta said.

"It's the second room on the right down the hall. You'll be across from the bathroom."

"Do I have to share the bathroom with you?" she asked Jimmy.

"Yeah, but we can draw straws to see who gets to use it first. I can't compete with all of you females and the boys, too."

"Don't be giving me that crap!" I said. "I'm always the one who has to juggle the schedule so I can get in there when I need to."

Anna yelled, "Sounds like something's boiling over on the stove!"

"Scheist!" I said. "The potatoes." I went running to the stove and lifted the lid. The boiling water was sloshing over the edges of the pot and making spitting noises on the burner. I was able to get to the control to turn it down, but when I moved the pot off the burner, I got splashed. I let out a yip.

"You okay?" Retta asked.

"I just need to put some ice on it real quick."

Retta went running to the refrigerator, opened the freezer door, and came to me with the ice cube tray.

"Take it over there to the sink." I pointed.

She hurried to the sink, turned on the water, and ran it over the ice cubes. They spilled out into the sink. I grabbed one and held it on my hand, which was already turning red and blistering.

"That looks way too familiar," Retta said.

It took me a couple of beats before I realized she was talking about the burns she'd gotten on her hands when the fire claimed our Mount Pleasant farm.

"Oh my gosh! I'd forgotten about that," I said.

"Wish I could forget it." She held her hands out, and I could see the scars that riddled her fingers and slashed across the backs and palms of both of her hands.

"Not too pretty, huh?"

"Oh, Retta. I never even thought about you having scars like that. I guess I never paid any attention to your hands when we've been together since that day."

"They don't hurt; they just look like Hell."

She had plugged the sink with the sink strainer and had run cold water into it. The ice cubes were floating. "Put your hand in there for a few minutes. It'll make the burn hurt less."

I did what she said, and she was right.

"Do I need to be concerned about what's going on?" Anna asked.

"No," Retta said.

"It's just superficial," I assured her.

"That's good to know," Anna sounded happy with the answer.

"That was a good supper, woman," Jimmy said to me as he pushed himself away from the table.

"Dad," Lloyd said, "you know it's called dinner now, right?"

"My apologies," Jimmy said. "I have mistakenly been callin' it supper since I was born, and I get reprimanded for it every time I slip up."

"Yeah, get with the times, old man," Retta said.

I said, "Well, I don't care what you call it, as long as you think it was good." I pushed myself up and started to gather the dishes.

"No, no," said Anna. "You're a wounded cook. I think the other people at this table should be responsible for cleaning up."

"Really, Anna, it's just a minor bur…"

"I don't care if it's just a passing memory," Retta said. "You aren't doing the dishes. Looks to me like there are five other capable people here who can make light work of all this." She rose from her chair and said, "All right, troops. Let's get this stuff cleaned up."

In no time, the table was clear, the kitchen was spotless, and everyone was in the living room rubbing their bellies.

"Why did I eat that much?" Jimmy asked no one in particular.

"'Cause it was good, Dad," Craig said. He looked over at Retta and said, "Mom doesn't usually cook that good when it's just for us."

"Craig!" Jimmy said.

"It's true," I defended Craig. "They're lucky to get a bologna sandwich some nights."

"Well I, for one, like bologna sandwiches," Anna said. "It's pretty much a staple in our house."

"And speaking of that, how are Bill and Rachel?"

"In a word—old," she said. "I don't know how much longer Rachel's gonna be able to tend to Bill and me and herself, too. It worries me."

"Is that why you want to get your back taken care of?" I asked.

"That's one of the reasons. I just feel like it's time. I've heard some good things about new surgical methods, and I feel like I owe it to everyone to pay back anything I can for all the care you've given me over the years."

"You owe us nothing," Retta said. "This has to be for you, or it isn't gonna be at all."

We all agreed.

Jimmy said, "Let's get a good night's sleep 'fore we talk about this any farther. That discussion could go on for hours, and with tomorrow bein' Monday, Helmi and I have to go to work. Whadda ya say we table it till tomorrow afternoon?"

"Okay by me," Anna said.

"Me too," Retta said.

"Me three," Lloyd added.

"Me four," Craig piped up.

"How 'bout we just watch Ed Sullivan and let our food settle. I hope the channel comes in tonight," Jimmy said.

We watched Ed introduce Johnny Cash, Wayne and Shuster, Shelley Winters, and a group of bell-ringing musicians called The Bizarro Brothers, along with some new talents only Lloyd and Craig were familiar with. When it was over, I excused myself so I could get into the bathroom first!

❖❖❖

With only a week left before Christmas, we needed to get a tree. So Monday afternoon when Jimmy got home, he and the boys and Retta went looking for a nice one. There were plenty of pine trees on our extra property between the house and the main road, and one of them was bound to make a nice Christmas tree.

I wouldn't be getting home till after six o'clock, so dinner was going to be a little less spectacular than the night before; I was planning to fry up some hamburgers and warm up a couple of boxes of frozen peas. But when I got home, I discovered that Retta had made a meatloaf out of the hamburger I'd thawed, and she had baked it with little potatoes and carrots all around it. She was just finishing a big bowl of tossed salad with vinegar and oil dressing and homemade croutons when I walked in the door.

"When did you learn to cook?" I asked her.

"I like it. Didn't know it until about two years ago."

"WOW!" I said. "How long can you stay?"

The meal was excellent, and not just because I didn't have to cook it. I'd had a somewhat tough day, and I was on call for that night. So Retta's little surprise was more than appreciated.

After supper we discussed Anna's plans to go to the Mayo Clinic. She knew a whole lot more about what to expect than I was able to find in the library, so I really wasn't much help when it came to making suggestions. Truth be known, I think Anna really only needed me to give her the go-ahead. She probably just wanted to hear someone say, "Do it!"

The next night we got out the Christmas tree decorations, and before long, it was lit and making the house look festive. The boys did most of the decorating, and Lloyd got to put the star on the top.

I recognized that star from my childhood. "Where did that star come from?" I asked. I turned to Retta. "Is that the one we used on the top of the tree when we were growing up?"

She sighed. "No. It's just like it, though. I was at an antique store in Frankfort and just happened to see it. I recognized it, too, and decided to bring it here for Christmas."

"What a wonderful gift!" I said. "Papa always put it on the treetop because he was the only one tall enough to do it without standing on a chair. And now we have Lloyd to do it."

Of course, Lloyd had never known his grandpa, and Anna was too young to remember much about Papa, so it didn't mean a lot to them. But to the rest of us, Christmas was going to be extra special that year each time we looked up at the star on the top of that tree.

"YOU CAN HANDLE THIS"

Link came to visit in late June. "I come bearing gifts!" he said as he came through the door. "Well, gift." He was carrying a beautifully decorated cake that said: GO BUCKEYES! He laughed. "You should have seen the looks I got when I asked the woman at the bakery in St. Ignace to write that on there."

It had taken him two days to get to our place; he had stopped in Ann Arbor to visit the University of Michigan campus. "Never hurts to check out the competition," he said. Then he proceeded to Grayling, where he stayed all night. He went to Hartwick Pines State Park first thing in the morning. It is dedicated to a representation of the life of Michigan's lumberjacks. The displays include a bunkhouse, the dining hall, the camp store, and much of the equipment that had been used to cut and haul the white pine that grew so abundantly in Michigan. The state had yielded so much, in fact, that the harvested trees could have covered the entire United States with a one-inch-thick white pine floor!

But he hadn't liked crossing the bridge. "I was more scared of that than when I proposed to Dorothea," he said.

"Yeah, the height can be a bit intimidatin'," Jimmy told him. "But at least ya didn't have to take a ferry."

"I might have been less afraid of that."

I said, "Not when you get out into the middle of the straits and can't see land anywhere around you because of the rain or snow or fog. And it seems like it's always windy in the straits."

We had a good time taking him to some of the typical tourist haunts. He appeared to enjoy them immensely, especially the Iroquois Point Lighthouse, which was only six miles west of our home. That was the first one he'd ever seen up close. "I never thought about living someplace where a lighthouse was so close. I guess I always pictured them out on some desolate point of land, miles from civilization."

"Most of them used to be; civilization has slowly crept up on them. But you can still find a few that are way off the beaten track," I told him.

I took him to work with me one day in order to show him what and who I worked with. He said, "You've got a great facility for what your practice is set up for." That made me feel good, and I know Aune was as pleased as punch to hear it.

When it was time for Link to head back to Columbus, however, he got a little bit choked up. "I wish Dorothea could have seen this, too. I think she'd have liked it. I couldn't imagine why you'd want to live here," he said, "until I got here and saw how beautiful it is…when the sun shines."

We had stepped out onto the backdoor stoop to see Link off when he said, "I've been doing a lot of traveling lately. I've decided not to stay in Columbus. I want to live somewhere new." He nervously played with the zipper on this jacket. "I thought about maybe changing climates—either to someplace much warmer or much colder, and now that I've been here, I can honestly say it appeals to me. Who knows… you may have a new neighbor within the next few months." Then he thanked us and went to his car. He honked as he drove away.

"That's one lonely man," Jimmy said.

I didn't know what to say. I just stared at the back of Link's car as it disappeared.

"No comment?" Jimmy asked.

I hung my head. I was afraid I'd cry if I spoke.

Jimmy put his arm around me and said, "C'mon. Let's go in and finish up that cake he brought us."

❖❖❖

The next few years passed by quickly. Anna had her surgery at the Mayo Clinic; she struggled with the recuperation period, but she managed to stand nearly straight up and see things from a different perspective for the first time in her life. On the downside, she was in constant pain and had to take pain relievers several times every day. She hated the way they made her feel. But in typical Anna fashion, she said, "I made the choice to trade one thing for another, and even though I'm not happy with my mental state, I'm thrilled beyond belief that I finally get to see things the way everyone else does."

Bill and Rachel Neidhart had both died within two weeks of one another shortly before Anna's surgery. It was unfortunate that very few people could be there when they were buried. Jimmy and I and Mary were the only ones who traveled any distance to be with Anna for the burial. The only others in attendance were a few people from the church Bill and Rachel had attended for so many years. Mary had made it clear to Anna that she would like to help her after the surgery and insisted that Anna live in the guest house behind Mary's home in Flint, which Anna proceeded to make her permanent home. I think she and Mary truly enjoyed each other's company.

Jimmy continued his job at the Pickford dairy farm, even when the owner died and the farm traded hands. He never griped about getting up and going to work. In November of 1961 he went deer hunting for the first time since the accident. But he didn't travel very far to do it; he joined a friend of his in Rudyard and shot a deer from a blind that sat in the back of one of the man's fields. When Jimmy came home that day, he was ecstatic. "One shot, Helmi! One shot! I thought maybe I'd forgotten how to shoot, but it came back to me like I'd just done it yesterday." It was a nice buck, too, and once again, we had venison in the freezer.

Lloyd graduated from high school in 1962. He went through the military conscription process, but he was exempt from serving because of his feet, which were enormous and had lots of problems. They were not fit to become those of a military man. Jokingly, of course, Jimmy told him it was really because the military didn't have shoes big enough to fit him. Lloyd made regular visits to a podiatrist in Petoskey who told him he might one day need to have surgery to remove some of the growths that had appeared on his feet.

Following graduation, Lloyd wasted no time before moving downstate to Owosso where he worked to get his license as a train engineer. He drove trains on a short-line railway that passed through Owosso, and his best friend was the dispatcher at that station. The man was twice Lloyd's age, but that didn't seem to matter to Lloyd. As far as he was concerned, anyone who had railroading experience was among the best people on earth. The man's name was Arturo, a Belgian gentleman who had been responsible for engineering some of the trains that were forced to carry deported Jews to the concentration camps in Germany during World War II. Oh, the stories he told! Lloyd, of course, repeated every one of them to Jimmy and me when we talked on the phone.

Craig was every bit as handsome as his father had been at that age, though his coloring was light, like mine, as opposed to his father's dark hair and eyes. The boy practically had to fight the girls off, though I'm afraid he didn't always try too hard. We warned him about the possible outcomes of his "extracurricular activities."

He developed into quite an athlete and became the quarterback for the Brimley football team in his junior and senior years of high school. Unfortunately, there weren't enough boys in the school to have an offensive team and a defensive team; all the players had to cover both, and as a result, their record was pretty bad. But Craig didn't seem to care; he merely enjoyed "the thrill of the game," as he called it. He registered with the United States Coast Guard when he turned seventeen, planning to become an active recruit after his graduation in 1968.

It was evident that Craig and I shared some of the same genes, because I, too, was perfectly happy with what I did, no matter what the conditions. It didn't matter to me if the weather was frigid or sweltering, the days long or short, or the cases difficult or easy. I loved my life doing veterinary work. I loved the animals, I loved the staff at the clinic, and I loved most of my clients (the ones I didn't love so much, I took with a grain of salt).

Retta's pet store boomed, and she opened another one on the outskirts of Traverse City. She was turning out to be not only an entrepreneur extraordinaire, but also a well-liked employer. Nearly everyone who worked for her stayed at the job; she had a very low employee turnover rate. And she decided to sell puppies and kittens, but she made sure she knew each of the breeders; she refused to buy animals from puppy or kitten mills. Her tenacity paid off, and the satellite store moved into downtown Traverse City where she made money hand-over-fist, always passing along the profits to her employees. Smart woman!

Bella had become the person in charge of nursing at the children's hospital in Chicago. She did very little hands-on work with the patients, but she visited every one of them during their stay and appeared to be well liked by all of her coworkers. We kept in touch, but the closeness I had with my other sisters was just not there with Bella.

Dora continued her career as an artist. She had ventured away from portraiture and into a branch of modern art that was completely foreign to Jimmy and me. She was obsessed with color. Though we didn't understand the paintings she produced, art aficionados obviously did, because she was selling her work right and left. When I asked her about Stephen Spicer, she said, "He's strictly small potatoes." I hoped her jump from anonymity to stardom in the art sector didn't come to a crashing halt with the next change that became popular. The woman she lived with, Trina McAlister, had become her lover. Dora informed us she had realized she was decidedly gay. I worried about her all the time.

❖❖❖

In the midst of football season during Craig's senior year at Brimley High, he came to Jimmy and me and said, "I need to talk to you about a job. I gotta make a big decision, and I'd like to get some input from you guys."

"Ya think we're smart enough to help ya out?" Jimmy asked.

Craig gave him a look that must have sent the message, *Can you be any more annoying?*

"How 'bout tonight after supper?" Jimmy asked.

"K," Craig answered and loped off. He'd grown almost as tall as Lloyd, though *his* growth spurts had happened in small sequences.

Following our dinner of chicken patty sandwiches and lima beans, we cleared the table and got down to business.

"So what's up?" Jimmy asked.

Craig shifted in his chair and looked down at the placemat. He began rolling up the edges of it from both sides, then unrolling it. I knew something big was about to come out of his mouth. "Amanda's pregnant, and she says it's mine." Amanda had been his most recent girlfriend, though he didn't appear to be enraptured by her.

Jimmy just sat there, looking at him. I knew he was gritting his teeth, because I could see the tendons in his jaws moving in and out.

"You figured out a way to take care of it?" he asked Craig.

"That's what I want to talk to you about," Craig answered.

"Is she important enough to ya that ya wanna stick with her?" Jimmy asked.

Craig sighed and looked away. "Not really."

"So you're sayin' you aren't gonna marry her. Are you plannin' on supportin' her and the baby when it's born?"

Craig said, still not looking at either of us, "I wanna take care of things like helpin' out with all the hospital bills and stuff even before the baby comes, like doctor's office bills and...what am I gonna do 'bout all of that?"

Up to that point I had remained silent. I reached over and pulled the placemat away from him, and he looked up at me. His eyes filled with tears.

"You know your dad and I will stand behind whatever decision you make," I said, and I reached over and put my hand on Jimmy's arm, but he pulled it away. His face was getting redder by the second. I was afraid he was going to explode.

"Look," Craig said. "I know I messed up." He ran his hand through his thick light brown hair and sat back in the chair, closing his eyes. A single tear drifted down his left cheek. He wiped at it with a vengeance. In a voice that was barely audible he said, "I just don't know what to do."

"Welcome to the real world, son," Jimmy said.

"Let's take this one step at a time," I said. "When's the baby due?"

"I think somewhere around March or April."

I swallowed the lump that had been building up in my throat. *Stay calm. You're the adult here. Show him how much you love him. Don't make things any harder for him than they are right now.* I looked over at Jimmy. He must have been thinking something along the same lines, because what could have developed into full-fledged rage seemed to have disappeared from his face.

Jimmy asked, "The job you get isn't somethin' you want to do for the rest of your life, right?"

"Right. I just need to do somethin' to make some money before I leave for the Coast Guard."

Jimmy sat there, eyes diverted toward the other end of the room, just like Papa used to do when he was preparing to say something important. Eventually Jimmy turned to Craig, took a deep breath, and gradually blew it out between puckered lips. "The sooner the better. The thing I can tell you without a doubt is that it isn't gonna get any better between you and Amanda before she has that baby. So if you want to take care of things, now's the time for you to get started. Don't wait. I understand that you'll be startin' at minimum wage, but that'll grow if you show your boss you're worth what the company's willin' to pay to keep you, which means you'll be makin' better money by the time the baby's born."

Craig nodded. "Make's sense, and that's pretty much what I was thinkin', too."

"Here's where the hard part comes in," Jimmy said. "You need to go to her parents and tell 'em what your plans are."

Craig sucked in a lungful of air. "But I don't even know if she's told her parents?"

"Then find out," I said. "You aren't alone in this, you know. Amanda's part of it, too. And she can't keep it from them if she's already four months along. Believe me when I tell you things will be much easier if you work together through this."

"Yeah, but Amanda hates me now. I don't think she'll sit still for me to talk to her, and definitely not her parents."

"Make it happen," Jimmy said. "Do whatever you have to to get her to listen to ya. You're a smart kid. You can figure out a way to get her to understand the situation. She won't be able to tell ya 'no' if she understands that you *want* to help. Same way with her parents. They'll have to know, and your mom and I will have to become a part of this, too. We'll have to talk to her parents. You got us tied up in the rope the minute you hung yourself."

The tears flowed from Craig's eyes like a waterfall. "I didn't even think about that," he said, putting his head down on his arm on the table. "How could I have been so stupid?"

"You're not the first and won't be the last kid who ever got in over his head," Jimmy said. He dug his handkerchief out of his pocket and handed it to Craig. "Just like your mom said, we're gonna be here for ya, whatever ya choose to do. We won't abandon ya just because ya messed up."

I said, "You have a lot to think about, more than you ever thought you had before you came to us about this. But at least you can be sure we'll help you through it."

"Thanks, Mom." He blew his nose and handed the handkerchief back to Jimmy.

Jimmy backed away and put both hands up. "I don't want that thing! Ya tryin' to make me to gag?"

That caused a hint of a smile to cross Craig's face.

Jimmy got up out of his chair, went around behind Craig and put him in a headlock. "Crazy kid," he said and did a Dutch rub on Craig's head. "Come to me whenever you need to." Then he left the room.

I looked over at my son, the boy I'd given birth to just as Amanda would be doing one day in the future, and my heart did the funniest thing: it crumpled into a tight little ball and, at the same time, felt like it swelled up several sizes. "You're a Butcher and a Schnier. You have the integrity of both your father and your grandfather. Do what you feel is right, not what you think is easy. You can handle this." I got up from my chair, walked around to him, reached my arms out as if I were going to hug him, and put him in a headlock. He laughed.

Craig followed his dad's advice and got a job working for a local restaurant. He started out doing grunt work part time in the kitchen, not having a lot of hours to invest because of his school work, football practice after school, and the games. But he was so handsome, the owner knew he'd be popular with all the ladies and would probably be a draw for female customers if he waited tables. When the owner asked Craig if he'd like to try his hand at it as soon as football season was over, Craig jumped at the chance, knowing that if he did a good job, he'd get big tips in addition to a waiter's paltry wage.

On March 28 of 1968, Craig became a father, albeit in title only. Amanda had a girl and named her Melissa. Amanda decided to keep the baby, and her mother decided to help her raise it. Craig sent ten percent of his pay to Amanda every week. And he never made that first complaint about doing so.

Jimmy and I went to bed early that night. Jimmy was lying there with his hands behind his head, as usual, staring at the ceiling, and I was finishing up the last of an article I'd been reading in some magazine. I turned out the light and lay down, waiting for Jimmy to start a conversation.

"We're grandparents, ya know," he said quietly.

I smiled, and a little chuckle escaped my lips.

He turned and looked at me.

"I know, it's not really funny. I just can't help but laugh over it all. It was such an ordeal in the beginning, and now it's just kind of passé. I don't feel like a granny."

"Yeah, I understand that. I'm no grampa, either. Ya s'pose we'll ever be *real* grandparents?"

"You mean the kind that babysit all the time and spend all of their money on their grandkids and take them places like Disneyland and…" I stopped.

Jimmy's face was all scrunched up like he'd taken a big bite out of a lemon. "God, I hope not!"

We both burst out laughing, and we heard Craig's voice from across the hall, "Hey! Keep it down in there. I gotta go to school tomorrow!"

Graduation that June was short and sweet, considering Craig's senior class consisted of only twenty-one students. There was no baccalaureate service, just the graduation ceremony that was held on the football field. Craig had insisted that we throw a graduation party. "Everybody's mom and dad are doing it," he had said.

We had a party, but only a few of the graduates and some of our friends were in attendance. Craig and his closest buddies were party hopping from one house to another. Luckily the weather was nice, and the few people who came to our house sat on lawn chairs and enjoyed the view. We had plenty of snacks left over.

Craig was among the newly enlisted personnel who went to Coast Guard recruit training at the CG Training Center in Cape May, New Jersey, for eight weeks. While there, he achieved high scores on his ASVAB tests (Armed Services Vocational Aptitude Battery), allowing him to go directly to an "A" School after graduation from boot camp without having to await orders to attend advanced training. Just like his brother, he was a hard worker, and Jimmy and I were extremely proud of our sons. In addition to Lloyd being a train engineer, Craig ended up becoming an EMT (Emergency Medical Technician).

THE PROFUNDITY OF AGING

In 1969 The Ohio State University Buckeye Football Team was playing Southern California in the Rose Bowl. Jimmy and I invited Link and Retta to come up and watch it with us. Link was now living in Traverse City. I had introduced him to Retta a few months back, and the two of them seemed to hit it off. Of course, Link was many years her senior—as much a father figure as a friend—but it didn't seem to matter to either of them. They enjoyed each other's company.

Link had made the move north, but he said, "I just couldn't settle in the U.P. knowing I'd have to travel the bridge every time I want to visit a big city. So I moved to a big city instead. As long as someone else is driving, it doesn't bother me to cross," so Retta picked him up and brought him along for the game.

"You should have seen him," she teased. "He did the entire five miles with his eyes closed."

"I did not!" he protested. "I opened them long enough to take one look at Mackinac Island."

We all got a good laugh out of that.

OSU won the game 27-16, so we drank a victory toast to the Buckeyes with a bottle of champagne we'd had in the cupboard for several years, probably left over from one of the boys' graduations, and a cake that Link had brought that said, of course, GO BUCKEYES! We talked and laughed and had a really good time, even Link. It appeared that he had overcome his loneliness by making friends with quite a few people in Traverse City. And he had met most of them at the TC Symphony.

"I didn't know you preferred high-class music," Jimmy said.

"I love it...always have. I studied violin when I was young. Played in the high school orchestra and went on to play in a civic orchestra in Columbus."

"Wow!" Retta said. "A musical veterinarian."

"Yeah, but I gave it up for cows, pigs, sheep, and horses," he said.

"But I never stopped going to the symphony. I'm glad there's a pretty good one in TC."

"Did you and Doro…" I stopped short.

"It's okay," Link said. "I can talk about her without having a meltdown. And yes, she loved it as much as I did. We also went to a lot of plays and operas."

"I think I'm out-cultured here," Jimmy said. "Even Helmi can play the piano."

"You don't play any instrument?" Link asked Jimmy.

As seriously as he could, Jimmy nodded and said, "I play the radio."

It was during that same year that I became aware of my past starting to disappear: the last weekly issue of *The Saturday Evening Post* was published in the United States after one-hundred and forty-seven years, Dwight Eisenhower died, and the Beatles did their last public performance. Could I possibly be getting old? I would be fifty in less than a year… nearly half a century had gone by. I didn't feel old; I still felt like I was in my twenties (well, maybe my thirties). On the upside, Neil Armstrong walked on the moon, the first ever heart transplant was performed, and the very first U.S. troops were withdrawn from Vietnam. Life was moving on around me.

I remember asking Jimmy, "Do you ever feel like time's passing and we're not a part of it?"

"I never thought about it like that."

"What do you mean 'like that'?"

"I mean, everybody gets older every day," he said. "And the days turn into years. That's just the way life is, and we're all a part of it. It's been goin' on since humans have inhabited the earth. It's not any different now, and it's not gonna be any different for a looooong time to come. Unless, of course, we blow ourselves up with atomic bombs."

I was dumbfounded. In the first place, I really didn't figure Jimmy ever contemplated such things, so I was surprised by his answer. And secondly, I was taken back by the fact that he so readily accepted that philosophy. "Do you ever wish we could change the passage of time?"

"Nope. It's not somethin' we can do, so I can't see the point of wastin' even a minute thinkin' 'bout it?"

"You're right. I need to think about other, more optimistic things."

"Good girl."

But I couldn't get the whole aging process out of my mind. *My sons are both grown. My attitude changed when I realized they won't be living in our house anymore; I've been less intent on the details of my home life and have put more emphasis on my job. Have I been ig-*

noring Jimmy? I looked over at him, sitting in front of the TV, and suddenly I felt the need to comfort him, nurture him, make him aware of how much I loved him.

I got up from my usual seat at the opposite end of the couch and sat down beside him, snuggling up to him like a puppy would to its mother when it was scared or worried.

"What's this?" he asked.

"I just want to be close."

"Any closer and you'll be on the other side of me."

"I'm sorry if I've ignored you," I said.

I waited for him to reply, but he didn't say anything. It was the first time he'd ever seemed distant to me, and that bothered me. *You're making way too much of this, Helmi,* I told myself. But deep down, I was concerned that our togetherness, even our intimacy, had lost some of its intensity.

At work the next day I recognized that my concentration on the matters at hand was less than it should have been. My mind kept wandering at will. I called my doctor's office and made an appointment to talk to him about what I was experiencing. Maybe there was an actual medical reason for it. I knew that depression often accompanied aging, and I also knew there were medications that could help people get through it.

Four days later I went to the doctor. I hadn't told Jimmy I was going. Our doctor's name was Adam Salisbury, and he was one of the nicest doctors I'd ever had the occasion to meet, next to Doc Weiser, of course, even though I had only been a child when he saw to my medical needs. I still had the highest respect for him because of the way he had cared for my family. Dr. Salisbury reminded me of him, and I felt totally at ease in his company.

After spending nearly a quarter of an hour with me, he announced, "You're in the first stages of menopause."

My face went red, not because of any embarrassment by him speaking my problem aloud, but because I had not even considered it. There I was, a woman in the medical field, and the very fact that I was going through something as common as menopause had never crossed my mind.

"Cheese and crackers," I said.

"What?" he asked.

I shook my head. "Just an expression. I don't know why I failed to think about that," I said. Then I smiled. "You know, I feel better already just knowing it's something natural, normal."

"There is definitely some depression rearing its ugly head," he said. "How about taking a mild antidepressant to help you get through it. It won't be a particularly strong one, just something that will put your serotonin back to where you can handle things. And you might end up needing some HRT."

"Which is…?"

"Hormone replacement therapy. Depends on how rough it becomes for you to get through the whole thing."

I thanked him profusely and left feeling better than I had for several weeks. I knew the medication would be the perfect thing to put me back on track. On the way back to work, I thought, *That was so simple.*

When I told Jimmy what my problem had been recently, he smiled and said, "I kinda thought that might be at the heart of the matter. But it's hard to believe you didn't see it. Actually, it's kinda funny, you bein' a doctor an' all."

"You should have seen my face when Dr. Salisbury told me. I was embarrassed because I hadn't thought of it. And you won't believe what came out of my mouth."

He thought for a moment, then he asked, "Did it have anything to do with cheese and crackers?"

"You never fail to fascinate me," I said, shaking my head.

We both survived the passing of my youth, and in 1976, Craig called to tell me he and Lloyd were going to take a trip to Europe together. Arturo's stories about the Belgian railway system had always fascinated Lloyd, and he thought it would be fun to take the train from Brussels to Antwerp with his brother. They very seldom did anything together, but they called each other at least once a month; I knew that because they called Jimmy and me every couple of weeks and told us about some of their conversations with each other.

Neither of them had married. Lloyd was totally satisfied to drive the trains, and Craig was totally satisfied to "play the field." Neither Jimmy nor I ever felt deprived because we had no grandchildren, though Lloyd and Craig came home every year for Christmas. Our lives were filled with each other and our boys and my sisters and our friends, and we were happy with that.

Jimmy was no longer working at the dairy farm. He had decided he wanted to stay closer to home and was working a couple of days a week at the hardware store in Brimley. He tried to walk to and from the job the first couple of days after he'd been hired, but climbing the hill each morning was more than he could bear. He'd had his prosthesis replaced twice, but even with the newest methods of attaching it, the pressure of walking up that steep grade was more than he could tolerate. He told the doctors, "These new-fangled things are great for kids, but us old-timers just don't have the wherewithal to overcome the pain." As a result, he drove to and from the store, even though it was less than half a mile, and he spent a lot more time inside the house than outside.

I was putting the supper dishes away. "Do you think we need to consider moving to a smaller place?" I asked him. He'd been talking about how much more difficult it had become to do the outdoor things, especially during the winter.

He sighed. "I don't wanna move. I love it here, Helmi. We could probably afford to hire somebody else to do the stuff I can't."

He was truly a man after my own heart. "I think that's about the best idea you've ever had."

"And while we're at it," he said, "what would you think of havin' somebody come in here once a week to do the house cleanin'?"

I had to grab hold of the kitchen counter to keep myself from collapsing. "You just keep coming up with these solutions like you've been thinking about this for a while."

I looked expectantly at him. "Well…have you?"

A smile crept over his face. "Maybe a little."

The next day he made some calls while I was at work and set up a man and his son to do the yard work and a maid to come in every Friday to clean. He said he knew a guy there in town who did snow removal. "He comes into the store nearly every day, so I'll talk to 'im when I go into work the day after tomorrow. We won't need 'im for a while, though, I hope."

It was only the first of July, and it had been hot and dry for over three weeks. The grass was brown and dead-looking, and the lake was down a few inches. The DNR had required most places to cancel their Fourth of July fireworks because of the high danger of fire. The Soo was having theirs, however, because they set them off from a pier on the east side of the locks, and the fireworks exploded right out over the river. So we took our mosquito repellant and a blanket and headed to a grassy area a couple of blocks from the launch site. When we got there, the place was packed. I guess everyone had the same idea.

August came and went, and in mid-September Lloyd and Craig booked a flight to Belgium. They planned to see a bit of Germany while they were there, as well, if time and the weather permitted.

I couldn't wait to see their photos and hear all about the trip. If it had been possible, I'd have hidden in one of their suitcases just so I could see the country where Papa and Uncle Herman had been born. Of course, it was no longer the Germany they had known, but the thought of walking on the same soil where they had trod gave me chills.

Jimmy and I were eating breakfast, dallying over a second cup of coffee before I had to leave for work, when the phone rang. We both just sat there, looking at the phone, wondering which of us would get it. Jimmy finally reached back over his head and grabbed the portable phone from its recharging base.

"Hello," he said, sounding as though he were glad to hear whomever was on the other end of the line, even though he had no idea who it might be.

"Speaking," he said as the smile melted from his face, and he stood up. "I'm sorry. Could you repeat that?" he asked. His entire body went limp, and he sort of stumbled; I thought he was going to fall, so I jumped up and ran to him. He put his arm up and stopped me. He was breathing heavily.

"When?" he asked. There was a long silence. Finally he said, "Oh, my God."

I didn't know what was going on. His body language told me it was something very bad. I grabbed a chair and slid it over behind him. He sat down as if his legs couldn't hold him up another second. He put his head in his free hand. Then he said, "Thank you," and dropped the phone in his lap. His phone hand joined the one over his face.

I was ready to panic. My mind raced with possibilities. I pulled another chair next to his and sat down.

"Tell me," I said.

He was sobbing, his shoulders heaving, his breathing sporadic.

"Tell me, Jimmy. Tell me."

Then he raised his face to the ceiling and wailed; it was a sound I would never have expected from him. "Our boys. Both of them."

"Oh, God." I stood up and began pacing. I couldn't breathe.

Jimmy tried to talk. "The train…derailed…just outside of Brussels. All the passengers…every one of them…"

"No, NO, NO!" I shouted.

We sat there for a long time. I remember getting up and going to the bedroom where I pulled open the top drawer of the dresser, grabbed the entire stack of Jimmy's folded handkerchiefs, and went back into the kitchen. Neither of us talked.

Jimmy finally rose and went into the bathroom. I moved to the couch and sat cross legged on one end. I felt completely spent, like I'd just finished a marathon. When Jimmy came back, he'd changed from his pajamas into his clothes. He sat down beside me. "I can't help but wonder if fate had somethin' to do with it," he said. "What if things were changed just one tiny bit? What if just one person on that train had done something different? What if the engineer sneezed at precisely the wrong moment? What if Lloyd and Craig had missed that train?"

"We can do the 'what ifs' till the cows come home, but it won't bring our boys back," I said without emotion.

The phone rang. I answered it; it was Shirley. "Are ya runnin' late today?" she asked.

That brought me back to the present. "Oh shit! Sorry. I should have called you earlier. We just got some bad news and are trying to make heads or tails of it. I'm not sure when I'll be in."

"Oh. What should I tell Aune? He's kind of in a bind. Got two emergency calls already, one from Dafter. Aune thought maybe you could catch that one before you come in, if you have what you need in your truck."

I started to cry again. "Shirley, someone called us from Belgium. Lloyd and Craig…there was a train derailment…they were both…" I couldn't go on.

"Oh my gosh! Are they all right?" she asked.

"No. Everyone on the train was killed." Another wave of devastation passed over me, and I had to put the phone down to dry my face and blow my nose.

I picked the phone back up, but Jimmy took it from me. "This is Jimmy," he said. "We'll call ya back." He pushed the OFF button.

"Thank you," I said. "But I really need to help Aune. There have been two emergency calls already this morning, and…"

"…and you just lost both of your sons. Your only children. I'm sorry, Helmi, but I think that might out-trump somebody losin' a calf or…or…"

"I get it," I said. "I guess there needs to be two of me today."

The phone rang again, and I reached toward it. "Don't answer it," Jimmy snapped.

I drew my hand back. "I have to. It might be Aune, and I need to explain…"

"You don't need to explain anything," Jimmy said. "Helmi, we're talkin' 'bout our children here. Our boys. We've lost 'em. We need some time to let it sink in that we aren't ever gonna talk to 'em again. We'll never get another phone call from 'em. Lloyd won't…" he broke down again, and in a thick voice, he said, "Lloyd won't ever put the star on the top of the Christmas tree again."

YEARS OF RECUPERATION

Unlike so many people who drift apart when they lose children, Jimmy and I became even closer over the following years. His whole outlook on life changed, too. He lived every day as if it might be his last.

My life was never boring; the life of a veterinarian never is. I saw new ailments and situations all the time. Some of them were so foreign to me, I had to figure out ways—sometimes unorthodox ones—to fix them. I think I enjoyed that the most about my job.

One of our clients had decided to help a baby moose that he'd found abandoned in the woods behind his barn. He watched it for two days before he was certain the mother wasn't coming back to care for it. Then when he tried to stand it up to take it into the barn, it wouldn't—or couldn't—walk. So he called Chippewa County Veterinarians. I was in the office manning the phones while Shirley took a break. When she came back, I told her, "I'm gonna have to make a run to Avery Cameron's place. He's got a baby moose that's been abandoned and can't seem to walk."

"Moose? We don't get a whole lot of calls about those around here. What're you gonna do with it?"

"I'm trying to figure that out. My first thought is that its mother hasn't really abandoned it, though Avery says he's watched it for two days, and there's no sign of the mother. It hasn't gotten up." I was already looking through some of the *Wild Animal Care* magazines Aune had accumulated over the years. So far I'd come up empty for ideas. Computers were proving to be a great source of information for that kind of situation, but unfortunately the Internet was not supported well enough to rely on it where our office was located.

As I was putting the magazines back onto the bookshelf, I spotted a pamphlet that had been written and distributed by the DNR. It was called, "Let Nature Take Its Course…Or Not?" So I pulled it out and found a small blurb about feeding baby moose. Bingo! Of course, it was promoting the practice of leaving abandoned wildlife alone, as chances are, the mother is probably nearby. But it also said, "…a baby [moose] usually nurses from the mother for 4 to 6 weeks. In the rare case that abandonment is assured, the baby can be fed alfalfa hay (it will not be able to digest regular field hay) and broccoli. Ample water and twigs should be made available, as this is a moose's main fare." It explained that the word "moose" means twig-eater.

I had found some good information to relay to Avery, but I didn't know the age of the baby, nor was I certain it wasn't in bad general health. *I guess that's what I'll find out when I get there.* I told Shirley what I'd found and then said, "I'll be back in about an hour. If Aune calls needing help with the Walters' Angus castrations, beep me and I'll go over there after."

"Okay. Good luck. Oh, and be sure to take some pictures."

"Good idea." I picked up the office camera and stuffed the DNR pamphlet into the back pocket of my coveralls. I had no idea what I'd find when I got to Avery's place.

"Yo!" Avery called and waved when I pulled up to his barn. "I put the moose in there." He motioned to the door at the end of the barn. "Had to carry it. Must only weigh about 15 pounds."

"Couldn't get it to walk, eh?" I asked.

"Not a step. Legs won't hold it up."

We went to the barn where Avery had it lying on a nice bed of straw. The little thing was trying its best to call for its mama, but it was so weak, the call could barely be heard. I sighed and said, "Doesn't look good, Avery. But I found some information in this pamphlet." I pulled it out of my pocket and let him read what I'd already discovered.

He scratched his head. "Broccoli. Would never have thought of that."

"I'm hoping it got some colostrum from the mother before she departed. You say you haven't seen her?"

"Not hide nor hair. No new tracks, neither. She probably got poached or hit by a car and wandered off and died. I haven't had a chance to do much searching."

I checked its gums and eyelids for color; they were pink, so it wasn't anemic. "Have you tried to get it to drink water?"

"Yeah, and it took plenty. First I tried to get it to drink from a bucket, but it wouldn't put its nose down in there, so I brought out some water in a dishpan, and it sucked it up like a sponge."

"Good. Let me take a listen," I said as I pulled my stethoscope out from under the neck of my coveralls. I listened to the baby's heart, lungs, and gut. Surprisingly, the heart and lungs sounded good, but the gut had hardly any noises coming from it.

"There's not much going on in the poor little critter's belly. I know it has to be super hungry."

"Can it drink cow's milk?"

I shook my head. "Not enough milk fat or solids." I said. "I'm gonna give it a little bit of calcium and selenium; there's not much selenium in our greenery in this neck of the woods, as you well know. And a lack of calcium could be what's keeping it from walking. It looks to me like it's just malnutrition. I think it's old enough not to have to nurse from the mother in order to live. Go buy some broccoli and alfalfa. And don't skimp on the water. It'll need a lot."

We talked about the dry spring we'd had that year and about his old Dodge truck and about his daughter-in-law's new business in the Soo—she'd opened a consignment shop. I told him I'd try to get there to see what she has on the racks, but I secretly doubted there would be anything for someone my age. All the while I was snapping pictures to take back for the others to see.

About a week passed, and I called Avery to ask after the moose.

"I think you hit the nail on the head about it just being hungry and needing the minerals," Avery said. "It ate like it might never see food again. Then one day it just got up and walked away," he said. "I haven't seen it since, so I'm hoping it's gonna be okay. Unfortunately, it isn't gonna find any broccoli in the woods." He chuckled.

When I hung up, Billie was on the other line. She put the caller on hold and went to the file cabinet. She returned to the phone empty-handed and took a message, then she hung up and looked at me with a strange expression on her face.

I looked back at her with a "what now?" expression on *my* face.

"It's a big Angus bull over in Kelden," she said. "I can't find a chart with the peoples' name on it; don't think we've ever seen any of their animals before. The woman who called said their name was—are you ready for this?—Schovajsa." She held the note out to me so I could see the name.

"I'm glad you pronounced it. I'd sure never know that was the pronunciation based on the spelling."

"It's Czechoslovakian. I had to ask her to spell it," Billie said. "She doesn't have any accent, so I'm guessing either she's a natural American citizen, or she's been in the U.S. long enough to have lost her accent."

"So what's the problem with the bull?" I asked.

"Has a big tear in his left flank. Doing a lot of bleeding."

"Is it walking okay?"

She shrugged her shoulders. "Doesn't want to leave its place in the pasture. Tries to headbutt anybody who comes near it."

I heaved a great big sigh.

"I can try to get hold of Aune," Billie said.

"He's pretty well tied up with those pregnancy checks he's doing. The Laitenens have a good-sized herd," I said. "I'm gonna try to tackle this by myself." I looked down at the note she'd handed me. There was a phone number, so I thanked Billie and told her I'd call the Schovajsas back and find out some of the particulars before I proceeded.

I found out that the place was a communal farm; four families had combined their livestock, and they all participated in caring for the fields that surrounded the main house and barns. The woman I talked to said she and her husband and their six children had come from Czechoslovakia in the mid-1940s and started farming around Kelden. When some other Czech families found out there was a Czech family already there, they all got together and decided to turn it into one big farm. She was the matriarch, but to me she sounded like a teenager. I was eager to see the place and what they'd done with it.

"It sounds to me like your bull has a mind of his own, and I'm going to need some help sedating him," I told her.

"There are eleven able-bodied men around here. You think that'll be enough? Oh, and we have a squeeze chute."

"How close is the bull to the chute?"

"That's the problem. The chute's at the barn; the bull's in the field behind the barn, and he won't let anyone get near him."

"Okay. As long as there are enough strong people to help tie up his legs after he's sedated, I can use the blow gun to bring him down." I got directions and then told her, "I'll be out in about 45 minutes."

I smiled. It had been a long time since I'd gotten to use the blow gun, and I really liked using it. Aune had been a bit hesitant about buying one for the clinic, but I convinced him it was exactly what we needed for cases like this. I had been good at hitting my target when I was in college, so I had no doubt that I'd be working on that bull within a couple of hours.

I was pleasantly surprised when I got to the farm. It was clean, and the buildings had recently been painted. There were no old pieces of farm equipment lying around with grass growing up around and through them, and no free-range chickens blocked the drive as I pulled up to the place! The house was attractive and had flower beds strategically placed in the front yard. A trio of large weeping willows hung gracefully over a pond in the side yard. A big hairy Newfoundland came bounding around the house barking a greeting, tail wagging, when I got out. A thin, white-haired elderly man who walked with a cane came through the front door. I hollered, "Hello!" He raised his arm in greeting fashion and called the dog's name, but I didn't catch

Dar Bagby

it. The dog immediately stopped barking, came up to me, and slobbered all over one leg of my coveralls. I petted him, and he decided I was all right. The man came to the back of the truck and shook my hand.

"I'm Dr. Butcher," I said. "You have a beautiful farm here."

"Thank you. Glad you here. Bad cut on bull. Need help to sew up." He had obviously not lost his accent, but he could speak enough English to be able to get his point across. Another man came out of the house. He was three times the size of the elderly man and only about twenty-five years old. He looked like one of the Olympic weightlifters I'd seen on TV.

"Hi, I'm Aksel."

"Dr. Butcher," I said as I shook his hand. "Understand you have a bull that's in need of some stitches."

"Yeah. He's a big one, though. You'll need plenty of sedative to bring him down."

"I understand he isn't interested in being friendly."

"You understand correctly. He became pretty agitated when we tried to get close to him."

"You know his weight?"

"Nineteen hundred and fifty pounds."

"Whew! That's no little boy," I said.

"What can we do to help?" Aksel asked.

"You can round up everyone who's capable of doing some heavy lifting. I'll be darting the bull, and it'll take upwards of twenty minutes for the sedation to take effect. When it does, we'll have to work fast to get him into a position where I can see the wound and work on it. Point me in the right direction, and I'll gather up some stuff and head that way."

"You don't need to walk. We'll take the Mule."

I did a momentary pause. "The Mule?" I was picturing myself getting up onto a mule with my arms full of everything I needed, including the dart gun. Then I heard the noise of an engine coming out from behind the barn. I turned and saw a Kawasaki Mule ATV coming toward me.

I burst out laughing. "For a moment there, Aksel, I was thinking you meant…"

He interrupted me, "…the animal, not the vehicle." He laughed along with me.

The man driving the Mule got out from behind the steering wheel, reached out his hand, and said, "Glad you were able to come so soon. We have a pretty nasty bull who needs a little TLC."

I shook his hand and said, "Dr. Butcher. I'll see if I can get him fixed up for you."

"What can I put in the Mule for you?"

I handed him some of the things I knew I'd need. "I didn't bring but one length of rope. We're gonna need several more, I'm sure. Normally, we'd be able to manhandle the legs, but with a bruiser like yours, it'll be much safer if we can do any necessary restraining with ropes."

Aksel said, "I'll get some from the shed."

"There are also a couple in the barn. They might be better; they are heavier," the second man said.

"You're probably right," Aksel said and then turned to me. "And by the way, this is my cousin Rafa."

I nodded to Rafa and said, "Nice to make your acquaintance."

Aksel left to gather up the ropes, and Rafa and I finished loading everything else into the bed of the Mule. Rafa was tall and muscular. He had darkly tanned skin, as if he spent most of his time in the sun.

Rafa said, "We can go on and make our way to the field where the bull is hiding. He thinks we do not know he is there. After we tried to subdue him earlier, he took off and went through the gate into the farthest corner of the north field." Rafa must have been in his early-to-mid thirties. He had the slightest bit of accent, not bad, but enough to tell his first language was not English.

He took off at a pretty good clip, wasting no time in getting me to within about fifty yards of the bull before stopping and allowing the Mule to idle. "Look at him," Rafa pointed toward a small stand of trees whose branches were dangling over the edge of the field. The bull was under the trees. "He does not know what is in store." Rafa smiled. "How close do you need to be?"

"As close as possible," I said.

"Twenty feet?"

"That'd be perfect. Just keep this thing in gear so we can make a fast getaway if he decides to charge."

"I will do that." Rafa slowly crept up toward the amazingly large beast who watched us without blinking. He knew something was up. He was shiny black with a head the size of Wisconsin! We finally got close enough for me to see the wound on his left rear flank. It was oozing blood that was running down his leg. Much more bleeding, and I wouldn't need to use the blow gun—he'd pass out from blood loss.

I whispered, "Looks like he's severed a main blood vessel. That's a lot of blood for just a skin tear."

Rafa whispered back, "We do not know what happened. Kaia, my daughter, came running into the barn and said our big bull was bleeding on his leg."

"It's a good thing she saw it. He could be down and not found until it was too late."

Rafa continued to creep up to the bull little by little until we were well within range for me to dart him. I filled the syringe with the right amount of sedative and stuffed the whole thing into the blow gun.

"If you can go a little to the left so I have a straight shot out my side, it'll be perfect," I whispered.

"You got it." Rafa slowly turned the Mule.

I put the blow gun to my lips and gave a big puff. The dart hit the bull in exactly the right spot…and bounced off.

"Schiest!" I said. "Oh, pardon me," I whispered to Rafa.

He laughed quietly.

"That one didn't stick. I'll have to try again." I filled another syringe and pushed it into the gun. "Wish me luck," I whispered.

The bull had turned and was facing the other direction, his right flank exposed to me. I blew harder this time. The needle stuck, and I could see the plunger depress. "Yes!" I whispered.

I looked over at Rafa. He was grinning. "Not bad…for a woman!"

I knew he was teasing. "Thank you," I whispered. "You should see the way I blow bubble gum!"

Rafa laughed right out loud, then caught himself and put his hand over his mouth.

"Now we wait," I whispered.

Within a couple more minutes, Aksel came up beside us on a smaller ATV without a bed. He had several ropes over his shoulder, which he dropped to the ground beside the Mule. In a whisper he said, "Hauke, Wen, and Kevin will be here in a few minutes. How long do we have till the bull's down?"

"Probably about ten minutes from the looks of him," I said. "And we don't need to whisper any longer. He knows we're here, and he's more concerned about staying awake than he is with us."

"Okay. Did you get everything you need from your truck?"

I got out of the Mule and went around to the back to check. "I think I have it all, thanks, but I could use a bucket of water. Can you manage to bring it on that four-wheeler?" He gave me a thumbs-up and took off.

The bull was no longer paying any attention to us. His head was hanging pretty low, and his tail had stopped twitching. Within the next three or four minutes, he lay down. I was glad he was in the shade. The noonday sun was getting pretty warm.

The other three men arrived right on time, and they were followed by Aksel with the bucket of water. "Here's the plan," I said. "I'll go make sure he's out, then you guys can put the ropes on his legs. He'll need to be on his right side. The front legs should be stretched out in front of him. The right rear one needs to be pulled back. The left rear—the one with the wound—needs to be stretched forward as far as possible; two of you should be on that rope. If he decides to pull away from us, he'll do it with that leg first. Please be careful of those hooves. They're lethal."

I quietly made my way up to the brute. His head was resting on his left front leg. His eyes were glazed over, but they followed me as I walked in front of him. When I reached his left rear leg, I gave it a kick with my foot. No response. "Okay, guys. Get a move on. He won't be out for very long."

After supervising the roping, I leaned over him and proceeded to clean up the wound. There was a pretty big blood vessel that had to be sutured to stop the bleeding. Then I was able to slather it with antibiotic ointment and close the skin flap. The whole process took about fifteen minutes, and the bull was beginning to show signs of waking up.

I gave the bull a shot of additional antibiotic in his hindquarters and walked away from him. "Time to untie his feet. He's coming out from under the sedation." Without a sound, the five men slipped the ropes off the bull's hooves and came over to where I was standing.

"Let's get out of here and let him come around by himself. I don't particularly want to be in his way when he's ready to stand up." I turned to go back to the Mule, but my foot caught on a tree root, and I lost my balance. Everything I had in my arms went flying, and I went down, hard, my back landing on a rock.

"Oof." The fall knocked the wind out of me.

The next thing I knew, I was lying in the bed of the Mule, and all five of the men were talking at once, trying to wake me up. I started to sit up, but my back was aching so bad I couldn't. Aksel leaned down and asked me, "Can you move your legs?"

I looked up at him like he was crazy. *Of course I can move my legs,* I thought. I lifted my right knee, then my left.

"Wiggle your toes," he said.

I wiggled them inside my boots, but no one could see them move.

"Remove her boots," he ordered one of the men, and one of them did.

"Do it again," he said to me. I wiggled them again, and this time I knew he could tell that they were moving. He backed away and said, "You aren't paralyzed. Back injuries can fool you. Can you sit up?" He was sweating, and his breaths were rapid and shallow. I had obviously given him a good scare.

I managed to get up on my elbows, but sitting all the way up was not a possibility at the moment.

"Did I actually black out?" I asked.

"Yeah, but I think it was just because you had the wind knocked out of you," Aksel said.

"Thank you for getting me into the Mule. Would you mind helping me sit up?"

Two of the men sat me up by raising me by my shoulders. I groaned as I tried to twist from side to side. "I'll bet that's gonna leave me grunting and groaning for a few days."

Rafa asked, "Would you like a ride back to your clinic? One of us can drive your truck, and another will follow."

I was beginning to move a little easier. "I think I'll be all right," I said. "But thanks for the offer. I'm sorry I created such a fracas. I guess I just lost my balance when I tripped over that root. And how's the bull?"

They all looked at each other, then they started to laugh. Five men were roaring with laughter, and I had been the source. One of them said something in a foreign language, which I assumed was Czechoslovakian, and they all laughed even harder.

Aksel leaned down to me and, in the midst of his hilarity, said, "It amuses them that you're concerned with the bull more than yourself, I think."

I paused for a moment, then said, "No one answered my question. How's the bull?"

And they all roared again.

I didn't know if they'd ever be able to get close enough to that bull to give it antibiotics, so I asked them if the bull ever came into the barn.

"For what?" one of them asked. "The cows are in the fields this time of year, and that is where the bull will be."

"I was hoping you could lure him into the squeeze chute and give him antibiotic injections."

They all looked at each other, but not one of them volunteered a reply.

"Will it even be worth leaving these with you?" I asked.

"Just a minute," Aksel said. He turned to the others and spoke to them in their language. They hemmed and hawed, but Aksel finally turned to me and said, "We may be able to lure him into the barn with a female. He'll follow her into the chute, but I don't think it'll work more than once."

"That's okay," I said. "One dose is better than none. It should be given day after tomorrow. He's had enough to get him through another day before the chance of infection takes over. If you need me to bring you more syringes, just let me know." I filled one syringe and handed it to one of them. They all thanked me and went back to their business, except for Aksel.

"Thank you so much for helping us," he said. "He's a very special bull; we had him brought in from Kansas. He's here so we can raise the best steaks this side of the Mississippi. There's a five-star restaurant in Detroit that buys our meat, and if we can provide the best meat in the state, we'll be set for many years to come."

"I understand. Best of luck to you. And please, if you need anything else, call us. I'm not the only vet there, so one of us should be available whenever you need something."

It was early afternoon. I got back to the clinic and gave all the information to Shirley, who created a chart for the farm.

"You're walking kind of funny," Shirley said. "You okay?"

"Yeah. I took a tumble and landed on a rock. I'm gonna be stiff for a few days."

That was an understatement.

When I got home that night, I told Jimmy I needed to lie down for a few minutes before starting dinner. He asked if I'd had a bad day.

"You might say that," I said. He followed me into the bedroom, and while I was changing my clothes, he was telling me about the moose he'd seen swimming in the lake out in front of our place.

"Was it very big?"

"No, it was just a young one." I wondered if it could have been the one Avery Cameron had wanted to save.

When I took off my shirt, Jimmy stopped dead and said, "Holy Man, Helmi! What happened to your back?"

"I fell on a rock."

"It must have been the size of a basketball. Have you seen the bruise you have?"

"No, I haven't taken time to look at it." I closed the bedroom door; there was a full-length mirror on the back of it. I arranged my body so I could turn my head and see my backside. I did a double take. Then my mouth dropped open. "I didn't have any idea it was that bad," I said. "Now I know why it hurts."

Jimmy said, "Cheese and crackers!"

In 1982 Anna had another surgery on her back; new methods had become popular with people who had previously been through what Anna had, and the outcomes were about eighty percent positive—Anna included—from those who had decided to undergo the up-to-date procedure. She and Mary and Retta made several trips to our place following the surgery. Anna got to take in our view firsthand and said, "I'm jealous. I'd sure like to wake up and look at this every day. No offense, Mary, but this is just a wee bit prettier than waking up and seeing the back of your house."

"No offense taken," Mary said. "I'd rather wake up to this, too. You sure have it nice, Helmi. You and Jimmy made the right call when you moved up here."

"I think so, too," I said as I was disappearing out the door on my way to work. This would be my last year as a full-time vet. I was planning to go to a part-time schedule after my sixty-second birthday in November. "See you all this evening!" I shouted as the door banged shut.

Aune had retired, and a new vet, Dr. Randy Garrish, now owned the practice. Since I was the senior vet, I was in charge, but Dr. Garrish, who was half my age, had bought the place from Aune, so he was the actual owner and had the final say in all the financial matters. Aune had, of course, given me first refusal to buy the business, but I turned him down. "I love the work, but I don't want the extra headaches of being a business owner," I had told him. I wondered if one of Uncle Herman's genes had infiltrated my system!

Dr. John Napoleon was in charge of the small animal clinic and had a new vet tech working with him. Billie had moved on shortly after Aune sold the place. We all thought she and Aune had something going on the side, but when she quit, she moved to Virginia, so our little theory was shot down.

Shirley was still working. She and I were about the same age, within a year or two of each other, and we got along so well, it made the workplace pleasant for both of us. I was glad she was still there. Garrish had hired a couple of receptionists who helped Shirley with the phone and filing, but Shirley was the office manager and ran a pretty tight ship. That was another reason I liked her.

Jimmy was still working two days a week at the hardware store. He had decided that being home most of the time wasn't all bad, even when there was a houseful of women to argue with. That only happened when Retta, Anna, Mary, and Lizzy visited. But his protests were only show; he loved having them there as much as I did.

We had overcome the deep grief of losing Lloyd and Craig, though it took a long time before we could speak of it without shedding tears. As Jimmy's and my closeness grew, and as we became more involved in the lives of our relatives and friends, we felt like a close-knit family once again.

"GOOD NIGHT, HELMI"

Two years went by like two minutes, and it was suddenly 1984. I was working only two days a week, and Jimmy was working only two half-days a week at the hardware store. Without any kids at home, neither of us was getting as much exercise as we should have, and as a result, both of us had put on extra pounds.

"I just got off the scales, Jimmy, and I definitely need to do something to lose this," I said, holding onto the spare tire that had taken up residence around my midsection.

"I don't mind that extra love handle," Jimmy said. "But I'm not sure you're real happy with my paunch."

"I don't mind it one bit. But I think, for the sake of good health, we should both do some working out. There's a new gym in the Soo, and they're offering a special on new memberships," I said.

Jimmy didn't answer; he simply looked off into the distance and sighed.

"I'm sure they have programs specifically for people with…with special needs like yours."

"You mean programs for old decrepit cripples?" he said.

I could sense he wasn't being humorous; he was feeling sorry for himself.

"Suit yourself, but I'm gonna check the place out. You'll be sorry when I look like I'm thirty again and all the men aren't able to take their eyes off me."

"I can't take my eyes off you now, and I don't care that you aren't thirty," Jimmy said. He wasn't smiling.

"It might make you feel better."

"I don't think much of anything's gonna make me feel better," he said.

I frowned. "Whadda you mean?"

"I mean I just don't feel good." He was practically shouting.

"Are you sick?"

"No, Helmi. I just mean I don't feel *good* anymore. I'm tired. I have no energy. I don't wanna do anything."

"Exercise will change that. At least, that's what everybody says."

"Who's everybody?" he asked. "Sounds like a buncha hooey to me. Probably just propaganda put out by the gyms that are after our money."

It was time to change the subject. "Ben Martin called me today. You remember him?"

"The jockey?"

"Yeah. He's going to be riding in one of the races that's run before the actual Kentucky Derby."

Silence.

"He was hired by one of the horse owners who has a horse entered in the Derby, but the guy's using some hot-shot jockey from Florida on that horse."

More silence.

"At least Ben has his foot in the door," I said.

Still no response.

"Did you hear me, Jimmy?"

"Uh-huh."

I sighed. "I'm gonna go take a bath."

Nothing.

"Jimmy?"

"I heard ya," he said without looking up.

While I was lounging in the tub, I was thinking about Jimmy's apparent lack of interest in having a conversation. It was unlike him to be so unresponsive. There must have been something on his mind. Something either I wasn't supposed to know about or something he thought I wouldn't be interested in. *Okay, Helmi, just let it drop. You're doing that thing where you keep trying to make something out of nothing.* But that explanation just didn't fill the bill.

That night, when we went to bed, I said, "How about going to visit Retta?"

"For what?"

"No special reason," I shrugged. "I'd just like to see her. Thought you might, too."

"You should go by yourself," he said. "That way we won't have to stay in a motel room." He was lying there with his arms behind his head, his usual pre-sleep position. "And you two hens can do all the cluckin' and cacklin' you want to without feelin' like ya have to entertain me."

"Retta would never forgive me if I showed up without you," I said.

"I'm nothin' to her," he said. "She just puts up with me 'cause I'm her sister's husband."

I sat straight up in the bed and turned so I was facing Jimmy. "James Butcher! Either you tell me what's eating you, or I'll… I'll…" I had nothing.

Jimmy shook his head and rolled over onto his side, away from me. "Good night, Helmi."

I didn't even get a good-night kiss. *What am I missing? After all these years I should be able to identify the problem. And there is definitely a problem.* I lay down with my back to him, knowing full well that I wouldn't be going to sleep very quickly because I had to figure out what was going on inside his head.

Three days passed, then a week, then two weeks, and Jimmy remained in a foul mood. I called Retta when he was at work.

"Hey, big sis. Good to hear from you. What's up?" she asked.

I loved that she sounded so upbeat. "I just needed to hear your voice, for one thing."

"And…?" she asked.

"And I need to know what to do with a puppy that has a big chip on his shoulder."

"You have a puppy?"

"Not the four-legged kind; the two-legged kind."

"Ohhh. He's no puppy. Sounds to me like he's the big dog who's decided he's tired of leading the pack," she said.

I paused in thought for a moment. "Holy whah! I think you just solved the mystery."

"So Jimmy's going through the old 'I'm no good to anyone anymore. I'm just an old fart who isn't worth his salt. Nobody loves me; everybody hates me. I'm gonna go eat worms.'"

I sat there, completely stunned by Retta's insight.

"You still there, Helmi?"

"How could you possibly have known that about him? You don't even have a husband," I said.

"Well, rub it in, why don't ya?"

"No, seriously, why do you know the answer, and I'm living with the man—right beside him, day in and day out—and I haven't been able to put my finger on what's wrong?"

"You're too close to it," she said. "Can't see the forest for the trees. Don't you read the tabloids? They have an explanation for everything."

"I can't believe you waste your time and money on that crap," I said.

"Hey, call it what you want, but it was that crap that made me able to tell you what the problem is."

"Retta to the rescue," I said. "Now you have to tell me how to fix it."

"It'll cost you. I don't offer free advice."

"Name your price," I said. "I'm willing to give up the house and the front porch if it'll make my life bearable again."

"He needs positive reinforcement. I know it sounds like something you'd do to treat the same ailment in a little kid, but I'll bet you dollars to donuts that you'll see a big difference in a matter of days," she said.

"It's certainly worth a try. I'm about ready to start putting arsenic in his morning coffee."

"Too obvious," Retta said. "The police would figure it out before you could make a clean get-away."

We ended up talking about nothing in particular for the next twenty minutes. Then I realized I was probably keeping her from important work-related matters, so I told her I needed to go. "Thanks for keeping me on the straight and narrow," I said before hanging up.

I made a quick trip to the meat market in the Soo for a couple of thick-cut pork chops, which I planned to serve with au gratin potatoes, corn on the cob, and my homemade coleslaw. I also figured I'd bake a red velvet cake with buttercream frosting for dessert. I knew Jimmy couldn't remain sullen with all of his favorite things on the menu.

He came home early; instead of getting off work at four, he was home at a little after two. "Well, it's final," he said. "As of today, I no longer have a job."

I frowned.

"No, I didn't get fired. The store's closin' up."

"For good?"

He nodded.

"How long has this been in the works?" I asked.

"Prob'ly a long time. I've known 'bout it for almost a month."

"So you knew this was coming?"

He looked right into my eyes and said, "I'm sorry, Helmi. I shoulda told ya right off. I guess I thought that if I didn't say it out loud, it wouldn't be true. But now that I know it is, I wanna apologize for bein' such a horse's ass over the last two or three weeks. I just felt like I wasn't needed anymore. Like someone was tellin' me I'm useless. And the worst part is, it didn't do me any good at all; it just made things bad for you. I wanna make it up to ya, and I'm gonna start by askin' ya out. How 'bout we go to dinner at that new place in St. Ignace? If we leave here at about four, that'll put us there 'fore the worst of the supper crowd—'scuse me—*dinner* crowd gets there." He smiled. It was the first time I'd seen him do that in at least three weeks.

I hugged him and told him I'd been really worried about him.

"I'd love to go to *dinner* with a man who can still turn heads when he walks into a room."

I put the pork chops in the freezer and stashed the cake mix in the pantry.

"I like to cook," Jimmy said on the way to the restaurant. "I just never took the initiative. How 'bout if I take over in the kitchen for dinner on the days when you're workin'?"

I think my smile stretched from one end of the U.P. to the other. "Oh, Jimmy, that would be one of the nicest things you could possibly do for me."

"I'll even take over doin' the grocery shoppin' for us. You put whatever you want on the list for the nights you'll be cookin', and I'll get whatever you need and whatever I want for my nights," he said.

"Great plan!" I said. I could hear the relief in my voice, and I think he could hear it, as well. And the plan worked perfectly.

❖❖❖

By the time 1985 rolled around, I was ready to say goodbye to my life as a veterinarian. I left the clinic with mixed emotions, however. I couldn't help but think back on all the years I had wanted to be a vet. It began when I was only a child, then I put in those five long years at OSU, and I was finally able to realize my dream at the clinic in Rudyard. Now I was leaving all those years behind and embarking on a new venture, that of becoming a retired wife.

I didn't have any of the feelings Jimmy had experienced when he was faced with no longer being employed. Maybe because I'd had the perfect job for me throughout my employable years. Maybe because I'd never thought about doing anything else. At any rate, I was happy to become Jimmy's full-time live-in partner. And that was enough for me.

As time traveled on, I kept noticing that Jimmy was moving slower. He kept rubbing his right leg, and he even developed the tiniest hint of a limp, probably unnoticeable to anyone else. It worried me; he reminded me of his dad. He fell asleep at the drop of a hat. If we sat down to watch TV, he drifted off. If we went to a movie, he slept through most of it. He went to bed earlier and earlier, and he slept later and later. I finally came to the conclusion that it was normal for a man who had been through what he had, and he'd handled it with much more ferocity and positivity than I ever could have. I felt the utmost respect for him, and I loved him more and more with each passing day.

❖❖❖

Retta and Anna came to visit us as often as Retta's schedule would allow, and Mary came with them once in a while. She was busy with her grandchildren and great grandchildren most of the time. Lizzy and Walter had moved to Saginaw, and of course, Mary was thrilled to no end. I had never been around a woman who loved children more than she did.

Jimmy and I made some trips to both Frankfort and Flint, but riding had become hard on Jimmy. He never complained, but I knew it wasn't easy for him to pretend that he didn't have one prosthetic leg and bad arthritis in the other, as well as in his elbows and neck. His right leg had become bowed out, and the doctor had put him on some pretty strong anti-inflammatories.

In early June of 1992 Retta came to visit. She said she'd asked Anna to come, too. "She turned me down," Retta said. "I couldn't get a decent answer from her as to why, but I'm thinking maybe she's been having some more back problems."

"Oh, no," I said. That was something I could have gone without hearing. "What makes you think so?"

"Mary says she's been moping around a lot and doesn't come out of her house except when she absolutely *has* to. And when she does come out, she's usually bent over more than usual. You think the surgery could have worked its magic. and now it's beginning to fail?" Retta asked.

"Hmm. I don't know. I haven't kept up on it. Why don't we look on the Internet and see what it says?" I asked.

"I tried to find something, but they only talk about how good it is."

"It has been a lot of years since Anna's surgery," I said. "Do you suppose it's giving up? I know that happens with a lot of the joint replacement surgeries they're doing now."

"Don't ask me," Retta said. "You're the one who knows about all that medical stuff."

"Used to know. It changes so fast now, Retta, I can't keep up with any of it anymore."

"Nor do you have to," she assured me. "Let's call Anna. Maybe we can at least make her smile."

We called, and she definitely sounded thrilled to hear our voices. "I just came back from the doctor," she said, "and she told me I could have a minor procedure done that will relieve some of the pain I've been having."

"Super!" I said. "When does she propose to do it?"

"It's nothing I'd have to stay in the hospital a long time for. She said she could do it as soon as next week. I told her I'd like to chew on what she said and that I'd give her a call back. Of course, I'll have to make special arrangements to get there and back and probably have some help here at home for a couple of days, just till the incision heals up. She wants to make sure I have someone who can check the wound for infection."

"You know I'd be glad to do that," I said.

"I figured as much, but I'm not totally convinced I want to have it done."

"What's keeping you from saying 'yes'?" Retta asked.

"Well…" Anna paused. "It's another one of those things that's not always one-hundred percent failsafe. You know. There's a possibility that it could make things worse, or at least not do any good at all. And then I'll have wasted all that money and…"

"Don't worry about the money," Retta and I both said at the same time.

"Anna, you put up with pain and inconvenience your whole life until you had that surgery. Why would you want to go through all of that again?" I asked.

"Yeah, ditto," Retta added.

"I know. I know. It's just, there's a really big risk because they have to manipulate things around the spinal cord. And that scares me."

"Wow. I understand," I said.

"Is that what you meant when you said it's not totally failsafe?"

"Yep," Anna said.

"In that case, I think you're probably right about being concerned. It's your body, and you have the right to make the final decisions about it."

"Freedom of choice," Retta said.

"I'll have to do some more thinking about it," Anna said. "But thanks for being willing to talk to me about it."

"Any time," Retta and I said.

We hung up.

"Did you get the feeling she's not telling us everything?" Retta asked me.

"I know she wasn't being totally up-front. I could hear it in her voice."

"Yeah, and her explanations sounded kind of vague."

"I guess we'll just have to let her make the final decision. She's a big girl now," I said.

"Maybe in age, but she's still our baby sister," Retta said.

❖❖❖

Later that month, while Jimmy and I were eating our breakfast, the phone rang. I answered.

"Is this Helmi?" a female voice asked.

"Yes, it is."

"This is Trina McAlister."

My brain searched through a few databases before picking out Dora's roommate. That set off some bells and whistles.

"Yes, hi."

"I'm afraid I have some bad news."

I wasn't sure how many more jolts my heart could stand.

"Oh dear," was all I could muster.

"It's about Dora."

"Yes?" I could barely hear my own voice.

"She's been in the hospital for several days."

"What's the problem?" I asked, afraid to hear the answer.

"She became terribly anemic, so they did a lot of testing, and they found a hole in her aorta. The blood was being pumped directly out into her body. Of course, her body tried to fight back, and she…"

"Yes. I understand the condition. I've been in the medical field for, well, that's immaterial." I said.

"She told me you'd know," Trina said. "Her twin sister didn't need the explanation, either."

"Where is Dora? I mean, what hospital?"

"She started out at Greene Memorial Hospital in Xenia, but they moved her to Miami Valley in Dayton since that facility can better cope with the problem."

"Is she in ICU?"

"Yes. She cannot have any visitors at this time. The staff there feels she is too vulnerable to infection with her compromised immune system."

"How did her immune system become compromised?" I asked.

"Her AIDS," Trina said matter-of-factly. "I was under the impression that you knew."

"No. No, I had no idea." My brain was racing, trying to piece together the parts of the puzzle that would explain the how and where and when of Dora's disease. "Do you have the number of the hospital?" I asked.

"Of course. But you will not be able to talk to Dora. At least not right now."

"I understand. I just want to talk to someone at the nurse's station and get the particulars about talking to her doctor and so forth."

"Yes, that would probably be best under the current circumstances." She gave me the hospital number and told me the doctor's name. She also told me to feel free to call her anytime.

"Thank you for contacting me, Trina. I know we've never spoken more than an occasional 'Hello,' but I appreciate all you've done for my sister. She depends greatly on you."

"Thank you, but it is truly my pleasure to do what I can for someone who is as talented as your lovely sister."

When I hung up the phone, I was surprised at how calm I was. I went back to the table and sat down, systematically pushing my plateful of unfinished eggs and sausage away from me.

"So...?" Jimmy asked.

"It's Dora."

"I gather she's in trouble?"

I took a deep breath and said, "She has AIDS."

"What?"

"But that's only the half of it. She also has a hole in her aorta."

"Good God!" Jimmy exploded. "What are we gonna do, Helmi?"

I didn't have an answer. Jimmy was waiting for me to say something, but my mind was blank. "I can't talk about this right now," I said. "I need to think." I poured myself another cup of coffee, stirred in milk and sugar, and stepped outside. I didn't want to get my slippers dirty, so I slid them off my feet and walked barefoot to the waterfront.

The coolness of the grass felt good on my soles, and the clear air felt good in my lungs. The sun had cleared the eastern horizon and was climbing toward a few puffs of clouds that hung above it. The water in the bay was calm and reflected the blue sky on a surface as smooth as glass. A mosquito buzzed my left ear, and I half-heartedly swatted at it.

I gazed out over the bay to the point of land that reached out toward the east, separating our little bay from the much bigger Whitefish Bay where the freighters made their way to Marquette or Two Harbors or Duluth or Superior or Thunder Bay. I could see the hills of Canada as clearly as if there were no air between us and them. There were little dots of orange on the shoreline, reflections of the sun off the windows of the Canadian cabins.

This was my home. I felt more comfortable here than anyplace else I'd ever lived. I wondered if Dora felt the same way about Yellow Springs; I wondered if, in fact, she even took the time to feel such things. I knew I'd never be able to ask her. I knew she'd be gone before I had the chance.

A feeling of serenity overtook my body. Strange as it was, considering the clamor of thoughts banging around inside me—Anna getting worse, Dora at Death's door, Jimmy becoming more and more unable to tackle life's daily tests—I felt a quietness inside. And I knew it was this place that was allowing me to see everything in a tranquil state. I could take in the big picture and still cope with what I was being handed. I knew I'd always feel that way about Brimley.

Jimmy appeared beside me. "You need to talk?"

I shook my head.

He put his arm around me, and we stood there, just the two of us, enjoying the view and the intertwining aromas of pine and fresh water and coffee and a hint of wood smoke from last night's campfires around the bay. And we smiled.

Dora left the world that day.

THE WORLD STOPPED SPINNING

Retta came to visit us twice, once following Dora's death and again for Thanksgiving. She did not come to our place for Christmas; she visited Mary and Anna in the hopes of helping to make the holidays easier for the two of them. They weren't handling Dora's death well. I had offered to go along, but Retta said, "No. You need to be with Jimmy, and he doesn't need to be traipsing all over the state." She was right.

Dora wanted no one to make the trip to Ohio upon her death; it was one of her wishes. She asked only that everyone say a special prayer for all the people in the world who were suffering from AIDS. She had known she was going to die months before Trina ever informed me of her condition. Dora had also requested cremation but no burial. Trina had called me the day after Dora died and read Dora's wishes to me, at Dora's request: "She'll (Helmi) understand how important it is to me to be sure she knows what I'd like when I go." Dora was right; I did need to understand...it helped me get through, and get past, the whole ordeal.

Jimmy hadn't gotten any better by early 1993; he was still tired all the time, and he spent a lot of time either in bed or sitting in front of the TV without his prosthesis in place. He said it bothered him, but he was in no hurry to get it replaced again. "I can get by with this one as long as I don't have to do a whole lot of walking."

Finally, I had to broach the subject. "Are you all right? I worry about you."

"Yeah, I'm okay. Why?"

"Well, you just seem to be so tired all the time. I want to make sure there isn't something wrong. You know...physically."

"Like what?"

"I don't know. There are lots of things that could be contributing to your tiredness, I guess."

He closed his eyes. "I'm worn out, Helmi. I don't have any energy. I can't seem to rev up my engine. It's like, no matter how hard I press on the gas pedal, the old motor won't respond."

"Let's get out of here for a while," I said. "Go someplace we've always wanted to go."

He was quiet. Then he sighed a long, deep sigh. "I can't. I'll never be able to do it. Just the thought of it makes me feel exhausted."

"You wouldn't have to do anything. I can drive. I'll make all the arrangements…or we could fly! How about…"

But he cut me off. "Forget it. I can't. I'm sorry, but it's just too much to think about." Then he strapped on his prosthesis, got up, and disappeared down the hall.

I sat on the couch wondering how I would feel if I'd been through all that he had. *The man lost one leg, and his other leg hurts him all the time. He's never again going to be what he considers a "whole man," and I know that weighs heavily on him. I can't help but wonder if I've expected too much from him all these years. But I didn't want him to feel like I wasn't confident in his abilities, even with what he's been through. Have I been too hard on him?*

I waited until I heard him finish in the bathroom and cross the hall into the bedroom, then I turned off the TV and got ready for bed. I was mentally drained. I lay down and put my head on his shoulder. He raised his arm, and I snuggled my shoulder into his armpit, resting my head on his chest. I could hear and feel his heart beating, slowly and faintly. He had been almost asleep when I got into bed, so the calm, relaxed sound made sense to me.

"I love you," I whispered.

He did not reply; he was asleep.

I awoke at about seven-thirty a.m. I slid out from under the covers and quietly put my feet into my slippers. I grabbed my robe from the back of the door, and I made sure I held onto the doorknob so it didn't click when it latched. Then I went into the kitchen and put on a pot of coffee. I put some milk and sugar into a mug and waited for the pot to finish dripping. Then I poured the mug full, watching the milk change the coffee's dark color to a lighter one as they mixed.

I sat down on the couch and picked up the book I'd been reading, but I had trouble concentrating on it; I read the same paragraph three times and still didn't comprehend what the words were telling me. So I went back into the kitchen and mixed up some muffins. I put them into the oven. They were one of the few things I'd learned to bake without creating a smoke screen in the kitchen. They made the whole house smell good.

By nine o'clock the muffins were getting cold, so I ate one with my third mug of coffee, even though two mugs were usually my limit. The house was always so quiet when I got up before Jimmy, though that seldom happened. He was usually up and dressed and either in the kitchen or outside doing something when I crawled out of my warm nest. But I was glad to know he was sleeping late that morning. He needed it.

At about nine-forty-five I crept into the bedroom to get my clothes; I'd take them into the bathroom and dress in there. I was really surprised by the fact that he was still asleep. I didn't remember him ever sleeping that late. He usually said, "I don't know how anybody can waste the best parta their day."

I smiled down at him in the half-light/half-dark room, a mere sliver of daylight filtering through a gap in the curtains. He looked so peaceful. I put my hand gently over the one he had above his head. It felt cold. *He's probably had it there long enough that the blood has drained out of it.* Then I looked down at his other hand resting outside the blanket that was covering his chest; the blanket wasn't moving. There was no up-and-down motion. I watched it for a full minute, but it didn't move. *I think he has sleep apnea. That's why he's been so tired!*

I wondered if I should wake him. I put my ear down to his chest. I could hear nothing. No breath sounds. No heartbeat. I lifted my head and looked at his face, then I touched it. His eyes didn't move under his eyelids, and his beautiful dark lashes were motionless. His skin offered no warmth.

I was dreaming; that had to be it. I was having a horrible nightmare. Then, without warning, something inside me snapped. It was like a rubber band being stretched until it could no longer resist the strain, and it broke. There was an explosion inside my head. And a woman began screaming. *Why doesn't someone help that poor woman? Make her stop screaming!*

❖❖❖

I sat there on the bed—it must have been for hours—looking at my Jimmy, my love, my reason for living. But time no longer mattered, because for me, the world had stopped spinning. At some point I rose and called Retta. I simply said, "Come. Please." And I hung up.

❖❖❖

Following all the hubbub that a death creates, I stood at the foot of Jimmy's and my bed. Retta came in and stood there beside me. She put her arm around my shoulder.

I said, "Dr. Salisbury told me it was as if his heart had only been given so many beats, and that night he used them up."

She asked me, "Why do you torture yourself? You should come away from this spot. All it does is conjure up memories."

"I love the memories," I said. "I need to remember Jimmy's

face." I began to cry for the first time since the funeral service. "He told me his dad closed the upstairs in their house—nailed the door shut—after his mother died. Jimmy said he couldn't remember her face, and that bothered him his whole life. Maybe if he'd been able to get up those stairs, her face would have been waiting for him, smiling down at him. I want to make sure I can remember Jimmy's face every minute of every day of the rest of my life."

Retta pulled me close. She was now my rock.

OLD FRIENDS, NEW FRIENDS

For a time, I counted Jimmy's passing in days. But as life went on, as it has a will to do, I began counting it in weeks and months, and eventually in years. During 1993 we lost Bella; she died of a brain aneurysm, alone in her apartment on the outskirts of Chicago. We buried her in the cemetery in Mt. Pleasant. According to Retta, Bella had become re-infatuated with our family—not the present one, but the one she remembered from the past—and wanted to spend eternity with Mama and Papa in the cemetery in Mount Pleasant. I was surprised to see some of her friends from the children's hospital at her funeral. She must have been greatly loved and greatly respected, or at the very least, greatly appreciated.

I put up a tree every Christmas, albeit only four feet tall, and every time I put the star on the top I thought of Papa and Lloyd. Those were some outstanding memories. And of course, they led me to others, which led me to others, and so on, ad infinitum. Christmas was always happy for me; I made it that way. I didn't want to think about unhappy things, only good ones, and that's exactly what I did.

Retta and I went to Mary's for Christmas in 1993, and we had a lovely brunch at her home. Lizzy and Walter were there, too, on Christmas Eve, but they didn't stay for the evening meal; Mary and Retta and I were on our own for that one. Mary was extremely quiet, contrary to the way Retta and I were behaving. We were all watching *A Christmas Story* on TV and guffawing over every little thing in the movie. Mary, on the other hand, was extremely quiet.

"Is everything all right, Mary?" I asked.

"Yes, of course," she said unconvincingly. "I'm so glad the two of you are staying. I didn't want to have to get up tomorrow morning and know that I would be alone."

"That makes two of us," I said.

"Three," Retta added.

"I hope I can make it through to 1994," Mary said.

"What do you mean?" I asked her.

Retta muted the volume on the TV.

"I'm just not feeling myself, and I think my time is coming very soon." She was going to be ninety-six in January.

"All the more reason to live it up," Retta said. "Don't let the bastards get you down!"

Mary smiled. "You always had such an unmistakable way of putting things, Retta."

I snorted. "Unmistakable, huh? I think I like that." Retta had always reminded me of Granny Nan in that she didn't mince words and simply "told it like it was."

Before Retta and I were able to return to our homes the day after Christmas, we ended up taking Mary to the hospital. She appeared to be fading rapidly.

"Sometimes the elderly just give up," the doctor said. "I've seen it happen more than once. When they make up their minds to leave this world, they somehow manage to accomplish it."

"Is there anything really wrong with her?" Retta asked.

The doctor shook her head. "It's entirely mental. Granted, she has some varicose veins in her legs, and she has alopecia, but those aren't reasons for her to be on her deathbed. Her heart's better than you'd expect for someone her age, and her mental capacity is above normal. She has no signs of renal, liver, or gastroenterology problems, no blood disorders or bad arthritis. She simply has herself convinced that it's time for her to pass on. And try as we might, that's not going to change. Believe me, I'd treat anything I thought was treatable. But I can't do a thing for what she has…or doesn't have."

"How sad," I said. "She was always so happy-go-lucky."

"Yes, it even attacks people of her demeanor. No one has been able to come up with a reason why it happens. It just does."

Mary made it through January and her ninety-sixth birthday. But early in February, she went to bed one night and simply didn't wake up the next day.

Anna finally chose to have her surgery in 1994, which went very well. But a staph infection overtook her so quickly and so completely, the hospital physicians were unable to contain it, and she died a year to the day after Bella. Anna would "sleep" beside Bella in the Mt. Pleasant cemetery; I thought it suitable since Bella had taken such good care of Anna when she was growing up.

About a year later, I got a letter from Link's daughter-in-law saying he had passed away. In the letter she said, "His last words were about the good times he and Dorothea had spent with you at OSU. He loved you dearly, Helmi." I wrote back and told her that I had always felt a special fondness for the two of them, as well, and that, without them, I might never have made it to my graduation. I was somewhat perplexed over the fact that Retta had not told me of Link's passing. I found out later that she had not known. It seems they had drifted apart. According to Retta, Link had fallen back into a depressed state, and it had worsened to the point where he wouldn't even talk to anyone but his daughter-in-law in the year preceding his death.

In 1995 Aune Halvorsen and Shirley were added to the list, as were Betty and Gene Downs, such good friends who gave so willingly of their time to care for us and our boys when Jimmy was recuperating after the accident. Those four years from 1992 to 1995 had been tough ones. Yet through them all, Jimmy's memory never took a back seat. He was always foremost in my thoughts.

My back began to bother me during the winter of 1996, so I went to see Dr. Salisbury about it. He asked me several questions and determined I should see a neurosurgeon, so he had his nurse set me up with one in Petoskey, Dr. Jacobowski, who was not only highly intelligent but also had an impeccable bedside manner. X-rays were done right in his office, and he brought them into the room and showed me. I had told him I'd been a veterinarian, so he knew I'd better understand my condition if I saw it on film. I also told him about the fall I had taken at the Czech families' farm, and he said that was a surefire way of bringing on the disc problems. He put me on anti-inflammatories, saying that was the best place to start. He also said I could end up having to go through surgery at some point later on.

"You do understand that I'm already seventy-five years old," I said.

"As long as you are healthy and deemed well enough to undergo anesthesia, we can do the surgery. But let's not get ahead of ourselves here. You're still a good way off from having to be cut on. We have lots of options. Surgery's a last resort."

From Petoskey, I drove on down to Traverse City to pay a surprise visit to Retta. I knew she would be in the TC store instead of in Frankfort. When I walked in, I could see her talking to someone in the back of the store, probably a customer, so I kept myself hidden behind one of the shelves where I could see her without her knowing I was there. When she finished her discussion with the customer, I made my way behind her and said, "Excuse me, Ma'am, but I'd like to take a look at your exotics. I think maybe a tarantula."

Retta turned and saw me and, without missing a beat, said, "I'm so sorry. Someone left the tarantula cage open, and we've not been able to find them. I'm sure they're running around here somewhere."

"Ew!" I said, and we both laughed. I whispered, "I hope none of your customers heard you say that."

"Oh, shit!" She looked around the store. "So do I." Then she hugged me. "What brings you down here to the big city?"

"Had an appointment with a neurosurgeon in Petoskey and thought I'd just come on down, since I was only an hour away."

"Neuro...that's a spine guy, right?"

"Yep. Gave me some pills for my bad back."

"Are they fun pills?"

"Not really. Just some anti-inflammatories. But he said he'd give me a prescription for the good stuff if I get to the point where I feel like I need them."

"Let's see..." She put both hands out to the side and moved them up and down like a scale. "Anti-inflammatories...bad pain and fun pills..."

"I'm opting for the prior, not the latter," I told her.

"Yeah, less pain's better than fun pills."

"I have a surprise," I said.

"Please don't make me guess. I hate that game," she said.

I reached into my purse and pulled out two tickets, holding them in front of her briefly. "I discovered Canada."

She paused, looking at me like I had lost my last bit of sanity. "What?"

"I finally decided to cross the International Bridge and drive around in a foreign country. It was great! We need to go shopping there sometime."

"Is that what the tickets are for?"

"No! The tickets are for a ride on the Algoma Central Snow Train to Agawa Canyon."

Retta's face turned white, and she exhaled like someone had punched her in the stomach.

"Did I say something I shouldn't have?" I asked.

"You said 'train.' I didn't think you'd ever want to ride one after..." She stopped and looked at me, dumbfounded.

"Yes, I said 'train.' And it doesn't bother me that we'd be taking a ride on one. We can't hold the Belgian rail system accountable for every train in the world."

"Wow! You have really bucked up for this, Helmi. I'm proud of you."

I shrugged. "Are you interested?"

She looked at the tickets again. She checked the date and said, "I have that week off."

"You'll have the rest of your life off by then. You can't keep it from me any longer; I know you're retiring, and it's about time, I might add."

"Who have you been talking to?"

"Not important. I just had to make sure before I paid for the tickets."

She grinned. "What if I don't want to go?"

"I figure I can always advertise in the newspaper and maybe find some other aging woman who's up for some rip-roaring fun."

"Some other *aging* woman?"

"You're a senior now, you know." I said. "No use trying to deny it."

She sighed. "So what do we do on this train?"

"We get to eat our lunch in the dining car, and we can take as many photos as we can possibly stand, because the train cars all have windows on both sides. And we get to cross the trestle over the Montreal River. Wait till you see the pictures on the Internet. It's mind-boggling."

"And we're doing this in the middle of winter? Lots of snow?"

"I hope so," I said.

"Well, I'm in," she said, a smile curling from one side of her face to the other.

"Look out, Agawa Canyon. Here we come!"

She looked at her watch. "I'll be finished here in about twenty minutes. Why don't you go sit in my office, then we can go someplace for dinner. How's that sound?"

"Wonderful. Italian?"

"Buon appetito!" she said, kissing her fingers.

I finally listed the Brimley house in the spring and sold it within nine weeks. It was clean and in good repair, and once the prospective buyers saw the view, they were hooked.

I began packing. At one point I boxed up Jimmy's tools, his accumulation of bookmarks (he'd gotten one at the library every time he checked out a book, and I don't think he ever threw one away), the books he'd bought but never passed on to someone else, and his jewelry box; that was the hardest to part with. He'd planned to give it to Lloyd and Craig when he died so they could divide up the rings and watches and tie clips and…that would have been the natural order of things, but it hadn't worked out that way, so it was not to be.

I never told anyone, not even Retta, that I saved Jimmy's unwashed pillowcase. I kept it in a plastic bag in the drawer of my nightstand and would occasionally take it out and hold it up to my nose. I swore I could smell his scent on it, and it carried me into a beautiful place for a few fleeting moments. Even after the scent had disappeared, I would still sniff it and be able to recall Jimmy's face, and that put me in a good mood, even on my worst days.

I'd found a perfect one-bedroom apartment in the Soo, not unlike Retta's place in Frankfort. It was close to all the places I'd be frequenting: the grocery, the library, a filling station, my doctor's office, my hairdresser, my pharmacy, and several restaurants. It looked out over the Ste. Mary's River, so I could relax and watch the freighters as they silently glided back and forth between Lake Huron and Lake Superior, their holds full and making them ride low in the water, or empty, allowing them to tower above the shoreline. Their whistle talk had always made the corners of my mouth turn up, and that was a good thing.

I was talking on the phone to a friend of mine about moving. "Aren't you going to miss Brimley?" she asked.

"Of course, I am," I said. "But I don't need to break my back trying to keep up with a property that's way too big for one person to take care of. Besides, this house needs a family in it."

"You could hire people to do everything. Or do you…" she paused.

"Do I what?"

"Do you need to go where you're not reminded of Jimmy all the time?"

"Retta suggested the same thing. But that's not why I'm moving. My memories of my life in Brimley will never fade. We raised our two sons here, and I had some of my happiest times in this house. Why would I not want to be reminded of that?"

"But when you move, those reminders won't be at the new place," she said.

"I'm taking the good memories with me."

My apartment had a patch of grass between the building and the river, so I took to feeding the ducks that frequently flew in to search for bugs and to rest before flying off to their evening roosting place. I still loved ducks and took great joy in watching them. I came to find out that the flock I watched didn't leave during the winter. Instead, they stayed right there, waddling around in the snow…so long as I had corn to feed them.

Each year between Christmas and the end of March, the ships stopped going through the locks because of ice build-up in the shipping channels and the river. I almost felt lonely without their whistles and the occasional "whump-whump-whumping" of their propellers, but I had made some new friends around town, and they kept my mind trained on other things. They taught me to play bridge, cribbage, and euchre (euchre was, by far, my favorite).

One of my friends, Jeannie, shared my love of the arts. We attended most of the plays at Lake Superior State University, and we went to all the Sault Symphony concerts, some of them on our side of the river and some on the Canadian side. I couldn't sit through a single concert without thinking of Link.

Another friend, Peg, and I went swimming in the public pool at Rudyard High School once a week. We even took a water aerobics class there; I hoped it would help my back pain. And besides, it was fun returning once a week to the area where I had spent so much of my life, and it reminded me that I was now living a pleasant life, a calm life, a life no longer filled with schedules and having to fix other people's problems.

At a local Christmas craft show I picked up ideas for doing some crafting of my own. I was smitten with the things in one crafter's booth in particular. The man and woman who had made the items were Colleen and Parker Townsend. Both were highly talented and had been displaying and selling their items all over the state of Michigan for years. She and I became friends on a level close to what Retta and I shared. Though Colleen was ten years younger than I, we still hit it off like sisters; she even reminded me a little bit of Retta. We shared the same sense of humor and the same love of envisioning and making things with our own hands.

I also became interested in birdwatching (other than ducks). I spent hours on the grassy spot between my building and the river with binoculars in hand, a bird identification book beside me, and a notepad in my lap. I kept records of every bird I saw and could positively identify. I drove to the Seney National Wildlife Refuge at least once a month to watch nature in its most natural form, and I discovered that it was the place I wanted my ashes to be deposited. Red pines abound there, and I knew Retta would find the right one under which I could be happy spending eternity. I took her there a couple of times, and she agreed that it was a perfect fit for me.

All in all, I was very happy—and busy—living in the Soo. Oh, I wished Jimmy could have spent it with me, but I knew he wouldn't have been physically able to do all the things I was lucky enough to be able to accomplish. I missed his wit, his smirk, his touch, and most of all, the way he made me smile. But I think he would have been proud of me for not slowing down and for keeping myself entertained.

I looked down at the ring he had given me the evening before he had left for deer camp, that fateful trip, and I couldn't hold back the tears. I was usually able to control them, but for some reason I was feeling lonely right then. I suspected it was because I'd had a difficult day—my back pain hadn't let up. I didn't want to have to take pain killers because I wouldn't be able to drive under their influence. And driving was something I was not prepared to give up; it didn't matter to me that I was going to turn eighty in four months.

Colleen and I spent several of our "crafting parties for two," as we called our sessions, making Christmas ornaments out of glass. We had gone to Lansing one Saturday and taken a crash course in creating various types of leaded-glass art at the glass dealer's there, the biggest in the state. We took the information home and put our own spin on things, so when Christmas got there, my tree was decorated completely with homemade leaded-glass ornaments.

I think Jimmy would have liked it.

PEACE

The Schnier family was down to just Retta and I. Lizzy was gone, as was Walter. They had both died within a few months of one another in Costa Rica, where one of their grandchildren had a job. He had convinced them to move there because the cost of living was so low.

My back had slowly become worse over the years. Dr. Jacobowski said my job had probably been the greatest factor in promoting my condition. It seems that the stress of everyday movements had caused little tears in the outer walls of my discs near the nerves, and that had been causing my pain. I had experienced numbness and tingling in my legs, and I realized I was having a lot of muscle weakness and occasional spasms. But as the years had crept by, the discs had bulged and slipped out of place, causing severe, nagging pain when I moved. It was the worst when I sat, bent, lifted something, or twisted; it was much less painful when I was lying down.

I had been through months of physical therapy in the hopes that it would make my back stronger and more flexible, but that had not been the case. The doctor had suggested steroid shots to ease the pain, but I reacted badly to them. It was at that point that he decided I'd need surgery to fuse the bones in my spine after he removed the bad discs.

Retta and I discussed the problems associated with surgery at my age, and decided it was too risky, even though I was in good health otherwise. We both knew my recovery would be a long and difficult endeavor, so we opted for a hospital bed to be moved into my apartment. That way I could recline most of the time, the only somewhat comfortable position I could tolerate.

The doctor had made the arrangements for the hospital bed to be moved in one afternoon, and Retta said, "Helmi, I know you're going to disagree with what I'm about to say, but it's something I really want. So please don't make it hard for me."

I looked at her and smiled, knowing full well what she was about to say. "How much time's left on your lease?"

"Well, that pretty much blew the surprise," she said and laughed.

"It's no surprise. If I were in your shoes, I'd want to do the same thing."

Her face turned red; I had rarely seen her blush. "Actually, as of tomorrow, I don't have a place to live unless I move in with you." She looked down at the floor. Then she lifted her eyes to me, the whites showing around the bottoms like some sad puppy dog.

"Of course, you can stay with me. I couldn't be happier that you want to. You'll have your own bed since I'll be sleeping in that hospital contraption. But you'll have to fight me for the TV remote."

The corners of her mouth went from barely turning up to nearly touching her ears. She was happy, and that thrilled me.

We got on well together. Her move into my apartment was something that appeared to be good for both of us. She cooked and cleaned, keeping us well fed and the apartment well polished. We rarely disagreed about anything other than the occasional minor clash about what to watch on TV. I, of course, wanted to watch every available show about veterinarians, and she was knee-deep into watching programs about space and the universe. But through the process of give and take, we managed to placate each other's preferences. And I loved her even more than I thought possible.

One day while I was looking through a magazine Retta had grabbed at the pharmacy when she was picking up our medications, I came across an article about saying goodbye to relatives. *I don't need to read that one*, I thought. *I've had plenty of experience at doing that*. But for some reason, I decided to read it anyway. My eyes were opened to a subject that had never crossed my mind: Retta had been through all of the deaths I had seen, and now she would most likely go through one more.

Throughout all my years, I had endured every loss of my family, the losses of my homes, and the deaths of Retta's and my mutual friends; the list was long. But Retta had been through the loss of all of them as well. They hadn't been only my losses, but hers, too. And now she was the one looking at losing another. Unless she was involved in some freak accident, she'd be the last of the Schniers.

My heart broke. I was as sad as I had ever been, thinking about her being alone. And yet, here she was, caring for me. I called to her, and she came jauntily into the room.

"Watcha need?" she asked, wiping her hands on a dish towel.

I couldn't speak around the lump in my throat at that moment, so I motioned for her to come over to the side of the bed. Her brow furrowed, but she walked over, and I took her hand. I looked up into her eyes.

"Helmi?"

I swallowed and said, "I'm okay. I just realized something that has evaded me for, well, my whole life." I had to swallow again, but this time tears came trickling down my face at the same time.

"What's evaded you?" she sat down on the edge of the chair she always sat in when we were playing cards or looking at something in the newspaper or a magazine. She threw the dish towel over her shoulder—such a typical Retta move.

I explained to her what I had just come to realize, and she said, "But, Helmi, you're the one all the rest of us depended on. You took the brunt of everything that happened to us. The rest of us were merely onlookers. You didn't have anyone; you were alone, way up here." She extended her arm up over her head. "We always knew where to find you…up here." She moved her arm, reaching upward, emphasizing the height of her hand.

"But when I go, you'll be alone," I said. "You'll have been through everything I went through, and then more."

She settled back in the chair. "You have it wrong, Helmi. I might be the last to go, though we don't know that for sure. But my passing will only be a statistic. Yours will be a monumental event in the history of our family."

I was overcome with emotion. I looked at Retta sitting beside me, holding my hand. The chaos inside my head vanished, and a satisfying peace settled over me.

EPILOGUE

Three days have passed, and Britta Bonbright, my attorney, has returned. I seem to have beaten the odds by remaining "of sound mind" long enough to consciously sign the *Wilhelmina Butcher Revocable Trust* for what I can safely say is the final time. I'm ready to rest, now, so I need to make sure Old Man Death has been informed of that.

I included a personal letter to Retta in my trust; it's a reminder of the arrangements I've requested following my death. She isn't merely my only living sister; she's the sister with whom I've been closest throughout my life. She was close to Jimmy, too, and during our most recent chats has joined me in reminiscing about her affection for him.

Jimmy. No other man ever came close to filling the void he left. Oh, I enjoyed the company of other men, but there was no comparison to the level of adoration shared between Jimmy and me. Not a day goes by that I don't think about him, about us, and about our boys.

Included in the letter to Retta is a poem for Jimmy. The poem became a part of me when I was 14 years old; I found it when looking through a book of poetry in the Mount Pleasant High School library. I don't remember ever sharing it with him. And I had no idea it would become a wellspring of serenity for me in Jimmy's absence. Retta will understand.

> *O love, that wilt not let me go,*
> *I rest my weary soul in thee.*
> *I give thee back the life I owe*
> *That, in thine ocean depths, its flow*
> *May richer, fuller be.*
>
> *O light, that followest all my way,*
> *I yield my flickering torch to thee.*
> *My heart restores its borrowed ray*
> *That, in thy sunshine's glow, its day*
> *May brighter, fairer be.*

> *O joy, you seek me through the pain.*
> *I cannot close my heart to thee.*
> *I trace the rainbow through the rain*
> *And feel the promise is not vain.*
> *Then morn shall tearless be.*
> **George Matheson**

And so it is that I have managed to satisfy all the requirements of passing on, according to Britta. She is unaware, however, that these last three days have allowed me to replay the fondest—and the foulest—milestones of my seasons on this earth. I can now take comfort in knowing I'll soon breathe my last and welcome the end.

Hey, Old Man, don't make me wait much longer.

HELMI'S FAMILY

Nancy "Granny Nan" Deacon
 born 09.10.1850; died 12.07.1941
Buster Deacon (Nancy's husband)
 born (?); died 1891
Heinrich "Papa" Schnier
 born 10.29.1886; died 05.08.1934
Violet Deacon "Mama" Schnier
 born 01.20.1891; died 03.08.1934
 Heinrich and Violet's children
 Wilhelmina "Helmi" Schnier Butcher
  born 11.13.1920; died (?)
 Josephina "Yosie" Schnier
  born 04.18.1922; died 12.31.1950
 Isabella "Bella" Schnier
  born 12.12.1923; died 1993
 Isadora "Dora" Schnier
  born 12.12.1923; died 06.1992
 Margaretta "Retta" Schnier
  born 08.06.1926; died (?)
 Marcelina "Celine" Schnier
  born 05.20.1928; died 08.1933
 Veronica "Ronnie" Schnier
  born 09.22.1931; died 09.1953
 Cynthianna "Anna" Schnier
  born 02.26.1933; died 1994
 Alexander Schnier
  stillborn 03.08.1934
 Aloysius Schnier
  born 03.08.1934; died 03.28.1934

James "Jimmy" Butcher (Helmi's husband)
    born 04.08.1917; died 01.06.1993
    Helmi and Jimmy's children
    Herman Lloyd Butcher
        born 12.13.1943; died 09.1976
    Craig Wendell Butcher
        born 08.30.1950; died 09.1976

Lavern Deacon Gounaris (Violet's sister)
    born 1876; died 1939
Julius Gounaris (Lavern's husband)
    born (?); died 1931
Herrmann "Uncle Herman" Schnier (Heinrich's brother)
    born 04.03.1880; died 02.1959
Mary Blodgett Schnier (Uncle Herman's wife)
    born 01.1897; died 02.1994
Lizzy (Mary's daughter)
    born (?); died 2020
James "Butch" Butcher (Jimmy's father)
    born (?); died 08.09.1941

OTHERS WHO IMPACTED HELMI'S LIFE

Betsy (a pet dog in Oklahoma and Michigan)
Torvin Setters, Atty (attorney in Beaver City, Oklahoma)
Eber "Doc" and Naomi Weiser, and son Robert (neighbors in Oklahoma)
Afton and Belinda (worked for the Gounarises in Chicago)
Duane Linley (childhood friend)
Mr. Zellers (real estate agent in Mount Pleasant)
Mrs. Matsen (Sunday school teacher)
Bill and Rachel Neidhart (neighbors in Isabella County)
Doc Barrett. MD (family doctor in Mount Pleasant)
Miss Michaels (teacher in the one-room school)
Miss Welch (teacher who took over for Miss Michaels)
Jim and Alice Chaney (friends of Violet and Heinrich)
Jacob Miller (Amish man)
Two-Tone (a pet dog in Michigan)
Mr. Watkins (banker in Mount Pleasant)

Dr. Pauley, DVM (veterinarian in Weidman)
Sandra (taught Helmi to read music)
Lillian Andrews (piano teacher)
Dr. D.K. "Link" Lincoln, DVM, PhD (veterinarian, professor at OSU, and lifelong friend)
Dorothea Lincoln (Link's wife, professor at OSU)
Dr. Aldridge, DVM, PhD (Dorothea's father, veterinarian, professor emeritus at OSU)
Liv, Millie, Wanda, Eileen, Hannah, Shinju, Penelope (roommates and acquaintances at OSU)
Isaac Miller (Jacob Miller's son)
Stephen Spicer (Dora's artist friend)
Trina McAlister (Dora's life partner)
Dr. Tom Bell, DVM (retired owner of the vet clinic in Rudyard)
Dr. Aune Halvorsen, DVM (second owner of the vet clinic)
Shirley (office manager at the vet clinic)
Andy Atkinson (owned rental cabins in Brimley)
Wil Devers (Retta's husband)
Gene and Betty Downs (close friends in Brimley)
Sheila Benjamin (Lloyd and Craig's babysitter in Rudyard)
Arturo (dispatcher at the rail yard in Owosso)
Ben Martin (a favorite client)
Walter (Lizzy's husband)
Sergeant Avery Dickerson (Chicago Police Department)
Dr. John Napoleon, DVM (small-animal veterinarian)
Billie White (vet tech)
Dr. Adam Salisbury, MD (family doctor in Sault Ste. Marie)
Dr. Randy Garrish, DVM (third owner of the vet clinic)
Dr. Jacobowski, MD, NSG (neurosurgeon in Petoskey)
Colleen and Parker Townsend, Jeannie, Peg, (friends in the Soo)

CPSIA information can be obtained
at www.ICGtesting.com
Printed in the USA
FFHW011311221119
56071555-62079FF